THE DARK TOWER

WOLVES OF THE CALLA

By Stephen King and published by
Hodder & Stoughton

FICTION:

Carrie

'Salem's Lot

The Shining

Night Shift

The Stand

Christine

The Talisman (with Peter Straub)

Pet Sematary

It

Misery

The Tommyknockers

The Dark Half

Four Past Midnight

Needful Things

Gerald's Game

Dolores Claiborne

Nightmares and Dreamscapes

Insomnia

Rose Madder

Desperation

The Dark Tower I: The Gunslinger

The Dark Tower II: The Drawing of the Three

The Dark Tower III: The Waste Lands

The Dark Tower IV: Wizard and Glass

The Dark Tower V: Wolves of the Calla

The Dark Tower VI: Song of Susannah

The Dark Tower VII: The Dark Tower

Bag of Bones

The Girl Who Loved Tom Gordon

Hearts in Atlantis

Dreamcatcher

Everything's Eventual

From a Buick 8

By Stephen King as Richard Bachman

Thinner

The Running Man

The Bachman Books

The Regulators

NON-FICTION:

On Writing (A Memoir of the Craft)

STEPHEN KING

THE DARK TOWER V

WOLVES OF THE CALLA

Illustrated by Bernie Wrightson

HODDER &
STOUGHTON

Grateful acknowledgement is made for permission to reprint
excerpts from the following copyrighted material:

'Someone Saved My Life Tonight' by Elton John and Bernie Taupin © 1975
Happenstance Limited and Rouge Booze, Inc.
All Rights in U.S. administered by WB MUSIC CORP.
All Rights outside U.S. administered by Muziekuitgeverij Artemis B.V.
All Rights Reserved. Used By Permission
WARNER BROS. PUBLICATIONS U.S. INC., Miami, FL 33014

'The Wandering Boy' © Song/ATV Tunes LLC.
All rights administered by Sony/ATV Music Publishing, 8 Music Square West,
Nashville, TN 37203. All rights reserved. Used by permission.

'The Magnificent Seven'
MGM Consumer Products, a division of Metro-Goldwyn-Mayer Home
Entertainment LLC, a wholly owned subsidiary of Metro-Goldwyn-Mayer Studios Inc.

First published in Great Britain in 2003 by Hodder and Stoughton
A division of Hodder Headline

This edition published in 2005

1 3 5 7 9 10 8 6 4 2

A CIP catalogue record for this title is available from the British Library

ISBN 0 340 82716 5

Typeset in Centaur by Palimpsest Book Production Limited,
Polmont, Stirlingshire

Printed and bound in Great Britain by
Clays Ltd, St Ives plc

Hodder and Stoughton
A division of Hodder Headline
338 Euston Road
London NW1 3BH

This book is for Frank Muller,
who hears the voices in my head.

CONTENTS

PART THREE
THE WOLVES

EPILOGUE
THE DOORWAY CAVE

ILLUSTRATIONS

THE FINAL ARGUMENT

Wolves of the Calla is the fifth volume of a longer tale inspired by Robert Browning's narrative poem 'Childe Roland to the Dark Tower Came.' The sixth, *Song of Susannah*, will be published in 2004. The seventh and last, *The Dark Tower*, will be published later that same year.

The first volume, *The Gunslinger*, tells how Roland Deschain of Gilead pursues and at last catches Walter, the man in black — he who pretended friendship with Roland's father but actually served the Crimson King in far-off End-World. Catching the half-human Walter is for Roland a step on the way to the Dark Tower, where he hopes the quickening destruction of Mid-World and the slow death of the Beams may be halted or even reversed. The subtitle of this novel is RESUMPTION.

The Dark Tower is Roland's obsession, his grail, his only reason for living when we meet him. We learn of how Marten tried, when Roland was yet a boy, to see him sent west in disgrace, swept from the board of the great game. Roland, however, lays Marten's plans at nines, mostly due to his choice of weapon in his manhood test.

Steven Deschain, Roland's father, sends his son and two friends (Cuthbert Allgood and Alain Johns) to the seacoast barony of Mejis, mostly to place the boy beyond Walter's reach. There Roland meets and falls in love with Susan Delgado, who has fallen afoul a witch. Rhea of the Cöos is jealous of the girl's beauty, and particularly dangerous because she has obtained one of the great glass balls known as the Bends o' the Rainbow . . . or the Wizard's Glasses. There are thirteen of these in all, the most powerful and dangerous being Black Thirteen. Roland and his friends have many adventures in Mejis, and although they escape with their lives (and the pink Bend o' the Rainbow), Susan Delgado, the lovely girl at the window, is burned at the stake. This tale is told in the fourth volume, *Wizard and Glass*. The subtitle of this novel is REGARD.

In the course of the tales of the Tower we discover that the gunslinger's world is related to our own in fundamental and terrible ways. The first of these links is revealed when Jake, a boy from the New York of 1977, meets Roland at a desert way station long years after the death of Susan Delgado. There are doors between Roland's world and our own, and one of them is death. Jake finds himself in this desert way station after being pushed into Forty-third Street and run over by a car. The car's driver was a man named Enrico Balazar. The pusher was a criminal sociopath named Jack Mort, Walter's representative on the New York level of the Dark Tower.

Before Jake and Roland reach Walter, Jake dies again . . . this time because the gunslinger, faced with an agonizing choice between this symbolic son and the Dark Tower, chooses the Tower. Jake's last words before plunging into the abyss are 'Go, then – there are other worlds than these.'

The final confrontation between Roland and Walter occurs near the Western Sea. In a long night of palaver, the man in black tells Roland's future with a Tarot deck of strange device. Three cards – the Prisoner, the Lady of Shadows, and Death ('but not for you, gunslinger') – are especially called to Roland's attention.

The Drawing of the Three, subtitled RENEWAL, begins on the shore of the Western Sea not long after Roland awakens from his confrontation with Walter. The exhausted gunslinger is attacked by a horde of carnivorous 'lobstrosities,' and before he can escape, he has lost two fingers of his right hand and has been seriously infected. Roland resumes his trek along the shore of the Western Sea, although he is sick and possibly dying.

On his walk he encounters three doors standing freely on the beach. These open into New York at three different *whens*. From 1987, Roland draws Eddie Dean, a prisoner of heroin. From 1964, he draws Odetta Susannah Holmes, a woman who lost her legs when a sociopath named Jack Mort pushed her in front of a subway train. She is the Lady of Shadows, with a violent 'other' hidden in her brain. This hidden woman, the violent and crafty Detta Walker, is determined to kill both Roland and Eddie when the gunslinger draws her into Mid-World.

Roland thinks that perhaps he has drawn three in just Eddie and Odetta, since Odetta is really two personalities, yet when Odetta and Detta merge as one into Susannah (largely thanks to Eddie Dean's love and courage), the gunslinger knows it's not so. He knows something else, as well: he is being tormented by thoughts of Jake, the boy who spoke of other worlds at the time of his death.

The Waste Lands, subtitled REDEMPTION, begins with a paradox: to Roland, Jake seems both alive and dead. In the New York of the late 1970s, Jake Chambers is haunted by the same question: alive or dead? Which is he? After killing a gigantic bear named either Mir (so called by the old people who went in fear of it) or Shardik (by the Great Old Ones who built it),

Roland, Eddie, and Susannah backtrack the beast and discover the Path of the Beam known as Shardik to Maturin, Bear to Turtle. There were once six of these Beams, running between the twelve portals which mark the edges of Mid-World. At the point where the Beams cross, at the center of Roland's world (and all worlds), stands the Dark Tower, the nexus of all *where* and *when*.

By now Eddie and Susannah are no longer prisoners in Roland's world. In love and well on the way to becoming gunslingers themselves, they are full participants in the quest and follow Roland, the last seppe-sai (death-seller), along the Path of Shardik, the Way of Maturin.

In a speaking ring not far from the Portal of the Bear, time is mended, paradox is ended, and the *real* third is drawn. Jake reenters Mid-World at the end of a perilous rite where all four — Jake, Eddie, Susannah, and Roland — remember the faces of their fathers and acquit themselves honorably. Not long after, the quartet becomes a quintet, when Jake befriends a billy-bumbler. Bumblers, which look like a combination of badger, raccoon, and dog, have a limited speaking ability. Jake names his new friend Oy.

The way of the pilgrims leads them toward the city of Lud, where the degenerate survivors of two old factions carry on an endless conflict. Before reaching the city, in the little town of River Crossing, they meet a few ancient survivors of the old days. They recognize Roland as a fellow survivor of those days before the world moved on, and honor him and his companions. The Old People also tell them of a monorail train which may still run from Lud and into the waste lands, along the Path of the Beam and toward the Dark Tower.

Jake is frightened by this news but not surprised; before being drawn from New York, he obtained two books from a bookstore owned by a man with the thought-provoking name of Calvin Tower. One is a book of riddles with the answers torn out. The other, *Charlie the Choo-Choo*, is a children's story with dark echoes of Mid-World. For one thing, the word *char* means *death* in the High Speech Roland grew up speaking in Gilead.

Aunt Talitha, the matriarch of River Crossing, gives Roland a silver cross to wear, and the travelers go their course. While crossing the dilapidated bridge which spans the River Send, Jake is abducted by a dying (and very dangerous) outlaw named Gasher. Gasher takes his young prisoner underground to the Tick-Tock Man, the last leader of the faction known as the Grays.

While Roland and Oy go after Jake, Eddie and Susannah find the Cradle of Lud, where Blaine the Mono awakes. Blaine is the last aboveground tool of a vast computer system that lies beneath Lud, and Blaine has only one remaining interest: riddles. It promises to take the travelers to the monorail's final stop . . . *if* they can pose it a riddle it cannot solve. Otherwise, Blaine says, their trip will end in death: *charyou tree*.

Roland rescues Jake, leaving the Tick-Tock Man for dead. Yet Andrew Quick is not dead. Half-blind, hideously wounded about the face, he is rescued by a man who calls himself Richard Fannin. Fannin, however, also identifies himself as the Ageless Stranger; a demon of whom Roland has been warned.

The pilgrims continue their journey from the dying city of Lud, this time by monorail. The fact that the actual mind running the mono exists in computers falling farther and farther behind them will make no difference one way or the other when the pink bullet jumps the decaying tracks somewhere along the Path of the Beam at a speed in excess of eight hundred miles an hour. Their one chance of survival is to pose Blaine a riddle which the computer cannot answer.

At the beginning of *Wizard and Glass*, Eddie does indeed pose such a riddle, destroying Blaine with a uniquely human weapon: illogic. The mono comes to a stop in a version of Topeka, Kansas, which has been emptied by a disease called 'superflu.' As they recommence their journey along the Path of the Beam (now on an apocalyptic version of Interstate 70), they see disturbing signs. ALL HAIL THE CRIMSON KING, advises one. WATCH FOR THE WALKIN DUDE, advises another. And, as alert readers will know, the Walkin Dude has a name very similar to Richard Fannin.

After telling his friends the story of Susan Delgado, Roland and his friends come to a palace of green glass which has been constructed across I-70, a palace that bears a strong resemblance to the one Dorothy Gale sought in *The Wizard of Oz*. In the throne-room of this great castle they encounter not Oz the Great and Terrible but the Tick-Tock Man, the great city of Lud's final refugee. With Tick-Tock dead, the *real* Wizard steps forward. It's Roland's ancient nemesis, Marten Broadcloak, known in some worlds as Randall Flagg, in others as Richard Fannin, in others as John Farson (the Good Man). Roland and his friends are unable to kill this apparition, who warns them one final time to give up their quest for the Tower ('Only misfires against *me*, Roland, old fellow,' he tells the gunslinger), but they are able to banish him.

After a final trip into the Wizard's Glass and a final dreadful revelation

– that Roland of Gilead killed his own mother, mistaking her for the witch named Rhea – the wanderers find themselves once more in Mid-World and once more on the Path of the Beam. They take up their quest again, and it is here that we will find them in the first pages of *Wolves of the Calla*.

This argument in no way summarizes the first four books of the *Tower* cycle; if you have not read those books before commencing this one, I urge you to do so or to put this one aside. These books are but parts of a single long tale, and you would do better to read them from beginning to end rather than starting in the middle.

Mister, we deal in lead.
  — Steve McQueen, in *The Magnificent Seven*

First comes smiles, then lies. Last is gunfire.
  — Roland Deschain, of Gilead

The blood that flows through you
flows through me,
when I look in any mirror,
it's your face that I see.
Take my hand,
lean on me,
We're almost free,
Wandering boy.
  — Rodney Crowell

RESISTANCE

19

PROLOGUE:
ROONT

1

Tian was blessed (though few farmers would have used such a word) with three patches: River Field, where his family had grown rice since time out of mind; Roadside Field, where ka-Jaffords had grown sharproot, pumpkin, and corn for those same long years and generations; and Son of a Bitch, a thankless tract which mostly grew rocks, blisters, and busted hopes. Tian wasn't the first Jaffords determined to make something of the twenty acres behind the home place; his Gran-pere, perfectly sane in most other respects, had been convinced there was gold there. Tian's Ma had been equally positive it would grow porin, a spice of great worth. Tian's particular insanity was madrigal. Of course madrigal would grow in Son of a Bitch. *Must* grow there. He'd gotten hold of a thousand seeds (and a dear penny they had cost him) that were now hidden beneath the floor-boards of his bedroom. All that remained before planting next year was to break ground in Son of a Bitch. This chore was easier spoken of than accomplished.

Clan Jaffords was blessed with livestock, including three mules, but a man would be mad to try using a mule out in Son of a Bitch; the beast unlucky enough to draw such duty would likely be lying legbroke or stung to death by noon of the first day. One of Tian's uncles had almost met this latter fate some years before. He had come running back to the home place, screaming at the top of his lungs and pursued by huge mutie wasps with stingers the size of nails.

They had found the nest (well, Andy had found it; Andy wasn't bothered by wasps no matter how big they were) and burned it with kerosene, but there might be others. And there were holes. Yer-bugger, plenty o' *them*, and you couldn't burn holes, could you? No. Son of a Bitch sat on what the old folks called 'loose ground.' It was consequently possessed of almost as many holes as rocks, not to mention at least one cave that puffed out draughts of nasty, decay-smelling air. Who knew what boggarts and speakies might lurk down its dark throat?

And the worst holes weren't out where a man (or a mule) could see them. Not at all, sir, never think so. The leg-breakers were always concealed in innocent-seeming nestles of weeds and high grass. Your mule would step in, there would come a bitter crack like a snapping branch, and then the damned thing would be lying there on the ground, teeth bared, eyes rolling, braying its agony at the sky. Until you put it out of its misery, that was, and stock was valuable in Calla Bryn Sturgis, even stock that wasn't precisely threaded.

Tian therefore plowed with his sister in the traces. No reason not to. Tia was roont, hence good for little else. She was a big girl — the roont ones often grew to prodigious size — and she was willing, Man Jesus love her. The Old Fella had made her a Jesus-tree, what he called a *crusie-fix*, and she wore it everywhere. It swung back and forth now, thumping against her sweating skin as she pulled.

The plow was attached to her shoulders by a rawhide harness. Behind her, alternately guiding the plow by its old ironwood handles and his sister by the hame-traces, Tian grunted and yanked and pushed when the blade of the plow dropped down and verged on becoming stuck. It was the end of Full Earth but as hot as midsummer here in Son of a Bitch; Tia's overalls were dark and damp and stuck to her long and meaty thighs. Each time Tian tossed his head to get his hair out of his eyes, sweat flew out of the mop in a spray.

'Gee, ye bitch!' he cried. 'Yon rock's a plow-breaker, are ye blind?'

Not blind; not deaf, either; just roont. She heaved to the left, and hard. Behind her, Tian stumbled forward with a neck-snapping jerk and barked his shin on another rock, one he hadn't seen and the plow had, for a wonder, missed. As he felt the first warm trickles of blood running down to his ankle, he wondered (and not for the first time) what madness it was that always got the Jaffordses out here. In his deepest heart he had an idea that madrigal would sow no more than the porin had before it, although you could grow devil-grass; yar, he could've bloomed all twenty acres with that shit, had he wanted. The trick was to keep it *out*, and it was always New Earth's first chore. It—

The plow rocked to the right and then jerked forward, almost pulling his arms out of their sockets. '*Arr!*' he cried. 'Go easy, girl! I can't grow em back if you pull em out, can I?'

Tia turned her broad, sweaty, empty face up to a sky full of low-hanging clouds and honked laughter. Man Jesus, but she even *sounded* like a donkey. Yet it was laughter, human laughter. Tian wondered, as he sometimes couldn't help doing, if that laughter *meant* anything. Did she understand some of what he was saying, or did she only respond to his tone of voice? Did any of the roont ones—

'Good day, sai,' said a loud and almost completely toneless voice from behind him. The owner of the voice ignored Tian's scream of surprise. 'Pleasant days, and may they be long upon the earth. I am here from a goodish wander and at your service.'

Tian whirled around, saw Andy standing there – all seven feet of him – and was then almost jerked flat as his sister took another of her large lurching steps forward. The plow's hame-traces were pulled from his hands and flew around his throat with an audible snap. Tia, unaware of this potential disaster, took another sturdy step forward. When she did, Tian's wind was cut off. He gave a whooping, gagging gasp and clawed at the straps. All of this Andy watched with his usual large and meaningless smile.

Tia jerked forward again and Tian was pulled off his feet. He landed on a rock that dug savagely into the cleft of his buttocks, but at least he could breathe again. For the moment, anyway. Damned unlucky field! Always had been! Always would be!

Tian snatched hold of the leather strap before it could pull tight around his throat again and yelled, 'Hold, ye bitch! Whoa up if you don't want me to twist yer great and useless tits right off the front of yer!'

Tia halted agreeably enough and looked back to see what was what. Her smile broadened. She lifted one heavily muscled arm – it glowed with sweat – and pointed. 'Andy!' she said. 'Andy's come!'

'I ain't blind,' Tian said and got to his feet, rubbing his bottom. Was that part of him also bleeding? Good Man Jesus, he had an idea it was.

'Good day, sai,' Andy said to her, and tapped his metal throat three times with his three metal fingers. 'Long days and pleasant nights.'

Although Tia had surely heard the standard response to this – *And may you have twice the number* – a thousand times or more, all she could do was once more raise her broad idiot's face to the sky and honk her donkey laugh. Tian felt a surprising moment of pain, not in his arms or throat or outraged ass but in his heart. He vaguely remembered her as a little girl: as pretty and quick as a dragonfly, as smart as ever you could wish. Then—

But before he could finish the thought, a premonition came. He felt a sinking in his heart. *The news* would *come while I'm out here*, he thought. *Out in this godforsaken patch where nothing is well and all luck is bad*. It was time, wasn't it? *Overtime*.

'Andy,' he said.

'Yes!' Andy said, smiling. 'Andy, your friend! Back from a goodish wander and at your service. Would you like your horoscope, sai Tian? It is Full Earth. The moon is red, what is called the Huntress Moon in Mid-World that was. A friend will call! Business affairs prosper! You will have two ideas, one good and one bad—'

'The bad one was coming out here to turn this field,' Tian said. 'Never mind my goddam horoscope, Andy. Why are you here?'

Andy's smile probably could not become troubled – he was a robot, after all, the last one in Calla Bryn Sturgis or for miles and wheels around – but to Tian it seemed to *grow* troubled, just the same. The robot looked like a young child's stick-figure of an adult, impossibly tall and impossibly thin. His legs and arms were silvery. His head was a stainless-steel barrel with electric eyes. His body, no more than a cylinder, was gold. Stamped in the middle – what would have been a man's chest – was this legend:

NORTH CENTRAL POSITRONICS, LTD.
IN ASSOCIATION WITH LaMERK INDUSTRIES
PRESENTS

ANDY

Design: MESSENGER (Many Other Functions)
Serial # DNF-44821-V-63

Why or how this silly thing had survived when all the rest of the robots were gone – gone for generations – Tian neither knew nor cared. You were apt to see him anywhere in the Calla (he would not venture beyond its borders) striding on his impossibly thin silver legs, looking everywhere, occasionally clicking to himself as he stored (or perhaps purged – who knew?) information. He sang songs, passed on gossip and rumor from one end of town to the other – a tireless walker was Andy the Messenger Robot – and seemed to enjoy the giving of horoscopes above all things, although there was general agreement in the village that they meant little.

He had one other function, however, and that meant much.

'Why are ye here, ye bag of bolts and beams? Answer me! Is it the Wolves? Are they coming from Thunderclap?'

Tian stood there looking up into Andy's stupid smiling metal face, the sweat growing cold on his skin, praying with all his might that the foolish thing would say no, then offer to tell his horoscope again, or perhaps to sing 'The Green Corn A-Dayo,' all twenty or thirty verses.

But all Andy said, still smiling, was: 'Yes, sai.'

'Christ and the Man Jesus,' Tian said (he'd gotten an idea from the Old Fella that those were two names for the same thing, but had never bothered pursuing the question). 'How long?'

'One moon of days before they arrive,' Andy replied, still smiling.

'From full to full?'

'Close enough, sai.'

Thirty days, then, give or take one. Thirty days to the Wolves. And there was no sense hoping Andy was wrong. No one kenned how the robot could know they were coming out of Thunderclap so far in advance of their arrival, but he *did* know. And he was never wrong.

'Fuck you for your bad news!' Tian cried, and was furious at the waver he heard in his own voice. 'What use are you?'

'I'm sorry that the news is bad,' Andy said. His guts clicked audibly, his eyes flashed a brighter blue, and he took a step backward. 'Would you not like me to tell your horoscope? This is the end of Full Earth, a time particularly propitious for finishing old business and meeting new people—'

'And fuck your false prophecy, too!' Tian bent, picked up a clod of earth, and threw it at the robot. A pebble buried in the clod clanged off Andy's metal hide. Tia gasped, then began to cry. Andy backed off another step, his shadow trailing out long in Son of a Bitch field. But his hateful, stupid smile remained.

'What about a song? I have learned an amusing one from the Manni far north of town; it is called "In Time of Loss, Make God Your Boss".' From somewhere deep in Andy's guts came the wavering honk of a pitch-pipe, followed by a ripple of piano keys. 'It goes—'

Sweat rolling down his cheeks and sticking his itchy balls to his thighs. The stink-smell of his own foolish obsession. Tia blatting her stupid face at the sky. And this idiotic, bad-news-bearing robot getting ready to sing him some sort of Manni hymn.

'Be quiet, Andy.' He spoke reasonably enough, but through clamped teeth.

'Sai,' the robot agreed, then fell mercifully silent.

Tian went to his bawling sister, put his arm around her, smelled the large (but not entirely unpleasant) smell of her. No obsession there, just the smell of work and obedience. He sighed, then began to stroke her trembling arm.

'Quit it, ye great bawling cunt,' he said. The words might have been ugly but the tone was kind in the extreme, and it was tone she responded to. She began to quiet. Her brother stood with the flare of her hip pushing into him just below his ribcage (she was a full foot taller), and any passing stranger would likely have stopped to look at them, amazed by the similarity of face and the great dissimilarity of size. The resemblance, at least, was honestly come by: they were twins.

He soothed his sister with a mixture of endearments and profanities – in the years since she had come back roont from the east, the two modes of expression were much the same to Tian Jaffords – and at last she ceased her weeping. And when a rustie flew across the sky, doing loops and giving out the usual series of ugly blats, she pointed and laughed.

A feeling was rising in Tian, one so foreign to his nature that he didn't even recognize it. 'Isn't right,' he said. 'Nossir. By the Man Jesus and all the gods that be, it isn't.' He looked to the east, where the hills rolled away into a rising membranous darkness that might have been clouds but wasn't. It was the edge of Thunderclap.

'Isn't right what they do to us.'

'Sure you wouldn't like to hear your horoscope, sai? I see bright coins and a beautiful dark lady.'

'The dark ladies will have to do without me,' Tian said, and began pulling the harness off his sister's broad shoulders. 'I'm married, as I'm sure ye very well know.'

'Many a married man has had his jilly,' Andy observed. To Tian he sounded almost smug.

'Not those who love their wives.' Tian shouldered the harness (he'd made it himself, there being a marked shortage of tack for human beings in most livery barns) and turned toward the home place. 'And not farmers, in any case. Show me a farmer who can afford a jilly and I'll kiss your shiny ass. Garn, Tia. Lift em up and put em down.'

'Home place?' she asked.

'That's right.'

'Lunch at home place?' She looked at him in a muddled, hopeful way. 'Taters?' A pause. '*Gravy?*'

'Shore,' Tian said. 'Why the hell not?'

Tia let out a whoop and began running toward the house. There was something almost awe-inspiring about her when she ran. As their father had once observed, not long before the fall that carried him off, 'Bright or dim, that's a lot of meat in motion.'

Tian walked slowly after her, head down, watching for the holes which his sister seemed to avoid without even looking, as if some deep part of her had mapped the location of each one. That strange new feeling kept growing and growing. He knew about anger — any farmer who'd ever lost cows to the milk-sick or watched a summer hailstorm beat his corn flat knew plenty about that — but this was deeper. This was rage, and it was a new thing. He walked slowly, head down, fists clenched. He wasn't aware of Andy following along behind him until the robot said, 'There's other news, sai. Northwest of town, along the Path of the Beam, strangers from Out-World—'

'Bugger the Beam, bugger the strangers, and bugger your good self,' Tian said. 'Let me be, Andy.'

Andy stood where he was for a moment, surrounded by the rocks and weeds and useless knobs of Son of a Bitch, that thankless tract of Jaffords land. Relays inside him clicked. His eyes flashed. And he decided to go and talk to the Old Fella. The Old Fella never told him to bugger his good self. The Old Fella was always willing to hear his horoscope.

And he was *always* interested in strangers.

Andy started toward town and Our Lady of Serenity.

2

Zalia Jaffords didn't see her husband and sister-in-law come back from Son of a Bitch; didn't hear Tia plunging her head repeatedly into the rain-barrel outside the barn and then blowing moisture off her lips like a horse. Zalia was on the south side of the house, hanging out wash and keeping an eye on the children. She wasn't aware that Tian was back until she saw him looking out the kitchen window at her. She was surprised to see him there at all and much more than surprised by the look of him. His face was ashy pale except for two bright blots of color high up on his cheeks and a third glaring in the center of his forehead like a brand.

She dropped the few pins she was still holding back into her clothes basket and started for the house.

'Where goin, Maw?' Heddon called, and 'Where goin, Maw-Maw?' Hedda echoed.

'Never mind,' she said. 'Just keep a eye on your ka-babbies.'

'*Why*-yyy?' Hedda whined. She had that whine down to a science. One of these days she would draw it out a little too long and her mother would clout her right down dead.

'Because ye're the oldest,' she said.

'But—'

'Shut your mouth, Hedda Jaffords.'

'We'll watch em, Ma,' Heddon said, Always agreeable was her Heddon; probably not quite so bright as his sister, but bright wasn't everything. Far from it. 'Want us to finish hanging the wash?'

'*Hed*-donnnn . . .' From his sister. That irritating whine again. But Zalia had no time for them. She just took one glance at the others: Lyman and Lia, who were five, and Aaron, who was two. Aaron sat naked in the dirt, happily chunking two stones together. He was the rare singleton, and how the women of the village envied her on account of him! Because Aaron would always be safe. The others, however, Heddon and Hedda . . . Lyman and Lia . . .

She suddenly understood what it might mean, him back at the house in the middle of the day like this. She prayed to the gods it wasn't so, but when she came into the kitchen and saw the way he was looking out at the kiddies, she became almost sure it was.

'Tell me it isn't the Wolves,' she said in a dry and frantic voice. 'Say it ain't.'

''Tis,' Tian replied. 'Thirty days, Andy says — moon to moon. And on that Andy's never—'

Before he could go on, Zalia Jaffords clapped her hands to her temples and shrieked. In the side yard, Hedda jumped up. In another moment she would have been running for the house, but Heddon held her back.

'They won't take any as young as Lyman and Lia, will they?' she asked him. 'Hedda or Heddon, maybe, but surely not my little ones? Why, they won't see their sixth for another half-year!'

'The Wolves have taken em as young as three, and you know it,' Tian said. His hands opened and closed, opened and closed. That feeling inside him continued to grow – the feeling that was deeper than mere anger.

She looked at him, tears spilling down her face.

'Mayhap it's time to say no.' Tian spoke in a voice he hardly recognized as his own.

'How can we?' she whispered. 'How in the name of the gods can we?'

'Dunno,' he said. 'But come here, woman, I beg ya.'

She came, throwing one last glance over her shoulder at the five children in the back yard – as if to make sure they were still all there, that no Wolves had taken them yet – and then crossed the living room. Gran-pere sat in his corner chair by the dead fire, head bent over, dozing and drizzling from his folded, toothless mouth.

From this room the barn was visible. Tian drew his wife to the window and pointed. 'There,' he said. 'Do you mark em, woman? Do you see em very well?'

Of course she did. Tian's sister, six and a half feet tall, now standing with the straps of her overalls lowered and her big breasts sparkling with water as she splashed them from the rain barrel. Standing in the barn doorway was Zalman, Zalia's very own brother. Almost seven feet tall was he, big as Lord Perth, tall as Andy, and as empty of face as the girl. A strapping young man watching a strapping young woman with her breasts out on show like that might well have been sporting a bulge in his pants, but there was none in Zally's. Nor ever would be. He was roont.

She turned back to Tian. They looked at each other, a man and a woman not roont, but only because of dumb luck. So far as either of them knew, it could just as easily have been Zal and Tia standing in here and watching Tian and Zalia out by the barn, grown large of body and empty of head.

'Of course I see,' she told him. 'Does thee think I'm blind?'

'Don't it sometimes make you wish you was?' he asked. 'To see em so?'

Zalia made no reply.

'Not right, woman. Not right. Never has been.'

'But since time out of mind—'

'Bugger time out of mind, too!' Tian cried. 'They's children! *Our* children!'

'Would you have the Wolves burn the Calla to the ground, then? Leave us all with our throats cut and our eyes fried in our heads? For it's happened before. You know it has.'

He knew, all right. But who would put matters right, if not the men of Calla Bryn Sturgis? Certainly there were no authorities, not so much as a sheriff, either high or low, in these parts. They were on their own. Even long ago, when the Inner Baronies had glowed with light and order, they would have seen precious little sign of that bright-life out here. These were the borderlands, and life here had always been strange. Then the Wolves had begun coming and life had grown far stranger. How long ago had it begun? How many generations? Tian didn't know, but he thought 'time out of mind' was too long. The Wolves had been raiding into the borderland villages when Gran-pere was young, certainly – Gran-pere's own twin had been snatched as the two of them sat in the dust, playing at jacks. 'Dey tuk im cos he closer to de rud,' Gran-pere had told them (many times). 'If Ah come out of dee house firs' dat day, Ah be closer to de rud an dey take *me*, God is good!' Then he would kiss the wooden crucie the Old Fella had given him, hold it skyward, and cackle.

Yet Gran-pere's own Gran-pere had told him that in *his* day – which would have been five or perhaps even six generations back, if Tian's calculations were right – there had been no Wolves sweeping out of Thunderclap on their gray horses. Once Tian had asked the old man, *And did all but a few of the babbies come in twos back then? Did any of the old folks ever say?* Granpere had considered this long, then had shaken his head. No, he couldn't remember what the old-timers had ever said about that, one way or the other.

Zalia was looking at him anxiously. 'Ye're in no mood to think of such things, I wot, after spending your morning in that rocky patch.'

'My frame of mind won't change when they come or who they'll take,' Tian said.

'Ye'll not do something foolish, T, will you? Something foolish and all on your own?'

'No,' he said.

No hesitation. *He's already begun to lay plans*, she thought, and allowed herself a thin gleam of hope. Surely there was nothing Tian could do against the Wolves – nothing *any* of them could do – but he was far from stupid. In a farming village where most men could think no further than planting the next row (or planting their stiffies on Saturday night), Tian was something of an anomaly. He could write his name; he could write words that said I LOVE YOU ZALLIE (and had won her by so doing, even though she couldn't read them there in the dirt); he could add the numbers and also call them back from big to small, which he said was even more difficult. Was it possible . . .?

Part of her didn't want to complete that thought. And yet, when she turned her mother's heart and mind to Hedda and Heddon, Lia and Lyman, part of her wanted to hope. 'What, then?'

'I'm going to call a Town Gathering. I'll send the feather.'

'Will they come?'

'When they hear this news, every man in the Calla will turn up. We'll talk it over. Mayhap they'll want to fight this time. Mayhap they'll want to fight for their babbies.'

From behind them, a cracked old voice said, 'Ye foolish killin.'

Tian and Zalia turned, hand in hand, to look at the old man. *Killin* was a harsh word, but Tian judged the old man was looking at them — at *him* — kindly enough.

'Why d'ye say so, Gran-pere?' he asked.

'Men'd go forrad from such a meetin as ye plan on and burn down half the countryside, were dey in drink,' the old man said. 'Men sober—' He shook his head. 'Ye'll never move such.'

'I think this time you might be wrong, Grand-pere,' Tian said, and Zalia felt cold terror squeeze her heart. And yet buried in it, warm, was that hope.

3

There would have been less grumbling if he'd given them at least one night's notice, but Tian wouldn't do that. They didn't have the luxury of even a single fallow night. And when he sent Heddon and Hedda with the feather, they *did* come. He'd known they would.

The Calla's Gathering Hall stood at the end of the village high street, beyond Took's general store and cater-corner from the town Pavilion, which was now dusty and dark with the end of summer. Soon enough the ladies of the town would begin decorating it for Reap, but they'd never made a lot of Reaping Night in the Calla. The children always enjoyed seeing the stuffy-guys thrown on the fire, of course, and the bolder fellows would steal their share of kisses as the night itself approached, but that was about it. Your fripperies and festivals might do for Mid-World and In-World, but this was neither. Out here they had more serious things to worry about than Reaping Day Fairs.

Things like the Wolves.

Some of the men — from the well-to-do farms to the west and the three ranches to the south — came on horses. Eisenhart of the Rocking B even brought his rifle and wore crisscrossed ammunition bandoliers. (Tian Jaffords doubted if the bullets were any good, or that the ancient rifle would fire even if some of them were.) A delegation of the Manni-folk came crammed into a bucka drawn by a pair of mutie geldings — one with three eyes, the other with a pylon of raw pink flesh poking out of its back. Most of the Calla men came on donks and burros, dressed in their white pants and long, colorful shirts. They knocked their dusty sombreros back on the tugstrings with callused thumbs as they stepped into the Gathering Hall, looking uneasily at each other. The benches were of plain pine. With no womenfolk and none of the roont ones, the men filled fewer than thirty of the ninety benches. There was some talk, but no laughter at all.

Tian stood out front with the feather now in his hands, watching the sun as it sank toward the horizon, its gold steadily deepening to a color that was like infected blood. When it touched the land, he took one more look up the high street. It was empty except for three or four roont fellas sitting on the steps of Took's. All of them huge and good for nothing more than yanking rocks out of the ground. He saw no more men, no more approaching donkeys. He took a deep breath, let it out, then drew in another and looked up at the deepening sky.

'Man Jesus, I don't believe in you,' he said. 'But if you're there, help me now. Tell God thankee.'

Then he went inside and closed the Gathering Hall doors a little harder than was strictly necessary. The talk stopped. A hundred and forty men, most of them farmers, watched him walk to the front of the hall, the wide legs of his white pants swishing, his shor'boots clacking on the hardwood floor. He had expected to be terrified by this point, perhaps even to find himself speechless. He was a farmer, not a stage performer or a politician. Then he thought of his children, and when he looked up at the men, he found he had no trouble meeting their eyes. The feather in his hands did not tremble. When he spoke, his words followed each other easily, naturally, and coherently. They might not do as he hoped they would — Gran-pere could be right about that — but they looked willing enough to listen.

'You all know who I am,' he said as he stood there with his hands clasped around the reddish feather's ancient stalk. 'Tian Jaffords, son of Luke, husband of Zalia Hoonik that was. She and I have five, two pairs and a singleton.'

Low murmurs at that, most probably having to do with how lucky Tian and Zalia were to have their Aaron. Tian waited for the voices to die away.

'I've lived in the Calla all my life. I've shared your khef and you have shared mine. Now hear what I say, I beg.'

'We say thankee-sai,' they murmured. It was little more than a stock response, yet Tian was encouraged.

'The Wolves are coming,' he said. 'I have this news from Andy. Thirty days from moon to moon and then they're here.'

More low murmurs. Tian heard dismay and outrage, but no surprise. When it came to spreading news, Andy was extremely efficient.

'Even those of us who can read and write a little have almost no paper to write on,' Tian said, 'so I cannot tell ye with any real certainty when last they came. There are no records, ye ken, just one mouth to another. I know I was well-breeched, so it's longer than twenty years—'

'It's twenty-four,' said a voice in the back of the room.

'Nay, twenty-three,' said a voice closer to the front. Reuben Caverra stood up. He was a plump man with a round, cheerful face. The cheer was gone from it now, however, and it showed only distress. 'They took Ruth, my sissa, hear me, I beg.'

A murmur – really no more than a vocalized sigh of agreement – came from the men sitting crammed together on the benches. They could have spread out, but had chosen shoulder-to-shoulder instead. Sometimes there was comfort in discomfort, Tian reckoned.

Reuben said, 'We were playing under the big pine in the front yard when they came. I made a mark on that tree each year after. Even after they brung her back, I went on with em. It's twenty-three marks and twenty-three years.' With that he sat down.

'Twenty-three or twenty-four, makes no difference,' Tian said. 'Those who were kiddies when the Wolves came last time have grown up since and had kiddies of their own. There's a fine crop here for those bastards. A fine crop of children.' He paused, giving them a chance to think of the next idea for themselves before speaking it aloud. '*If* we let it happen,' he said at last. 'If we let the Wolves take our children into Thunderclap and then send them back to us roont.'

STEPHEN KING

'What the hell else can we do?' cried a man sitting on one of the middle benches. 'They's not human!' At this there was a general (and miserable) mumble of agreement.

One of the Manni stood up, pulling his dark-blue cloak tight against his bony shoulders. He looked around at the others with baleful eyes. They weren't mad, those eyes, but to Tian they looked a long league from reasonable. 'Hear me, I beg,' he said.

'We say thankee-sai.' Respectful but reserved. To see a Manni in town was a rare thing, and here were eight, all in a bunch. Tian was delighted they had come. If anything would underline the deadly seriousness of this business, the appearance of the Manni would do it.

The Gathering Hall door opened and one more man slipped inside. He wore a long black coat. There was a scar on his forehead. None of the men, including Tian, noticed. They were watching the Manni.

'Hear what the Book of Manni says: When the Angel of Death passed over Ayjip, he killed the firstborn in every house where the blood of a sacrificial lamb hadn't been daubed on the doorposts. So says the Book.'

'Praise the Book,' said the rest of the Manni.

'Perhaps we should do likewise,' the Manni spokesman went on. His voice was calm, but a pulse beat wildly in his forehead. 'Perhaps we should turn these next thirty days into a festival of joy for the wee ones, and then put them to sleep, and let their blood out upon the earth. Let the Wolves take their corpses into the east, should they desire.'

'You're insane,' Benito Cash said, indignant and at the same time almost laughing. 'You and all your kind. We ain't gonna kill our babbies!'

'Would the ones that come back not be better off dead?' the Manni responded. 'Great useless hulks! Scooped-out shells!'

'Aye, and what about their brothers and sisters?' asked Vaughn Eisenhart. 'For the Wolves only take one out of every two, as ye very well know.'

A second Manni rose, this one with a silky-white beard flowing down over his breast. The first one sat down. The old man, Henchick, looked around at the others, then at Tian. 'You hold the feather, young fella — may I speak?'

Tian nodded for him to go ahead. This wasn't a bad start at all. Let them fully explore the box they were in, explore it all the way to the corners. He was confident they'd see there were only two alternatives, in the end: let the Wolves take one of every pair under the age of puberty, as they always had, or stand and fight. But to see that, they needed to understand that all other ways out were dead ends.

The old man spoke patiently. Sorrowfully, even. "Tis a terrible idea, aye. But think 'ee this, sais: if the Wolves were to come and find us childless, they might leave us alone ever after."

'Aye, so they might,' one of the smallhold farmers rumbled — his name was Jorge Estrada. 'And so they might not. Manni-sai, would you really kill a whole town's children for what *might* be?'

A strong rumble of agreement ran through the crowd. Another small-holder, Garrett Strong, rose to his feet. His pug-dog's face was truculent. His thumbs were hung in his belt. 'Better we all kill ourselves,' he said. 'Babbies and grown-ups alike.'

The Manni didn't look outraged at this. Nor did any of the other blue-cloaks around him. 'It's an option,' the old man said. 'We would speak of it if others would.' He sat down.

'Not me,' Garrett Strong said. 'It'd be like cuttin off your damn head to save shaving, hear me, I beg.'

There was laughter and a few cries of *Hear you very well*. Garrett sat back down, looking a little less tense, and put his head together with Vaughn Eisenhart. One of the other ranchers, Diego Adams, was listening in, his black eyes intent.

Another smallholder rose — Bucky Javier. He had bright little blue eyes in a small head that seemed to slope back from his goatee'd chin. 'What if we left for awhile?' he asked. 'What if we took our children and went back west? All the way to the west branch of the Big River, mayhap?'

There was a moment of considering silence at this bold idea. The west branch of the Whye was almost all the way back to Mid-World . . . where, according to Andy, a great palace of green glass had lately appeared and even more lately disappeared again. Tian was about to respond himself when Eben Took, the storekeeper, did it for him. Tian was relieved. He hoped to be silent as long as possible. When they were talked out, he'd tell them what was left.

'Are ye mad?' Eben asked. 'Wolves'd come in, see us gone, and burn all to the ground — farms and ranches, crops and stores, root and branch. What would we come back to?'

'And what if they came after *us*?' Jorge Estrada chimed in. 'Do'ee think we'd be hard to follow, for such as the Wolves? They'd burn us out as Took says, ride our backtrail, and take the kiddies anyway!'

Louder agreement. The stomp of shor'boots on the plain pine floor-boards. And a few cries of *Hear him, hear him!*

'Besides,' Neil Faraday said, standing and holding his vast and filthy sombrero in front of him, 'they never steal *all* our children.' He spoke in a frightened let's-be-reasonable tone that set Tian's teeth on edge. It was this counsel he feared above all others. Its deadly-false call to reason.

One of the Manni, this one younger and beardless, uttered a sharp and contemptuous laugh. 'Ah, one saved out of every two! And that make it all right, does it? God bless thee!' He might have said more, but Henchick clamped a gnarled hand on the young man's arm. The young one said no more, but he didn't lower his head submissively, either. His eyes were hot, his lips a thin white line.

'I don't mean it's right,' Neil said. He had begun to spin his sombrero in a way that made Tian feel a little dizzy. 'But we have to face the realities, don't we? Aye. And they *don't* take em all. Why, my daughter, Georgina, she's just as apt and canny—'

'Yar, and yer son George is a great empty-headed galoot,' Ben Slightman said. Slightman was Eisenhart's foreman, and he did not suffer fools lightly. He took off his spectacles, wiped them with a bandanna, and set them back on his face. 'I seen him settin on the steps in front of Tooky's when I rode downstreet. Seen him very well. Him and some others equally empty-brained.'

'But—'

'I know,' Slightman said. 'It's a hard decision. Some empty-brained's maybe better than all dead.' He paused. 'Or all taken instead of just half.'

Cries of *Hear him* and *Say thankee* as Ben Slightman sat down.

'They always leave us enough to go on with, don't they?' asked a small-hold farmer whose place was just west of Tian's, near the edge of the Calla. His name was Louis Haycox, and he spoke in a musing, bitter tone of voice. Below his mustache, his lips curved in a smile that didn't have much humor in it. 'We won't kill our children,' he said, looking at the Manni. 'All God's grace to ye, gentlemen, but I don't believe even *you* could do so, came it right down to the killin-floor. Or not all of ye. We can't pull up bag and baggage and go west – or in any other direction – because we leave our farms behind. They'd burn us out, all right, and come after the children just the same. They need em, gods know why.

'It always comes back to the same thing: we're farmers, most of us. Strong when our hands are in the soil, weak when they ain't. I got two kiddies of my own, four years old, and I love em both well. Should hate to lose either. But I'd give one to keep the other. And my farm.' Murmurs of agreement met this. 'What other choice do we have? I say this: it would be the world's worst mistake to anger the Wolves. Unless, of course, we can stand against them. If 'twere possible, I'd stand. But I just don't see how it is.'

Tian felt his heart shrivel with each of Haycox's words. How much of his thunder had the man stolen? Gods and the Man Jesus!

Wayne Overholser got to his feet. He was Calla Bryn Sturgis's most successful farmer, and had a vast sloping belly to prove it. 'Hear me, I beg.'

'We say thankee-sai,' they murmured.

'Tell you what we're going to do,' he said, looking around. 'What we *always* done, that's what. Do any of you want to talk about standing against the Wolves? Are any of you that mad? With what? Spears and rocks, a few bows and bahs? Maybe four rusty old sof' calibers like that?' He jerked a thumb toward Eisenhart's rifle.

'Don't be making fun of my shooting-iron, son,' Eisenhart said, but he was smiling ruefully.

'They'll come and they'll take the children,' Overholser said, looking around. '*Some* of em. Then they'll leave us alone again for a generation or even longer. So it is, so it has been, and I say leave it alone.'

Disapproving rumbles rose at this, but Overholser waited them out.

'Twenty-three years or twenty-four, it don't matter,' he said when they were quiet again. 'Either way it's a long time. A long time of *peace*. Could be you've forgotten a few things, folks. One is that children are like any other crop. God always sends more. I know that sounds hard. But it's how we've lived and how we have to go on.'

Tian didn't wait for any of the stock responses. If they went any further down this road, any chance he might have to turn them would be lost. He raised the opopanax feather and said, 'Hear what I say! Would ye hear, I beg!'

'Thankee-sai,' they responded. Overholser was looking at Tian distrustfully.

And you're right to look at me so, the farmer thought. *For I've had enough of such cowardly common sense, so I have.*

'Wayne Overholser is a smart man and a successful man,' Tian said, 'and I hate to speak against his position for those reasons. And for another, as well: he's old enough to be my Da'.'

''Ware he *ain't* your Da',' Garrett Strong's only farmhand – Rossiter, his name was — called out, and there was general laughter. Even Overholser smiled at this jest.

'Son, if ye truly hate to speak agin me, don't ye do it,' Overholser said. He continued to smile, but only with his mouth.

'I must, though,' Tian said. He began to walk slowly back and forth in front of the benches. In his hands, the rusty-red plume of the opopanax feather swayed. Tian raised his voice slightly so they'd understand he was no longer speaking just to the big farmer.

'I must *because* sai Overholser is old enough to be my Da'. *His* children are grown, do ye kennit, and so far as I know there were only two to begin with, one girl and one boy.' He paused, then shot the killer. 'Born two years apart.' Both singletons, in other words. Both safe from the Wolves, although he didn't need to say it right out loud. The crowd murmured.

Overholser flushed a bright and dangerous red. 'That's a rotten goddamned thing to say! My get's got nothing to do with this whether single or double! Give me that feather, Jaffords. I got a few more things to say.'

But the boots began to thump down on the boards, slowly at first, then picking up speed until they rattled like hail. Overholser looked around angrily, now so red he was nearly purple.

'I'd speak!' he shouted. 'Would'ee not hear me, I beg?'

Cries of *No, no* and *Not now* and *Jaffords has the feather* and *Sit and listen* came in response. Tian had an idea sai Overholser was learning — and remarkably late in the game — that there was often a deep-running resentment of a village's richest and most successful. Those less fortunate or less canny (most of the time they amounted to the same) might tug their hats off when the rich folk passed in their buckas or lowcoaches, they might send a slaughtered pig or cow as a thank-you when the rich folk loaned their hired hands to help with a house- or barn-raising, the well-to-do might be cheered at Year End Gathering for helping to buy the piano that now sat in the Pavilion's *musica*. Yet the men of the Calla tromped their shor'boots to drown Overholser out with a certain savage satisfaction.

Overholser, unused to being balked in such a way — flabbergasted, in fact — tried one more time. '*I'd have the feather, do ye, I beg!*'

'No,' Tian said. 'Later if it does ya, but not now.'

There were actual *cheers* at this, mostly from the smallest of the small-hold farmers and some of their hands. The Manni did not join in. They were now drawn so tightly together that they looked like a dark blue inkstain in the middle of the hall. They were clearly bewildered by this turn. Vaughn Eisenhart and Diego Adams, meanwhile, moved to flank Overholser and speak low to him.

You've got a chance, Tian thought. *Better make the most of it.*

He raised the feather and they quieted.

'Everyone will have a chance to speak,' he said. 'As for me, I say this: we can't go on this way, simply bowing our heads and standing quiet when the Wolves come and take our children. They—'

'They always return them,' a hand named Farren Posella said timidly.

'*They return husks!*' Tian cried, and there were a few cries of *Hear him*. Not enough, however, Tian judged. Not enough by far. Not yet.

He lowered his voice again. He did not want to harangue them. Overholser had tried that and gotten nowhere, a thousand acres or not.

'They return husks. And what of us? What is this doing to us? Some might say nothing, that the Wolves have always been a part of our life in Calla Bryn Sturgis, like the occasional cyclone or earthshake. Yet that is not true. They've been coming for six generations, at most. But the Calla's been here a thousand years and more.'

The old Manni with the bony shoulders and baleful eyes half-rose. 'He says true, *folken*. There were farmers here – and Manni-folk among em – when the darkness in Thunderclap hadn't yet come, let alone the Wolves.'

They received this with looks of wonder. Their awe seemed to satisfy the old man, who nodded and sat back down.

'So in time's greater course, the Wolves are almost a new thing,' Tian said. 'Six times have they come over mayhap a hundred and twenty or a hundred and forty years. Who can say? For as ye ken, time has softened, somehow.'

A low rumble. A few nods.

'In any case, once a generation,' Tian went on. He was aware that a hostile contingent was coalescing around Overholser, Eisenhart, and Adams. Ben Slightman might or might not be with them – probably was. These men he would not move even if he were gifted with the tongue of an angel. Well, he could do without them, maybe. If he caught the rest. 'Once a generation they come, and how many children do they take? Three dozen? Four?

'Sai Overholser may not have babbies this time, but *I* do – not one set of twins but two. Heddon and Hedda, Lyman and Lia. I love all four, but in a month of days, two of them will be taken away. And when those two come back, they'll be roont. Whatever spark there is that makes a complete human being, it'll be out forever.'

Hear him, hear him swept through the room like a sigh.

'How many of you have twins with no hair except that which grows on their heads?' Tian demanded. 'Raise yer hands!'

Six men raised their hands. Then eight. A dozen. Every time Tian began to think they were done, another reluctant hand went up. In the end, he counted twenty-two hands, and of course not everyone who had children was here. He could see that Overholser was dismayed by such a large count. Diego Adams had his hand raised, and Tian was pleased to see he'd moved away a little bit from Overholser, Eisenhart, and Slightman. Three of the Manni had their hands up. Jorge Estrada. Louis Haycox. Many others he knew, which was not surprising, really; he knew almost every one of these men. Probably all save for a few wandering fellows working smallhold farms for short wages and hot dinners.

'Each time they come and take our children, they take a little more of our hearts and our souls,' Tian said.

'Oh come on now, son,' Eisenhart said. 'That's laying it on a bit th—'

'Shut up, Rancher,' a voice said. It belonged to the man who had come late, he with the scar on his forehead. It was shocking in its anger and contempt. 'He's got the feather. Let him speak out to the end.'

Eisenhart whirled around to mark who had spoken to him so. He saw, and made no reply. Nor was Tian surprised.

'Thankee, Pere,' Tian said evenly. 'I've almost come to the end. I keep thinking of trees. You can strip the leaves of a strong tree and it will live. Cut its bark with many names and it will grow its skin over them again. You can even take from the heartwood and it will live. But if you take of the heartwood again and again and again, there will come a time when even the strongest tree must die. I've seen it happen on my farm, and it's an ugly thing. They die from the inside out. You can see it in the leaves as they turn yellow from the trunk to the tips of the branches. And that's what the Wolves are doing to this little village of ours. What they're doing to our Calla.'

'Hear him!' cried Freddy Rosario from the next farm over. 'Hear him very well!' Freddy had twins of his own, although they were still on the tit and so probably safe.

Tian went on, 'You say that if we stand and fight, they'll kill us all and burn the Calla from east-border to west.'

'*Yes*,' Overholser said. 'So I do say. Nor am I the only one.' From all around him came rumbles of agreement.

'Yet each time we simply stand by with our heads lowered and our hands open while the Wolves take what's dearer to us than any crop or house or barn, they scoop a little more of the heart's wood from the tree that is this village!' Tian spoke strongly, now standing still with the feather raised high in one hand. 'If we don't stand and fight soon, we'll be dead anyway! This is what I say, Tian Jaffords, son of Luke! If we don't stand and fight soon, we'll be roont ourselves!'

Loud cries of *Hear him!* Exuberant stomping of shor'boots. Even some applause.

George Telford, another rancher, whispered briefly to Eisenhart and Overholser. They listened, then nodded. Telford rose. He was silver-haired, tanned, and handsome in the weatherbeaten way women seemed to like.

'Had your say, son?' he asked kindly, as one might ask a child if he had played enough for one afternoon and was ready for his nap.

'Yar, reckon,' Tian said. He suddenly felt dispirited. Telford wasn't a rancher on a scale with Vaughn Eisenhart, but he had a silver tongue. Tian had an idea he was going to lose this, after all.

'May I have the feather, then?'

Tian thought of holding onto it, but what good would it do? He'd said his best. Had tried. Perhaps he and Zalia should pack up the kids and go out west themselves, back toward the Mids. Moon to moon before the Wolves came, according to Andy. A person could get a hell of a head start on trouble in thirty days.

He passed the feather.

'We all appreciate young sai Jaffords's passion, and certainly no one doubts his courage,' George Telford said. He spoke with the feather held against the left side of his chest, over his heart. His eyes roved the audience, seeming to make eye contact — *friendly* eye contact — with each man. 'But we have to think of the kiddies who'd be left as well as those who'd be taken, don't we? In fact, we have to protect *all* the kiddies, whether they be twins, triplets, or singletons like sai Jaffords's Aaron.'

Telford turned to Tian now.

'What will you tell your children as the Wolves shoot their mother and mayhap set their Gran-pere on fire with one of their light-sticks? What can you say to make the sound of those shrieks all right? To sweeten the smell of burning skin and burning crops? That it's *souls* we're a-saving? Or the heart's wood of some make-believe *tree*?'

He paused, giving Tian a chance to reply, but Tian had no reply to make. He'd almost had them . . . but he'd left Telford out of his reckoning. Smooth-voiced sonofabitch Telford, who was also far past the age when he needed to be concerned about the Wolves calling into his dooryard on their great gray horses.

Telford nodded, as if Tian's silence was no more than he expected, and turned back to the benches. 'When the Wolves come,' he said, 'they'll come with fire-hurling weapons – the light-sticks, ye ken – and guns, and flying metal things. I misremember the name of those—'

'The buzz-balls,' someone called.

'The sneetches,' called someone else.

'Stealthies!' called a third.

Telford was nodding and smiling gently. A teacher with good pupils. 'Whatever they are, they fly through the air, seeking their targets, and when they lock on, they put forth whirling blades as sharp as razors. They can strip a man from top to toe in five seconds, leaving nothing around him but a circle of blood and hair. Do not doubt me, *for I have seen it happen.*'

'*Hear him, hear him well!*' the men on the benches shouted. Their eyes had grown huge and frightened.

'The Wolves themselves are terrible fearsome,' Telford went on, moving smoothly from one campfire story to the next. 'They look sommat like men, and yet they are *not* men but something bigger and far more awful. And those they serve in far Thunderclap are more terrible by far. Vampires, I've heard. Men with the heads of birds and animals, mayhap. Broken-helm undead ronin. Warriors of the Scarlet Eye.'

The men muttered. Even Tian felt a cold scamper of rats' paws up his back at the mention of the Eye.

'The Wolves I've seen; the rest I've been told,' Telford went on. 'And while I don't believe it all, I believe much. But never mind Thunderclap and what may den there. Let's stick to the Wolves. The Wolves are our problem, and problem enough. Especially when they come armed to the teeth!' He shook his head, smiling grimly. 'What would we do? Perhaps we could knock them from their greathorses with hoes, sai Jaffords? D'ee think?'

Derisive laughter greeted this.

'We have no weapons that can stand against them,' Telford said. He was now dry and businesslike, a man stating the bottom line. 'Even if we had such, we're farmers and ranchers and stockmen, not fighters. We—'

'Stop that yellow talk, Telford. You ought to be ashamed of yourself.'

Shocked gasps greeted this chilly pronouncement. There were cracking backs and creaking necks as men turned to see who had spoken. Slowly, then, as if to give them exactly what they wanted, the white-haired late-comer in the long black coat and turned-around collar rose from the bench at the very back of the room. The scar on his forehead — it was in the shape of a cross — was bright in the light of the kerosene lamps.

It was the Old Fella.

Telford recovered himself with relative speed, but when he spoke, Tian thought he still looked shocked. 'Beg pardon, Pere Callahan, but I have the feather—'

'To hell with your heathen feather and to hell with your cowardly counsel,' Pere Callahan said. He walked down the center aisle, stepping with the grim gait of arthritis. He wasn't as old as the Manni elder, nor *nearly* so old as Tian's Gran-pere (who claimed to be the oldest person not only here but in Calla Lockwood to the south), and yet he seemed somehow older than both. Older than the ages. Some of this no doubt had to do with the haunted eyes that looked out at the world from below the scar on his forehead (Zalia claimed it had been self-inflicted). More had to do with the *sound* of him. Although he had been here enough years to build his strange Man Jesus church and convert half the Calla to his way of spiritual thinking, not even a stranger would have been fooled into believing Pere Callahan was *from* here. His alienness was in his flat and nasal speech and in the often obscure slang he used ('street-jive,' he called it). He had undoubtedly come from one of those other worlds the Manni were always babbling about, although he never spoke of it and Calla Bryn Sturgis was now his home. He had the sort of dry and unquestionable authority that made it difficult to dispute his right to speak, with or without the feather.

Younger than Tian's Gran-pere he might be, but Pere Callahan was still the Old Fella.

4

Now he surveyed the men of Calla Bryn Sturgis, not even glancing at George Telford. The feather sagged in Telford's hand. He sat down on the first bench, still holding it.

Callahan began with one of his slang-terms, but they were farmers and no one needed to ask for an explanation.

'This is chickenshit.'

He surveyed them longer. Most would not return his look. After a moment, even Eisenhart and Adams dropped their eyes. Overholser kept his head up, but under the Old Fella's hard gaze, the rancher looked petulant rather than defiant.

'Chickenshit,' the man in the black coat and turned-around collar repeated, enunciating each syllable. A small gold cross gleamed below the notch in the backwards collar. On his forehead, that other cross – the one Zalia believed he'd carved in his flesh with his own thumbnail in partial penance for some awful sin – glared under the lamps like a tattoo.

'This young man isn't one of my flock, but he's right, and I think you all know it. You know it in your hearts. Even you, Mr Overholser. And you, George Telford.'

'Know no such thing,' Telford said, but his voice was weak and stripped of its former persuasive charm.

'All your lies will cross your eyes, that's what my mother would have told you.' Callahan offered Telford a thin smile Tian wouldn't have wanted pointed in his direction. And then Callahan *did* turn to him. 'I never heard it put better than you put it tonight, boy. Thankee-sai.'

Tian raised a feeble hand and managed an even more feeble smile. He felt like a character in a silly festival play, saved at the last moment by some improbable supernatural intervention.

'I know a bit about cowardice, may it do ya,' Callahan said, turning to the men on the benches. He raised his right hand, misshapen and twisted by some old burn, looked at it fixedly, then dropped it to his side again. 'I have personal experience, you might say. I know how one cowardly decision leads to another . . . and another . . . and another . . . until it's too late to turn around, too late to change. Mr Telford, I assure you the tree of which young Mr Jaffords spoke is not make-believe. The Calla is in dire danger. Your *souls* are in danger.'

'Hail Mary, full of grace,' said someone on the left side of the room, 'the Lord is with thee. Blessed is the fruit of thy womb, J—'

'Bag it,' Callahan snapped. 'Save it for Sunday.' His eyes, blue sparks in their deep hollows, studied them. 'For this night, never mind God and Mary and the Man Jesus. Never mind the light-sticks and the buzz-bugs of the Wolves, either. You must fight. You're the men of the Calla, are you not?

Then *act* like men. Stop behaving like dogs crawling on their bellies to lick the boots of a cruel master.'

Overholser went dark red at that, and began to stand. Diego Adams grabbed his arm and spoke in his ear. For a moment Overholser remained as he was, frozen in a kind of crouch, and then he sat back down. Adams stood up.

'Sounds good, *padrone*,' Adams said in his heavy accent. 'Sounds brave. Yet there are still a few questions, mayhap. Haycox asked one of em. How can ranchers and farmers stand against armed killers?'

'By hiring armed killers of our own,' Callahan replied.

There was a moment of utter, amazed silence. It was almost as if the Old Fella had lapsed into another language. At last Diego Adams said – cautiously, 'I don't understand.'

'Of course you don't,' the Old Fella said. 'So listen and gain wisdom. Rancher Adams and all of you, listen and gain wisdom. Not six days' ride nor' west of us, and bound southeast along the Path of the Beam, come three gunslingers and one 'prentice.' He smiled at their amazement. Then he turned to Slightman. 'The 'prentice isn't much older than your boy Ben, but he's already as quick as a snake and as deadly as a scorpion. The others are quicker and deadlier by far. I have it from Andy, who's seen them. You want hard calibers? They're at hand. I set my watch and warrant on it.'

This time Overholser made it all the way to his feet. His face burned as if with a fever. His great pod of a belly trembled. 'What children's good-night story is this?' he asked. 'If there ever were such men, they passed out of existence with Gilead. And Gilead has been dust in the wind for a thousand years.'

There were no mutterings of support or dispute. No mutterings of any kind. The crowd was still frozen, caught in the reverberation of that one mythic word: *gunslingers*.

'You're wrong,' Callahan said, 'but we don't need to fight over it. We can go and see for ourselves. A small party will do, I think. Jaffords here . . . myself . . . and what about you, Overholser? Want to come?'

'*There ain't no gunslingers!*' Overholser roared.

Behind him, Jorge Estrada stood up. 'Pere Callahan, God's grace on you—'

'—and you, Jorge.'

'—but even if there *were* gunslingers, how could three stand against forty or sixty? And not forty or sixty normal men, but forty or sixty *Wolves*?'

'Hear him, he speaks sense!' Eben Took, the storekeeper, called out.

'And why would they fight for us?' Estrada continued. 'We make it from year to year, but not much more. What could we offer them, beyond a few hot meals? And what man agrees to die for his dinner?'

'*Hear him, hear him!*' Telford, Overholser, and Eisenhart cried in unison. Others stamped rhythmically up and down on the boards.

The Old Fella waited until the stomping had quit, and then said: 'I have books in the Rectory. Half a dozen.'

Although most of them knew this, the thought of books — all that paper — still provoked a general sigh of wonder.

'According to one of them, gunslingers were forbidden to take reward. Supposedly because they descend from the line of Arthur Eld.'

'The Eld! The Eld!' the Manni whispered, and several raised fists into the air with the first and fourth fingers pointed. *Hook em horns*, the Old Fella thought. *Go, Texas.* He managed to stifle a laugh, but not the smile that rose on his lips.

'Are ye speaking of hardcases who wander the land, doing good deeds?' Telford asked in a gently mocking voice. 'Surely you're too old for such tales, Pere.'

'Not hardcases,' Callahan said patiently, '*gunslingers.*'

'How can three men stand against the Wolves, Pere?' Tian heard himself ask.

According to Andy, one of the gunslingers was actually a woman, but Callahan saw no need to muddy the waters further (although an impish part of him wanted to, just the same). 'That's a question for their dinh, Tian. We'll ask him. And they wouldn't just be fighting for their suppers, you know. Not at all.'

'What else, then?' Bucky Javier asked.

Callahan thought they would want the thing that lay beneath the floorboards of his church. And that was good, because that thing had awakened. The Old Fella, who had once run from a town called Jerusalem's Lot in another world, wanted to be rid of it. If he wasn't rid of it soon, it would kill him.

Ka had come to Calla Bryn Sturgis. Ka like a wind.

'In time, Mr Javier,' Callahan said. 'All in good time, sai.'

Meantime, a whisper had begun in the Gathering Hall. It slipped along the benches from mouth to mouth, a breeze of hope and fear.

Gunslingers.

Gunslingers to the west, come out of Mid-World.

And it was true, God help them. Arthur Eld's last deadly children, moving toward Calla Bryn Sturgis along the Path of the Beam. Ka like a wind.

'Time to be men,' Pere Callahan told them. Beneath the scar on his forehead, his eyes burned like lamps. Yet his tone was not without compassion. 'Time to stand up, gentlemen. Time to stand and be true.'

PART ONE
TODASH

CHAPTER I

THE FACE ON
THE WATER

1

Time is a face on the water: this was a proverb from the long-ago, in far-off Mejis. Eddie Dean had never been there.

Except he had, in a way. Roland had carried all four of his companions – Eddie, Susannah, Jake, Oy – to Mejis one night, storying long as they camped on I-70, the Kansas Turnpike in a Kansas that never was. That night he had told them the story of Susan Delgado, his first love. Perhaps his only love. And how he had lost her.

The saying might have been true when Roland had been a boy not much older than Jake Chambers, but Eddie thought it was even truer now, as the world wound down like the mainspring in an ancient watch. Roland had told them that even such basic things as the points of the compass could no longer be trusted in Mid-World; what was dead west today might be *south*west tomorrow, crazy as that might seem. And time had likewise begun to soften. There were days Eddie could have sworn were forty hours long, some of them followed by nights (like the one on which Roland had taken them to Mejis) that seemed even longer. Then there would come an afternoon when it seemed you could almost see darkness bloom as night rushed over the horizon to meet you. Eddie wondered if time had gotten lost.

They had ridden (and riddled) out of a city called Lud on Blaine the Mono. *Blaine is a pain,* Jake had said on several occasions, but he – or it – turned out to be quite a bit more than just a pain; Blaine the Mono had been utterly mad. Eddie killed it with illogic ('Somethin you're just naturally good at, sugar,' Susannah told him), and they had detrained in a Topeka which wasn't quite part of the world from which Eddie, Susannah, and Jake had come. Which was good, really, because this world – one in which the Kansas City pro baseball team was called The Monarchs, Coca-Cola was called Nozz-A-La, and the big Japanese car-maker was Takuro rather than Honda – had been overwhelmed by some sort of plague which had killed damn near everyone. *So stick* that *in your Takuro Spirit and drive it*, Eddie thought.

The passage of time had seemed clear enough to him through all of this. During much of it he'd been scared shitless – he guessed all of them had been, except maybe for Roland – but yes, it had seemed real and clear. He'd not had that feeling of time slipping out of his grasp even when they'd been walking up I-70 with bullets in their ears, looking at the frozen traffic and listening to the warble of what Roland called a thinny.

But after their confrontation in the glass palace with Jake's old friend the Tick-Tock Man and Roland's old friend (Flagg . . . or Marten . . . or – just perhaps – Maerlyn), time had changed.

Not right away, though. We traveled in that damned pink ball . . . saw Roland kill his mother by mistake . . . and when we came back . . .

Yes, that was when it had happened. They had awakened in a clearing perhaps thirty miles from the Green Palace. They had still been able to see it, but all of them had understood that it was in another world. Someone – or some force – had carried them over or through the thinny and back to the Path of the Beam. Whoever or whatever it had been, it had actually been considerate enough to pack them each a lunch, complete with Nozz-A-La sodas and rather more familiar packages of Keebler cookies.

Near them, stuck on the branch of a tree, had been a note from the being Roland had just missed killing in the Palace: 'Renounce the Tower. This is your last warning.' Ridiculous, really. Roland would no more renounce the Tower than he'd kill Jake's pet billy-bumbler and then roast him on a spit for dinner. *None* of them would renounce Roland's Dark Tower. God help them, they were in it all the way to the end.

We got some daylight left, Eddie had said on the day they'd found Flagg's warning note. *You want to use it, or what?*

Yes, Roland of Gilead had replied. *Let's use it.*

And so they had, following the Path of the Beam through endless open fields that were divided from each other by belts of straggly, annoying underbrush. There had been no sign of people. Skies had remained low and cloudy day after day and night after night. Because they followed the Path of the Beam, the clouds directly above them sometimes roiled and broke open, revealing patches of blue, but never for long. One night they opened long enough to disclose a full moon with a face clearly visible on it: the nasty, complicitous squint-and-grin of the Peddler. That made it late summer by Roland's reckoning, but to Eddie it looked like half-past no time at all, the grass mostly listless or outright dead, the trees (what few there were) bare, the bushes scrubby and brown. There was little game, and for the first time in weeks — since leaving the forest ruled by Shardik, the cyborg bear — they sometimes went to bed with their bellies not quite full.

Yet none of that, Eddie thought, was quite as annoying as the sense of having lost hold of time itself: no hours, no days, no weeks, no *seasons*, for God's sake. The moon might have told Roland it was the end of summer, but the world around them looked like the first week of November, dozing sleepily toward winter.

Time, Eddie had decided during this period, was in large part created by external events. When a lot of interesting shit was happening, time seemed to go by fast. If you got stuck with nothing but the usual boring shit, it slowed down. And when *everything* stopped happening, time apparently quit altogether. Just packed up and went to Coney Island. Weird but true.

Had everything stopped happening? Eddie considered (and with nothing to do but push Susannah's wheelchair through one boring field after another, there was plenty of time for consideration). The only peculiarity he could think of since returning from the Wizard's Glass was what Jake called the Mystery Number, and that probably meant nothing. They'd needed to solve a mathematical riddle in the Cradle of Lud in order to gain access to Blaine, and Susannah had suggested the Mystery Number was a holdover from that. Eddie was far from sure she was right, but hey, it was a theory.

And really, what could be so special about the number nineteen? Mystery Number, indeed. After some thought, Susannah had pointed out it was prime, at least, like the numbers that had opened the gate between them and Blaine the Mono. Eddie had added that it was the only one that came between eighteen and twenty every time you counted. Jake had laughed at that and told him to stop being a jerk. Eddie, who had been sitting close to the campfire and carving a rabbit (when it was done, it would join the cat and dog already in his pack), told Jake to quit making fun of his only real talent.

2

They might have been back on the Path of the Beam five or six weeks when they came to a pair of ancient double ruts that had surely once been a road. It didn't follow the Path of the Beam exactly, but Roland swung them onto it anyway. It bore closely enough to the Beam for their purposes, he said. Eddie thought being on a road again might refocus things, help them to shake that maddening becalmed-in-the-Horse-Latitudes feeling, but it didn't. The road carried them up and across a rising series of fields like steps. They finally topped a long north–south ridge. On the far side, their road descended into a dark wood. Almost a fairy-tale wood, Eddie thought as they passed into its shadows. Susannah shot a small deer on their second day in the forest (or maybe it was the third day . . . or the fourth), and the meat was delicious after a steady diet of vegetarian gunslinger burritos, but there were no orcs or trolls in the deep glades, and no elves – Keebler or otherwise. No more deer, either.

'I keep lookin for the candy house,' Eddie said. They'd been winding their way through the great old trees for several days by then. Or maybe it had been as long as a week. All he knew for sure was that they were still reasonably close to the Path of the Beam. They could see it in the sky . . . and they could feel it.

'What candy house is this?' Roland asked. 'Is it another tale? If so, I'd hear.'

Of course he would. The man was a glutton for stories, especially those that led off with a 'Once upon a time when everyone lived in the forest.' But the way he listened was a little odd. A little off. Eddie had mentioned this to Susannah once, and she'd nailed it with a single stroke, as she often did. Susannah had a poet's almost uncanny ability to put feelings into words, freezing them in place.

'That's cause he doesn't listen all big-eyed like a kid at bedtime,' she said. 'That's just how you *want* him to listen, honeybunch.'

'And how *does* he listen?'

'Like an anthropologist,' she had replied promptly. 'Like an anthropologist tryin to figure out some strange culture by their myths and legends.'

She was right. And if Roland's way of listening made Eddie uncomfortable, it was probably because in his heart, Eddie felt that if anyone should be listening like scientists, it should be him and Suze and Jake. Because they came from a far more sophisticated where and when. Didn't they?

Whether they did or didn't, the four had discovered a great number of stories that were common to both worlds. Roland knew a tale called 'Diana's Dream' that was eerily close to 'The Lady or the Tiger,' which all three exiled New Yorkers had read in school. The tale of Lord Perth was similar to the Bible story of David and Goliath. Roland had heard many tales of the Man Jesus, who died on the cross to redeem the sins of the world, and told Eddie, Susannah, and Jake that Jesus had His fair share of followers in Mid-World. There were also songs common to both worlds. 'Careless Love' was one. 'Hey Jude' was another, although in Roland's world, the first line of this song was 'Hey Jude, I see you, lad.'

Eddie passed at least an hour telling Roland the story of Hansel and Gretel, turning the wicked child-eating witch into Rhea of the Cöos almost without thinking of it. When he got to the part about her trying to fatten the children up, he broke off and asked Roland: 'Do you know this one? A version of this one?'

'No,' Roland said, 'but it's a fair tale. Tell it to the end, please.'

Eddie did, finishing with the required *They lived happily ever after*, and the gunslinger nodded. 'No one ever *does* live happily ever after, but we leave the children to find that out for themselves, don't we?'

'Yeah,' Jake said.

Oy was trotting at the boy's heel, looking up at Jake with the usual expression of calm adoration in his gold-ringed eyes. 'Yeah,' the bumbler said, copying the boy's rather glum inflection exactly.

Eddie threw an arm around Jake's shoulders. 'Too bad you're over here instead of back in New York,' he said. 'If you were back in the Apple, Jakey-boy, you'd probably have your own child psychiatrist by now. You'd be working on these issues about your parents. Getting to the heart of your unresolved conflicts. Maybe getting some good drugs, too. Ritalin, stuff like that.'

'On the whole, I'd rather be here,' Jake said, and looked down at Oy.

'Yeah,' Eddie said. 'I don't blame you.'

'Such stories are called "fairy tales,"' Roland mused.

'Yeah,' Eddie replied.

'There were no fairies in this one, though.'

'No,' Eddie agreed. 'That's more like a category name than anything else.

In our world you got your mystery and suspense stories . . . your science fiction stories . . . your Westerns . . . your fairy tales. Get it?'

'Yes,' Roland said. 'Do people in your world always want only one story-flavor at a time? Only one taste in their mouths?'

'I guess that's close enough,' Susannah said.

'Does no one eat stew?' Roland asked.

'Sometimes at supper, I guess,' Eddie said, 'but when it comes to enter-tainment, we *do* tend to stick with one flavor at a time, and don't let any one thing touch another thing on your plate. Although it sounds kinda boring when you put it that way.'

'How many of these fairy tales would you say there are?'

With no hesitation — and certainly no collusion — Eddie, Susannah, and Jake all said the same word at exactly the same time: 'Nineteen!' And a moment later, Oy repeated it in his hoarse voice: 'Nie-teen!'

They looked at each other and laughed, because 'nineteen' had become a kind of jokey catchword among them, replacing 'bumhug,' which Jake and Eddie had pretty much worn out. Yet the laughter had a tinge of uneasi-ness about it, because this business about nineteen had gotten a trifle weird. Eddie had found himself carving it on the side of his most recent wooden animal, like a brand: *Hey there, Pard, welcome to our spread! We call it the Bar-Nineteen.* Both Susannah and Jake had confessed to bringing wood for the evening fire in armloads of nineteen pieces. Neither of them could say why; it just felt right to do it that way, somehow.

Then there was the morning Roland had stopped them at the edge of the wood through which they were now traveling. He had pointed at the sky, where one particularly ancient tree had reared its hoary branches. The shape those branches made against the sky was the number nineteen. Clearly nineteen. They had all seen it, but Roland had seen it first.

Yet Roland, who believed in omens and portents as routinely as Eddie had once believed in lightbulbs and Double-A batteries, had a tendency to dismiss his ka-tet's odd and sudden infatuation with the number. They had grown close, he said, as close as any ka-tet could, and so their thoughts, habits, and little obsessions had a tendency to spread among them all, like a cold. He believed that Jake was facilitating this to a certain degree.

'You've got the touch, Jake,' he said. 'I'm not sure that it's as strong in you as it was in my old friend Alain, but by the gods I believe it may be.'

'I don't know what you're talking about,' Jake had replied, frowning in puzzlement. Eddie did — sort of — and guessed that Jake would know, in time. If time ever began passing in a normal way again, that was.

And on the day Jake brought the muffin-balls, it did.

3

They had stopped for lunch (more uninteresting vegetarian burritos, the deermeat now gone and the Keebler cookies little more than a sweet memory) when Eddie noticed that Jake was gone and asked the gunslinger if he knew where the kid had gotten off to.

'Peeled off about half a wheel back,' Roland said, and pointed along the road with the two remaining fingers of his right hand. 'He's all right. If he wasn't, we'd all feel it.' Roland looked at his burrito, then took an unenthusiastic bite.

Eddie opened his mouth to say something else, but Susannah got there first. 'Here he is now. Hi there, sugar, what you got?'

Jake's arms were full of round things the size of tennis balls. Only these balls would never bounce true; they had little horns sticking up from them. When the kid got closer, Eddie could smell them, and the smell was wonderful — like fresh-baked bread.

'I think these might be good to eat,' Jake said. 'They smell like the fresh sourdough bread my mother and Mrs Shaw — the housekeeper — got at Zabar's.' He looked at Susannah and Eddie, smiling a little. 'Do you guys know Zabar's?'

'*I* sure do,' Susannah said. 'Best of everything, mmm-*hmmm*. And they *do* smell fine. You didn't eat any yet, did you?'

'No way.' He looked questioningly at Roland.

The gunslinger ended the suspense by taking one, plucking off the horns, and biting into what was left. 'Muffin-balls,' he said. 'I haven't seen any in gods know how long. They're wonderful.' His blue eyes were gleaming. 'Don't want to eat the horns; they're not poison but they're sour. We can fry them, if there's a little deerfat left. That way they taste almost like meat.'

'Sounds like a good idea,' Eddie said. 'Knock yourself out. As for me, I think I'll skip the mushroom muff-divers, or whatever they are.'

'They're not mushrooms at all,' Roland said. 'More like a kind of ground berry.'

Susannah took one, nibbled, then helped herself to a bigger bite. 'You don't want to skip these, sweetheart,' she said. 'My Daddy's friend, Pop Mose, would have said "These are *prime*."' She took another of the muffin-balls from Jake and ran a thumb over its silky surface.

'Maybe,' he said, 'but there was this book I read for a report back in high school – I think it was called *We Have Always Lived in the Castle* – where this nutty chick poisoned her whole family with things like that.' He bent toward Jake, raising his eyebrows and stretching the corners of his mouth in what he hoped was a creepy smile. 'Poisoned her whole family and they died in *AG-o-ny!*'

Eddie fell off the log on which he had been sitting and began to roll around on the needles and fallen leaves, making horrible faces and choking sounds. Oy ran around him, yipping Eddie's name in a series of high-pitched barks.

'Quit it,' Roland said. 'Where did you find these, Jake?'

'Back there,' he said. 'In a clearing I spotted from the path. It's *full* of these things. Also, if you guys are hungry for meat . . . I know I am . . . there's all kinds of sign. A lot of the scat's fresh.' His eyes searched Roland's face. 'Very . . . fresh . . . scat.' He spoke slowly, as if to someone who wasn't fluent in the language.

A little smile played at the corners of Roland's mouth. 'Speak quiet but speak plain,' he said. 'What worries you, Jake?'

When Jake replied, his lips barely made the shapes of the words. 'Men watching me while I picked the muffin-balls.' He paused, then added: 'They're watching us now.'

Susannah took one of the muffin-balls, admired it, then dipped her face as if to smell it like a flower. 'Back the way we came? To the right of the road?'

'Yes,' Jake said.

Eddie raised a curled fist to his mouth as if to stifle a cough, and said: 'How many?'

'I think four.'

'Five,' Roland said. 'Possibly as many as six. One's a woman. Another a boy not much older than Jake.'

Jake looked at him, startled. Eddie said, 'How long have they been there?'

'Since yesterday,' Roland said. 'Cut in behind us from almost dead east.'

'And you didn't tell us?' Susannah asked. She spoke rather sternly, not bothering to cover her mouth and obscure the shapes of the words.

Roland looked at her with the barest twinkle in his eye. 'I was curious as to which of you would smell them out first. Actually, I had my money on you, Susannah.'

She gave him a cool look and said nothing. Eddie thought there was more than a little Detta Walker in that look, and was glad not to be on the receiving end.

'What do we do about them?' Jake asked.

'For now, nothing,' the gunslinger said.

Jake clearly didn't like this. 'What if they're like Tick-Tock's ka-tet? Gasher and Hoots and those guys?'

'They're not.'

'How do you know?'

'Because they would have set on us already and they'd be fly-food.'

There seemed no good reply to that, and they took to the road again. It wound through deep shadows, finding its way among trees that were centuries old. Before they had been walking twenty minutes, Eddie heard the sound of their pursuers (or shadowers): snapping twigs, rustling underbrush, once even a low voice. Slewfeet, in Roland's terminology. Eddie was disgusted with himself for remaining unaware of them for so long. He also wondered what yon cullies did for a living. If it was tracking and trapping, they weren't very good at it.

Eddie Dean had become a part of Mid-World in many ways, some so subtle he wasn't consciously aware of them, but he still thought of distances in miles instead of wheels. He guessed they'd come about fifteen from the spot where Jake rejoined them with his muffin-balls and his news when Roland called it a day. They stopped in the middle of the road, as they always did since entering the forest; that way the embers of their campfire stood little chance of setting the woods on fire.

Eddie and Susannah gathered a nice selection of fallen branches while Roland and Jake made a little camp and set about cutting up Jake's trove of muffin-balls. Susannah rolled her wheelchair effortlessly over the duff under the ancient trees, piling her selections in her lap. Eddie walked nearby, humming under his breath.

'Lookit over to your left, sugar,' Susannah said.

He did, and saw a distant orange blink. A fire.

'Not very good, are they?' he asked.

'No. Truth is, I feel a little sorry for em.'

'Any idea what they're up to?'

'Unh-unh, but I think Roland's right — they'll tell us when they're ready. Either that or decide we're not what they want and just sort of fade away. Come on, let's go back.'

'Just a second.' He picked up one more branch, hesitated, then took yet another. Then it was right. 'Okay,' he said.

As they headed back, he counted the sticks he'd picked up, then the ones in Susannah's lap. The total came to nineteen in each case.

'Suze,' he said, and when she glanced over at him: 'Time's started up again.'

She didn't ask him what he meant, only nodded.

4

Eddie's resolution about not eating the muffin-balls didn't last long; they just smelled too damned good sizzling in the lump of deerfat Roland (thrifty, murderous soul that he was) had saved away in his scuffed old purse. Eddie took his share on one of the ancient plates they'd found in Shardik's woods and gobbled them.

'These are as good as lobster,' he said, then remembered the monsters on the beach that had eaten Roland's fingers. 'As good as Nathan's hotdogs is what I meant to say. And I'm sorry for teasing you, Jake.'

'Don't worry about it,' Jake said, smiling. 'You never tease hard.'

'One thing you should be aware of,' Roland said. He was smiling — he smiled more these days, quite a lot more — but his eyes were serious. 'All of you. Muffin-balls sometimes bring very lively dreams.'

'You mean they make you stoned?' Jake asked, rather uneasily. He was thinking of his father. Elmer Chambers had enjoyed many of the weirder things in life.

'Stoned? I'm not sure I—'

'Buzzed. High. Seeing things. Like when you took the mescaline and went into the stone circle where that thing almost . . . you know, almost hurt me.'

Roland paused for a moment, remembering. There had been a kind of succubus imprisoned in that ring of stones. Left to its own devices, she undoubtedly would have initiated Jake Chambers sexually, then fucked him to death. As matters turned out, Roland had made it speak. To punish him, it had sent him a vision of Susan Delgado.

'Roland?' Jake was looking at him anxiously.

'Don't concern yourself, Jake. There are mushrooms that do what you're thinking of — change consciousness, heighten it — but not muffin-balls. These are berries, just good to eat. If your dreams are particularly vivid, just remind yourself you *are* dreaming.'

Eddie thought this a very odd little speech. For one thing, it wasn't like Roland to be so tenderly solicitous of their mental health. Not like him to waste words, either.

Things have started again and he knows it, too, Eddie thought. *There was a little time-out there, but now the clock's running again. Game on, as they say.*

'We going to set a watch, Roland?' Eddie asked.

'Not by my warrant,' the gunslinger said comfortably, and began rolling himself a smoke.

'You really don't think they're dangerous, do you?' Susannah said, and raised her eyes to the woods, where the individual trees were now losing themselves in the general gloom of evening. The little spark of campfire they'd noticed earlier was now gone, but the people following them were still there. Susannah felt them. When she looked down at Oy and saw him gazing in the same direction, she wasn't surprised.

'I think that may be their problem,' Roland said.

'What's *that* supposed to mean?' Eddie asked, but Roland would say no more. He simply lay in the road with a rolled-up piece of deerskin beneath his neck, looking up at the dark sky and smoking.

Later, Roland's ka-tet slept. They posted no watch and were undisturbed.

5

The dreams, when they came, were not dreams at all. They all knew this except perhaps for Susannah, who in a very real sense was not there at all that night.

My God, I'm back in New York, Eddie thought. And, on the heels of this: Really *back in New York. This is really happening.*

It was. He was in New York. On Second Avenue.

That was when Jake and Oy came around the corner from Fifty-fourth Street. 'Hey, Eddie,' Jake said, grinning. 'Welcome home.'

Game on, Eddie thought. *Game on.*

CHAPTER II

NEW YORK GROOVE

1

Jake fell asleep looking into pure darkness — no stars in that cloudy night sky, no moon. As he drifted off, he had a sensation of falling that he recognized with dismay: in his previous life as a so-called normal child he'd often had dreams of falling, especially around exam time, but these had ceased since his violent rebirth into Mid-World.

Then the falling feeling was gone. He heard a brief chiming melody that was somehow *too* beautiful: three notes and you wanted it to stop, a dozen and you thought it would kill you if it didn't. Each chime seemed to make his bones vibrate. *Sounds Hawaiian, doesn't it?* he thought, for although the chiming melody was nothing like the sinister warble of the thinny, somehow it was.

It was.

Then, just when he truly believed he could bear it no longer, the terrible, gorgeous tune stopped. The darkness behind his closed eyes suddenly lit up a brilliant dark red.

He opened them cautiously on strong sunlight.

And gaped.

At New York.

Taxis bustled past, gleaming bright yellow in the sunshine. A young black man wearing Walkman earphones strolled by Jake, bopping his sandaled feet a little bit to the music and going 'Cha-da-ba, cha-da-*bow!*' under his breath. A jackhammer battered Jake's eardrums. Chunks of cement dropped into a dumptruck with a crash that echoed from one cliff-face of buildings to another. The world was a-din with racket. He had gotten used to the deep silences of Mid-World without even realizing it. No, more. Had come to love them. Still, this noise and bustle had its attractions, and

Jake couldn't deny it. Back in the New York groove. He felt a little grin stretch his lips.

'Ake! Ake!' cried a low, rather distressed voice.

Jake looked down and saw Oy sitting on the sidewalk with his tail curled neatly around him. The billy-bumbler wasn't wearing little red booties and Jake wasn't wearing the red Oxfords (thank God), but this was still very like their visit to Roland's Gilead, which they had reached by traveling in the pink Wizard's Glass. The glass ball that had caused so much trouble and woe.

No glass this time . . . he'd just gone to sleep. But this was no dream. It was more intense than any dream he'd ever had, and more textured. Also . . .

Also, people kept detouring around him and Oy as they stood to the left of a midtown saloon called Kansas City Blues. While Jake was making this observation, a woman actually stepped *over* Oy, hitching up her straight black skirt a bit at the knee in order to do so. Her preoccupied face (*I'm just one more New Yorker minding my business, so don't screw with me* was what that face said to Jake) never changed.

They don't see us, but somehow they sense us. And if they can sense us, we must really be here.

The first logical question was Why? Jake considered this for a moment, then decided to table it. He had an idea the answer would come. Meantime, why not enjoy New York while he had it?

'Come on, Oy,' he said, and walked around the corner. The billy-bumbler, clearly no city boy, walked so close to him that Jake could feel his breath feathering against his ankle.

Second Avenue, he thought. Then: *My God—*

Before he could finish the thought, he saw Eddie Dean standing outside of the Barcelona Luggage store, looking dazed and more than a little out of place in old jeans, a deerskin shirt, and deerskin moccasins. His hair was clean, but it hung to his shoulders in a way that suggested no professional had seen to it in quite some time. Jake realized he himself didn't look much better; he was also wearing a deerskin shirt and, on his lower half, the battered remains of the Dockers he'd had on the day he left home for good, setting sail for Brooklyn, Dutch Hill, and another world.

Good thing no one can see us, Jake thought, then decided that wasn't true. If people could see them, they'd probably get rich on spare change before noon. The thought made him grin. 'Hey, Eddie,' he said. 'Welcome home.'

Eddie nodded, looking bemused. 'See you brought your friend.'

Jake reached down and gave Oy an affectionate pat. 'He's my version of the American Express Card. I don't go home without him.'

Jake was about to go on – he felt witty, bubbly, full of amusing things to say – when someone came around the corner, passed them without looking (as everyone else had), and changed everything. It was a kid wearing Dockers that looked like Jake's because they *were* Jake's. Not the pair he had on now, but they were his, all right. So were the sneakers. They were the ones Jake had lost in Dutch Hill. The plaster-man who guarded the door between the worlds had torn them right off his feet.

The boy who had just passed them was John Chambers, it was *him*, only this version looked soft and innocent and painfully young. *How did you survive?* he asked his own retreating back. *How did you survive the mental stress of losing your mind, and running away from home, and that horrible house in Brooklyn? Most of all, how did you survive the doorkeeper? You must be tougher than you look.*

Eddie did a doubletake so comical that Jake laughed in spite of his own shocked surprise. It made him think of those comic-book panels where Archie or Jughead is trying to look in two directions at the same time. He looked down and saw a similar expression on Oy's face. Somehow that made the whole thing even funnier.

'What the *fuck*?' Eddie asked.

'Instant replay,' Jake said, and laughed harder. It came out sounding goofy as shit, but he didn't care. He *felt* goofy. 'It's like when we watched Roland in the Great Hall of Gilead, only this is New York and it's May 31st 1977! It's the day I took French Leave from Piper! Instant replay, baby!'

'French—?' Eddie began, but Jake didn't give him a chance to finish. He was struck by another realization. Except *struck* was too mild a word. He was *buried* by it, like a man who just happens to be on the beach when a tidal wave rolls in. His face blazed so brightly that Eddie actually took a step back.

'The rose!' he whispered. He felt too weak in the diaphragm to speak any louder, and his throat was as dry as a sandstorm. 'Eddie, *the rose!*'

'What about it?'

'This is the day I see it!' He reached out and touched Eddie's forearm with a trembling hand. 'I go to the bookstore . . . then to the vacant lot. I think there used to be a delicatessen—'

Eddie was nodding and beginning to look excited himself. 'Tom and Jerry's Artistic Deli, corner of Second and Forty-sixth—'

'The deli's gone but the rose is there! That me walking down the street is going to see it, *and we can see it, too!*'

At that, Eddie's own eyes blazed. 'Come on, then,' he said. 'We don't want to lose you. Him. Whoever the fuck.'

'Don't worry,' Jake said. 'I know where he's going.'

2

The Jake ahead of them — New York Jake, spring-of-1977 Jake — walked slowly, looking everywhere, clearly digging the day. Mid-World Jake remembered exactly how that boy had felt: the sudden relief when the arguing voices in his mind

(*I died!*)

(*I didn't!*) had finally stopped their squabbling. Back by the board fence that had been, where the two businessmen had been playing tic-tac-toe with a Mark Cross pen. And, of course, there had been the relief of being away from the Piper School and the insanity of his Final Essay for Ms Avery's English class. The Final Essay counted a full twenty-five per cent toward each student's final grade, Ms Avery had made that perfectly clear, and Jake's had been gibberish. The fact that his teacher had later given him an A+ on it didn't change that, only made it clear that it wasn't just him; the whole world was losing its shit, going nineteen.

Being out from under all that — even for a little while — had been great. Of course he was digging the day.

Only the day's not quite right, Jake thought — the Jake walking along behind his old self. *Something about it . . .*

He looked around but couldn't figure it out. Late May, bright summer sun, lots of strollers and window-shoppers on Second Avenue, plenty of taxis, the occasional long black limo; nothing wrong with any of this.

Except there was.

Everything was wrong with it.

3

Eddie felt the kid twitch his sleeve. 'What's wrong with this picture?' Jake asked.

Eddie looked around. In spite of his own adjustment problems (his involved coming back to a New York that was clearly a few years behind his when), he knew what Jake meant. Something *was* wrong.

He looked down at the sidewalk, suddenly sure he wouldn't have a shadow. They'd lost their shadows like the kids in one of the stories . . . one of the nineteen fairy tales . . . or was it maybe something newer, like *The Lion, The Witch, and The Wardrobe* or *Peter Pan*? One of what might be called the Modern Nineteen?

Didn't matter in any case, because their shadows were there.

Shouldn't be, though, Eddie thought. *Shouldn't be able to see our shadows when it's this dark.*

Stupid thought. It *wasn't* dark. It was *morning*, for Christ's sake, a bright May morning, sunshine winking off the chrome of passing cars and the windows of the stores on the east side of Second Avenue brightly enough to make you squint your eyes. Yet still it seemed somehow dark to Eddie, as if all this were nothing but fragile surface, like the canvas backdrop of a stage set. 'At rise we see the Forest of Arden.' Or a Castle in Denmark. Or the Kitchen of Willy Loman's House. In this case we see Second Avenue, midtown New York.

Yes, like that. Only behind this canvas you wouldn't find the workshop and storage areas of backstage but only a great bulging darkness. Some vast dead universe where Roland's Tower had already fallen.

Please let me be wrong, Eddie thought. *Please let this just be a case of culture shock or the plain old heebie-jeebies.*

He didn't think it was.

'How'd we get here?' he asked Jake. 'There was no door . . .' He trailed off, and then asked with some hope: 'Maybe it *is* a dream?'

'No,' Jake said. 'It's more like when we traveled in the Wizard's Glass. Except this time there was no ball.' A thought struck him. 'Did you hear music, though? Chimes? Just before you wound up here?'

Eddie nodded. 'It was sort of overwhelming. Made my eyes water.'

'Right,' Jake said. 'Exactly.'

Oy sniffed a fire hydrant. Eddie and Jake paused to let the little guy lift his leg and add his own notice to what was undoubtedly an already crowded bulletin board. Ahead of them, that other Jake – Kid Seventy-seven – was still walking slowly and gawking everywhere. To Eddie he looked like a tourist from Michigan. He even craned up to see the tops of the buildings, and Eddie had an idea that if the New York Board of Cynicism caught you doing that, they took away your Bloomingdale's charge card. Not that he was complaining; it made the kid easy to follow.

And just as Eddie was thinking that, Kid Seventy-seven disappeared.

'Where'd you go? Christ, where'd you go?'

'Relax,' Jake said. (At his ankle, Oy added his two cents' worth: 'Ax!') The kid was grinning. 'I just went into the bookstore. The . . . um . . . Manhattan Restaurant of the Mind, it's called.'

'Where you got *Charlie the Choo-Choo* and the riddle book?'

'Right.'

Eddie loved the mystified, dazzled grin Jake was wearing. It lit up his whole face. 'Remember how excited Roland got when I told him the owner's name?'

Eddie did. The owner of The Manhattan Restaurant of the Mind was a fellow named Calvin Tower.

'Hurry up,' Jake said. 'I want to watch.'

Eddie didn't have to be asked twice. He wanted to watch, too.

4

Jake stopped in the doorway to the bookstore. His smile didn't fade, exactly, but it faltered.

'What is it?' Eddie asked. 'What's wrong?'

'Dunno. Something's different, I think. It's just . . . so much has happened since I was here . . .'

He was looking at the chalkboard in the window, which Eddie thought was actually a very clever way of selling books. It looked like the sort of thing you saw in diners, or maybe the fish markets.

TODAY'S SPECIALS

From Mississippi! Pan-Fried William Faulkner
Hardcovers Market Price
Vintage Library Paperbacks 75c each

From Maine! Chilled Stephen King
Hardcovers Market Price
Book Club Bargains
Paperbacks 75c each

From California! Hard-Boiled Raymond Chandler
Hardcovers Market Price
Paperbacks 7 for $5.00

Eddie looked beyond this and saw that other Jake – the one without the tan or the look of hard clarity in his eyes – standing at a small display table. Kiddie books. Probably both the Nineteen Fairy Tales and the Modern Nineteen.

Quit it, he told himself. *That's obsessive-compulsive crap and you know it.*

Maybe, but good old Jake Seventy-seven was about to make a purchase from that table which had gone on to change – and very likely to save – their lives. He'd worry about the number nineteen later. Or not at all, if he could manage it.

'Come on,' he told Jake. 'Let's go in.'

The boy hung back.

'What's the matter?' Eddie asked. 'Tower won't be able to see us, if that's what you're worried about.'

'*Tower* won't be able to,' Jake said, 'but what if *he* can?' He pointed at his other self, the one who had yet to meet Gasher and Tick-Tock and the old people of River Crossing. The one who had yet to meet Blaine the Mono and Rhea of the Cöos.

Jake was looking at Eddie with a kind of haunted curiosity. 'What if I see *myself*?'

Eddie supposed that might really happen. Hell, *anything* might happen. But that didn't change what he felt in his heart. 'I think we're supposed to go in, Jake.'

'Yeah . . .' It came out in a long sigh. 'I do, too.'

5

They went in and they weren't seen and Eddie was relieved to count twenty-one books on the display table that had attracted the boy's notice. Except, of course, when Jake picked up the two he wanted — *Charlie the Choo-Choo* and the riddle book — that left nineteen.

'Find something, son?' a mild voice inquired. It was a fat fellow in an open-throated white shirt. Behind him, at a counter that looked as if it might have been filched from a turn-of-the-century soda fountain, a trio of old guys were drinking coffee and nibbling pastries. A chessboard with a game in progress sat on the marble counter.

'The guy sitting on the end is Aaron Deepneau,' Jake whispered. 'He's going to explain the riddle about Samson to me.'

'Shh!' Eddie said. He wanted to hear the conversation between Calvin Tower and Kid Seventy-seven. All of a sudden that seemed very important . . . only why was it so fucking *dark* in here?

Except it's not dark at all. The east side of the street gets plenty of sun at this hour, and with the door open, this place is getting all of it. How can you say it's dark?

Because it somehow was. The sunlight — the *contrast* of the sunlight — only made it worse. The fact that you couldn't exactly *see* that darkness made it worse still . . . and Eddie realized a terrible thing: these people were in danger. Tower, Deepneau, Kid Seventy-seven. Probably him and Mid-World Jake and Oy, as well.

All of them.

6

Jake watched his other, younger self take a step back from the bookshop owner, his eyes widening in surprise. *Because his name is Tower,* Jake thought. *That's what surprised me. Not because of Roland's Tower, though — I didn't know about that yet — but because of the picture I put on the last page of my Final Essay.*

He had pasted a photo of the Leaning Tower of Pisa on the last page, then had scribbled all over it with a black Crayola, darkening it as best he could.

Tower asked him his name. Seventy-seven Jake told him and Tower joked around with him a little. It was good joking-around, the kind you got from adults who really didn't mind kids.

'Good handle, pard,' Tower was saying. 'Sounds like the footloose hero in a Western novel – the guy who blows into Black Fork, Arizona, cleans up the town, and then travels on. Something by Wayne D. Overholser, maybe . . .'

Jake took a step closer to his old self (part of him was thinking what a wonderful sketch all this would make on *Saturday Night Live*), and his eyes widened slightly. 'Eddie!' He was still whispering, although he knew the people in the bookstore couldn't—

Except maybe on some level they could. He remembered the lady back on Fifty-fourth Street, twitching her skirt up at the knee so she could step over Oy. And now Calvin Tower's eyes shifted slightly in his direction before going back to the other version of him.

'Might be good not to attract unnecessary attention,' Eddie muttered in his ear.

'I know,' Jake said, 'but look at *Charlie the Choo-Choo*, Eddie!'

Eddie did, and for a moment saw nothing – except for Charlie himself, of course: Charlie with his headlight eye and not-quite-trustworthy cowcatcher grin. Then Eddie's eyebrows went up.

'I thought *Charlie the Choo-Choo* was written by a lady named Beryl Evans,' he whispered.

Jake nodded. 'I did, too.'

'Then who's this—' Eddie took another look. 'Who's this Claudia y Inez Bachman?'

'I have no idea,' Jake said. 'I never heard of her in my life.'

7

One of the old men at the counter came sauntering toward them. Eddie and Jake drew away. As they stepped back, Eddie's spine gave a cold little wrench. Jake was very pale, and Oy was giving out a series of low, distressed whines. Something was wrong here, all right. In a way they *had* lost their shadows. Eddie just didn't know how.

Kid Seventy-seven had taken out his wallet and was paying for the two books. There was some more talk and good-natured laughter, then he headed for the door. When Eddie started after him, Mid-World Jake grabbed his arm. 'No, not yet – I come back in.'

'I don't care if you alphabetize the whole place,' Eddie said. 'Let's wait out on the sidewalk.'

Jake thought about this, biting his lip, then nodded. They headed for the door, then stopped and moved aside as the other Jake returned. The riddle book was open. Calvin Tower had lumbered over to the chessboard on the counter. He looked around with an amiable smile.

'Change your mind about that cup of coffee, O Hyperborean Wanderer?'

'No, I wanted to ask you—'

'This is the part about Samson's Riddle,' Mid-World Jake said. 'I don't think it matters. Although the Deepneau guy sings a pretty good song, if you want to hear it.'

'I'll pass,' Eddie said. 'Come on.'

They went out. And although things on Second Avenue were still wrong – that sense of endless dark behind the scenes, behind the very *sky* – it was somehow better than in The Manhattan Restaurant of the Mind. At least there was fresh air.

'Tell you what,' Jake said. 'Let's go down to Second and Forty-sixth right now.' He jerked his head toward the version of him listening to Aaron Deepneau sing. 'I'll catch up with us.'

Eddie considered it, then shook his head.

Jake's face fell a little. 'Don't you want to see the rose?'

'You bet your ass I do,' Eddie said. 'I'm wild to see it.'

'Then—'

'I don't feel like we're done here yet. I don't know why, but I don't.'

Jake – the Kid Seventy-seven version of him – had left the door open when he went back inside; and now Eddie moved into it. Aaron Deepneau was telling Jake a riddle they would later try on Blaine the Mono: What can run but never walks, has a mouth but never talks. Mid-World Jake, meanwhile, was once more looking at the notice board in the bookstore window (*Pan-Fried William Faulkner, Hard-Boiled Raymond Chandler*). He wore a frown of the kind that expresses doubt and anxiety rather than ill temper.

'That sign's different, too,' he said.

'How?'

'I can't remember.'

'Is it important?'

Jake turned to him. The eyes below the furrowed brow were haunted. 'I don't know. It's another riddle. I *hate* riddles!'

Eddie sympathized. *When is a Beryl not a Beryl?* 'When it's a Claudia,' he said.

'Huh?'

'Never mind. Better step back, Jake, or you're going to run into yourself.'

Jake gave the oncoming version of John Chambers a startled glance, then did as Eddie suggested. And when Kid Seventy-seven started on down Second Avenue with his new books in his left hand, Mid-World Jake gave Eddie a tired smile. 'I *do* remember one thing,' he said. 'When I left this bookstore, I was sure I'd never come here again. But I did.'

'Considering that we're more ghosts than people, I'd say that's debatable.' Eddie gave the back of Jake's neck a friendly scruff. 'And if you *have* forgotten something important, Roland might be able to help you remember. He's good at that.'

Jake grinned at this, relieved. He knew from personal experience that the gunslinger really *was* good at helping people remember. Roland's friend Alain might have been the one with the strongest ability to touch other minds and his friend Cuthbert had gotten all the sense of humor in that particular ka-tet, but Roland had developed over the years into one *hell* of a hypnotist. He could have made a fortune in Las Vegas.

'Can we follow me now?' Jake asked. 'Check out the rose?' He looked up and down Second Avenue — a street that was somehow bright and dark at the same time — with a kind of unhappy perplexity. 'Things are probably better there. The rose makes everything better.'

Eddie was about to say okay when a dark gray Lincoln Town Car pulled up in front of Calvin Tower's bookshop. It parked by the yellow curb in front of a fire hydrant with absolutely no hesitation. The front doors opened, and when Eddie saw who was getting out from behind the wheel, he seized Jake's shoulder.

'Ow!' Jake said. 'Man, that hurts!'

Eddie paid no attention. In fact the hand on Jake's shoulder clamped down even tighter.

'Christ,' Eddie whispered. 'Dear Jesus Christ, what's this? What in hell is *this?*'

8

Jake watched Eddie go past pale to ashy gray. His eyes were bulging from their sockets. Not without difficulty, Jake pried the clamping hand off his shoulder. Eddie made as if to point with that hand, but didn't seem to have the strength. It fell against the side of his leg with a little thump.

The man who had gotten out on the passenger side of the Town Car walked around to the sidewalk while the driver opened the rear curbside door. Even to Jake their moves looked practiced, almost like steps in a dance. The man who got out of the back seat was wearing an expensive suit, but that didn't change the fact that he was basically a dumpy little guy with a potbelly and black hair going gray around the edges. *Dandruffy* black hair, from the look of his suit's shoulders.

To Jake, the day suddenly felt darker than ever. He looked up to see if the sun had gone behind a cloud. It hadn't, but it almost seemed to him that there was a black corona forming around its brilliant circle, like a ring of mascara around a startled eye.

Half a block farther downtown, the 1977 version of him was glancing in the window of a restaurant, and Jake could remember the name of it: Chew Chew Mama's. Not far beyond it was Tower of Power Records, where he would think *Towers are selling cheap today*. If that version of him had looked back, he would have seen the gray Town Car . . . but he hadn't. Kid Seventy-seven's mind was fixed firmly on the future.

'It's Balazar,' Eddie said.

'What?'

Eddie was pointing at the dumpy guy, who had paused to adjust his Sulka tie. The other two now stood flanking him. They looked simultaneously relaxed and watchful.

'Enrico Balazar. And looking much younger. God, he's almost middle-aged!'

'It's 1977,' Jake reminded him. Then, as the penny dropped: 'That's the guy you and Roland *killed*?' Eddie had told Jake the story of the shoot-out at Balazar's club in 1987, leaving out the gorier parts. The part, for instance, where Kevin Blake had lobbed the head of Eddie's brother into Balazar's office in an effort to flush Eddie and Roland into the open. Henry Dean, the great sage and eminent junkie.

'Yeah,' Eddie said. 'The guy Roland and I killed. And the one who was driving, that's Jack Andolini. Old Double-Ugly, people used to call him, although never to his face. He went through one of those doors with me just before the shooting started.'

'Roland killed him, too. Didn't he?'

Eddie nodded. It was simpler than trying to explain how Jack Andolini had happened to die blind and faceless beneath the tearing claws and ripping jaws of the lobstrosities on the beach.

'The other bodyguard's George Biondi. Big Nose. I killed him myself. *Will* kill him. Ten years from now.' Eddie looked as if he might faint at any second.

'Eddie, are you okay?'

'I guess so. I guess I have to be.' They had drawn away from the book-shop's doorway. Oy was still crouched at Jake's ankle. Down Second Avenue, Jake's other, earlier self had disappeared. *I'm running by now*, Jake thought. *Maybe jumping over the UPS guy's dolly. Sprinting all-out for the delicatessen, because I'm sure that's the way back to Mid-World. The way back to* him.

Balazar peered at his reflection in the window beside the TODAY'S SPECIALS display-board, gave the wings of hair above his ears one last little fluff with the tips of his fingers, then stepped through the open door. Andolini and Biondi followed.

'Hard guys,' Jake said.

'The hardest,' Eddie agreed.

'From Brooklyn.'

'Well, yeah.'

'Why are hard guys from Brooklyn visiting a used-book store in Manhattan?'

'I think that's what we're here to find out. Jake, did I hurt your shoulder?'

'I'm okay. But I don't really want to go back in there.'

'Neither do I. So let's go.'

They went back into The Manhattan Restaurant of the Mind.

9

Oy was still at Jake's heel and still whining. Jake wasn't crazy about the sound, but he understood it. The smell of fear in the bookstore was palpable. Deepneau sat beside the chessboard, gazing unhappily at Calvin Tower and the newcomers, who didn't look much like bibliophiles in search of the elusive signed first edition. The other two old guys at the counter were drinking the last of their coffee in big gulps, with the air of fellows who have just remembered important appointments elsewhere.

Cowards, Jake thought with a contempt he didn't recognize as a relatively new thing in his life. *Lowbellies. Being old forgives some of it, but not all of it.*

'We just have a couple of things to discuss, Mr Toren,' Balazar was saying. He spoke in a low, calm, reasonable voice, without even a trace of accent. 'Please, if we could step back into your office—'

'We don't have business,' Tower said. His eyes kept drifting to Andolini. Jake supposed he knew why. Jack Andolini looked the ax-wielding psycho in a horror movie. 'Come July fifteenth, we might have business. *Might.* So we could talk after the Fourth. I guess. If you wanted to.' He smiled to show he was being reasonable. 'But now? Gee, I just don't see the point. It's not even June yet. And for your information my name's not—'

'He doesn't see the point,' Balazar said. He looked at Andolini; looked at the one with the big nose; raised his hands to his shoulders, then dropped them. *What's wrong with this world of ours?* the gesture said. 'Jack? George? This man took a check from me — the amount before the decimal point was a one followed by five zeroes — and now he says he doesn't see the point of talking to me.'

'Unbelievable,' Biondi said. Andolini said nothing. He simply looked at Calvin Tower, muddy brown eyes peering out from beneath the unlovely bulge of his skull like mean little animals peering out of a cave. With a face like that, Jake supposed, you didn't have to talk much to get your point across. The point being intimidation.

'*I* want to talk to *you,*' Balazar said. He spoke in a patient, reasonable tone of voice, but his eyes were fixed on Tower's face with a terrible intensity. 'Why? Because my employers in this matter *want* me to talk to you. That's good enough for me. And do you know what? I think you can afford five minutes of chit-chat for your hundred grand. Don't you?'

'The hundred thousand is gone,' Tower said bleakly. 'As I'm sure you and whoever hired you must know.'

'That's of no concern to me,' Balazar said. 'Why would it be? It was your money. What concerns me is whether or not you're going to take us out back. If not, we'll have to have our conversation right here, in front of the whole world.'

The whole world now consisted of Aaron Deepneau, one billy-bumbler, and a couple of expatriate New Yorkers none of the men in the bookstore could see. Deepneau's counter-buddies had run like the lowbellies they were.

Tower made one last try. 'I don't have anyone to mind the store. Lunch-hour is coming up, and we often have quite a few browsers during—'

'This place doesn't do fifty dollars a day,' Andolini said, 'and we all know it, Mr Toren. If you're really worried you're going to miss a big sale, let *him* run the cash register for a few minutes.'

For one horrible second, Jake thought the one Eddie had called 'Old Double-Ugly' meant none other than John 'Jake' Chambers. Then he realized Andolini was pointing past him, at Deepneau.

Tower gave in. Or Toren. 'Aaron?' he asked. 'Do you mind?'

'Not if you don't,' Deepneau said. He looked troubled. 'Sure you want to talk with these guys?'

Biondi gave him a look. Jake thought Deepneau stood up under it remarkably well. In a weird way, he felt proud of the old guy.

'Yeah,' Tower said. 'Yeah, it's fine.'

'Don't worry, he won't lose his butthole virginity on our account,' Biondi said, and laughed.

'Watch your mouth, you're in a place of scholarship,' Balazar said, but Jake thought he smiled a little. 'Come on, Toren. Just a little chat.'

'That's not my name! I had it legally changed on—'

'Whatever,' Balazar said soothingly. He actually patted Tower's arm. Jake was still trying to get used to the idea that all this ... all this *melodrama* ... had happened after he'd left the store with his two new books (new to him, anyway) and resumed his journey. That it had all happened behind his back.

'A squarehead's always a squarehead, right, boss?' Biondi asked jovially. 'Just a Dutchman. Don't matter what he calls himself.'

Balazar said, 'If I want you to talk, George, I'll tell you what I want you to say. Have you got that?'

'Okay,' Biondi said. Then, perhaps after deciding that didn't sound quite enthusiastic enough: 'Yeah! Sure.'

'Good.' Balazar, now holding the arm he had patted, guided Tower toward the back of the shop. Books were piled helter-skelter here; the air was heavy with the scent of a million musty pages. There was a door marked EMPLOYEES ONLY. Tower produced a ring of keys, and they jingled slightly as he picked through them.

'His hands are shaking,' Jake murmured.

Eddie nodded. 'Mine would be, too.'

Tower found the key he wanted, turned it in the lock, opened the door. He took another look at the three men who had come to visit him – hard guys from Brooklyn – then led them into the back room. The door closed behind them, and Jake heard the sound of a bolt being shot across. He doubted Tower himself had done that.

Jake looked up into the convex anti-shoplifting mirror mounted in the corner of the shop, saw Deepneau pick up the telephone beside the cash register, consider it, then put it down again.

'What do we do now?' Jake asked Eddie.

'I'm gonna try something,' Eddie said. 'I saw it in a movie once.' He stood in front of the closed door, then tipped Jake a wink. 'Here I go. If I don't do anything but bump my head, feel free to call me an asshole.'

Before Jake could ask him what he was talking about, Eddie walked into the door. Jake saw his eyes close and his mouth tighten in a grimace. It was the expression of a man who expects to take a hard knock.

Only there *was* no hard knock. Eddie simply passed through the door. For one moment his moccasin-clad foot was sticking out, and then it went through, too. There was a low rasping sound, like a hand being passed over rough wood.

Jake bent down and picked Oy up. 'Close your eyes,' he said.

'Eyes,' the bumbler agreed, but continued to look at Jake with that expression of calm adoration. Jake closed his own eyes, squinting them shut. When he opened them again, Oy was mimicking him. Without wasting any time, Jake walked into the door with the EMPLOYEES ONLY sign on it. There was a moment of darkness and the smell of wood. Deep in his head, he heard a couple of those disturbing chimes again. Then he was through.

10

It was a storage area much bigger than Jake had expected – almost as big as a warehouse and stacked high with books in every direction. He guessed that some of those stacks, held in place by pairs of upright beams that provided shoring rather than shelving, had to be fourteen or sixteen feet high. Narrow, crooked aisles ran between them. In a couple he saw rolling platforms that made him think of the portable boarding ramps you saw in smaller airports. The smell of old books was the same back here as in front, but ever so much stronger, almost overwhelming. Above them hung a scattering of shaded lamps that provided yellowish, uneven illumination. The shadows of Tower, Balazar, and Balazar's friends leaped grotesquely on the wall to their left. Tower turned that way, leading his visitors to a corner that really was an office: there was a desk with a typewriter and a Rolodex on it, three old filing cabinets, and a wall covered with various pieces of paperwork. There was a calendar with some nineteenth-century guy on the May sheet Jake didn't recognize . . . and then he did. Robert Browning. Jake had quoted him in his Final Essay.

Tower sat down in the chair behind his desk, and immediately seemed sorry he'd done that. Jake could sympathize. The way the other three crowded around him couldn't have been very pleasant. Their shadows jumped up the wall behind the desk like the shadows of gargoyles.

Balazar reached into his suitcoat and brought out a folded sheet of paper. He opened it and put it down on Tower's desk. 'Recognize this?'

Eddie moved forward. Jake grabbed at him. 'Don't go close! They'll sense you!'

'I don't care,' Eddie said. 'I need to see that paper.'

Jake followed, not knowing what else to do. Oy stirred in his arms and whined. Jake shushed him curtly, and Oy blinked. 'Sorry, buddy,' Jake said, 'but you have to keep quiet.'

Was the 1977 version of him in the vacant lot yet? Once inside it, that earlier Jake had slipped somehow and knocked himself unconscious. Had that happened yet? No sense wondering. Eddie was right. Jake didn't like it, but he knew it was true: they were supposed to be *here*, not there, and they were supposed to see the paper Balazar was now showing Calvin Tower.

11

Eddie got the first couple of lines before Jack Andolini said, 'Boss, I don't like this. Something feels hinky.'

Balazar nodded. 'I agree. Is someone back here with us, Mr Toren?' He still sounded calm and courteous, but his eyes were everywhere, assessing this large room's potential for concealment.

'No,' Tower said. 'Well, there's Sergio; he's the shop cat. I imagine he's back here somew—'

'This ain't no shop,' Biondi said, 'it's a hole you pour money into. One of those chi-chi designers'd have trouble making enough to cover the overhead on a joint this big, and a *bookstore*? Man, who are you kidding?'

Himself, that's who, Eddie thought. *He's been kidding himself.*

As if this thought had summoned them, those terrible chimes began again. The hoods gathered in Tower's storeroom office didn't hear them, but Jake and Oy did; Eddie could read it on their distressed faces. And suddenly this room, already dim, began to grow dimmer still.

We're going back, Eddie thought. *Jesus, we're going back! But not before—*

He bent forward between Andolini and Balazar, aware that both men were looking around with wide, wary eyes, not caring. What he cared about was the paper. Someone had hired Balazar first to get it signed (probably) and then to shove it under Tower / Toren's nose when the time was right (certainly). In most cases, *Il Roche* would have been content to send a couple of his hard boys — what he called his 'gentlemen' — on an errand like that. This job, however, was important enough to warrant his personal attention. Eddie wanted to know why.

MEMORANDUM OF AGREEMENT

This document constitutes a Pact of Agreement between Mr Calvin Tower, **a New York State resident, owning real property which is principally** a vacant lot, **identified as Lot #298 and Block #19, located** . . .

Those chimes wriggled through his head again, making him shiver. This time they were louder. The shadows drew thicker, leaping up the storage room's walls. The darkness Eddie had sensed out on the street was breaking through. They might be swept away, and that would be bad. They might be drowned in it, and that would be worse, of course it would, being drowned in darkness would surely be an awful way to go.

And suppose there were *things* in that darkness? Hungry things like the doorkeeper?

There are. That was Henry's voice. For the first time in almost two months. Eddie could imagine Henry standing just behind him and grinning a sallow junkie's grin: all bloodshot eyes and yellow, uncared-for teeth. *You know there are. But when you hear the chimes, you got to go, bro, as I think you know.*

'Eddie!' Jake cried. 'It's coming back! Do you hear it?'

'Grab my belt,' Eddie said. His eyes raced back and forth over the paper in Tower's pudgy hands. Balazar, Andolini, and Big Nose were still looking around. Biondi had actually drawn his gun.

'Your—?'

'Maybe we won't be separated,' Eddie said. The chimes were louder than ever, and he groaned. The words of the agreement blurred in front of him. Eddie squinted his eyes, bringing the print back together:

> **. . . identified as Lot #298 and Block #19, located in** Manhattan, **New York City, on** 46th **Street and** 2nd **Avenue, and** Sombra Corporation, **a corporation doing business within the State of New York.**
>
> **On this day of** July 15, 1976, Sombra **is paying a non-returnable sum of** $100,000.00 **to** Calvin Tower, **receipt of which is acknowledged in regard to this property. In consideration thereof,** Calvin Tower **agrees not to . . .**

July 15th, 1976. Not quite a year ago.

Eddie felt the darkness sweeping down on them, and tried to cram the rest of it through his eyes and into his brain: enough, maybe, to make sense of what was going on here. If he could do that, it would be at least a step toward figuring out what all this meant to them.

If the chimes don't drive me crazy. If the things in the darkness don't eat us on the way back.

'Eddie!' Jake. And terrified, by the sound. Eddie ignored him.

> **. . . Calvin** Tower **agrees not to sell or lease or otherwise encumber the property during a** one-year **period commencing on the date hereof and ending on** July 15, 1977. **It is understood that the** Sombra Corporation **shall have first right of purchase on the abovementioned property, as defined below.**
>
> **During this period,** Calvin Tower **will fully preserve and protect** Sombra Corporation's **stated interest in the abovementioned Property and will permit no liens or other encumbrances . . .**

There was more, but now the chimes were hideous, head-bursting. For just one moment Eddie understood — hell, could almost *see* — how thin this world had become. All of the worlds, probably. As thin and worn as his own jeans. He caught one final phrase from the agreement: ... **if these conditions are met, will have the right to sell or otherwise dispose of the property to** Sombra **or any other party**. Then the words were gone, everything was gone, spinning into a black whirlpool. Jake held onto Eddie's belt with one hand and Oy with the other. Oy was barking wildly now, and Eddie had another confused image of Dorothy being swirled away to the Land of Oz.

There *were* things in the darkness: looming shapes behind weird phosphorescent eyes, the sort of things you saw in movies about exploring the deepest cracks of the ocean floor. Except in those movies, the explorers were always inside a steel diving-bell, while he and Jake—

The chimes grew to an ear-splitting volume. Eddie felt as if he had been jammed headfirst into the works of Big Ben as it was striking midnight. He screamed without hearing himself. And then it was gone, everything was all gone — Jake, Oy, Mid-World — and he was floating somewhere beyond the stars and the galaxies.

Susannah! he cried. *Where are you, Suze?*

No answer. Only darkness.

CHAPTER III

MIA

1

Once upon a time, back in the sixties (before the world moved on), there had been a woman named Odetta Holmes, a pleasant and really quite socially conscious young woman who was wealthy, good-looking, and perfectly willing to look out for the other guy. (Or gal.) Without even realizing it, this woman shared her body with a far less pleasant creature named Detta Walker. Detta did not give a tin shit for the other guy (or gal). Rhea of the Cöos would have recognized Detta, and called her sister. On the other side of Mid-World, Roland of Gilead, the last gunslinger, had drawn this divided woman to him and had created a third, who was far better, far stronger, than either of the previous two. This was the woman with whom Eddie Dean had fallen in love. She called him husband, and thus herself by the name of his father. Having missed the feminist squabbles of later decades, she did this quite happily. If she did not call herself Susannah Dean with pride as well as happiness, it was only because her mother had taught her that pride goeth before a fall.

Now there was a fourth woman. She had been born out of the third in yet another time of stress and change. She cared nothing for Odetta, Detta, or Susannah; she cared for nothing save the new chap who was on his way. The new chap needed to be fed. The banqueting hall was near. That was what mattered and all that mattered.

This new woman, every bit as dangerous in her own way as Detta Walker had been, was Mia. She bore the name of no man's father, only the word that in the High Speech means *mother*.

2

She walked slowly down long stone corridors toward the place of feasting. She walked past the rooms of ruin, past the empty naves and niches, past forgotten galleries where the apartments were hollow and none was the number. Somewhere in this castle stood an old throne drenched in ancient blood. Somewhere ladderways led to bone-walled crypts that went gods knew how deep. Yet there *was* life here; life and rich food. Mia knew this as well as she knew the legs under her and the textured, many-layered skirt swishing against them. Rich food. Life for you and for your crop, as the saying went. And she was so hungry now. Of course! Wasn't she eating for two?

She came to a broad staircase. A sound, faint but powerful, rose up to her: the beat-beat-beat of slo-trans engines buried in the earth below the deepest of the crypts. Mia cared nothing for them, nor for North Central Positronics, Ltd., which had built them and set them in motion tens of thousands of years before. She cared nothing for the dipolar computers, or the doors, or the Beams, or the Dark Tower which stood at the center of everything.

What she cared about was the smells. They drifted up to her, thick and wonderful. Chicken and gravy and roasts of pork dressed in suits of crackling fat. Sides of beef beaded with blood, wheels of moist cheese, huge Calla Fundy shrimp like plump orange commas. Split fish with staring black eyes, their bellies brimming with sauce. Great pots of jambalaya and fanata, the vast *caldo largo* stews of the far south. Add to this a hundred fruits and a thousand sweets, and still you were only at the beginning! The appetizers! The first mouthfuls of the first course!

Mia ran quickly down the broad central staircase, the skin of her palm skimming silkily along the bannister, her small slippered feet stuttering on the steps. Once she'd had a dream that she had been pushed in front of an underground train by an awful man, and her legs had been cut off at the knee. But dreams were foolish. Her feet were there, and the legs above them, weren't they? Yes! And so was the babe in her belly. The chap, wanting to be fed. He was hungry, and so was she.

3

From the foot of the stairs, a wide corridor floored with polished black marble ran ninety feet to a pair of tall double doors. Mia hurried that way. She saw her reflection floating below her, and the electric flambeaux that burned in the depths of the marble like torches underwater, but she did not see the man who came along behind her, descending the sweeping curve of the stairs not in dress pumps but in old and range-battered boots. He wore faded jeans and a shirt of blue chambray instead of court clothes. One gun, a pistol with a worn sandalwood grip, hung at his left side, the holster tied down with rawhide. His face was tanned and lined and weathered. His hair was black, although now seeded with growing streaks of white. His eyes were his most striking feature. They were blue and cold and steady. Detta Walker had feared no man, not even this one, but she had feared those shooter's eyes.

There was a foyer just before the double doors. It was floored with red and black marble squares. The wood-paneled walls were hung with faded portraits of old lords and ladies. In the center was a statue made of entwined rose marble and chrome steel. It seemed to be a knight errant with what might have been a sixgun or a short sword raised above his head. Although the face was mostly smooth — the sculptor had done no more than hint at the features — Mia knew who it was, right enough. Who it must be.

'I salute thee, Arthur Eld,' she said, and dropped her deepest curtsy. 'Please bless these things I'm about to take to my use. And to the use of my chap. Good evening to you.' She could not wish him long days upon the earth, for his days — and those of most of his kind — were gone. Instead she touched her smiling lips with the tips of her fingers and blew him a kiss. Having made her manners, she walked into the dining hall.

It was forty yards wide and seventy yards long, that room. Brilliant electric torches in crystal sheaths lined both sides. Hundreds of chairs stood in place at a vast ironwood table laden with delicacies both hot and cold. There was a white plate with delicate blue webbing, a *forspecial* plate, in front of each chair. The chairs were empty, the forspecial banquet plates were empty, and the wineglasses were empty, although the wine to fill them stood in golden buckets at intervals along the table, chilled and ready. It was as she had known it would be, as she had seen it in her fondest, clearest imaginings, as she had found it again and again, and would find it as long as she (and the chap) needed it. Wherever she found herself, this castle was near. And if there was a smell of dampness and ancient mud, what of that? If there were scuttering sounds from the shadows under the table — mayhap the sound of rats or even fortnoy weasels — why should she care? Abovetable, all was lush and lighted, fragrant and ripe and ready for taking. Let the shadows belowtable take care of themselves. That was none of her business, no, none of hers.

'Here comes Mia, daughter of none!' she called gaily to the silent room with its hundred aromas of meats and sauces and creams and fruits. 'I am hungry and I will be fed! Moreover, I'll feed my chap! If anyone would say against me, let him step forward! Let me see him very well, and he me!'

No one stepped forward, of course. Those who might once have banqueted here were long gone. Now there was only the deep and sleepy beat of the slo-trans engines (and those faint and unpleasant scampering sounds from the Land of Undertable). Behind her, the gunslinger stood quietly, watching. Nor was it for the first time. He saw no castle but he saw her; he saw her very well.

'Silence gives consent!' she called. She pressed her hand to her belly, which had begun to protrude outward. To curve. Then, with a laugh, she cried: 'Aye, so it does! Here comes Mia to the feast! May it serve both her and the chap who grows inside her! May it serve them very well!'

And she did feast, but not in one place and never from one of the plates. She hated the plates, the white-and-blue *forspecials*. She didn't know why and didn't care to know. What she cared about was the food. She walked along the table like a woman at the world's grandest buffet, taking things with her fingers and tossing them into her mouth, sometimes chewing meat hot and tender right off the bone before slinging the joints back onto their serving platters. A few times she missed these and the chunks of meat would go rolling across the white linen tablecloth, leaving splotches of juice in nose-bleed stains. One of these rolling roasts overturned a gravy-boat. One smashed a crystal serving dish filled with cranberry jelly. A third rolled clean off the far side of the table, where Mia heard something drag it underneath. There was a brief, squealing squabble, followed by a howl of pain as something sank its teeth into something else. Then silence. It was brief, though, and soon broken by Mia's laughter. She wiped her greasy fingers on her bosom, doing it slowly. Enjoying the way the stains of the mixed meats and juices spread on the expensive silk. Enjoying the ripening curves of her breasts and the feel of her nipples under her fingertips, rough and hard and excited.

She made her way slowly down the table, talking to herself in many voices, creating a kind of lunatic chitchat.

How they hangin, honey?

Oh they hanging just fine, thank you so much for asking, Mia.

Do you really believe that Oswald was working alone when he shot Kennedy?

Never in a million years, darling — that was a CIA job the whole way. Them, or those honky millionaires from the Alabama steel crescent.

Bombingham, Alabama, honey, ain't it the truth?

Have you heard the new Joan Baez record?

My God, yes, doesn't she sing like an angel? I hear that she and Bob Dylan are going to get themselves married . . .

And on and on, chitter and chatter. Roland heard Odetta's cultured voice and Detta's rough but colorful profanity. He heard Susannah's voice, and many others, as well. How many women in her head? How many person-alities, formed and half-formed? He watched her reach over the empty plates that weren't there and empty glasses (also not there), eating directly from the serving platters, chewing everything with the same hungry relish, her face gradually picking up the shine of grease, the bodice of her gown (which he did not see but sensed) darkening as she wiped her fingers there again and again, squeezing the cloth, matting it against her breasts — these motions were too clear to mistake. And at each stop, before moving on, she would seize the empty air in front of her and throw a plate he could not see either on the floor at her feet or across the table at a wall that must exist in her dream.

'*There!*' she'd scream in the defiant voice of Detta Walker. '*There, you nasty old Blue Lady, I done broke it again! I broke yo' fuckin plate, and how do you like it? How do you like it now?*'

Then, stepping to the next place, she might utter a pleasant but restrained little trill of laughter and ask so-and-so how their boy so-and-so was coming along down there at Morehouse, and wasn't it wonderful to have such a fine school for people of color, just the most *wonderful! . . . thing!* And how is your Mamma, dear? Oh I am so *sorry* to hear it, we'll all be praying for her recovery.

Reaching across another of those make-believe plates as she spoke. Grabbing up a great tureen filled with glistening black roe and lemon rinds. Lowering her face into it like a hog dropping its face into the trough. Gobbling. Raising her face again, smiling delicately and demurely in the glow of the electric torches, the fish eggs standing out like black sweat on her brown skin, dotting her cheeks and her brow, nestling around her nostrils like clots of old blood — *Oh yes, I think we are making wonderful progress, folks like that Bull Connor are living in the sunset years now, and the best revenge on them is that they know it* — and then she would throw the tureen backward over her head like a crazed volleyball player, some of the roe raining down in her hair (Roland could almost see it), and when the tureen smashed against the stone, her polite isn't-this-a-wonderful-party face would cramp into a ghoulish Detta Walker snarl and she might scream, '*Dere, you nasty old Blue Lady, how dat feel? You want to stick some of dat caviar up yo dry-ass cunt, you go on and do it! You go right on! Dat be fine, sho!*'

And then she would move on to the next place. And the next. And the next. Feeding herself in the great banquet hall. Feeding herself and feeding her chap. Never turning to see Roland at all. Never realizing that this place did not, strictly speaking, even exist.

4

Eddie and Jake had been far from Roland's mind and concerns as the four of them (five, if Oy was counted) bedded down after feasting on the fried muffin-balls. He had been focused on Susannah. The gunslinger was quite sure she would go wandering again tonight, and again he would follow after her when she did. Not to see what she was up to; he knew in advance what it would be.

No, his chief purpose had been protection.

Early that afternoon, around the time Jake had returned with his armload of food, Susannah had begun to show signs Roland knew: speech that was clipped and short, movements that were a little too jerky to be graceful, an absent tendency to rub at her temple or above her left eyebrow, as if there was a pain there. Did Eddie not see those signs? Roland wondered. Eddie had been a dull observer indeed when Roland first met him, but he had changed greatly since then, and . . .

And he loved her. *Loved* her. How could he and not see what Roland saw? The signs weren't quite as obvious as they had been on the beach at the edge of the Western Sea, when Detta was preparing to leap forward and wrest control from Odetta, but they were there, all right, and not so different, at that.

On the other hand, Roland's mother had had a saying, *love stumbles*. It could be that Eddie was simply too close to her to see. *Or doesn't want to*, Roland thought. *Doesn't want to face the idea that we might have to go through that whole business again. The business of making her face herself and her divided nature.*

Except this time it wasn't about *her*. Roland had suspected this for a long time — since before their palaver with the people of River Crossing, in fact, — and now he knew. No, it wasn't about *her*.

And so he'd lain there, listening to their breathing lengthen as they dropped off one by one: Oy, then Jake, then Susannah. Eddie last.

Well . . . not *quite* last. Faintly, very faintly, Roland could hear a murmur of conversation from the folk on the other side of yonder south hill, the ones who were trailing them and watching them. Nerving themselves to step forward and make themselves known, very likely. Roland's ears were sharp, but not quite sharp enough to pick out what they were saying. There were perhaps half a dozen murmured exchanges before someone uttered a loud shushing hiss. Then there was silence, except for the low, intermittent snuffling of the wind in the treetops. Roland lay still, looking up into the darkness where no stars shone, waiting for Susannah to rise. Eventually she did.

But before that, Jake, Eddie, and Oy went todash.

5

Roland and his mates had learned about todash (what there was to learn) from Vannay, the tutor of court in the long-ago when they had been young. They had been a quintet to begin with: Roland, Alain, Cuthbert, Jamie, and Wallace, Vannay's son. Wallace, fiercely intelligent but ever sickly, had died of the falling sickness, sometimes called king's evil. Then they had been four, and under the umbrella of true ka-tet. Vannay had known it as well, and that knowing was surely part of his sorrow.

Cort taught them to navigate by the sun and stars; Vannay showed them compass and quadrant and sextant and taught them the mathematics necessary to use them. Cort taught them to fight. With history, logic problems, and tutorials on what he called 'the universal truths,' Vannay taught them how they could sometimes avoid having to do so. Cort taught them to kill if they had to. Vannay, with his limp and his sweet but distracted smile, taught them that violence worsened problems far more often than it solved them. He called it the hollow chamber, where all true sounds became distorted by echoes.

He taught them physics — what physics there was. He taught them chemistry — what chemistry was left. He taught them to finish such sentences as 'That tree is like a' and 'When I'm running I feel as happy as a' and 'We couldn't help laughing because.' Roland hated these exercises, but Vannay wouldn't let him slip away from them. 'Your imagination is a poor thing, Roland,' the tutor told him once — Roland might have been eleven at the time. 'I will not let you feed it short rations and make it poorer still.'

He had taught them the Seven Dials of Magic, refusing to say if he believed in any of them, and Roland thought it was tangential to one of these lessons that Vannay had mentioned todash. Or perhaps you capitalized it, perhaps it was Todash. Roland didn't know for sure. He knew that Vannay had spoken of the Manni sect, people who were far travelers. And hadn't he also mentioned the Wizard's Rainbow?

Roland thought yes, but he had twice had the pink bend o' the rainbow in his own possession, once as a boy and once as a man, and although he had traveled in it both times — with his friends on the second occasion — it had never taken him todash.

Ah, but how would you know? he asked himself. *How would you know, Roland, when you were inside it?*

Because Cuthbert and Alain would have told him, that was why.

Are you sure?

Some feeling so strange as to be unidentifiable rose in the gunslinger's bosom — was it indignation? horror? perhaps even a sense of betrayal? — as he realized that no, he *wasn't* sure. All he knew was that the ball had taken him deep into itself, and he had been lucky to ever get out again.

There's no ball here, he thought, and again it was that other voice — the dry, implacable voice of his old limping tutor, whose grief for his only son had never really ended — that answered him, and the words were the same:

Are you sure?

Gunslinger, are you sure?

6

It started with a low crackling sound. Roland's first thought was the camp-fire: one of them had gotten some green fir boughs in there, the coals had finally reached them, and they were producing that sound as the needles smoldered. But—

The sound grew louder, became a kind of electric buzzing. Roland sat up and looked across the dying fire. His eyes widened and his heart began to speed up.

Susannah had turned from Eddie, had drawn away a little, too. Eddie had reached out and so had Jake. Their hands touched. And, as Roland looked at them, they commenced fading in and out of existence in a series of jerky pulses. Oy was doing the same thing. When they were gone, they were replaced by a dull gray glow that approximated the shapes and posi-tions of their bodies, as if something was holding their places in reality. Each time they came back, there would be that crackling buzz. Roland could see their closed eyelids ripple as the balls rolled beneath.

Dreaming. But not *just* dreaming. This was todash, the passing between two worlds. Supposedly the Manni could do it. And supposedly some pieces of the Wizard's Rainbow could *make* you do it, whether you wanted to or not. One piece of it in particular.

They could get caught between and fall, Roland thought. *Vannay said that, too. He said that going todash was full of peril.*

What else had he said? Roland had no time to recall, for at that moment Susannah sat up, slipped the soft leather caps Roland had made her over the stumps of her legs, then hoisted herself into her wheelchair. A moment later she was rolling toward the ancient trees on the north side of the road. It was directly away from the place where the watchers were camped; there was that much to be grateful for.

Roland stayed where he was for a moment, torn. But in the end, his course was clear enough. He couldn't wake them up while they were in the todash state; to do so would be a horrible risk. All he could do was follow Susannah, as he had on other nights, and hope she didn't get herself into trouble.

You might also do some thinking about what happens next. That was Vannay's dry, lecturely voice. Now that his old tutor was back, he apparently meant to stay for awhile. *Reason was never your strong point, but you must do it, nevertheless. You'll want to wait until your visitors make themselves known, of course — until you can be sure of what they want — but eventually, Roland, you must act. Think first, however. Sooner would be better than later.*

Yes, sooner was always better than later.

There was another loud, buzzing crackle. Eddie and Jake were back, Jake lying with his arm curled around Oy, and then they were gone again, nothing left where they had been but a faint ectoplasmic shimmer. Well, never mind. His job was to follow Susannah. As for Eddie and Jake, there would be water if God willed it.

Suppose you come back here and they're gone? It happens, Vannay said so. What will you tell her if she wakes and finds them both gone, her husband and her adopted son?

It was nothing he could worry about now. Right now there was Susannah to worry about, Susannah to keep safe.

7

On the north side of the road, old trees with enormous trunks stood at considerable distances from each other. Their branches might entwine and create a solid canopy overhead, but at ground level there was plenty of room for Susannah's wheelchair, and she moved along at a good pace, weaving between the vast ironwoods and pines, rolling downhill over a fragrant duff of mulch and needles.

Not Susannah. Not Detta or Odetta, either. This one calls herself Mia.

Roland didn't care if she called herself Queen o' Green Days, as long as she came back safe, and the other two were still there when she did.

He began to smell a brighter, fresher green: reeds and water-weeds. With it came the smell of mud, the thump of frogs, the sarcastic *hool! hool!* salute of an owl, the splash of water as something jumped. This was followed by a thin shriek as something died, maybe the jumper, maybe the jumped-upon. Underbrush began to spring up in the duff, first dotting it and then crowding it out. The tree-cover thinned. Mosquitoes and chiggers whined. Binnie-bugs stitched the air. The bog-smells grew stronger.

The wheels of the chair had passed over the duff without leaving any trace. As duff gave way to straggling low growth, Roland began to see broken twigs and torn-off leaves marking her passage. Then, as she reached the more or less level low ground, the wheels began to sink into the increasingly soft earth. Twenty paces farther on, he began to see liquid seeping into the tracks. She was too wise to get stuck, though — too crafty. Twenty paces beyond the first signs of seepage, he came to the wheelchair itself, abandoned. Lying on the seat were her pants and shirt. She had gone on into the bog naked save for the leather caps that covered her stumps.

Down here there were ribbons of mist hanging over puddles of standing water. Grassy hummocks rose; on one, wired to a dead log that had been planted upright, was what Roland at first took for an ancient stuffy-guy. When he got closer, he saw it was a human skeleton. The skull's forehead had been smashed inward, leaving a triangle of darkness between the staring sockets. Some sort of primitive war-club had made that wound, no doubt, and the corpse (or its lingering *spirit*) had been left to mark this as the edge of some tribe's territory. They were probably long dead or moved on, but caution was ever a virtue. Roland drew his gun and continued after the woman, stepping from hummock to hummock, wincing at the occasional jab of pain in his right hip. It took all his concentration and agility to keep up with her. Partly this was because she hadn't Roland's interest in staying as dry as possible. She was as naked as a mermaid and moved like one, as comfortable in the muck and swamp-ooze as on dry land. She crawled over the larger hummocks, slid through the water between them, pausing every now and then to pick off a leech. In the darkness, the walking and sliding seemed to merge into a single slithering motion that was eely and disturbing.

She went on perhaps a quarter of a mile into the increasingly oozy bog with the gunslinger following patiently along behind her. He kept as quiet as possible, although he doubted if there was any need; the part of her that saw and felt and thought was far from here.

At last she came to a halt, standing on her truncated legs and holding to tough tangles of brush on either side in order to keep her balance. She looked out over the black surface of a pond, head up, body still. The gunslinger couldn't tell if the pond was big or small; its borders were lost in the mist. Yet there was light here, some sort of faint and unfocused radiance which seemed to lie just beneath the surface of the water itself, perhaps emanating from submerged and slowly rotting logs.

She stood there, surveying this muck-crusted woodland pond like a queen surveying a . . . a what? What did she see? A banquet hall? That was what he had come to believe. Almost to see. It was a whisper from her mind to his, and it dovetailed with what she said and did. The banqueting hall was her mind's ingenious way of keeping Susannah apart from Mia as it had kept Odetta apart from Detta all those years. Mia might have any number of reasons for wanting to keep her existence a secret, but surely the greatest of these had to do with the life she carried inside her.

The chap, she called it.

Then, with a suddenness that still startled him (although he had seen this before, as well), she began to hunt, slipping in eerie splashless silence first along the edge of the pond and then a little way out into it. Roland watched her with an expression that contained both horror and lust as she knitted and wove her way in and out of the reeds, between and over the tussocks. Now, instead of picking the leeches off her skin and throwing them away, she tossed them into her mouth like pieces of candy. The muscles in her thighs rippled. Her brown skin gleamed like wet silk. When she turned (Roland had by this time stepped behind a tree and become one of the shadows), he could clearly see the way her breasts had ripened.

The problem, of course, extended beyond 'the chap.' There was Eddie to consider, as well. *What the hell's wrong with you, Roland?* Roland could hear him saying. *That might be our kid. I mean, you can't know for sure that it isn't. Yeah, yeah, I know something had her while we were yanking Jake through, but that doesn't necessarily mean . . .*

On and on and on, blah-blah-blah as Eddie himself might say, and why? Because he loved her and would want the child of their union. And because arguing came as naturally to Eddie Dean as breathing. Cuthbert had been the same.

In the reeds, the naked woman's hand pistoned forward and seized a good-sized frog. She squeezed and the frog popped, squirting guts and a shiny load of eggs between her fingers. Its head burst. She lifted it to her mouth and ate it greedily down while its greenish-white rear legs still twitched, licking the blood and shiny ropes of tissue from her knuckles. Then she mimed throwing something down and cried out '*How you like that, you stinkin Blue Lady?*' in a low, guttural voice that made Roland shiver. It was Detta Walker's voice. Detta at her meanest and craziest.

With hardly a pause she moved on again, questing. Next it was a small fish . . . then another frog . . . and then a real prize: a water-rat that squeaked and writhed and tried to bite. She crushed the life out of it and stuffed it into her mouth, paws and all. A moment later she bent her head down and regurgitated the waste — a twisted mass of fur and splintered bones.

Show him this, then — always assuming that he and Jake get back from whatever adventure they're on, that is. And say, 'I know that women are supposed to have strange cravings when they carry a child, Eddie, but doesn't this seem a little too strange? Look at her, questing through the reeds and ooze like some sort of human alligator. Look at her and tell me she's doing that in order to feed your child. Any human child.'

Still he would argue. Roland knew it. What he *didn't* know was what Susannah herself might do when Roland told her she was growing something that craved raw meat in the middle of the night. And as if this business wasn't worrisome enough, now there was todash. And strangers who had come looking for them. Yet the strangers were the least of his problems. In fact, he found their presence almost comforting. He didn't know what they wanted, and yet he *did* know. He had met them before, many times. At bottom, they always wanted the same thing.

8

Now the woman who called herself Mia began to talk as she hunted. Roland was familiar with this part of her ritual as well, but it chilled him nevertheless. He was looking right at her and it was still hard to believe all those different voices could be coming from the same throat. She asked herself how she was. She told herself she was doing fine, thank you so *vereh* much. She spoke of someone named Bill, or perhaps it was Bull. She asked after someone's mother. She asked someone about a place called Morehouse, and then in a deep, gravelly voice — a man's voice, beyond doubt — she told herself that she didn't go to Morehouse or *no* house. She laughed raucously at this, so it must have been some sort of joke. She introduced herself several times (as she had on other nights) as Mia, a name Roland knew well from his early life in Gilead. It was almost a holy name. Twice she curtsied, lifting invisible skirts in a way that tugged at the gunslinger's heart — he had first seen that sort of curtsy in Mejis, when he and his friends Alain and Cuthbert had been sent there by their fathers.

She worked her way back to the edge of the

(*hall*)

pond, glistening and wet. She stayed there without moving for five minutes, then ten. The owl uttered its derisive salute again — *hool!* — and as if in response, the moon came out of the clouds for a brief look around. When it did, some small animal's bit of shady concealment disappeared. It tried to dart past the woman. She snared it faultlessly and plunged her face into its writhing belly. There was a wet crunching noise, followed by several smacking bites. She held the remains up in the moonlight, her dark hands and wrists darker with its blood. Then she tore it in half and bolted down the remains. She gave a resounding belch and rolled herself back into the water. This time she made a great splash, and Roland knew tonight's banqueting was done. She had even eaten some of the binnie-bugs, snatching them effortlessly out of the air. He could only hope nothing she'd taken in would sicken her. So far, nothing had.

While she made her rough toilet, washing off the mud and blood, Roland retreated back the way he'd come, ignoring the more frequent pains in his hip and moving with all his guile. He had watched her go through this three times before, and once had been enough to see how gruesomely sharp her senses were while in this state.

He paused at her wheelchair, looking around to make sure he'd left no trace of himself. He saw a bootprint, smoothed it away, then tossed a few leaves over it for good measure. Not too many; too many might be worse than none at all. With that done, he headed back toward the road and their camp, not hurrying anymore. She would pause for a little housekeeping of her own before going on. What would Mia see as she was cleaning Susannah's wheelchair, he wondered? Some sort of small, motorized cart? It didn't matter. What did was how clever she was. If he hadn't awakened with a need to make water just as she left on one of her earlier expeditions, he quite likely still wouldn't know about her hunting trips, and he was supposed to be clever about such things.

Not as clever as she, maggot. Now, as if the ghost of Vannay were not enough, here was Cort to lecture him. *She's shown you before, hasn't she?*

Yes. She had shown him cleverness as three women. Now there was this fourth.

9

When Roland saw the break in the trees ahead — the road they'd been following, and the place where they'd camped for the night — he took two long, deep breaths. These were meant to steady him and didn't succeed very well.

Water if God wills it, he reminded himself. *About the great matters, Roland, you have no say.*

Not a comfortable truth, especially for a man on a quest such as his, but one he'd learned to live with.

He took another breath, then stepped out. He released the air in a long, relieved sigh as he saw Eddie and Jake lying deeply asleep beside the dead fire. Jake's right hand, which had been linked with Eddie's left when the gunslinger had followed Susannah out of camp, now circled Oy's body.

The bumbler opened one eye and regarded Roland. Then he closed it again.

Roland couldn't hear her coming, but sensed her just the same. He lay down quickly, rolled over onto his side, and put his face in the crook of his elbow. And from this position he watched as the wheelchair rolled out of the trees. She had cleaned it quickly but well. Roland couldn't see a single spot of mud. The spokes gleamed in the moonlight.

She parked the chair where it had been before, slipped out of it with her usual grace, and moved across to where Eddie lay. Roland watched her approach her husband's sleeping form with some anxiety. Anyone, he thought, who had met Detta Walker would have felt that anxiety. Because the woman who called herself *mother* was simply too close to what Detta had been.

Lying completely still, like one in sleep's deepest sling, Roland prepared himself to move.

Then she brushed the hair back from the side of Eddie's face and kissed the hollow of his temple. The tenderness in that gesture told the gunslinger all he needed to know. It was safe to sleep. He closed his eyes and let the darkness take him.

CHAPTER IV

PALAVER

1

When Roland woke in the morning, Susannah was still asleep but Eddie and Jake were up. Eddie had built a small new fire on the gray bones of the old one. He and the boy sat close to it for the warmth, eating what Eddie called gunslinger burritos. They looked both excited and worried.

'Roland,' Eddie said, 'I think we need to talk. Something happened to us last night—'

'I know,' Roland said. 'I saw. You went todash.'

'Todash?' Jake asked. 'What's that?'

Roland started to tell them, then shook his head. 'If we're going to palaver, Eddie, you'd better wake Susannah up. That way we won't have to double back over the first part.' He glanced south. 'And hopefully our new friends won't interrupt us until we've had our talk. They're none of this.' But already he was wondering about that.

He watched with more than ordinary interest as Eddie shook Susannah awake, quite sure but by no means positive that it *would* be Susannah who opened her eyes. It was. She sat up, stretched, ran her fingers through her tight curls. 'What's your problem, honeychile? I was good for another hour, at least.'

'We need to talk, Suze,' Eddie said.

'All you want, but not quite yet,' she said. '*God*, but I'm stiff.'

'Sleeping on hard ground'll do it every time,' Eddie said.

Not to mention hunting naked in the bogs and damps, Roland thought.

'Pour me some water, sug.' She held out her palms, and Eddie filled them with water from one of the skins. She dashed this over her cheeks and into her eyes, gave out a little shivery cry, and said, 'Cold.'

'Old!' Oy said.

'Not yet,' she told the bumbler, 'but you give me a few more months like the last few, and I *will* be. Roland, you Mid-World folks know about coffee, right?'

77

Roland nodded. 'From the plantations of the Outer Arc. Down south.'

'If we come across some, we'll hook it, won't we? You promise me, now.'

'I promise,' Roland said.

Susannah, meanwhile, was studying Eddie. 'What's going on? You boys don't look so good.'

'More dreams,' Eddie said.

'Me too,' Jake said.

'Not dreams,' the gunslinger said. 'Susannah, how did *you* sleep?'

She looked at him candidly. Roland did not sense even the shadow of a lie in her answer. 'Like a rock, as I usually do. One thing all this traveling *is* good for – you can throw your damn Nembutal away.'

'What's this toadish thing, Roland?' Eddie asked.

'Todash,' he said, and explained it to them as well as he could. What he remembered best from Vannay's teachings was how the Manni spent long periods fasting in order to induce the right state of mind, and how they traveled around, looking for exactly the right spot in which to induce the todash state. This was something they determined with magnets and large plumb-bobs.

'Sounds to me like these guys would have been right at home down in Needle Park,' Eddie said.

'Anywhere in Greenwich Village,' Susannah added.

'"Sounds Hawaiian, doesn't it?"' Jake said in a grave, deep voice, and they all laughed. Even Roland laughed a little.

'Todash is another way of traveling,' Eddie said when the laughter had stopped. 'Like the doors. And the glass balls. Is that right?'

Roland started to say yes, then hesitated. 'I think they might all be variations of the same thing,' he said. 'And according to Vannay, the glass balls – the pieces of the Wizard's Rainbow – make going todash easier. Sometimes *too* easy.'

Jake said, 'We really flickered on and off like . . . like lightbulbs? What you call sparklights?'

'Yes – you appeared and disappeared. When you were gone, there was a dim glow where you'd been, almost as if something were holding your place for you.'

'Thank God if it was,' Eddie said. 'When it ended . . . when those chimes started playing again and we kicked loose . . . I'll tell you the truth, I didn't think we were going to get back.'

'Neither did I,' Jake said quietly. The sky had clouded over again, and in the dull morning light, the boy looked very pale. 'I lost you.'

'I was never so glad to see anyplace in my life as I was when I opened my eyes and saw this little piece of road,' Eddie said. 'And you beside me, Jake. Even Rover looked good to me.' He glanced at Oy, then over at Susannah. 'Nothing like this happened to you last night, hon?'

'We'd have seen her,' Jake said.

'Not if she todashed off to someplace else,' Eddie said.

Susannah shook her head, looking troubled. 'I just slept the night away. As I told you. What about you, Roland?'

'Nothing to report,' Roland said. As always, he would keep his own counsel until his instinct told him it was time to share. And besides, what he'd said wasn't exactly a lie. He looked keenly at Eddie and Jake. 'There's trouble, isn't there?'

Eddie and Jake looked at each other, then back at Roland. Eddie sighed. 'Yeah, probably.'

'How bad? Do you know?'

'I don't think we do. Do we, Jake?'

Jake shook his head.

'But I've got some ideas,' Eddie went on, 'and if I'm right, we've got a problem. A *big* one.' He swallowed. Hard. Jake touched his hand, and the gunslinger was concerned to see how quickly and firmly Eddie took hold of the boy's fingers.

Roland reached out and drew Susannah's hand into his own. He had a brief vision of that hand seizing a frog and squeezing the guts out of it. He put it out of his mind. The woman who had done that was not here now.

'Tell us,' he said to Eddie and Jake. 'Tell us everything. We would hear it all.'

'Every word,' Susannah agreed. 'For your fathers' sakes.'

2

They recounted what had happened to them in the New York of 1977. Roland and Susannah listened, fascinated, as they told of following Jake to the bookstore, and of seeing Balazar and his gentlemen pull up in front.

'Huh!' Susannah said. 'The very same bad boys! It's almost like a Dickens novel.'

'Who is Dickens, and what is a novel?' Roland asked.

'A novel's a long story set down in a book,' she said. 'Dickens wrote about a dozen. He was maybe the best who ever lived. In his stories, folks in this big city called London kept meeting people they knew from other places or long ago. I had a teacher in college who hated the way that always happened. He said Dickens's stories were full of easy coincidences.'

'A teacher who either didn't know about ka or didn't believe in it,' Roland said.

Eddie was nodding. 'Yeah, this is ka, all right. No doubt.'

'I'm more interested in the woman who wrote *Charlie the Choo-Choo* than this storyteller Dickens,' Roland said. 'Jake, I wonder if you'd—'

'I'm way ahead of you,' Jake said, unbuckling the straps of his pack. Almost reverently, he slid out the battered book telling the adventures of Charlie the locomotive and his friend, Engineer Bob. They all looked at the cover. The name below the picture was still Beryl Evans.

'Man,' Eddie said. 'That is so weird. I mean, I don't want to get side-tracked, or anything . . .' He paused, realizing he had just made a railroading pun, then went on. Roland wasn't very interested in puns and jokes, anyway. '. . . but that is *weird*. The one Jake bought — Jake Seventy-seven — was by Claudia something Bachman.'

'Inez,' Jake said. 'Also, there was a *y*. A lowercase *y*. Any of you know what that means?'

None of them did, but Roland said there had been names like it in Mejis. 'I believe it was some sort of added honorific. And I'm not sure it *is* to the side. Jake, you said the sign in the window was different from before. How?'

'I can't remember. But you know what? I think if you hypnotized me again — you know, with the bullet — I could.'

'And in time I may,' Roland said, 'but this morning time is short.'

Back to that again, Eddie thought. *Yesterday it hardly existed, and now it's short. But it's all about time, somehow, isn't it? Roland's old days, our old days, and these new days. These dangerous new days.*

'Why?' Susannah asked.

'Our friends,' Roland said, and nodded to the south. 'I have a feeling they'll be making themselves known to us soon.'

'*Are* they our friends?' Jake asked.

'That really *is* to the side,' Roland said, and again wondered if that were really true. 'For now, let's turn the mind of our khef to this Bookstore of the Mind, or whatever it's called. You saw the harriers from the Leaning Tower greensticking the owner, didn't you? This man Tower, or Toren.'

'Pressuring him, you mean?' Eddie asked. 'Twisting his arm?'

'Yes.'

'Sure they were,' Jake said.

'Were,' Oy put in. 'Sure were.'

'Bet you anything that Tower and Toren are really the same name,' Susannah said. 'That *toren*'s Dutch for "tower."' She saw Roland getting ready to speak, and held up her hand. 'It's the way folks often do things in our bit of the universe, Roland – change the foreign name to one that's more . . . well . . . American.'

'Yeah,' Eddie said. 'So Stempowicz becomes Stamper . . . Yakov becomes Jacob . . . or . . .'

'Or Beryl Evans becomes Claudia y Inez Bachman,' Jake said. He laughed but didn't sound very amused.

Eddie picked a half-burned stick out of the fire and began to doodle with it in the dirt. One by one the Great Letters formed: C . . . L . . . A . . . U. 'Big Nose even *said* Tower was Dutch. "A squarehead's always a square-head, right, boss?"' He looked at Jake for confirmation. Jake nodded, then took the stick and continued on with it: D . . . I . . . A.

'Him being Dutch makes a lot of sense, you know,' Susannah said. 'At one time, the Dutch owned most of Manhattan.'

'You want another Dickens touch?' Jake asked. He wrote y in the dirt after CLAUDIA, then looked up at Susannah. 'How about the haunted house where I came through into this world?'

'The Mansion,' Eddie said.

'The Mansion in *Dutch Hill*,' Jake said.

'Dutch Hill. Yeah, that's right. Goddam.'

'Let's go to the core,' Roland said. 'I think it's the agreement paper you saw. And you felt you *had* to see it, didn't you?'

Eddie nodded.

'Did your need feel like a part of following the Beam?'

'Roland, I think it *was* the Beam.'

'The way to the Tower, in other words.'

'Yeah.' Eddie said. He was thinking about the way clouds flowed along the Beam, the way shadows bent along the Beam, the way every twig of every tree seemed to turn in its direction. *All things serve the Beam*, Roland had told them, and Eddie's need to see the paper Balazar had put in front of Calvin Tower had felt like a need, harsh and imperative.

'Tell me what it said.'

Eddie bit his lip. He didn't feel as scared about this as he had about carving the key which had ultimately allowed them to rescue Jake and pull him through to this side, but it was close. Because, like the key, this was important. If he forgot something, worlds might crash.

'Man, I can't remember it all, not word for word—'

Roland made an impatient gesture. 'If I need that, I'll hypnotize you and *get* it word for word.'

'Do you think it matters?' Susannah asked.

'I think it *all* matters,' Roland said.

'What if hypnosis doesn't work on me?' Eddie asked. 'What if I'm not, like, a good subject?'

'Leave that to me,' Roland said.

'Nineteen,' Jake said abruptly. They all turned toward him. He was looking at the letters he and Eddie had drawn in the dirt beside the dead campfire. 'Claudia y Inez Bachman. Nineteen letters.'

3

Roland considered for a moment, then let it pass. If the number nineteen *was* somehow part of this, its meaning would declare itself in time. For now there were other matters.

'The paper,' he said. 'Let's stay with that for now. Tell me everything about it you can remember.'

'Well, it was a legal agreement, with the seal at the bottom and everything.' Eddie paused, struck by a fairly basic question. Roland *probably* got this part of it – he'd been a kind of law enforcement officer, after all – but it wouldn't hurt to be sure. 'You know about lawyers, don't you?'

Roland spoke in his driest tone. 'You forget that I came from Gilead, Eddie. The most inner of the Inner Baronies. We had more merchants and farmers and manufactors than lawyers, I think, but the count would have been close.'

Susannah laughed. 'You make me think of a scene from Shakespeare,

Roland. Two characters — might have been Falstaff and Prince Hal, I'm not sure — are talkin about what they're gonna do when they win the war and take over. And one of em says, "First we'll kill all the lawyers."'

'It would be a fairish way to start,' Roland said, and Eddie found his thoughtful tone rather chilling. Then the gunslinger turned to him again. 'Go on. If you can add anything, Jake, please do. And relax, both of you, for your fathers' sakes. For now I only want a sketch.'

Eddie supposed he'd known that, but hearing Roland say it made him feel better. 'All right. It was a Memorandum of Agreement. That was right at the top, in big letters. At the bottom it said *Agreed to*, and there were two signatures. One was Calvin Tower. The other was Richard someone. Do you remember, Jake?'

'Sayre,' Jake said. 'Richard Patrick Sayre.' He paused briefly, lips moving, then nodded. 'Nineteen letters.'

'And what did it say, this agreement?' Roland asked.

'Not all that much, if you want to know the truth,' Eddie said. 'Or that's what it seemed like to me, anyway. Basically it said that Tower owned a vacant lot on the corner of Forty-sixth Street and Second Avenue—'

'*The* vacant lot,' Jake said. 'The one with the rose in it.'

'Yeah, that one. Anyway, Tower signed this agreement on July 15th, 1976. Sombra Corporation gave him a hundred grand. What he gave them, so far as I could tell, was a promise not to sell the lot to anyone but Sombra for the next year, to take care of it — pay the taxes and such — and then to give Sombra first right of purchase, assuming he hasn't sold it to them by then, anyway. Which he hadn't when we were there, but the agreement still had a month and a half to run.'

'Mr Tower said the hundred thousand was all spent,' Jake put in.

'Was there anything in the agreement about this Sombra Corporation having a topping privilege?' Susannah asked.

Eddie and Jake thought it over, exchanged a glance, then shook their heads.

'Sure?' Susannah asked.

'Not quite, but *pretty* sure,' Eddie said. 'You think it matters?'

'I don't know,' Susannah said. 'The kind of agreement you're talking about . . . well, without a topping privilege, it just doesn't seem to make sense. What does it boil down to, when you stop to think about it? "I, Calvin Tower, agree to think about selling you my vacant lot. You pay me a hundred thousand dollars and I'll think about it for a whole year. When I'm not drinking coffee and playing chess with my friends, that is. And when the year's up, maybe I'll sell it to you and maybe I'll keep it and maybe I'll just auction it off to the highest bidder. And if you don't like it, sweetcheeks, you just go spit."'

'You're forgetting something,' Roland said mildly.

'What?' Susannah asked.

'This Sombra is no ordinary law-abiding combination. Ask yourself if an ordinary law-abiding combination would hire someone like Balazar to carry their messages.'

'You have a point,' Eddie said. 'Tower was *mucho* scared.'

'Anyway,' Jake said, 'it makes at least a few things clearer. The sign I saw in the vacant lot, for instance. This Sombra Company also got the right to "advertise forthcoming projects" there for their hundred thousand. Did you see that part, Eddie?'

'I think so. Right after the part about Tower not permitting any liens or encumbrances on his property, because of Sombra's "stated interest," wasn't it?'

'Right,' Jake said. 'The sign I saw in the lot said . . .' He paused, thinking, then raised his hands and looked between them, as if reading a sign only he could see: 'MILLS CONSTRUCTION AND SOMBRA REAL ESTATE ASSOCIATES ARE CONTINUING TO REMAKE THE FACE OF MANHATTAN. And then, COMING SOON, TURTLE BAY LUXURY CONDOMINIUMS.'

'So that's what they want it for,' Eddie said. 'Condos. But—'

'What are condominiums?' Susannah asked, frowning. 'It sounds like some newfangled kind of spice rack.'

'It's a kind of co-op apartment deal,' Eddie said. 'They probably had em in your when, but by a different name.'

'Yeah,' Susannah said with some asperity. 'We called em co-ops. Or sometimes we went *way* downtown and called em apartment buildings.'

'It doesn't matter because it was never about condos,' Jake said. 'Never about the building the sign said they were going to put there, for that matter. All that's only, you know . . . shoot, what's the word?'

'Camouflage?' Roland suggested.

Jake grinned. 'Camuflage, yeah. It's about the *rose*, not the building! And they can't get at it until they own the ground it grows on. I'm sure of it.'

'You may be right about the building's not meaning anything,' Susannah said, 'but that Turtle Bay name has a certain resonance, wouldn't you say?'

She looked at the gunslinger. 'That part of Manhattan is *called* Turtle Bay, Roland.'

He nodded, unsurprised. The Turtle was one of the twelve Guardians, and almost certainly stood at the far end of the Beam upon which they now traveled.

'The people from Mills Construction might not know about the rose,' Jake said, 'but I bet the ones from Sombra Corporation do.' His hand stole into Oy's fur, which was thick enough at the billy-bumbler's neck to make his fingers disappear entirely. 'I think that somewhere in New York City – in some business building, probably in Turtle Bay on the East Side – there's a door marked SOMBRA CORPORATION. And someplace behind that door there's *another* door. The kind that takes you here.'

For a minute they sat thinking about it – about worlds spinning on a single axle in dying harmony – and no one said anything.

4

'Here's what I think is happening,' Eddie said. 'Suze, Jake, feel free to step in if you think I'm getting it wrong. This guy Cal Tower's some sort of custodian for the rose. He may not know it on a conscious level, but he must be. Him and maybe his whole family before him. It explains the name.'

'Only he's the last,' Jake said.

'You can't be sure of that, hon,' Susannah said.

'No wedding ring,' Jake responded, and Susannah nodded, giving him that one, at least provisionally.

'Maybe at one time there were lots of Torens owning lots of New York property,' Eddie said, 'but those days are gone. Now the only thing standing between the Sombra Corporation and the rose is one nearly broke fat guy who changed his name. He's a . . . what do you call someone who loves books?'

'A bibliophile,' Susannah said.

'Yeah, one of those. And George Biondi may not be Einstein, but he said at least one smart thing while we were eavesdropping. He said Tower's place wasn't a real shop but just a hole you poured money into. What's going on with him is a pretty old story where we come from, Roland. When my Ma used to see some rich guy on TV – Donald Trump, for instance—'

'Who?' Susannah asked.

'You don't know him, he would've been just a kid back in '64. And it doesn't matter. "Shirtsleeves to shirtsleeves in three generations," my mother would tell us. "It's the American way, boys."

'So here's Tower, and he's sort of like Roland -- the last of his line. He sells off a piece of property here and a piece there, making his taxes, making his house payments, keeping up with the credit cards and the doctor bills, paying for his stock. And yeah, I'm making this up . . . except somehow it doesn't feel that way.'

'No,' Jake said. He spoke in a low, fascinated voice. 'It doesn't.'

'Perhaps you shared his khef,' Roland said. 'More likely, you touched him. As my old friend Alain used to. Go on, Eddie.'

'And every year he tells himself the bookstore'll turn around. Catch on, maybe, the way things in New York sometimes do. Get out of the red and into the black and then he'll be okay. And finally there's only one thing left to sell: lot two-ninety-eight on Block Nineteen in Turtle Bay.'

'Two-nine-eight adds up to nineteen,' Susannah said. 'I wish I could decide if that means something or if it's just Blue Car Syndrome.'

'What's Blue Car Syndrome?' Jake asked.

'When you buy a blue car, you see blue cars everywhere.'

'Not here, you don't,' Jake said.

'Not here,' Oy put in, and they all looked at him. Days, sometimes whole weeks would go by, and Oy would do nothing but give out the occasional echo of their talk. Then he would say something that might almost have been the product of original thought. But you didn't know. Not for sure. Not even Jake knew for sure.

The way we don't know for sure about nineteen, Susannah thought, and gave the bumbler a pat on the head. Oy responded with a companionable wink.

'He holds onto that lot until the bitter end,' Eddie said. 'I mean hey, he doesn't even own the crappy building his bookstore's in, he only leases it.'

Jake took over. 'Tom and Jerry's Artistic Deli goes out of business, and Tower has it torn down. Because part of him wants to sell the lot. That part of him says he'd be crazy not to.' Jake fell silent for a moment, thinking about how some thoughts came in the middle of the night. Crazy thoughts, crazy ideas, and voices that wouldn't shut up. 'But there's *another* part of him, another voice—'

'The voice of the Turtle,' Susannah put in quietly.

'Yes, the Turtle or the Beam,' Jake agreed. 'They're probably the same thing. And this voice tells him he has to hold onto it at all costs.' He looked at Eddie. 'Do you think he knows about the rose? Do you think he goes down there sometimes and looks at it?'

'Does a rabbit shit in the woods?' Eddie responded. 'Sure he goes. And sure he *knows*. On some level he *must* know. Because a corner lot in Manhattan . . . how much would a thing like that be worth, Susannah?'

'In my time, probably a million bucks,' she said. 'By 1977, God knows. Three? Five?' She shrugged. 'Enough to let sai Tower go on selling books at a loss for the rest of his life, provided he was reasonably careful about how he invested the principal.'

Eddie said, 'Everything about this shows how reluctant he is to sell. I mean Suze already pointed out how little Sombra got for their hundred grand.'

'But they *did* get something,' Roland said. 'Something very important.'

'A foot in the door,' Eddie said.

'You say true. And now, as the term of their agreement winds down, they send your world's version of the Big Coffin Hunters. Hard-caliber boys. If greed or necessity doesn't compel Tower to sell them the land with the rose on it, they'll terrify him into it.'

'Yeah,' Jake said. And who would stand on Tower's side? Maybe Aaron Deepneau. Maybe no one. 'So what do we do?'

'Buy it ourselves,' Susannah said promptly. 'Of course.'

5

There was a moment of thunderstruck silence, and then Eddie nodded thoughtfully. 'Sure, why not? The Sombra Corporation doesn't have a topping privilege in their little agreement — they probably tried, but Tower wouldn't go for it. So sure, we'll buy it. How many deerskins do you think he'll want? Forty? Fifty? If he's a real hard bargainer, maybe we can throw in some relics from the Old People. You know, cups and plates and arrowheads. They'd be conversation pieces at cocktail parties.'

Susannah was looking at him reproachfully.

'Okay, maybe not so funny,' Eddie said. 'But we have to face the facts, hon. We're nothing but a bunch of dirty ass pilgrims currently camped out in some other reality — I mean, this isn't even Mid-World anymore.'

'Also,' Jake said apologetically, 'we weren't even really there, at least not the way you are when you go through one of the doors. They sensed us, but basically we were invisible.'

'Let's take one thing at a time,' Susannah said. 'As far as money goes, I have plenty. If we could get at it, that is.'

'How much?' Jake asked. 'I know that's sort of impolite — my mother'd faint if she heard me ask someone that, but—'

'We've come a little bit too far to worry about being polite,' Susannah said. 'Truth is, honey, I don't exactly know. My dad invented a couple of new dental processes that had to do with capping teeth, and he made the most of it. Started a company called Holmes Dental Industries and handled the financial side mostly by himself until 1959.'

'The year Mort pushed you in front of the subway train,' Eddie said.

She nodded. 'That happened in August. About six weeks later, my father had a heart attack — the first of many. Some of it was probably stress over what happened to me, but I won't own all of it. He was a hard driver, pure and simple.'

'You don't have to own *any* of it,' Eddie said. 'I mean, it's not as if you *jumped* in front of that subway car, Suze.'

'I know. But how you feel and how long you feel it doesn't always have a lot to do with objective truth. With Mama gone, it was my job to take care of him and I couldn't handle it — I could never completely get the idea that it was my fault out of my head.'

'Gone days,' Roland said, and without much sympathy.

'Thanks, sug,' Susannah said dryly. 'You have *such* a way of puttin things in perspective. In any case, my Dad turned over the financial side of the company to his accountant after that first heart attack — an old friend named Moses Carver. After my Dad passed, Pop Mose took care of things for me. I'd guess that when Roland yanked me out of New York and into this charming piece of nowhere, I might have been worth eight or ten million dollars. Would that be enough to buy Mr Tower's lot, always assuming he'd sell it to us?'

'He probably *would* sell it for deerskins, if Eddie's right about the Beam,' Roland said. 'I believe a deep part of Mr Tower's mind and spirit — the ka that made him hold onto the lot for so long in the first place — has been waiting for us.'

'Waiting for the cavalry,' Eddie said with a trace of a grin. 'Like Fort Ord in the last ten minutes of a John Wayne movie.'

Roland looked at him, unsmiling. 'He's been waiting for the White.'

Susannah held her brown hands up to her brown face and looked at them. 'Then I guess he isn't waiting for me,' she said.

'Yes,' Roland said, 'he is.' And wondered, briefly, what color that other one was. Mia.

'We need a door,' Jake said.

'We need at least two,' Eddie said. 'One to deal with Tower, sure. But before we can do that, we need one to go back to Susannah's *when*. And I mean as close to when Roland took her as we can possibly get. It'd be a bummer to go back to 1977, get in touch with this guy Carver, and discover he had Odetta Holmes declared legally dead in 1971. That the whole estate had been turned over to relatives in Green Bay or San Berdoo.'

'Or to go back to 1968 and discover Mr Carver was gone,' Jake said. 'Funneled everything into his own accounts and retired to the Costa del Sol.'

Susannah was looking at him with a shocked oh-my-lands expression that would have been funny under other circumstances. 'Pop Mose'd never do such a thing! Why, he's my godfather!'

Jake looked embarrassed. 'Sorry. I read lots of mystery novels – Agatha Christie, Rex Stout, Ed McBain – and stuff like that happens in them all the time.'

'Besides,' Eddie said, 'big money can do weird things to people.'

She gave him a cold and considering glance that looked strange, almost alien, on her face. Roland, who knew something Eddie and Jake didn't, thought it a frog-squeezing look. 'How would *you* know?' she asked. And then, almost at once, 'Oh, sugar, I'm sorry. That was uncalled-for.'

'It's okay,' Eddie said. He smiled. The smile looked stiff and unsure of itself. 'Heat of the moment.' He reached out, took her hand, squeezed it. She squeezed back. The smile on Eddie's face grew a little, started to look as if it belonged there.

'It's just that I know Moses Carver. He's as honest as the day is long.'

Eddie raised his hand – not signaling belief so much as an unwillingness to go any further down that path.

'Let me see if I understand your idea,' Roland said. 'First, it depends upon our ability to go back to your world of New York at not just one point of when, but two.'

There was a pause while they parsed that, and then Eddie nodded. 'Right. 1964, to start with. Susannah's been gone a couple of months, but nobody's given up hope or anything like that. She strolls in, everybody claps. Return of the prodigal daughter. We get the dough, which might take a little time—'

'The hard part's apt to be getting Pop Mose to let go of it,' Susannah said. 'When it comes to money in the bank, that man got a tight grip. And I'm pretty sure that in his heart, he still sees me as eight years old.'

'But legally it's yours, right?' Eddie asked. Roland could see that he was still proceeding with some caution. Hadn't quite got over that crack – How would *you* know? – just yet. And the look that had gone with it. 'I mean, he can't stop you from taking it, can he?'

'No, honey,' she said. 'My Dad and Pop Mose made me a trust fund, but it went moot in 1959, when I turned twenty-five.' She turned her eyes – dark eyes of amazing beauty and expression – upon him. 'There. You don't need to devil me about my age anymore, do you? If you can subtract, you can figure it out for yourself.'

'It doesn't matter,' Eddie said. 'Time is a face on the water.'

Roland felt gooseflesh run up his arms. Somewhere – perhaps in a glaring, blood-colored field of roses still far from here – a rustie had just walked over his grave.

6

'Has to be cash,' Jake said in a dry, businesslike tone.

'Huh?' Eddie looked away from Susannah with an effort.

'Cash,' Jake repeated. 'No one'd honor a check, even a cashier's check, that was thirteen years old. Especially not one for millions of dollars.'

'How do you know stuff like that, sug?' Susannah asked.

Jake shrugged. Like it or not (usually he didn't), he was Elmer Chambers's son. Elmer Chambers wasn't one of the world's good guys – Roland would never call him part of the White – but he had been a master of what network execs called 'the kill.' *A Big Coffin Hunter in TV Land*, Jake thought. Maybe that was a little unfair, but saying that Elmer Chambers knew how to play the angles was definitely *not* unfair. And yeah, he was Jake, son of Elmer. He hadn't forgotten the face of his father, although he had times when he wished that wasn't so.

'Cash, by all means cash,' Eddie said, breaking the silence. 'A deal like this has to be cash. If there's a check, we cash it in 1964, not 1977. Stick it in a gym-bag – did they have gym-bags in 1964, Suze? Never mind. Doesn't matter. We stick it in a bag and take it to 1977. Doesn't have to be the same day Jake bought *Charlie the Choo-Choo* and *Riddle-De-Dum*, but it ought to be close.'

'And it can't be after July fifteenth of '77,' Jake put in.

'God, no,' Eddie agreed. 'We'd be all too likely to find Balazar'd persuaded Tower to sell, and there we'd be, bag of cash in one hand, thumbs up our asses, and big grins on our faces to pass the time of day.'

There was a moment of silence – perhaps they were considering this lurid image – and then Roland said, 'You make it sound very easy, and why not? To you three, the concept of doorways between this world and your world of tack-sees and astin and fottergrafs seems almost as mundane as riding a mule would to me. Or strapping on a sixgun. And there's good reason for you to feel that way. Each of you has been through one of these doors. Eddie has actually gone both ways – into this world and then back into his own.'

'I gotta tell you that the return trip to New York wasn't much fun,' Eddie said. 'Too much gunplay.' *Not to mention my brother's severed head rolling across the floor of Balazar's office.*

'Neither was getting through the door on Dutch Hill,' Jake added.

Roland nodded, ceding these points without yielding his own. 'All my life I've accepted what you said the first time I knew you, Jake – what you said when you were dying.'

Jake looked down, pale and without answer. He did not like to recall that (it was mercifully hazy in any case), and knew that Roland didn't, either. *Good!* he thought. *You* shouldn't *want to remember! You let me drop! You let me die!*

'You said there were other worlds than these,' Roland said, 'and there are. New York in all its multiple whens is only one of many. That we are drawn there again and again has to do with the rose. I have no doubt of that, nor do I doubt that in some way I do not understand the rose *is* the Dark Tower. Either that or—'

'Or it's another door,' Susannah murmured. 'One that opens on the Dark Tower itself.'

Roland nodded. 'The idea has done more than cross my mind. In any case, the Manni know of these other worlds, and in some fashion have dedicated their lives to them. They believe todash to be the holiest of rites and most exalted of states. My father and his friends have long known of the glass balls; this I have told you. That the Wizard's Rainbow, todash, and these magical doors may all be much the same is something we have guessed.'

'Where you going with this, sug?' Susannah asked.

'I'm simply reminding you that I have wandered long,' Roland said. 'Because of changes in time — a *softening* of time which I know you all have felt — I've quested after the Dark Tower for over a thousand years, sometimes skipping over whole generations the way a sea-bird may cruise from one wave-top to the next, only wetting its feet in the foam. Never in all this time did I come across one of these doors between the worlds until I came to the ones on the beach at the edge of the Western Sea. I had no idea what they were, although I could have told you something of todash and the bends o' the rainbow.'

Roland looked at them earnestly.

'You speak as though my world were as filled with magical doorways as yours is with . . .' He thought about it. '. . . with airplanes or stage-buses. That's not so.'

'Where we are now isn't the same as anywhere you've been before, Roland,' Susannah said. She touched his deeply tanned wrist, her fingers gentle. 'We're not in your world anymore. You said so yourself, back in that version of Topeka where Blaine finally blew his top.'

'Agreed,' Roland said. 'I only want you to realize that such doors may be far more rare than you realize. And now you're speaking not of one but two. Doors you can aim in time, the way you'd aim a gun.'

I do not aim with my hand, Eddie thought, and shivered a little. 'When you put it that way, Roland, it *does* sound a little iffy.'

'Then what do we do next?' Jake asked.

'I might be able to help you with that,' a voice said.

They all turned, only Roland without surprise. He had heard the stranger when he arrived, about halfway through their palaver. Roland did turn with interest, however, and one look at the man standing twenty feet from them on the edge of the road was enough to tell him that the newcomer was either from the world of his new friends, or from one right next door.

'Who are you?' Eddie asked.

'Where are your friends?' Susannah asked.

'Where are you from?' Jake asked. His eyes were alight with eagerness.

The stranger wore a long black coat open over a dark shirt with a notched collar. His hair was long and white, sticking up on the sides and in front as if scared. His forehead was marked with a T-shaped scar. 'My friends are still back there a little piece,' he said, and jerked a thumb over his shoulder at the woods in a deliberately nonspecific way. 'I now call Calla Bryn Sturgis my home. Before that, Detroit, Michigan, where I worked in a homeless shelter, making soup and running AA meetings. Work I knew quite well. Before that – for a short while – Topeka, Kansas.'

He observed the way the three younger ones started at that with a kind of interested amusement.

'Before that, New York City. And before *that*, a little town called Jerusalem's Lot, in the state of Maine.'

7

'You're from our side,' Eddie said. He spoke in a kind of sigh. 'Holy God, you're really from our side!'

'Yes, I think I am,' the man in the turned-around collar said. 'My name is Donald Callahan.'

'You're a priest,' Susannah said. She looked from the cross that hung around his neck – small and discreet, but gleaming gold – to the larger, cruder one that scarred his forehead.

Callahan shook his head. 'No more. Once. Perhaps one day again, with the blessing, but not now. Now I'm just a man of God. May I ask . . . when are you from?'

'1964,' Susannah said.

'1977,' Jake said.

'1987,' Eddie said.

Callahan's eyes gleamed at that. '1987. And I came here in 1983, counting as we did then. So tell me something, young man, something very important. Had the Red Sox won the World Series yet when you left?'

Eddie threw back his head and laughed. The sound was both surprised and cheerful. 'No, man, sorry. They came within one out of it last year – at Shea Stadium this was, against the Mets – and then this guy named Bill Buckner who was playing first base let an easy grounder get through his wickets. He'll never live it down. Come on over here and sit down, what do you say? There's no coffee, but Roland – that's this beat-up-lookin guy on my right, – makes a pretty fair cup of woods tea.'

Callahan turned his attention to Roland and then did an amazing thing: dropped to one knee, lowered his head slightly, and put his fist against his scarred brow. 'Hile, gunslinger, may we be well-met on the path.'

'Hile,' Roland said. 'Come forward, good stranger, and tell us of your need.'

Callahan looked up at him, surprised.

Roland looked back at him calmly, and nodded. 'Well-met or ill, it may be you will find what you seek.'

'And you may also,' Callahan said.

'Then come forward,' Roland said. 'Come forward and join our palaver.'

8

'Before we really get going, can I ask you something?'

This was Eddie. Beside him, Roland had built up the fire and was rummaging in their combined gunna for the little earthen pot – an artifact of the Old People – in which he liked to brew tea.

'Of course, young man.'

'You're Donald Callahan.'

'Yes.'

'What's your *middle* name?'

Callahan cocked his head a little to the side, raised one eyebrow, then smiled. 'Frank. After my grandfather. Does it signify?'

Eddie, Susannah, and Jake shared a look. The thought that went with it flowed effortlessly among them: Donald Frank Callahan. Equals nineteen.

'It *does* signify,' Callahan said.

'Perhaps,' Roland said. 'Perhaps not.' He poured water for the tea, manipulating the waterskin easily.

'You seem to have suffered an accident,' Callahan said, looking at Roland's right hand.

'I make do,' Roland said.

'Gets by with a little help from his friends, you might say,' Jake added, not smiling.

Callahan nodded, not understanding and knowing he need not: they were ka-tet. He might not know that particular term, but the term didn't matter. It was in the way they looked at each other and moved around each other.

'You know my name,' Callahan said. 'May I have the pleasure of knowing yours?'

They introduced themselves: Eddie and Susannah Dean, of New York; Jake Chambers, of New York; Oy of Mid-World; Roland Deschain, of Gilead that was. Callahan nodded to each in turn, raising his closed fist to his forehead.

'And to you comes Callahan, of the Lot,' he said when the introductions were done. 'Or so I was. Now I guess I'm just the Old Fella. That's what they call me in the Calla.'

'Won't your friends join us?' Roland said. 'We haven't a great deal to eat, but there's always tea.'

'Perhaps not just yet.'

'Ah,' Roland said, and nodded as if he understood.

'In any case, we've eaten well,' Callahan said. 'It's been a good year in the Calla – until now, anyway – and we'll be happy to share what we have.' He paused, seemed to feel he had gone too far too fast, and added: 'Mayhap. If all goes well.'

'If,' Roland said. 'An old teacher of mine used to call it the only word a thousand letters long.'

Callahan laughed. 'Not bad! In any case, we're probably better off for food than you are. We also have fresh muffin-balls – Zalia found em – but I suspect you know about those. She said the patch, although large, had a picked-over look.'

'Jake found them,' Roland said.

'Actually, it was Oy,' Jake said, and stroked the bumbler's head. 'I guess he's sort of a muffin-hound.'

'How long have you known we were here?' Callahan asked.

'Two days.'

Callahan contrived to look both amused and exasperated. 'Since we cut your trail, in other words. And we tried to be so crafty.'

'If you didn't think you needed someone craftier than you are, you wouldn't have come,' Roland said.

Callahan sighed. 'You say true, I say thankya.'

'Do you come for aid and succor?' Roland asked. There was only mild curiosity in his voice, but Eddie Dean felt a deep, deep chill. The words seemed to hang there, full of resonance. Nor was he alone in feeling that. Susannah took his right hand. A moment later Jake's hand crept into Eddie's left.

'That is not for me to say.' Callahan sounded suddenly hesitant and unsure of himself. Afraid, maybe.

'Do you know you come to the line of Eld?' Roland asked in that same curiously gentle voice. He stretched a hand toward Eddie, Susannah, and Jake. Even toward Oy. 'For these are mine, sure. As I am theirs. We are round, and roll as we do. And you know what we are.'

'*Are* you?' Callahan asked. 'Are you *all*?'

Susannah said, 'Roland, what are you getting us into?'

'Naught be zero, naught be free,' he said. 'I owe not you, nor you owe me. At least for now. They have not decided to ask.'

They will, Eddie thought. Dreams of the rose and the deli and little todash-jaunts aside, he didn't think of himself as particularly psychic, but he didn't *need* to be psychic to know that they – the people from whom this Callahan had come as representative – *would* ask. Somewhere chestnuts had fallen into a hot fire, and Roland was supposed to pull them out.

But not *just* Roland.

You've made a mistake here, Pops, Eddie thought. *Perfectly understandable, but a mistake, all the same. We're not the cavalry. We're not the posse. We're not gunslingers. We're just three lost souls from the Big Apple who—*

But no. No. Eddie had known who they were since River Crossing, when the old people had knelt in the street to Roland. Hell, he'd known since the woods (what he still thought of as Shardik's Woods), where Roland had taught them to aim with the eye, shoot with the mind, kill with the heart. Not three, not four. One. That Roland should finish them so, *complete* them so, was horrible. He was filled with poison and had kissed them with his poisoned lips. He had made them gunslingers, and had Eddie really thought there was no work left for the line of Arthur Eld in this mostly empty and husked-out world? That they would simply be allowed to toddle along the Path of the Beam until they got to Roland's Dark Tower and fixed whatever was wrong there? Well, guess again.

It was Jake who said what was in Eddie's mind, and Eddie didn't like the look of excitement in the boy's eyes. He guessed plenty of kids had gone off to plenty of wars with that same excited gonna-kick-some-ass look on their faces. Poor kid didn't know he'd been poisoned, and that made him pretty dumb, because no one should have known better.

'They will, though,' he said. 'Isn't that true, Mr Callahan? They will ask.'

'I don't know,' Callahan said. 'You'd have to convince them . . .'

He trailed off, looking at Roland. Roland was shaking his head.

'That's not how it works,' the gunslinger said. 'Not being from Mid-World you may not know that, but that's not how it works. Convincing isn't what we do. We deal in lead.'

Callahan sighed deeply, then nodded. 'I have a book. *Tales of Arthur*, it's called.'

Roland's eyes gleamed. '*Do* you? Do you, indeed? I would like to see such a book. I would like it very well.'

'Perhaps you shall,' Callahan said. 'The stories in it are certainly not much like the tales of the Round Table I read as a boy, but . . .' He shook his head. 'I understand what you're saying to me, let's leave it at that. There are three questions, am I right? And you just asked me the first.'

'Three, yes,' Roland said. 'Three is a number of power.'

Eddie thought, *If you want to try a real* number of power, *Roland old buddy, try* nineteen.

'And all three must be answered yes.'

Roland nodded. 'And if they are, you may ask no more. We may be cast on, sai Callahan, but no man may cast us back. Make sure your people'— he nodded toward the woods south of them— 'understand that.'

'Gunslinger—'

'Call me Roland. We're at peace, you and I.'

'All right, Roland. Hear me well, do ya, I beg. (For so we say in the Calla.) We who come to you are only half a dozen. We six cannot decide. Only the Calla can decide.'

'Democracy,' Roland said. He pushed his hat back from his forehead, rubbed his forehead, and sighed.

'But if we six agree – especially sai Overholser—' He broke off, looking rather warily at Jake. 'What? Did I say something?'

Jake shook his head and motioned Callahan to continue.

'If we six agree, it's pretty much a done deal.'

Eddie closed his eyes, as if in bliss. 'Say it again, pal.'

Callahan eyed him, puzzled and wary. 'What?'

'Done deal. Or anything from your where and when.' He paused. 'Our side of the big ka.'

Callahan considered this, then began to grin. 'I didn't know whether to shit or go blind,' he said. 'I went on a bender, broke the bank, kicked the bucket, blew my top, walked on thin ice, rode the pink horse down nightmare alley. Like that?'

Roland looked puzzled (perhaps even a little bored), but Eddie Dean's face was a study in bliss. Susannah and Jake seemed caught somewhere between amusement and a kind of surprised, recollective sadness.

'Keep em coming, pal,' Eddie said hoarsely, and made a *come on, man* gesture with both hands. He sounded as if he might have been speaking through a throatful of tears. 'Just keep em coming.'

'Perhaps another time,' Callahan said gently. 'Another time we may sit and have our own palaver about the old places and ways of saying. Baseball, if it do ya. Now, though, time is short.'

'In more ways than you know, maybe,' Roland said. 'What would you have of us, sai Callahan? And now you must speak to the point, for I've told you in every way I can that we are not wanderers your friends may interview, then hire or not as they do their farmhands or saddle-tramps.'

'For now I ask only that you stay where you are and let me bring them to you,' he said. 'There's Tian Jaffords, who's really responsible for us being out here, and his wife, Zalia. There's Overholser, the one who most needs to be convinced that we need you.'

'*We* won't convince him or anyone,' Roland said.

'I understand,' Callahan said hastily. 'Yes, you've made that perfectly clear. And there's Ben Slightman and his boy, Benny. Ben the Younger is an odd case. His sister died four years ago, when she and Benny were both ten. No one knows if that makes Ben the Younger a twin or a singleton.' He stopped abruptly. 'I've wandered. I'm sorry.'

Roland gestured with an open palm to show it was all right.

'You make me nervous, hear me I beg.'

'You don't need to beg us nothing, sugar,' Susannah said.

Callahan smiled. 'It's only the way we speak. In the Calla, when you meet someone, you may say, "How from head to feet, do ya, I beg?" And the answer, "I do fine, no rust, tell the gods thankee-sai." You haven't heard this?'

They shook their heads. Although some of the words were familiar, the overall expressions only underlined the fact that they had come to somewhere else, a place where talk was strange and customs perhaps stranger.

'What matters,' Callahan said, 'is that the borderlands are terrified of creatures called the Wolves, who come out of Thunderclap once a generation and steal the children. There's more to it, but that's the crux. Tian Jaffords, who stands to lose not just one child this time but two, says no more, the time has come to stand and fight. Others — men like Overholser — say doing that would be disaster. I think Overholser and those like him would have carried the day, but your coming has changed things.' He leaned forward earnestly. 'Wayne Overholser isn't a bad man, just a frightened man. He's the biggest farmer in the Calla, and so he has more to lose than some of the rest. But if he could be convinced that we might drive the Wolves off . . . that we could actually win against them . . . I believe he might also stand and fight.'

'I told you—' Roland began.

'You don't convince,' Callahan broke in. 'Yes, I understand. I do. But if they see you, hear you speak, and then convince themselves . . .?'

Roland shrugged. 'There'll be water if God wills it, we say.'

Callahan nodded. 'They say it in the Calla, too. May I move on to another, related matter?'

Roland raised his hands slightly – as if, Eddie thought, to tell Callahan it was his nickel.

For a moment the man with the scar on his brow said nothing. When he did speak, his voice had dropped. Eddie had to lean forward to hear him. 'I have something. Something you want. That you may need. It has reached out to you already, I think.'

'Why do you say so?' Roland asked.

Callahan wet his lips and then spoke a single word: 'Todash.'

9

'What about it?' Roland asked. 'What about todash?'

'Haven't you gone?' Callahan looked momentarily unsure of himself. 'Haven't *any* of you gone?'

'Say we have,' Roland said. 'What's that to you, and to your problem in this place you call the Calla?'

Callahan sighed. Although it was still early in the day, he looked tired. 'This is harder than I thought it would be,' he said, 'and by quite a lot. You are considerably more – what's the word? – trig, I suppose. More trig than I expected.'

'You expected to find nothing but saddle-tramps with fast hands and empty heads, isn't that about the size of it?' Susannah asked. She sounded angry. 'Well, joke's on you, honeybunch. Anyway, we may be tramps, but we got no saddles. No need for saddles with no horses.'

'We've brought you horses,' Callahan said, and that was enough. Roland didn't understand everything, but he thought he now had enough to clarify the situation quite a bit. Callahan had known they were coming, known how many they were, known they were walking instead of riding. Some of those things could have been passed on by spies, but not all. And todash . . . knowing that some or all of them had gone todash . . .

'As for empty heads, we may not be the brightest four on the planet, but—' She broke off suddenly, wincing. Her hands went to her stomach.

'Suze?' Eddie asked, instantly concerned. 'Suze, what is it? You okay?'

'Just gas,' she said, and gave him a smile. To Roland that smile didn't look quite real. And he thought he saw tiny lines of strain around the corners of her eyes. 'Too many muffin-balls last night.' And before Eddie could ask her any more questions, Susannah turned her attention back to Callahan. 'You got something else to say, then say it, sugar.'

'All right,' Callahan said. 'I have an object of great power. Although you are still many wheels from my church in the Calla, where this object is hidden, I think it's already reached out to you. Inducing the todash state is only one of the things it does.' He took a deep breath and let it out. 'If you will render us — for the Calla is my town now, too, ye ken, where I hope to finish my days and then be buried — the service I beg, I will give you this . . . this thing.'

'For the last time, I'd ask you to speak no more so,' Roland said. His tone was so harsh that Jake looked around at him with dismay. 'It dishonors me and my an-tet. We're bound to do as you ask, if we judge your Calla in the White and those you call Wolves as agents of the outer dark: Beam-breakers, if you ken. We may take *no* reward for our services, and you must not offer. If one of your own mates were to speak so — the one you call Tian or the one you call Overholser—'

(Eddie thought to correct the gunslinger's pronunciation and then decided to keep his mouth shut — when Roland was angry, it was usually best to stay silent.)

'—that would be different. They know nothing but legends, mayhap. But you, sai, have at least one book which should have taught you better. I told you we deal in lead, and so we do. But that doesn't make us hired guns.'

'All right, all right—'

'As for what you have,' Roland said, his voice rising and overriding Callahan's, 'you'd be rid of it, would you not? It terrifies you, does it not?

Even if we decide to ride on past your town, you'd beg us to take it with us, would you not? *Would you not?*'

'Yes,' Callahan said miserably. 'You speak true and I say thankee. But . . . it's just that I heard a bit of your palaver . . . enough to know you want to go back . . . to pass over, as the Manni say . . . and not just to one place but two . . . or maybe more . . . and time . . . I heard you speak of aiming time like a gun . . .'

Jake's face filled with understanding and horrified wonder. 'Which one is it?' he asked. 'It can't be the pink one from Mejis, because Roland went inside it, it never sent him todash. So which one?'

A tear spilled down Callahan's right cheek, then another. He wiped them away absently. 'I've never dared handle it, but I've seen it. Felt its power. Christ the Man Jesus help me, I have Black Thirteen under the floorboards of my church. And it's come alive. Do you understand me?' He looked at them with his wet eyes. '*It's come alive.*'

Callahan put his face in his hands, hiding it from them.

10

When the holy man with the scar on his forehead left to get his trailmates, the gunslinger stood watching him go without moving. Roland's thumbs were hooked into the waistband of his old patched jeans, and he looked as if he could stand that way well into the next age. The moment Callahan was out of sight, however, he turned to his own mates and made an urgent, almost bearish, clutching gesture at the air: *Come to me.* As they did, Roland squatted on his hunkers. Eddie and Jake did the same (and to Susannah, hunkers were almost a way of life). The gunslinger spoke almost curtly.

'Time is short, so tell me, each of you, and don't shilly-shally: honest or not?'

'Honest,' Susannah said at once, then gave another little wince and rubbed beneath her left breast.

'Honest,' said Jake.

'Onnes,' said Oy, although he had not been asked.

'Honest,' Eddie agreed, 'but look.' He took an unburned twig from the edge of the campfire, brushed away a patch of pine-duff, and wrote in the black earth underneath:

Calla Callahan

'Live or Memorex?' Eddie said. Then, seeing Susannah's confusion: 'Is it a coincidence, or does it mean something?'

'Who knows?' Jake asked. They were all speaking in low tones, heads together over the writing in the dirt. 'It's like nineteen.'

'I think it's only a coincidence,' Susannah said. 'Surely not *everything* we encounter on our path is ka, is it? I mean, these don't even *sound* the same.' And she pronounced them, *Calla* with the tongue up, making the broad-*a* sound, *Callahan* with the tongue down, making a much sharper *a*-sound. '*Calla*'s Spanish in our world . . . like many of the words you remember from Mejis, Roland. It means street or square, I think . . . don't hold me to it, because high school Spanish is far behind me now. But if I'm right, using the word as a prefix for the name of a town — or a whole series of them, as seems to be the case in these parts — makes pretty good sense. Not perfect, but pretty good. Callahan, on the other hand . . .' She shrugged. 'What is it? Irish? English?'

'It's sure not Spanish,' Jake said. 'But the nineteen thing—'

'Piss on nineteen,' Roland said rudely. 'This isn't the time for number games. He'll be back here with his friends in short order, and I would speak to you an-tet of another matter before he does.'

'Do you think he could possibly be right about Black Thirteen?' Jake asked.

'Yes,' Roland said. 'Based just on what happened to you and Eddie last night, I think the answer is yes. Dangerous for us to have such a thing if he *is* right, but have it we must. I fear these Wolves out of Thunderclap will if we don't. Never mind, that need not trouble us now.'

Yet Roland looked very troubled indeed. He turned his regard toward Jake.

'You started when you heard the big farmer's name. So did you, Eddie, although you concealed it better.'

'Sorry,' Jake said. 'I have forgotten the face of—'

'Not even a bit have you,' Roland said. 'Unless I have, as well. Because I've heard the name myself, and recently. I just can't remember where.' Then, reluctantly: 'I'm getting old.'

'It was in the bookstore,' Jake said. He took his pack, fiddled nervously with the straps, undid them. He flipped the pack open as he spoke. It was as if he had to make sure *Charlie the Choo-Choo* and *Riddle-De-Dum* were still there, still real. 'The Manhattan Restaurant of the Mind. It's so weird. Once it happened to me and once I *watched* it happen to me. That'd make a pretty good riddle all by itself.'

Roland made a rapid rotating gesture with his diminished right hand, telling him to go on and be quick.

'Mr Tower introduced himself,' Jake said, 'and then I did the same. Jake Chambers, I said. And *he* said—'

'"Good handle, partner,"' Eddie broke in. 'That's what he said. Then he said Jake Chambers sounded like the name of the hero in a Western novel.'

'"The guy who blows into Black Fork, Arizona, cleans up the town, then moves on,"' Jake quoted. 'And then he said, "Something by Wayne D. Overholser, maybe."' He looked at Susannah and repeated it. '*Wayne D. Overholser.* And if you tell me *that's* a coincidence, Susannah . . .' He broke into a sunny, sudden grin. 'I'll tell you to kiss my white-boy ass.'

Susannah laughed. 'No need of that, sass-box. I don't believe it's a co-incidence. And when we meet Callahan's farmer friend, I intend to ask him what his middle name is. I set my warrant that it'll not only begin with D, it'll be something like Dean or Dane, just four letters—' Her hand went back to the place below her breast. 'This *gas!* My! What I wouldn't give for a roll of Tums or even a bottle of—' She broke off again. 'Jake, what is it? What's wrong?'

Jake was holding *Charlie the Choo-Choo* in his hands, and his face had gone dead white. His eyes were huge, shocked. Beside him, Oy whined uneasily. Roland leaned over to look, and his eyes also widened.

'Good gods,' he said.

Eddie and Susannah looked. The title was the same. The picture was the same: an anthropomorphic locomotive puffing up a hill, its cowcatcher wearing a grin, its headlight a cheerful eye. But the yellow letters across the bottom, Story and Pictures by Beryl Evans, were gone. There was no credit line there at all.

Jake turned the book and looked at the spine. It said *Charlie the Choo-Choo* and McCauley House, Publishers. Nothing else.

South of them now, the sound of voices. Callahan and his friends, approaching. Callahan from the Calla. Callahan of the Lot, he had also called himself.

'Title page, sugar,' Susannah said. 'Look there, quick.'

Jake did. Once again there was only the title of the story and the publisher's name, this time with a colophon.

'Look at the copyright page,' Eddie said.

Jake turned the page. Here, on the verso of the title page and beside the recto where the story began, was the copyright information. Except there *was* no information, not really.

Copyright 1936,

it said. Numbers which added up to nineteen.

The rest was blank.

CHAPTER V

OVERHOLSER

1

Susannah was able to observe a good deal on that long and interesting day, because Roland gave her the chance and because, after her morning's sickness passed off, she felt wholly herself again.

Just before Callahan and his party drew within earshot, Roland murmured to her, 'Stay close to me, and not a word from you unless I prompt it. If they take you for my sh'veen, let it be so.'

Under other circumstances, she might have had something pert to say about the idea of being Roland's quiet little side-wife, his nudge in the night, but there was no time this morning, and in any case, it was far from a joking matter; the seriousness in his face made that clear. Also, the part of the faithful, quiet second appealed to her. In truth, *any* part appealed to her. Even as a child, she had rarely been so happy as when pretending to be someone else.

Which probably explains all there is about you worth knowing, sugar, she thought.

'Susannah?' Roland asked. 'Do you hear me?'

'Hear you well,' she told him. 'Don't you worry about me.'

'If it goes as I want, they'll see you little and you'll see them much.'

As a woman who'd grown up black in mid-twentieth-century America (Odetta had laughed and applauded her way through Ralph Ellison's *Invisible Man*, often rocking back and forth in her seat like one who has been visited by a revelation), Susannah knew exactly what he wanted. And would give it to him. There was a part of her – a spiteful Detta Walker part – that would always resent Roland's ascendancy in her heart and mind, but for the most part she recognized him for what he was: the last of his kind. Maybe even a hero.

2

Watching Roland make the introductions (Susannah was presented dead last, after Jake, and almost negligently), she had time to reflect on how fine she felt now that the nagging gas-pains in her left side had departed. Hell, even the lingering headache had gone its way, and *that* sucker had been hanging around — sometimes in the back of her head, sometimes at one temple or the other, sometimes just above her left eye, like a migraine waiting to hatch — for a week or more. And of course there were the mornings. Every one found her feeling nauseated and with a bad case of jelly-leg for the first hour or so. She never vomited, but for that first hour she always felt on the verge of it.

She wasn't stupid enough to mistake such symptoms, but had reason to know they meant nothing. She just hoped she wouldn't embarrass herself by swelling up as her Mama's friend Jessica had done, not once but twice. Two false pregnancies, and in both cases that woman had looked ready to bust out twins. Triplets, even. But of course Jessica Beasley's periods had stopped, and that made it all too easy for a woman to believe she was with child. Susannah knew she wasn't pregnant for the simplest of reasons: she was still menstruating. She had begun a period on the very day they had awakened back on the Path of the Beam, with the Green Palace twenty-five or thirty miles behind them. She'd had another since then. Both courses had been exceptionally heavy, necessitating the use of many rags to soak up the dark flow, and before then her menses had always been light, some months no more than a few of the spots her mother called 'a lady's roses.' Yet she didn't complain, because before her arrival in this world, her periods had usually been painful and sometimes excruciating. The two she'd had since returning to the Path of the Beam hadn't hurt at all. If not for the soaked rags she'd carefully buried to one side of their path or the other, she wouldn't have had a clue that it was her time of the month. Maybe it was the purity of the water.

Of course she knew what all this was about; it didn't take a rocket scientist, as Eddie sometimes said. The crazy, scrambled dreams she couldn't recall, the weakness and nausea in the mornings, the transient headaches, the strangely fierce gas attacks and occasional cramps all came down to the same thing: she wanted his baby. More than anything else in the world, she wanted Eddie Dean's chap growing in her belly.

What she *didn't* want was to puff up in a humiliating false pregnancy.

Never mind all that now, she thought as Callahan approached with the others. *Right now you've got to watch. Got to see what Roland and Eddie and Jake don't see. That way nothing gets dropped.* And she felt she could do that job very well.

Really, she had never felt finer in her life.

3

Callahan came first. Behind him were two men, one who looked about thirty and another who looked to Susannah nearly twice that. The older man had heavy cheeks that would be jowls in another five years or so, and lines carving their courses from the sides of his nose down to his chin. 'I-want lines,' her father would have called them (and Dan Holmes had had a pretty good set of his own). The younger man wore a battered sombrero, the older a clean white Stetson that made Susannah want to smile — it looked like the kind of hat the good guy would wear in an old black-and-white Western movie. Still, she guessed a lid like that didn't come cheap, and she thought the man wearing it had to be Wayne Overholser. 'The big farmer,' Roland had called him. The one that had to be convinced, according to Callahan.

But not by us, Susannah thought, which was sort of a relief. The tight mouth, the shrewd eyes, and most of all those deep-carved lines (there was another slashed vertically into his brow, just above the eyes) suggested sai Overholser would be a pain in the ass when it came to convincing.

Just behind these two — specifically behind the younger of the two — there came a tall, handsome woman, probably not black but nonetheless nearly as dark-skinned as Susannah herself. Bringing up the rear was an earnest-looking man in spectacles and farmer's clothes and a likely looking boy probably two or three years older than Jake. The resemblance between this pair was impossible to miss; they had to be Slightman the Elder and Younger.

Boy may be older than Jake in years, she thought, *but he's got a soft look about him, all the same.* True, but not necessarily a bad thing. Jake had seen far too much for a boy not yet in his teens. *Done* too much, as well.

Overholser looked at their guns (Roland and Eddie each wore one of the big revolvers with the sandalwood grips; the .44 Ruger from New York City hung under Jake's arm in what Roland called a docker's clutch), then at Roland. He made a perfunctory salute, his half-closed fist skimming somewhere at least close to his forehead. There was no bow. If Roland was offended by this, it didn't show on his face. Nothing showed on his face but polite interest.

'Hile, gunslinger,' the man who had been walking beside Overholser said, and this one actually dropped to one knee, with his head down and his brow resting on his fist. 'I am Tian Jaffords, son of Luke. This lady is my wife, Zalia.'

'Hile,' Roland said. 'Let me be Roland to you, if it suits. May your days be long upon the earth, sai Jaffords.'

'Tian. Please. And may you and your friends have twice the—'

'I'm Overholser,' the man in the white Stetson broke in brusquely. 'We've come to meet you – you and your friends – at the request of Callahan and young Jaffords. I'd pass the formalities and get down to business as soon as possible, do ya take no offense, I beg.'

'Ask pardon but that's not quite how it is,' Jaffords said. 'There was a meeting, and the men of the Calla voted—'

Overholser broke in again. He was, Susannah thought, just that kind of man. She doubted he was even aware he was doing it. 'The town, yes. The Calla. I've come along with every wish to do right by my town and my neighbors, but this is a busy time for me, none busier—'

'Charyou tree,' Roland said mildly, and although Susannah knew a deeper meaning for this phrase, one that made her back prickle, Overholser's eyes lit up. She had her first inkling then of how this day was going to go.

'Come reap, yessir, say thankee.' Off to one side, Callahan was gazing into the woods with a kind of studied patience. Behind Overholser, Tian Jaffords and his wife exchanged an embarrassed glance. The Slightmans only waited and watched. 'You understand that much, anyway.'

'In Gilead we were surrounded by farms and freeholds,' Roland said. 'I got my share of hay and corn in barn. Aye, and sharproot, too.'

Overholser was giving Roland a grin that Susannah found fairly offensive. It said, *We know better than that, don't we, sai? We're both men of the world, after all.* 'Where are you from really, sai Roland?'

'My friend, you need to see an audiologist,' Eddie said.

Overholser looked at him, puzzled. 'Beg-my-ear?'

Eddie made a *there, you see?* gesture and nodded. 'Exactly what I mean.'

'Be still, Eddie,' Roland said. Still as mild as milk. 'Sai Overholser, we may take a moment to exchange names and speak a good wish or two, surely.

For that is how civilized, kindly folk behave, is it not?' Roland paused – a brief, underlining pause – and then said, 'With harriers it may be different, but there are no harriers here.'

Overholser's lips pressed together and he looked hard at Roland, ready to take offense. He saw nothing in the gunslinger's face that offered it, and relaxed again. 'Thankee,' he said. 'Tian and Zalia Jaffords, as told—'

Zalia curtsied, spreading invisible skirts to either side of her battered corduroy pants.

'—and here are Ben Slightman the Elder and Benny the Younger.'

The father raised his fist to his forehead and nodded. The son, his face a study in awe (it was mostly the guns, Susannah surmised), bowed with his right leg out stiffly in front of him and the heel planted.

'The Old Fella you already know,' Overholser finished, speaking with exactly the sort of offhand contempt at which Overholser himself would have taken deep offense, had it been directed toward his valued self. Susannah supposed that when you were the big farmer, you got used to talking just about any way you wanted. She wondered how far he might push Roland before discovering that he hadn't been pushing at all. Because some men couldn't be pushed. They might go along with you for awhile, but then—

'These are my trailmates,' Roland said. 'Eddie Dean and Jake Chambers, of New York. And this is Susannah.' He gestured at her without turning in her direction. Overholser's face took on a knowing, intensely male look Susannah had seen before. Detta Walker had had a way of wiping that look off men's faces that she didn't believe sai Overholser would care for at all.

Nonetheless, she gave Overholser and the rest of them a demure little smile and made her own invisible-skirts curtsy. She thought hers as graceful in its way as the one made by Zalia Jaffords, but of course a curtsy didn't look quite the same when you were missing your lower legs and feet. The newcomers had marked the part of her that was gone, of course, but their feelings on that score didn't interest her much. She *did* wonder what they thought of her wheelchair, though, the one Eddie had gotten her in Topeka, where Blaine the Mono had finished up. These folks would never have seen the like of it.

Callahan may have, she thought. *Because Callahan's from our side. He—*

The boy said, 'Is that a bumbler?'

'Hush, do ya,' Slightman said, sounding almost shocked that his son had spoken.

'That's okay,' Jake said. 'Yeah, he's a bumbler. Oy, go to him.' He pointed at Ben the Younger. Oy trotted around the campfire to where the newcomer stood and looked up at the boy with his gold-ringed eyes.

'I never saw a tame one before,' Tian said. 'Have heard of em, of course, but the world has moved on.'

'Mayhap not all of it has moved on,' Roland said. He looked at Overholser. 'Mayhap some of the old ways still hold.'

'Can I pat him?' the boy asked Jake. 'Will he bite?'

'You can and he won't.'

As Slightman the Younger dropped on his hunkers in front of Oy, Susannah certainly hoped Jake was right. Having a billy-bumbler chomp off this kid's nose would not set them on in any style at all.

But Oy suffered himself to be stroked, even stretching his long neck up so he could sample the odor of Slightman's face. The boy laughed. 'What did you say his name was?'

Before Jake could reply, the bumbler spoke for himself. 'Oy!'

They all laughed. And as simply as that they were together, well-met on this road that followed the Path of the Beam. The bond was fragile, but even Overholser sensed it. And when he laughed, the big farmer looked as if he might be a good enough fellow. Maybe frightened, and pompous to be sure, but there was something there.

Susannah didn't know whether to be glad or afraid.

4

'I'd have a word alone with 'ee, if it does ya,' Overholser said. The two boys had walked off a little distance with Oy between them, Slightman the Younger asking Jake if the bumbler could count, as he'd heard some of them could.

'I think not, Wayne,' Jaffords said at once. 'It was agreed we'd go back to our camp, break bread, and explain our need to these folk. And then, if they agreed to come further—'

'I have no objection to passing a word with sai Overholser,' Roland said, 'nor will you, sai Jaffords, I think. For is he not your dinh?' And then, before Tian could object further (or deny it): 'Give these folks tea, Susannah. Eddie, step over here with us a bit, if it do ya fine.'

This phrase, new to all their ears, came out of Roland's mouth sounding perfectly natural. Susannah marveled at it. If she had tried saying that, she would have sounded as if she were sucking up.

'We have food south aways,' Zalia said timidly. 'Food and graf and coffee. Andy—'

'We'll eat with pleasure, and drink your coffee with joy,' Roland said. 'But have tea first, I beg. We'll only be a moment or two, won't we, sai?'

Overholser nodded. His look of stern unease had departed. So had his stiffness of body. From the far side of the road (close to where a woman named Mia had slipped into the woods only the night before), the boys laughed as Oy did something clever – Benny with surprise, Jake with obvious pride.

Roland took Overholser's arm and led him a little piece up the road. Eddie strolled with them. Jaffords, frowning, made as if to go with them anyway. Susannah touched his shoulder. 'Don't,' she said in a low voice. 'He knows what he's doing.'

Jaffords looked at her doubtfully for a moment, then came with her. 'P'raps I could build that fire up for you a bit, sai,' Slightman the Elder said with a kindly look at her diminished legs. 'For I see a few sparks yet, so I do.'

'If you please,' Susannah said, thinking how wonderful all this was. How wonderful, how strange. Potentially deadly as well, of course, but she had come to learn that also had its charms. It was the possiblity of darkness that made the day seem so bright.

5

Up the road about forty feet from the others, the three men stood together. Overholser appeared to be doing all the talking, sometimes gesturing violently to punctuate a point. He spoke as if Roland were no more than some gunbunny hobo who happened to come drifting down the road with a few no-account friends riding drogue behind him. He explained to Roland that Tian Jaffords was a fool (albeit a well-meaning one) who did not understand the facts of life. He told Roland that Jaffords had to be restrained, cooled off, not only in his best interests but in those of the entire Calla. He insisted to Roland that if anything *could* be done, Wayne Overholser, son of Alan, would be first in line to do it; he'd never shirked a chore in his life, but to go against the Wolves was madness. And, he added, lowering his voice, speaking of madness, there was the Old Fella. When he kept to his church and his rituals, he was fine. In such things, a little madness made a fine sauce. This, however, was summat different. Aye, and by a long hike.

Roland listened to it all, nodding occasionally. He said almost nothing. And when Overholser was finally finished, Calla Bryn Sturgis's big farmer simply looked with a kind of fixed fascination at the gunman who stood before him. Mostly at those faded blue eyes.

'Are ye what ye say?' he asked finally. 'Tell me true, sai.'

'I'm Roland of Gilead,' the gunslinger said.

'From the line of Eld? Ye do say it?'

'By watch and by warrant,' Roland said.

'But Gilead . . .' Overholser paused. 'Gilead's long gone.'

'I,' Roland said, 'am not.'

'Would ye kill us all, or cause us to be killed? Tell me, I beg.'

'What would *you*, sai Overholser? Not later; not a day or a week or a moon from now, but at this minute?'

Overholser stood a long time, looking from Roland to Eddie and then back to Roland again. Here was a man not used to changing his mind; if he did so, it would hurt him like a rupture. From down the road came the laughter of the boys as Oy fetched something Benny had thrown – a stick almost as big as the bumbler was himself.

'I'd listen,' Overholser said at last. 'I'd do that much, gods help me, and say thankee.'

'In other words he explained all the reasons why it was a fool's errand,' Eddie told her later, 'and then did exactly what Roland wanted him to do. It was like magic.'

'Sometimes Roland *is* magic,' she said.

6

The Calla's party had camped in a pleasant hilltop clearing not far south of the road but just enough off the Path of the Beam so that the clouds hung still and moveless in the sky, seemingly close enough to touch. The way there through the woods had been carefully marked; some of the blazes

Susannah saw were as big as her palm. These people might be crackerjack farmers and stockmen, but it was clear the woods made them uneasy.

'May I spell ye on that chair a bit, young man?' Overholser asked Eddie as they began the final push upslope. Susannah could smell roasting meat and wondered who was tending to the cooking if the entire Callahan-Overholser party had come out to meet them. Had the woman mentioned someone named Andy? A servant, perhaps? She had. Overholser's personal? Perhaps. Surely a man who could afford a Stetson as grand as the one now tipped back on his head could afford a personal.

'Do ya,' Eddie said. He didn't quite dare to add 'I beg' (*Still sounds phony to him*, Susannah thought), but he moved aside and gave over the wheelchair's push-handles to Overholser. The farmer was a big man, it was a fair slope, and now he was pushing a woman who weighed close on to a hundred and thirty pounds, but his breathing, although heavy, remained regular.

'Might I ask you a question, sai Overholser?' Eddie asked.

'Of course,' Overholser replied.

'What's your middle name?'

There was a momentary slackening of forward motion; Susannah put this down to mere surprise. 'That's an odd 'un, young fella; why d'ye ask?'

'Oh, it's a kind of hobby of mine,' Eddie said. 'In fact, I tell fortunes by em.'

Careful, Eddie, careful, Susannah thought, but she was amused in spite of herself.

'Oh, aye?'

'Yes,' Eddie said. 'You, now. I'll bet your middle name begins with—' he seemed to calculate— 'with the letter *D*.' Only he pronounced it *Deh*, in the fashion of the Great Letters in the High Speech. 'And I'd say it's short. Five letters? Maybe only four?'

The slackening of forward push came again. 'Devil say please!' Overholser exclaimed. 'How'd you know? Tell me!'

Eddie shrugged. 'It's no more than counting and guessing, really. In truth, I'm wrong almost as often as I'm right.'

'More often,' Susannah said.

'Tell ya my middle name's Dale,' Overholser said, 'although if anyone ever explained me why, it's slipped my mind. I lost my folks when I was young.'

'Sorry for your loss,' Susannah said, happy to see that Eddie was moving away. Probably to tell Jake she'd been right about the middle name: Wayne Dale Overholser. Equals nineteen.

'Is that young man trig or a fool?' Overholser asked Susannah. 'Tell me, I beg, for I canna' tell myself.'

'A little of both,' she said.

'No question about this push-chair, though, would you say? It's trig as a compass.'

'Say thankya,' she said, then gave a small inward sigh of relief. It had come out sounding all right, probably because she hadn't exactly planned on saying it.

'Where did it come from?'

'Back on our way a good distance,' she said. This turn of the conversation did not please her much. She thought it was Roland's job to tell their history (or not tell it). He was their dinh. Besides, what was told by only one could not be contradicted. Still, she thought she could say a little more. 'There's a thinny. We came from the other side of that, where things are much different.' She craned around to look at him. His cheeks and neck had flushed, but really, she thought, he was doing very well for a man who had to be deep into his fifties. 'Do you know what I'm talking about?'

'Yar,' he said, hawked, and spat off to the left. 'Not that I've seen or heard it myself, you understand. I never wander far; too much to do on the farm. Those of the Calla aren't woodsy people as a rule, anyway, do ya kennit.'

Oh yes, I think I kennit, Susannah thought, spying another blaze roughly the size of a dinner plate. The unfortunate tree so marked would be lucky to survive the coming winter.

'Andy's told of the thinny many and many-a. Makes a sound, he says, but can't tell what it is.'

'Who's Andy?'

'Ye'll meet him for y'self soon enough, sai, Are'ee from this Calla York, like yer friends?'

'Yes,' she said, again on her guard. He swung her wheelchair around a hoary old ironwood. The trees were sparser now, and the smell of cooking much stronger. Meat . . . and coffee. Her stomach rumbled.

'And they be not gunslingers,' Overholser said, nodding at Jake and Eddie. 'You'll not tell me so, surely.'

'You must decide that for yourself when the time comes,' Susannah said.

He made no reply for a few moments. The wheelchair rumbled over a rock outcropping. Ahead of them, Oy padded along between Jake and Benny Slightman, who had made friends with boyhood's eerie speed. She wondered if it was a good idea. For the two boys were different. Time might show them how much, and to their sorrow.

'He scared me,' Overholser said. He spoke in a voice almost too low to hear. As if to himself. ''T were his eyes, I think. Mostly his eyes.'

'Would you go on as you have, then?' Susannah asked. The question was far from as idle as she hoped it sounded, but she was still startled by the fury of his response.

'Are 'ee mad, woman? Course not – not if I saw a way out of the box we're in. Hear me well! That boy' —he pointed at Tian Jaffords, walking ahead of them with his wife— 'that boy as much as accused me of running yella. Had to make sure they all knew I didn't have any children of the age the Wolves fancy, aye. Not like *he* has, kennit. But do 'ee think I'm a fool that can't count the cost?'

'Not me,' Susannah said, calmly.

'But do *he*? I halfway think so.' Overholser spoke as a man does when pride and fear are fighting it out in his head. 'Do I want to give the babbies to the Wolves? Babbies that're sent back roont to be a drag on the town ever after? No! But neither do I want some hardcase to lead us all to blunder wi' no way back!'

She looked over her shoulder at him and saw a fascinating thing. He now wanted to say yes. To find a reason to say yes. Roland had brought him that far, and with hardly a word. Had only . . . well, had only looked at him.

There was movement in the corner of her eye. 'Holy *Christ*!' Eddie cried. Susannah's hand darted for a gun that wasn't there. She turned forward in the chair again. Coming down the slope toward them, moving with a prissy care that she couldn't help find amusing even in her startlement, was a metal man at least seven feet high.

Jake's hand had gone to the docker's clutch and the butt of the gun that hung there.

'Easy, Jake!' Roland said.

The metal man, eyes flashing blue, stopped in front of them. It stood perfectly still for perhaps ten seconds, plenty of time for Susannah to read what was stamped on its chest. *North Central Positronics*, she thought, *back for another curtain call. Not to mention LaMerk Industries.*

Then the robot raised one silver arm, placing a silver hand against its stainless-steel forehead. 'Hile, gunslinger, come from afar,' it said. 'Long days and pleasant nights.'

Roland raised his fingers to his own forehead. 'May you have twice the number, Andy-sai.'

'Thankee.' Clickings from its deep and incomprehensible guts. Then it leaned forward toward Roland, blue eyes flashing brighter. Susannah saw Eddie's hand creep to the sandalwood grip of the ancient revolver he wore. Roland, however, never flinched.

'I've made a goodish meal, gunslinger. Many good things from the fullness of the earth, aye.'

'Say thankee, Andy.'

'May it do ya fine.' The robot's guts clicked again. 'In the meantime, would you perhaps care to hear your horoscope?'

CHAPTER VI

THE WAY OF THE ELD

1

At around two in the afternoon of that day, the ten of them sat down to what Roland called a rancher's dinner. 'During the morning chores, you look forward with love,' he told his friends later. 'During the evening ones, you look back with nostalgia.'

Eddie thought he was joking, but with Roland you could never be completely sure. What humor he had was dry to the point of desiccation.

It wasn't the best meal Eddie had ever had, the banquet put on by the old people in River Crossing still held pride of place in that regard, but after weeks in the woods, subsisting on gunslinger burritos (and shitting hard little parcels of rabbit turds maybe twice a week), it was fine fare indeed. Andy served out whopping steaks done medium rare and smothered in mushroom gravy. There were beans on the side, wrapped things like tacos, and roasted corn. Eddie tried an ear of this and found it tough but tasty. There was coleslaw which, Tian Jaffords was at pains to tell them, had been made by his own wife's hands. There was also a wonderful pudding called strawberry cosy. And of course there was coffee. Eddie guessed that, among the four of them, they must have put away at least a gallon. Even Oy had a little. Jake put down a saucer of the dark, strong brew. Oy sniffed, said 'Coff!' and then lapped it up quickly and efficiently.

There was no serious talk during the meal ('Food and palaver don't mix' was but one of Roland's many little nuggets of wisdom), and yet Eddie learned a great deal from Jaffords and his wife, mostly about how life was lived out here in what Tian and Zalia called 'the borderlands.' Eddie hoped Susannah (sitting by Overholser) and Jake (with the youngster Eddie was already coming to think of as Benny the Kid) were learning half as much. He would have expected Roland to sit with Callahan, but Callahan sat with no one. He took his food off a little distance from all of them, blessed himself, and ate alone. Not very much, either. Mad at Overholser for taking over the show, or just a loner by nature? Hard to tell on such short notice, but if someone had put a gun to his head, Eddie would have voted for the latter.

What struck Eddie with the most force was how goddam *civilized* this part of the world was. It made Lud, with its warring Grays and Pubes, look like the Cannibal Isles in a boy's sea-story. These people had roads, law enforcement, and a system of government that made Eddie think of New England town meetings. There was a Town Gathering Hall and a feather which seemed to be some sort of authority symbol. If you wanted to call a meeting, you had to send the feather around. If enough people touched it when it came to their place, there was a meeting. If they didn't, there wasn't. Two people were sent to carry the feather, and their count was trusted without question. Eddie doubted if it would work in New York, but for a place like this it seemed a fine way to run things.

There were at least seventy other Callas, stretching in a mild arc north and south of Calla Bryn Sturgis. Calla Bryn Lockwood to the south and Calla Amity to the north were also farms and ranches. They also had to endure the periodic depredations of the Wolves. Farther south were Calla Bryn Bouse and Calla Staffel, containing vast tracts of ranchland, and Jaffords said they suffered the Wolves as well . . . at least he thought so. Farther north, Calla Sen Pinder and Calla Sen Chre, which were farms and sheep.

'Farms of a good size,' Tian said, 'but they're smaller as ye go north, kennit, until ye're in the lands where the snows fall — so I'm told; I've never seen it myself — and wonderful cheese is made.'

'Those of the north wear wooden shoes, or so 'tis said,' Zalia told Eddie, looking a little wistful. She herself wore scuffed clodhoppers called shor'-boots.

The people of the Callas traveled little, but the roads were there if they wanted to travel, and trade was brisk. In addition to them, there was the Whye, sometimes called Big River. This ran south of Calla Bryn Sturgis all the way to the South Seas, or so 'twas said. There were mining Callas and manufacturing Callas (where things were made by steam-press and even, aye, by electricity) and even one Calla devoted to nothing but pleasure: gambling and wild, amusing rides, and . . .

But here Tian, who had been talking, felt Zalia's eyes on him and went back to the pot for more beans. And a conciliatory dish of his wife's slaw.

'So,' Eddie said, and drew a curve in the dirt. 'These are the borderlands. The Callas. An arc that goes north and south for . . . how far, Zalia?'

''Tis men's business, so it is,' she said. Then, seeing her own man was still at the embering fire, inspecting the pots, she leaned forward a bit toward Eddie. 'Do you speak in miles or wheels?'

'A little of both, but I'm better with miles.'

She nodded. 'Mayhap two thousand miles so' —she pointed north— 'and twice that, *so.*' To the south. She remained that way, pointing in opposite directions, then dropped her arms, clasped her hands in her lap, and resumed her former demure pose.

'And these towns . . . these Callas . . . stretch the whole way?'

'So we're told, if it please ya, and the traders *do* come and go. Northwest of here, the Big River splits in two. We call the east branch Devar-Tete Whye – the Little Whye, you might say. Of course we see more river-travel from the north, for the river flows north to south, do ya see.'

'I do. And to the east?'

She looked down. 'Thunderclap,' she said in a voice Eddie could barely hear. 'None go there.'

'Why?'

'It's dark there,' said she, still not looking up from her lap. Then she raised an arm. This time she pointed in the direction from which Roland and his friends had come. Back toward Mid-World. 'There,' she said, 'the world is ending. Or so we're told. And there . . .' She pointed east and now raised her face to Eddie's. 'There, in Thunderclap, it's *already* ended. In the middle are we, who only want to go our way in peace.'

'And do you think it will happen?'

'No.' And Eddie saw she was crying.

2

Shortly after this, Eddie excused himself and stepped into a copse of trees for a personal moment. When he rose from his squat, reaching for some leaves with which to clean himself, a voice spoke from directly behind him.

'Not those, sai, do it please ya. Those be poison flurry. Wipe with those and how you'll itch.'

Eddie jumped and wheeled around, grabbing the waistband of his jeans with one hand and reaching for Roland's gunbelt, hanging from the branch of a nearby tree, with the other. Then he saw who had spoken – or *what* – and relaxed a little.

'Andy, it's not really kosher to creep up behind people when they're taking a dump.' Then he pointed to a thatch of low green bushes. 'What about those? How much trouble will I get into if I wipe with those?'

There were pauses and clicks.

'What?' Eddie asked. 'Did I do something wrong?'

'No,' Andy said. 'I'm simply processing information, sai. *Kosher*: unknown word. *Creeping up*: I didn't, I walked, if it do ye fine. *Taking a dump*: likely slang for the excretion of—'

'Yeah,' Eddie said, 'that's what it is. But listen – if you didn't creep up on me, Andy, how come I didn't hear you? I mean, there's *underbrush*. Most people make noise when they go through underbrush.'

'I am not a person, sai,' Andy said. Eddie thought he sounded smug.

'Guy, then. How can a big guy like you be so quiet?'

'Programming,' Andy said. 'Those leaves will be fine, do ya.'

Eddie rolled his eyes, then grabbed a bunch. 'Oh yeah. Programming. Sure. Should have known. Thankee-sai, long days, kiss my ass and go to heaven.'

'Heaven,' said Andy. 'A place one goes after death; a kind of paradise. According to the Old Fella, those who go to heaven sitteth at the right hand of God the Father Almighty, forever and ever.'

'Yeah? Who's gonna sit at his left hand? All the Tupperware salesmen?'

'Sai, I don't know. *Tupperware* is an unknown word to me. Would you like your horoscope?'

'Why not?' Eddie said. He started back toward the camp, guided by the sounds of laughing boys and a barking billy-bumbler. Andy towered beside him, shining even beneath the cloudy sky and seeming to not make a sound. It was eerie.

'What's your birth date, sai?'

Eddie thought he might be ready for this one. 'I'm Goat Moon,' he said, then remembered a little more. 'Goat with beard.'

'Winter's snow is full of woe, winter's child is strong and wild,' said Andy. Yes, that was smugness in its voice, all right.

'Strong and wild, that's me,' Eddie said. 'Haven't had a real bath in over a month, you better believe I'm strong and wild. What else do you need, Andy old guy? Want to look at my palm, or anything?'

'That will not be necessary, sai Eddie.' The robot sounded unmistakably happy and Eddie thought, *That's me, spreading joy wherever I go. Even robots love me. It's my ka.* 'This is Full Earth, say we all thankya. The moon is red, what is called the Huntress Moon in Mid-World that was. You will travel, Eddie! You will travel far! You and your friends! This very night you return to Calla New York. You will meet a dark lady. You—'

'I want to hear more about this trip to New York,' Eddie said, stopping. Just ahead was the camp. He was close enough so he could see people moving around. 'No joking around, Andy.'

'You will go todash, sai Eddie! You and your friends. You must be careful. When you hear the *kammen* – the chimes, ken ya well – you must all concentrate on each other. To keep from getting lost.'

'How do you know this stuff?' Eddie asked.

'Programming,' Andy said. 'Horoscope is done, sai. No charge.' And then, what struck Eddie as the final capping lunacy: 'Sai Callahan – the Old Fella, ye ken – says I have no license to tell fortunes, so must never charge.'

'Sai Callahan says true,' Eddie said, and then, when Andy started forward again: 'But stay a minute, Andy. Do ya, I beg.' It was absolutely weird how quickly that started to sound okay.

Andy stopped willingly enough and turned toward Eddie, his blue eyes glowing. Eddie had roughly a thousand questions about todash, but he was currently even more curious about something else.

'You know about these Wolves.'

'Oh, yes. I told sai Tian. He was wroth.' Again Eddie detected something like smugness in Andy's voice . . . but surely that was just the way it struck him, right? A robot – even one that had survived from the old days – couldn't enjoy the discomforts of humans? Could it?

Didn't take you long to forget the mono, did it, sugar? Susannah's voice asked in his head. Hers was followed by Jake's. *Blaine's a pain.* And then, just his own: *If you treat this guy like nothing more than a fortune-telling machine in a carnival arcade, Eddie old boy, you deserve whatever you get.*

'Tell me about the Wolves,' Eddie said.

'What would you know, sai Eddie?'

'Where they come from, for a start. The place where they feel like they can put their feet up and fart right out loud. Who they work for. Why they take the kids. And why the ones they take come back ruined.' Then another question struck him. Perhaps the most obvious. 'Also, how do you know when they're coming?'

Clicks from inside Andy. A lot of them this time, maybe a full minute's worth. When Andy spoke again, its voice was different. It made Eddie think about Officer Bosconi, back in the neighborhood. Brooklyn Avenue, that was Bosco Bob's beat. If you just met him, walking along the street and twirling his nightstick, Bosco talked to you like you were a human being and so was he — howya doin, Eddie, how's your mother these days, how's your goodfornothin bro, are you gonna sign up for PAL Middlers, okay, seeya at the gym, stay off the smokes, have a good day. But if he thought maybe you'd done something, Bosco Bob turned into a guy you didn't want to know. That Officer Bosconi didn't smile, and the eyes behind his glasses were like puddle ice in February (which just happened to be the Time o' the Goat, over here on this side of the Great Whatever). Bosco Bob had never hit Eddie, but there were a couple of times — once just after some kids lit Woo Kim's Market on fire — when he felt sure that bluesuit mothafuck *would* have hit him, if Eddie had been stupid enough to smart off. It wasn't schizophrenia — at least not of the pure Detta/Odetta kind — but it was close. There were two versions of Officer Bosconi. One of them was a nice guy. The other one was a cop.

When Andy spoke again, it no longer sounded like your well-meaning but rather stupid uncle, the one who believed the alligator-boy and Elvis-is-alive-in-Buenos Aires stories *Inside View* printed were absolutely true. This Andy sounded emotionless and somehow dead.

Like a *real* robot, in other words.

'What's your password, sai Eddie?'

'Huh?'

'Password. You have ten seconds. Nine . . . eight . . . seven . . .'

Eddie thought of spy movies he'd seen. 'You mean I say something like "The roses are blooming in Cairo" and *you* say "Only in Mrs Wilson's garden" and then *I* say—'

'Incorrect password, sai Eddie . . . two . . . one . . . zero.' From within Andy came a low thudding sound which Eddie found singularly unpleasant. It sounded like the blade of a sharp cleaver passing through meat and into the wood of the chopping block beneath. He found himself thinking for the first time about the Old People, who had surely built Andy (or maybe the people before the Old People, call them the Really Old People — who knew for sure?). Not people Eddie himself would want to meet, if the last remainders in Lud had been any example.

'You may retry once,' said the cold voice. It bore a resemblance to the one that had asked Eddie if Eddie would like his horoscope told, but that was the best you could call it — a resemblance. 'Would you retry, Eddie of New York?'

Eddie thought fast. 'No,' he said, 'that's all right. The info's restricted, huh?'

Several clicks. Then: '*Restricted:* confined, kept within certain set limits, as information in a given document or q-disc; limited to those authorized to use that information; those authorized announce themselves by giving the password.' Another pause to think and then Andy said, 'Yes, Eddie. That info's restricted.'

'Why?' Eddie asked.

He expected no answer, but Andy gave him one. 'Directive Nineteen.'

Eddie clapped him on his steel side. 'My friend, that don't surprise me at all. Directive Nineteen it is.'

'Would you care to hear an expanded horoscope, Eddie-sai?'

'Think I'll pass.'

'What about a tune called "The Jimmy Juice I Drank Last Night"? It has many amusing verses.' The reedy note of a pitch-pipe came from somewhere in Andy's diaphragm.

Eddie, who found the idea of many amusing verses somehow alarming, increased his pace toward the others. 'Why don't we just put that on hold?' he said. 'Right now I think I need another cup of coffee.'

'Give you joy of it, sai,' Andy said. To Eddie he sounded rather forlorn. Like Bosco Bob when you told him you thought you'd be too busy for PAL League that summer.

3

Roland sat on a stone outcrop, drinking his own cup of coffee. He listened to Eddie without speaking himself, and with only one small change of expression: a minute lift of the eyebrows at the words Directive Nineteen.

Across the clearing from them, Slightman the Younger had produced a kind of bubble-pipe that made extraordinarily tough bubbles. Oy chased them, popped several with his teeth, then began to get the hang of what Slightman seemed to want, which was for him to herd them into a fragile little pile of light. The bubble-pile made Eddie think of the Wizard's

Rainbow, those dangerous glass balls. And did Callahan really have one? The worst of the bunch?

Beyond the boys, at the edge of the clearing, Andy stood with his silver arms folded over the stainless-steel curve of his chest. Waiting to clean up the meal he had hauled to them and then cooked, Eddie supposed. The perfect servant. He cooks, he cleans, he tells you about the dark lady you'll meet. Just don't expect him to violate Directive Nineteen. Not without the password, anyway.

'Come over to me, folks, would you?' Roland asked, raising his voice slightly. 'Time we had a bit of palaver. Won't be long, which is good, at least for us, for we've already had our own, before sai Callahan came to us, and after awhile talk sickens, so it does.'

They came over and sat near him like obedient children, those from the Calla and those who were from far away and would go beyond here perhaps even farther.

'First I'd hear what you know of these Wolves. Eddie tells me Andy may not say how he comes by what he knows.'

'You say true,' Slightman the Elder rumbled. 'Either those who made him or those who came later have mostly gagged him on that subject, although he always warns us of their coming. On most other subjects, his mouth runs everlastingly.'

Roland looked toward the Calla's big farmer. 'Will you set us on, sai Overholser?'

Tian Jaffords looked disappointed not to be called on. His woman looked disappointed for him. Slightman the Elder nodded as if Roland's choice of speaker was only to be expected. Overholser himself did not puff up as Eddie might have guessed. Instead he looked down at his own crossed legs and scuffed shor'boots for thirty seconds or so, rubbing at the side of his face, thinking. The clearing was so quiet Eddie could hear the minute rasp of the farmer's palm on two or three days' worth of bristles. At last he sighed, nodded, and looked up at Roland.

'Say thankee. Ye're not what I expected, I must say. Nor your tet.' Overholser turned to Tian. 'Ye were right to haul us out here, Tian Jaffords. This is a meeting we needed to have, and I say thankee.'

'It wasn't me got you out here,' Jaffords said. 'Was the Old Fella.'

Overholser nodded to Callahan. Callahan nodded back, then sketched the shape of a cross in the air with his scarred hand — as if to say, Eddie thought, that it wasn't him, either, but God. Maybe so, but when it came to pulling coals out of a hot fire, he'd put two dollars on Roland of Gilead for every one he put on God and the Man Jesus, those heavenly gunslingers.

Roland waited, his face calm and perfectly polite.

Finally Overholser began to talk. He spoke for nearly fifteen minutes, slowly but always to the point. There was the business of the twins, to begin with. Residents of the Calla realized that children birthed in twos were the exception rather than the rule in other parts of the world and at other times in the past, but in their area of the Grand Crescent it was the singletons, like the Jaffordses' Aaron, who were the rarities. The *great* rarities.

And, beginning perhaps a hundred and twenty years ago (or mayhap a hundred and fifty; with time the way it was, such things were impossible to pin down with any certainty), the Wolves had begun their raids. They did not come exactly once every generation; that would have been each twenty years or so, and it was longer than that. Still, it was *close* to that.

Eddie thought of asking Overholser and Slightman how the Old People could have shut Andy's mouth concerning the Wolves if the Wolves had been raiding out of Thunderclap for less than two centuries, then didn't bother. Asking what couldn't be answered was a waste of time, Roland would have said. Still, it was interesting, wasn't it? Interesting to wonder when someone (or some*thing*) had last programmed Andy the Messenger (Many Other Functions).

And why.

The children, Overholser said, one of each set between the ages of perhaps three and fourteen, were taken east, into the land of Thunderclap. (Slightman the Elder put his arm around his boy's shoulders during this part of the tale, Eddie noticed.) There they remained for a relatively short period of time – mayhap four weeks, mayhap eight. Then most of them would be returned. The assumption made about those few who did not return was that they had died in the Land of Darkness, that whatever evil rite was performed on them killed a few instead of just ruining them.

The ones who came back were at best biddable idiots. A five-year-old would return with all his hard-won talk gone, reduced to nothing but babble and reaching for the things he wanted. Diapers which had been left forgotten two or three years before would go back on and might stay on until such a roont child was ten or even twelve.

'Yer-bugger, Tia *still* pisses herself one day out of every six, and can be counted on to shit herself once a moon, as well,' Jaffords said.

'Hear him,' Overholser agreed gloomily. 'My own brother, Welland, was much the same until he died. And of course they have to be watched more or less constant, for if they get something they like, they'll eat it until they bust. Who's watching yours, Tian?'

'My cuz,' Zalia said before Tian could speak. 'Heddon n Hedda can help a little now, as well; they've come to a likely enough age—' She stopped and seemed to realize what she was saying. Her mouth twisted and she fell silent. Eddie guessed he understood. Heddon and Hedda could help now, yes. Next year, one of them would still be able to help. The other one, though . . .

A child taken at the age of ten might come back with a few rudiments of language left, but would never get much beyond that. The ones who were taken oldest were somehow the worst, for they seemed to come back with some vague understanding of what had been done to them. What had been stolen from them. These had a tendency to cry a great deal, or to simply creep off by themselves and peer into the east, like lost things. As if they might see their poor brains out there, circling like birds in the dark sky. Half a dozen such had even committed suicide over the years. (At this, Callahan once more crossed himself.)

The roont ones remained childlike in stature as well as in speech and behavior until about the age of sixteen. Then, quite suddenly, most of them sprouted to the size of young giants.

'Ye can have no idea what it's like if ye haven't seen it and been through it,' Tian said. He was looking into the ashes of the fire. 'Ye can have no idea of the pain it causes them. When a babby cuts his teeth, ye ken how they cry?'

'Yes,' Susannah said.

Tian nodded. 'It's as if their whole bodies are teething, kennit.'

'Hear him,' Overholser said. 'For sixteen or eighteen months, all my brother did was sleep and eat and cry and grow. I can remember him crying even *in* his sleep. I'd get out of my bed and go across to him and there'd be a whispering sound from inside his chest and legs and head. 'Twere the sound of his bones growing in the night, hear me.'

Eddie contemplated the horror of it. You heard stories about giants — fee-fi-fo-fum, and all that — but until now he'd never considered what it might be like to *become* a giant. *As if their whole bodies are teething*, Eddie thought, and shivered.

'A year and a half, no longer than that and it were done, but I wonder how long it must seem to them, who're brought back with no more sense of time than birds or bugs.'

'Endless,' Susannah said. Her face was very pale and she sounded ill. 'It must seem endless.'

'The whispering in the nights as their bones grow,' Overholser said. 'The headaches as their *skulls* grow.'

'Zalman screamed one time for nine days without stopping,' Zalia said. Her voice was expressionless, but Eddie could see the horror in her eyes; he could see it very well. 'His cheekbones pushed up. You could see it happening. His forehead curved out and out, and if you held an ear close to it you could hear the skull creaking as it spread. It sounded like a tree-branch under a weight of ice.

'Nine days he screamed. Nine. Morning, noon, and in the dead of night. Screaming and screaming. Eyes gushing water. We prayed to all the gods there were that he'd go hoarse – that he'd be stricken dumb, even – but none such happened, say thankee. If we'd had a gun, I believe we would have slew him as he lay on his pallet just to end his pain. As it was, my good old Da' was ready to slit 'een's thr'ut when it stopped. His bones went on yet awhile – his skellington, do ya – but his head was the worst of it and it finally stopped, tell gods thankya, and Man Jesus too.'

She nodded toward Callahan. He nodded back and raised his hand toward her, outstretched in the air for a moment. Zalia turned back to Roland and his friends.

'Now I have five of my own,' she said. 'Aaron's safe, and say thankee, but Heddon and Hedda's ten, a prime age. Lyman and Lia's only five, but five's old enough. Five's . . .'

She covered her face with her hands and said no more.

4

Once the growth-spurt was finished, Overholser said, some of them could be put to work. Others – the majority – weren't able to manage even such rudimentary tasks as pulling stumps or digging postholes. You saw these sitting on the steps of Took's General Store or sometimes walking across the countryside in gangling groups, young men and women of enormous height, weight, and stupidity, sometimes grinning at each other and babbling, sometimes only goggling up at the sky.

They didn't mate, there was that to be grateful for. While not all of them grew to prodigious size and their mental skills and physical abilities might vary somewhat, there seemed to be one universal: they came back sexually dead. 'Beggin your pardon for the crudity,' Overholser said, 'but I don't b'lieve my brother Welland had so much as a piss-hardon after they brought him back. Zalia? Have you ever seen your brother with a . . . you know . . .'

Zalia shook her head.

'How old were you when they came, sai Overholser?' Roland asked.

'First time, ye mean. Welland and I were nine.' Overholser now spoke rapidly. It gave what he said the air of a rehearsed speech, but Eddie didn't think that was it. Overholser was a force in Calla Bryn Sturgis; he was, God save us and stone the crows, the big farmer. It was hard for him to go back in his mind to a time when he'd been a child, small and powerless and terrified. 'Our Ma and Pa tried to hide us away in the cellar. So I've been told, anyway. I remember none of it, m'self, to be sure. Taught myself not to, I s'pose. Yar, quite likely. Some remember better'n others, Roland, but all the tales come to the same: one is took, one is left behind. The one took comes back roont, maybe able to work a little but dead in the b'low the waist. Then . . . when they get in their thirties . . .'

When they reached their thirties, the roont twins grew abruptly, shockingly old. Their hair turned white and often fell completely out. Their eyes dimmed. Muscles that had been prodigious (as Tia Jaffords's and Zalman Hoonik's were now) went slack and wasted away. Sometimes they died peacefully, in their sleep. More often, their endings weren't peaceful at all. The sores came, sometimes out on the skin but more often in the stomach or the head. In the brain. All died long before their natural span would have been up, had it not been for the Wolves, and many died as they had grown from the size of normal children to that of giants: screaming in pain. Eddie wondered how many of these idiots, dying of what sounded to him like terminal cancer, were simply smothered or perhaps fed some strong sedative that would take them far beyond pain, far beyond sleep. It wasn't the sort of question you asked, but he guessed the answer would have been many. Roland sometimes used the word *delah*, always spoken with a light toss of the hand toward the horizon.

Many.

The visitors from the Calla, their tongues and memories untied by distress, might have gone on for some time, piling one sorry anecdote on another, but Roland didn't allow them to. 'Now speak of the Wolves, I beg. How many come to you?'

'Forty,' Tian Jaffords said.

'Spread across the whole Calla?' Slightman the Elder asked. 'Nay, more than forty.' And to Tian, slightly apologetic: 'You were no more'n nine y'self last time they came, Tian. I were in my young twenties. Forty in town, maybe, but more came to the outlying farms and ranches. I'd say sixty in all, Roland-sai, maybe eighty.'

Roland looked at Overholser, eyebrows raised.

'It's been twenty-three years, ye mind,' Overholser said, 'but I'd call sixty about right.'

'You call them Wolves, but what are they really? Are they men? Or something else?'

Overholser, Slightman, Tian, Zalia: for a moment Eddie could feel them sharing khef, could almost hear them. It made him feel lonely and left-out, the way you did when you saw a couple kissing on a streetcorner, wrapped in each other's arms or looking into each other's eyes, totally lost in each other's regard. Well, he didn't have to feel that way anymore, did he? He had his own ka-tet, his own khef. Not to mention his own woman.

Meanwhile, Roland was making the impatient little finger-twirling gesture with which Eddie had become so familiar. *Come on, folks*, it said, *day's wasting*.

'No telling for sure what they are,' Overholser said. 'They *look* like men, but they wear masks.'

'Wolf-masks,' Susannah said.

'Aye, lady, wolf-masks, gray as their horses.'

'Do you say all come on gray horses?' Roland asked.

The silence was briefer this time, but Eddie still felt that sense of khef and ka-tet, minds consulting via something so elemental it couldn't even rightly be called telepathy; it was more elemental than telepathy.

'Yer-bugger!' Overholser said, a slang term that seemed to mean *You bet your ass, don't insult me by asking again*. 'All on gray horses. They wear gray pants that look like skin. Black boots with cruel big steel spurs. Green cloaks and hoods. And the masks. We know they're masks because they've been found left behind. They look like steel but rot in the sun like flesh, buggerdly things.'

'Ah.'

Overholser gave him a rather insulting head-cocked-to-one side look, the sort that asked *Are you foolish or just slow?* Then Slightman said: 'Their horses ride like the wind. Some have ta'en one babby before the saddle and another behind.'

'Do you say so?' Roland asked.

Slightman nodded emphatically. 'Tell gods thankee.' He saw Callahan again make the sign of the cross in the air and sighed. 'Beg pardon, Old Fella.'

Callahan shrugged. 'You were here before I was. Call on all the gods you like, so long as you know I think they're false.'

'And they come out of Thunderclap,' Roland said, ignoring this last.

'Aye,' Overholser said. 'You can see where it lies over that way about a hundred wheels.' He pointed southeast. 'For we come out of the woods on the last height of land before the Crescent. Ye can see all the Eastern Plain from there, and beyond it a great darkness, like a rain cloud on the horizon. 'Tis said, Roland, that in the far long ago, you could see mountains over there.'

'Like the Rockies from Nebraska,' Jake breathed.

Overholser glanced at him. 'Beg pardon, Jake-soh?'

'Nothing,' Jake said, and gave the big farmer a small, embarrassed smile. Eddie, meanwhile, filed away what Overholser had called him. Not sai but soh. Just something else that was interesting.

'We've heard of Thunderclap,' Roland said. His voice was somehow terrifying in its lack of emotion, and when Eddie felt Susannah's hand creep into his, he was glad of it.

''Tis a land of vampires, boggarts, and taheen, so the stories say,' Zalia told them. Her voice was thin, on the verge of trembling. 'Of course the stories are old—'

'The stories are true,' Callahan said. His own voice was harsh, but Eddie heard the fear in it. Heard it very well. 'There *are* vampires — other things as well, very likely — and Thunderclap's their nest. We might speak more of this another time, gunslinger, if it does ya. For now, only hear me, I beg: of vampires I know a good deal. I don't know if the Wolves take the Calla's children to them — I rather think not — but yes, there *are* vampires.'

'Why do you speak as if I doubt?' Roland asked.

Callahan's eyes dropped. 'Because many do. I did myself. I doubted much and . . .' His voice cracked. He cleared his throat, and when he finished, it was almost in a whisper. '. . . and it was my undoing.'

Roland sat quiet for several moments, hunkered on the soles of his ancient boots with his arms wrapped around his bony knees, rocking back and forth a little. Then, to Overholser: 'What o' the clock do they come?'

'When they took Welland, my brother, it was morning,' the farmer said. 'Breakfast not far past. I remember, because Welland asked our Ma if he could take his cup of coffee into the cellar with him. But last time . . . the time they come and took Tian's sister and Zalia's brother and so many others . . .'

'I lost two nieces and a nephew,' Slightman the Elder said.

'That time wasn't long after the noon-bell from the Gathering Hall. We know the day because *Andy* knows the day, and that much he tells us. Then we hear the thunder of their hooves as they come out of the east and see the rooster-tail of dust they raise—'

'So you know when they're coming,' Roland said. 'In fact, you know three ways: Andy, the sound of their hoofbeats, the rise of their dust.'

Overholser, taking Roland's implication, had flushed a dull brick color up the slopes of his plump cheeks and down his neck. 'They come armed, Roland, do ya. With guns — rifles as well as the revolvers yer own tet carries, grenados, too — and other weapons, as well. Fearsome weapons of the Old People. Light-sticks that kill at a touch, flying metal buzz-balls called drones or sneetches. The sticks burn the skin black and stop the heart — electrical, maybe, or maybe—'

Eddie heard Overholser's next word as *ant-NOMIC*. At first he thought the man was trying to say anatomy. A moment later he realized it was probably 'atomic.'

'Once the drones smell you, they follow no matter how fast you run,' Slightman's boy said eagerly, 'or how much you twist and turn. Right, Da'?'

'Yer-bugger,' Slightman the Elder said. 'Then sprout blades that whirl around so fast you can't see em and they cut you apart.'

'All on gray horses,' Roland mused. 'Every one of em the same color. What else?'

Nothing, it seemed. It was all told. They came out of the east on the day Andy foretold, and for a terrible hour — perhaps longer — the Calla was filled with the thunderous hoofbeats of those gray horses and the screams of desolated parents. Green cloaks swirled. Wolf-masks that looked like metal and rotted in the sun like skin snarled. The children were taken. Sometimes a few pair were overlooked and left whole, suggesting that the Wolves' prescience wasn't perfect. Still, it must have been pretty goddam good, Eddie thought, because if the kids were moved (as they often were) or hidden at home (as they almost *always* were), the Wolves found them anyway, and in short order. Even at the bottom of sharproot piles or haystacks they were found. Those of the Calla who tried to stand against them were shot, fried by the light-sticks — lasers of some kind? — or cut to pieces by the flying drones. When trying to imagine these latter, he kept recalling a bloody little film Henry had dragged him to. *Phantasm*, it had been called. Down at the old Majestic. Corner of Brooklyn and Markey Avenue. Like too much of his old life, the Majestic had smelled of piss and popcorn and the kind of wine that came in brown bags. Sometimes there were needles in the aisles. Not good, maybe, and yet sometimes — usually at night, when sleep was long in coming — a deep part of him still cried for the old life of which the Majestic had been a part. Cried for it as a stolen child might cry for his mother.

The children were taken, the hoofbeats receded the way they had come, and that was the end of it.

'No, can't be,' Jake said. 'They must bring them back, don't they?'

'No,' Overholser said. 'The roont ones come back on the train, hear me, there's a great junkpile of em I could show 'ee, and— What? What's wrong?' Jake's mouth had fallen open, and he'd lost most of his color.

'We had a bad experience on a train not so very long ago,' Susannah said. 'The trains that bring your children back, are they monos?'

They weren't. Overholser, the Jaffords, and the Slightmans had no idea what a mono was, in fact. (Callahan, who had been to Disneyland as a teenager, did.) The trains which brought the children back were hauled by plain old locomotives (*hopefully none of them named Charlie*, Eddie thought), driverless and attached to one or perhaps two open flatcars. The children were huddled on these. When they arrived they were usually crying with fear (from sunburns as well, if the weather west of Thunderclap was hot and clear), covered with food and their own drying shit, and dehydrated into the bargain. There was no station at the railhead, although Overholser opined there might have been, centuries before. Once the children had been offloaded, teams of horses were used to pull the short trains from the rusty railhead. It occurred to Eddie that they could figure out the number of times the Wolves had come by counting the number of junked engines, sort of like figuring out the age of a tree by counting the rings on the stump.

'How long a trip for them, would you guess?' Roland asked. 'Judging from their condition when they arrive?'

Overholser looked at Slightman, then at Tian and Zalia. 'Two days? Three?'

They shrugged and nodded.

'Two or three days,' Overholser said to Roland, speaking with more confidence than was perhaps warranted, judging from the looks of the others. 'Long enough for sunburns, and to eat most of the rations they're left—'

'Or paint themselves with em,' Slightman grunted.

'—but not long enough to die of exposure,' Overholser finished. 'If ye'd judge from that how far they were taken from the Calla, all I can say is I wish 'ee joy of the riddle, for no one knows what speed the train draws when it's crossing the plains. It comes slow and stately enough to the far side of the river, but that means little.'

'No,' Roland agreed, 'it doesn't.' He considered. 'Twenty-seven days left?'

'Twenty-six now,' Callahan said quietly.

'One thing, Roland,' Overholser said. He spoke apologetically, but his jaw was jutting. Eddie thought he'd backslid to the kind of guy you could dislike on sight. If you had a problem with authority figures, that was, and Eddie always had.

Roland raised his eyebrows in silent question.

'We haven't said yes.' Overholser glanced at Slightman the Elder, as if for support, and Slightman nodded agreement.

'Ye must ken we have no way of knowing y' are who you say y' are,' Slightman said, rather apologetically. 'My family had no books growing up, and there's none out at the ranch – I'm foreman of Eisenhart's Rocking B – except for the stockline books, but growing up I heard as many tales of Gilead and gunslingers and Arthur Eld as any other boy . . . heard of Jericho Hill and such blood-and-thunder tales of pretend . . . but I never heard of a gunslinger missing two of his fingers, or a brown-skinned woman gunslinger, or one who won't be old enough to shave for years yet.'

His son looked shocked, and in an agony of embarrassment as well. Slightman looked rather embarrassed himself, but pushed on.

'I cry your pardon if what I say offends, indeed I do—'

'Hear him, hear him well,' Overholser rumbled. Eddie was starting to think that if the man's jaw jutted out much further, it would snap clean off.

'—but any decision we make will have long echoes. Ye must see it's so. If we make the wrong one, it could mean the death of our town, and all in it.'

'I can't believe what I'm hearing!' Tian Jaffords cried indignantly. 'Do you think 'ese're a fraud? Good gods, man, have 'ee not *looked* at him? Do 'ee not have—'

His wife grasped his arm hard enough to pinch white marks into his farmer's tan with the tips of her fingers. Tian looked at her and fell quiet, though his lips were pressed together tightly.

Somewhere in the distance, a crow called and a rustie answered in its slightly shriller voice. Then all was silent. One by one they turned to Roland of Gilead to see how he would reply.

5

It was always the same, and it made him tired. They wanted help, but they also wanted references. A parade of witnesses, if they could get them. They wanted rescue without risk, just to close their eyes and be saved.

Roland rocked slowly back and forth with his arms wrapped around his knees. Then he nodded to himself and raised his head. 'Jake,' he said. 'Come to me.'

Jake glanced at Benny, his new friend, then got up and walked across to Roland. Oy walked at his heel, as always.

'Andy,' Roland said.

'Sai?'

'Bring me four of the plates we ate from.' As Andy did this, Roland spoke to Overholser: 'You're going to lose some crockery. When gunslingers come to town, sai, things get broken. It's a simple fact of life.'

'Roland, I don't think we need—'

'Hush now,' Roland said, and although his voice was gentle, Overholser hushed at once. 'You've told your tale; now we tell ours.'

Andy's shadow fell over Roland. The gunslinger looked up and took the plates, which hadn't been rinsed and still gleamed with grease. Then he turned to Jake, where a remarkable change had taken place. Sitting with Benny the Kid, watching Oy do his small clever tricks and grinning with pride, Jake had looked like any other boy of twelve — carefree and full of the old Dick, likely as not. Now the smile had fallen away and it was hard to tell just what his age might have been. His blue eyes looked into Roland's, which were of almost the same shade. Beneath his shoulder, the Ruger Jake had taken from his father's desk in another life hung in its docker's clutch. The trigger was secured with a rawhide loop which Jake now loosened without looking. It took only a single tug.

'Say your lesson, Jake, son of Elmer, and be true.'

Roland half-expected either Eddie or Susannah to interfere, but neither did. He looked at them. Their faces were as cold and grave as Jake's. Good.

Jake's voice was also without expression, but the words came out hard and sure.

'I do not aim with my hand; he who aims with his hand has forgotten the face of his father. I aim with my eye. I do not shoot with my hand—'

'I don't see what this—' Overholser began.

'Shut up,' Susannah said, and pointed a finger at him.

Jake seemed not to have heard. His eyes never left Roland's. The boy's right hand lay on his upper chest, the fingers spread. 'He who shoots with his hand has forgotten the face of his father. I shoot with my mind. I do not kill with my gun; he who kills with his gun has forgotten the face of his father.'

Jake paused. Drew in breath. And let it out speaking.

'I kill with my heart.'

'Kill these,' Roland remarked, and with no more warning than that, slung all four of the plates high into the air. They rose, spinning and separating, black shapes against the white sky.

Jake's hand, the one resting on his chest, became a blur. It pulled the Ruger from the docker's clutch, swung it up, and began pulling the trigger while Roland's hand was still in the air. The plates did not seem to explode one after the other but rather all at once. The pieces rained down on the clearing. A few fell into the fire, puffing up ash and sparks. One or two clanged off Andy's steel head.

Roland snatched upward, open hands moving in a blur. Although he had given them no command, Eddie and Susannah did the same, did it even while the visitors from Calla Bryn Sturgis cringed, shocked by the loudness of the gunfire. And the speed of the shots.

'Look here at us, do ya, and say thankee,' Roland said. He held out his hands. Eddie and Susannah did the same. Eddie had caught three pottery shards. Susannah had five (and a shallow cut on the pad of one finger). Roland had snatched a full dozen pieces of falling shrapnel. It looked like almost enough to make a whole plate, were the pieces glued back together.

The six from the Calla stared, unbelieving. Benny the Kid still had his hands over his ears; now he lowered them slowly. He was looking at Jake as one might look at a ghost or an apparition from the sky.

'My . . . *God*,' Callahan said. 'It's like a trick in some old Wild West show.'

'It's no trick,' Roland said, 'never think it. It's the Way of the Eld. We are of that an-tet, khef and ka, watch and warrant. Gunslingers, do ya. And now I'll tell you what we will do.' His eyes sought Overholser's. 'What we *will* do, I say, for no man bids us. Yet I think nothing I say will discomfort you too badly. If mayhap it does—' Roland shrugged. *If it does, too bad,* that shrug said.

He dropped the pottery shards between his boots and dusted his hands.

'If those had been Wolves,' he said, 'there would have been fifty-six left to trouble you instead of sixty. Four of them lying dead on the ground before you could draw a breath. Killed by a boy.' He gazed at Jake. 'What you would *call* a boy, mayhap.' Roland paused. 'We're used to long odds.'

'The young fella's a breathtaking shot, I'd grant ye,' said Slightman the Elder. 'But there's a difference between clay dishes and Wolves on horseback.'

'For you, sai, perhaps. Not for us. Not once the shooting starts. When the shooting starts, we kill what moves. Isn't that why you sought us?'

'Suppose they can't be shot?' Overholser asked. 'Can't be laid low by even the hardest of hard calibers?'

'Why do you waste time when time is short?' Roland asked evenly. 'You *know* they can be killed or you never would have come out here to us in the first place. I didn't ask, because the answer is self-evident.'

Overholser had once more flushed dark red. 'Cry your pardon,' he said.

Benny, meanwhile, continued to stare at Jake with wide eyes, and Roland felt a minor pang of regret for both boys. They might still manage some sort of friendship, but what had just happened would change it in fundamental ways, turn it into something quite unlike the usual lighthearted khef boys shared. Which was a shame, because when Jake wasn't being called upon to be a gunslinger, he was still only a child. Close to the age Roland himself had been when the test of manhood had been thrust on him. But he would not be young much longer, very likely. And it was a shame.

'Listen to me now,' Roland said, 'and hear me very well. We leave you shortly to go back to our own camp and take our own counsel. Tomorrow, when we come to your town, we'll put up with one of you—'

'Come to Seven-Mile,' Overholser said. 'We'll have you and say thankee, Roland.'

'Our place is much smaller,' Tian said, 'but Zalia and I—'

'We'd be so pleased to have 'ee,' Zalia said. She had flushed as deeply as Overholser. 'Aye, we would.'

Roland said, 'Do you have a house as well as a church, sai Callahan?'

Callahan smiled. 'I do, and tell God thankya.'

'We might stay with you on our first night in Calla Bryn Sturgis,' Roland said. 'Could we do that?'

'Sure, and welcome.'

'You could show us your church. Introduce us to its mysteries.'

Callahan's gaze was steady. 'I'd welcome the chance to do that.'

'In the days after,' Roland said, smiling, 'we shall throw ourselves on the hospitality of the town.'

'You'll not find it wanting,' Tian said. 'That I promise ye.' Overholser and Slightman were nodding.

'If the meal we've just eaten is any sign, I'm sure that's true. We say thankee, sai Jaffords; thankee one and all. For a week we four will go about your town, poking our noses here and there. Mayhap a bit longer, but likely a week. We'll look at the lay of the land and the way the buildings are set on it. Look with an eye to the coming of these Wolves. We'll talk to folk, and folk will talk to us – those of you here now will see to that, aye?'

Callahan was nodding. 'I can't speak for the Manni, but I'm sure the rest will be more than willing to talk to you about the Wolves. God and Man Jesus knows they're no secret. And those of the Crescent are frightened to death of them. If they see a chance you might be able to help us, they'll do all you ask.'

'The Manni will speak to me as well,' Roland said. 'I've held palaver with them before.'

'Don't be carried away with the Old Fella's enthusiasm, Roland,' Overholser said. He raised his plump hands in the air, a gesture of caution. 'There are others in town you'll have to convince—'

'Vaughn Eisenhart, for one,' said Slightman.

'Aye, and Eben Took, do ya,' Overholser said. 'The General Store's the only thing his name's on, ye ken, but he owns the boarding house and the restaurant out front of it . . . as well's a half-interest in the livery . . . and loan-paper on most of the smallholds hereabouts.

'When it comes to the smallholds, 'ee mustn't neglect Bucky Javier,'

Overholser rumbled. 'He ain't the biggest of em, but only because he gave away half of what he had to his young sister when she married.' Overholser leaned toward Roland, his face alight with a bit of town history about to be passed on. 'Roberta Javier, Bucky's sissa, she's lucky,' he said. 'When the Wolves came last time, she and her twin brother were but a year old. So they were passed over.'

'Bucky's own twin brother was took the time before,' Slightman said. 'Bully's dead now almost four year. Of the sickness. Since then, there ain't enough Bucky can do for those younger two. But you should talk to him, aye. Bucky's not got but eighty acre, yet he's trig.'

Roland thought, *They still don't see.*

'Thank you,' he said. 'What lies directly ahead for us comes down to looking and listening, mostly. When it's done, we'll ask that whoever is in charge of the feather take it around so that a meeting can be called. At that meeting, we'll tell you if the town can be defended and how many men we'll want to help us, if it can be done.'

Roland saw Overholser puffing up to speak and shook his head at him.

'It won't be many we'd want, in any case,' he said. 'We're gunslingers, not an army. We think differently, act differently, than armies do. We might ask for as many as five to stand with us. Probably fewer — only two or three. But we might need more to help us prepare.'

'Why?' Benny asked.

Roland smiled. 'That I can't say yet, son, because I haven't seen how things are in your Calla. But in cases like this, surprise is always the most potent weapon, and it usually takes many people to prepare a good surprise.'

'The greatest surprise to the Wolves,' Tian said, 'would be if we fought at all.'

'Suppose you decide the Calla *can't* be defended?' Overholser asked. 'Tell me that, I beg.'

'Then I and my friends will thank you for your hospitality and ride on,' Roland said, 'for we have our own business farther along the Path of the Beam.' He observed Tian's and Zalia's crestfallen faces for a moment, then said: 'I don't think that's likely, you know. There's usually a way.'

'May the meeting receive your judgment favorably,' Overholser said.

Roland hesitated. This was the point where he could hammer the truth home, should he want to. If these people still believed a tet of gunslingers would be bound by what farmers and ranchers decided in a public meeting, they really *had* lost the shape of the world as it once was. But was that so bad? In the end, matters would play out and become part of his long history. Or not. If not, he would finish his history and his quest in Calla Bryn Sturgis, moldering beneath a stone. Perhaps not even that; perhaps he'd finish in a dead heap somewhere east of town, he and his friends with him, so much rotting meat to be picked over by the crows and the rusties. Ka would tell. It always did.

Meanwhile, they were looking at him.

Roland stood up, wincing at a hard flare of pain in his right hip as he did so. Taking their cues from him, Eddie, Susannah, and Jake also got to their feet.

'We're well-met,' Roland said. 'As for what lies ahead, there will be water if God wills it.'

Callahan said, 'Amen.'

CHAPTER VII

TODASH

1

'Gray horses,' Eddie said.

'Aye,' Roland agreed.

'Fifty or sixty of them, all on gray horses.'

'Aye, so they did say.'

'And didn't think it the least bit strange,' Eddie mused.

'No. They didn't seem to.'

'Is it?'

'Fifty or sixty horses, all the same color? I'd say so, yes.'

'These Calla-folk raise horses themselves.'

'Aye.'

'Brought some for us to ride.' Eddie, who had never ridden a horse in his life, was grateful that at least had been put off, but didn't say so.

'Aye, tethered over the hill.'

'You know that for a fact?'

'Smelled em. I imagine the robot had the keeping of them.'

'Why would these folks take fifty or sixty horses, all the same shade, as a matter of course?'

'Because they don't really think about the Wolves or anything to do with them,' Roland said. 'They're too busy being afraid, I think.'

Eddie whistled five notes that didn't quite make a melody. Then he said, 'Gray horses.'

Roland nodded. 'Gray horses.'

They looked at each other for a moment, then laughed. Eddie loved it when Roland laughed. The sound was dry, as ugly as the calls of those giant blackbirds he called rusties . . . but he loved it. Maybe it was just that Roland laughed so seldom.

It was late afternoon. Overhead, the clouds had thinned enough to turn a pallid blue that was almost the color of sky. The Overholser party had returned to their camp. Susannah and Jake had gone back along the forest road to pick more muffin-balls. After the big meal they'd packed away, none of them wanted anything heavier. Eddie sat on a log, whittling. Beside him sat Roland, with all their guns broken down and spread out before him on a piece of deerskin. He oiled the pieces one by one, holding each bolt and cylinder and barrel up to the daylight for a final look before setting it aside for reassembly.

'You told them it was out of their hands,' Eddie said, 'but they didn't ken that any more than they did the business about all those gray horses. And you didn't press it.'

'Only would have distressed them,' Roland said. 'There was a saying in Gilead: let evil wait for the day on which it must fall.'

'Uh-huh,' Eddie said. 'There was a saying in Brooklyn: You can't get snot off a suede jacket.' He held up the object he was making. It would be a top, Roland thought, a toy for a baby. And again he wondered how much Eddie might know about the woman he lay down with each night. The *women*. Not on the top of his mind, but underneath. 'If you decide we *can* help them, then we *have* to help them. That's what Eld's Way really boils down to, doesn't it?'

'Yes,' Roland said.

'And if we can't get any of them to stand with us, we stand alone.'

'Oh, I'm not worried about that,' Roland said. He had a saucer filled with light, sweet gun-oil. Now he dipped the corner of a chamois rag into it, picked up the spring-clip of Jake's Ruger, and began to clean it. 'Tian Jaffords would stand with us, come to that. Surely he has a friend or two who'd do the same regardless of what their meeting decides. In a pinch, there's his wife.'

'And if we get them both killed, what about their kids? They have five. Also, I think there's an old guy in the picture. One of em's Grampy. They probably take care of him, too.'

Roland shrugged. A few months ago, Eddie would have mistaken that gesture – and the gunslinger's expressionless face – for indifference. Now he knew better. Roland was as much a prisoner of his rules and traditions as Eddie had ever been of heroin.

'What if *we* get killed in this little town, screwing around with these Wolves?' Eddie asked. 'Isn't your last thought gonna be something like, "I can't believe what a putz I was, throwing away my chance to get to the Dark Tower in order to take up for a bunch of snotnose brats." Or similar sentiments.'

'Unless we stand true, we'll never get within a thousand miles of the Tower,' Roland said. 'Would you tell me you don't feel that?'

Eddie couldn't, because he did. He felt something else, as well: a species of bloodthirsty eagerness. He actually wanted to fight again. Wanted to have a few of these Wolves, whatever they were, in the sights of one of Roland's big revolvers. There was no sense kidding himself about the truth: he wanted to take a few scalps.

Or wolf-masks.

'What's really troubling you, Eddie? I'd have you speak while it's just you and me.' The gunslinger's mouth quirked in a thin, slanted smile. 'Do ya, I beg.'

'Shows, huh?'

Roland shrugged and waited.

Eddie considered the question. It was a *big* question. Facing it made him feel desperate and inadequate, pretty much the way he'd felt when faced with the task of carving the key that would let Jake Chambers through into their world. Only then he'd had the ghost of his big brother to blame, Henry whispering deep down in his head that he was no good, never had been, never would be. Now it was just the enormity of what Roland was asking. Because everything was troubling him, everything was wrong. *Everything.* Or maybe *wrong* was the wrong word, and by a hundred and eighty degrees. Because in another way things seemed too *right*, too perfect, too . . .

'Arrrggghh,' Eddie said. He grabbed bunches of hair on both sides of his head and pulled. 'I can't think of a way to say it.'

'Then say the first thing that comes into your mind. Don't hesitate.'

'Nineteen,' Eddie said. 'This whole deal has gone nineteen.'

He fell backward onto the fragrant forest floor, covered his eyes, and kicked his feet like a kid doing a tantrum. He thought: *Maybe killing a few Wolves will set me right. Maybe that's all it will take.*

2

Roland gave him a full minute by count and then said, 'Do you feel better?'

Eddie sat up. 'Actually I do.'

Roland nodded, smiling a little. 'Then can you say more? If you can't, we'll let it go, but I've come to respect your feelings, Eddie – far more than you realize – and if you'd speak, I'd hear.'

What he said was true. The gunslinger's initial feelings for Eddie had wavered between caution and contempt for what Roland saw as his weakness of character. Respect had come more slowly. It had begun in Balazar's office, when Eddie had fought naked. Very few men Roland had known could have done that. It had grown with his realization of how much Eddie was like Cuthbert. Then, on the mono, Eddie had acted with a kind of desperate creativity that Roland could admire but never equal. Eddie Dean was possessed of Cuthbert Allgood's always puzzling and sometimes annoying sense of the ridiculous; he was also possessed of Alain Johns's deep flashes of intuition. Yet in the end, Eddie was like neither of Roland's old friends. He was sometimes weak and self-centered, but possessed of deep reservoirs of courage and courage's good sister, what Eddie himself sometimes called 'heart.'

But it was his intuition Roland wanted to tap now.

'All right, then,' Eddie said. 'Don't stop me. Don't ask questions. Just listen.'

Roland nodded. And hoped Susannah and Jake wouldn't come back, at least not just yet.

'I look in the sky – up there where the clouds are breaking right this minute – and I see the number nineteen written in blue.'

Roland looked up. And yes, it was there. He saw it, too. But he also saw a cloud like a turtle, and another hole in the thinning dreck that looked like a gunnywagon.

'I look in the trees and see nineteen. Into the fire, see nineteen. Names make nineteen, like Overholser's and Callahan's. But that's just what I can *say*, what I can *see*, what I can get hold of.' Eddie was speaking with desperate speed, looking directly into Roland's eyes. 'Here's another thing. It has to do with todash. I know you guys sometimes think everything reminds me of getting high, and maybe that's right, but Roland, going todash is like being stoned.'

Eddie always spoke to him of these things as if Roland had never put anything stronger than graf into his brain and body in all his long life, and that was far from the truth. He might remind Eddie of this at another time, but not now.

'Just being here in your world is like going todash. Because . . . ah, man, this is hard . . . Roland, everything here is real, but it's not.'

Roland thought of reminding Eddie this wasn't *his* world, not anymore – for him the city of Lud had been the end of Mid-World and the beginning of all the mysteries that lay beyond – but again kept his mouth closed.

Eddie grasped a handful of duff, scooping up fragrant needles and leaving five black marks in the shape of a hand on the forest floor. 'Real,' he said. 'I can feel it and smell it.' He put the handful of needles to his mouth and ran out his tongue to touch them. 'I can taste it. And at the same time, it's as unreal as a nineteen you might see in the fire, or that cloud in the sky that looks like a turtle. Do you understand what I'm saying?'

'I understand it very well,' Roland murmured.

'The people are real. You . . . Susannah . . . Jake . . . that guy Gasher who snatched Jake . . . Overholser and the Slightmans. But the way stuff from my world keeps showing up over here, that's *not* real. It's not sensible or logical, either, but that's not what I mean. *It's just not real.* Why do people over here sing "Hey Jude"? I don't know. That cyborg bear, Shardik – where do I know that name from? Why did it remind me of rabbits? All that shit about the Wizard of Oz, Roland – all that happened to us, I have no doubt of it, but at the same time it doesn't seem real to me. It seems like todash. Like nineteen. And what happens after the Green Palace? Why, we walk into the woods, just like Hansel and Gretel. There's a road for us to walk on. Muffin-balls for us to pick. Civilization has ended. Everything is coming unraveled. You told us so. We saw it in Lud. Except guess what? It's not! Booya, assholes, gotcha again!'

Eddie gave a short laugh. It sounded shrill and unhealthy. When he brushed his hair back from his forehead, he left a dark smear of forest earth on his brow.

'The joke is that, out here a billion miles from nowhere, we come upon a storybook town. Civilized. Decent. The kind of folks you feel you know. Maybe you don't like em all – Overholser's a little hard to swallow – but you feel you know em.'

Eddie was right about that, too, Roland thought. He hadn't even seen Calla Bryn Sturgis yet, and already it reminded him of Mejis. In some ways that seemed perfectly reasonable – farming and ranching towns the world over bore similarities to each other – but in other ways it was disturbing. Disturbing as *hell*. The sombrero Slightman had been wearing, for instance. Was it possible that here, thousands of miles from Mejis, the men should wear similar hats? He supposed it might be. But was it likely that Slightman's sombrero should remind Roland so strongly of the one worn by Miguel, the old *mozo* at Seafront in Mejis, all those years before? Or was that only his imagination?

As for that, Eddie says I have none, he thought.

'The storybook town has a fairy tale problem,' Eddie was continuing. 'And so the storybook people call on a band of movie-show heroes to save them from the fairy tale villains. I know it's real – people are going to die, very likely, and the blood will be real, the screams will be real, the crying afterward will be real – but at the same time there's something about it that feels no more real than stage scenery.'

'And New York?' Roland asked. 'How did that feel to you?'

'The same,' Eddie said. 'I mean, think about it. Nineteen books left on the table after Jake took *Charlie the Choo-Choo* and the riddle book . . . and then, out of all the hoods in New York, *Balazar* shows up! *That* fuck!'

'Here, here, now!' Susannah called merrily from behind them. 'No profanity, boys.' Jake was pushing her up the road, and her lap was full of muffin-balls. They both looked cheerful and happy. Roland supposed that eating well earlier in the day had something to do with it.

Roland said, 'Sometimes that feeling of unreality goes away, doesn't it?'

'It's not exactly unreality, Roland. It—'

'Never mind splitting nails to make tacks. Sometimes it goes away. Doesn't it?'

'Yes,' Eddie said. 'When I'm with her.'

He went to her. Bent. Kissed her. Roland watched them, troubled.

3

The light was fading out of the day. They sat around the fire and let it go. What little appetite they'd been able to muster had been easily satisfied by the muffin-balls Susannah and Jake had brought back to camp. Roland had been meditating on something Slightman had said, and more deeply than was probably healthy. Now he pushed it aside still half-chewed and said, 'Some of us or all of us may meet later tonight in the city of New York.'

'I only hope I get to go this time,' Susannah said.

'That's as ka will,' Roland said evenly. 'The important thing is that you stay together. If there's only one who makes the journey, I think it's apt to be you who goes, Eddie. If only one makes the journey, that one should stay exactly where he . . . or mayhap *she* . . . is until the bells start again.'

'The *kammen*,' Eddie said. 'That's what Andy called em.'

'Do you all understand that?'

They nodded, and looking into their faces, Roland realized that each one of them was reserving the right to decide what to do when the time came, based upon the circumstances. Which was exactly right. They were either gunslingers or they weren't, after all.

He surprised himself by uttering a brief snort of a laugh.

'What's so funny?' Jake asked.

'I was just thinking that long life brings strange companions,' Roland said.

'If you mean us,' Eddie said, 'lemme tell you something, Roland – you're not exactly Norman Normal yourself.'

'I suppose not,' Roland said. 'If it's a group that crosses – two, a trio, perhaps all of us – we should join hands when the chimes start.'

'Andy said we had to concentrate on each other,' Eddie said. 'To keep from getting lost.'

Susannah surprised them all by starting to sing. Only to Roland, it sounded more like a galley-chorus – a thing made to be shouted out verse by verse – than an actual song. Yet even without a real tune to carry, her voice was melodious enough: '*Children, when ye hear the music of the clarinet . . . Children, when ye hear the music of the flute! Children, when ye hear the music of the tam-bou-rine . . . Ye must bow down and wor-ship the iyyy-DOL!*'

'What is it?'

'A field-chant,' she said. 'The sort of thing my grandparents and great-grandparents might have sung while they were picking ole massa's cotton. But times change.' She smiled. 'I first heard it in a Greenwich Village coffee-house, back in 1962. And the man who sang it was a white blues-shouter named Dave Van Ronk.'

'I bet Aaron Deepneau was there, too,' Jake breathed. 'Hell, I bet he was sitting at the next damn *table*.'

Susannah turned to him, surprised and considering. 'Why do you say so, sugar?'

Eddie said, 'Because he overheard Calvin Tower saying this guy Deepneau had been hanging around the Village since . . . what'd he say, Jake?'

'Not the Village, Bleecker Street,' Jake said, laughing a little. 'Mr Tower said Mr Deepneau was hanging around Bleecker Street back before Bob

Dylan knew how to blow more than open G on his Hohner. That must be a harmonica.'

'It is,' Eddie said, 'and while I might not bet the farm on what Jake's saying, I'd go a lot more than pocket-change. Sure, Deepneau was there. It wouldn't even surprise me to find out that Jack Andolini was tending the bar. Because that's just how things work in the Land of Nineteen.'

'In any case,' Roland said, 'those of us who cross should stay together. And I mean within a hand's reach, all the time.'

'I don't think I'll be there,' Jake said.

'Why do you say so, Jake?' the gunslinger asked, surprised.

'Because I'll never fall asleep,' Jake said. 'I'm too excited.'

But eventually they all slept.

4

He knows it's a dream, something brought on by no more than Slightman's chance remark, and yet he can't escape it. Always look for the back door, *Cort used to tell them, but if there's a back door in this dream, Roland cannot find it.* I heard of Jericho Hill and such blood-and-thunder tales of pretend, *that was what Eisenhart's foreman had said, only Jericho Hill had seemed real enough to Roland. Why would it not? He had been there. It had been the end of them. The end of a whole world.*

The day is suffocatingly hot; the sun reaches its roofpeak and then seems to stay there, as if the hours have been suspended. Below them is a long sloping field filled with great gray-black stone faces, eroded statues left by people who are long gone, and Grissom's men advance relentlessly among them as Roland and his final few companions withdraw ever upward, shooting as they go. The gunfire is constant, unending, the sound of bullets whining off the stone faces a shrill counterpoint that sinks into their heads like the bloodthirsty whine of mosquitoes. Jamie DeCurry has been killed by a sniper, perhaps Grissom's eagle-eyed son or Grissom himself. With Alain the end was far worse; he was shot in the dark the night before the final battle by his two best friends, a stupid error, a horrible death. There was no help. DeMullet's column was ambushed and slaughtered at Rimrocks and when Alain rode back after midnight to tell them, Roland and Cuthbert . . . the sound of their guns . . . and oh, when Alain cried out their names—

And now they're at the top and there's nowhere left to run. Behind them to the east is a shale-crumbly drop to the Salt — what five hundred miles south of here is called the Clean Sea. To the west is the hill of the stone faces, and Grissom's screaming, advancing men.

Roland and his own men have killed hundreds, but there are still two thousand left, and that's a conservative estimate. Two thousand men, their howling faces painted blue, some armed with guns and even a few with Bolts — against a dozen. That's all that's left of them now, here at the top of Jericho Hill, under the burning sky. Jamie dead, Alain dead under the guns of his best friends — stolid, dependable Alain, who could have ridden on to safety but chose not to — and Cuthbert has been shot. How many times? Five? Six? His shirt is soaked crimson to his skin. One side of his face has been drowned in blood; the eye on that side bulges sightlessly on his cheek. Yet he still has Roland's horn, the one which was blown by Arthur Eld, or so the stories did say. He will not give it back. 'For I blow it sweeter than you ever did,' he tells Roland, laughing. 'You can have it again when I'm dead. Neglect not to pluck it up, Roland, for it's your property.'

Cuthbert Allgood, who had once ridden into the Barony of Mejis with a rook's skull mounted on the pommel of his saddle. 'The lookout,' he had called it, and talked to it just as though it were alive, for such was his fancy and sometimes he drove Roland half-mad with his foolishness, and here he is under the burning sun, staggering toward him with a smoking revolver in one hand and Eld's Horn in the other, blood-bolted and half-blinded and dying . . . but still laughing. Ah dear gods, laughing and laughing.

'Roland!' he cries. 'We've been betrayed! We're outnumbered! Our backs are to the sea! We've got em right where we want em! Shall we charge?'

And Roland understands he is right. If their quest for the Dark Tower is really to end here on Jericho Hill — betrayed by one of their own and then overwhelmed by this barbaric remnant of John Farson's army — then let it end splendidly.

'Aye!' he shouts. 'Aye, very well. Ye of the castle, to me! Gunslingers, to me! To me, I say!'

'As for gunslingers, Roland,' Cuthbert says, 'I am here. And we are the last.'

Roland first looks at him, then embraces him under that hideous sky. He can feel Cuthbert's burning body, its suicidal trembling thinness. And yet he's laughing. Bert is still laughing.

'All right,' Roland says hoarsely, looking around at his few remaining men. 'We're going into them. And will accept no quarter.'

'Nope, no quarter, absolutely none,' Cuthbert says.

'We will not accept their surrender if offered.'

'Under no circumstances!' Cuthbert agrees, laughing harder than ever. 'Not even should all two thousand lay down their arms.'

'Then blow that fucking horn.'

Cuthbert raises the horn to his bloody lips and blows a great blast — the final blast, for when it drops from his fingers a minute later (or perhaps it's five, or ten; time has no meaning in that final battle), Roland will let it lie in the dust. In his grief and bloodlust he will forget all about Eld's Horn.

'And now, my friends — hile!'

'Hile!' the last dozen cry beneath that blazing sun. It is the end of them, the end of Gilead, the end of everything, and he no longer cares. The old red fury, dry and maddening, is settling over his mind, drowning all thought. One last time, then, *he thinks.* Let it be so.

'To me!' cries Roland of Gilead. 'Forward! For the Tower!'

'The Tower!' Cuthbert cries out beside him, reeling. He holds Eld's Horn up to the sky in one hand, his revolver in the other.

'No prisoners!' Roland screams. 'NO PRISONERS!'

They rush forward and down toward Grissom's blue-faced horde, he and Cuthbert in the lead, and as they pass the first of the great gray-black faces leaning in the high grass, spears and bolts and bullets flying all around them, the chimes begin. It is a melody far beyond beautiful; it threatens to tear him to pieces with its stark loveliness.

Not now, *he thinks,* ah, gods, not now — let me finish it. Let me finish it with my friend at my side and have peace at last. Please.

He reaches for Cuthbert's hand. For one moment he feels the touch of his friend's blood-sticky fingers, there on Jericho Hill where his brave and laughing existence was snuffed out . . . and then the fingers touching his are gone. Or rather, his have melted clean through Bert's. He is falling, he is falling, the world is darkening, he is falling, the chimes are playing, the kammen *are playing ('Sounds Hawaiian, doesn't it?') and he is falling, Jericho Hill is gone, Eld's Horn is gone, there's darkness and red letters in the darkness, some are Great Letters, enough so he can read what they say, the words say—*

5

They said DON'T WALK. Although, Roland saw, people were crossing the street in spite of the sign. They would take a quick look in the direction of the flowing traffic, and then go for it. One fellow crossed in spite of an oncoming yellow tack-see. The tack-see swerved and blared its horn. The walking man yelled fearlessly at it, then shot up the middle finger of his right-hand and shook it after the departing vehicle. Roland had an idea that this gesture probably did not mean long days and pleasant nights.

It was night in New York City, and although there were people moving everywhere, none were of his ka-tet. Here, Roland admitted to himself, was one contingency he had hardly expected: that the one person to show up would be him. Not Eddie, but him. Where in the name of all the gods was he supposed to go? And what was he supposed to do when he got there?

Remember your own advice, he thought. '*If you show up alone,*' you told them, '*stay where you are.*'

But did that mean to just roost on . . . he looked up at the green street-sign . . . on the corner of Second Avenue and Fifty-fourth Street, doing nothing but watching a sign change from DON'T WALK in red to WALK in white?

While he was pondering this, a voice called out from behind him, high and delirious with joy. '*Roland! Sugarbunch! Turn around and see me! See me very well!*'

Roland turned, already knowing what he would see, but smiling all the same. How terrible to relive that day at Jericho Hill, but what an antidote was this – Susannah Dean, flying down Fifty-fourth Street toward him, laughing and weeping with joy, her arms held out.

'*My legs!*' She was screaming it at the top of her voice. '*My legs! I have my legs back! Oh Roland, honeydoll, praise the Man Jesus, I HAVE MY LEGS BACK!*'

6

She threw herself into his embrace, kissing his cheek, his neck, his brow, his nose, his lips, saying it over and over again: 'My legs, oh Roland do you see, I can walk, I can *run*, I have my legs, praise God and all the saints, *I have my legs back.*'

'Give you every joy of them, dear heart,' Roland said. Falling into the patois of the place in which he had lately found himself was an old trick of his – or perhaps it was habit. For now it was the patois of the Calla. He supposed if he spent much time here in New York, he'd soon find himself waving his middle finger at tack-sees.

But I'd always be an outsider, he thought. *Why, I can't even say aspirin. Every time I try, the word comes out wrong.*

She took his right hand, dragged it down with surprising force, and placed it on her shin. 'Do you feel it?' she demanded. 'I mean, I'm not just imagining it, am I?'

Roland laughed. 'Did you not run to me as if with wings on em like Raf? Yes, Susannah.' He put his left hand, the one with all the fingers, on her left leg. 'One leg and two legs, each with a foot below them.' He frowned. 'We ought to get you some shoes, though.'

'Why? This is a dream. It has to be.'

He looked at her steadily, and slowly her smile faded.

'Not? Really not?'

'We've gone todash. We are really here. If you cut your foot, Mia, you'll have a cut foot tomorrow, when you wake up aside the campfire.'

The other name had come out almost — but not quite — on its own. Now he waited, all his muscles wire-tight, to see if she would notice. If she did, he'd apologize and tell her he'd gone todash directly from a dream of someone he'd known long ago (although there had only been one woman of any importance after Susan Delgado, and her name had not been Mia).

But she *didn't* notice, and Roland wasn't much surprised.

Because she was getting ready to go on another of her hunting expeditions — as Mia — when the kammen *rang. And unlike Susannah, Mia has legs. She banquets on rich foods in a great hall, she talks with all her friends, she didn't go to Morehouse or to no house, and she has legs. So this one has legs. This one is both women, although she doesn't know it.*

Suddenly Roland found himself hoping that they wouldn't meet Eddie. He might sense the difference even if Susannah herself didn't. And that could be bad. If Roland had had three wishes, like the foundling prince in a child's bedtime story, right now all three would have been for the same thing: to get through this business in Calla Bryn Sturgis before Susannah's pregnancy — *Mia's* pregnancy — became obvious. Having to deal with both things at the same time would be hard.

Perhaps impossible.

She was looking at him with wide, questioning eyes. Not because he'd called her by a name that wasn't hers, but because she wanted to know what they should do next.

'It's your city,' he said. 'I would see the bookstore. And the vacant lot.' He paused. 'And the rose. Can you take me?'

'Well,' she said, looking around, 'it's my city, no doubt about that, but Second Avenue sure doesn't look like it did back in the days when Detta got her kicks shoplifting in Macy's.'

'So you can't find the bookstore and the vacant lot?' Roland was disappointed but far from desolate. There would be a way. There was always a—

'Oh, no problem there,' she said. 'The streets are the same. New York's just a grid, Roland, with the avenues running one way and the streets the other. Easy as pie. Come on.'

The sign had gone back to DON'T WALK, but after a quick glance uptown,

Susannah took his arm and they crossed Fifty-fourth to the other side. Susannah strode fearlessly in spite of her bare feet. The blocks were short but crowded with exotic shops. Roland couldn't help goggling, but his lack of attention seemed safe enough; although the sidewalks were crowded, no one crashed into them. Roland could hear his bootheels clopping on the sidewalk, however, and could see the shadows they were casting in the light of the display windows.

Almost here, he thought. *Were the force that brought us any more powerful, we would be here.*

And, he realized, the force might indeed grow stronger, assuming that Callahan was right about what was hidden under the floor of his church. As they drew closer to the town and to the source of the thing doing this . . .

Susannah twitched his arm. Roland stopped immediately. 'Is it your feet?' he asked.

'No,' she said, and Roland saw she was frightened. 'Why is it so *dark*?'

'Susannah, it's night.'

She gave his arm an impatient shake. 'I know that, I'm not blind. Can't you . . .' She hesitated. 'Can't you *feel* it?'

Roland realized he could. For one thing, the darkness on Second Avenue really wasn't dark at all. The gunslinger still couldn't comprehend the prodigal way in which these people of New York squandered the things those of Gilead had held most rare and precious. Paper; water; refined oil; artificial light. This last was everywhere. There was the glow from the store windows (although most were closed, the displays were still lit), the even harsher glow from a popkin-selling place called Blimpie's, and over all this, peculiar orange electric lamps that seemed to drench the very air with light. Yet Susannah was right. There was a black feel to the air in spite of the orange lamps. It seemed to surround the people who walked this street. It made him think about what Eddie had said earlier: *This whole deal has gone nineteen.*

But this darkness, more felt than seen, had nothing to do with nineteen. You had to subtract six in order to understand what was going on here. And for the first time, Roland really believed Callahan was right.

'Black Thirteen,' he said.

'What?'

'It's brought us here, sent us todash, and we feel it all around us. It's not the same as when I flew inside the grapefruit, but it's *like* that.'

'It feels bad,' she said, speaking low.

'It *is* bad,' he said. 'Black Thirteen's very likely the most terrible object from the days of Eld still remaining on the face of the earth. Not that the Wizard's Rainbow was from then; I'm sure it existed even before—'

'Roland! Hey, Roland! Suze!'

They looked up and in spite of his earlier misgivings, Roland was immensely relieved to see not only Eddie, but Jake and Oy, as well. They were about a block and a half farther along. Eddie was waving. Susannah waved back exuberantly. Roland grabbed her arm before she started to run, which was clearly her intention.

'Mind your feet,' he said. 'You don't need to pick up some sort of infection and carry it back to the other side.'

They compromised at a rapid walk. Eddie and Jake, both shod, ran to meet them. Pedestrians moved out of their way without looking, or even breaking their conversations, Roland saw, and then observed that wasn't quite true. There was a little boy, surely no older than three, walking sturdily along next to his mother. The woman seemed to notice nothing, but as Eddie and Jake swung around them, the toddler watched with wide, wondering eyes . . . and then actually stretched out a hand, as if to stroke the briskly trotting Oy.

Eddie pulled ahead of Jake and arrived first. He held Susannah out at arm's length, looking at her. His expression, Roland saw, was really quite similar to that of the tot.

'Well? What do you think, sugar?' Susannah spoke nervously, like a woman who has come home to her husband with some radical new hairdo.

'A definite improvement,' Eddie said. 'I don't need em to love you, but they're way beyond good and into the land of excellent. Christ, now you're an inch taller than I am!'

Susannah saw this was true and laughed. Oy sniffed at the ankle that hadn't been there the last time he'd seen this woman, and then he laughed, too. It was an odd barky-bark of a sound, but quite clearly a laugh for all that.

'Like your legs, Suze,' Jake said, and the perfunctory quality of this compliment made Susannah laugh again. The boy didn't notice; he had already turned to Roland. 'Do you want to see the bookstore?'

'Is there anything to see?'

Jake's face clouded. 'Actually, not much. It's closed.'

'I would see the vacant lot, if there's time before we're sent back,' Roland said. 'And the rose.'

'Do they hurt?' Eddie asked Susannah. He was looking at her closely indeed.

'They feel fine,' she said, laughing. '*Fine*.'

'You look different.'

'I bet!' she said, and executed a little barefoot jig. It had been moons and moons since she had last danced, but the exultancy she so clearly felt made up for any lack of grace. A woman wearing a business suit and swinging a briefcase bore down on the ragged little party of wanderers, then abruptly veered off, actually taking a few steps into the street to get around them. 'You bet I do, I got *legs!*'

'Just like the song says,' Eddie told her.

'Huh?'

'Never mind,' he said, and slipped an arm around her waist. But again Roland saw him give her that searching, questioning look. *But with luck he'll leave it alone*, Roland thought.

And that was what Eddie did. He kissed the corner of her mouth, then turned to Roland. 'So you want to see the famous vacant lot and the even more famous rose, huh? Well, so do I. Lead on, Jake.'

7

Jake led them down Second Avenue, pausing only long enough so they could all take a quick peek into The Manhattan Restaurant of the Mind. No one was wasting light in this shop, however, and there really wasn't much to see. Roland was hoping for a look at the menu sign, but it was gone.

Reading his mind in the matter-of-fact way of people who share khef, Jake said, 'He probably changes it every day.'

'Maybe,' Roland said. He looked in through the window a moment longer, saw nothing but darkened shelves, a few tables, and the counter Jake had mentioned – the one where the old fellows sat drinking coffee and playing this world's version of Castles. Nothing to see, but something to feel, even through the glass: despair and loss. If it had been a smell, Roland thought, it would have been sour and a bit stale. The smell of failure. Maybe of good dreams that never grew. Which made it the perfect lever for someone like Enrico '*Il Roche*' Balazar.

'Seen enough?' Eddie asked.

'Yes. Let's go.'

8

For Roland, the eight-block journey from Second and Fifty-fourth to Second and Forty-sixth was like visiting a country in which he had until that moment only half-believed. *How much stranger must it be for Jake?* he wondered. The bum who'd asked the boy for a quarter was gone, but the restaurant he'd been sitting near was there: Chew Chew Mama's. This was on the corner of Second and Fifty-second. A block farther down was the record store, Tower of Power. It was still open – according to an overhead clock that told the time in large electric dots, it was only fourteen minutes after eight in the evening. Loud sounds were pouring out of the open door. Guitars and drums. This world's music. It reminded him of the sacrificial music played by the Grays, back in the city of Lud, and why not? This *was* Lud, in some twisted, otherwhere-and-when way. He was sure of it.

'It's the Rolling Stones,' Jake said, 'but not the one that was playing on the day I saw the rose. That one was "Paint It Black."'

'Don't you recognize this one?' Eddie asked.

'Yeah, but I can't remember the title.'

'Oh, but you should,' Eddie said. 'It's "Nineteenth Nervous Breakdown."'

Susannah stopped, looked around. 'Jake?'

Jake nodded. 'He's right.'

Eddie, meanwhile, had fished a piece of newspaper from the security-gated doorway next to Tower of Power Records. A section of *The New York Times*, in fact.

'Hon, didn't your Ma ever teach you that gutter-trolling is generally not practiced by the better class of people?' Susannah asked.

Eddie ignored her. 'Look at this,' he said. 'All of you.'

Roland bent close, half-expecting to see news of another great plague, but there was nothing so shattering. At least not as far as he could tell.

'Read me what it says,' he asked Jake. 'The letters swim in and out of my mind. I think it's because we're todash – caught in between—'

'RHODESIAN FORCES TIGHTEN HOLD ON MOZAMBIQUE VILLAGES,' Jake read. 'TWO CARTER AIDES PREDICT A SAVING OF BILLIONS IN WELFARE PLAN. And down here, CHINESE DISCLOSE THAT 1976 QUAKE WAS DEADLIEST IN FOUR CENTURIES. Also—'

'Who's Carter?' Susannah asked. 'Is he the President before . . . *Ronald Reagan*?' She garnished the last two words with a large wink. Eddie had so far been unable to convince her that he was serious about Reagan's being President. Nor would she believe Jake when the boy told her he knew it sounded crazy, but the idea was at least faintly plausible because Reagan had been governor of California. Susannah had simply laughed at this and nodded, as if giving him high marks for creativity. She knew Eddie had talked Jake into backing up his fish story, but she would not be hooked. She supposed she could see Paul Newman as President, maybe even Henry Fonda, who had looked presidential enough in *Fail-Safe*, but the host of *Death Valley Days*? Not on your bottom.

'Never mind Carter,' Eddie said. 'Look at the *date*.'

Roland tried, but it kept swimming in and out. It would almost settle into Great Letters that he could read, and then fall back into gibberish. 'What is it, for your father's sake?'

'June second,' Jake said. He looked at Eddie. 'But if time's the same here and over on the other side, shouldn't it be June *first*?'

'But it's *not* the same,' Eddie said grimly. 'It's *not*. Time goes by faster on this side. Game on. And the game-clock's running fast.'

Roland considered. 'If we come here again, it's going to be later each time, isn't it?'

Eddie nodded.

Roland went on, talking to himself as much as to the others. 'Every minute we spend on the other side — the Calla side — a minute and *a half* goes by over here. Or maybe two.'

'No, not two,' Eddie said. 'I'm sure it's not going double-time.' But his uneasy glance back down at the date on the newspaper suggested he wasn't sure at all.

'Even if you're right,' Roland said, 'all we can do now is go forward.'

'Toward the fifteenth of July,' Susannah said. 'When Balazar and his gentlemen stop playing nice.'

'Maybe we ought to just let these Calla-folk do their own thing,' Eddie said. 'I hate to say that, Roland, but maybe we should.'

'We can't do that, Eddie.'

'Why not?'

'Because Callahan's got Black Thirteen,' Susannah said. 'Our help is his price for turning it over. And we need it.'

Roland shook his head. 'He'll turn it over in any case — I thought I was clear about that. He's terrified of it.'

'Yeah,' Eddie said. 'I got that feeling, too.'

'We have to help them because it's the Way of Eld,' Roland told Susannah. 'And because the way of ka is always the way of duty.'

He thought he saw a glitter far down in her eyes, as though he'd said something funny. He supposed he had, but Susannah wasn't the one he had amused. It had been either Detta or Mia who found those ideas funny. The question was which one. Or had it been both?

'I hate how it feels here,' Susannah said. 'That *dark* feeling.'

'It'll be better at the vacant lot,' Jake said. He started walking, and the others followed. 'The rose makes everything better. You'll see.'

9

When Jake crossed Fiftieth, he began to hurry. On the downtown side of Forty-ninth, he began to jog. At the corner of Second and Forty-eighth, he began to run. He couldn't help it. He got a little WALK help at Forty-eighth, but the sign on the post began to flash red as soon as he reached the far curb.

'Jake, wait up!' Eddie called from behind him, but Jake didn't. Perhaps couldn't. Certainly Eddie felt the pull of the thing; so did Roland and Susannah. There was a hum rising in the air, faint and sweet. It was everything the ugly black feeling around them was not.

To Roland the hum brought back memories of Mejis and Susan Delgado. Of kisses shared in a mattress of sweet grass.

Susannah remembered being with her father when she was little, crawling up into his lap and laying the smooth skin of her cheek against the rough weave of his sweater. She remembered how she would close her eyes and breathe deeply of the smell that was his smell and his alone: pipe tobacco and wintergreen and the Musterole he rubbed into his wrists, where the arthritis first began to bite him at the outrageous age of twenty-five. What these smells meant to her was that everything was all right.

Eddie found himself remembering a trip to Atlantic City when he'd been very young, no more than five or six. Their mother had taken them, and at one point in the day she and Henry had gone off to get ice cream cones. Mrs Dean had pointed at the boardwalk and had said, *You put your fanny right there, Mister Man, and keep it there until we get back.* And he did. He could have sat there all day, looking down the slope of the beach at the gray pull and flow of the ocean. The gulls rode just above the foam, calling to each other. Each time the waves drew back, they left a slick expanse of wet brown sand so bright he could hardly look at it without squinting. The sound of the waves was both large and lulling. *I could stay here forever,* he remembered thinking. *I could stay here forever because it's beautiful and peaceful and . . . and all right. Everything here is all right.*

That was what all five of them felt most strongly (for Oy felt it, too): the sense of something that was wonderfully and beautifully all right.

Roland and Eddie grasped Susannah by the elbows without so much as an exchanged glance. They lifted her bare feet off the sidewalk and carried her. At Second and Forty-seventh the traffic was against them, but Roland threw up a hand at the oncoming headlights and cried, *'Hile! Stop in the name of Gilead!'*

And they did. There was a scream of brakes, a crump of a front fender meeting a rear one, and the tinkle of falling glass, but they stopped. Roland and Eddie crossed in a spotlight glare of headlights and a cacophony of horns, Susannah between them with her restored (and already very dirty) feet three inches off the ground. Their sense of happiness and rightness grew stronger as they approached the corner of Second Avenue and Forty-sixth Street. Roland felt the hum of the rose racing deliriously in his blood.

Yes, Roland thought. *By all the gods, yes. This is it. Perhaps not just a doorway to the Dark Tower, but the Tower itself. Gods, the strength of it! The pull of it! Cuthbert, Alain, Jamie — if only you were here!*

Jake stood on the corner of Second and Forty-sixth, looking at a board fence about five feet high. Tears were streaming down his cheeks. From the darkness beyond the fence came a strong harmonic humming. The sound of many voices, all singing together. Singing one vast open note. *Here is yes,* the voices said. *Here is you may. Here is the good turn, the fortunate meeting, the fever that broke just before dawn and left your blood calm. Here is the wish that came true and the understanding eye. Here is the kindness you were given and thus learned to pass on. Here is the sanity and clarity you thought were lost. Here, everything is all right.*

Jake turned to them. 'Do you feel it?' he asked. 'Do you?'

Roland nodded. So did Eddie.

'Suze?' the boy asked.

'It's almost the loveliest thing in the world, isn't it?' she said. *Almost,* Roland thought. *She said almost.* Nor did he miss the fact that her hand went to her belly and stroked as she said it.

10

The posters Jake remembered were there — Olivia Newton-John at Radio City Music Hall, G. Gordon Liddy and the Grots at a place called the Mercury Lounge, a horror movie called *War of the Zombies*, NO TRESPASSING. But—

'*That's* not the same,' he said, pointing at a graffito in dusky pink. 'It's the same color, and the printing looks like the same person did it, but when I was here before, it was a poem about the Turtle. "See the TURTLE of enormous girth, on his shell he holds the earth." And then something about following the Beam.'

Eddie stepped closer and read this: 'Oh SUSANNAH-MIO, divided girl of mine, Done parked her RIG in the DIXIE PIG, in the year of '99.' He looked at Susannah. 'What in the hell does *that* mean? Any idea, Suze?'

She shook her head. Her eyes were very large. Frightened eyes, Roland thought. But which woman was frightened? He couldn't tell. He only knew that Odetta Susannah Holmes had been divided from the beginning, and that 'mio' was very close to Mia. The hum coming from the darkness behind the fence made it hard to think of these things. He wanted to go to the source of the hum right now. *Needed* to, as a man dying of thirst needs to go to water.

'Come on,' Jake said. 'We can climb right over. It's easy.'

Susannah looked down at her bare, dirty feet, and took a step backward. 'Not me,' she said. 'I can't. Not without shoes.'

Which made perfect sense, but Roland thought there was more to it than that. Mia didn't *want* to go in there. Mia understood something dreadful might happen if she did. To her, and to her baby. For a moment he was on the verge of forcing the issue, of letting the rose take care of both the thing growing inside her and her troublesome new personality, one so strong that Susannah had shown up here with Mia's legs.

No, Roland. That was Alain's voice. Alain, who had always been strongest in the touch. *Wrong time, wrong place.*

'I'll stay with her,' Jake said. He spoke with enormous regret but no hesitation, and Roland was swept by his love for the boy he had once allowed to die. That vast voice from the darkness beyond the fence sang of that love; he heard it. And of simple forgiveness rather than the difficult forced march of atonement? He thought it was.

'No,' she said. 'You go on, honeybunch. I'll be fine.' She smiled at them. 'This is my city too, you know. I can look out for myself. And besides—' She lowered her voice as if confiding a great secret. 'I think we're kind of invisible.'

Eddie was once again looking at her in that searching way, as if to ask her how she could *not* go with them, bare feet or no bare feet, but this time Roland wasn't worried. Mia's secret was safe, at least for the time being; the call of the rose was too strong for Eddie to be able to think of much else. He was wild to get going.

'We should stay together,' Eddie said reluctantly. 'So we don't get lost going back. You said so yourself, Roland.'

'How far is it from here to the rose, Jake?' Roland asked. It was hard to talk with that hum singing in his ears like a wind. Hard to think.

'It's pretty much in the middle of the lot. Maybe thirty yards, but probably less.'

'The second we hear the chimes,' Roland said, 'we run for the fence and Susannah. All three of us. Agreed?'

'Agreed,' Eddie said.

'All three of us and Oy,' Jake said.

'No, Oy stays with Susannah.'

Jake frowned, clearly not liking this. Roland hadn't expected him to. 'Jake, Oy also has bare feet . . . and didn't you say there was broken glass in there?'

'Ye-eahh . . .' Drawn-out. Reluctant. Then Jake dropped to one knee and looked into Oy's gold-ringed eyes. 'Stay with Susannah, Oy.'

'Oy! Ay!' *Oy stay.* It was good enough for Jake. He stood up, turned to Roland, and nodded.

'Suze?' Eddie asked. 'Are you sure?'

'Yes.' Emphatic. No hesitation. Roland was now almost sure it was Mia in control, pulling the levers and turning the dials. *Almost.* Even now he wasn't positive. The hum of the rose made it impossible to be positive of anything except that everything — *everything* — could be all right.

Eddie nodded, kissed the corner of her mouth, then stepped to the board fence with its odd poem: Oh SUSANNAH-MIO, divided girl of mine. He laced his fingers together into a step. Jake was into it, up, and gone like a breath of breeze.

'Ake!' Oy cried, and then was silent, sitting beside one of Susannah's bare feet.

'You next, Eddie,' Roland said. He laced his remaining fingers together, meaning to give Eddie the same step Eddie had given Jake, but Eddie simply grabbed the top of the fence and vaulted over. The junkie Roland had first met in a jet plane coming into Kennedy Airport could never have done that.

Roland said, 'Stay where you are. Both of you.' He could have meant the woman and the billy-bumbler, but it was only the woman he looked at.

'We'll be fine,' she said, and bent to stroke Oy's silky fur. 'Won't we, big guy?'

'Oy!'

'Go see your rose, Roland. While you still can.'

Roland gave her a last considering look, then grasped the top of the fence. A moment later he was gone, leaving Susannah and Oy alone on the most vital and vibrant streetcorner in the entire universe.

11

Strange things happened to her as she waited.

Back the way they'd come, near Tower of Power Records, a bank clock alternately flashed the time and temperature: 8:27, 64. 8:27, 64. 8:27, 64. Then, suddenly, it was flashing 8:34, 64. 8:34, 64. She never took her eyes off it, she would swear to that. Had something gone wrong with the sign's machinery?

Must've, she thought. *What else could it be?* Nothing, she supposed, but why did everything suddenly feel different? Even *look* different? *Maybe it was my machinery that went wrong.*

Oy whined and stretched his long neck toward her. As he did, she realized why things looked different. Besides somehow slipping seven uncounted minutes by her, the world had regained its former, all-too-familiar perspective. A *lower* perspective. She was closer to Oy because she was closer to the ground. The splendid lower legs and feet she'd been wearing when she had opened her eyes on New York were gone.

How had it happened? And when? In the missing seven minutes?

Oy whined again. This time it was almost a bark. He was looking past her, in the other direction. She turned that way. Half a dozen people were crossing Forty-sixth toward them. Five were normal. The sixth was a white-faced woman in a moss splotched dress. The sockets of her eyes were empty and black. Her mouth hung open seemingly all the way down to her breastbone, and as Susannah watched, a green worm crawled over the lower lip. Those crossing with her gave her her own space, just as the other pedestrians on Second Avenue had given Roland and his friends theirs. Susannah guessed that in both cases, the more normal promenaders sensed something out of the ordinary and steered clear. Only this woman wasn't todash.

This woman was dead.

12

The hum rose and rose as the three of them stumbled across the trash- and brick-littered wilderness of the vacant lot. As before, Jake saw faces in every angle and shadow. He saw Gasher and Hoots; Tick-Tock and Flagg; he saw Eldred Jonas's gunbunnies, Depape and Reynolds; he saw his mother and father and Greta Shaw, their housekeeper, who looked a little like Edith Bunker on TV and who always remembered to cut the crusts off his sand- wiches. Greta Shaw who sometimes called him 'Bama, although that was a secret, just between them.

Eddie saw people from the old neighborhood: Jimmie Polio, the kid with the clubfoot, and Tommy Fredericks, who always got so excited watching the street stickball games that he made faces and the kids called him Halloween Tommy. There was Skipper Brannigan, who would have picked a fight with Al Capone himself, had Capone shown sufficient bad judg- ment to come to their neighborhood, and Csaba Drabnik, the Mad Fuckin Hungarian. He saw his mother's face in a pile of broken bricks, her glim- mering eyes recreated from the broken pieces of a soft-drink bottle. He saw her friend, Dora Bertollo (all the kids on the block called her Tits Bertollo because she had really big ones, big as fuckin watermelons). And of course he saw Henry. Henry standing far back in the shadows, watching him. Only Henry was smiling instead of scowling, and he looked straight. Holding out one hand and giving Eddie what looked like a thumbs-up. *Go on*, the rising hum seemed to whisper, and now it whispered in Henry Dean's voice. *Go on, Eddie, show em what you're made of. Didn't I tell those other guys? When we were out behind Dahlie's smokin Jimmie Polio's cigarettes, didn't I tell em? 'My little bro could talk the devil into settin himself on fire,' I said. Didn't I?* Yes. Yes he had.

And that's the way I always felt, the hum whispered. *I always loved you. Sometimes I put you down, but I always loved you. You were my little man.*

Eddie began to cry. And these were good tears.

Roland saw all the phantoms of his life in this shadowed, brick-strewn ruin, from his mother and his cradle-amah right up to their visitors from Calla Bryn Sturgis. And as they walked, that sense of rightness grew. A feeling that all his hard decisions, all the pain and loss and spilled blood, had not been for nothing, after all. There was a reason. There was a purpose. There was life and love. He heard it all in the song of the rose, and he too began to cry. Mostly with relief. Getting here had been a hard journey. Many had died. Yet here they lived; here they sang with the rose. His life had not all been a dry dream after all.

They joined hands and stumbled forward, helping each other to avoid the nail-studded boards and the holes into which an ankle could plunge and twist and perhaps break. Roland didn't know if one could break a bone while in the todash state, but he had no urge to find out.

'This is worth everything,' he said hoarsely.

Eddie nodded. 'I'll never stop now. Might not stop even if I die.'

Jake gave him a thumb-and-forefinger circle at that, and laughed. The sound was sweet in Roland's ears. It was darker in here than it had been on the street, but the orange streetlights on Second and Forty-sixth were strong enough to provide at least some illumination. Jake pointed at a sign lying in a pile of boards. 'See that? It's the deli sign. I pulled it out of the weeds. That's why it is where it is.' He looked around, then pointed in another direction. 'And look!'

This sign was still standing. Roland and Eddie turned to read it. Although neither of them had seen it before, they both felt a strong sense of *déjà vu*, nonetheless.

**MILLS CONSTRUCTION AND SOMBRA REAL ESTATE ASSOCIATES
ARE CONTINUING TO REMAKE THE FACE OF MANHATTAN!
COMING SOON TO THIS LOCATION:
TURTLE BAY LUXURY CONDOMINIUMS!
CALL 661–6712 FOR INFORMATION!
*YOU WILL BE SO GLAD YOU DID!***

As Jake had told them, the sign looked old, in need of either refreshment or outright replacement. Jake had remembered the graffito which had been sprayed across the sign, and Eddie remembered it from Jake's story, not because it meant anything to him but simply because it was odd. And there it was, just as reported: BANGO SKANK. Some long-gone tagger's calling card.

'I think the telephone number on the sign's different,' Jake said.

'Yeah?' Eddie asked. 'What was the old one?'

'I don't remember.'

'Then how can you be sure this one's different?'

In another place and at another time, Jake might have been irritated by these questions. Now, soothed by the proximity of the rose, he smiled, instead. 'I don't know. I guess I can't. But it sure seems different. Like the sign in the bookstore window.'

Roland barely heard. He was walking forward over the piles of bricks and boards and smashed glass in his old cowboy boots, his eyes brilliant even in the shadows. He had seen the rose. There was something lying beside it, in the spot where Jake had found his version of the key but Roland paid this no heed. He only saw the rose, growing from a clump of grass that had been stained purple with spilled paint. He dropped to his knees before it. A moment later Eddie joined him on his left, Jake on his right.

The rose was tightly furled against the night. Then as they knelt there, the petals began to open, as if in greeting. The hum rose all around them, like a song of angels.

13

At first Susannah was all right. She held on despite the fact that she had lost over a foot and a half of herself — the self that had arrived here, anyway — and was now forced into her old familiar (and hatefully subservient) posture, half-kneeling and half-sitting on the filthy sidewalk. Her back was propped against the fence surrounding the vacant lot. A sardonic thought crossed her mind — *All I need's a cardboard sign and a tin cup.*

She held on even after seeing the dead woman cross Forty-sixth Street. The singing helped — what she understood to be the voice of the rose. Oy helped, too, crowding his warmth close to her. She stroked his silky fur, using the reality of him as a steadying-point. She told herself again and again that she was *not* insane. All right, she'd lost seven minutes. *Maybe.* Or maybe the guts inside that newfangled clock down there had just hiccupped.

All right, she'd seen a dead woman crossing the street. *Maybe.* Or maybe she'd just seen some strung-out junkie, God knew there was no shortage of them in New York—

A junkie with a little green worm crawling out of her mouth?

'I could have imagined that part,' she said to the bumbler. 'Right?'

Oy was dividing his nervous attention between Susannah and the rushing headlights, which might have looked to him like large, predatory animals with shining eyes. He whined nervously.

'Besides, the boys'll be back soon.'

'Oys,' the bumbler agreed, sounding hopeful.

Why didn't I just go in with em? Eddie would have carried me on his back, God knows he's done it before, both with the harness and without it.

'I couldn't,' she whispered. 'I just couldn't.'

Because some part of her was frightened of the rose. Of getting too close to it. Had that part been in control during the missing seven minutes? Susannah was afraid it had been. If so, it was gone now. Had taken back its legs and just walked off on them into New York, circa 1977. Not good. But it had taken her fear of the rose with it, and that *was* good. She didn't want to be afraid of something that felt so strong and so wonderful.

Another personality? Are you thinking the lady who brought the legs was another person-ality?

Another version of Detta Walker, in other words?

The idea made her feel like screaming. She thought she now understood how a woman would feel if, five years or so after an apparently successful cancer operation, the doctor told her a routine X-ray had picked up a shadow on her lung.

'Not again,' she murmured in a low, frantic voice as a fresh group of pedestrians schooled past. They all moved away from the board fence a little, although it reduced the space between them considerably. 'No, not again. It can't be. I'm whole. I'm . . . I'm *fixed.*'

How long had her friends been gone?

She looked downstreet at the flashing clock. It said 8:42, but she wasn't sure she could trust it. It felt longer than that. Much longer. Maybe she should call to them. Just give a halloo. How y'all doin in there?

No. No such thing. You're a gunslinger, girl. At least that's what he *says. What he thinks. And you're not going to change what he thinks by hollering like a schoolgirl just seen a garter snake under a bush. You're just going to sit here and wait. You can do it. You've got Oy for company and you—*

Then she saw the man standing on the other side of the street. Just standing there beside a newsstand. He was naked. A ragged Y-cut, sewn up with large black industrial stitches, began at his groin, rose, and branched at his sternum. His empty eyes gazed at her. Through her. Through the world.

Any possibility that this might have been only a hallucination ended when Oy began to bark. He was staring directly across at the naked dead man.

Susannah gave up her silence and began to scream for Eddie.

14

When the rose opened, disclosing the scarlet furnace within its petals and the yellow sun burning at the center, Eddie saw everything that mattered.

'Oh my Lord,' Jake sighed from beside him, but he might have been a thousand miles away.

Eddie saw great things and near misses. Albert Einstein as a child, not quite struck by a runaway milk-wagon as he crossed a street. A teenage boy named Albert Schweitzer getting out of a bathtub and not quite stepping on the cake of soap lying beside the pulled plug. A Nazi *Oberleutnant* burning a piece of paper with the date and place of the D-Day invasion written on it. He saw a man who intended to poison the entire water supply of Denver die of a heart attack in a roadside rest stop on I-80 in Iowa with a bag of McDonald's french fries on his lap. He saw a terrorist wired up with explosives suddenly turn away from a crowded restaurant in a city that might have been Jerusalem. The terrorist had been transfixed by nothing more than the sky, and the thought that it arced above the just and unjust alike. He saw four men rescue a little boy from a monster whose entire head seemed to consist of a single eye.

But more important than any of these was the vast, accretive weight of small things, from planes which hadn't crashed to men and women who had come to the correct place at the perfect time and thus founded generations. He saw kisses exchanged in doorways and wallets returned and men who had come to a splitting of the way and chosen the right fork. He saw a thousand random meetings that weren't random, ten thousand right decisions, a hundred thousand right answers, a million acts of unacknowledged kindness. He saw the old people of River Crossing and Roland kneeling in the dust for Aunt Talitha's blessing; again heard her giving it freely and gladly. Heard her telling him to lay the cross she had given him at the foot of the Dark Tower and speak the name of Talitha Unwin at the far end of the earth. He saw the Tower itself in the burning folds of the rose and for a moment understood its purpose: how it distributed its lines of force to all the worlds that were and held them steady in time's great helix. For every brick that landed on the ground instead of some little kid's head, for every tornado that missed the trailer park, for every missile that didn't fly, for every hand stayed from violence, there was the Tower.

And the quiet, singing voice of the rose. The song that promised all might be well, all might be well, that all manner of things might be well.

But something's wrong with it, he thought.

There was a jagged dissonance buried in the hum, like bits of broken glass. There was a nasty flickering purple glare in its hot heart, some cold light that did not belong there.

'There are two hubs of existence,' he heard Roland say. '*Two!*' Like Jake, he could have been a thousand miles away. 'The Tower . . . and the rose. Yet they are the same.'

'The same,' Jake agreed. His face was painted with brilliant light, dark red and bright yellow. Yet Eddie thought he could see that other light, as well – a flickering purple reflection like a bruise. Now it danced on Jake's forehead, now on his cheek, now it swam in the well of his eye; now gone, now reappearing at his temple like the physical manifestation of a bad idea.

'What's wrong with it?' Eddie heard himself ask, but there was no answer. Not from Roland or Jake, not from the rose.

Jake raised one finger and began to count. Counting petals, Eddie saw. But there was really no need to count. They all knew how many petals there were.

'We *must* have this patch,' Roland said. 'Own it and then protect it. Until the Beams are reestablished and the Tower is made safe again. Because while the Tower weakens, this is what holds everything together. And this is weakening, too. It's sick. Do you feel it?'

Eddie opened his mouth to say of course he felt it, and that was when Susannah began to scream. A moment later Oy joined his voice to hers, barking wildly.

Eddie, Jake, and Roland looked at each other like sleepers awakened from the deepest of dreams. Eddie made it to his feet first. He turned and stumbled back toward the fence and Second Avenue, shouting her name. Jake followed, pausing only long enough to snatch something out of the snarl of burdocks where the key had been before.

Roland spared one final, agonized look at the wild rose growing so bravely here in this tumbled wasteland of bricks and boards and weeds and litter. It had already begun to furl its petals again, hiding the light that blazed within.

I'll come back, he told it. *I swear by the gods of all the worlds, by my mother and father and my friends that were, that I'll come back.*

Yet he was afraid.

Roland turned and ran for the board fence, picking his way through the tumbled litter with unconscious agility in spite of the pain in his hip. As he ran, one thought returned to him and beat at his mind like a heart: *Two. Two hubs of existence. The rose and the Tower. The Tower and the rose.*

All the rest was held between them, spinning in fragile complexity.

15

Eddie threw himself over the fence, landed badly and asprawl, leaped to his feet, and stepped in front of Susannah without even thinking. Oy continued to bark.

'Suze! What? What is it?' He reached for Roland's gun and found nothing. It seemed that guns did not go todash.

'There!' she cried, pointing across the street. 'There! Do you see him? Please, Eddie, *please tell me you see him!*'

Eddie felt the temperature of his blood plummet. What he saw was a naked man who had been cut open and then sewed up again in what could only be an autopsy tattoo. Another man — a living one — bought a paper at the nearby newsstand, checked for traffic, then crossed Second Avenue. Although he was shaking open the paper to look at the headline as he did it, Eddie saw the way he swerved around the dead man. *The way people swerved around us*, he thought.

'There was another one, too,' she whispered. 'A woman. She was walking. And there was a worm. I saw a worm c-c-crawling—'

'Look to your right,' Jake said tightly. He was down on one knee, stroking Oy back to quietness. In his other hand he held a crumpled pink something. His face was as pale as cottage cheese.

They looked. A child was wandering slowly toward them. It was only possible to tell it was a girl because of the red-and-blue dress she wore. When she got closer, Eddie saw that the blue was supposed to be the ocean. The red blobs resolved themselves into little candy-colored sailboats. Her head had been squashed in some cruel accident, squashed until it was wider than it was long. Her eyes were crushed grapes. Over one pale arm was a white plastic purse. A little girl's best I'm-going-to-the-car-accident-and-don't-know-it purse.

Susannah drew in breath to scream. The darkness she had only sensed earlier was now almost visible. Certainly it was palpable; it pressed against her like earth. Yet she would scream. She *must* scream. Scream or go mad.

'Not a sound,' Roland of Gilead whispered in her ear. 'Do not disturb her, poor lost thing. For your life, Susannah!' Susannah's scream expired in a long, horrified sigh.

'They're dead,' Jake said in a thin, controlled voice. 'Both of them.'

'The vagrant dead,' Roland replied. 'I heard of them from Alain Johns's father. It must have been not long after we returned from Mejis, for after that there wasn't much more time before everything . . . what is it you say, Susannah? Before everything "went to hell in a handbasket." In any case, it was Burning Chris who warned us that if we ever went todash, we might see vags.' He pointed across the street where the naked dead man still stood. 'Such as him yonder have either died so suddenly they don't yet understand what's happened to them, or they simply refuse to accept it. Sooner or later they *do* go on. I don't think there are many of them.'

'Thank God,' Eddie said. 'It's like something out of a George Romero zombie movie.'

'Susannah, what happened to your legs?' Jake asked.

'I don't know,' she said. 'One minute I had em, and the next minute I was the same as before.' She seemed to become aware of Roland's gaze and turned toward him. 'You see somethin funny, sugar?'

'We are ka-tet, Susannah. Tell us what really happened.'

'What the hell are you trying to imply?' Eddie asked him. He might have had said more, but before he could get started, Susannah grasped his arm.

'Caught me out, didn't you?' she asked Roland. 'All right, I'll tell you. According to that fancy dot-clock down there, I lost seven minutes while I was waiting for you boys. Seven minutes and my fine new legs. I didn't want to say anything because . . .' She faltered, then went on. 'Because I was afraid I might be losing my mind.'

That's not what you're afraid of, Roland thought. *Not exactly.*

Eddie gave her a brief hug and a kiss on the cheek. He glanced nervously across the street at the nude corpse (the little girl with the squashed head had, thankfully, wandered off down Forty-sixth Street toward the United Nations), then back at the gunslinger. 'If what you said before is true, Roland, this business of time slipping its cogs is very bad news. What if instead of just seven minutes, it slips three months? What if the next time we get back here, Calvin Tower's sold his lot? We can't let that happen. Because that rose, man ... that rose ...' Tears had begun to slip out of Eddie's eyes.

'It's the best thing in the world,' Jake said, low.

'In all the worlds,' Roland said. Would it ease Eddie and Jake to know that this particular time-slip had probably been in Susannah's head? That Mia had come out for seven minutes, had a look around, and then dived back into her hole like Punxsutawney Phil on Groundhog Day? Probably not. But he saw one thing in Susannah's haggard face: she either knew what was going on, or suspected very strongly. *It must be hellish for her*, he thought.

'We have to do better than this if we're really going to change things,' Jake said. 'This way we're not much better than vags ourselves.'

'We have to get to '64, too,' Susannah said. 'If we're going to get hold of my dough, that is. Can we, Roland? If Callahan's got Black Thirteen, will it work like a door?'

What it will work is mischief, Roland thought. *Mischief and worse.* But before he could say that (or anything else), the todash chimes began. The pedestrians on Second Avenue heard them no more than they saw the pilgrims gathered by the board fence, but the corpse across the street slowly raised his dead hands and placed them over his dead ears, his mouth turning down in a grimace of pain. And then they could see through him.

'Hold onto each other,' Roland said. 'Jake, get your hand into Oy's fur, and *deep!* Never mind if it hurts him!'

Jake did as Roland said, the chimes digging deep into his head. Beautiful but painful.

'Like a root canal without Novocain,' Susannah said. She turned her head and for one moment she could see through the board fence. It had become transparent. Beyond it was the rose, its petals now closed but still giving off its own quietly gorgeous glow. She felt Eddie's arm slip around her shoulders.

'Hold on, Suze – whatever you do, hold on.'

She grasped Roland's hand. For a moment longer she could see Second Avenue, and then everything was gone. The chimes ate up the world and she was flying through blind darkness with Eddie's arm around her and Roland's hand squeezing her own.

16

When the darkness let them go, they were almost forty feet down the road from their camp. Jake sat up slowly, then turned to Oy. 'You all right, boy?'

'Oy.'

Jake patted the bumbler's head. He looked around at the others. All here. He sighed, relieved.

'What's this?' Eddie asked. He had taken Jake's other hand when the chimes began. Now, caught in their interlocked fingers, was a crumpled pink object. It felt like cloth; it also felt like metal.

'I don't know,' Jake said.

'You picked it up in the lot, just after Susannah screamed,' Roland said. 'I saw you.'

Jake nodded. 'Yeah. I guess maybe I did. Because it was where the key was, before.'

'What is it, sugar?'

'Some kind of bag.' He held it by the straps. 'I'd say it was my bowling bag, but that's back at the lanes, with my ball inside it. Back in 1977.'

'What's written on the side?' Eddie asked.

But they couldn't make it out. The clouds had closed in again and there was no moonlight. They walked back to their camp together, slowly, shaky as invalids, and Roland built up the fire. Then they looked at the writing on the side of the rose-pink bowling bag.

NOTHING BUT STRIKES AT MID-WORLD LANES

was what it said.

'That's not right,' Jake said. 'Almost, but not quite. What it says on my bag is NOTHING BUT STRIKES AT MID-*TOWN* LANES. Timmy gave it to me one day when I bowled a two-eighty-two. He said I wasn't old enough for him to buy me a beer.'

'A bowling gunslinger,' Eddie said, and shook his head. 'Wonders never cease, do they?'

Susannah took the bag and ran her hands over it. 'What kind of weave is this? Feels like metal. And it's *heavy*.'

Roland, who had an idea what the bag was for — although not who or what had left it for them — said, 'Put it in your knapsack with the books, Jake. And keep it very safe.'

'What do we do next?' Eddie asked.

'Sleep,' Roland said. 'I think we're going to be very busy for the next few weeks. We'll have to take our sleep when and where we find it.'

'But—'

'Sleep,' Roland said, and spread out his skins.

Eventually they did, and all of them dreamed of the rose. Except for Mia, who got up in the night's last dark hour and slipped away to feast in the great banquet hall. And there she feasted very well.

She was, after all, eating for two.

PART TWO
TELLING TALES

CHAPTER I
THE PAVILION

1

If anything about the ride into Calla Bryn Sturgis surprised Eddie, it was how easily and naturally he took to horseback. Unlike Susannah and Jake, who had both ridden at summer camp, Eddie had never even *petted* a horse. When he'd heard the clop of approaching hooves on the morning after what he thought of as Todash Number Two, he'd felt a sharp pang of dread. It wasn't the riding he was afraid of, or the animals themselves; it was the possibility – hell, the strong *probability* – of looking like a fool. What kind of gunslinger had never ridden a horse?

Yet Eddie still found time to pass a word with Roland before they came. 'It wasn't the same last night.'

Roland raised his eyebrows.

'It wasn't nineteen last night.'

'What do you mean?'

'I don't know what I mean.'

'I don't know, either,' Jake put in, 'but he's right. Last night New York felt like the real deal. I mean, I know we were todash, but still . . .'

'Real,' Roland had mused.

And Jake, smiling, said: 'Real as roses.'

2

The Slightmans were at the head of the Calla's party this time, each leading a pair of mounts by long hacks. There was nothing very intimidating about the horses of Calla Bryn Sturgis; certainly they weren't much like the ones Eddie had imagined galloping along the Drop in Roland's tale of long-ago Mejis. These beasts were stubby, sturdy-legged creatures with shaggy coats and large, intelligent eyes. They were bigger than Shetland ponies, but a very long cast from the fiery-eyed stallions he had been expecting. Not only had they been saddled, but a proper bedroll had been lashed to each mount.

As Eddie walked toward his (he didn't need to be told which it was, he knew: the roan), all his doubts and worries fell away. He only asked a single question, directed at Ben Slightman the Younger after examining the stirrups. 'These are going to be too short for me, Ben — can you show me how to make them longer?'

When the boy dismounted to do it himself, Eddie shook his head. 'It'd be best if I learned,' he said. And with no embarrassment at all.

As the boy showed him, Eddie realized he didn't really need the lesson. He saw how it was done almost as soon as Benny's fingers flipped up the stirrup, revealing the leather tug in back. This wasn't like hidden, subconscious knowledge, and it didn't strike him as anything supernatural, either. It was just that, with the horse a warm and fragrant reality before him, he understood how everything worked. He'd only had one experience exactly like this since coming to Mid-World, and that had been the first time he'd strapped on one of Roland's guns.

'Need help, sugar?' Susannah asked.

'Just pick me up if I go off on the other side,' he grunted, but of course he didn't do any such thing. The horse stood steady, swaying just the slightest bit as Eddie stepped into the stirrup and then swung into the plain black ranchhand's saddle.

Jake asked Benny if he had a poncho. The foreman's son looked doubtfully up at the cloudy sky. 'I really don't think it's going to rain,' he'd said. 'It's often like this for days around Reaptide—'

'I want it for Oy.' Perfectly calm, perfectly certain. *He feels exactly like I do,* Eddie thought. *As if he's done this a thousand times before.*

The boy drew a rolled oilskin from one of his saddlebags and handed it to Jake, who thanked him, put it on, and then tucked Oy into the capacious pocket which ran across the front like a kangaroo's pouch. There wasn't a single protest from the bumbler, either. Eddie thought: *If I told Jake I'd expected Oy to trot along behind us like a sheepdog, would he say, 'He always rides like this'? No . . . but he might think it.*

As they set off, Eddie realized what all this reminded him of: stories he'd heard of reincarnation. He had tried to shake the idea off, to reclaim the practical, tough-minded Brooklyn boy who had grown up in Henry Dean's shadow, and wasn't quite able to do it. The thought of reincarnation might have been less unsettling if it had come to him head-on, but it didn't. What he thought was that he couldn't be from Roland's line, simply couldn't. Not unless Arthur Eld had at some point stopped by Co-Op City, that was. Like maybe for a redhot and a piece of Dahlie Lundgren's fried dough. Stupid to project such an idea from the ability to ride an obviously docile horse without lessons. Yet the idea came back at odd moments through the day, and had followed him down into sleep last night: the Eld. The line of the Eld.

3

They nooned in the saddle, and while they were eating popkins and drinking cold coffee, Jake eased his mount in next to Roland's. Oy peered at the gunslinger with bright eyes from the front pocket of the poncho. Jake was feeding the bumbler pieces of his popkin, and there were crumbs caught in Oy's whiskers.

'Roland, may I speak to you as dinh?' Jake sounded slightly embarrassed.

'Of course.' Roland drank coffee and then looked at the boy, interested, all the while rocking contentedly back and forth in the saddle.

'Ben – that is, both Slightmans, but mostly the kid – asked if I'd come and stay with them. Out at the Rocking B.'

'Do you want to go?' Roland asked.

The boy's cheeks flushed thin red. 'Well, what I thought is that if you guys were in town with the Old Fella and I was out in the country – south of town, you ken – then we'd get two different pictures of the place. My Dad says you don't see anything very well if you only look at it from one viewpoint.'

'True enough,' Roland said, and hoped neither his voice nor his face would give away any of the sorrow and regret he suddenly felt. Here was a boy who was now ashamed of being a boy. He had made a friend and the friend had invited him to stay over, as friends sometimes do. Benny had undoubtedly promised that Jake could help him feed the animals, and perhaps shoot his bow (or his bah, if it shot bolts instead of arrows). There would be places Benny would want to share, secret places he might have gone to with his twin in other times. A platform in a tree, mayhap, or a fishpond in the reeds special to him, or a stretch of riverbank where pirates of eld were reputed to have buried gold and jewels. Such places as boys go. But a large part of Jake Chambers was now ashamed to want to do such things. This was the part that had been despoiled by the doorkeeper in Dutch Hill, by Gasher, by the Tick-Tock Man. And by Roland himself, of course. Were he to say no to Jake's request now, the boy would very likely never ask again. And never resent him for it, which was even worse. Were he to say yes in the wrong way – with even the slightest trace of indulgence in his voice, for instance – the boy would change his mind.

The boy. The gunslinger realized how much he wanted to be able to go on calling Jake that, and how short the time to do so was apt to be. He had a bad feeling about Calla Bryn Sturgis.

'Go with them after they dine us in the Pavilion tonight,' Roland said. 'Go and do ya fine, as they say here.'

'Are you sure? Because if you think you might need me—'

'Your father's saying is a good one. My old teacher—'

'Cort or Vannay?'

'Cort. He used to tell us that a one-eyed man sees flat. It takes two eyes, set a little apart from each other, to see things as they really are. So aye. Go with them. Make the boy your friend, if that seems natural. He seems likely enough.'

'Yeah,' Jake said briefly. But the color was going down in his cheeks again. Roland was pleased to see this.

'Spend tomorrow with him. And his friends, if he has a gang he goes about with.'

Jake shook his head. 'It's far out in the country. Ben says that Eisenhart's got plenty of help around the place, and there are some kids his age, but he's not allowed to play with them. Because he's the foreman's son, I guess.'

Roland nodded. This did not surprise him. 'You'll be offered graf tonight in the Pavilion. Do you need me to tell you it's iced tea once we're past the first toast?'

Jake shook his head.

Roland touched his temple, his lips, the corner of one eye, his lips again. 'Head clear. Mouth shut. See much. Say little.'

Jake grinned briefly and gave him a thumbs-up. 'What about you?'

'The three of us will stay with the priest tonight. I'm in hopes that tomorrow we may hear his tale.'

'And see . . .' They had fallen a bit behind the others, but Jake still lowered his voice. 'See what he told us about?'

'That I don't know,' Roland said. 'The day after tomorrow, we three will ride out to the Rocking B. Perhaps noon with sai Eisenhart and have a bit of palaver. Then, over the next few days, the four of us will have a look at this town, both the inner and the outer. If things go well for you at the ranch, Jake, I'd have you stay there as long as you like and as much as they'll have you.'

'Really?' Although he kept his face well (as the saying went), the gunslinger thought Jake was very pleased by this.

'Aye. From what I make out – what I *ken* – there's three big bugs in Calla Bryn Sturgis. Overholser's one. Took, the storekeeper, is another. The third one's Eisenhart. I'd hear what you make of him with great interest.'

'You'll hear,' Jake said. 'And thankee-sai.' He tapped his throat three times. Then his seriousness broke into a broad grin. A boy's grin. He urged his horse into a trot, moving up to tell his new friend that yes, he might stay the night, yes, he could come and play.

4

'Holy wow,' Eddie said. The words came out low and slow, almost the exclamation of an awestruck cartoon character. But after nearly two months in the woods, the view warranted an exclamation. And there was the element of surprise. At one moment they'd just been clopping along the forest trail, mostly by twos (Overholser rode alone at the head of the group, Roland alone at its tail). At the next the trees were gone and the land itself fell away to the north, south, and east. They were thus presented with a sudden, breathtaking, stomach-dropping view of the town whose children they were supposed to save.

Yet at first, Eddie had no eyes at all for what was spread out directly below him, and when he glanced at Susannah and Jake, he saw they were also looking beyond the Calla. Eddie didn't have to look around at Roland to know he was looking beyond, too. *Definition of a wanderer*, Eddie thought, *a guy who's always looking beyond*.

'Aye, quite the view, we tell the gods thankee,' Overholser said complacently; and then, with a glance at Callahan, 'Man Jesus as well, a' course, all gods is one when it comes to thanks, so I've heard, and 'tis a good enough saying.'

He might have prattled on. Probably did; when you were the big farmer, you usually got to have your say, and all the way to the end. Eddie took no notice. He had returned his attention to the view.

Ahead of them, beyond the village, was a gray band of river running south. The branch of the Big River known as Devar-Tete Whye, Eddie remembered. Where it came out of the forest, the Devar-Tete ran between steep banks, but they lowered as the river entered the first cultivated fields, then fell away entirely. He saw a few stands of palm trees, green and improbably tropical. Beyond the moderate-sized village, the land west of the river was a brilliant green shot through everywhere with more gray. Eddie was sure that on a sunny day, that gray would turn a brilliant blue, and that when the sun was directly overhead, the glare would be too bright to look at. He was looking at rice-fields. Or maybe you called them paddies.

Beyond them and east of the river was desert, stretching for miles. Eddie could see parallel scratches of metal running into it, and made them for railroad tracks.

And beyond the desert – or obscuring the rest of it – was simple blackness. It rose into the sky like a vapory wall, seeming to cut into the low-hanging clouds.

'Yon's Thunderclap, sai,' Zalia Jaffords said.

Eddie nodded. 'Land of the Wolves. And God knows what else.'

'Yer-bugger,' Slightman the Younger said. He was trying to sound bluff and matter-of-fact, but to Eddie he looked plenty scared, maybe on the verge of tears. But the Wolves wouldn't take him, surely – if your twin died, that made you a singleton by default, didn't it? Well, it had certainly worked for Elvis Presley, but of course the King hadn't come from Calla Bryn Sturgis. Or even Calla Lockwood to the south.

'Naw, the King was a Mis'sippi boy,' Eddie said, low.

Tian turned in his saddle to look at him. 'Beg your pardon, sai?'

Eddie, not aware that he'd spoken aloud, said: 'I'm sorry. I was talking to myself.'

Andy the Messenger Robot (Many Other Functions) came striding back up the path from ahead of them in time to hear this. 'Those who hold conversation with themselves keep sorry company. This is an old saying of the Calla, sai Eddie, don't take it personally, I beg.'

'And, as I've said before and will undoubtedly say again, you can't get snot off a suede jacket, my friend. An old saying from Calla Bryn Brooklyn.'

Andy's innards clicked. His blue eyes flashed. '*Snot*: mucus from the nose. Also a disrespectful or supercilious person. *Suede*: this is a leather product which—'

'Never mind, Andy,' Susannah said. 'My friend is just being silly. He does this quite frequently.'

'Oh yes,' Andy said. 'He is a child of winter. Would you like me to tell your horoscope, Susannah-sai? You will meet a handsome man! You will have two ideas, one bad and one good! You will have a dark-haired—'

'Get out of here, idiot,' Overholser said. 'Right into town, straight line, no wandering. Check that all's well at the Pavilion. No one wants to hear your goddamned horoscopes, begging your pardon, Old Fella.'

Callahan made no reply. Andy bowed, tapped his metal throat three times, and set off down the trail, which was steep but comfortingly wide. Susannah watched him go with what might have been relief.

'Kinda hard on him, weren't you?' Eddie asked.

'He's but a piece of machinery,' Overholser said, breaking the last word into syllables, as if speaking to a child.

'And he *can* be annoying,' Tian said. 'But tell me, sais, what do you think of our Calla?'

Roland eased his horse in between Eddie's and Callahan's. 'It's very beautiful,' he said. 'Whatever the gods may be, they have favored this place. I see corn, sharproot, beans, and . . . potatoes? Are those potatoes?'

'Aye, spuds, do ya,' Slightman said, clearly pleased by Roland's eye.

'And yon's all that gorgeous rice,' Roland said.

'All smallholds by the river,' Tian said, 'where the water's sweet and slow. And we know how lucky we are. When the rice comes ready – either to plant or to harvest – all the women go together. There's singing in the fields, and even dancing.'

'Come-come-commala,' Roland said. At least that was what Eddie heard.

Tian and Zalia brightened with surprise and recognition. The Slightmans exchanged a glance and grinned. 'Where did you hear The Rice Song?' the Elder asked. 'When?'

'In my home,' said Roland. 'Long ago. Come-come-commala, rice come a-falla.' He pointed to the west, away from the river. 'There's the biggest farm, deep in wheat. Yours, sai Overholser?'

'So it is, say thankya.'

'And beyond, to the south, more farms ... and then the ranches. That one's cattle ... that one sheep ... that one cattle ... more cattle ... more sheep ...'

'How can you tell the difference from so far away?' Susannah asked.

'Sheep eat the grass closer to the earth, lady-sai,' Overholser said. 'So where you see the light brown patches of earth, that's sheep-graze land. The others — what you'd call ocher, I guess — that's cattle-graze.'

Eddie thought of all the Western movies he'd seen at the Majestic: Clint Eastwood, Paul Newman, Robert Redford, Lee Van Cleef. 'In my land, they tell legends of range-wars between the ranchers and the sheep-farmers,' he said. 'Because, it was told, the sheep ate the grass too close. Took even the roots, you ken, so it wouldn't grow back again.'

'That's plain silly, beg your pardon,' Overholser said. 'Sheep do crop grass close, aye, but then we send the cows over it to water. The manure they drop is full of seed.'

'Ah,' Eddie said. He couldn't think of anything else. Put that way, the whole idea of range wars seemed exquisitely stupid.

'Come on,' Overholser said. 'Daylight's wasting, do ya, and there's a feast laid on for us at the Pavilion. The whole town'll be there to meet you.'

And to give us a good looking-over, too, Eddie thought.

'Lead on,' Roland said. 'We can be there by late day. Or am I wrong?'

'Nup,' Overholser said, then drove his feet into his horse's sides and yanked its head around (just looking at this made Eddie wince). He headed down the path. The others followed.

5

Eddie never forgot their first encounter with those of the Calla; that was one memory always within easy reach. Because everything that happened had been a surprise, he supposed, and when everything's a surprise, experience takes on a dreamlike quality. He remembered the way the torches changed when the speaking was done — their strange, varied light. He remembered Oy's unexpected salute to the crowd. The upturned faces and his suffocating panic and his anger at Roland. Susannah hoisting herself onto the piano bench in what the locals called the *musica*. Oh yeah, that memory always. You bet. But even more vivid than this memory of his beloved was that of the gunslinger.

Of Roland dancing.

But before any of these things came the ride down the Calla's high street, and his sense of foreboding. His premonition of bad days on the way.

6

They reached the town proper an hour before sunset. The clouds parted and let through the day's last red light. The street was empty. The surface was oiled dirt. The horses' hooves made muffled thuds on the wheel-marked hardpack. Eddie saw a livery stable, a place called the Travelers' Rest that seemed a combination lodging-house and eating-house, and, at the far end of the street, a large two-story that just about had to be the Calla's Gathering Hall. Off to the right of this was the flare of torches, so he supposed there were people waiting there, but at the north end of town where they entered there were none.

The silence and the empty board sidewalks began to give Eddie the creeps. He remembered Roland's tale of Susan's final ride into Mejis in the back of a cart, standing with her hands tied in front of her and a noose around her neck. *Her* road had been empty, too. At first. Then, not far from the intersection of the Great Road and the Silk Ranch Road, Susan and her captors had passed a single farmer, a man with what Roland had called lamb-slaughterer's eyes. Later she would be pelted with vegetables and sticks, even with stones, but this lone farmer had been first, standing there with his handful of cornshucks, which he had tossed almost gently at her as she passed on her way to . . . well, on her way to *charyou tree*, the Reap Fair of the Old People.

As they rode into Calla Bryn Sturgis, Eddie kept expecting that man, those lamb-slaughterer's eyes, and the handful of cornshucks. Because this town felt bad to him. Not evil — evil as Mejis had likely been on the night of Susan Delgado's death — but bad in a simpler way. Bad as in bad luck, bad choices, bad omens. Bad ka, maybe.

He leaned toward Slightman the Elder. 'Where in the heck is everyone, Ben?'

'Yonder,' Slightman said, and pointed to the flare of the torches.

'Why are they so quiet?' Jake asked.

'They don't know what to expect,' Callahan said. 'We're cut off here. The outsiders we *do* see from time to time are the occasional peddler, harrier, gambler . . . oh, and the lake-boat marts sometimes stop in high summer.'

'What's a lake-boat mart?' Susannah asked.

Callahan described a wide flatboat, paddlewheel-driven and gaily painted, covered with small shops. These made their slow way down the Devar-Tete Whye, stopping to trade at the Callas of the Middle Crescent until their goods were gone. Shoddy stuff for the most part, Callahan said, but Eddie wasn't sure he trusted him entirely, at least on the subject of the lake-boat marts; he spoke with the almost unconscious distaste of the longtime religious.

'And the other outsiders come to steal their children,' Callahan concluded. He pointed to the left, where a long wooden building seemed to take up almost half the high street. Eddie counted not two hitching rails or four, but eight. *Long* ones. 'Took's General Store, may it do ya fine,' Callahan said, with what might have been sarcasm.

They reached the Pavilion. Eddie later put the number present at seven or eight hundred, but when he first saw them — a mass of hats and bonnets and boots and work-roughened hands beneath the long red light of that day's evening sun — the crowd seemed enormous, untellable.

They will *throw shit at us*, he thought. *Throw shit at us and yell* 'Charyou tree.' The idea was ridiculous but also strong.

The Calla-folk moved back on two sides, creating an aisle of green grass which led to a raised wooden platform. Ringing the Pavilion were torches caught in iron cages. At that point, they still all flared a quite ordinary yellow. Eddie's nose caught the strong reek of oil.

Overholser dismounted. So did the others of his party. Eddie, Susannah, and Jake looked at Roland. Roland sat as he was for a moment, leaning slightly forward, one arm cast across the pommel of his saddle, seeming lost in his own thoughts. Then he took off his hat and held it out to the crowd. He tapped his throat three times. The crowd murmured. In appreciation or surprise? Eddie couldn't tell. Not anger, though, definitely not anger, and that was good. The gunslinger lifted one booted foot across the saddle and lightly dismounted. Eddie left his horse more carefully, aware of all the eyes on him. He'd put on Susannah's harness earlier, and now he stood next to her mount, back-to. She slipped into the harness with the ease of long practice. The crowd murmured again when they saw her legs were missing from just above the knees.

Overholser started briskly up the path, shaking a few hands along the way. Callahan walked directly behind him, occasionally sketching the sign of the cross in the air. Other hands reached out of the crowd to secure the horses. Roland, Eddie, and Jake walked three abreast. Oy was still in the wide front pocket of the poncho Benny had loaned Jake, looking about with interest.

Eddie realized he could actually smell the crowd — sweat and hair and sunburned skin and the occasional splash of what the characters in the Western movies usually called (with contempt similar to Callahan's for the lake-boat marts) 'foo-foo water.' He could also smell food: pork and beef, fresh bread, frying onions, coffee and graf. His stomach rumbled, yet he wasn't hungry. No, not really hungry. The idea that the path they were walking would disappear and these people would close in on them wouldn't leave his mind. They were so *quiet*! Somewhere close by he could hear the first nightjars and whippoorwills tuning up for evening.

Overholser and Callahan mounted the platform. Eddie was alarmed to see that none of the others of the party which had ridden out to meet them did. Roland walked up the three broad wooden steps without hesitation, however. Eddie followed, conscious that his knees were a little weak.

'You all right?' Susannah murmured in his ear.

'So far.'

To the left of the platform was a round stage with seven men on it, all dressed in white shirts, blue jeans, and sashes. Eddie recognized the instruments they were holding, and although the mandolin and banjo made him think their music would probably be of the shitkicking variety, the sight of them was still reassuring. They didn't hire bands to play at human sacrifices, did they? Maybe just a drummer or two, to wind up the spectators.

Eddie turned to face the crowd with Susannah on his back. He was dismayed to see that the aisle that had begun where the high street ended was indeed gone now. Faces tilted up to look at him. Women and men, old and young. No expression on those faces, and no children among them. These were faces that spent most of their time out in the sun and had the cracks to prove it. That sense of foreboding would not leave him.

Overholser stopped beside a plain wooden table. On it was a large billowy feather. The farmer took it and held it up. The crowd, quiet to begin with, now fell into a silence so disquietingly deep that Eddie could hear the rattling rales in some old party's chest as he or she breathed.

'Put me down, Eddie,' Susannah said quietly. He didn't like to, but he did.

'I'm Wayne Overholser of Seven-Mile Farm,' Overholser said, stepping to the edge of the stage with the feather held before him. 'Hear me now, I beg.'

'We say thankee-sai,' they murmured.

Overholser turned and held one hand out to Roland and his tet, standing there in their travel-stained clothes (Susannah didn't stand, exactly, but rested between Eddie and Jake on her haunches and one propped hand). Eddie thought he had never felt himself studied more eagerly.

'We men of the Calla heard Tian Jaffords, George Telford, Diego Adams, and all others who would speak at the Gathering Hall,' Overholser said. 'There I did speak myself. "They'll come and take the children," I said, meaning the Wolves, a'course, "then they'll leave us alone again for a generation or more. So 'tis, so it's been, I say leave it alone." I think now those words were mayhap a little hasty.'

A murmur from the crowd, soft as a breeze.

'At this same meeting we heard Pere Callahan say there were gunslingers north of us.'

Another murmur. This one was a little louder. *Gunslingers . . . Mid-World . . . Gilead.*

'It was taken among us that a party should go and see. These are the folk we found, do ya. They claim to be . . . what Pere Callahan said they were.' Overholser now looked uncomfortable. Almost as if he were suppressing a fart. Eddie had seen this expression before, mostly on TV, when politicians faced with some fact they couldn't squirm around were forced to backtrack. 'They claim to be of the gone world. Which is to say . . .'

Go on, Wayne, Eddie thought, *get it out. You can do it.*

'. . . which is to say of Eld's line.'

'Gods be praised!' some woman shrieked. 'Gods've sent em to save our babbies, so they have!'

There were shushing sounds. Overholser waited for quiet with a pained look on his face, then went on. 'They can speak for themselves — and must — but I've seen enough to believe they may be able to help us with our problem. They carry good guns — you see em — and they can use em. Set my watch and warrant on it, and say thankya.'

This time the murmur from the crowd was louder, and Eddie sensed goodwill in it. He relaxed a little.

'All right, then, let em stand before 'ee one by one, that ye might hear their voices and see their faces very well. This is their dinh.' He lifted a hand to Roland.

The gunslinger stepped forward. The red sun set his left cheek on fire; the right was painted yellow with torchglow. He put out one leg. The thunk of the worn bootheel on the boards was very clear in the silence; Eddie for no reason thought of a fist knocking on a coffintop. He bowed deeply, open palms held out to them. 'Roland of Gilead, son of Steven,' he said. 'The Line of Eld.'

They sighed.

'May we be well-met.' He stepped back, and glanced at Eddie.

This part he could do. 'Eddie Dean of New York,' he said. 'Son of Wendell.' *At least that's what Ma always claimed*, he thought. And then, unaware he was going to say it: 'The Line of Eld. The ka-tet of Nineteen.'

He stepped back, and Susannah moved forward to the edge of the plat-form. Back straight, looking out at them calmly, she said, 'I am Susannah Dean, wife of Eddie, daughter of Dan, the Line of Eld, the ka-tet of Nineteen, may we be well-met and do ya fine.' She curtsied, holding out her pretend skirts.

At this there was both laughter and applause.

While she spoke her piece, Roland bent to whisper a brief something in Jake's ear. Jake nodded and then stepped forward confidently. He looked very young and very handsome in the day's end light.

He put out his foot and bowed over it. The poncho swung comically forward with Oy's weight. 'I am Jake Chambers, son of Elmer, the Line of Eld, the ka-tet of the Ninety and Nine.'

Ninety-nine? Eddie looked at Susannah, who offered him a very small shrug. *What's this ninety-nine shit?* Then he thought what the hell. He didn't know what the ka-tet of Nineteen was, either, and he'd said it himself.

But Jake wasn't done. He lifted Oy from the pocket of Benny Slightman's poncho. The crowd murmured at the sight of him. Jake gave Roland a quick glance — *Are you sure?* it asked — and Roland nodded.

At first Eddie didn't think Jake's furry pal was going to do anything. The people of the Calla — the *folken* — had gone completely quiet again, so quiet that once again the evensong of the birds could be heard clearly.

Then Oy rose up on his rear legs, stuck one of them forward, and actu-ally bowed over it. He wavered but kept his balance. His little black paws were held out with the palms up, like Roland's. There were gasps, laughter, applause. Jake looked thunderstruck.

'Oy!' said the bumbler. 'Eld! Thankee!' Each word clear. He held the bow a moment longer, then dropped onto all fours and scurried briskly back to Jake's side. The applause was thunderous. In one brilliant, simple stroke, Roland (for who else, Eddie thought, could have taught the bumbler to do that) had made these people into their friends and admirers. For tonight, at least.

So that was the first surprise: Oy bowing to the assembled Calla *folken* and declaring himself an-tet with his traveling-mates. The second came hard on its heels. 'I'm no speaker,' Roland said, stepping forward again. 'My tongue tangles worse than a drunk's on Reap-night. But Eddie will set us on with a word, I'm sure.'

This was Eddie's turn to be thunderstruck. Below them, the crowd applauded and stomped appreciatively on the ground. There were cries of *Thankee-sai* and *Speak you well* and *Hear him, hear him*. Even the band got into the act, playing a flourish that was ragged but loud.

He had time to shoot Roland a single frantic, furious look: *What in the blue fuck are you doing to me?* The gunslinger looked back blandly, then folded his arms across his chest.

The applause was fading. So was his anger. It was replaced by terror. Overholser was watching him with interest, arms crossed in conscious or unconscious imitation of Roland. Below him, Eddie could see a few individual faces at the front of the crowd: the Slightmans, the Jaffordses. He looked in the other direction and there was Callahan, blue eyes narrowed. Above them, the ragged cruciform scar on his forehead seemed to glare.

What the hell am I supposed to say to them?

Better say somethin, Eds, his brother Henry spoke up. *They're waiting.*

'Cry your pardon if I'm a little slow getting started,' he said. 'We've come miles and wheels and more miles and wheels, and you're the first folks we've seen in many a—'

Many a what? Week, month, year, decade?

Eddie laughed. To himself he sounded like the world's biggest idiot, a fellow who couldn't be trusted to hold his own dick at watering-time, let alone a gun. 'In many a blue moon.'

They laughed at that, and *hard*. Some even applauded. He had touched the town's funnybone without even realizing it. He relaxed, and when he did he found himself speaking quite naturally. It occurred to him, just in passing, that not so long ago the armed gunslinger standing in front of these seven hundred frightened, hopeful people had been sitting in front of the TV in nothing but a pair of yellowing underpants, eating Cheetos, done up on heroin, and watching *Yogi Bear*.

'We've come from afar,' he said, 'and have far yet to go. Our time here will be short, but we'll do what we can, hear me, I beg.'

'Say on, stranger!' someone called. 'You speak fair!'

Yeah? Eddie thought. *News to me, fella.*

A few cries of *Aye* and *Do ya*.

'The healers in my barony have a saying,' Eddie told them. '"First, do no harm."' He wasn't sure if this was a lawyer-motto or a doctor-motto, but he'd heard it in quite a few movies and TV shows, and it sounded pretty good. 'We would do no harm here, do you ken, but no one ever pulled a bullet, or even a splinter from under a kid's fingernail, without spilling some blood.'

There were murmurs of agreement. Overholser, however, was poker-faced, and in the crowd Eddie saw looks of doubt. He felt a surprising flush of anger. He had no right to be angry at these people, who had done them absolutely no harm and had refused them absolutely nothing (at least so far), but he was, just the same.

'We've got another saying in the barony of New York,' he told them. '"There ain't no free lunch." From what we know of your situation, it's serious. Standing up against these Wolves would be dangerous. But some-times doing nothing just makes people feel sick and hungry.'

'Hear him, hear him!' the same someone at the back of the crowd called out. Eddie saw Andy the robot back there, and near him a large wagon full of men in voluminous cloaks of either black or dark blue. Eddie assumed that these were the Manni-folk.

'We'll look around,' Eddie said, 'and once we understand the problem, we'll see what can be done. If we think the answer's nothing, we'll tip our hats to you and move along.' Two or three rows back stood a man in a battered white cowboy hat. He had shaggy white eyebrows and a white mustache to match. Eddie thought he looked quite a bit like Pa Cartwright on that old TV show, *Bonanza*. This version of the Cartwright patriarch looked less than thrilled with what Eddie was saying.

'If we can help, we'll help,' he said. His voice was utterly flat now. 'But we won't do it alone, folks. Hear me, I beg. Hear me very well. You better be ready to stand up for what you want. You better be ready to fight for the things you'd keep.'

With that he stuck out a foot in front of him — the moccasin he wore didn't produce the same fist-on-coffintop thud, but Eddie thought of it, all the same — and bowed. There was dead silence. Then Tian Jaffords began to clap. Zalia joined him. Benny also applauded. His father nudged him, but the boy went on clapping, and after a moment Slightman the Elder joined in.

Eddie gave Roland a burning look. Roland's own bland expression didn't change. Susannah tugged the leg of his pants and Eddie bent to her.

'You did fine, sugar.'

'No thanks to *him*.' Eddie nodded at Roland. But now that it was over, he felt surprisingly good. And talking was really not Roland's thing, Eddie knew that. He could do it when he had no backup, but he didn't care for it.

So now you know what you are, he thought. *Roland of Gilead's mouthpiece.*

And yet was that so bad? Hadn't Cuthbert Allgood had the job long before him?

Callahan stepped forward. 'Perhaps we could set them on a bit better than we have, my friends — give them a proper Calla Bryn Sturgis welcome.'

He began to applaud. The gathered *folken* joined in immediately this time. The applause was long and lusty. There were cheers, whistles, stamping feet (the foot-stamping a little less than satisfying without a wood floor to amplify the sound). The musical combo played not just one flourish but a whole series of them. Susannah grasped one of Eddie's hands. Jake grasped the other. The four of them bowed like some rock group at the end of a particularly good set, and the applause redoubled.

At last Callahan quieted it by raising his hands. 'Serious work ahead, folks,' he said. 'Serious things to think about, serious things to do. But for now, let's eat. Later, let's dance and sing and be merry!' They began to applaud again and Callahan quieted them again. 'Enough!' he cried, laughing. 'And you Manni at the back, I know you haul your own rations, but there's no reason on earth for you not to eat and drink what you have with us. Join us, do ya! May it do ya fine!'

May it do us all fine, Eddie thought, and still that sense of foreboding wouldn't leave him. It was like a guest standing on the outskirts of the party, just beyond the glow of the torches. And it was like a sound. A bootheel on a wooden floor. A fist on the lid of a coffin.

7

Although there were benches and long trestle tables, only the old folks ate their dinners sitting down. And a famous dinner it was, with literally two hundred dishes to choose among, most of them homely and delicious. The doings began with a toast to the Calla. It was proposed by Vaughn Eisenhart, who stood with a bumper in one hand and the feather in the other. Eddie thought this was probably the Crescent's version of the National Anthem.

'May she always do fine!' the rancher cried, and tossed off his cup of graf in one long swallow. Eddie admired the man's throat, if nothing else; Calla Bryn Sturgis graf was so hard that just smelling it made his eyes water.

'*DO YA!*' the *folken* responded, and cheered, and drank.

At that moment the torches ringing the Pavilion went the deep crimson of the recently departed sun. The crowd oohed and aahed and applauded. As technology went, Eddie didn't think it was such of a much – certainly not compared to Blaine the Mono, or the dipolar computers that ran Lud – but it cast a pretty light over the crowd and seemed to be non-toxic. He applauded with the rest. So did Susannah. Andy had brought her wheelchair and unfolded it for her with a compliment (he also offered to tell her about the handsome stranger she would soon meet). Now she wheeled her way amongst the little knots of people with a plate of food on her lap, chatting here, moving on, chatting there and moving on again. Eddie guessed she'd been to her share of cocktail parties not much different from this, and was a little jealous of her aplomb.

Eddie began to notice children in the crowd. Apparently the *folken* had decided their visitors weren't going to just haul out their shooting irons and start a massacre. The oldest kids were allowed to wander about on their own. They traveled in the protective packs Eddie recalled from his own childhood, scoring massive amounts of food from the tables (although not even the appetites of voracious teenagers could make much of a dent in that bounty). They watched the outlanders, but none quite dared approach.

The youngest children stayed close to their parents. Those of the painful 'tween age clustered around the slide, swings, and elaborate monkey-bar construction at the very far end of the Pavilion. A few used the stuff, but most of them only watched the party with the puzzled eyes of those who are somehow caught just wrongways. Eddie's heart went out to them. He could see how many pairs there were – it was eerie – and guessed that it was these puzzled children, just a little too old to use the playground equipment unselfconsciously, who would give up the greatest number to the Wolves . . . if the Wolves were allowed to do their usual thing, that was. He saw none of the 'roont' ones, and guessed they had deliberately been kept apart, lest they cast a pall on the gathering. Eddie could understand that, but hoped they were having a party of their own somewhere. (Later he found that this was exactly the case – cookies and ice cream behind Callahan's church.)

Jake would have fit perfectly into the middle group of children, had he been of the Calla, but of course he wasn't. And he'd made a friend who suited him perfectly: older in years, younger in experience. They went about from table to table, grazing at random. Oy trailed at Jake's heels contentedly enough, head always swinging from side to side. Eddie had no doubt whatever that if someone made an aggressive move toward Jake of New York (or his new friend, Benny of the Calla), that fellow would find himself missing a couple of fingers. At one point Eddie saw the two boys look at each other, and although not a word passed between them, they burst out laughing at exactly the same moment. And Eddie was reminded so forcibly of his own childhood friendships that it hurt.

Not that Eddie was allowed much time for introspection. He knew from Roland's stories (and from having seen him in action a couple of times) that the gunslingers of Gilead had been much more than peace officers. They had also been messengers, accountants, sometimes spies, once in awhile even executioners. More than anything else, however, they had been diplomats. Eddie, raised by his brother and his friends with such nuggets of wisdom as *Why can't you eat me like your sister does* and *I fucked your mother and she sure was fine*, not to mention the ever-popular *I don't shut up I grow up, and when I look at you I throw up*, would never have thought himself a diplomat, but on the whole he thought he handled himself pretty well. Only Telford was hard, and the band shut him up, say thankya.

God knew it was a case of sink or swim; the Calla-folk might be frightened of the Wolves, but they weren't shy when it came to asking how Eddie and the others of his tet would handle them. Eddie realized Roland had done him a very big favor, making him speak in front of the entire bunch of them. It had warmed him up a little for this.

He told all of them the same things, over and over. It would be impossible to talk strategy until they had gotten a good look at the town. Impossible to tell how many men of the Calla would need to join them.

Time would show. They'd peek at daylight. There would be water if God willed it. Plus every other cliché he could think of. (It even crossed his mind to promise them a chicken in every pot after the Wolves were vanquished, but he stayed his tongue before it could wag so far.) A small-hold farmer named Jorge Estrada wanted to know what they'd do if the Wolves decided to light the village on fire. Another, Garrett Strong, wanted Eddie to tell them where the children would be kept safe when the Wolves came. 'For we can't leave em here, you must kennit very well,' he said. Eddie, who realized he kenned very little, sipped at his graf and was noncommittal. A fellow named Neil Faraday (Eddie couldn't tell if he was a smallhold farmer or just a hand) approached and told Eddie this whole thing had gone too far. 'They never take *all* the children, you know,' he said. Eddie thought of asking Faraday what he'd make of someone who said, 'Well, only *two* of them raped my wife,' and decided to keep the comment to himself. A dark-skinned, mustached fellow named Louis Haycox introduced himself and told Eddie he had decided Tian Jaffords was right. He'd spent many sleepless nights since the meeting, thinking it over, and had finally decided that he would stand and fight. If they wanted him, that was. The combination of sincerity and terror Eddie saw in the man's face touched him deeply. This was no excited kid who didn't know what he was doing but a full-grown man who probably knew all too well.

So here they came with their questions and there they went with no real answers, but looking more satisfied even so. Eddie talked until his mouth was dry, then exchanged his wooden cup of graf for cold tea, not wanting to get drunk. He didn't want to eat any more, either; he was stuffed. But still they came. Cash and Estrada. Strong and Echeverria. Winkler and Spalter (cousins of Overholser's, they said). Freddy Rosario and Farren Posella . . . or was it Freddy Posella and Farren Rosario?

Every ten or fifteen minutes the torches would change color again. From red to green, from green to orange, from orange to blue. The jugs of graf circulated. The talk grew louder. So did the laughter. Eddie began to hear more frequent cries of *Yer-bugger* and something that sounded like *Dive-down!*, always followed by laughter.

He saw Roland speaking with an old man in a blue cloak. The old fellow had the thickest, longest, whitest beard Eddie had ever seen outside of a TV Bible epic. He spoke earnestly, looking up into Roland's weatherbeaten face. Once he touched the gunslinger's arm, pulled it a little. Roland listened, nodded, said nothing — not while Eddie was watching him, anyway. *But he's interested*, Eddie thought. *Oh yeah — old long tall and ugly's hearing something that interests him a lot.*

The musicians were trooping back to the bandstand when someone else stepped up to Eddie. It was the fellow who had reminded him of Pa Cartwright.

'George Telford,' he said. 'May you do well, Eddie of New York.' He gave his forehead a perfunctory tap with the side of his fist, then opened the hand and held it out. He wore rancher's headgear — a cowboy hat instead of a farmer's sombrero — but his palm felt remarkably soft, except for a line of callus running along the base of his fingers. *That's where he holds the reins*, Eddie thought, *and when it comes to work, that's probably it.*

Eddie gave a little bow. 'Long days and pleasant nights, sai Telford.' It crossed his mind to ask if Adam, Hoss, and Little Joe were back at the Ponderosa, but he decided again to keep his wiseacre mouth shut.

'May 'ee have twice the number, son, twice the number.' He looked at the gun on Eddie's hip, then up at Eddie's face. His eyes were shrewd and not particularly friendly. 'Your dinh wears the mate of that, I ken.'

Eddie smiled, said nothing.

'Wayne Overholser says yer ka-babby put on quite a shooting exhibition with another 'un. I believe yer wife's wearing it tonight?'

'I believe she is,' Eddie said, not much caring for that ka-babby thing. He knew very well that Susannah had the Ruger. Roland had decided it would be better if Jake didn't go armed out to Eisenhart's Rocking B.

'Four against forty'd be quite a pull, wouldn't you say?' Telford asked. 'Yar, a hard pull that'd be. Or mayhap there might be sixty come in from the east; no one seems to remember for sure, and why would they? Twenty-three years is a long time of peace, tell God aye and Man Jesus thankya.'

Eddie smiled and said a little more nothing, hoping Telford would move along to another subject. Hoping Telford would go away, actually.

No such luck. Pissheads always hung around: it was almost a law of nature. 'Of course four *armed* against forty ... or sixty ... would be a sight better than three armed and one standing by to raise a cheer. Especially four armed with hard calibers, may you hear me.'

'Hear you just fine,' Eddie said. Over by the platform where they had been introduced, Zalia Jaffords was telling Susannah something. Eddie thought Suze also looked interested. *She gets the farmer's wife, Roland gets the Lord of the fuckin Rings, Jake gets to make a friend, and what do I get? A guy who looks like Pa Cartwright and cross-examines like Perry Mason.*

'*Do* you have more guns?' Telford asked. 'Surely you must have more, if you think to make a stand against the Wolves. Myself, I think the idea's madness; I've made no secret of it. Vaughn Eisenhart feels the same—'

'Overholser felt that way and changed his mind,' Eddie said in a just-passing-the-time kind of way. He sipped tea and looked at Telford over the rim of his cup, hoping for a frown. Maybe even a brief look of exasperation. He got neither.

'Wayne the Weathervane,' Telford said, and chuckled. 'Yar, yar, swings this way and that. Wouldn't be too sure of him yet, young sai.'

Eddie thought of saying, *If you think this is an election you better think again*, and then didn't. Mouth shut, see much, say little.

'Do 'ee have speed-shooters, p'raps?' Telford asked. 'Or grenados?'

'Oh well,' Eddie said, 'that's as may be.'

'I never heard of a woman gunslinger.'

'No?'

'Or a boy, for that matter. Even a 'prentice. How are we to know you are who you say you are? Tell me, I beg.'

'Well, that's a hard one to answer,' Eddie said. He had taken a strong dislike to Telford, who looked too old to have children at risk.

'Yet people will want to know,' Telford said. 'Certainly before they bring the storm.'

Eddie remembered Roland's saying *We may be cast on but no man may cast us back*. It was clear they didn't understand that yet. Certainly Telford didn't. Of course there were questions that had to be answered, and answered yes; Callahan had mentioned that and Roland had confirmed it. Three of them. The first was something about aid and succor. Eddie didn't think those questions had been asked yet, didn't see how they could have been, but he didn't think they would be asked in the Gathering Hall when the time came. The answers might be given by little people like Posella and Rosario, who didn't even know what they were saying. People who *did* have children at risk.

'Who are you really?' Telford asked. 'Tell me, I beg.'

'Eddie Dean, of New York. I hope you're not questioning my honesty. I hope to *Christ* you're not doing that.'

Telford took a step back, suddenly wary. Eddie was grimly glad to see it. Fear wasn't better than respect, but by God it was better than nothing. 'Nay, not at all, my friend! Please! But tell me this — have you ever used the gun you carry? Tell me, I beg.'

Eddie saw that Telford, although nervous of him, didn't really believe it. Perhaps there was still too much of the old Eddie Dean, the one who really *had* been of New York, in his face and manner for this rancher-sai to believe it, but Eddie didn't think that was it. Not the bottom of it, anyway. Here was a fellow who'd made up his mind to stand by and watch creatures from Thunderclap take the children of his neighbors, and perhaps a man like that simply couldn't believe in the simple, final answers a gun allowed. Eddie had come to know those answers, however. Even to love them. He remembered their single terrible day in Lud, racing Susannah in her wheelchair under a gray sky while the god-drums pounded. He remembered Frank and Luster and Topsy the Sailor; thought of a woman named Maud kneeling to kiss one of the lunatics Eddie had shot to death. What had she said? *You shouldn't've shot Winston, for 'twas his birthday.* Something like that.

'I've used this one and the other one and the Ruger as well,' he said. 'And don't you ever speak to me that way again, my friend, as if the two of us were on the inside of some funny joke.'

'If I offended in any way, gunslinger, I cry your pardon.'

Eddie relaxed a little. *Gunslinger.* At least the silver-haired son of a bitch had the wit to say so even if he might not believe so.

The band produced another flourish. The leader slipped his guitar-strap over his head and called, 'Come on now, you all! That's enough food! Time to dance it off and sweat it out, so it is!'

Cheers and yipping cries. There was also a rattle of explosions that caused Eddie to drop his hand, as he had seen Roland drop his on a good many occasions.

'Easy, my friend,' Telford said. 'Only little bangers. Children setting off Reap-crackers, you ken.'

'So it is,' Eddie said. 'Cry your pardon.'

'No need.' Telford smiled. It was a handsome Pa Cartwright smile, and in it Eddie saw one thing clear: this man would never come over to their side. Not that was, until and unless every Wolf out of Thunderclap lay dead for the town's inspection in this very Pavilion. And if that happened, he would claim to have been with them from the very first.

8

The dancing went on until moonrise, and that night the moon showed clear. Eddie took his turn with several ladies of the town. Twice he waltzed with Susannah in his arms, and when they danced the squares, she turned and crossed – allamand left, allamand right – in her wheelchair with pretty precision. By the ever-changing light of the torches, her face was damp and delighted. Roland also danced, gracefully but (Eddie thought) with no real enjoyment or flair for it. Certainly there was nothing in it to prepare them for what ended the evening. Jake and Benny Slightman had wandered off on their own, but once Eddie saw them kneeling beneath a tree and playing a game that looked suspiciously like mumblety-peg.

When the dancing was done, there was singing. This began with the band itself – a mournful love-ballad and then an up-tempo number so deep in the Calla's patois that Eddie couldn't follow the lyric. He didn't have to in order to know it was at least mildly ribald; there were shouts and laughter from the men and screams of glee from the ladies. Some of the older ones covered their ears.

After these first two tunes, several people from the Calla mounted the bandstand to sing. Eddie didn't think any of them would have gotten very far on *Star Search*, but each was greeted warmly as they stepped to the front of the band and were cheered lustily (and in the case of one pretty young matron, lust*fully*) as they stepped down. Two girls of about nine, obviously identical twins, sang a ballad called 'Streets of Campara' in perfect, aching harmony, accompanied by just a single guitar which one of them played. Eddie was struck by the rapt silence in which the *folken* listened. Although most of the men were now deep in drink, not a single one of these broke the attentive quiet. No baby-bangers went off. A good many (the one named Haycox among them) listened with tears streaming down their faces. If asked earlier, Eddie would have said of course he understood the emotional weight beneath which this town was laboring. He hadn't. He knew that now.

When the song about the kidnapped woman and the dying cowboy ended, there was a moment of utter silence – not even the nightbirds cried. It was followed by wild applause. Eddie thought, *If they showed hands on what to do about the Wolves right now, not even Pa Cartwright would dare vote to stand aside.*

The girls curtsied and leaped nimbly down to the grass. Eddie thought that would be it for the night, but then, to his surprise, Callahan climbed on stage.

He said, 'Here's an even sadder song my mother taught me,' and then launched into a cheerful Irish ditty called 'Buy Me Another Round You Booger You.' It was at least as dirty as the one the band had played earlier, but this time Eddie could understand most of the words. He and the rest of the town gleefully joined in on the last line of every verse: *Before y'ez put me in the ground, buy me another round, you booger you!*

Susannah rolled her wheelchair over to the gazebo and was helped up during the round of applause that followed the Old Fella's song. She spoke briefly to the three guitarists and showed them something on the neck of one of the instruments. They all nodded. Eddie guessed they either knew the song or a version of it.

The crowd waited expectantly, none more so than the lady's husband. He was delighted but not entirely surprised when she voyaged upon 'Maid of Constant Sorrow,' which she had sometimes sung on the trail. Susannah was no Joan Baez, but her voice was true, full of emotion. And why not? It was the song of a woman who has left her home for a strange place. When she finished, there was no silence, as after the little girls' duet, but a round of honest, enthusiastic applause. There were cries of *Yar!* and *Again!* and *More staves!* Susannah offered no more staves (for she'd sung all the ones she knew) but gave them a deep curtsy, instead. Eddie clapped until his hands hurt, then stuck his fingers in the corners of his mouth and whistled.

And then – the wonders of this evening would never end, it seemed – Roland himself was climbing up as Susannah was handed carefully down.

Jake and his new pal were at Eddie's side. Benny Slightman was carrying Oy. Until tonight Eddie would have said the bumbler would have bitten anyone not of Jake's ka-tet who tried that.

'Can he sing?' Jake asked.

'News to me if he can, kiddo,' Eddie said. 'Let's see.' He had no idea what to expect, and was a little amused at how hard his heart was thumping.

9

Roland removed his holstered gun and cartridge belt. He handed them down to Susannah, who took them and strapped on the belt high at the waist. The cloth of her shirt pulled tight when she did it, and for a moment Eddie thought her breasts looked bigger. Then he dismissed it as a trick of the light.

The torches were orange. Roland stood in their light, gunless and as slim-hipped as a boy. For a moment he only looked out over the silent, watching faces, and Eddie felt Jake's hand, cold and small, creep into his own. There was no need for the boy to say what he was thinking, because Eddie was thinking it himself. Never had he seen a man who looked so lonely, so far from the run of human life with its fellowship and warmth. To see him here, in this place of fiesta (for it was a fiesta, no matter how desperate the business that lay behind it might be), only underlined the truth of him: he was the last. There was no other. If Eddie, Susannah, Jake, and Oy were of his line, they were only a distant shoot, far from the trunk. Afterthoughts, almost. Roland, however . . . Roland . . .

Hush, Eddie thought. *You don't want to think about such things. Not tonight.*

Slowly, Roland crossed his arms over his chest, narrow and tight, so he could lay the palm of his right hand on his left cheek and the palm of his left hand on his right cheek. This meant zilch to Eddie, but the reaction from the seven hundred or so Calla-folk was immediate: a jubilant, approving roar that went far beyond mere applause. Eddie remembered a Rolling Stones concert he'd been to. The crowd had made that same sound when the Stones' drummer, Charlie Watts, began to tap his cowbell in a syncopated rhythm that could only mean 'Honky Tonk Woman.'

Roland stood as he was, arms crossed, palms on cheeks, until they quieted. 'We are well-met in the Calla,' he said. 'Hear me, I beg.'

'*We say thankee!*' they roared. And '*Hear you very well!*'

Roland nodded and smiled. 'But I and my friends have been far and we have much yet to do and see. Now while we bide, will you open to us if we open to you?'

Eddie felt a chill. He felt Jake's hand tighten on his own. *It's the first of the questions*, he thought.

Before the thought was completed, they had roared their answer: '*Aye, and thankee!*'

'Do you see us for what we are, and accept what we do?'

There goes the second one, Eddie thought, and now it was him squeezing Jake's hand. He saw Telford and the one named Diego Adams exchange a dismayed, knowing look. The look of men suddenly realizing that the deal is going down right in front of them and they are helpless to do anything about it. *Too late, boys*, Eddie thought.

'Gunslingers!' someone shouted. 'Gunslingers fair and true, say thankee! Say thankee in God's name!'

Roars of approval. A thunder of shouts and applause. Cries of *thankee* and *aye* and even *yer-bugger*.

As they quieted, Eddie waited for him to ask the last question, the most important one: *Do you seek aid and succor?*

Roland didn't ask it. He said merely, 'We'd go our way for tonight, and put down our heads, for we're tired. But I'd give 'ee one final song and a little step-toe before we leave, so I would, for I believe you know both.'

A jubilant roar of agreement met this. They knew it, all right.

'I know it myself, and love it,' said Roland of Gilead. 'I know it of old, and never expected to hear "The Rice Song" again from any lips, least of all from my own. I am older now, so I am, and not so limber as I once was. Cry your pardon for the steps I get wrong—'

'Gunslinger, we say thankee!' a woman called. 'Such joy we feel, aye!'

'And do I not feel the same?' the gunslinger asked gently. 'Do I not give you joy from my joy, and water I carried with the strength of my arm and my heart?'

'*Give you to eat of the green-crop,*' they chanted as one, and Eddie felt his back prickle and his eyes tear up.

'Oh my God,' Jake sighed. 'He knows so *much* . . .'

'Give you joy of the rice,' Roland said.

He stood for a moment longer in the orange glow, as if gathering his strength, and then he began to dance something that was caught between a jig and a tap routine. It was slow at first, very slow, heel and toe, heel and toe. Again and again his bootheels made that fist-on-coffintop sound, but now it had rhythm. *Just* rhythm at first, and then, as the gunslinger's feet began to pick up speed, it was more than rhythm: it became a kind of jive. That was the only word Eddie could think of, the only one that seemed to fit.

Susannah rolled up to them. Her eyes were huge, her smile amazed. She clasped her hands tightly between her breasts. 'Oh, Eddie!' she breathed. 'Did you know he could do this? Did you have any slightest idea?'

'No,' Eddie said. 'No idea.'

10

Faster moved the gunslinger's feet in their battered and broken old boots. Then faster still. The rhythm becoming clearer and clearer, and Jake suddenly realized he *knew* that beat. Knew it from the first time he'd gone todash in New York. Before meeting Eddie, a young black man with Walkman earphones on his head had strolled past him, bopping his sandaled feet and going 'Cha-da-ba, cha-da-*bow!*' under his breath. And that was the rhythm Roland was beating out on the bandstand, each *Bow!* accomplished by a forward kick of the leg and a hard skip of the heel on wood.

Around them, people began to clap. Not on the beat, but on the off-beat. They were starting to sway. Those women wearing skirts held them out and swirled them. The expression Jake saw on all the faces, oldest to youngest, was the same: pure joy. *Not just that,* he thought, and remembered a phrase his English teacher had used about how some books make us feel. *the ecstasy of perfect recognition.*

Sweat began to gleam on Roland's face. He lowered his crossed arms and started clapping. When he did, the Calla-*folken* began to chant one word over and over on the beat: '*Come! . . . Come! . . . Come! . . . Come!*' It occurred to Jake that this was the word some kids used for jizz, and he suddenly doubted if that was mere coincidence.

Of course it's not. Like the black guy bopping to that same beat. It's all the Beam, and it's all nineteen.

'*Come! . . . Come! . . . Come!*'

Eddie and Susannah had joined in. Benny had joined in. Jake abandoned thought and did the same.

11

In the end, Eddie had no real idea what the words to 'The Rice Song' might have been. Not because of the dialect, not in Roland's case, but because they spilled out too fast to follow. Once, on TV, he'd heard a tobacco auctioneer in South Carolina. This was like that. There were hard rhymes, soft rhymes, off-rhymes, even rape-rhymes — words that didn't rhyme at all but were forced to for a moment within the borders of the song. It *wasn't* a song, not really; it was like a chant, or some delirious streetcorner hip-hop. That was the closest Eddie could come. And all the while, Roland's feet pounded out their entrancing rhythm on the boards; all the while the crowd clapped and chanted *Come, come, come, come.*

What Eddie *could* pick out went like this:

*Come-come-commala
Rice come a-falla
I-sissa-'ay a-bralla
Dey come a-folla
Down come a-rivva
Or-i-za we kivva
Rice be a green-o
See all we seen-o
Seen-o the green-o
Come-come-commala!*

*Come-come-commala
Rice come a-falla
Deep inna walla
Grass come-commala
Under the sky-o
Grass green n high-o
Girl n her fella
Lie down togetha
They slippy 'ay slide-o
Under 'ay sky-o
Come-come-commala
Rice come a-falla!*

At least three more verses followed these two. By then Eddie had lost track of the words, but he was pretty sure he got the idea: a young man and woman, planting both rice and children in the spring of the year. The song's tempo, suicidally speedy to begin with, sped up and up until the words were nothing but a jargon-spew and the crowd was clapping so rapidly their hands were a blur. And the heels of Roland's boots had disappeared entirely. Eddie would have said it was impossible for anyone to dance at that speed, especially after having consumed a heavy meal.

Slow down, Roland, he thought. *It's not like we can call 911 if you vapor-lock.*

Then, on some signal neither Eddie, Susannah, nor Jake understood, Roland and the Calla-*folken* stopped in mid-career, threw their hands to the sky, and thrust their hips forward, as if in coitus. '*COMMALA!*' they shouted, and that was the end.

Roland swayed, sweat pouring down his cheeks and brow . . . and tumbled off the stage into the crowd. Eddie's heart took a sharp upward lurch in his chest. Susannah cried out and began to roll her wheelchair forward. Jake stopped her before she could get far, grabbing one of the push-handles.

'I think it's part of the show!' he said.

'Yar, I'm pretty sure it is, too,' Benny Slightman said.

The crowd cheered and applauded. Roland was conveyed through them and above them by willing upraised arms. His own arms were raised to the stars. His chest heaved like a bellows. Eddie watched in a kind of hilarious disbelief as the gunslinger rolled toward them as if on the crest of a wave.

'Roland sings, Roland dances, and to top it all off,' he said, 'Roland stage-dives like Joey Ramone.'

'What are you talking about, sugar?' Susannah asked.

Eddie shook his head. 'Doesn't matter. But nothing can top that. It's *got* to be the end of the party.'

It was.

12

Half an hour later, four riders moved slowly down the high street of Calla Bryn Sturgis. One was wrapped in a heavy *salide*. Frosty plumes came from their mouths and those of their mounts on each exhale. The sky was filled with a cold strew of diamond-chips, Old Star and Old Mother brightest among them. Jake had already gone his way with the Slightmans to Eisenhart's Rocking B. Callahan led the other three travelers, riding a bit ahead of them. But before leading them anywhere, he insisted on wrapping Roland in the heavy blanket.

'You say it's not even a mile to your place—' Roland began.

'Never mind your blather,' Callahan said. 'The clouds have rolled away, the night's turned nigh-on cold enough to snow, and you danced a commala such as I've never seen in my years here.'

'How many years would that be?' Roland asked.

Callahan shook his head. 'I don't know. Truly, gunslinger, I don't. I know well enough when I came here – that was the winter of 1983, nine years after I left the town of Jerusalem's Lot. Nine years after I got this.' He raised his scarred hand briefly.

'Looks like a burn,' Eddie remarked.

Callahan nodded, but said no more on the subject. 'In any case, time over here is different, as you all must very well know.'

'It's in drift,' Susannah said. 'Like the points of the compass.'

Roland, already wrapped in the blanket, had seen Jake off with a word ... and with something else, as well. Eddie heard the clink of metal as something passed from the hand of the gunslinger to that of the 'prentice. A bit of money, perhaps.

Jake and Benny Slightman rode off into the dark side by side. When Jake turned and offered a final wave, Eddie had returned it with a surprising pang. *Christ, you're not his father,* he thought. That was true, but it didn't make the pang go away.

'Will he be all right, Roland?' Eddie had expected no other answer but yes, had wanted nothing more than a bit of balm for that pang. So the gunslinger's long silence alarmed him.

At long last Roland replied, 'We'll hope so.' And on the subject of Jake Chambers, he would say no more.

13

Now here was Callahan's church, a low and simple log building with a cross mounted over the door.

'What name do you call it, Pere?' Roland asked.

'Our Lady of Serenity.'

Roland nodded. 'Good enough.'

'Do you feel it?' Callahan asked. 'Do any of you feel it?' He didn't have to say what he was talking about.

Roland, Eddie, and Susannah sat quietly for perhaps an entire minute. At last Roland shook his head.

Callahan nodded, satisfied. 'It sleeps.' He paused, then added: 'Tell God thankya.'

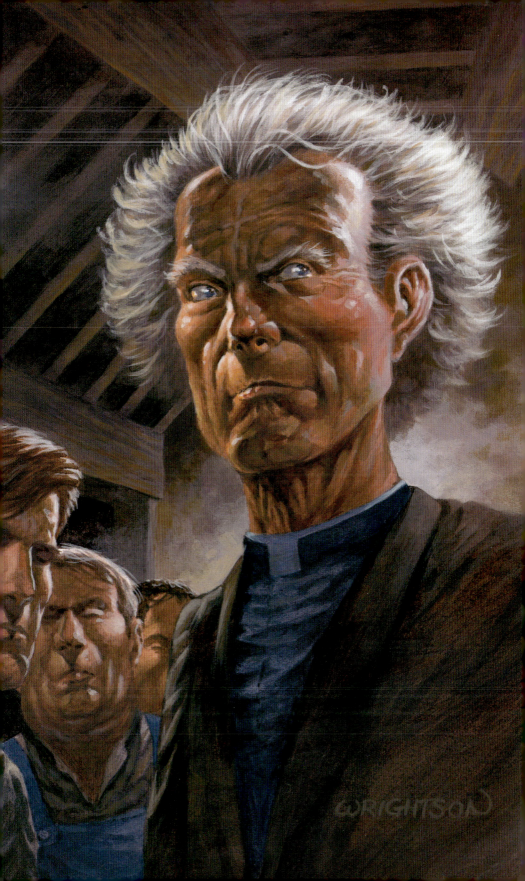

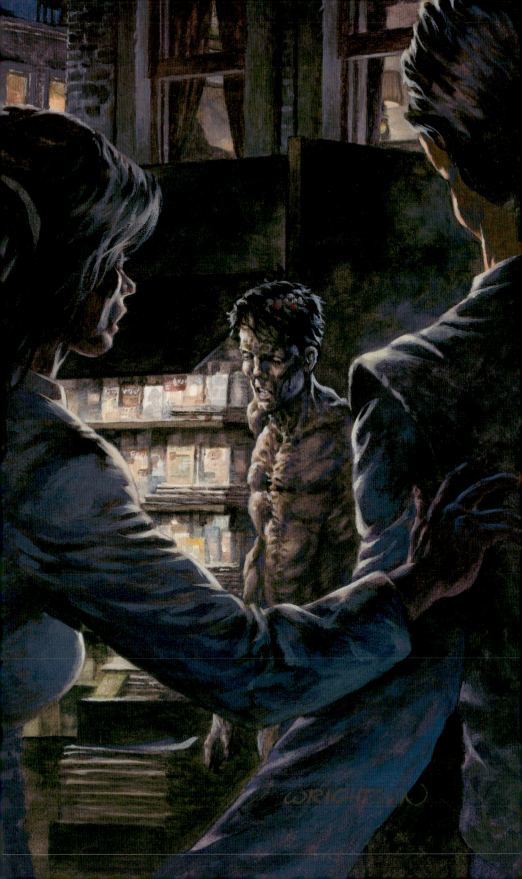

'*Something's* there, though,' Eddie said. He nodded toward the church. 'It's like a . . . I don't know, a weight, almost.'

'Yes,' Callahan said. 'Like a weight. It's awful. But tonight it sleeps. God be thanked.' He sketched a cross in the frosty air.

Down a plain dirt track (but smooth, and bordered with carefully tended hedges) was another log building. Callahan's house, what he called the rectory.

'Will you tell us your story tonight?' Roland said.

Callahan glanced at the gunslinger's thin, exhausted face and shook his head. 'Not a word of it, sai. Not even if you were fresh. Mine is no story for starlight. Tomorrow at breakfast, before you and your friends are off on your errands – would that suit?'

'Aye,' Roland said.

'What if it wakes up in the night?' Susannah asked, and cocked her head toward the church. 'Wakes up and sends us todash?'

'Then we'll go,' Roland said.

'You've got an idea what to do with it, don't you?' Eddie asked.

'Perhaps,' Roland said. They started down the path to the house, including Callahan among them as naturally as breathing.

'Anything to do with that old Manni guy you were talking to?' Eddie asked.

'Perhaps,' Roland repeated. He looked at Callahan. 'Tell me, Pere, has it ever sent *you* todash? You know the word, don't you?'

'I know it,' Callahan said. 'Twice. Once to Mexico. A little town called Los Zapatos. And once . . . I think . . . to the Castle of the King. I believe that I was very lucky to get back, that second time.'

'What King are you talking about?' Susannah asked. 'Arthur Eld?'

Callahan shook his head. The scar on his forehead glared in the starlight. 'Best not to talk about it now,' he said. 'Not at night.' He looked at Eddie sadly. 'The Wolves are coming. Bad enough. Now comes a young man who tells me the Red Sox lost the World Series again . . . to the *Mets*?'

'Afraid so,' Eddie said, and his description of the final game – a game that made little sense to Roland, although it sounded a bit like Points, called Wickets by some – carried them up to the house. Callahan had a housekeeper. She was not in evidence but had left a pot of hot chocolate on the hob.

While they drank it, Susannah said: 'Zalia Jaffords told me something that might interest you, Roland.'

The gunslinger raised his eyebrows.

'Her husband's grandfather lives with them. He's reputed to be the oldest man in Calla Bryn Sturgis. Tian and the old man haven't been on good terms in years – Zalia isn't even sure what they're pissed off about, it's that old – but Zalia gets on with him very well. She says he's gotten quite senile over the last couple of years, but he still has his bright days. And he claims to have seen one of these Wolves. Dead.' She paused. 'He claims to have killed it himself.'

'My soul!' Callahan exclaimed. 'You don't say so!'

'I do. Or rather, Zalia did.'

'That,' Roland said, 'would be a tale worth hearing. Was it the last time the Wolves came?'

'No,' Susannah said. 'And not the time before, when even Overholser would have been not long out of his clouts. The time before that.'

'If they come every twenty-three years,' Eddie said, 'that's almost seventy years ago.'

Susannah nodded. 'But he was a man grown, even then. He told Zalia that a moit of them stood out on the West Road and waited for the Wolves to come. I don't know how many a moit might be—'

'Five or six,' Roland said. He was nodding over his chocolate.

'Anyway, Tian's Gran-pere was among them. And they killed one of the Wolves.'

'What was it?' Eddie asked. 'What did it look like with its mask off?'

'She didn't say,' Susannah replied. 'I don't think he told her. But we ought to—'

A snore arose, long and deep. Eddie and Susannah turned, startled. The gunslinger had fallen asleep. His chin was on his breastbone. His arms were crossed, as if he'd drifted off to sleep still thinking of the dance. And the rice.

14

There was only one extra bedroom, so Roland bunked in with Callahan. Eddie and Susannah were thus afforded a sort of rough honeymoon: their first night together by themselves, in a bed and under a roof. They were not too tired to take advantage of it. Afterward, Susannah passed immediately into sleep. Eddie lay awake a little while. Hesitantly, he sent his mind out in the direction of Callahan's tidy little church, trying to touch the thing that lay within. Probably a bad idea, but he couldn't resist at least trying. There was nothing. Or rather, a nothing in front of a something.

I could wake it up, Eddie thought. *I really think I could.*

Yes, and someone with an infected tooth could rap it with a hammer, but why would you?

We'll have to wake it up eventually. I think we're going to need it.

Perhaps, but that was for another day. It was time to let this one go.

Yet for awhile Eddie was incapable of doing that. Images flashed in his mind, like bits of broken mirror in bright sunlight. The Calla, lying spread out below them beneath the cloudy sky, the Devar-Tete Whye a gray ribbon. The green beds at its edge: rice come a-falla. Jake and Benny Slightman looking at each other and laughing without a word passed between them to account for it. The aisle of green grass between the high street and the Pavilion. The torches changing color. Oy, bowing and speaking (*Eld! Thankee!*) with perfect clarity. Susannah singing: 'I've known sorrow all my days.'

Yet what he remembered most clearly was Roland standing slim and gunless on the boards with his arms crossed at the chest and his hands pressed against his cheeks; those faded blue eyes looking out at the *folken.* Roland asking questions, two of three. And then the sound of his boots on the boards, slow at first, then speeding up. Faster and faster, until they were a blur in the torchlight. Clapping. Sweating. Smiling. Yet his *eyes* didn't smile, not those blue bombardier's eyes; they were as cold as ever.

Yet how he had danced! Great God, how he had danced in the light of the torches.

Come-come-commala, rice come a-falla, Eddie thought.

Beside him, Susannah moaned in some dream.

Eddie turned to her. Slipped his hand beneath her arm so he could cup her breast. His last thought was for Jake. They had better take care of him out at that ranch. If they didn't, they were going to be one sorry-ass bunch of cowpunchers.

Eddie slept. There were no dreams. And beneath them as the night latened and the moon set, this borderland world turned like a dying clock.

CHAPTER II
DRY TWIST

1

Roland awoke from another vile dream of Jericho Hill in the hour before dawn. The horn. Something about Arthur Eld's horn. Beside him in the big bed, the Old Fella slept with a frown on his face, as if caught in his own bad dream. It creased his broad brow zigzag, breaking the arms of the cross scarred into the skin there.

It was pain that had wakened Roland, not his dream of the horn spilling from Cuthbert's hand as his old friend fell. The gunslinger was caught in a vise of it from the hips all the way down to his ankles. He could visualize the pain as a series of bright and burning rings. This was how he paid for his outrageous exertions of the night before. If that was all, all would have been well, but he knew there was more to this than just having danced the commala a little too enthusiastically. Nor was it the rheumatiz, as he had been telling himself these last few weeks, his body's necessary period of adjustment to the damp weather of this fall season. He was not blind to the way his ankles, especially the right one, had begun to thicken. He had observed a similar thickening of his knees, and although his hips still looked fine, when he placed his hands on them, he could feel the way the right one was changing under the skin. No, not the rheumatiz that had afflicted Cort so miserably in his last year or so, keeping him inside by his fire on rainy days. This was something worse. It was arthritis, the bad kind, the *dry* kind. It wouldn't be long before it reached his hands. Roland would gladly have fed his right one to the disease, if that would have satisfied it; he had taught it to do a good many things since the lobstrosities had taken the first two fingers, but it was never going to be what it was. Only ailments didn't work that way, did they? You couldn't placate them with sacrifices. The arthritis would come when it came and go where it wanted to go.

I might have a year, he thought, lying in bed beside the sleeping religious from Eddie and Susannah and Jake's world. *I might even have two.*

No, not two. Probably not even one. What was it Eddie sometimes said? *Quit kidding yourself.* Eddie had a lot of sayings from his world, but that was a particularly good one. A particularly *apt* one.

Not that he would cry off the Tower if Old Bone-Twist Man took his ability to shoot, saddle a horse, cut a strip of rawhide, even to chop wood for a campfire, so simple a thing as that; no, he was in it until the end. But he didn't relish the picture of riding along behind the others, dependent upon them, perhaps tied to his saddle with the reins because he could no longer hold the pommel. Nothing but a drag-anchor. One they wouldn't be able to pull up if and when fast sailing was required.

If it gets to that, I'll kill myself.

But he wouldn't. That was the truth. *Quit kidding yourself.*

Which brought Eddie to mind again. He needed to talk to Eddie about Susannah, and right away. This was the knowledge with which he had awakened, and perhaps worth the pain. It wouldn't be a pleasant talk, but it had to be done. It was time Eddie knew about Mia. She would find it more difficult to slip away now that they were in a town – in a house – but she would have to, just the same. She could argue with her baby's needs and her own cravings no more than Roland could argue with the bright rings of pain which circled his right hip and knee and both ankles but had so far spared his talented hands. If Eddie wasn't warned, there might be terrible trouble. More trouble was something they didn't need now; it might sink them.

Roland lay in the bed, and throbbed, and watched the sky lighten. He was dismayed to see that brightness no longer bloomed dead east; it was a little off to the south, now.

Sunrise was also in drift.

2

The housekeeper was good-looking, about forty. Her name was Rosalita Munoz, and when she saw the way Roland walked to the table, she said: 'One cup coffee, then you come with me.'

Callahan cocked his head at Roland when she went to the stove to get the pot. Eddie and Susannah weren't up yet. The two of them had the kitchen to themselves. 'How bad is it with you, sir?'

'It's only the rheumatiz,' Roland said. 'Goes through all my family on my father's side. It'll work out by noon, given bright sunshine and dry air.'

'I know about the rheumatiz,' Callahan said. 'Tell God thankya it's no worse.'

'I do.' And to Rosalita, who brought heavy mugs of steaming coffee, 'I tell you thankya, as well.'

She put down the cups, curtsied, and then regarded him shyly and gravely. 'I never saw the rice-dance kicked better, sai.'

Roland smiled crookedly. 'I'm paying for it this morning.'

'I'll fix you,' she said. 'I've a cat-oil, special to me. It'll first take the pain and then the limp. Ask Pere.'

Roland looked at Callahan, who nodded.

'Then I'll take you up on it. Thankee-sai.'

She curtsied again, and left them.

'I need a map of the Calla,' Roland said when she was gone. 'It doesn't have to be great art, but it has to be accurate, and true as to distance. Can you draw one for me?'

'Not at all,' Callahan said composedly. 'I cartoon a little, but I couldn't draw you a map that would take you as far as the river, not even if you put a gun to my head. It's just not a talent I have. But I know two that could help you there.' He raised his voice. 'Rosalita! Rosie! Come to me a minute, do ya!'

3

Twenty minutes later, Rosalita took Roland by the hand, her grip firm and dry. She led him into the pantry and closed the door. 'Drop yer britches, I beg,' she said. 'Be not shy, for I doubt you've anything I haven't seen before, unless men are built summat different in Gilead and the Inners.'

'I don't believe they are,' Roland said, and let his pants fall.

The sun was now up but Eddie and Susannah were still down. Roland was in no hurry to wake them. There would be plenty of early days ahead – and late evenings, too, likely – but this morning let them enjoy the peace of a roof over their heads, the comfort of a feather mattress beneath their bodies, and the exquisite privacy afforded by a door between their secret selves and the rest of the world.

Rosalita, a bottle of pale, oily liquid in one hand, drew in a hiss over her full lower lip. She looked at Roland's right knee, then touched his right hip with her left hand. He flinched away a bit from the touch, although it was gentleness itself.

She raised her eyes to him. They were so dark a brown they were almost black. 'This isn't rheumatiz. It's arthritis. The kind that spreads fast.'

'Aye, where I come from some call it dry twist,' he said. 'Not a word of it to the Pere, or to my friends.'

Those dark eyes regarded him steadily. 'You won't be able to keep this a secret for long.'

'I hear you very well. Yet while I can keep the secret, I *will* keep the secret. And you'll help me.'

'Aye,' she said. 'No fear. I'll bide 'ee.'

'Say thankya. Now, will that help me?'

She looked at the bottle and smiled. 'Aye. It's mint and spriggum from the swamp. But the secret's the cat's bile that's in it — not but three drops in each bottle, ye ken. They're the rock-cats that come in out of the desert, from the direction of the great darkness.' She tipped up the bottle and poured a little of the oily stuff into her palm. The smell of the mint struck Roland's nose at once, followed by some other smell, a lower smell, which was far less pleasant. Yes, he reckoned that could be the bile of a puma or a cougar or whatever they meant by a rock-cat in these parts.

When she bent and rubbed it into his kneecaps, the heat was immediate and intense, almost too strong to bear. But when it moderated a bit, there was more relief than he would have dared hope for.

When she had finished anointing him, she said: 'How be your body now, gunslinger-sai?'

Instead of answering with his mouth, he crushed her against his lean, undressed body and hugged her tightly. She hugged him back with an artless lack of shame and whispered in his ear, 'If 'ee are who 'ee say 'ee are, 'ee mustn't let 'un take the babbies. No, not a single one. Never mind what the big bugs like Eisenhart and Telford might say.'

'We'll do the best we can,' he said.

'Good. Thankya.' She stepped back, looked down. 'One part of 'ee has no arthritis, nor rheumatiz, either. Looks quite lively. Perhaps a lady might look at the moon tonight, gunslinger, and pine for company.'

'Perhaps she'll find it,' Roland said. 'Will you give me a bottle of that stuff to take on my travels around the Calla, or is it too dear?'

'Nay, not too dear,' she said. In her flirting, she had smiled. Now she looked grave again. 'But will only help 'ee a little while, I think.'

'I know,' Roland said. 'And no matter. We spread the time as we can, but in the end the world takes it all back.'

'Aye,' she said. 'So it does.'

4

When he came out of the pantry, buckling his belt, he finally heard stirring in the other room. The murmur of Eddie's voice followed by a sleepy peal of female laughter. Callahan was at the stove, pouring himself fresh coffee. Roland went to him and spoke rapidly.

'I saw pokeberries on the left of your drive between here and your church.'

'Yes, and they're ripe. Your eyes are sharp.'

'Never mind my eyes, do ya. I would go out to pick my hat full. I'd have Eddie join me while his wife perhaps cracks an egg or three. Can you manage that?'

'I believe so, but—'

'Good,' Roland said, and went out.

5

By the time Eddie came, Roland had already half-filled his hat with the orange berries, and also eaten several good handfuls. The pain in his legs and hips had faded with amazing rapidity. As he picked, he wondered how much Cort would have paid for a single bottle of Rosalita Munoz's cat-oil.

'Man, those look like the wax fruit our mother used to put out on a doily every Thanksgiving,' Eddie said. 'Can you really eat them?'

Roland picked a pokeberry almost as big as the tip of his own finger and popped it into Eddie's mouth. 'Does that taste like wax, Eddie?'

Eddie's eyes, cautious to begin with, suddenly widened. He swallowed, grinned, and reached for more. 'Like cranberries, only sweeter. I wonder if Suze knows how to make muffins? Even if she doesn't, I bet Callahan's housekeeper—'

'Listen to me, Eddie. Listen closely and keep a rein on your emotions. For your father's sake.'

Eddie had been reaching for a bush that was particularly heavy with poke-berries. Now he stopped and simply looked at Roland, his face expressionless. In this early light, Roland could see how much older Eddie looked. How much he had grown up was really extraordinary.

'What is it?'

Roland, who had held this secret in his own counsel until it seemed more complex than it really was, was surprised at how quickly and simply it was told. And Eddie, he saw, wasn't completely surprised.

'How long have you known?'

Roland listened for accusation in this question and heard none. 'For certain? Since I first saw her slip into the woods. Saw her eating . . .' Roland paused '. . . what she was eating. Heard her speaking with people who weren't there. I've suspected much longer. Since Lud.'

'And didn't tell me.'

'No.' Now the recriminations would come, and a generous helping of Eddie's sarcasm. Except they didn't.

'You want to know if I'm pissed, don't you? If I'm going to make this a problem.'

'Are you?'

'No. I'm not angry, Roland. Exasperated, maybe, and I'm scared to fuckin death for Suze, but why would I be angry with you? Aren't you the dinh?' It was Eddie's turn to pause. When he spoke again, he was more specific. It wasn't easy for him, but he got it out. 'Aren't you *my* dinh?'

'Yes,' Roland said. He reached out and touched Eddie's arm. He was astounded by his desire — almost his need — to explain. He resisted it. If Eddie could call him not just dinh but *his* dinh, he ought to behave as dinh. What he said was, 'You don't seem exactly stunned by my news.'

'Oh, I'm surprised,' Eddie said. 'Maybe not stunned, but . . . well . . .' He picked berries and dropped them into Roland's hat. 'I saw some things, okay? Sometimes she's too pale. Sometimes she winces and grabs at herself, but if you ask her, she says it's just gas. And her boobs are bigger. I'm sure of it. But Roland, she's still having her period! A month or so ago I saw her burying the rags, and they were bloody. *Soaked.* How can that be? If she caught pregnant when we pulled Jake through — while she was keeping the demon of the circle occupied — that's got to be four months at least, and probably five. Even allowing for the way time slips around now, it's *gotta* be.'

Roland nodded. 'I know she's been having her monthlies. And that's proof conclusive it isn't your baby. The thing she's carrying scorns her woman's blood.' Roland thought of her squeezing the frog in her fist, popping it. Drinking its black bile. Licking it from her fingers like syrup.

'Would it . . .' Eddie made as if to eat one of the pokeberries, decided against it, and tossed it into Roland's hat instead. Roland thought it would be a while before Eddie felt the stirrings of true appetite again. 'Roland, would it even *look* like a human baby?'

'Almost surely not.'

'What, then?'

And before he could stay them, the words were out. 'Better not to name the devil.'

Eddie winced. What little color remained in his face now left it.

'Eddie? Are you all right?'

'No,' Eddie said. 'I am most certainly not all right. But I'm not gonna faint like a girl at an Andy Gibb concert, either. What are we going to do?'

'For the time being, nothing. We have too many other things to do.'

'Don't we just,' Eddie said. 'Over here, the Wolves come in twenty-four days, if I've got it figured right. Over there in New York, who knows what day it is? The sixth of June? The tenth? Closer to July fifteenth than it was yesterday, that's for sure. But Roland — if what she's got inside her isn't human, we can't be sure her pregnancy will go nine months. She might pop it in six. Hell, she might pop it tomorrow.'

Roland nodded and waited. Eddie had gotten this far; surely he would make it the rest of the way.

And he did. 'We're stuck, aren't we?'

'Yes. We can watch her, but there's not much else we can do. We can't even keep her still in hopes of slowing things down, because she'd very likely guess why we were doing it. And we need her. To shoot when the time comes, but before that, we'll have to train some of these people with whatever weapons they feel comfortable with. It'll probably turn out to be bows.' Roland grimaced. In the end he had hit the target in the North Field with enough arrows to satisfy Cort, but he had never cared for bow and arrow or bah and bolt. Those had been Jamie DeCurry's choice of weapons, not his own.

'We're really gonna go for it, aren't we?'

'Oh yes.'

And Eddie smiled. Smiled in spite of himself. He was what he was. Roland saw it and was glad.

6

As they walked back to Callahan's rectory-house, Eddie asked: 'You came clean with me, Roland, why not come clean with her?'

'I'm not sure I understand you.'

'Oh, I think you do,' Eddie said.

'All right, but you won't like the answer.'

'I've heard all sorts of answers from you, and I couldn't say I've cared for much more than one in five.' Eddie considered. 'Nah, that's too generous. Make it one in fifty.'

'The one who calls herself Mia — which means *mother* in the High Speech — kens she's carrying a child, although I doubt she kens what kind of a child.'

Eddie considered this in silence.

'Whatever it is, Mia thinks of it as her baby, and she'll protect it to the limit of her strength and life. If that means taking over Susannah's body — the way Detta Walker sometimes took over Odetta Holmes — she'll do it if she can.'

'And probably she could,' Eddie said gloomily. Then he turned directly to Roland. 'So what I think you're saying — correct me if I've got it wrong — is that you don't want to tell Suze she might be growing a monster in her belly because it might impair her efficiency.'

Roland could have quibbled about the harshness of his judgment, but chose not to. Essentially, Eddie was right.

As always when he was angry, Eddie's street accent became more pronounced. It was almost as though he were speaking through his nose instead of his mouth. 'And if anything changes over the next month or so — if she goes into labor and pops out the Creature from the Black Lagoon, for instance — she's gonna be completely unprepared. Won't have a clue.'

Roland stopped about twenty feet from the rectory-house. Inside the window, he could see Callahan talking to a couple of young people, a boy and a girl. Even from here he could see they were twins.

'Roland?'

'You say true, Eddie. Is there a point? If so, I hope you'll get to it. Time is no longer just a face on the water, as you yourself pointed out. It's become a precious commodity.'

Again he expected a patented Eddie Dean outburst complete with phrases such as *kiss my ass* or *eat shit and die*. Again, no such outburst came. Eddie was looking at him, that was all. Steadily and a little sorrowfully. Sorry for Susannah, of course, but also for the two of them. The two of them standing here and conspiring against one of the tet.

'I'm going to go along with you,' Eddie said, 'but not because you're the dinh, and not because one of those two is apt to come back brainless from Thunderclap.' He pointed to the pair of kids the Old Fella was talking to in his living room. 'I'd trade every kid in this town for the one Suze is carrying. If it *was* a kid. My kid.'

'I know you would,' Roland said.

'It's the rose I care about,' Eddie said. 'That's the only thing worth risking her for. But even so, you've got to promise me that if things go wrong — if she goes into labor, or if this Mia chick starts taking over — we'll try to save her.'

'I would always try to save her,' Roland said, and then had a brief, nightmare image — brief but very clear — of Jake dangling over the drop under the mountains.

'You swear that?' Eddie asked.

'Yes,' Roland said. His eyes met those of the younger man. In his mind, however, he saw Jake falling into the abyss.

7

They reached the rectory door just as Callahan was ushering the two young people out. They were, Roland thought, very likely the most gorgeous children he had ever seen. Their hair was black as coal, the boy's shoulder-length, the girl's bound by a white ribbon and falling all the way to her bottom. Their eyes were dark, perfect blue. Their skin was creamy-pale, their lips a startling, sensuous red. There were faint spatters of freckles on their cheeks. So far as Roland could tell, the spatters were also identical. They looked from him to Eddie and then back to Susannah, who leaned in the kitchen doorway with a dish-wiper in one hand and a coffee cup in the other. Their shared expression was one of curious wonder. He saw caution in their faces, but no fear.

'Roland, Eddie, I'd like you to meet the Tavery twins, Frank and Francine. Rosalita fetched them – the Taverys live not half a mile away, do ya. You'll have your map by this afternoon, and I doubt if you'll ever have seen a finer one in all your life. It's but one of the talents they have.'

The Tavery twins made their manners, Frank with a bow and Francine with a curtsy.

'You do us well and we say thankya,' Roland told them.

An identical blush suffused their astoundingly creamy complexions; they muttered their thanks and prepared to slip away. Before they could, Roland put an arm around each narrow but well-made pair of shoulders and led the twins a little way down the walk. He was taken less by their perfect child's beauty than by the piercing intelligence he saw in their blue eyes. He had no doubt they would make his map; he also had no doubt that Callahan had had Rosalita fetch them as a kind of object lesson, were one still needed: with no interference, one of these beautiful children would be a grizzling idiot a month from now.

'Sai?' Frank asked. Now there *was* a touch of worry in his voice.

'Fear me not,' Roland said, 'but hear me well.'

8

Callahan and Eddie watched Roland walk the Tavery twins slowly along the rectory's flagstoned path and toward the dirt drive. Both men shared the same thought: Roland looked like a benevolent gran-pere.

Susannah joined them, watched, then plucked Eddie's shirt. 'Come with me a minute.'

He followed her into the kitchen. Rosalita was gone and they had it to themselves. Susannah's brown eyes were enormous, shining.

'What is it?' he asked her.

'Pick me up.'

He did.

'Now kiss me quick, while you have the chance.'

'Is that all you want?'

'Isn't it enough? It better be, Mister Dean.'

He kissed her, and willingly, but couldn't help marking how much larger her breasts were as they pressed against him. When he drew his face away from hers, he found himself looking for traces of the other one in her face. The one who called herself Mother in the High Speech. He saw only Susannah, but he supposed that from now on he would be condemned to look. And his eyes kept trying to go to her belly. He tried to keep them away, but it was as if they were weighted. He wondered how much that was between them would change now. It was not a pleasant speculation.

'Is that better?' he asked.

'Much.' She smiled a little, and then the smile faded. 'Eddie? Is something wrong?'

He grinned and kissed her again. 'You mean other than that we're all probably gonna die here? Nope. Nothing at all.'

Had he lied to her before? He couldn't remember, but he didn't think so. And even if he had, he had never done so with such baldness. With such calculation.

This was bad.

9

Ten minutes later, rearmed with fresh mugs of coffee (and a bowl of poke-berries), they went out into the rectory's small back yard. The gunslinger lifted his face into the sun for a moment, relishing its weight and heat. Then he turned to Callahan. 'We three would hear your story now, Pere, if you'd tell it. And then mayhap stroll up to your church and see what's there.'

'I want you to take it,' Callahan said. 'It hasn't desecrated the church, how could it when Our Lady was never consecrated to begin with? But it's changed it for the worse. Even when the church was still a-building. I felt the spirit of God inside it. No more. That thing has driven it out. I want you to take it.'

Roland opened his mouth to say something noncommittal, but Susannah spoke before he could. 'Roland? You all right?'

He turned to her. 'Why, yes. Why would I not be?'

'You keep rubbing your hip.'

Had he been? Yes, he saw, he had. The pain was creeping back already, in spite of the warm sun, in spite of Rosalita's cat-oil. The dry twist.

'It's nothing,' he told her. 'Just a touch of the rheumatiz.'

She looked at him doubtfully, then seemed to accept. *This is a hell of a way to start*, Roland thought, *with at least two of us keeping secrets. We can't go on so. Not for long.*

He turned to Callahan. 'Tell us your tale. How you came by your scars, how you came here, and how you came by Black Thirteen. We would hear every word.'

'Yes,' Eddie murmured.

'Every word,' Susannah echoed.

All three of them looked at Callahan – the Old Fella, the religious who would allow himself to be called Pere but not priest. His twisted right hand went to the scar on his forehead and rubbed at it. At last he said: ''Twas the drink. That's what I believe now. Not God, not devils, not predestination, not the company of saints. 'Twas the drink.' He paused, thinking, then smiled at them. Roland remembered Nort, the weed-eater in Tull who had been brought back from the dead by the man in black. Nort had smiled like that. 'But if God made the world, then God made the drink. And that is also His will.'

Ka, Roland thought.

Callahan sat quiet, rubbing the scarred crucifix on his forehead, gathering his thoughts. And then he began to tell his story.

CHAPTER III
THE PRIEST'S TALE
(NEW YORK)

1

It was the drink, that was what he came to believe when he finally stopped it and clarity came. Not God, not Satan, not some deep psychosexual battle between his blessed mither and his blessed Da'. Just the drink. And was it surprising that whiskey should have taken him by the ears? He was Irish, he was a priest, one more strike and you're out.

From seminary in Boston he'd gone to a city parish in Lowell, Massachusetts. His parishioners had loved him (he wouldn't refer to them as his flock, flocks were what you called seagulls on their way to the town dump), but after seven years in Lowell, Callahan had grown uneasy. When talking to Bishop Dugan in the Diocese office, he had used all the correct buzzwords of the time to express this unease: anomie, urban malaise, an increasing lack of empathy, a sense of disconnection from the life of the spirit. He'd had a nip in the bathroom before his appointment (followed by a couple of Wintergreen Life Savers, no fool he), and had been particularly eloquent that day. Eloquence does not always proceed from belief, but often proceeds from the bottle. And he was no liar. He *had* believed what he was saying that day in Dugan's study. Every word. As he believed in Freud, the future of the Mass spoken in English, the nobility of Lyndon Johnson's War on Poverty, and the idiocy of his widening war in Vietnam: waist-deep in the Wide Muddy, and the big fool said to push on, as the old folk-tune had it. He believed in large part because those ideas (if they *were* ideas and not just cocktail-party chatter) had been currently trading high on the intellectual Big Board. Social Conscience is up two and a third, Hearth and Home down a quarter but still your basic blue-chip stock. Later it all became simpler. Later he came to understand that he wasn't drinking too much because he was spiritually unsettled but spiritually unsettled because he was drinking too much. You wanted to protest, to say *that* couldn't be it, or not *just* that, it was too simple. But it *was* that, just that. God's voice is still and small, the voice of a sparrow in a cyclone, so said the prophet Isaiah, and we all say thankya. It's hard to hear a small voice clearly if you're shitass drunk most of the time. Callahan left America for Roland's world before the computer revolution spawned the acronym GIGO – garbage in, garbage out – but in plenty of time to hear someone at an AA meeting observe that if you put an asshole on a plane in San Francisco and flew him to the east coast, the same asshole got off in Boston. Usually with four or five drinks under his belt. But that was later. In 1964 he had believed what he believed, and plenty of people had been anxious to help him find his way. From Lowell he had gone to Spofford, Ohio, a suburb of Dayton. There he stayed for five years, and then he began to feel restless again. Consequently, he began to talk the talk again. The kind the Diocesan Office listened to. The kind that got you moved on down the line. Anomie. Spiritual disconnection (this time from his suburban parishioners). Yes, they liked him (and he liked them), but something still seemed to be wrong. And there *was* something wrong, mostly in the quiet bar on the corner (where everybody *also* liked him) and in the liquor cabinet in the rectory living room. Beyond small doses, alcohol is a toxin, and Callahan was poisoning himself on a nightly basis. It was the poison in his system, not the state of the world or that of his own soul, which was bringing him down. Had it always been that obvious? Later (at another AA meeting) he'd heard a guy refer to alcoholism and addiction as the elephant in the living room: how could you miss it? Callahan hadn't told him, he'd still been in the first ninety days of sobriety at that point and that meant he was supposed to just sit there and be quiet ('Take the cotton out of your ears and stick it in your mouth,' the old-timers advised, and we all say thankya), but he *could* have told him, yes indeed. You could miss the elephant if it was a *magic* elephant, if it had the power – like The Shadow – to cloud men's minds. To actually make you believe that your problems were spiritual and mental but absolutely not boozical. Good Christ, just the alcohol-related loss of the REM sleep was enough to screw you up righteously, but somehow you never thought of that while you were active. Booze turned your thought-processes into something akin to that circus routine where all the clowns come piling out of the little car. When you looked back in sobriety, the things you'd said and done made you wince ('I'd sit in a bar solving all the problems of the world, then not be able to find my car in the parking lot,' one fellow at a meeting remembered, and we all say thankya). The things you *thought* were even worse. How could you spend the morning puking and the afternoon believing you were having a spiritual crisis? Yet he had. And his superiors had, possibly because more than a few of them were having their own problems with the magic elephant. Callahan began thinking that a smaller church, a rural parish, would put him back in touch with God and himself. And so, in the spring of 1969, he found himself in New England again. Northern New England, this time. He had set up shop – bag and baggage, crucifix and chasuble – in the pleasant little town of Jerusalem's Lot, Maine. There he had finally met real evil. Looked it in the face.

And flinched.

2

'A writer came to me,' he said. 'A man named Ben Mears.'

'I think I read one of his books,' Eddie said. '*Air Dance*, it was called. About a man who gets hung for the murder his brother committed?'

Callahan nodded. 'That's the one. There was also a teacher named Matthew Burke, and they both believed there was a vampire at work in 'Salem's Lot, the kind who makes other vampires.'

'Is there any other kind?' Eddie asked, remembering about a hundred movies at the Majestic and maybe a thousand comic books purchased at (and sometimes stolen from) Dahlie's.

'There is, and we'll get there, but never mind that now. Most of all, there was a boy who believed. He was about the same age as your Jake. They didn't convince me – not at first – but *they* were convinced, and it was hard to stand against their belief. Also, *something* was going on in The Lot, that much was certain. People were disappearing. There was an atmosphere of terror in the town. Impossible to describe it now, sitting here in the sun, but it was there. I had to officiate at the funeral of another boy. His name was Daniel Glick. I doubt he was this vampire's first victim in The Lot, and he certainly wasn't the last, but he was the first one who turned up dead. On the day of Danny Glick's burial, my life changed, somehow. And I'm not talking about the quart of whiskey a day anymore, either. Something changed in my *head*. I felt it. Like a switch turning. And although I haven't had a drink in years, that switch is still turned.'

Susannah thought: *That's when you went todash, Father Callahan.*

Eddie thought: *That's when you went nineteen, pal. Or maybe it's ninety-nine. Or maybe it's both, somehow.*

Roland simply listened. His mind was clear of reflection, a perfect receiving machine.

'The writer, Mears, had fallen in love with a town girl named Susan Norton. The vampire took her. I believe he did it partly because he could, and partly to punish Mears for daring to form a group – a ka-tet – that would try to hunt him. We went to the place the vampire had bought, an old wreck called the Marsten House. The thing staying there went by the name of Barlow.'

Callahan sat, considering, looking through them and back to those old days. At last he resumed.

'Barlow was gone, but he'd left the woman. And a letter. It was addressed to all of us, but was directed principally to me. The moment I saw her lying there in the cellar of the Marsten House I understood it was all true. The doctor with us listened to her chest and took her blood pressure, though, just to be sure. No heartbeat. Blood pressure zero. But when Ben pounded the stake into her, she came alive. The blood flowed. She screamed, over and over. Her hands . . . I remembered the shadows of her hands on the wall . . .'

Eddie's hand gripped Susannah's. They listened in a horrified suspension that was neither belief nor disbelief. This wasn't a talking train powered by malfunctioning computer circuits, nor men and women who had reverted to savagery. This was something akin to the unseen demon that had come to the place where they had drawn Jake. Or the doorkeeper in Dutch Hill.

'What did he say to you in his note, this Barlow?' Roland asked.

'That my faith was weak and I would undo myself. He was right, of course. By then the only thing I really believed in was Bushmill's. I just didn't know it. *He* did, though. Booze is also a vampire, and maybe it takes one to know one.

'The boy who was with us became convinced that this prince of vampires meant to kill his parents next, or turn them. For revenge. The boy had been taken prisoner, you see, but he escaped and killed the vampire's half-human accomplice, a man named Straker.'

Roland nodded, thinking this boy sounded more and more like Jake. 'What was his name?'

'Mark Petrie. I went with him to his house, and with all the considerable power my church affords: the cross, the stole, the holy water, and of course the Bible. But I had come to think of these things as symbols, and that was my Achilles' heel. Barlow was there. He had Petrie's parents. And then he had the boy. I held up my cross. It glowed. It hurt him. He screamed.' Callahan smiled, recalling that scream of agony. The look of it chilled Eddie's heart. 'I told him that if he hurt Mark, I'd destroy him, and at that moment I could have done it. He knew it, too. His response was that before I did, he'd rip the child's throat out. And *he* could have done it.'

'Mexican standoff,' Eddie murmured, remembering a day by the Western Sea when he had faced Roland in a strikingly similar situation. 'Mexican standoff, baby.'

'What happened?' Susannah asked.

Callahan's smile faded. He was rubbing his scarred right hand the way the gunslinger had rubbed his hip, without seeming to realize it. 'The vampire made a proposal. He would let the boy go if I'd put down the crucifix I held. We'd face each other unarmed. His faith against mine. I agreed. God help me, I agreed. The boy'

3

The boy is gone, like an eddy of dark water.

Barlow seems to grow taller. His hair, swept back from his brow in the European manner, seems to float around his skull. He's wearing a dark suit and a bright red tie, impeccably knotted, and to Callahan he seems part of the darkness that surrounds him. Mark Petrie's parents lie dead at his feet, their skulls crushed.

'Fulfill your part of the bargain, shaman.'

But why should he? Why not drive him off, settle for a draw this night? Or kill him outright? Something is wrong with the idea, terribly wrong, but he cannot pick out just what it is. Nor will any of the buzzwords that have helped him in previous moments of crisis be of any help to him here. This isn't anomie, lack of empathy, or the existential grief of the twentieth century; this is a vampire. *And—*

And his cross, which had been glowing fiercely, is growing dark.

Fear leaps into his belly like a confusion of hot wires. Barlow is walking toward him across the Petrie kitchen, and Callahan can see the thing's fangs very clearly because Barlow is smiling. It is a winner's smile.

Callahan takes a step backward. Then two. Then his buttocks strike the edge of the table, and the table pushes back against the wall, and then there is nowhere left to go.

'Sad to see a man's faith fail,' says Barlow, and reaches out.

Why should he not reach out? The cross Callahan is holding up is now dark. Now it's nothing but a piece of plaster, a cheap piece of rickrack his mother bought in a Dublin souvenir shop, probably at a scalper's price. The power it had sent ramming up his arm, enough spiritual voltage to smash down walls and shatter stone, is gone.

Barlow plucks it from his fingers. Callahan cries out miserably, the cry of a child who suddenly realizes the bogeyman has been real all along, waiting patiently in the closet for its chance. And now comes a sound that will haunt him for the rest of his life, from New York and the secret highways of America to the AA meetings in Topeka where he finally sobered up to the final stop in Detroit to his life here, in Calla Bryn Sturgis. He will remember that sound when his forehead is scarred and he fully expects to be killed. He will remember it when he is killed. The sound is two dry snaps as Barlow breaks the arms of the cross, and the meaningless thump as he throws what remains on the floor. And he'll also remember the cosmically ludicrous thought which came, even as Barlow reached for him: God, I need a drink.

4

The Pere looked at Roland, Eddie, and Susannah with the eyes of one who is remembering the absolute worst moment of his life. 'You hear all sorts of sayings and slogans in Alcoholics Anonymous. There's one that recurs to me whenever I think of that night. Of Barlow taking hold of my shoulders.'

'What?' Eddie asked.

'Be careful what you pray for,' Callahan said. 'Because you just might get it.'

'You got your drink,' Roland said.

'Oh yes,' Callahan said. 'I got my drink.'

5

Barlow's hands are strong, implacable. As Callahan is drawn forward, he suddenly understands what is going to happen. Not death. Death would be a mercy compared to this.

No, please no, he tries to say, but nothing comes out of his mouth but one small, whipped moan.

'Now, priest,' the vampire whispers.

Callahan's mouth is pressed against the reeking flesh of the vampire's cold throat. There is no anomie, no social dysfunction, no ethical or racial ramifications. Only the stink of death and one vein, open and pulsing with Barlow's dead, infected blood. No sense of existential loss, no postmodern grief for the death of the American value system, not even the religio-psychological guilt of Western man. Only the effort to hold his breath forever, or twist his head away, or both. He cannot. He holds on for what seems like aeons, smearing the blood across his cheeks and forehead and chin like war paint. To no avail. In the end he does what all alcoholics must do once the booze has taken them by the ears: he drinks.

Strike three. You're out.

6

'The boy got away. There was that much. And Barlow let me go. Killing me wouldn't have been any fun, would it? No, the fun was in letting me live.

'I wandered for an hour or more, through a town that was less and less there. There aren't many Type One vampires, and that's a blessing because a Type One can cause one hell of a lot of mayhem in an extremely short period of time. The town was already half-infected, but I was too blind – too *shocked* – to realize it. And none of the new vampires approached me. Barlow had set his mark on me as surely as God set his mark on Cain before sending him off to dwell in the land of Nod. His watch and his warrant, as you'd say, Roland.

'There was a drinking fountain in the alley beside Spencer's Drugs, the sort of thing no Public Health Office would have sanctioned a few years later, but back then there was one or two in every small town. I washed Barlow's blood off my face and neck there. Tried to wash it out of my hair, too. And then I went to St Andrews, my church. I'd made up my mind to pray for a second chance. Not to the God of the theologians who believe that everything holy and unholy ultimately comes from inside us, but to the old God. The one who proclaimed to Moses that he should not suffer a witch to live and gave unto his own son the power to raise from the dead. A second chance is all I wanted. My life for that.

'By the time I got to St Andrews, I was almost running. There were three doors going inside. I reached for the middle one. Somewhere a car back-fired, and someone laughed. I remember those sounds very clearly. It's as if they mark the border of my life as a priest of the Holy Roman Catholic Church.'

'What happened to you, sugar?' Susannah asked.

'The door rejected me,' Callahan said. 'It had an iron handle, and when I touched it, fire came out of it like a reverse stroke of lightning. It knocked me all the way down the steps and onto the cement path. It did this.' He raised his scarred right hand.

'And that?' Eddie asked, and pointed to his forehead.

'No,' Callahan said. 'That came later. I picked myself up. Walked some more. Wound up at Spencer's again. Only this time I went in. Bought a bandage for my hand. And then, while I was paying, I saw the sign. Ride The Big Gray Dog.'

'He means Greyhound, sugar,' Susannah told Roland. 'It's a nationwide bus company.'

Roland nodded and twirled a finger in his go-on gesture.

'Miss Coogan told me the next bus went to New York, so I bought a ticket on that one. If she'd told me it went to Jacksonville or Nome or Hot Burgoo, South Dakota, I would have gone to one of those places. All I wanted to do was get out of that town. I didn't care that people were dying and worse than dying, some of them my friends, some of them my parishioners. I just wanted to get *out*. Can you understand that?'

'Yes,' Roland said with no hesitation. 'Very well.'

Callahan looked into his face, and what he saw there seemed to reassure him a little. When he continued, he seemed calmer.

'Loretta Coogan was one of the town spinsters. I must have frightened her, because she said I'd have to wait for the bus outside. I went out. Eventually the bus came. I got on and gave the driver my ticket. He took his half and gave me my half. I sat down. The bus started to roll. We went under the flashing yellow blinker at the middle of town, and that was the first mile. The first mile on the road that took me here. Later on — maybe four-thirty in the morning, still dark outside — the bus stopped in'

7

'Hartford,' the bus driver says. 'This is Hartford, Mac. We got a twenty-minute rest stop. Do you want to go in and get a sandwich or something?'

Callahan fumbles his wallet out of his pocket with his bandaged hand and almost drops it. The taste of death is in his mouth, a moronic, mealy taste like a spoiled apple. He needs something to take away that taste, and if nothing will take it away something to change it, and if nothing will change it at least something to cover it up, the way you might cover up an ugly gouge in a wood floor with a piece of cheap carpet.

He holds out a twenty to the bus driver and says, 'Can you get me a bottle?'

'Mister, the rules—'

'And keep the change, of course. A pint would be fine.'

'I don't need nobody cutting up on my bus. We'll be in New York in two hours. You can get anything you want once we're there.' The bus driver tries to smile. 'It's Fun City, you know.'

Callahan — he's no longer Father Callahan, the flash of fire from the doorhandle answered that question, at least — adds a ten to the twenty. Now he's holding out thirty dollars. Again he tells the driver a pint would be fine, and he doesn't expect any change. This time the driver, not an idiot, takes the money. 'But don't you go cutting up on me,' he repeats. 'I don't need nobody cutting up on my bus.'

Callahan nods. No cutting up, that's a big ten-four. The driver goes into the combination grocery store–liquor store–short-order restaurant that exists here on the rim of Hartford, on the rim of morning, under yellow hi-intensity lights. There are secret highways in America, highways in hiding. This place stands at one of the entrance ramps leading into that network of darkside roads, and Callahan senses it. It's in the way the Dixie cups and crumpled cigarette packs blow across the tarmac in the pre-dawn wind. It whispers from the sign on the gas pumps, the one that says PAY FOR GAS IN ADVANCE AFTER SUNDOWN. It's in the teenage boy across the street, sitting on a porch stoop at four-thirty in the morning with his head in his arms, a silent essay in pain. The secret highways are out close, and they whisper to him. 'Come on, buddy,' they say. 'Here is where you can forget everything, even the name they tied on you when you were nothing but a naked, blatting baby still smeared with your mother's blood. They tied a name to you like a can to a dog's tail, didn't they? But you don't need to drag it around here. Come. Come on.' But he goes nowhere. He's waiting for the bus driver, and pretty soon the bus driver comes back, and he's got a pint of Old Log Cabin in a brown paper sack. This is a brand Callahan knows well, a pint of the stuff probably goes for two dollars and a quarter out here in the boonies, which means the bus driver has just earned himself a twenty-eight-dollar tip, give or take. Not bad. But it's the

American way, isn't it? Give a lot to get a little. And if the Log Cabin will take that terrible taste out of his mouth — much worse than the throbbing in his burned hand — it will be worth every penny of the thirty bucks. Hell, it would be worth a C-note.

'No cutting up,' the driver says. 'I'll put you out right in the middle of the Cross Bronx Expressway if you start cutting up. I swear to God I will.'

By the time the Greyhound pulls into the Port Authority, Don Callahan is drunk. But he doesn't cut up; he simply sits quietly until it's time to get off and join the flow of six o'clock humanity under the cold fluorescent lights: the junkies, the cabbies, the shoeshine boys, the girls who'll blow you for ten dollars, the boys dressed up as girls who'll blow you for five dollars, the cops twirling their nightsticks, the dope dealers carrying their transistor radios, the blue-collar guys who are just coming in from New Jersey, Callahan joins them, drunk but quiet; the nightstick-twirling cops do not give him so much as a second glance. The Port Authority air smells of cigarette smoke and joysticks and exhaust. The docked buses rumble. Everyone here looks cut loose. Under the cold white fluorescents, they all look dead.

No, *he thinks, walking under a sign reading* TO STREET. *Not dead, that's wrong.* Undead.

8

'Man,' Eddie said. 'You been to the wars, haven't you? Greek, Roman, and Vietnam.'

When the Old Fella began, Eddie had been hoping he'd gallop through his story so they could go into the church and look at whatever was stashed there. He hadn't expected to be touched, let alone shaken, but he had been. Callahan knew stuff Eddie thought no one else could possibly know: the sadness of Dixie cups rolling across the pavement, the rusty hopelessness of that sign on the gas pumps, the look of the human eye in the hour before dawn.

Most of all about how sometimes you had to have it.

'The wars? I don't know,' Callahan said. Then he sighed and nodded. 'Yes, I suppose so. I spent that first day in movie theaters and that first night in Washington Square Park. I saw that the other homeless people covered themselves up with newspapers, so that's what I did. And here's an example of how life — the quality of life and the texture of life — seemed to have changed for me, beginning on the day of Danny Glick's burial. You won't understand right away, but bear with me.' He looked at Eddie and smiled.

'And don't worry, son, I'm not going to talk the day away. Or even the morning.'

'You go on and tell it any old way it does ya fine,' Eddie said.

Callahan burst out laughing. 'Say thankya! Aye, say thankya big! What I was going to tell you is that I'd covered my top half with the *Daily News* and the headline said HITLER BROTHERS STRIKE IN QUEENS.'

'Oh my God, the Hitler Brothers,' Eddie said. 'I remember them. Couple of morons. They beat up . . . what? Jews? Blacks?'

'Both,' Callahan said. 'And carved swastikas on their foreheads. They didn't have a chance to finish mine. Which is good, because what they had in mind after the cutting was a lot more than a simple beating. And that was years later, when I came back to New York.'

'Swastika,' Roland said. 'The sigul on the plane we found near River Crossing? The one with David Quick inside it?'

'Uh-huh,' Eddie said, and drew one in the grass with the toe of his boot. The grass sprang up almost immediately, but not before Roland saw that yes, the mark on Callahan's forehead could have been meant to be one of those. If it had been finished.

'On that day in late October of 1975,' Callahan said, 'the Hitler Brothers were just a headline I slept under. I spent most of that second day in New York walking around and fighting the urge to score a bottle. There was part of me that wanted to fight instead of drink. To try and atone. At the same time, I could feel Barlow's blood working into me, getting in deeper and deeper. The world smelled different, and not better. Things *looked* different, and not better. And the taste of him came creeping back into my mouth, a taste like dead fish or rotten wine.

'I had no hope of salvation. Never think it. But atonement isn't about salvation, anyway. Not about heaven. It's about clearing your conscience here on earth. And you can't do it drunk. I didn't think of myself as an alcoholic, not even then, but I *did* wonder if he'd turned me into a vampire. If the sun would start to burn my skin, and I'd start looking at ladies' necks.' He shrugged, laughed. 'Or maybe gentlemen's. You know what they say about the priesthood; we're just a bunch of closet queers running around and shaking the cross in people's faces.'

'But you weren't a vampire,' Eddie said.

'Not even a Type Three. Nothing but unclean. On the outside of everything. Cast away. Always smelling his stink and always seeing the world the way things like him must see it, in shades of gray and red. Red was the only bright color I was allowed to see for years. Everything else was just a whisper.

'I guess I was looking for a ManPower office — you know, the day-labor company? I was still pretty rugged in those days, and of course I was a lot younger, as well.

'I didn't find ManPower. What I *did* find was a place called Home. This was on First Avenue and Forty-seventh Street, not far from the UN.'

Roland, Eddie, and Susannah exchanged a look. Whatever Home was, it had existed only two blocks from the vacant lot. *Only it wouldn't have been vacant back then*, Eddie thought. *Not back in 1975. In '75 it would still have been Tom and Jerry's Artistic Deli, Party Platters Our Specialty*. He suddenly wished Jake were here. Eddie thought that by now the kid would have been jumping up and down with excitement.

'What kind of shop was Home?' Roland asked.

'Not a shop at all. A shelter. A *wet* shelter. I can't say for sure that it was the only one in Manhattan, but I bet it was one of the very few. I didn't know much about shelters then — just a little bit from my first parish — but as time went by, I learned a great deal. I saw the system from both sides. There were times when I was the guy who ladled out the soup at six P.M. and passed out the blankets at nine; at other times I was the guy who drank the soup and slept under the blankets. After a head-check for lice, of course.

'There are shelters that won't let you in if they smell booze on your breath. And there are ones where they'll let you in if you claim you're at least two hours downstream from your last drink. There are places — a few — that'll let you in pissyassed drunk, as long as they can search you at the door and get rid of all your hooch. Once that's taken care of, they put you in a special locked room with the rest of the low-bottom guys. You can't slip out to get another drink if you change your mind, and you can't scare the folks who are less soaked than you are if you get the dt's and start seeing bugs come out of the walls. No women allowed in the lockup; they're too apt to get raped. It's just one of the reasons more homeless women die in the streets than homeless men. That's what Lupe used to say.'

'Lupe?' Eddie asked.

'I'll get to him, but for now, suffice it to say that he was the architect of Home's alcohol policy. At Home, they kept the *booze* in lockup, not the drunks. You could get a shot if you needed one, and if you promised to be quiet. Plus a sedative chaser. This isn't recommended medical procedure

— I'm not even sure it was legal, since neither Lupe nor Rowan Magruder were doctors — but it seemed to work. I came in sober on a busy night, and Lupe put me to work. I worked free for the first couple of days, and then Rowan called me into his office, which was roughly the size of a broom closet. He asked me if I was an alcoholic. I said no. He asked me if I was wanted by the police. I said no. He asked if I was on the run from anything. I said yes, from myself. He asked me if I wanted to work, and I started to cry. He took that as a yes.

'I spent the next nine months — until June of 1976 — working at Home. I made the beds, I cooked in the kitchen, I went on fund-raising calls with Lupe or sometimes Rowan, I took drunks to AA meetings in the Home van, I gave shots of booze to guys that were shaking too badly to hold the glasses themselves. I took over the books because I was better at it than Magruder or Lupe or any of the other guys who worked there. Those weren't the happiest days of my life, I'd never go that far, and the taste of Barlow's blood never left my mouth, but they were days of grace. I didn't think a lot. I just kept my head down and did whatever I was asked to do. I started to heal.

'Sometime during that winter, I realized that I'd started to change. It was as if I'd developed a kind of sixth sense. Sometimes I heard chiming bells. Horrible, yet at the same time sweet. Sometimes, when I was on the street, things would start to look dark even if the sun was shining. I can remember looking down to see if my shadow was still there. I'd be positive it wouldn't be, but it always was.'

Roland's ka-tet exchanged a glance.

'Sometimes there was an olfactory element to these fugues. It was a bitter smell, like strong onions all mixed with hot metal. I began to suspect that I had developed a form of epilepsy.'

'Did you see a doctor?' Susannah asked.

'I did not. I was afraid of what else he might find. A brain tumor seemed most likely. What I did was keep my head down and keep working. And then one night I went to a movie in Times Square. It was a revival of two Clint Eastwood Westerns. What they used to call Spaghetti Westerns?'

'Yeah,' Eddie said.

'I started hearing the bells. The chimes. And smelling that smell, stronger than ever. All this was coming from in front of me, and to the left. I looked there and saw two men, one rather elderly, the other younger. They were easy enough to pick out, because the place was three-quarters empty. The younger man leaned close to the older man. The older man never took his eyes off the screen, but he put his arm around the younger man's shoulders. If I'd seen that on any other night, I would have been pretty positive what was going on, but not that night. I watched. And I started to see a kind of dark blue light, first just around the younger man, then around both of them. It was like no other light I'd ever seen. It was like the darkness I felt sometimes on the street, when the chimes started to play in my head. Like the smell. You knew those things weren't there, and yet they were. And I understood. I didn't accept it – that came later – but I understood. The younger man was a vampire.'

He stopped, thinking about how to tell his tale. How to lay it out.

'I believe there are at least three types of vampires at work in our world. I call them Types One, Two, and Three. Type Ones are rare. Barlow was a Type One. They live very long lives, and may spend extended periods – fifty years, a hundred, maybe two hundred – in deep hibernation. When they're active, they're capable of making new vampires, what we call the undead. These undead are Type Twos. They are also capable of making new vampires, but they aren't cunning.' He looked at Eddie and Susannah. 'Have you seen *Night of the Living Dead*?'

Susannah shook her head. Eddie nodded.

'The undead in that movie were zombies, utterly brain-dead. Type Two vampires are more intelligent than that, but not much. They can't go out during the daylight hours. If they try, they are blinded, badly burned, or killed. Although I can't say for sure, I believe their life-spans are usually short. Not because the change from living and human to undead and vampire shortens life, but because the existences of Type Two vampires are extremely perilous.

'In most cases – this is what I believe, not what I know – Type Two vampires create other Type Two vampires, in a relatively small area. By this phase of the disease – and it *is* a disease – the Type One vampire, the king vampire, has usually moved on. In 'Salem's Lot, they actually killed the son of a bitch, one of what might have been only a dozen in the entire world.

'In other cases, Type Twos create Type Threes. Type Threes are like mosquitoes. They can't create more vampires, but they can feed. And feed. And feed.'

'Do they catch AIDS?' Eddie asked. 'I mean, you know what that is, right?'

'I know, although I never heard the term until the spring of 1983, when

I was working at the Lighthouse Shelter in Detroit and my time in America had grown short. Of course we'd known for almost ten years that there was *something*. Some of the literature called it GRID — Gay-Related Immune Deficiency. In 1982 there started to be newspaper articles about a new disease called "Gay Cancer," and speculations that it might be catching. On the street some of the men called it Fucksore Disease, after the blemishes it left. I don't believe that vampires die of it, or even get sick from it. But they can have it. And they can pass it on. Oh, yes. And I have *reason* to think that.' Callahan's lips quivered, then firmed.

'When this vampire-demon made you drink his blood, he gave you the ability to see these things,' Roland said.

'Yes.'

'All of them, or just the Threes? The little ones?'

'The little ones,' Callahan mused, then voiced a brief and humorless laugh. 'Yes. I like that. In any case, Threes are all I've ever seen, at least since leaving Jerusalem's Lot. But of course Type Ones like Barlow are very rare, and Type Twos don't last long. Their very hunger undoes them. They're always ravenous. Type Threes, however, can go out in daylight. And they take their principal sustenance from food, just as we do.'

'What did you do that night?' Susannah asked. 'In the theater?'

'Nothing,' Callahan said. 'My whole time in New York — my *first* time in New York — I did nothing until April. I wasn't sure, you see. I mean, my *heart* was sure, but my head refused to go along. And all the time, there was interference from the most simple thing of all: I was a dry alcoholic. An alcoholic is also a vampire, and that part of me was getting thirstier and thirstier, while the rest of me was trying to deny my essential nature. So I told myself I'd seen a couple of homosexuals canoodling in the movies, nothing more than that. As for the rest of it — the chimes, the smell, the dark-blue light around the young one — I convinced myself it was epilepsy, or a holdover from what Barlow had done to me, or both. And of course about Barlow I was right. His blood was awake inside me. It *saw*.'

'It was more than that,' Roland said.

Callahan turned to him.

'You went todash, Pere. Something was calling you from this world. The thing in your church, I suspect, although it would not have been in your church when you first knew of it.'

'No,' Callahan said. He was regarding Roland with wary respect. 'It was not. How do you know? Tell me, I beg.'

Roland did not. 'Go on,' he said. 'What happened to you next?'

'Lupe happened next,' Callahan said.

9

His last name was Delgado.

Roland registered only a moment of surprise at this — a widening of the eyes — but Eddie and Susannah knew the gunslinger well enough to understand that even this was extraordinary. At the same time they had become almost used to these coincidences that could not possibly be coincidences, to the feeling that each one was the click of some great turning cog.

Lupe Delgado was thirty-two, an alcoholic almost five one-day-at-a-time years from his last drink, and had been working at Home since 1974. Magruder had founded the place, but it was Lupe Delgado who invested it with real life and purpose. During his days, he was part of the maintenance crew at the Plaza Hotel, on Fifth Avenue. Nights, he worked at the shelter. He had helped to craft Home's 'wet' policy, and had been the first person to greet Callahan when he walked in.

'I was in New York a little over a year that first time,' Callahan said, 'but by March of 1976, I had . . .' He paused, struggling to say what all three of them understood from the look on his face. His skin had flushed rosy except for where the scar lay; that seemed to glow an almost preternatural white by comparison.

'Oh, okay, I suppose you'd say that by March I'd fallen in love with him. Does that make me a queer? A faggot? I don't know. They say we all are, don't they? Some do, anyway. And why not? Every month or two there seemed to be another story in the paper about a priest with a penchant for sticking his hand up the altar boys' skirts. As for myself, I had no reason to think of myself as queer. God knows I wasn't immune to the turn of a pretty female leg, priest or not, and molesting the altar boys never crossed my mind. Nor was there ever anything physical between Lupe and me. But I loved him, and I'm not just talking about his mind or his dedication or his ambitions for Home. Not just because he'd chosen to do his real work among the poor, like Christ, either. There was a physical attraction.'

Callahan paused, struggled, then burst out: 'God, he was beautiful. *Beautiful!*'

'What happened to him?' Roland asked.

'He came in one snowy night in late March. The place was full, and the natives were restless. There had already been one fistfight, and we were still picking up from that. There was a guy with a full-blown fit of the dt's, and Rowan Magruder had him in back, in his office, feeding him coffee laced with whiskey. As I think I told you, we had no lockup room at Home. It was dinnertime, half an hour past, actually, and three of the volunteers hadn't come in because of the weather. The radio was on and a couple of women were dancing. "Feeding time in the zoo," Lupe used to say.

'I was taking off my coat, heading for the kitchen . . . this fellow named Frank Spinelli collared me . . . wanted to know about a letter of recommendation I'd promised to write him . . . there was a woman, Lisa somebody, who wanted help with one of the AA steps, "Make a list of those we had harmed" . . . there was a young guy who wanted help with a job application, he could read a little but not write . . . something starting to burn on the stove . . . complete confusion. And I liked it. It had a way of sweeping you up and carrying you along. But in the middle of it all, I stopped. There were no bells and the only aromas were drunks' b.o. and burning food . . . but that light was around Lupe's neck like a collar. And I could see marks there. Just little ones. No more than nips, really.

'I stopped, and I must have reeled, because Lupe came hurrying over. And then I *could* smell it, just faintly: strong onions and hot metal. I must have lost a few seconds, too, because all at once the two of us were in the corner by the filing cabinet where we keep the AA stuff and he was asking me when I last ate. He knew I sometimes forgot to do that.

'The smell was gone. The blue glow around his neck was gone. And those little nips, where something had bitten him, they were gone, too. Unless the vampire's a real guzzler, the marks go in a hurry. But I knew. It was no good asking him who he'd been with, or when, or where. Vampires, even Type Threes — *especially* Type Threes, maybe — have their protective devices. Pond-leeches secrete an enzyme in their saliva that keeps the blood flowing while they're feeding. It also numbs the skin, so unless you actually see the thing on you, you don't know what's happening. With these Type Three vampires, it's as if they carry a kind of selective, short-term amnesia in their saliva.

'I passed it off somehow. Told him I'd just felt light-headed for a second or two, blamed it on coming out of the cold and into all the noise and light and heat. He accepted it but told me I had to take it easy. "You're too valuable to lose, Don," he said, and then he kissed me. Here.' Callahan touched his right cheek with his scarred right hand. 'So I guess I lied when I said there was nothing physical between us, didn't I? There was that one kiss. I can still remember exactly how it felt. Even the little prickle of fine stubble on his upper lip . . . here.'

'I'm so very sorry for you,' Susannah said.

'Thank you, my dear,' he said. 'I wonder if you know how much that means? How wonderful it is to have condolence from one's own world? It's like being a castaway and getting news from home. Or fresh water from a spring after years of stale bottled stuff.' He reached out, took her hand in both of his, and smiled. To Eddie, something in that smile looked forced, or even false, and he had a sudden ghastly idea. What if Pere Callahan was smelling a mixture of bitter onions and hot metal right now? What if he was seeing a blue glow, not around Susannah's neck like a collar, but around her stomach like a belt?

Eddie looked at Roland, but there was no help there. The gunslinger's face was expressionless.

'He had AIDS, didn't he?' Eddie asked. 'Some gay Type Three vampire bit your friend and passed it on to him.'

'Gay,' Callahan said. 'Do you mean to tell me that stupid word actually . . .' He trailed off, shaking his head.

'Yep,' Eddie said. 'The Red Sox still haven't won the Series and homos are gays.'

'Eddie!' Susannah said.

'Hey,' Eddie said, 'do you think it's easy being the one who left New York last and forgot to turn off the lights? Cause it's not. And let me tell you, I'm feeling increasingly out of date myself.' He turned back to Callahan. 'Anyway, that *is* what happened, isn't it?'

'I think so. You have to remember that I didn't know a great deal myself at that time, and was denying and repressing what I *did* know. With great vigor, as President Kennedy used to say. I saw the first one — the first "little one" — in that movie theater in the week between Christmas and New Year's of 1975.' He gave a brief, barking laugh. 'And now that I think back, that theater was called the Gaiety. Isn't that surprising?' He paused, looking into their faces with some puzzlement. 'It's not. You're not surprised at all.'

'Coincidence has been cancelled, honey,' Susannah said. 'What we're living in these days is more like the Charles Dickens version of reality.'

'I don't understand you.'

'You don't need to, sug. Go on. Tell your tale.'

The Old Fella took a moment to find the dropped thread, then went on.

'I saw my first Type Three in late December of 1975. By that night about three months later when I saw the blue glow around Lupe's neck, I'd come across half a dozen more. Only one of them at prey. He was down in an East Village alley with another guy. He – the vampire – was standing like this.' Callahan rose and demonstrated, arms out, palms propped against an invisible wall. 'The other one – the victim – was between his propped arms, facing him. They could have been talking. They could have been kissing. But I knew – I *knew* – that it wasn't either one.

'The others . . . I saw a couple in restaurants, both of them eating alone. That glow was all over their hands and their faces – smeared across their lips like . . . like electric blueberry juice – and the burned-onion smell hung around them like some kind of perfume.' Callahan smiled briefly. 'It strikes me how every description I try to make has some kind of simile buried in it. Because I'm not just trying to describe them, you know, I'm trying to understand them. Still trying to understand them. To figure out how there could have been this other world, this secret world, there all the time, right beside the one I'd always known.'

Roland's right, Eddie thought. *It's todash. Got to be. He doesn't know it, but it is. Does that make him one of us? Part of our ka-tet?*

'I saw one in line at Marine Midland Bank, where Home did its business,' Callahan said. 'Middle of the day. I was in the Deposit line, this woman was in Withdrawals. That light was all around her. She saw me looking at her and smiled. Fearless eye contact. Flirty.' He paused. 'Sexy.'

'You knew them, because of the vampire-demon's blood in you,' Roland said. 'Did they know you?'

'No,' Callahan said promptly. 'If they'd been able to see me – to isolate me – my life wouldn't have been worth a dime. Although they *came* to know about me. That was later, though.

'My point is, I saw them. I knew they were there. And when I saw what had happened to Lupe, I knew what had been at him. They see it, too. Smell it. Probably hear the chimes, as well. Their victims are marked, and after that more are apt to come, like bugs to a light. Or dogs, all determined to piss on the same telephone pole.

'I'm sure that night in March was the first time Lupe was bitten, because I never saw that glow around him before . . . or the marks on the side of his throat, which looked like no more than a couple of shaving nicks. But he was bitten repeatedly after that. It had something to do with the nature of the business we were in, working with transients. Maybe drinking alcohol-laced blood is a cheap high for them. Who knows?

'In any case, it was because of Lupe that I made my first kill. The first of many. This was in April . . .'

10

This is April and the air has finally begun to feel and smell like spring. Callahan has been at Home since five, first writing checks to cover end-of-the-month bills, then working on his culinary specialty, which he calls Toads n Dumplins Stew. The meat is actually stewing beef, but the colorful name amuses him.

He has been washing the big steel pots as he goes along, not because he needs to (one of the few things there's no shortage of at Home is cooking gear) but because that's the way his mother taught him to operate in the kitchen: clean as you go.

He takes a pot to the back door, holds it against his hip with one hand, turns the knob with his other hand. He goes out into the alley, meaning to toss the soapy water into the sewer grating out there, and then he stops. Here is something he has seen before, down in the Village, but then the two men — the one standing against the wall, the one in front of him, leaning forward with his hands propped against the bricks — were only shadows. These two he can see clearly in the light from the kitchen, and the one leaning back against the wall, seemingly asleep with his head turned to the side, exposing his neck, is someone Callahan knows.

It is Lupe.

Although the open door has lit up this part of the alley, and Callahan has made no effort to be quiet — has, in fact, been singing Lou Reed's 'Take a Walk on the Wild Side' — neither of them notices him. They are entranced. The man in front of Lupe looks to be about fifty, well dressed in a suit and a tie. Beside him, an expensive Mark Cross briefcase rests on the cobbles. This man's head is thrust forward and tilted. His open lips are sealed against the right side of Lupe's neck. What's under there? Jugular? Carotid? Callahan doesn't remember, nor does it matter. The chimes don't play this time, but the smell is overwhelming, so rank that tears burst from his eyes and clear mucus immediately begins to drip from his nostrils. The two men opposite him blaze with that dark blue light, and Callahan can see it swirling in rhythmic pulses. That's their breathing, *he thinks.* It's their breathing, stirring that shit around. Which means it's real.

Callahan can hear, very faintly, a liquid smooching sound. It's the sound you hear in a movie when a couple is kissing passionately, really pouring it on.

He doesn't think about what he does next. He puts down the potful of sudsy, greasy water. It clanks loudly on the concrete stoop, but the couple leaning against the alley wall opposite don't stir; they remain lost in their dream. Callahan takes two steps backward into the kitchen. On the counter is the cleaver he's been using to cube the stew-beef. Its blade gleams brightly. He can see his face in it and thinks, Well at least I'm not one; my reflection's still there. Then he closes his hand around the rubber grip. He walks back out into the alley. He steps over the pot of soapy water. The air is mild and damp. Somewhere water is dripping. Somewhere a radio is blaring 'Someone Saved My Life Tonight.' Moisture in the air makes a halo around the light on the far side of the alley. It's April in New York, and ten feet from where Callahan — not long ago an ordained priest of the Catholic Church — stands, a vampire is taking blood from his prey. From the man with whom Donald Callahan has fallen in love.

'Almost had your hooks in me, din'tcha, dear?' Elton John sings, and Callahan steps forward, raising the cleaver. He brings it down and it sinks deep into the vampire's skull. The sides of the vampire's face push out like wings. He raises his head suddenly, like a predator that has just heard the approach of something bigger and more dangerous than he is. A moment later he dips slightly at the knees, as if meaning to pick up the briefcase, then seems to decide he can do without it. He turns and walks slowly toward the mouth of the alley. Toward the sound of Elton John, who is now singing 'Someone saved, someone saved, someone saved my lii-iife tonight.' The cleaver is still sticking out of the thing's skull. The handle waggles back and forth with each step like a stiff little tail. Callahan sees some blood, but not the ocean he would have expected. At that moment he is too deep in shock to wonder about this, but later he will come to believe that there is precious little liquid blood in these beings; whatever keeps them moving, it's more magical than the miracle of blood. Most of what was their blood has coagulated as firmly as the yolk of a hard-cooked egg.

It takes another step, then stops. Its shoulders slump. Callahan loses sight of its head when it sags forward. And then, suddenly, the clothes are collapsing, crumpling in on themselves, drifting down to the wet surface of the alley.

Feeling like a man in a dream, Callahan goes forward to examine them. Lupe Delgado stands against the wall, head back, eyes shut, still lost in whatever dream the vampire has cast over him. Blood trickles down his neck in small and unimportant streams.

Callahan looks at the clothes. The tie is still knotted. The shirt is still inside the suit-coat, and still tucked into the suit-pants. He knows that if he unzipped the fly of those suit-pants, he would see the underwear inside. He picks up one arm of the coat, mostly to confirm its emptiness by touch as well as sight, and the vampire's watch tumbles out of the sleeve and lands with a clink beside what looks like a class ring.

There is hair. There are teeth, some with fillings. Of the rest of Mr Mark Cross Briefcase, there is no sign.

Callahan gathers up the clothes. Elton John is still singing 'Someone Saved My Life Tonight,' but maybe that's not surprising. It's a pretty long song, one of those four-minute jobs, must be. He puts the watch on his own wrist and the ring on one of his own fingers, just for temporary safekeeping. He takes the clothes inside, walking past Lupe. Lupe's still lost in his dream. And the holes in his neck, little bigger than pinpricks to start with, are disappearing.

The kitchen is miraculously empty. Off it, to the left, is a door marked STORAGE. *Beyond it is a short hall with compartments on both sides. These are behind locked gates made of heavy chickenwire, to discourage pilferage. Canned goods on one side, dry goods on the other. Then clothes. Shirts in one compartment. Pants in another. Dresses and skirts in another. Coats in yet another. At the very end of the hall is a beat-up wardrobe marked* MISCEL-LANY. *Callahan finds the vampire's wallet and sticks it in his pocket, on top of his own. The two of them together make quite a lump. Then he unlocks the wardrobe and tosses in the vampire's unsorted clothes. It's easier than trying to take his ensemble apart, although he guesses that when the underwear is found inside the pants, there will be grumbling. At Home, used underwear is not accepted.*

'We may cater to the low-bottom crowd,' Rowan Magruder has told Callahan once, 'but we do have our standards.'

Never mind their standards now. There's the vampire's hair and teeth to think about. His watch, his ring, his wallet . . . and God, his briefcase and his shoes! They must still be out there!

Don't you dare complain, *he tells himself.* Not when ninety-five per cent of him is gone, just conveniently disappeared like the monster in the last reel of a horror movie. God's been with you so far – I think it's God – so don't you dare complain.

Nor does he. He gathers up the hair, the teeth, the briefcase, and takes them to the end of the alley, splashing through puddles, and tosses them over the fence. After a moment's consideration he throws the watch, wallet, and ring over, too. The ring sticks on his finger for a moment and he almost panics, but at last it comes off and over it goes – plink. *Someone will take care of this stuff for him. This is New York, after all. He goes back to Lupe and sees the shoes. They are too good to throw away, he thinks; there are years of wear left in those babies. He picks them up and walks back into the kitchen with them dangling from the first two fingers of his right hand. He's standing there with them by the stove when Lupe comes walking into the kitchen from the alley.*

'Don?' he asks. His voice is a little furry, the voice of someone who has just awakened from a sound sleep. It also sounds amused. He points at the shoes hooked over the tips of Callahan's fingers. 'Were you going to put those in the stew?'

'It might improve the flavor, but no, just in storage,' Callahan says. He is astounded by the calmness of his own voice. And his heart! Beating along at a nice regular sixty or seventy beats a minute. 'Someone left them out back. What have you been up to?'

Lupe gives him a smile, and when he smiles, he is more beautiful than ever. 'Just out there, having a smoke,' he says. 'It was too nice to come in. Didn't you see me?'

'As a matter of fact, I did,' Callahan said. 'You looked lost in your own little world, and I didn't want to interrupt you. Open the storage-room door for me, would you?'

Lupe opens the door. 'That looks like a really nice pair,' he says. 'Bally. What's someone doing, leaving Bally shoes for the drunks?'

'Someone must have changed his mind about them,' Callahan says. He hears the bells, that poison sweetness, and grits his teeth against the sound. The world seems to shimmer for a moment. Not now, he thinks. Ah, not now, please.

It's not a prayer, he prays little these days, but maybe something hears, because the sound of the chimes fades. The world steadies. From the other room someone is bawling for supper. Someone else is cursing. Same old same old. And he wants a drink. That's the same, too, only the craving is fiercer than it's ever been. He keeps thinking about how the rubber grip felt in his hand. The weight of the cleaver. The sound it made. And the taste is back in his mouth. The dead taste of Barlow's blood. That, too. What did the vampire say in the Petries' kitchen, after it had broken the crucifix his mother had given him? That it was sad to see a man's faith fail.

I'll sit in on the AA meeting tonight, he thinks, putting a rubber band around the Bally loafers and tossing them in with the rest of the footwear. Sometimes the meetings help. He never says, 'I'm Don and I'm an alcoholic,' but sometimes they help.

Lupe is so close behind him when he turns around that he gasps a little.

'Easy, boy,' Lupe says, laughing. He scratches his throat casually. The marks are still there, but they'll be gone in the morning. Still, Callahan knows the vampires see something. Or smell it. Or some damn thing.

'Listen,' he says to Lupe, 'I've been thinking about getting out of the city for a week or two. A little R and R. Why don't we go together? We could go upstate. Do some fishing.'

'Can't,' Lupe says. 'I don't have any vacation time coming at the hotel until June, and besides, we're shorthanded here. But if you want to go, I'll square it with Rowan. No problem.' Lupe looks at him closely. 'You could use some time off, looks like. You look tired. And you're jumpy.'

'Nah, it was just an idea,' Callahan says. He's not going anywhere. If he stays, maybe he can watch out for Lupe. And he knows something now. Killing them is no harder than swatting bugs on a wall. And they don't leave much behind. E-Z Kleen-Up, as they say in the TV ads. Lupe will be all right. The Type Threes like Mr Mark Cross Briefcase don't seem to kill their prey, or even change them. At least not that he can see, not over the short *term. But he will watch, he can do that much. He will mount a guard. It will be one small act of atonement for Jerusalem's Lot. And Lupe will be all right.*

11

'Except he wasn't,' Roland said. He was carefully rolling a cigarette from the crumbs at the bottom of his poke. The paper was brittle, the tobacco really not much more than dust.

'No,' Callahan agreed. 'He wasn't. Roland, I have no cigarette papers, but I can do you better for a smoke than that. There's good tobacco in the house, from down south. I don't use it, but Rosalita sometimes likes a pipe in the evening.'

'I'll take you up on that later and say thankya,' the gunslinger said. 'I don't miss it as much as coffee, but almost. Finish your tale. Leave nothing out, I think it's important we hear it all, but—'

'I know. Time is short.'

'Yes,' Roland said. 'Time is short.'

'Then briefly put, my friend contracted this disease – AIDS became the name of choice?'

He was looking at Eddie, who nodded.

'All right,' Callahan said. 'It's as good a name as any, I guess, although the first thing I think of when I hear that word is a kind of diet candy. You may know it doesn't always spread fast, but in my friend's case, it moved like a fire in straw. By mid-May of 1976, Lupe Delgado was very ill. He lost his color. He was feverish a lot of the time. He'd sometimes spend the whole night in the bathroom, vomiting. Rowan would have banned him from the kitchen, but he didn't need to – Lupe banned himself. And then the blemishes began to show up.'

'They called those Kaposi's sarcoma, I think,' Eddie said. 'A skin disease. Disfiguring.'

Callahan nodded. 'Three weeks after the blemishes started showing up, Lupe was in New York General. Rowan Magruder and I went to see him one night in late June. Up until then we'd been telling each other he'd turn it around, come out of it better than ever, hell, he was young and strong. But that night we knew the minute we were in the door that he was all through. He was in an oxygen tent. There were IV lines running into his arms. He was in terrible pain. He didn't want us to get close to him. It might be catching, he said. In truth, no one seemed to know much about it.'

'Which made it scarier than ever,' Susannah said.

'Yes. He said the doctors believed it was a blood disease spread by homosexual activity, or maybe by sharing needles. And what he wanted us to know, what he kept saying over and over again, was that he was clean, all the drug tests came back negative. "Not since nineteen-seventy," he kept saying. "Not one toke off one joint. I swear to God." We said we knew he was clean. We sat on either side of his bed and he took our hands.'

Callahan swallowed. There was an audible click in his throat.

'Our hands ... he made us wash them before we left. Just in case, he said. And he thanked us for coming. He told Rowan that Home was the best thing that ever happened to him. That as far as he was concerned, it really *was* home.

'I never wanted a drink as badly as I did that night, leaving New York General. I kept Rowan right beside me, though, and the two of us walked past all the bars. That night I went to bed sober, but I lay there knowing it was really just a matter of time. The first drink is the one that gets you drunk, that's what they say in Alcoholics Anonymous, and mine was somewhere close. Somewhere a bartender was just waiting for me to come in so he could pour it out.

'Two nights later, Lupe died.

'There must have been three hundred people at the funeral, almost all of them people who'd spent time in Home. There was a lot of crying and a lot of wonderful things said, some by folks who probably couldn't have walked a chalk line. When it was over, Rowan Magruder took me by the arm and said, "I don't know who you are, Don, but I know *what* you are — one hell of a good man and one hell of a bad drunk who's been dry for ... how long has it been?"

'I thought about going on with the bullshit, but it just seemed like too much work. "Since October of last year," I said.

'"You want one now," he said. "That's all over your face. So I tell you what: if you think taking a drink will bring Lupe back, you have my permission. In fact, come get me and we'll go down to the Blarney Stone together and drink up what's in my wallet first. Okay?"

'"Okay," I said.

'He said, "You getting drunk today would be the worst memorial to Lupe I could think of. Like pissing in his dead face."

'He was right, and I knew it. I spent the rest of that day the way I spent my second one in New York, walking around, fighting that taste in my mouth, fighting the urge to score a bottle and stake out a park bench. I remember being on Broadway, then over on Tenth Avenue, then way down at Park and Thirtieth. By then it was getting dark, cars going both ways on Park with their lights on. The sky all orange and pink in the west, and the streets full of this gorgeous long light.

'A sense of peace came over me, and I thought, "I'm going to win. Tonight at least, I'm going to win." And that was when the chimes started. The loudest ever. I felt as if my head would burst. Park Avenue shimmered in front of me and I thought, *Why, it's not real at all. Not Park Avenue, not any of it. It's just a gigantic swatch of canvas. New York is nothing but a backdrop painted on that canvas, and what's behind it? Why, nothing. Nothing at all. Just blackness.*

'Then things steadied again. The chimes faded . . . faded . . . finally gone. I started to walk, very slowly. Like a man walking on thin ice. What I was afraid of was that if I stepped too heavily, I might plunge right out of the world and into the darkness behind it. I know that makes absolutely no sense – hell, I knew it then – but knowing a thing doesn't always help. Does it?'

'No,' Eddie said, thinking of his days snorting heroin with Henry.

'No,' said Susannah.

'No,' Roland agreed, thinking of Jericho Hill. Thinking of the fallen horn.

'I walked one block, then two, then three. I started to think it was going to be okay. I mean, I might get the bad smell, and I might see a few Type Threes, but I could handle those things. Especially since the Type Threes didn't seem to recognize me. Looking at them was like looking through one-way glass at suspects in a police interrogation room. But that night I saw something much, much worse than a bunch of vampires.'

'You saw someone who was actually dead,' Susannah said.

Callahan turned to her with a look of utter, flabbergasted surprise. 'How . . . how do you . . .'

'I know because I've been todash in New York, too,' Susannah said. 'We all have. Roland says those are people who either don't know they've passed on or refuse to accept it. They're . . . what'd you call em, Roland?'

'The vagrant dead,' the gunslinger replied. 'There aren't many.'

'There were enough,' Callahan said, 'and *they* knew I was there. Mangled people on Park Avenue, one of them a man without eyes, one a woman missing the arm and leg on the right side of her body and burned all over, both of them looking at *me*, as if they thought I could . . . *fix* them, somehow.

'I ran. And I must have run one hell of a long way, because when I came back to something like sanity, I was sitting on the curb at Second Avenue and Nineteenth Street, head hung down, panting like a steam engine.

'Some old geezer came along and asked if I was all right. By then I'd caught enough of my breath to tell him that I was. He said that in that case I'd better move along, because there was an NYPD radio-car just a couple of blocks away and it was coming in our direction. They'd roust me for sure, maybe bust me. I looked the old guy in the eyes and said, "I've seen vampires. Killed one, even. And I've seen the walking dead. Do you think I'm afraid of a couple of cops in a radio-car?"

'He backed off. Said to keep away from him. Said I'd looked okay, so he tried to do me a favor. Said this was what he got. "In New York, no good deed goes unpunished," he said, and stomped off down the street like a kid having a tantrum.

'I started laughing. I got up off the curb and looked down at myself. My shirt was untucked all the way around. I had crud on my pants from running into something, I couldn't even remember what. I looked around, and there by all the saints and all the sinners was the Americano Bar. I found out later there are several of them in New York, but I thought then that one had moved down from the Forties just for me. I went inside, took the stool at the end of the bar, and when the bartender came down, I said, "You've been keeping something for me."

'"Is that so, my pal?" he said.

'"Yes," I said.

'"Well," he said, "you tell me what it is, and I'll get it for you."

'"It's Bushmill's, and since you've had it since last October, why don't you add the interest and make it a double."'

Eddie winced. 'Bad idea, man.'

'Right then it seemed like the finest idea ever conceived by the mind of mortal man. I'd forget Lupe, stop seeing dead people, perhaps even stop seeing the vampires . . . the mosquitoes, as I came to think of them.

'By eight o'clock I was drunk. By nine, I was very drunk. By ten, I was as drunk as I'd ever been. I have a vague memory of the barman throwing me out. A slightly better one of waking up the next morning in the park, under a blanket of newspapers.'

'Back to the beginning,' Susannah murmured.

'Aye, lady, back to the beginning, you say true, I say thankya. I sat up. I thought my head was going to split wide open. I put it down between my knees, and when it didn't explode, I raised it again. There was an old woman sitting on a bench about twenty yards away from me, just an old lady with a kerchief on her head feeding the squirrels from a paper bag filled with nuts. Only that blue light was crawling all over her cheeks and brow, going into and out of her mouth when she breathed. She was one of *them*. A mosquito. The walking dead were gone, but I could still see the Type Threes.

'Getting drunk again seemed like a logical response to this, but I had one small problem: no money. Someone had apparently rolled me while I was sleeping it off under my newspaper blanket, and there goes your ball-game.' Callahan smiled. There was nothing pleasant about it.

'That day I *did* find ManPower. I found it the next day, too, and the day after that. Then I got drunk. That became my habit during the Summer of the Tall Ships: work three days sober, usually shoving a wheelbarrow on some construction site or lugging big boxes for some company moving floors, then spend one night getting enormously drunk and the next day recovering. Then start all over again. Take Sundays off. That was my life in New York that summer. And everywhere I went, it seemed that I heard that Elton John song, "Someone Saved My Life Tonight." I don't know if that was the summer it was popular or not. I only know I heard it everywhere. Once I worked five days straight for Covay Movers. The Brother Outfit, they called themselves. For sobriety, that was my personal best that July. The guy in charge came up to me on the fifth day and asked me how I'd like to hire on full-time.

'"I can't," I said. "The day-labor contracts specifically forbid their guys from taking a steady job with any outside company for a month."

'"Ah, fuck that," he says, "everyone winks at that bullshit. What do you say, Donnie? You're a good man. And I got an idea you could do a little more than buck furniture up on the truck. You want to think about it tonight?"

'I thought about it, and thinking led back to drinking, as it always did that summer. As it always does for those of the alcoholic persuasion. Back to me sitting in some little bar across from the Empire State Building, listening to Elton John on the juke-box. "Almost had your hooks in me, din'tcha, dear?" And when I went back to work, I checked in with a different day-labor company, one that had never heard of the fucking Brother Outfit.'

Callahan spat out the word *fucking* in a kind of desperate snarl, as men do when vulgarity has become for them a kind of linguistic court of last resort.

'You drank, you drifted, you worked,' Roland said. 'But you had at least one other piece of business that summer, did you not?'

'Yes. It took me a little while to get going. I saw several of them – the woman feeding the squirrels in the park was only the first – but they weren't doing anything. I mean, I knew what they were, but it was still hard to kill them in cold blood. Then, one night in Battery Park, I saw another one feeding. I had a fold-out knife in my pocket by then, carried it everywhere. I walked up behind him while he was eating and stabbed him four times: once in the kidneys, once between the ribs, once high up in the back, once in the neck. I put all my strength into the last one. The knife came out the other side with the thing's Adam's apple skewered on it like a piece of steak on a shish kebab. Made a kind of ripping sound.'

Callahan spoke matter-of-factly, but his face had grown very pale.

'What had happened in the alley behind Home happened again – the guy disappeared right out of his clothes. I'd expected it, but of course I couldn't be sure until it actually happened.'

'One swallow does not make a summer,' Susannah said.

Callahan nodded. 'The victim was this kid of about fifteen, looked Puerto Rican or maybe Dominican. He had a boombox between his feet. I don't remember what it was playing, so it probably wasn't "Someone Saved My Life Tonight." Five minutes went by. I was about to start snapping my fingers under his nose or maybe patting his cheeks, when he blinked, staggered, shook his head, and came around. He saw me standing there in front of him and the first thing he did was grab his boombox. He held it to his chest, like it was a baby. Then he said, "What *joo* want, man?" I said I didn't want anything, not a single thing, no harm and no foul, but I *was* curious about those clothes lying beside him. The kid looked, then knelt down and started going through the pockets. I thought he'd find enough to keep him occupied – more than enough – and so I just walked away. And that was the second one. The third one was easier. The fourth one, easier still. By the end of August, I'd gotten half a dozen. The sixth was the woman I'd seen in the Marine Midland Bank. Small world, isn't it?

'Quite often I'd go down to First and Forty-seventh and stand across from Home. Sometimes I'd find myself there in the late afternoon, watching the drunks and the homeless people showing up for dinner. Sometimes Rowan would come out and talk to them. He didn't smoke, but he always kept cigarettes in his pockets, a couple of packs, and he'd pass them out until they were gone. I never made any particular effort to hide from him, but if he ever pegged me, I never saw any sign of it.'

'You'd probably changed by then,' Eddie said.

Callahan nodded. 'Hair down to my shoulders, and coming in gray. A beard. And of course I no longer took any pains about my clothes. Half of what I was wearing by then came from the vampires I'd killed. One of them was a bicycle messenger guy, and he had a *great* pair of motorcycle boots. Not Bally loafers, but almost new, and my size. Those things last forever. I've still got them.' He nodded toward the house. 'But I don't think any of that was why he didn't recognize me. In Rowan Magruder's business, dealing with drunks and hypes and homeless people who've got one foot in reality and the other in the Twilight Zone, you get used to seeing big changes in people, and usually not changes for the better. You teach yourself to see who's under the new bruises and the fresh coats of dirt. I think it was more like I'd become one of what you call the vagrant dead, Roland. Invisible to the world. But I think those people – those *former* people – must be tied to New York—'

'They never go far,' Roland agreed. His cigarette was done; the dry paper and crumbles of tobacco had disappeared up to his fingernails in two puffs. 'Ghosts always haunt the same house.'

'Of course they do, poor things. And I wanted to leave. Every day the sun would set a little earlier, and every day I'd feel the call of those roads, those highways in hiding, a little more strongly. Some of it might have been the fabled geographic cure, to which I believe I have already alluded. It's a wholly illogical but nonetheless powerful belief that things will change for the better in a new place; that the urge to self-destruct will magically disappear. Some of it was undoubtedly the hope that in another place, a *wider* place, there would be no more vampires or walking dead people to cope with. But mostly it was other things. Well . . . one very big thing.' Callahan smiled, but it was no more than a stretch of the lips exposing the gums. 'Someone had begun hunting me.'

'The vampires,' Eddie said.

'Ye-ess . . .' Callahan bit at his lip, then repeated it with a little more conviction. 'Yes. But not *just* the vampires. Even when that had to be the most logical idea, it didn't seem entirely right. I knew it wasn't the dead, at least; they could see me, but didn't care about me one way or another, except maybe for the hope that I might be able to fix them or put them out of their misery. But the Type Threes *couldn't* see me, as I've told you — not as the thing hunting them, anyway. And their attention spans are short, as if they're infected to some degree by the same amnesia they pass on to their victims.

'I first became aware that I was in trouble one night in Washington Square Park, not long after I killed the woman from the bank. That park had become a regular haunt of mine, although God knows I wasn't the only one. In the summer it was a regular open-air dormitory. I even had my own favorite bench, although I didn't get it every night . . . didn't even *go* there every night.

'On this particular evening — thundery and sultry and close — I got there around eight o'clock. I had a bottle in a brown bag and a book of Ezra Pound's Cantos. I approached the bench, and there, spray-painted across the back of another bench near mine, I saw a graffito that said HE COMES HERE. HE HAS A BURNED HAND.'

'Oh my Lord God,' Susannah said, and put a hand to her throat.

'I left the park at once and slept in an alley twenty blocks away. There was no doubt in my mind that I was the subject of that graffito. Two nights later I saw one on the sidewalk outside a bar on Lex where I liked to drink and sometimes have a sandwich if I was, as they say, in funds. It had been done in chalk and the foot-traffic had rubbed it to a ghost, but I could still read it. It said the same thing: HE COMES HERE. HE HAS A BURNED HAND. There were comets and stars around the message, as if whoever wrote it had actually tried to dress it up. A block down, spray-painted on a No Parking sign: HIS HAIR IS MOSTLY WHITE NOW. The next morning, on the side of a cross-town bus: HIS NAME MIGHT BE COLLINGWOOD. Two or three days after that, I started to see lost-pet posters around a lot of the places that had come to be my places — Needle Park, the Central Park West side of The Ramble, the City Lights bar on Lex, a couple of folk music and poetry clubs down in the Village.'

'*Pet* posters,' Eddie mused. 'You know, in a way that's brilliant.'

'They were all the same,' Callahan said. 'HAVE YOU SEEN OUR IRISH SETTER? HE IS A STUPID OLD THING BUT WE LOVE HIM. BURNED RIGHT FOREPAW. ANSWERS TO THE NAME OF KELLY, COLLINS, OR COLLINGWOOD. WE WILL PAY A VERY LARGE REWARD. And then a row of dollar signs.'

'Who would posters like that be aimed at?' Susannah asked.

Callahan shrugged. 'Don't know, exactly. The vampires, perhaps.'

Eddie was rubbing his face wearily. 'All right, let's see. We've got the Type

Three vampires . . . and the vagrant dead . . . and now this third group. The ones that went around putting up lost-pet posters that weren't about pets and writing stuff on buildings and sidewalks. Who were they?'

'The low men,' Callahan said. 'They call themselves that, sometimes, although there are women among them. Sometimes they call themselves regulators. A lot of them wear long yellow coats . . . but not all. A lot of them have blue coffins tattooed on their hands . . . but not all.'

'Big Coffin Hunters, Roland,' Eddie murmured.

Roland nodded but never took his eyes from Callahan. 'Let the man talk, Eddie.'

'What they are — what they *really* are — is soldiers of the Crimson King,' Callahan said. And he crossed himself.

12

Eddie started. Susannah's hand went back to her belly and began to rub. Roland found himself remembering their walk through Gage Park after they had finally escaped Blaine. The dead animals in the zoo. The run-to-riot rose garden. The carousel and the toy train. Then the metal road leading up to the even larger metal road which Eddie, Susannah, and Jake called a turnpike. There, on one sign, someone had slashed **WATCH FOR THE WALKIN DUDE**. And on another sign, decorated with the crude drawing of an eye, this message: **ALL HAIL THE CRIMSON KING!** 'You've heard of the gentleman, I see,' Callahan said dryly.

'Let's say he's left his mark where we could see it, too,' Susannah said.

Callahan nodded his head in the direction of Thunderclap. 'If your quest takes you there,' he said, 'you're going to see a hell of a lot more than a few signs spray-painted on a few walls.'

'What about you?' Eddie asked. 'What did you do?'

'First, I sat down and considered the situation. And decided that, no matter how fantastic or paranoid it might sound to an outsider, I really was being stalked, and not necessarily by Type Three vampires. Although of course I did realize that the people leaving the graffiti around and putting up the lost-pet posters wouldn't scruple to use the vampires against me.

'At this point, remember, I had no idea who this mysterious group could be. Back in Jerusalem's Lot, Barlow moved into a house that had seen terrible violence and was reputed to be haunted. The writer, Mears, said that an evil house had drawn an evil man. My best thinking in New York took me back to that idea. I began to think I'd drawn another king vampire, another Type One, the way the Marsten House had drawn Barlow. Right idea or wrong one (it turned out to be wrong), I found it comforting to know my brain, booze-soaked or not, was still capable of some logic.

'The first thing I had to decide was whether to stay in New York or run away. I knew if I *didn't* run, they'd catch up to me, and probably sooner rather than later. They had a description, with this as an especially good marker.' Callahan raised his burned hand. 'They *almost* had my name; would have it for sure in another week or two. They'd stake out all my regular stops, places where my scent had collected. They'd find people I'd talked to, hung out with, played checkers and cribbage with. People I'd worked with on my ManPower and Brawny Man jobs, too.

'This led me to a place I should have gotten to much sooner, even after a month of binge drinking. I realized they'd find Rowan Magruder and Home and all sorts of other people who knew me there. Part-time workers, volunteers, dozens of clients. Hell, after nine months, *hundreds* of clients.

'On top of that, there was the lure of those roads.' Callahan looked at Eddie and Susannah. 'Do you know there's a footbridge over the Hudson River to New Jersey? It's practically in the shadow of the GWB, a plank footbridge that still has a few wooden drinking troughs for cows and horses along one side.'

Eddie laughed the way a man will when he realizes one of his lower appendages is being shaken briskly. 'Sorry, Father, but that's impossible. I've been over the George Washington Bridge maybe five hundred times in my life. Henry and I used to go to Palisades Park all the time. There's no plank bridge.'

'There is, though,' Callahan said calmly. 'It goes back to the early nineteenth century, I should say, although it's been repaired quite a few times since then. In fact, there's a sign halfway across that says BICENTENNIAL REPAIRS COMPLETED 1975 BY LaMERK INDUSTRIES. I recalled that name the first time I saw Andy the robot. According to the plate on his chest, that's the company that made him.'

'We've seen the name before, too,' Eddie said. 'In the city of Lud. Only there it said LaMerk *Foundry*.'

'Different divisions of the same company, probably,' Susannah said.

Roland said nothing, only made that impatient twirling gesture with the remaining two fingers of his right hand: hurry up, hurry up.

'It's there, but it's hard to see,' Callahan said. 'It's in hiding. And it's only the first of the secret ways. From New York they radiate out like a spider's web.'

'Todash turnpikes,' Eddie murmured. 'Dig the concept.'

'I don't know if that's right or not,' Callahan said. 'I only know I saw extraordinary things in my wanderings over the next few years, and I also met a lot of good people. It seems almost an insult to call them normal people, or ordinary people, but they were both. And certainly they give such words as *normal* and *ordinary* a feel of nobility for me.

'I didn't want to leave New York without seeing Rowan Magruder again. I wanted him to know that maybe I *had* pissed in Lupe's dead face — I'd gotten drunk, surely enough — but I hadn't dropped my pants all the way down and done the other thing. Which is my too-clumsy way of saying I hadn't given up entirely. And that I'd decided not just to cower like a rabbit in a flashlight beam.'

Callahan had begun to weep again. He wiped at his eyes with the sleeves of his shirt. 'Also, I suppose I wanted to say goodbye to someone, and have someone say goodbye to me. The goodbyes we speak and the goodbyes we hear are the goodbyes that tell us we're still alive, after all. I wanted to give him a hug, and pass along the kiss Lupe had given me. Plus the same message: You're too valuable to lose. I—'

He saw Rosalita hurrying down the lawn with her skirt twitched up slightly at the ankle, and broke off. She handed him a flat piece of slate upon which something had been chalked. For a wild moment Eddie imagined a message flanked by stars and moons: LOST! ONE STRAY DOG WITH MANGLED FRONT PAW! ANSWERS TO THE NAME OF *ROLAND*! BAD-TEMPERED, PRONE TO BITE, *BUT WE LOVE HIM ANYWAY!!!*

'It's from Eisenhart,' Callahan said, looking up. 'If Overholser's the big farmer in these parts, and Eben Took's the big businessman, then you'd have to call Vaughn Eisenhart the big rancher. He says that he, Slightman Elder and Younger, and your Jake would meet us at Our Lady falls noon, if it do ya fine. It's hard to make out his shorthand, but I think he'd have you visit farms, smallholds, and ranches on your way back out to the Rocking B, where you'd spend the night. Does it do ya?'

'Not quite,' Roland said. 'I'd much like to have my map before I set off.'

Callahan considered this, then looked at Rosalita. Eddie decided the woman was probably a lot more than just a housekeeper. She had withdrawn out of earshot, but not all the way back to the house. *Like a good executive secretary*, he thought. The Old Fella didn't need to beckon her; she came forward at his glance. They spoke, and then Rosalita set off.

'I think we'll take our lunch on the church lawn,' Callahan said. 'There's a pleasant old ironwood there that'll shade us. By the time we're done, I'm sure the Tavery twins will have something for you.'

Roland nodded, satisfied.

Callahan stood up with a wince, put his hands in the small of his back, and stretched. 'And I have something to show you now,' he said.

'You haven't finished your story,' Susannah said.

'No,' Callahan agreed, 'but time has grown short. I can walk and talk at the same time, if you fellows can walk and listen.'

'We can do that,' Roland said, getting up himself. There was pain, but not a great deal of it. Rosalita's cat-oil was something to write home about. 'Just tell me two things before we go.'

'If I can, gunslinger, and do 'ee fine.'

'They of the signs: did you see them in your travels?'

Callahan nodded slowly. 'Aye, gunslinger, so I did.' He looked at Eddie and Susannah. 'Have you ever seen a color photo of people — one taken with a flash — where everyone's eyes are red?'

'Yeah,' Eddie said.

'Their eyes are like that. Crimson eyes. And your second question, Roland?'

'Are they the Wolves, Pere? These low men? These soldiers of the Crimson King? Are they the Wolves?'

Callahan hesitated a long time before replying. 'I can't say for sure,' he said at last. 'Not a hundred per cent, kennit. But I don't think so. Yet certainly they're kidnappers, although it's not just children they take.' He thought over what he'd said. 'Wolves of a kind, perhaps.' He hesitated, thought it over some more, then said it again: 'Aye, Wolves of a kind.'

CHAPTER IV

THE PRIEST'S TALE CONTINUED (HIGHWAYS IN HIDING)

1

The walk from the back yard of the rectory to the front door of Our Lady of Serenity was a short one, taking no more than five minutes. That was surely not enough time for the Old Fella to tell them about the years he had spent on the bum before seeing a news story in the Sacramento *Bee* which had brought him back to New York in 1981, and yet the three gunslingers heard the entire tale, nevertheless. Roland suspected that Eddie and Susannah knew what this meant as well as he did: when they moved on from Calla Bryn Sturgis — always assuming they didn't die here — there was every likelihood that Donald Callahan would be moving on with them. This was not just storytelling but khef, the sharing of water. And, leaving the touch, which was a different matter, to one side, khef could only be shared by those whom destiny had welded together for good or for ill. By those who were ka-tet.

Callahan said, 'Do you know how folks say, "We're not in Kansas anymore, Toto?"'

'The phrase has some vague resonance for us, sugar, yes,' Susannah said dryly.

'Does it? Yes, I see just looking at you that it does. Perhaps you'll tell me your own story someday. I have an idea it would put mine to shame. In any case, I knew I wasn't in Kansas anymore as I approached the far end of the footbridge. And it seemed that I wasn't entering New Jersey, either. At least not the one I'd always expected to find on the other side of the Hudson. There was a newspaper crumpled against the'

2

footrail of the bridge — which seems completely deserted except for him, although vehicle traffic on the big suspension bridge to his left is heavy and constant — and Callahan bends to pick it up. The cool wind blowing along the river ruffles his shoulder-length salt-and-pepper hair.

There's only one folded sheet, but the top of it's the front page of the Leabrook Register. *Callahan has never heard of Leabrook. No reason he should have, he's no New Jersey scholar, hasn't even been over there since arriving in Manhattan the previous year, but he always thought the town on the other side of the GWB was Fort Lee.*

Then his mind is taken over by the headlines. The one across the top seems right enough; RACIAL TENSIONS IN MIAMI EASE, *it reads. The New York papers have been full of these troubles over the last few days. But what to make of* WAR OF KITES CONTINUES IN TEANECK, HACKENSACK, *complete with a picture of a burning building? There's a photo of firemen arriving on a pumper, but they are all laughing! What to make of* PRESIDENT AGNEW SUPPORTS NASA TERRAFORM DREAM? *What to make of the item at the bottom, written in Cyrillic?*

What has happened to me? *Callahan asks himself. All through the business of the vampires and the walking dead — even through the appearance of lost-pet posters which clearly refer to him — he has never questioned his sanity. Now, standing on the New Jersey end of this humble (and most remarkable!) footbridge across the Hudson — this footbridge which is being utilized by no one except himself — he finally does. The idea of Spiro Agnew as President is enough all by itself, he thinks, to make anyone with a speck of political sense doubt his sanity. The man resigned in disgrace years ago, even before his boss did.*

What has happened to me? *he wonders, but if he's a raving lunatic imagining all of this, he really doesn't want to know.*

'Bombs away,' he says, and tosses the four-page remnant of the Leabrook Register *over the railing of the bridge. The breeze catches it and carries it away toward the George Washington.* That's reality, *he thinks,* right over there. Those cars, those trucks, those Peter Pan charter buses. *But then, among them, he sees a red vehicle that appears to be speeding along on a number of circular treads. Above the vehicle's body — it's about as long as a medium-sized schoolbus — a crimson cylinder is turning.* BANDY, *it says on one side.* BROOKS, *it says on the other.* BANDY BROOKS. *Or* BANDYBROOKS. *What the hell's Bandy Brooks? He has no idea. Nor has he ever seen such a vehicle in his life, and would not have believed such a thing — look at the* treads, *for heaven's sake — would have been allowed on a public highway.*

So the George Washington Bridge isn't the safe world, either. Or not anymore.

Callahan grabs the railing of the footbridge and squeezes down tightly as a wave of

dizziness courses through him, making him feel unsteady on his feet and unsure of his
balance. The railing feels real enough, wood warmed by the sun and engraved with thou-
sands of interlocking initials and messages. He sees DK L MB *in a heart. He sees* FREDDY
& HELENA = TRU LUV. *He sees* KILL ALL SPIX AND NIGERS, *the message flanked by*
swastikas, and wonders at verbal depletion so complete the sufferer cannot even spell his
favorite epithets. Messages of hate, messages of love, and all of them as real as the rapid
beating of his heart or the weight of the few coins and bills in the right front pocket of
his jeans. He takes a deep breath of the breeze, and that's real, too, right down to the tang
of diesel fuel.

This is happening to me, I know it is, *he thinks.* I am *not* in some psychi-
atric hospital's Ward 9. I am me, I am here, and I'm even sober – at least
for the time being – and New York is at my back. So is the town of
Jerusalem's Lot, Maine, with its uneasy dead. Before me is the weight of
America, with all its possibilities.

This thought lifts him, and is followed by one that lifts him even higher: not just one
America, perhaps, but a dozen . . . or a thousand . . . or a million. If that's Leabrook over
there instead of Fort Lee, maybe there's another version of New Jersey where the town on
the other side of the Hudson is Leeman or Leighman or Lee Bluffs or Lee Palisades or
Leghorn Village. Maybe instead of forty-two continental United States on the other side of
the Hudson, there are forty-two hundred, or forty-two thousand, all of them stacked in
vertical geographies of chance.

And he understands instinctively that this is almost certainly true. He has stumbled upon
a great, possibly endless, confluence of worlds. They are all America, but they are all different.
There are highways which lead through them, and he can see them.

He walks rapidly to the Leabrook end of the footbridge, then pauses again. Suppose I
can't find my way back? *he thinks.* Suppose I get lost and wander and never
find my way back to the America where Fort Lee is on the west side of
the George Washington Bridge and Gerald Ford (of all people!) is the
President of the United States?

And then he thinks: So what if I do? So fucking what?

When he steps off on the Jersey side of the footbridge he's grinning, truly lighthearted for
this first time since the day he presided over Danny Glick's grave in the town of Jerusalem's
Lot. A couple of boys with fishing poles are walking toward him. 'Would one of you young
fellows care to welcome me to New Jersey?' Callahan asks, grinning more widely than ever.

'Welcome to En-Jay, man,' one of them says, willingly enough, but both of them give
Callahan a wide berth and a careful look. He doesn't blame them, but it doesn't cut into
his splendid mood in the slightest. He feels like a man who has been let out of a gray and
cheerless prison on a sunny day. He begins to walk faster, not turning around to give the

skyline of Manhattan a single goodbye glance. Why would he? Manhattan is the past. The multiple Americas which lie ahead of him, those are the future.

He is in Leabrook. There are no chimes. Later there will be chimes and vampires; later there will be more messages chalked on sidewalks and sprayed on brick walls (not all about him, either). Later he will see the low men in their outrageous red Cadillacs and green Lincolns and purple Mercedes-Benz sedans, low men with red flashgun eyes, but not today. Today there is sunshine in a new America on the west side of a restored footbridge across the Hudson.

On Main Street he stops in front of the Leabrook Homestyle Diner and there is a sign in the window reading SHORT-ORDER COOK WANTED. Don Callahan short-ordered through most of his time at seminary and did more than his share of the same at Home on the East Side of Manhattan. He thinks he might fit right in here at the Leabrook Homestyle. Turns out he's right, although it takes three shifts before the ability to crack a pair of eggs one-handed onto the grill comes swimming back to him. The owner, a long drink of water named Dicky Rudebacher, asks Callahan if he has any medical problems — 'catching stuff,' he calls it — and nods simple acceptance when Callahan says he doesn't. He doesn't ask Callahan for any paperwork, not so much as a Social Security number. He wants to pay his new short-order off the books, if that's not a problem. Callahan assures him it is not.

'One more thing,' says Dicky Rudebacher, and Callahan waits for the shoe to drop. Nothing would surprise him, but all Rudebacher says is: 'You look like a drinking man.'

Callahan allows as how he has been known to take a drink.

'So have I,' Rudebacher says. 'In this business it's the way you protect your gahdam sanity. I ain't gonna smell your breath when you come in . . . if you come in on time. Miss coming in on time twice, though, and you're on your way to wherever. I ain't going to tell you that again.'

Callahan short-orders at the Leabrook Homestyle Diner for three weeks, and stays two blocks down at the Sunset Motel. Only it's not always the Homestyle, and it's not always the Sunset. On his fourth day in town, he wakes up in the Sunrise Motel, and the Leabrook Homestyle Diner is the Fort Lee Homestyle Diner. The Leabook Register which people have been leaving behind on the counter becomes the Fort Lee Register-American. He is not exactly relieved to discover Gerald Ford has reassumed the Presidency.

When Rudebacher pays him at the end of his first week — in Fort Lee — Grant is on the fifties, Jackson is on the twenties, and Alexander Hamilton is on the single ten in the envelope the boss hands him. At the end of the second week — in Leabrook — Abraham Lincoln is on the fifties and someone named Chadbourne is on the ten. It's still Andrew Jackson on the twenties, which is something of a relief. In Callahan's motel room, the bedcover is pink in Leabrook and orange in Fort Lee. This is handy. He always knows which version of New Jersey he's in as soon as he wakes up.

Twice he gets drunk. The second time, after closing, Dicky Rudebacher joins him and matches him drink for drink. 'This used to be a great country,' the Leabrook version of Rudebacher mourns, and Callahan thinks how great it is that some things don't change; the fundamental bitch and moans apply as time goes by.

But his shadow starts getting longer earlier each day, he has seen his first Type Three vampire waiting in line to buy a ticket at the Leabrook Twin Cinema, and one day he gives notice.

'Thought you told me you didn't have anything,' Rudebacher says to Callahan.

'Beg your pardon?'

'You've got a bad case of itchy-foot, my friend. It often goes with the other thing.' Rudebacher makes a bottle-tipping gesture with one dishwater-reddened hand. 'When a man catches itchy-foot late in life, it's often incurable. Tell you what, if I didn't have a wife that's still a pretty good lay and two kids in college, I might just pack me a bindle and join you.'

'Yeah?' Callahan asks, fascinated.

'September and October are always the worst,' Rudebacher says dreamily. 'You just hear it calling. The birds hear it, too, and go.'

'It?'

Rudebacher gives him a look that says don't be stupid. 'With them it's the sky. Guys like us, it's the road. Call of the open fuckin road. Guys like me, kids in school and a wife that still likes it more than just on Saturday night, they turn up the radio a little louder and drown it out. You're not gonna do that.' He pauses, looks at Callahan shrewdly. 'Stay another week? I'll bump you twenty-five bucks. You make a gahdam fine Monte Cristo.'

Callahan considers, then shakes his head. If Rudebacher was right, if it was only one road, maybe he would stay another week . . . and another . . . and another. But it's not just one. It's all of them, all those highways in hiding, and he remembers the name of his third-grade reader and bursts out laughing. It was called Roads to Everywhere.

'What's so funny?' Rudebacher asks sourly.

'Nothing,' Callahan says. 'Everything.' He claps his boss on the shoulder. 'You're a good man, Dicky. If I get back this way, I'll stop in.'

'You won't get back this way,' Dicky Rudebacher says, and of course he is right.

3

'I was five years on the road, give or take,' Callahan said as they approached his church, and in a way that was all he said on the subject. Yet they heard more. Nor were they surprised later to find that Jake, on his way into town with Eisenhart and the Slightmans, had heard some of it, too. It was Jake, after all, who was strongest in the touch.

Five years on the road, no more than that.

And all the rest, do ya ken: a thousand lost worlds of the rose.

4

He's five years on the road, give or take, only there's a lot more than one road and maybe, under the right circumstances, five years can be forever.

There is Route 71 through Delaware and apples to pick. There's a little boy named Lars with a broken radio. Callahan fixes it and Lars's mother packs him a great and wonderful lunch to go on with, a lunch that seems to last for days. There is Route 317 through rural Kentucky, and a job digging graves with a fellow named Pete Petacki who won't shut up. A girl comes to watch them, a pretty girl of seventeen or so, sitting on a rock wall with yellow leaves raining down all around her, and Pete Petacki speculates on what it would be like to have those long thighs stripped of the corduroys they're wearing and wrapped around his neck, what it would be like to be tongue-deep in jailbait. Pete Petacki doesn't see the blue light around her, and he certainly doesn't see the way her clothes drift to the ground like feathers later on, when Callahan sits beside her, then draws her close as she slips a hand up his leg and her mouth onto his throat, then thrusts his knife unerringly into the bulge of bone and nerve and gristle at the back of her neck. This is a shot he's getting very good at.

There is Route 19 through West Virginia, and a little road-dusty carnival that's looking for a man who can fix the rides and feed the animals. 'Or the other way around,' says Greg Chumm, the carny's greasy-haired owner. 'You know, feed the rides and fix the animals. Whatever floats ya boat.' And for awhile, when a strep infection leaves the carny shorthanded (they are swinging down south by now, trying to stay ahead of winter), he finds himself also playing Menso the ESP Wonder, and with surprising success. It is also as Menso that he first sees them, not vampires and not bewildered dead people but tall men with pale, watchful faces that are usually hidden under old-fashioned hats with brims or new-fashioned baseball hats with extra-long bills. In the shadows thrown by these hats, their eyes flare a dusky red, like the eyes of coons or polecats when you catch them in the beam of a flashlight, lurking around your trash barrels. Do they see him? The vampires (the Type Threes, at least) do not. The dead people do. And these men, with their hands stuffed into the pockets of their long yellow coats and their hardcase faces peering out from beneath their hats? Do they see? Callahan doesn't know for sure but decides to take no chances. Three days later, in the town of Yazoo City, Mississippi, he hangs up his black Menso tophat, leaves his greasy coverall on the floor of a pickup truck's camper cap, and blows Chumm's Traveling Wonder Show, not bothering with the formality of his final paycheck. On his way out of town, he sees a number of those pet posters nailed to telephone poles. A typical one reads:

LOST! SIAMESE CAT, 2 YRS OLD
ANSWERS TO THE NAME OF RUTA
SHE IS NOISY BUT FULL OF FUN
LARGE REWARD OFFERED
$$$$$$
DIAL 764, WAIT FOR BEEP, GIVE YOUR NUMBER
GOD BLESS YOU FOR HELPING

Who is Ruta? Callahan doesn't know. All he knows is that she is NOISY but FULL OF FUN. Will she still be noisy when the low men catch up to her? Will she still be full of fun?

Callahan doubts it.

But he has his own problems and all he can do is pray to the God in whom he no longer strictly believes that the men in the yellow coats won't catch up to her.

Later that day, thumbing on the side of Route 3 in Issaquena County under a hot gunmetal sky that knows nothing of December and approaching Christmas, the chimes come again. They fill his head, threatening to pop his eardrums and blow pinprick hemorrhages across the entire surface of his brain. As they fade, a terrible certainty grips him: they are coming. The men with the red eyes and big hats and long yellow coats are on their way.

Callahan bolts from the side of the road like a chaingang runaway, clearing the pond-scummy ditch like Superman: at a single bound. Beyond is an old stake fence overgrown with drifts of kudzu and what might be poison sumac. He doesn't care if it's poison sumac or not. He dives over the fence, rolls over in high grass and burdocks, and peers out at the highway through a hole in the foliage.

For a moment or two there's nothing. Then a white-over-red Cadillac comes pounding down Highway 3 from the direction of Yazoo City. It's doing seventy easy, and Callahan's peephole is small, but he still sees them with supernatural clarity: three men, two in what appear to be yellow dusters, the third in what might be a flight-jacket. All three are smoking: the Cadillac's closed cabin fumes with it.

They'll see me they'll hear me they'll sense me, *Callahan's mind yammers, and he forces it away from its own panicky wretched certainty,* yanks *it away. He forces himself to think of that Elton John song—'Someone saved, someone saved, someone saved my li-iife tonight . . .' and it seems to work. There is one terrible, heart-stopping moment when he thinks the Caddy is slowing — long enough for him to imagine them chasing him through this weedy, forgotten field, chasing him down, dragging him into an abandoned shed or barn — and then the Caddy roars over the next hill, headed for Natchez, maybe. Or Copiah. Callahan waits another ten minutes. 'Got to make sure they're not trickin on you, man,' Lupe might have said. But even as he waits, he knows this is only a formality. They're not trickin on him; they flat missed him. How? Why?*

The answer dawns on him slowly — an answer, at least, and he's damned if it doesn't feel like the right one. They missed him because he was able to slip into a different version of America as he lay behind the tangle of kudzu and sumac, peering out at Route 3. Maybe different in only a few small details — Lincoln on the one and Washington on the five instead of the other way around, let us say — but enough. Just enough. And that's good, because these guys aren't brain blasted, like the dead folks, or blind to him, like the bloodsucking folks. These people, whoever they are, are the most dangerous of all.

Finally, Callahan goes back out to the road. Eventually a black man in a straw hat and overalls comes driving along in an old beat-up Ford. He looks so much like a Negro farmer from a thirties movie that Callahan almost expects him to laugh and slap his knee and give out occasional cries of 'Yassuh, boss! Ain't dat de troof!' Instead, the black man engages him in a discussion about politics prompted by an item on National Public Radio, to which he is listening. And when Callahan leaves him, in Shady Grove, the black man gives him five dollars and a spare baseball cap.

'I have money,' Callahan says, trying to give back the five.

'A man on the run never has enough,' says the black man. 'And please don't tell me you're not on the run. Don't insult my intelligence.'

'I thank you,' Callahan says.

'De nada,' says the black man. 'Where are you going? Roughly speaking?'

'I don't have a clue,' Callahan replies, then smiles. 'Roughly speaking.'

5

Picking oranges in Florida. Pushing a broom in New Orleans. Mucking out horse-stalls in Lufkin, Texas. Handing out real estate brochures on streetcorners in Phoenix, Arizona. Working jobs that pay cash. Observing the ever-changing faces on the bills. Noting the different names in the papers. Jimmy Carter is elected President, but so are Ernest 'Fritz' Hollings and Ronald Reagan. George Bush is also elected President. Gerald Ford decides to run again and he is elected President. The names in the papers (those of the celebrities change the most frequently, and there are many he has never heard of) don't matter. The faces on the currency don't matter. What matters is the sight of a weathervane against a violent pink sunset, the sound of his heels on an empty road in Utah, the sound of the wind in the New Mexico desert, the sight of a child skipping rope beside a junked-out Chevrolet Caprice in Fossil, Oregon. What matters is the whine of the powerlines beside Highway 50 west of Elko, Nevada, and a dead crow in a ditch outside Rainbarrel Springs. Sometimes he's sober and sometimes he gets drunk. Once he lays up in an abandoned shed — this is just over the California state line from Nevada — and drinks for four days straight. It ends with seven hours of off-and-on vomiting. For the first hour or so, the puking is so constant and so violent he is convinced it will kill him. Later on, he can only wish it would. And when it's over, he swears to himself that he's done, no more booze for him, he's finally learned his lesson, and a week later he's drunk again and staring up at the strange stars behind the restaurant where he has hired on as a dishwasher. He is an animal in a trap and he doesn't care. Sometimes there are vampires and sometimes he kills them. Mostly he lets them live, because he's afraid of drawing attention to himself — the attention of the low men. Sometimes he asks himself what he thinks he's doing, where the hell he's going, and such questions are apt to send him in search of the next bottle in a hurry. Because he's really not going anywhere. He's just following the highways in hiding and dragging his trap along behind him, he's just listening to the call of those roads and going from one to the next. Trapped or not, sometimes he is happy; sometimes he sings in his chains like the sea. He wants to see the next weathervane standing against the next pink sunset. He wants to see the next silo crumbling at the end of some disappeared farmer's long-abandoned north field and see the next droning truck with TONOPAH GRAVEL or ASPLUNDH HEAVY CONSTRUCTION written on the side. He's in hobo heaven, lost in the split personalities of America. He wants to hear the wind in canyons and know that he's the only one who hears it. He wants to scream and hear the echoes run away. When the taste of Barlow's blood is too strong in his mouth, he wants to drink. And, of course, when he sees the lost-pet posters or the messages chalked on the sidewalks, he wants to move on. Out west he sees fewer of them, and neither his name nor his description is on any of them. From time to time he sees vampires cruising — give us this day our daily blood — but he leaves them be. They're mosquitoes, after all, no more than that.

In the spring of 1981 he finds himself rolling into the city of Sacramento in the back of what may be the oldest International-Harvester stake-bed truck still on the road in California. He's crammed in with roughly three dozen Mexican illegals, there is mescal and tequila and pot and several bottles of wine, they're all drunk and done up and Callahan is perhaps the drunkest of them all. The names of his companions come back to him in later years like names spoken in a haze of fever: Escobar . . . Estrado . . . Javier . . . Esteban . . . Rosario . . . Echeverria . . . Caverra. Are they all names he will later encounter in the Calla, or is that just a booze-hallucination? For that matter, what is he to make of his own name, which *is so close to that of the place where he finishes up?* Calla, Callahan. Calla, Callahan. *Sometimes, when he's long getting to sleep in his pleasant rectory bed, the two names chase each other in his head like the tigers in* Little Black Sambo.

Sometimes a line of poetry comes to him, a paraphrase from (he thinks) Archibald MacLeish's 'Epistle to Be Left in Earth.' It was not the voice of God but only the thunder. *That's not right, but it's how he remembers it.* Not God but the thunder. *Or is that only what he wants to believe? How many times has God been denied just that way?*

In any case, all of that comes later. When he rolls into Sacramento he's drunk and he's happy. There are no questions in his mind. He's even halfway happy the next day, hangover and all. He finds a job easily; jobs are everywhere, it seems, lying around like apples after a windstorm has gone through the orchard. As long as you don't mind getting your hands dirty, that is, or scalded by hot water or sometimes blistered by the handle of an ax or a shovel; in his years on the road no one has ever offered him a stockbroker's job.

The work he gets in Sacramento is unloading trucks at a block-long bed-and-mattress store called Sleepy John's. Sleepy John is preparing for his once-yearly Mattre$$ Ma$$acre, and all morning long Callahan and a crew of five other men haul in the kings and queens and doubles. Compared to some of the day-labor he's done over the last years, this job is a tit.

At lunch, Callahan and the rest of the men sit in the shade of the loading dock. So far as he can tell, there's no one in this crew from the International-Harvester, but he wouldn't swear to it; he was awfully drunk. All he knows for sure is that he's once again the only guy present with a white skin. All of them are eating enchiladas from Crazy Mary's down the road. There's a dirty old boombox sitting on a pile of crates, playing salsa. Two young men tango together while the others — Callahan included — put aside their lunches so they can clap along.

A young woman in a skirt and blouse comes out, watches the men dance disapprovingly, then looks at Callahan. 'You're anglo, right?' *she says.*

'Anglo as the day is long,' *Callahan agrees.*

'Then maybe you'd like this. Certainly no good to the rest of them.' *She hands him the newspaper — the Sacramento Bee — then looks at the dancing Mexicans.* 'Beaners,' *she says, and the subtext is in the tone: What can you do?*

Callahan considers rising to his feet and kicking her narrow can't-dance anglo ass for her, but it's noon, too late in the day to get another job if he loses this one. And even if he doesn't wind up in the calabozo *for assault, he won't get paid. He settles for giving her turned back the finger, and laughs when several of the men applaud. The young woman wheels, looks at them suspiciously, then goes back inside. Still grinning, Callahan shakes open the paper. The grin lasts until he gets to the page marked* NATIONAL BRIEFS, *then fades in a hurry. Between a story about a train derailment in Vermont and a bank robbery in Missouri, he finds this:*

AWARD-WINNING 'STREET ANGEL' CRITICAL

NEW YORK (AP) Rowan R. Magruder, owner and Chief Supervisor of what may be America's most highly regarded shelter for the homeless, alcoholic, and drug-addicted, is in critical condition after being assaulted by the so-called Hitler Brothers. The Hitler Brothers have been operating in the five boroughs of New York for at least eight years. According to police, they are believed responsible for over three dozen assaults and the deaths of two men. Unlike their other victims, Magruder is neither black nor Jewish, but he was found in a doorway not far from Home, the shelter he founded in 1968, with the Hitler Brothers' trademark swastika cut into his forehead. Magruder had also suffered multiple stab-wounds.

Home gained nationwide notice in 1977, when Mother Teresa visited, helped to serve dinner, and prayed with the clients. Magruder himself was the subject of a *Newsweek* cover story in 1980, when the East Side's so-called 'Street Angel' was named Manhattan's Man of the Year by Mayor Ed Koch.

A doctor familiar with the case rated Magruder's chances of pulling through as 'no higher than three in ten.' He said that, as well as being branded, Magruder was blinded by his assailants. 'I think of myself as a merciful man,' the doctor said, 'but in my opinion, the men who did this should be beheaded.'

Callahan reads the article again, wondering if this is 'his' Rowan Magruder or another one — a Rowan Magruder from a world where a guy named Chadbourne is on some of the greenbacks, say. He's somehow sure that it's his, and that he was meant to see this particular item. Certainly he is in what he thinks of as the 'real world' now, and it's not just the thin sheaf of currency in his wallet that tells him so. It's a feeling, a kind of tone. A truth. If so (and it is so, he knows it), how much he has missed out here on the hidden highways. Mother Teresa came to visit! Helped to ladle out soup! Hell, for all Callahan knows, maybe she cooked up a big old mess of Toads n Dumplins! Could've; the recipe was right there, Scotch-taped to the wall beside the stove. And an award! The cover of Newsweek! *He's pissed he didn't see that, but you don't see the news magazines very regularly when you're traveling with the carnival and fixing the Krazy Kups or mucking out the bull-stalls behind the rodeo in Enid, Oklahoma.*

He is so deeply ashamed that he doesn't even know *he's ashamed. Not even when Juan Castillo says, 'Why joo crine, Donnie?'*

'Am I?' he asks, and wipes underneath his eyes, and yeah, he is. He is crying. But he doesn't know it's for shame, not then. He assumes it's shock, and probably part of it is. 'Yeah, I guess I am.'

'Where joo goan?' Juan persists. 'Lunch break's almost over, man.'

'I have to leave,' Callahan says. 'I have to go back east.'

'You take off, they ain goan pay joo.'

'I know,' Callahan says. 'It's okay.'

And what a lie that is. Because nothing's okay.

Nothing.

6

'I had a couple of hundred dollars sewn into the bottom of my backpack,' Callahan said. They were now sitting on the steps of the church in the bright sunshine. 'I bought an airplane ticket back to New York. Speed was of the essence – of course – but that really wasn't the only reason. I had to get off those highways in hiding.' He gave Eddie a small nod. 'The todash turnpikes. They're as addictive as the booze—'

'More,' Roland said. He saw three figures coming toward them: Rosalita, shepherding the Tavery twins, Frank and Francine. The girl had a large sheet of paper in her hands and was carrying it out in front of her with an air of reverence that was almost comic. 'Wandering's the most addictive drug there is, I think, and every hidden road leads on to a dozen more.'

'You say true, I say thankya,' Callahan replied. He looked gloomy and sad and, Roland thought, a little lost.

'Pere, we'd hear the rest of your tale, but I'd have you save it until evening. Or tomorrow evening, if we don't get back until then. Our young friend Jake will be here shortly—'

'You know that, do you?' Callahan asked, interested but not disbelieving.

'Aye,' Susannah said.

'I'd see what you have in there before he comes,' Roland said. 'The story of how you came by it is part of *your* story, I think—'

'Yes,' Callahan said. 'It is. The *point* of my story, I think.'

'—and must wait its place. As for now, things are stacking up.'

'They have a way of doing that,' Callahan said. 'For months – sometimes even years, as I tried to explain to you – time hardly seems to exist. Then everything comes in a gasp.'

'You say true,' Roland said. 'Step over with me to see the twins, Eddie. I believe the young lady has her eye on you.'

'She can look as much as she wants,' Susannah said good-humoredly. 'Lookin's free. I might just sit here in the sun on these steps, Roland, if it's all the same to you. Been a long time since I rode, and I don't mind telling you that I'm saddle-sore. Not having any lower pins seems to put everything else out of whack.'

'Do ya either way,' Roland said, but he didn't mean it and Eddie knew he didn't. The gunslinger wanted Susannah to stay right where she was, for the time being. He could only hope Susannah wasn't catching the same vibe.

As they walked toward the children and Rosalita, Roland spoke to Eddie, low and quick. 'I'm going into the church with him by myself. Just know that it's not the both of you I want to keep away from whatever's in there. If it *is* Black Thirteen – and I believe it must be – it's best she not go near it.'

'Given her delicate condition, you mean. Roland, I would have thought Suze having a miscarriage would almost be something you'd want.'

Roland said: 'It's not a miscarriage that concerns me. I'm worried about Black Thirteen making the thing inside her even stronger.' He paused again. '*Both* things, mayhap. The baby and the baby's keeper.'

'Mia.'

'Yes, her.' Then he smiled at the Tavery twins. Francine gave him a perfunctory smile in return, saving full wattage for Eddie.

'Let me see what you've made, if you would,' Roland said.

Frank Tavery said, 'We hope it's all right. Might not be. We were afraid, do ya. It's such a wonderful piece of paper the missus gave us, we were afraid.'

'We drew on the ground first,' Francine said. 'Then in lightest char. 'Twas Frank did the final; my hands were all a-shake.'

'No fear,' Roland said. Eddie drew close and looked over his shoulder. The map was a marvel of detail, with the Town Gathering Hall and the common at the center and the Big River/Devar-Tete running along the left side of the paper, which looked to Eddie like an ordinary mimeo sheet. The kind available by the ream at any office supply store in America.

'Kids, this is absolutely terrific,' Eddie said, and for a moment he thought Francine Tavery might actually faint.

'Aye,' Roland said. 'You've done a great service. And now I'm going to do something that will probably look like blasphemy to you. You know the word?'

'Yes,' Frank said. 'We're Christians. "Thou shalt not take the name of the Lord thy God or His Son, the Man Jesus, in vain." But blasphemy is also to commit a rude act upon a thing of beauty.'

His tone was deeply serious, but he looked interested to see what blasphemy the outworlder meant to commit. His sister did, too.

Roland folded the paper — which they had almost dared not touch, in spite of their obvious skill — in half. The children gasped. So did Rosalita Munoz, although not quite as loudly.

'It's not blasphemy to treat it so because it's no longer just paper,' Roland said. 'It has become a tool, and tools must be protected. D'ye ken?'

'Yes,' they said, but doubtfully. Their confidence was at least partly restored by the care with which Roland stowed the folded map in his purse.

'Thankya big-big,' Roland said. He took Francine's hand in his left, Frank's in his diminished right. 'You may have saved lives with your hands and eyes.'

Francine burst into tears. Frank held his own back until he grinned. Then they overspilled and ran down his freckled cheeks.

7

Walking back to the church steps, Eddie said: 'Good kids. Talented kids.'

Roland nodded.

'Can you see one of them coming back from Thunderclap a drooling idiot?'

Roland, who could see it all too well, made no reply.

8

Susannah accepted Roland's decision that she and Eddie should stay outside the church with no argument, and the gunslinger found himself remembering her reluctance to enter the vacant lot. He wondered if part of her was afraid of the same thing he was. If that was the case, the battle — *her* battle — had already begun.

'How long before I come in and drag you out?' Eddie asked.

'Before *we* come in and drag you out?' Susannah corrected him.

Roland considered. It was a good question. He looked at Callahan, who stood on the top step in blue jeans and a plaid shirt rolled to the elbows. His hands were clasped in front of him. Roland saw good muscle on those forearms.

The Old Fella shrugged. 'It sleeps. There should be no problem. But—' He unlocked one of his gnarled hands and pointed at the gun on Roland's hip. 'I sh'd ditch that. Mayhap it sleeps with one eye open.'

Roland unbuckled the gunbelt and handed it to Eddie, who was wearing the other one. Then he unslung his purse and handed it to Susannah. 'Five minutes,' he said. 'If there's trouble, I might be able to call.' *Or I might not*, he didn't add.

'Jake should be here by then,' Eddie said.

'If they come, hold them out here,' Roland told him.

'Eisenhart and the Slightmans won't try to come in,' Callahan said. 'What worship they have is for Oriza. Lady Rice.' He grimaced to show what he thought of Lady Rice and the rest of the Calla's second-rate gods.

'Let's go, then,' Roland said.

9

It had been a long time since Roland Deschain had been afraid in the deeply superstitious way that goes with a believed religion. Since his childhood, perhaps. But fear fell upon him as soon as Pere Callahan opened the door of his modest wooden church and held it, gesturing for Roland to precede him inside.

There was a foyer with a faded rug on the floor. On the other side of the foyer, two doors stood open. Beyond them was a largish room with pews on each side and kneelers on the floor. At the room's far end was a raised platform and what Roland thought of as a lectern flanked by pots of white flowers. Their mild scent pervaded the still air. There were narrow windows of clear glass. Behind the lectern, on the far wall, was an iron-wood cross.

He could hear the Old Fella's secret treasure, not with his ears but with his bones. A steady low hum. Like the rose, that hum conveyed a sense of power, but it was like the rose in no other way. This hum spoke of colossal emptiness. A void like the one they had all sensed behind the surface reality of todash New York. A void that could become a voice.

Yes, this is what took us, he thought. *It took us to New York — one New York of many, according to Callahan's story — but it could take us anywhere or anywhen. It could take us . . . or it could fling us.*

He remembered the conclusion of his long palaver with Walter, in the place of the bones. He had gone todash then, too; he understood that now. And there had been a sense of growing, of *swelling,* until he had been bigger than the earth, the stars, the very universe itself. That power was here, in this room, and he was afraid of it.

Gods grant it sleep, he thought, but the thought was followed by an even more dismaying one: sooner or later they would have to wake it up. Sooner or later they would have to use it to get back to the New York whens they needed to visit.

There was a bowl of water on a stand beside the door. Callahan dipped his fingers, then crossed himself.

'You can do that now?' Roland murmured in what was little more than a whisper.

'Aye,' Callahan said. 'God has taken me back, gunslinger. Although I think only on what might be called "a trial basis." Do you ken?'

Roland nodded. He followed Callahan into the church without dipping his fingers in the font.

Callahan led him down the center aisle, and although he moved swiftly and surely, Roland sensed the man was as frightened as Roland was himself, perhaps more. The religious wanted to be rid of the thing, of course, there was that, but Roland still gave him high marks for courage.

On the far right side of the preacher's cove was a little flight of three steps. Callahan mounted them. 'No need for you to come up, Roland; you can see well enough from where you are. You'd not have it this minute, I ken?'

'Not at all,' Roland said. Now they *were* whispering.

'Good.' Callahan dropped to one knee. There was an audible pop as the joint flexed, and they both started at the sound. 'I'd not even touch the box it's in, if I don't have to. I haven't since I put it here. The hidey-hole I made myself, asking God's pardon for using a saw in His house.'

'Take it up,' Roland said. He was on complete alert, every sense drawn fine, feeling and listening for any slightest change in that endless void hum. He missed the weight of the gun on his hip. Did the people who came here to worship not sense the terrible thing the Old Fella had hidden here? He supposed they must not, or they'd stay away. And he supposed there was really no better place for such a thing; the simple faith of the parishioners might neutralize it to some degree. Might even soothe it and thus deepen its doze.

But it could wake up, Roland thought. *Wake up and send them all to the nineteen points of nowhere in the blink of an eye.* This was an especially terrible thought, and he turned his mind from it. Certainly the idea of using it to secure protection for the rose seemed more and more like a bitter joke. He had faced both men and monsters in his time, but had never been close to anything like this. The sense of its evil was terrible, almost unmanning. The sense of its malevolent emptiness was far, far worse.

Callahan pressed his thumb into the groove between two boards. There was a faint click and a section of the preacher's cove popped out of place. Callahan pulled the boards free, revealing a square hole roughly fifteen inches long and wide. He rocked back on his haunches, holding the boards across his chest. The hum was much louder now. Roland had a brief image of a gigantic hive with bees the size of waggons crawling sluggishly over it. He bent forward and looked into the Old Fella's hidey-hole.

The thing inside was wrapped in white cloth, fine linen from the look of it.

'An altar boy's surplice,' Callahan said. Then, seeing Roland didn't know the word: 'A thing to wear.' He shrugged. 'My heart said to wrap it up, and so I did.'

'Your heart surely said true,' Roland whispered. He was thinking of the bag Jake had brought out of the vacant lot, the one with NOTHING BUT STRIKES AT MID-WORLD LANES on the side. They would need it, aye and aye, but he didn't like to think of the transfer.

Then he put thought aside — fear as well — and folded back the cloth. Beneath the surplice, wrapped in it, was a wooden box.

Despite his fear, Roland reached out to touch that dark, heavy wood. *It will be like touching some lightly oiled metal*, he thought, and it was. He felt an erotic shiver shake itself deep inside him; it kissed his fear like an old lover and then was gone.

'This is black ironwood,' Roland whispered. 'I have heard of it but never seen it.'

'In my *Tales of Arthur*, it's called ghostwood,' Callahan whispered back.
'Aye? Is it so?'

Certainly the box had a ghostly air to it, as of something derelict which
had come to rest, however temporarily, after long wandering. The gunslinger
very much would have liked to give it a second caress – the dark, dense
wood begged his hand – but he had heard the vast hum of the thing inside
rise a notch before falling back to its former drone. *The wise man doesn't poke
a sleeping bear with a stick*, he told himself. It was true, but it didn't change
what he wanted. He did touch the wood once more, lightly, with just the
tips of his fingers, then smelled them. There was an aroma of camphor and
fire and – he would have sworn it – the flowers of the far north country,
the ones that bloom in the snow.

Three objects had been carved on top of the box: a rose, a stone, and
a door. Beneath the door was this:

$$\text{ᔑᓭᓫ ᐅ ᔑᓭ}$$

Roland reached out again. Callahan made a move forward, as if to stop
him, and then subsided. Roland touched the carving beneath the image of
the door. Again the hum beneath it rose – the hum of the black ball hidden
inside the box.

'Un . . .?' he whispered, and ran the ball of his thumb across the raised
symbols again. 'Un . . . found?' Not what he read but what his fingertips
heard.

'Yes, I'm sure that's what it says,' Callahan whispered back. He looked
pleased, but still grasped Roland's wrist and pushed it, wanting the
gunslinger's hand away from the box. A fine sweat had broken on his brow
and forearms. 'It makes sense, in a way. A leaf, a stone, an unfound door.
They're symbols in a book from my side. *Look Homeward, Angel*, it's called.'

A leaf, a stone, a door, Roland thought. *Only substitute* rose *for* leaf. *Yes. That
feels right.*

'Will you take it?' Callahan asked. Only his voice rose slightly now, out
of its whisper, and the gunslinger realized he was begging.

'You've actually seen it, Pere, have you?'

'Aye. Once. It's horrible beyond telling. Like the slick eye of a monster
that grew outside God's shadow. Will you take it, gunslinger?'

'Yes.'

'When?'

Faintly, Roland heard the chime of bells — a sound so beautifully hideous it made you want to grind your teeth against it. For a moment the walls of Pere Callahan's church wavered. It was as if the thing in the box had spoken to them: *Do you see how little it all matters? How quickly and easily I can take it all away, should I choose to do so? Beware, gunslinger! Beware, shaman! The abyss is all around you. You float or fall into it at my whim.*

Then the *kammen* were gone.

'When?' Callahan reached over the box in its hole and grasped Roland's shirt. *'When?'*

'Soon,' Roland said.

Too soon, his heart replied.

CHAPTER V

THE TALE OF
GRAY DICK

1

Now it's twenty-three, Roland thought that evening as he sat behind Eisenhart's Rocking B, listening to the boys shout and Oy bark. Back in Gilead, this sort of porch behind the main house, facing the barns and the fields, would have been called the work-stoop. *Twenty-three days until the Wolves. And how many until Susannah foals?*

A terrible idea concerning that had begun to form in his head. Suppose Mia, the new *she* inside Susannah's skin, were to give birth to her monstrosity on the very day the Wolves appeared? One wouldn't think that likely, but according to Eddie, coincidence had been cancelled. Roland thought he was probably right about that. Certainly there was no way to gauge the thing's period of gestation. Even if it had been a human child, nine months might no longer be nine months. Time had grown soft.

'Boys!' Eisenhart bawled. 'What in the name of the Man Jesus am I going to tell my wife if you kill yer sad selfs jumpin out of that barn?'

'We're okay!' Benny Slightman called. 'Andy won't let us get hurt!' The boy, dressed in bib overalls and barefooted, was standing in the open bay of the barn, just above the carved letters which said ROCKING B. 'Unless . . . do you really want us to stop, sai?'

Eisenhart glanced toward Roland, who saw Jake standing just behind Benny, impatiently waiting his chance to risk his bones. Jake was also dressed in bib overalls – a pair of his new friend's, no doubt – and the look of them made Roland smile. Jake wasn't the sort of boy you imagined in such clothes, somehow.

'It's nil to me, one way or the other, if that's what you want to know,' Roland said.

'Garn, then!' the rancher called. Then he turned his attention to the bits and pieces of hardware spread out on the boards. 'What do 'ee think? Will any of em shoot?'

Eisenhart had produced all three of his guns for Roland's inspection. The best was the rifle the rancher had brought to town on the night Tian Jaffords had called the meeting. The other two were pistols of the sort Roland and his friends had called 'barrel-shooters' as children, because of the oversized cylinders which had to be revolved with the side of the hand after each shot. Roland had disassembled Eisenhart's shooting irons with no initial comment. Once again he had set out gun-oil, this time in a bowl instead of a saucer.

'I said—'

'I heard you, sai,' Roland said. 'Your rifle is as good as I've seen this side of the great city. The barrel-shooters . . .' He shook his head. 'That one with the nickel plating might fire. The other you might as well stick in the ground. Maybe it'll grow something better.'

'Hate to hear you speak so,' Eisenhart said. 'These were from my Da' and his Da' before him and on back at least this many.' He raised seven fingers and one thumb. 'That's back to before the Wolves, ye ken. They was always kept together and passed to the likeliest son by dead-letter. When I got em instead of my elder brother, I was some pleased.'

'Did you have a twin?' Roland asked.

'Aye, Verna,' Eisenhart said. He smiled easily and often and did so now beneath his great graying bush of a mustache, but it was painful – the smile of a man who doesn't want you to know he's bleeding somewhere inside his clothes. 'She was lovely as dawn, so she was. Passed on these ten year or more. Went painful early, as the roont ones often do.'

'I'm sorry.'

'Say thankya.'

The sun was going down red in the southwest, turning the yard the color of blood. There was a line of rockers on the porch. Eisenhart was settled in one of them. Roland sat cross-legged on the boards, housekeeping Eisenhart's inheritance. That the pistols would probably never fire meant nothing to the gunslinger's hands, which had been trained to this work long ago and still found it soothing.

Now, with a speed that made the rancher blink, Roland put the weapons back together in a rapid series of clicks and clacks. He set them aside on a square of sheepskin, wiped his fingers on a rag, and sat in the rocker next to Eisenhart's. He guessed that on more ordinary evenings, Eisenhart and his wife sat out here side by side, watching the sun abandon the day.

Roland rummaged through his purse for his tobacco pouch, found it, and built himself a cigarette with Callahan's fresh, sweet tobacco. Rosalita had added her own present, a little stack of delicate cornshuck wraps she called 'pulls.' Roland thought they wrapped as good as any cigarette paper, and he paused a moment to admire the finished product before tipping the end into the match Eisenhart had popped alight with one horny thumb-nail. The gunslinger dragged deep and exhaled a long plume that rose but slowly in the evening air, which was still and surprisingly muggy for summer's end. 'Good,' he said, and nodded.

'Aye? May it do ya fine. I never got the taste for it myself.'

The barn was far bigger than the ranchhouse, at least fifty yards long and fifty feet high. The front was festooned with reap-charms in honor of the season; stuffy-guys with huge sharproot heads stood guard. From above the open bay over the main doors, the butt of the head-beam jutted. A rope had been fastened around this. Below, in the yard, the boys had built a good-sized stack of hay. Oy stood on one side of it, Andy on the other. They were both looking up as Benny Slightman grabbed the rope, gave it a tug, then retreated back into the loft and out of sight. Oy began to bark in anticipation. A moment later Benny came pelting forward with the rope wrapped in his fists and his hair flying out behind him.

'*Gilead and the Eld!*' he cried, and leaped from the bay. He swung into the red sunset air with his shadow trailing behind him.

'*Ben-Ben!*' Oy barked. '*Ben-Ben-Ben!*'

The boy let go, flew into the haystack, disappeared, then popped up laughing. Andy offered him a metal hand but Benny ignored it, flopping out onto the hardpacked earth. Oy ran around him, barking.

'Do they always call so at play?' Roland asked.

Eisenhart snorted laughter. 'Not at all! Usually it's a cry of Oriza, or Man Jesus, or "hail the Calla," or all three. Your boy's been filling Slightman's boy full of tales, thinks I.'

Roland ignored the slightly disapproving note in this and watched Jake reel in the rope. Benny lay on the ground, playing dead, until Oy licked his face. Then he sat up, giggling. Roland had no doubt that if the boy had gone off-course, Andy would have snagged him.

To one side of the barn was a remuda of work-horses, perhaps twenty in all. A trio of cowpokes in chaps and battered shor'boots were leading the last half-dozen mounts toward it. On the other side of the yard was a slaughter-pen filled with steers. In the following weeks they would be butchered and sent downriver on the trading boats.

Jake retreated into the loft, then came pelting forward. *'New York!'* he shouted. *'Times Square! Empire State Building! Twin Towers! Statue of Liberty!'* And he launched himself into space along the arc of the rope. They watched him disappear, laughing, into the pile of hay.

'Any particular reason you wanted your other two to stay with the Jaffordses?' Eisenhart asked. He spoke idly, but Roland thought this was a question that interested him more than a little.

'Best we spread ourselves around. Let as many as possible get a good look at us. Time is short. Decisions must be made.' All of which was true, but there was more, and Eisenhart probably knew it. He was shrewder than Overholser. He was also dead set against standing up to the Wolves — at least so far. This didn't keep Roland from liking the man, who was big and honest and possessed of an earthy countryman's sense of humor. Roland thought he might come around, if he could be shown they had a chance to win.

On their way out to the Rocking B, they had visited half a dozen small-hold farms along the river, where rice was the main crop. Eisenhart had performed the introductions good-naturedly enough. At each stop Roland had asked the two questions he had asked the previous night, at the Pavilion: *Will you open to us, if we open to you? Do you see us for what we are, and accept us for what we do?* All of them had answered yes. Eisenhart had also answered yes. But Roland knew better than to ask the third question of any. There was no need to, not yet. They still had over three weeks.

'We bide, gunslinger,' Eisenhart said. 'Even in the face of the Wolves, we bide. Once there was Gilead and now there's Gilead nummore — none knows better 'n you — but still we bide. If we stand against the Wolves, all that may change. To you and yours, what happens along the Crescent might not mean s'much as a fart in a high wind one way or t'other. If ye win and survive, you'll move along. If ye lose and die, we have nowhere to go.'

'But—'

Eisenhart raised his hand. 'Hear me, I beg. Would 'ee hear me?'

Roland nodded, resigned to it. And for him to speak was probably for the best. Beyond them, the boys were running back into the barn for another leap. Soon the coming dark would put an end to their game. The gunslinger wondered how Eddie and Susannah were making out. Had they spoken to Tian's Gran-pere yet? And if so, had he told them anything of value?

'Suppose they send fifty or even sixty, as they have before, many and many-a? And suppose we wipe them out? And then, suppose that a week or a month later, after you're gone, they send five *hundred* against us?'

Roland considered the question. As he was doing so, Margaret Eisenhart joined them. She was a slim woman, fortyish, small-breasted, dressed in jeans and a shirt of gray silk. Her hair, pulled back in a bun against her neck, was black threaded with white. One hand hid beneath her apron.

'That's a fair question,' she said, 'but this might not be a fair time to ask it. Give him and his friends a week, why don't you, to peek about and see what they may see.'

Eisenhart gave his sai a look that was half humorous and half irritated. 'Do I tell 'ee how to run your kitchen, woman? When to cook and when to wash?'

'Only four times a week,' said she. Then, seeing Roland rise from the rocker next to her husband's: 'Nay, sit still, I beg you. I've been in a chair this last hour, peeling sharproot with Edna, yon's auntie.' She nodded in Benny's direction. 'It's good to be on my feet.' She watched, smiling, as the boys swung out into the pile of hay and landed, laughing, while Oy danced and barked. 'Vaughn and I have never had to face the full horror of it before, Roland. We had six, all twins, but all grown in the time between. So we may not have all the understanding needed to make such a decision as you ask.'

'Being lucky doesn't make a man stupid,' Eisenhart said. 'Quite the contrary, is what I think. Cool eyes see clear.'

'Perhaps,' she said, watching the boys run back into the barn. They were bumping shoulders and laughing, each trying to get to the ladder first. 'Perhaps, aye. But the heart must call for its rights, too, and a man or woman who doesn't listen is a fool. Sometimes 'tis best to swing on the rope, even if it's too dark to see if the hay's there or not.'

Roland reached out and touched her hand. 'I couldn't have said better myself.'

She gave him a small, distracted smile. It was only a moment before she returned her attention to the boys, but it was long enough for Roland to see that she was frightened. Terrified, in fact.

'Ben, Jake!' she called. 'Enough! Time to wash and then come in! There's pie for those can eat it, and cream to go on top!'

Benny came to the open bay. 'My Da' says we can sleep in my tent over on the bluff, sai, if it's all right with you.'

Margaret Eisenhart looked at her husband. Eisenhart nodded. 'All right,' she said, 'tent it is and give you joy of it, but come in now if you'd have pie. Last warning! And wash first, mind 'ee! Hands *and* faces!'

'Aye, say thankya,' Benny said. 'Can Oy have pie?'

Margaret Eisenhart thudded the pad of her left hand against her brow, as if she had a headache. The right, Roland was interested to note, stayed beneath her apron. 'Aye,' she said, 'pie for the bumbler, too, as I'm sure he's Arthur Eld in disguise and will reward me with jewels and gold and the healing touch.'

'Thankee-sai,' Jake called. 'Could we have one more swing first? It's the quickest way down.'

'I'll catch them if they fly wrong, Margaret-sai,' Andy said. His eyes flashed blue, then dimmed. He appeared to be smiling. To Roland, the robot seemed to have two personalities, one old-maidish, the other harmlessly cozening. The gunslinger liked neither, and understood why perfectly. He'd come to mistrust machinery of all kinds, and especially the kind that walked and talked.

'Well,' Eisenhart said, 'the broken leg usually hides in the last caper, but have on, if ye must.'

They had on, and there were no broken legs. Both boys hit the haypile squarely, popped up laughing and looking at each other, then footraced for the kitchen with Oy running behind them. Appearing to herd them.

'It's wonderful how quickly children can become friends,' Margaret Eisenhart said, but she didn't look like one contemplating something wonderful. She looked sad.

'Yes,' Roland said. 'Wonderful it is.' He laid his purse across his lap, seemed on the verge of pulling the knot that anchored the laces, then didn't. 'Which are your men good with?' he asked Eisenhart. 'Bow or bah? For I know it's surely not the rifle or revolver.'

'We favor the bah,' Eisenhart said. 'Fit the bolt, wind it, aim it, fire it, 'tis done.'

Roland nodded. It was as he had expected. Not good, because the bah was rarely accurate at a distance greater than twenty-five yards, and that only on a still day. On one when a strong breeze was kicking up ... or, gods help us, a gale ...

But Eisenhart was looking at his wife. Looking at her with a kind of reluctant admiration. She stood with her eyebrows raised, looking back at her man. Looking him back a question. What was this? It surely had to do with the hand under the apron.

'Garn, tell im,' Eisenhart said. Then he pointed an almost-angry finger at Roland, like the barrel of a pistol. 'It changes nothing, though. Nothing! Say thankya!' This last with the lips drawn back in a kind of savage grin. Roland was more puzzled than ever, but he felt a faint stirring of hope. It might be false hope, probably would be, but anything was better than the worries and confusions – and the aches – that had beset him lately.

'Nay,' Margaret said with maddening modesty. ''Tis not my place to tell. To show, perhaps, but not to tell.'

Eisenhart sighed, considered, then turned to Roland. 'Ye danced the rice-dance,' he said, 'so ye know Lady Oriza.'

Roland nodded. The Lady of the Rice, in some places considered a goddess, in others a heroine, in some, both.

'And ye know how she did away with Gray Dick, who killed her father?'

Roland nodded again.

2

According to the story – a good one that he must remember to tell Eddie, Susannah, and Jake, when and if there was once more time for storytelling – Lady Oriza invited Gray Dick, a famous outlaw prince, to a vast dinner party in Waydon, her castle by the River Send. She wanted to forgive him for the murder of her father, she said, for she had accepted the Man Jesus into her heart and such was according to His teachings.

Ye'll get me there and kill me, be I stupid enough to come, said Gray Dick.

Nay, nay, said the Lady Oriza, never think it. All weapons will be left outside the castle. And when we sit in the banqueting hall below, there will be only me, at one end of the table, and thee, at the other.

You'll conceal a dagger in your sleeve or a *bola* beneath your dress, said Gray Dick. And if you don't, I will.

Nay, nay, said the Lady Oriza, never think it, for we shall both be naked.

At this Gray Dick was overcome with lust, for Lady Oriza was fair. It excited him to think of his prick getting hard at the sight of her bare breasts and bush, and no breeches on him to conceal his excitement from her maiden's eye. And he thought he understood why she would make such a proposal. *His haughty heart will undo him*, Lady Oriza told her maid (whose name was Marian and who went on to have many fanciful adventures of her own).

The Lady was right. *I've killed Lord Grenfall, wiliest lord in all the river baronies,* Gray Dick told himself. *And who is left to avenge him but one weak daughter?* (Oh, but she was fair.) *So she sues for peace. And maybe even for marriage, if she has audacity and imagination as well as beauty.*

So he accepted her offer. His men searched the banquet hall downstairs before he arrived and found no weapons — not on the table, not under the table, not behind the tapestries. What none of them could know was that for weeks before the banquet, Lady Oriza had practiced throwing a specially weighted dinner-plate. She did this for hours a day. She was athletically inclined to begin with, and her eyes were keen. Also, she hated Gray Dick with all her heart and had determined to make him pay no matter what the cost.

The dinner-plate wasn't just weighted; its rim had been sharpened. Dick's men overlooked this, as she and Marian had been sure they would. And so they banqueted, and what a strange banquet that must have been, with the laughing, handsome outlaw naked at one end of the table and the demurely smiling but exquisitely beautiful maiden thirty feet from him at the other end, equally naked. They toasted each other with Lord Grenfall's finest rough red. It infuriated the Lady to the point of madness to watch him slurp that exquisite country wine down as though it were water, scarlet drops rolling off his chin and splashing to his hairy chest, but she gave no sign; simply smiled coquettishly and sipped from her own glass. She could feel the weight of his eyes on her breasts. It was like having unpleasant bugs lumbering to and fro on her skin.

How long did this charade go on? Some tale-tellers had her putting an end to Gray Dick after the second toast. (His: *May your beauty ever increase.* Hers: *May your first day in hell last ten thousand years, and may it be the shortest.*) Others — the sort of spinners who enjoyed drawing out the suspense — recounted a meal of a dozen courses before Lady Oriza gripped the special plate, looking Gray Dick in the eyes and smiling at him while she turned it, feeling for the dull place on the rim where it would be safe to grip.

No matter how long the tale, it always ended the same way, with Lady Oriza flinging the plate. Little fluted channels had been carved on its underside, beneath the sharpened rim, to help it fly true. As it did, humming weirdly as it went, casting its fleeting shadow on the roast pork and turkey, the heaping bowls of vegetables, the fresh fruit piled on crystal serving dishes.

A moment after she flung the plate on its slightly rising course – her arm was still outstretched, her first finger and cocked thumb pointing at her father's assassin – Gray Dick's head flew out through the open door and into the foyer behind him. For a moment longer Gray Dick's body stood there with its penis pointing at her like an accusing finger. Then the dick shriveled and the Dick behind it crashed forward onto a huge roast of beef and a mountain of herbed rice.

Lady Oriza, whom Roland would hear referred to as the Lady of the Plate in some of his wanderings, raised her glass of wine and toasted the body. She said

3

'May your first day in hell last ten thousand years,' Roland murmured.

Margaret nodded. 'Aye, and let that one be the shortest. A terrible toast, but one I'd gladly give each of the Wolves. Each and every one!' Her visible hand clenched. In the fading red light she looked feverish and ill. 'We had six, do ya. An even half-dozen. Has he told you why none of them are here, to help with the Reaptide slaughtering and penning? Has he told you that, gunslinger?'

'Margaret, there's no need,' Eisenhart said. He shifted uncomfortably in his rocker.

'Ah, but mayhap there is. It goes back to what we were saying before. Mayhap ye pay a price for leaping, but sometimes ye pay a higher one for looking. Our children grew up free and clear, with no Wolves to worry about. I gave birth to my first two, Tom and Tessa, less than a month before they came last time. The others followed along, neat as peas out of a pod. The youngest be only fifteen, do ya not see it.'

'Margaret—'

She ignored him. 'But they'd not be s' lucky with their own children, and they knew it. And so they're gone. Some far north along the Arc, some far south. Looking for a place where the Wolves don't come.'

She turned to Eisenhart, and although she spoke to Roland, it was her husband she looked at as she had her final word.

'One of every two; that's the Wolves' bounty. That's what they take every twenty-some, for many and many-a. Except for us. They took *all* of our children. Every . . . single . . . one.' She leaned forward and tapped Roland's leg just above the knee with great emphasis. '*Do ya not see it.*'

Silence fell on the back porch. The condemned steers in the slaughter-pen mooed moronically. From the kitchen came the sound of boy-laughter following some comment of Andy's.

Eisenhart had dropped his head. Roland could see nothing but the extravagant bush of his mustache, but he didn't need to see the man's face to know that he was either weeping or struggling very hard not to.

'I'd not make 'ee feel bad for all the rice of the Arc,' she said, and stroked her husband's shoulder with infinite tenderness. 'And they come back betimes, aye, which is more than the dead do, except in our dreams. They're not so old that they don't miss their mother, or have how-do-ye-do-it questions for their Da'. But they're gone, nevertheless. And that's the price of safety, as ye must ken.' She looked down at Eisenhart for a moment, one hand on his shoulder and the other still beneath her apron. 'Now tell how angry with me you are,' she said, 'for I'd know.'

Eisenhart shook his head. 'Not angry,' he said in a muffled voice.

'And have 'ee changed your mind?'

Eisenhart shook his head again.

'Stubborn old thing,' she said, but she spoke with good-humored affection. 'Stubborn as a stick, aye, and we all say thankya.'

'I'm thinking about it,' he said, still not looking up. 'Still thinking, which is more than I expected at this late date – usually I make up my mind and there's the end of it.

'Roland, I understand young Jake showed Overholser and the rest of em some shooting out in the woods. Might be we could show you something right here that'd raise your eyebrows. Maggie, go in and get your Oriza.'

'No need,' she said, at last taking her hand from beneath her apron, 'for I brought it out with me, and here 'tis.'

4

It was a plate both Detta and Mia would have recognized, a blue plate with a delicate webbed pattern. A forspecial plate. After a moment Roland recognized the webbing for what it was: young oriza, the seedling rice plant. When sai Eisenhart tapped her knuckles on the plate, it gave out a peculiar high ringing. It looked like china, but wasn't. Glass, then? Some sort of glass?

He held his hand out for it with the solemn, respectful mien of one who knows and respects weapons. She hesitated, biting the corner of her lip. Roland reached into his holster, which he'd strapped back on before the noon meal outside the church, and pulled his revolver. He held it out to her, butt first.

'Nay,' she said, letting the word out on a long breath of sigh. 'No need to offer me your shooter as a hostage, Roland. I reckon if Vaughn trusts you at the house, I c'n trust you with my Oriza. But mind how you touch, or you'll lose another finger, and I think you could ill afford that, for I see you're already two shy on your right hand.'

A single look at the blue plate – the sai's Oriza – made it clear how wise that warning was. At the same time, Roland felt a bright spark of excitement and appreciation. It had been long years since he'd seen a new weapon of worth, and never one like this.

The plate was metal, not glass – some light, strong alloy. It was the size of an ordinary dinner-plate, a foot (and a bit more) in diameter. Three quarters of the edge had been sharpened to suicidal keenness.

'There's never a question of where to grip, even if ye're in a hurry,' Margaret said. 'For, do 'ee see—'

'Yes,' Roland said in a tone of deepest admiration. Two of the rice-stalks crossed in what could have been the Great Letter **Zn** , which by itself means both *zi* (eternity) and *now*. At the point where these stalks crossed (only a sharp eye would pick them out of the bigger pattern to begin with), the rim of the plate was not only dull but slightly thicker. Good to grip.

Roland turned the plate over. Beneath, in the center, was a small metal pod. To Jake, it might have looked like the plastic pencil-sharpener he'd taken to school in his pocket as a first-grader. To Roland, who had never seen a pencil-sharpener, it looked a little like the abandoned egg-case of some insect.

'That makes the whistling noise when the plate flies, do ya ken,' she said. She had seen Roland's honest admiration and was reacting to it, her color high and her eye bright. Roland had heard that tone of eager explanation many times before, but not for a long time now.

'It has no other purpose?'

'None,' she said. 'But it must whistle, for it's part of the story, isn't it?'

Roland nodded. Of course it was.

The Sisters of Oriza, Margaret Eisenhart said, was a group of women who liked to help others—

'And gossip amongst theirselves,' Eisenhart growled, but he sounded good-humored.

'Aye, that too,' she allowed.

They cooked for funerals and festivals (it was the Sisters who had put on the previous night's banquet at the Pavilion). They sometimes held sewing circles and quilting bees after a family had lost its belongings to fire or when one of the river-floods came every six or eight years and drowned the smallholders closest to Devar-Tete Whye. It was the Sisters who kept the Pavilion well-tended and the Town Gathering Hall well-swept on the inside and well-kept on the outside. They put on dances for the young people, and chaperoned them. They were sometimes hired by the richer folk ('Such as the Tooks and their kin, do ya,' she said) to cater wedding celebrations, and such affairs were always fine, the talk of the Calla for months after-ward, sure. Among themselves they *did* gossip, aye, she'd not deny it; they also played cards, and Points, and Castles.

'And you throw the plate,' Roland said.

'Aye,' said she, 'but ye must understand we only do it for the fun of the thing. Hunting's men's work, and they do fine with the bah.' She was stroking her husband's shoulder again, this time a bit nervously, Roland thought. He also thought that if the men really did do fine with the bah, she never would have come out with that pretty, deadly thing held under her apron in the first place. Nor would Eisenhart have encouraged her.

Roland opened his tobacco-pouch, took out one of Rosalita's cornshuck pulls, and drifted it toward the plate's sharp edge. The square of cornshuck fluttered to the porch a moment later, cut neatly in two. *Only for the fun of the thing*, Roland thought, and almost smiled.

'What metal?' he asked. 'Does thee know?'

She raised her eyebrows slightly at this form of address but didn't comment on it. 'Titanium is what Andy calls it. It comes from a great old factory building, far north, in Calla Sen Chre. There are many ruins there. I've never been, but I've heard the tales. It sounds spooky.'

Roland nodded. 'And the plates — how are they made? Does Andy do it?'

She shook her head. 'He can't or won't, I know not which. It's the ladies of Calla Sen Chre who make them, and send them to the Callas all round about. Although Divine is as far south as that sort of trading reaches, I think.'

'The ladies make these,' Roland mused. 'The *ladies*.'

'Somewhere there's a machine that still makes em, that's all it is,' Eisenhart said. Roland was amused at his tone of stiff defensiveness. 'Comes down to no more than pushing a button, I 'magine.'

Margaret, looking at him with a woman's smile, said nothing to this, either for or against. Perhaps she didn't know, but she certainly knew the politics that keep a marriage sweet.

'So there are Sisters north and south of here along the Arc,' Roland said. 'And all of them throw the plate.'

'Aye – from Calla Sen Chre to Calla Divine south of us. Farther south or north, I don't know. We like to help and we like to talk. We throw our plates once a month, in memory of how Lady Oriza did for Gray Dick, but few of us are any good at it.'

'Are *you* good at it, sai?'

She was silent, biting at the corner of her lip again.

'Show him,' Eisenhart growled. 'Show him and be done.'

5

They walked down the steps, the rancher's wife leading the way, Eisenhart behind her, Roland third. Behind them the kitchen door opened and banged shut.

'Gods-a-glory, missus Eisenhart's gonna throw the dish!' Benny Slightman cried gleefully. 'Jake! You won't believe it!'

'Send em back in, Vaughn,' she said. 'They don't need to see this.'

'Nar, let em look,' Eisenhart said. 'Don't hurt a boy to see a woman do well.'

'Send them back, Roland, aye?' She looked at him, flushed and flustered and very pretty. To Roland she looked ten years younger than when she'd come out on the porch, but he wondered how she'd fling in such a state. It was something he much wanted to see, because ambushing was brutal work, quick and emotional.

'I agree with your husband,' he said. 'I'd let them stay.'

'Have it as you like,' she said. Roland saw she was actually pleased, that she *wanted* an audience, and his hope grew. He thought it increasingly likely that this pretty middle-aged wife with her small breasts and salt-and-pepper hair had a hunter's heart. Not a gunslinger's heart, but at this point he would settle for a few hunters — a few *killers* — male or female.

She marched toward the barn. When they were fifty yards from the stuffy-guys flanking the barn door, Roland touched her shoulder and made her stop.

'Nay,' she said, 'this is too far.'

'I've seen you fling as far and half again,' her husband said, and stood firm in the face of her angry look. 'So I have.'

'Not with a gunslinger from the Line of Eld standing by my right elbow, you haven't,' she said, but she stood where she was.

Roland went to the barn door and took the grinning sharproot head from the stuffy on the left side. He went into the barn. Here was a stall filled with freshly picked sharproot, and beside it one of potatoes. He took one of the potatoes and set it atop the stuffy-guy's shoulders, where the sharproot had been. It was a good-sized spud, but the contrast was still comic; the stuffy-guy now looked like Mr Tinyhead in a carnival show or street-fair.

'Oh, Roland, no!' she cried, sounding genuinely shocked. 'I could never!'

'I don't believe you,' he said, and stood aside. 'Throw.'

For a moment he thought she wouldn't. She looked around for her husband. If Eisenhart had still been standing beside her, Roland thought, she would have thrust the plate into his hands and run for the house and never mind if he cut himself on it, either. But Vaughn Eisenhart had withdrawn to the foot of the steps. The boys stood above him, Benny Slightman watching with mere interest, Jake with closer attention, his brows drawn together and the smile now gone from his face.

'Roland, I—'

'None of it, missus, I beg. Your talk of leaping was all very fine, but now I'd see you do it. *Throw.*'

She recoiled a little, eyes widening, as if she had been slapped. Then she turned to face the barn door and drew her right hand above her left shoulder. The plate glimmered in the late light, which was now more pink than red. Her lips had thinned to a white line. For a moment all the world held still.

'*Riza!*' she cried in a shrill, furious voice, and cast her arm forward. Her hand opened, the index finger pointing precisely along the path the plate would take. Of all of them in the yard (the cowpokes had also stopped to watch), only Roland's eyes were sharp enough to follow the flight of the dish.

True! he exulted. *True as ever was!*

The plate gave a kind of moaning howl as it bolted above the dirt yard. Less than two seconds after it had left her hand, the potato lay in two pieces, one by the stuffy-guy's gloved right hand and the other by its left. The plate itself stuck in the side of the barn door, quivering.

The boys raised a cheer. Benny hoisted his hand as his new friend had taught him, and Jake slapped him a high five.

'Great going, sai Eisenhart!' Jake called.

'Good hit! Say thankya!' Benny added.

Roland observed the way the woman's lips drew back from her teeth at this hapless, well-meant praise — she looked like a horse that has seen a snake. 'Boys,' he said, 'I'd go inside now, were I you.'

Benny was bewildered. Jake, however, took another look at Margaret Eisenhart and understood. You did what you had to . . . and then the reaction set in. 'Come on, Ben,' he said.

'But—'

'Come *on*.' Jake took his new friend by the shirt and tugged him back toward the kitchen door.

Roland let the woman stay where she was for a moment, head down, trembling with reaction. Strong color still blazed in her cheeks, but everywhere else her skin had gone as pale as milk. He thought she was struggling not to vomit.

He went to the barn door, grasped the plate at the grasping-place, and pulled. He was astounded at how much effort it took before the plate first wiggled and then pulled loose. He brought it back to her, held it out. 'Thy tool.'

For a moment she didn't take it, only looked at him with a species of bright hate. 'Why do you mock me, Roland? How do 'ee know Vaughn took me from the Manni Clan? Tell us that, I beg.'

It was the rose, of course — an intuition left by the touch of the rose — and it was also the tale of her face, which was a womanly version of the old Henchick's. But how he knew what he knew was no part of this woman's business, and he only shook his head. 'Nay. But I do not mock thee.'

Margaret Eisenhart abruptly seized Roland by the neck. Her grip was dry and so hot her skin felt feverish. She pulled his ear to her uneasy, twitching mouth. He thought he could smell every bad dream she must have had since deciding to leave her people for Calla Bryn Sturgis's big rancher.

'I saw thee speak to Henchick last night,' she said. 'Will 'ee speak to him more? Ye will, won't you?'

Roland nodded, transfixed by her grip. The strength of it. The little puffs of air against his ear. Did a lunatic hide deep down inside everyone, even such a woman as this? He didn't know.

'Good. Say thankya. Tell him Margaret of the Redpath Clan does fine with her heathen man, aye, fine still.' Her grip tightened. 'Tell him she regrets *nothing*! Will 'ee do that for me?'

'Aye, lady, if you like.'

She snatched the plate from him, fearless of its lethal edge. Having it seemed to steady her. She looked at him from eyes in which tears swam, unshed. 'Is it the cave ye spoke of with my Da'? The Doorway Cave?'

Roland nodded.

'What would ye visit on us, ye chary gunstruck man?'

Eisenhart joined them. He looked uncertainly at his wife, who had endured exile from her people for his sake. For a moment she looked at him as though she didn't know him.

'I only do as ka wills,' Roland said.

'Ka!' she cried, and her lip lifted. A sneer transformed her good looks to an ugliness that was almost startling. It would have frightened the boys. 'Every troublemaker's excuse! Put it up your bum with the rest of the dirt!'

'I do as ka wills and so will you,' Roland said.

She looked at him, seeming not to comprehend. Roland took the hot hand that had gripped him and squeezed it, not quite to the point of pain. *'And so will you.'*

She met his gaze for a moment, then dropped her eyes. 'Aye,' she muttered. 'Oh aye, so do we all.' She ventured to look at him again. 'Will ye give Henchick my message?'

'Aye, lady, as I said.'

The darkening dooryard was silent except for the distant call of a rustie. The cowpokes still leaned at the remuda fence. Roland ambled over to them.

'Evening, gents.'

'Hope ya do well,' one said, and touched his forehead.

'May you do better,' Roland said. 'Missus threw the plate, and she threw it well, say aye?'

'Say thankya,' another of them agreed. 'No rust on the missus.'

'No rust,' Roland agreed. 'And will I tell you something now, gents? A word to tuck beneath your hats, as we do say?'

They looked at him warily.

Roland looked up, smiled at the sky. Then looked back at them. 'Set my watch and warrant on't. You might want to speak of it. Tell what you saw.'

They watched him cautiously, not liking to admit to this.

'Speak of it and I'll kill every one of you,' Roland said. 'Do you understand me?'

Eisenhart touched his shoulder. 'Roland, surely—'

The gunslinger shrugged his hand off without looking at him. 'Do you understand me?'

They nodded.

'And believe me?'

They nodded again. They looked frightened. Roland was glad to see it. They were right to be afraid. 'Say thankya.'

'Say thanks,' one of them repeated. He had broken a sweat.

'Aye,' said the second.

'Thankya big-big,' said the third, and shot a nervous stream of tobacco to one side.

Eisenhart tried again. 'Roland, hear me, I beg—'

But Roland didn't. His mind was alight with ideas. All at once he saw their course with perfect clarity. Their course on *this* side, at least. 'Where's the robot?' he asked the rancher.

'Andy? Went in the kitchen with the boys, I think.'

'Good. Do you have a stockline office in there?' He nodded toward the barn.

'Aye.'

'Let's go there, then. You, me, and your missus.'

'I'd like to take her into the house a bit,' Eisenhart said. *I'd like to take her anywhere that's away from you*, Roland read in his eyes.

'Our palaver won't be long,' Roland said, and with perfect honesty. He'd already seen everything he needed.

6

The stockline office only had a single chair, the one behind the desk. Margaret took it. Eisenhart sat on a footstool. Roland squatted on his hunkers with his back to the wall and his purse open before him. He had shown them the twins' map. Eisenhart hadn't immediately grasped what Roland had pointed out (might not grasp it even now), but the woman did. Roland thought it no wonder she hadn't been able to stay with the Manni. The Manni were peaceful. Margaret Eisenhart was not. Not once you got below her surface, at any rate.

'You'll keep this to yourselves,' he said.

'Or thee'll kill us, like our cowpokes?' she asked.

Roland gave her a patient look, and she colored beneath it.

'I'm sorry, Roland. I'm upset. It comes of throwing the plate in hot blood.'

Eisenhart put an arm around her. This time she accepted it gladly, and laid her head on his shoulder.

'Who else in your group can throw as well as that?' Roland asked. 'Any?'

'Zalia Jaffords,' she said at once.

'Say true?'

She nodded emphatically. 'Zalia could have cut that tater in two ten-for-ten, at twenty paces farther back.'

'Others?'

'Sarey Adams, wife of Diego. And Rosalita Munoz.'

Roland raised his eyebrows at that.

'Aye,' she said. 'Other than Zalia, Rosie's best.' A brief pause. 'And me, I suppose.'

Roland felt as if a huge weight had rolled off his back. He'd been convinced they'd somehow have to bring back weapons from New York or find them on the east side of the river. Now it looked as if that might not be necessary. Good. They had other business in New York — business involving Calvin Tower. He didn't want to mix the two unless he absolutely had to.

'I'd see you four women at the Old Fella's rectory-house. And *just* you four.' His eyes flicked briefly to Eisenhart, then back to Eisenhart's sai. 'No husbands.'

'Now wait just a damn minute,' Eisenhart said.

Roland held up his hand. 'Nothing's been decided yet.'

'It's the *way* it's not been decided I don't care for,' Eisenhart said.

'Hush a minute,' Margaret said. 'When would you see us?'

Roland calculated. Twenty-four days left, perhaps only twenty-three and still much left to see. And there was the thing hidden in the Old Fella's church, that to deal with, too. And the old Manni, Henchick . . .

Yet in the end, he knew, the day would come and things would play out with shocking suddenness. They always did. Five minutes, ten at most, and all would be finished, for good or ill.

The trick was to be ready when those few minutes came around.

'Ten days from now,' he said. 'In the evening. I'd see the four of you in competition, turn and turn about.'

'All right,' she said. 'That much we can do. But Roland . . . I'll not throw so much as a single plate or raise a single finger against the Wolves if my husband still says no.'

'I understand,' Roland said, knowing she would do as he said, like it or not. When the time came they all would.

There was one small window in the office wall, dirty and festooned with cobwebs but clear enough for them to be able to see Andy marching across the yard, his electric eyes flashing on and off in the deepening twilight. He was humming to himself.

'Eddie says robots are programmed to do certain tasks,' he said. 'Andy does the tasks you bid him?'

'Mostly, yes,' Eisenhart said. 'Not always. And he's not always around, ye ken.'

'Hard to believe he was built to do no more than sing foolish songs and tell horoscopes,' Roland mused.

'Perhaps the Old People gave him hobbies,' Margaret Eisenhart said, 'and now that his main tasks are gone — lost in time, do ya ken — he concentrates on the hobbies.'

'You think the Old People made him?'

'Who else?' Vaughn Eisenhart asked. Andy was gone now, and the back yard was empty.

'Aye, who else,' Roland said, still musing. 'Who else would have the wit and the tools? But the Old People were gone two thousand years before the Wolves began raiding into the Calla. Two thousand or more. So what I'd like to know is who or what programmed Andy not to talk about them, *except to tell you folks when they're coming*. And here's another question, not as interesting as that but still curious: why does he tell you that much if he cannot – or will not – tell you anything else?'

Eisenhart and his wife were looking at each other, thunderstruck. They'd not gotten past the first part of what Roland had said. The gunslinger wasn't surprised, but he was a little disappointed in them. Really, there was much here that was obvious. If, that was, one set one's wits to work. In fairness to the Eisenharts, Jaffordses, and Overholsers of the Calla, he supposed, straight thinking wasn't so easy when your babbies were at stake.

There was a knock at the door. Eisenhart called, 'Come!'

It was Ben Slightman. 'Stock's all put to bed, boss.' He took off his glasses and polished them on his shirt. 'And the boys're off with Benny's tent. Andy was stalkin em close, so that's well.' Slightman looked at Roland. 'It's early for rock-cats, but if one *were* to come, Andy'd give my boy at least one shot at it with his bah – he's been told so and comes back "Order recorded." If Benny were to miss, Andy'd get between the boys and the cat. He's programmed strictly for defense and we've never been able to change that, but if the cat were to keep coming—'

'Andy'd rip it to pieces,' Eisenhart said. He spoke with a species of gloomy satisfaction.

'Fast, is he?' Roland asked.

'Yer-bugger,' Slightman said. 'Don't look it, do he, all tall and gangly like he is? But aye, he can move like greased lightning when he wants to. Faster than any rock-cat. We believe he must run on ant-nomics.'

'Very likely,' Roland said absently.

'Never mind that,' Eisenhart said, 'but listen, Ben – why d'you suppose it is that Andy won't talk about the Wolves?'

'His programming—'

'Aye, but it's as Roland pointed out to us just before 'ee came in – and we should have seen it for ourselves long before this – if the Old People set him a-going and then the Old People died out or moved on ... *long* before the Wolves showed themselves ... do you see the problem?'

Slightman the Elder nodded, then put his glasses back on. 'Must have been something like the Wolves in the elden days, don't you think? Enough like em so Andy can't tell em apart. It's all I can figure.'

Is it really? Roland thought.

He produced the Tavery twins' map, opened it, and tapped an arroyo in the hill country northeast of town. It wound its way deeper and deeper into those hills before ending in one of the Calla's old garnet mines. This one was a shaft that went thirty feet into a hillside and then stopped. The place wasn't really much like Eyebolt Canyon in Mejis (there was no thinny in the arroyo, for one thing), but there was one crucial similarity: both were dead ends. And, Roland knew, a man will try to take service again from that which has served him once. That he should pick this arroyo, this dead-end mineshaft, for his ambush of the Wolves made perfect sense. To Eddie, to Susannah, to the Eisenharts, and now to the Eisenharts' foreman. It would make sense to Sarey Adams and Rosalita Munoz. It would make sense to the Old Fella. He would disclose this much of his plan to others, and it would make sense to them, as well.

And if things were left out? If some of what he said was a lie?

If the Wolves got wind of the lie and believed it?

That would be good, wouldn't it? Good if they lunged and snapped in the right direction, but at the wrong thing?

Yes, but I'll need to trust someone with the whole truth eventually. Who?

Not Susannah, because Susannah was now two again, and he didn't trust the other one.

Not Eddie, because Eddie might let something crucial slip to Susannah, and then Mia would know.

Not Jake, because Jake had become fast friends with Benny Slightman.

He was on his own again, and this condition had never felt more lonely to him.

'Look,' he said, tapping the arroyo. 'Here's a place you might think of, Slightman. Easy to get in, not so easy to get back out. Suppose we were to take all the children of a certain age and tuck them away safe in this little bit of a mine?'

He saw understanding begin to dawn in Slightman's eyes. Something else, too. Hope, maybe.

'If we hide the children, they know where,' Eisenhart said. 'It's as if they smell em, like ogres in a kid's cradle-story.'

'So I'm told,' Roland said. 'What I suggest is that we could use that.'

'Make em bait, you mean. Gunslinger, that's hard.'

Roland, who had no intention of putting the Calla's children in the abandoned garnet mine — or anywhere near it — nodded his head. 'Hard world sometimes, Eisenhart.'

'Say thankya,' Eisenhart replied, but his face was grim. He touched the map. 'Could work. Aye, could work . . . *if* ye could suck all the Wolves in.'

Wherever the children wind up, I'll need help putting them there, Roland thought.

There'll have to be people who know where to go and what to do. A plan. But not yet. For now I can play the game I'm playing. It's like Castles. Because someone's hiding.

Did he *know* that? He did not.

Did he smell it? Aye, he did.

Now it's twenty-four, Roland thought. *Twenty-four days until the Wolves.*

It would have to be enough.

CHAPTER VI

GRAN-PERE'S TALE

1

Eddie, a city boy to the core, was almost shocked by how much he liked the Jaffords place on the River Road. *I could live in a place like this*, he thought. *That'd be okay. It'd do me fine.*

It was a long log cabin, craftily built and chinked against the winter winds. Along one side there were large windows which gave a view down a long, gentle hill to the rice-fields and the river. On the other side was the barn and the dooryard, beaten dirt that had been prettied up with circular islands of grass and flowers and, to the left of the back porch, a rather exotic little vegetable garden. Half of it was filled with a yellow herb called madrigal, which Tian hoped to grow in quantity the following year.

Susannah asked Zalia how she kept the chickens out of the stuff, and the woman laughed ruefully, blowing hair back from her forehead. 'With great effort, that's how,' she said. 'Yet the madrigal *does* grow, you see, and where things grow, there's always hope.'

What Eddie liked was the way it all seemed to work together and produce a feeling of home. You couldn't exactly say what caused that feeling, because it was no one thing, but—

Yeah, there is one thing. And it doesn't have anything to do with the rustic log-cabin look of the place or the vegetable garden and the pecking chickens or the beds of flowers, either.

It was the kids. At first Eddie had been a little stunned by the number of them, produced for his and Suze's inspection like a platoon of soldiers for the eye of a visiting general. And by God, at first glance there looked like almost enough of them to *fill* a platoon . . . or a squad, at least.

'Them on the end're Heddon and Hedda,' Zalia said, pointing to the pair of dark blonds. 'They're ten. Make your manners, you two.'

Heddon sketched a bow, at the same time tapping his grimy forehead with the side of an even grimier fist. *Covering all the bases*, Eddie thought. The girl curtsied.

'Long nights and pleasant days,' said Heddon.

'That's *pleasant days* and *long lives*, dummikins,' Hedda stage-whispered, then curtsied and repeated the sentiment in what she felt was the correct manner. Heddon was too overawed by the outworlders to glower at his know-it-all sister, or even really to notice her.

'The two young 'uns is Lyman and Lia,' Zalia said.

Lyman, who appeared all eyes and gaping mouth, bowed so violently he nearly fell in the dirt. Lia actually did tumble over while making her curtsy. Eddie had to struggle to keep a straight face as Hedda picked her sister out of the dust, hissing.

'And this 'un,' she said, kissing the large baby in her arms, 'is Aaron, my little love.'

'Your singleton,' Susannah said.

'Aye, lady, so he is.'

Aaron began to struggle, kicking and twisting. Zalia put him down. Aaron hitched up his diaper and trotted off toward the side of the house, yelling for his Da'.

'Heddon, go after him and mind him,' Zalia said.

'Maw-Maw, *no!*' He sent her frantic eye-signals to the effect that he wanted to stay right here, listening to the strangers and eating them up with his eyes.

'Maw-Maw, *yes*,' Zalia said. 'Garn and mind your brother, Heddon.'

The boy might have argued further, but at that moment Tian Jaffords came around the corner of the cabin and swept the little boy up into his arms. Aaron crowed, knocked off his Da's straw hat, pulled at his Da's sweaty hair.

Eddie and Susannah barely noticed this. They had eyes only for the overall-clad giants following along in Jaffords's wake. Eddie and Susannah had seen maybe a dozen extremely large people on their tour of the small-hold farms along the River Road, but always at a distance. ('Most of em 're shy of strangers, do ye ken,' Eisenhart had said.) These two were less than ten feet away.

Man and woman or boy and girl? *Both at the same time*, Eddie thought. *Because their ages don't matter.*

The female, sweaty and laughing, had to be six-six, with breasts that looked twice as big as Eddie's head. Around her neck on a string was a wooden crucifix. The male had at least six inches on his sister-in-law. He looked at the newcomers shyly, then began sucking his thumb with one hand and squeezing his crotch with the other. To Eddie the most amazing thing about them wasn't their size but their eerie resemblance to Tian and Zalia. It was like looking at the clumsy first drafts of some ultimately successful work of art. They were so clearly idiots, the both of them, and so clearly, so *closely*, related to people who weren't. *Eerie* was the only word for them.

No, Eddie thought, *the word is roont*.

'This is my brother, Zalman,' Zalia said, her tone oddly formal.

'And my sister, Tia,' Tian added. 'Make your manners, you two galoots.'

Zalman just went ahead sucking one piece of himself and kneading the other. Tia, however, gave a huge (and somehow ducklike) curtsy. 'Long days long nights long earth!' she cried. '*WE GET TATERS AND GRAVY!*'

'Good,' Susannah said quietly. 'Taters and gravy is good.'

'*TATERS AND GRAVY IS GOOD!*' Tia wrinkled her nose, pulling her upper lip away from her teeth in a piglike sneer of good fellowship. '*TATERS AND GRAVY! TATERS AND GRAVY! GOOD OL' TATERS AND GRAVY!*'

Hedda touched Susannah's hand hesitantly. 'She go on like that all day unless you tell her shush, missus-sai.'

'Shush, Tia,' Susannah said.

Tia gave a honk of laughter at the sky, crossed her arms over her prodigious bosom, and fell silent.

'Zal,' Tian said. 'You need to go pee-pee, don't you?'

Zalia's brother said nothing, only continued squeezing his crotch.

'Go pee-pee,' Tian said. 'You go on behind the barn. Water the sharproot, say thankya.'

For a moment nothing happened. Then Zalman set off, moving in a wide, shambling gait.

'When they were young—' Susannah began.

'Bright as polished agates, the both of em,' Zalia said. 'Now she's bad and my brother's even worse.'

She abruptly put her hands over her face. Aaron gave a high laugh at this and covered his own face in imitation ('Peet-a-boo!' he called through his fingers), but both sets of twins looked grave. Alarmed, even.

'What's wrong 'it Maw-Maw?' Lyman asked, tugging at his father's pantsleg. Zalman, heedless of all, continued toward the barn, still with one hand in his mouth and the other in his crotch.

'Nothing, son. Your Maw-Maw's all right.' Tian put the baby down, then ran his arm across his eyes. 'Everything's fine. Ain't it, Zee?'

'Aye,' she said, lowering her hands. The rims of her eyes were red, but she wasn't crying. 'And with the blessing, what ain't fine will be.'

'From your lips to God's ear,' Eddie said, watching the giant shamble toward the barn. 'From your lips to God's ear.'

2

'Is he having one of his bright days, your Gran-pere?' Eddie asked Tian a few minutes later. They had walked around to where Tian could show Eddie the field he called Son of a Bitch, leaving Zalia and Susannah with all children great and small.

'Not so's you'd notice,' Tian said, his brow darkening. 'He ain't half-addled these last few years, and won't have nobbut to do with me, anyway. *Her*, aye, because she'll hand-feed him, then wipe the drool off his chin for him and tell him thankya. Ain't enough I got two great roont galoots to feed, is it? I've got to have that bad-natured old man, as well. Head's gone as rusty as an old hinge. Half the time he don't even know where he is, say any small-small!'

They walked, high grass swishing against their pants. Twice Eddie almost tripped over rocks, and once Tian seized his arm and led him around what looked like a right leg-smasher of a hole. *No wonder he calls it Son of a Bitch*, Eddie thought. And yet there were signs of cultivation. Hard to believe anyone could pull a plow through this mess, but it looked as if Tian Jaffords had been trying.

'If your wife's right, I think I need to talk to him,' Eddie said. 'Need to hear his story.'

'My Granda's got stories, all right. Half a thousand! Trouble is, most of em was lies from the start and now he gets em all mixed up together. His accent were always thick, and these last three years he's missing his last three teeth as well. Likely you won't be able to understand his nonsense to begin with. I wish you joy of him, Eddie of New York.'

'What the hell did he do to you, Tian?'

''Twasn't what he did to me but what he did to my Da'. That's a long story and nothing to do with this business. Leave it.'

'No, *you* leave it,' Eddie said, coming to a stop.

Tian looked at him, startled. Eddie nodded, unsmiling: you heard me.

He was twenty-five, already a year older than Cuthbert Allgood on his last day at Jericho Hill, but in this day's failing light he could have passed for a man of fifty. One of harsh certainty.

'If he's seen a dead Wolf, we need to debrief him.'

'I don't kennit, Eddie.'

'Yeah, but I think you ken my *point* just fine. Whatever you've got against him, put it aside. If we settle up with the Wolves, you have my permission to bump him into the fireplace or push him off the goddam roof. But for now, keep your sore ass to yourself. Okay?'

Tian nodded. He stood looking out across his troublesome north field, the one he called Son of a Bitch, with his hands in his pockets. When he studied it so, his expression was one of troubled greed.

'Do you think his story about killing a Wolf is so much hot air? If you really do, I won't waste my time.'

Grudgingly, Tian said: 'I'm more apt to believe that 'un than most of the others.'

'Why?'

'Well, he were tellin it ever since I were old enough to listen, and *that* 'un never changes much. Also . . .'. Tian's next words squeezed down, as if he were speaking them through gritted teeth. 'My Gran-pere never had no shortage of thorn and bark. If anyone would have had guts enough to go out on the East Road and stand against the Wolves – not to mention enough trum to get others to go with him – I'd bet my money on Jamie Jaffords.'

'Trum?'

Tian thought about how to explain it. 'If 'ee was to stick your head in a rock-cat's mouth, that'd take courage, wouldn't it?'

It would take idiocy was what Eddie thought, but he nodded.

'If 'ee was the sort of man could convince someone *else* to stick his head in a rock-cat's mouth, that'd make you trum. Your dinh's trum, ain't he?'

Eddie remembered some of the stuff Roland had gotten him to do, and nodded. Roland was trum, all right. He was trum as hell. Eddie was sure the gunslinger's old mates would have said the same.

'Aye,' Tian said, turning his gaze back to his field. 'In any case, if ye'd get something halfway sensible out of the old man, I'd wait until after supper. He brightens a bit once he's had his rations and half a pint of graf. And make sure my wife's sitting right beside you, where he can get an eyeful. I 'magine he'd try to have a good deal more than his eye on her, were he a younger man.' His face had darkened again.

Eddie clapped him on the shoulder. 'Well, he's not younger. *You* are. So lighten up, all right?'

'Aye.' Tian made a visible effort to do just that. 'What do 'ee think of my field, gunslinger? I'm going to plant it with madrigal next year. The yellow stuff ye saw out front.'

What Eddie thought was that the field looked like a heartbreak waiting to happen. He suspected that down deep Tian thought about the same; you didn't call your only unplanted field Son of a Bitch because you expected good things to happen there. But he knew the look on Tian's face. It was the one Henry used to get when the two of them were setting off to score. It was always going to be the best stuff this time, the best stuff ever. China White and never mind that Mexican Brown that made your head ache and your bowels run. They'd get high for a week, the best high ever, *mellow*, and then quit the junk for good. That was Henry's scripture, and it could have been Henry here beside him, telling Eddie what a fine cash crop madrigal was, and how the people who'd told him you couldn't grow it this far north would be laughing on the other side of their faces come next reap. And then he'd buy Hugh Anselm's field over on the far side of yon ridge ... hire a couple of extra men come reap, for the land 'd be gold for as far as you could see ... why, he might even quit the rice altogether and become a madrigal monarch.

Eddie nodded toward the field, which was hardly half-turned. 'Looks like slow plowing, though. You must have to be damned careful with the mules.'

Tian gave a short laugh. 'I'd not risk a mule out here, Eddie.'

'Then what——?'

'I plow my sister.'

Eddie's jaw dropped. 'You're shitting me!'

'Not at all. I'd plow Zal, too — he's bigger, as ye saw, and even stronger — but not as bright. More trouble than it's worth. I've tried.'

Eddie shook his head, feeling dazed. Their shadows ran out long over the lumpy earth, with its crop of weed and thistle. 'But ... man ... she's your *sister!*'

'Aye, and what else would she do all day? Sit outside the barn door and watch the chickens? Sleep more and more hours, and only get up for her taters and gravy? This is better, believe me. She don't mind it. It's tur'ble hard to get her to plow straight, even when there ain't a plow-buster of a rock or a hole every eight or ten steps, but she pulls like the devil and laughs like a loon.'

What convinced Eddie was the man's earnestness. There was no defensiveness in it, not that he could detect.

'Sides, she'll likely be dead in another ten year, anyway. Let her help while she can, I say. And Zalia feels the same.'

'Okay, but why don't you get Andy to do at least some of the plowing? I bet it'd go faster if you did. All you guys with the smallhold farms could share him, ever think of that? He could plow your fields, dig your wells, raise a barn roofbeam all by himself. And you'd save on taters and gravy.' He clapped Tian on the shoulder again. 'That's *got* to do ya fine.'

Tian's mouth quirked. 'It's a lovely dream, all right.'

'Doesn't work, huh? Or rather, *he* doesn't work.'

'Some things he'll do, but plowing fields and digging wells ain't among em. You ask him, and he'll ask *you* for your password. When you have no password to give him, he'll ask you if you'd like to retry. And then—'

'Then he tells you you're shit out of luck. Because of Directive Nineteen.'

'If you knew, why did you ask?'

'I knew he was that way about the Wolves, because I asked him. I didn't know it extended to all this other stuff.'

Tian nodded. 'He's really not much help, and he can be tiresome – if 'ee don't ken that now, ye will if 'ee stay long – but he *does* tell us when the Wolves are on their way, and for that we all say thankya.'

Eddie actually had to bite off the question that came to his lips. Why did they thank him when his news was good for nothing except making them miserable? Of course this time there might be more to it; this time Andy's news might actually lead to a change. Was that what Mr You-Will-Meet-An-Interesting-Stranger had been angling for all along? Getting the *folken* to stand up on their hind legs and fight? Eddie recalled Andy's decidedly smarmy smile and found such altruism hard to swallow. It wasn't fair to judge people (or even robots, maybe) by the way they smiled or talked, and yet everybody did it.

Now that I think about it, what about his voice? What about that smug little I-know-and-you-don't thing he's got going on? Or am I imagining that, too?

The hell of it was, he didn't know.

3

The sound of Susannah's singing voice accompanied by the giggles of the children — all children great and small — drew Eddie and Tian back around to the other side of the house.

Zalman was holding one end of what looked like a stock-rope. Tia had the other. They were turning it in lazy loops with large, delighted grins on their faces while Susannah, sitting propped on the ground, recited a skip-rope rhyme Eddie vaguely remembered. Zalia and her four older children were jumping in unison, their hair rising and falling. Baby Aaron stood by, his diaper now sagging almost to his knees. On his face was a huge, delighted grin. He made rope-twirling motions with one chubby fist.

"'Pinky Pauper came a-calling! Into sin that boy be falling! I caught him creeping, one-two-three, he's as wicked as can be!" Faster, Zalman! Faster, Tia! Come on, make em really jump to it!'

Tia spun her end of the rope faster at once, and a moment later Zalman caught up with her. This was apparently something he could do. Laughing, Susannah chanted faster.

"'Pinky Pauper took her measure! That bad boy done took her treasure! Four-five-six, we're up to seven, that bad boy won't go to heaven!" Yow, Zalia, I see your knees, girl! Faster, you guys! Faster!'

The four twins jumped like shuttlecocks, Heddon tucking his fists into his armpits and doing a buck and wing. Now that they had gotten over the awe which had made them clumsy, the two younger kids jumped in limber spooky harmony. Even their hair seemed to fly up in the same clumps. Eddie found himself remembering the Tavery twins, whose very freckles had looked the same.

"'Pinky . . . Pinky Pauper . . .'" Then she stopped. 'Shoo-fly, Eddie! I can't remember any more!'

'Faster, you guys,' Eddie said to the giants turning the skip-rope. They did as he said, Tia hee-hawing up at the fading sky. Eddie measured the spin of the rope with his eyes, moving backward and forward at the knees, timing it. He put his hand on the butt of Roland's gun to make sure it wouldn't fly free.

'Eddie Dean, you cain't *never!*' Susannah cried, laughing.

But the next time the rope flew up he did, jumping in between Hedda and Hedda's mother. He faced Zalia, whose face was flushed and sweating, jumping with her in perfect harmony, Eddie chanted the one verse that survived in his memory. To keep it in time, he had to go almost as fast as a county fair auctioneer. He didn't realize until later that he had changed the bad boy's name, giving it a twist that was pure Brooklyn.

'"Piggy Pecker pick my pocket, took my baby's silver locket, caught im sleepin eightnineteen, stole that locket back again!" *Go, you guys! Spin it!*'

They did, twirling the rope so fast it was almost a blur. In a world that now appeared to be going up and down on an invisible pogo-stick, he saw an old man with fly-away hair and grizzled sideburns come out on the porch like a hedgehog out of its hole, thumping along on an ironwood cane. *Hello, Gran-pere*, he thought, then dismissed the old man for the time being. All he wanted to do right now was keep his footing and not be the one who fucked the spin. As a little kid, he'd always loved jumping rope and always hated the idea that he had to give it over to the girls once he went to Roosevelt Elementary or be damned forever as a sissy. Later, in high school phys ed, he had briefly rediscovered the joys of jump-rope. But never had there been anything like this. It was as if he had discovered (or rediscovered) some practical magic that bound his and Susannah's New York lives to this other life in a way that required no magic doors or magic balls, no todash state. He laughed deliriously and began to scissor his feet back and forth. A moment later Zalia Jaffords was doing the same, mimicking him step for step. It was as good as the rice-dance. Maybe better, because they were all doing it in unison.

Certainly it was magic for Susannah, and of all the wonders ahead and behind, those few moments in the Jaffordses' dooryard always maintained their own unique luster. Not two of them jumping in tandem, not even four, but *six* of them, while the two great grinning idiots spun the rope as fast as their slab-like arms would allow.

Tian laughed and stomped his shor'boots and cried: 'That beats the drum! Don't it just! Yer-*bugger!*' And from the porch, his grandfather gave out a laugh so rusty that Susannah had to wonder how long ago he had laid that sound away in mothballs.

For another five seconds or so, the magic held. The jump-rope spun so rapidly the eye lost it and it existed as nothing but a whirring sound like a wing. The half-dozen within that whirring — from Eddie, the tallest, at Zalman's end, to pudgy little Lyman, at Tia's — rose and fell like pistons in a machine.

Then the rope caught on someone's heel — Heddon's, it looked like to

Susannah, although later all would take the blame so none had to feel bad – and they sprawled in the dust, gasping and laughing. Eddie, clutching his chest, caught Susannah's eye. 'I'm havin a heart attack, sweetheart, you better call 911.'

She hoisted herself over to where he lay and put her head down so she could kiss him. 'No, you're not,' she said, 'but you're attacking *my* heart, Eddie Dean. I love you.'

He gazed up at her seriously from the dust of the dooryard. He knew that however much she might love him, he would always love her more. And as always when he thought these things, the premonition came that ka was not their friend, that it would end badly between them.

If it's so, then your job is to make it as good as it can be for as long as it can be. Will you do your job, Eddie?

'With greatest pleasure,' he said.

She raised her eyebrows. 'Do ya?' she said, Calla-talk for *Beg pardon?*

'I do,' he said, grinning. 'Believe me, I do.' He put an arm around her neck, pulled her down, kissed her brow, her nose, and finally her lips. The twins laughed and clapped. The baby chortled. And on the porch, old Jamie Jaffords did the same.

4

All of them were hungry after their exercise, and with Susannah helping from her chair, Zalia Jaffords laid a huge meal on the long trestle table out behind the house. The view was a winner, in Eddie's opinion. At the foot of the hill was what he took to be some especially hardy type of rice, now grown to the height of a tall man's shoulder. Beyond it, the river glowed with sunset light.

'Set us on with a word, Zee, if 'ee would,' Tian said.

She looked pleased at that. Susannah told Eddie later that Tian hadn't thought much of his wife's religion, but that seemed to have changed since Pere Callahan's unexpected support of Tian at the Town Gathering Hall.

'Bow your heads, children.'

Four heads dropped – six, counting the big 'uns. Lyman and Lia had their eyes squinched so tightly shut that they looked like children suffering terrible headaches. They held their hands, clean and glowing pink from the pump's cold gush, out in front of them.

'Bless this food to our use, Lord, and make us grateful. Thank you for our company, may we do em fine and they us. Deliver us from the terror that flies at noonday and the one that creeps at night. We say thankee.'

'*Thankee!*' cried the children, Tia almost loudly enough to rattle the windows.

'Name of God the Father and His Son, the Man Jesus,' she said.

'*Man Jesus!*' cried the children. Eddie was amused to see that Gran-pere, who sported a crucifix nearly as large as those worn by Zalman and Tia, sat with his eyes open, peacefully picking his nose during the prayers.

'Amen.'

'*Amen!*'

'*TATERS!*' cried Tia.

5

Tian sat at one end of the long table, Zalia at the other. The twins weren't shunted off to the ghetto of a 'kiddie table' (as Susannah and her cousins always had been at family gatherings, and how she had hated that) but seated a-row on one side, with the older two flanking the younger pair. Heddon helped Lia; Hedda helped Lyman. Susannah and Eddie were seated side by side across from the kids, with one young giant to Susannah's left and the other to Eddie's right. The baby did fine first on his mother's lap and then, when he grew bored with that, on his father's. The old man sat next to Zalia, who served him, cut his meat small-small, and did indeed wipe his chin when the gravy ran down. Tian glowered at this in a sulky way which Eddie felt did him little credit, but he kept his mouth shut, except once to ask his grandfather if he wanted more bread.

'My arm still wuks if Ah do,' the old man said, and snatched up the bread-basket to prove it. He did this smartly for a gent of advanced years, then spoiled the impression of briskness by overturning the jam-cruet. 'Slaggit!' he cried.

The four children looked at each other with round eyes, then covered their mouths and giggled. Tia threw back her head and honked at the sky. One of her elbows caught Eddie in the ribs and almost knocked him off his chair.

'Wish 'ee wouldn't speak so in front of the children,' Zalia said, righting the cruet.

'Cry 'er pardon,' Gran-pere said. Eddie wondered if he would have managed such winning humility if his grandson had been the one to reprimand him.

'Let me help you to a little of that, Gran-pere,' Susannah said, taking the jam from Zalia. The old man watched her with moist, almost worshipful eyes.

'Ain't seen a true brown woman in oh Ah'd have to say forty year,' Gran-pere told her. 'Uster be they'd come on the lake-mart boats, but nummore.' When Gran-pere said *boats*, it came out *butts*.

'I hope it doesn't come as too much of a shock to find out we're still around,' Susannah said, and gave him a smile. The old fellow responded with a goaty, toothless grin.

The steak was tough but tasty, the corn almost as good as that in the meal Andy had prepared near the edge of the woods. The bowl of taters, although almost the size of a washbasin, needed to be refilled twice, the gravy boat three times, but to Eddie the true revelation was the rice. Zalia served three different kinds, and as far as Eddie was concerned, each one was better than the last. The Jaffordses, however, ate it almost absentmindedly, the way people drink water in a restaurant. The meal ended with an apple cobbler, and then the children were sent off to play. Gran-pere put on the finishing touch with a ringing belch. 'Say thankee,' he told Zalia, and tapped his throat three times. 'Fine as ever was, Zee.'

'It does me good to see you eat so, Dad,' she said.

Tian grunted, then said, 'Dad, these two would speak to you of the Wolves.'

'Just Eddie, if it do ya,' Susannah said with quick decisiveness. 'I'll help you clear the table and wash the dishes.'

'There's no need,' Zalia said. Eddie thought the woman was sending Susannah a message with her eyes — *Stay, he likes you* — but Susannah either didn't see it or elected to ignore it.

'Not at all,' she said, transferring herself to her wheelchair with the ease of long experience. 'You'll talk to my man, won't you, sai Jaffords?'

'All that 'us long ago and by the way,' the old man said, but he didn't look unwilling. 'Don't know if Ah kin. My mind dun't hold a tale like it uster.'

'But I'd hear what you do remember,' Eddie said. 'Every word.'

Tia honked laughter as if this were the funniest thing she'd ever heard. Zal did likewise, then scooped the last bit of mashed potato out of the bowl with a hand nearly as big as a cutting board. Tian gave it a brisk smack. 'Never do it, ye great galoot, how many times have 'ee been told?'

'Arright,' Gran-pere said. 'Ah'd talk a bit if ye'd listen, boy. What else kin Ah do 'ith meself these days 'cept clabber? Help me git back on the porch, fur them steps is a strake easier comin down than they is goin up. And if ye'd fatch my pipe, daughter-girl, that'd do me fine, for a pipe helps a man think, so it does.'

'Of course I will,' Zalia said, ignoring another sour look from her husband. 'Right away.'

6

'This were all long ago, ye must ken,' Gran-pere said once Zalia Jaffords had him settled in his rocker with a pillow at the small of his back and his pipe drawing comfortably. 'I canna say for a certain if the Wolves have come twice since or three times, for although I were nineteen reaps on earth then, I've lost count of the years between.'

In the northwest, the red line of sunset had gone a gorgeous ashes-of-roses shade. Tian was in the barn with the animals, aided by Heddon and Hedda. The younger twins were in the kitchen. The giants, Tia and Zalman, stood at the far edge of the dooryard, looking off toward the east, not speaking or moving. They might have been monoliths in a *National Geographic* photograph of Easter Island. Looking at them gave Eddie a moderate case of the creeps. Still, he counted his blessings. Gran-pere seemed relatively bright and aware, and although his accent was thick — almost a burlesque — he'd had no trouble following what the old man was saying, at least so far.

'I don't think the years between matter that much, sir,' Eddie said.

Gran-pere's eyebrows went up. He uttered his rusty laugh. 'Sir, yet! Been long and long sin' Ah heerd that! Ye must be from the northern folk!'

'I guess I am, at that,' Eddie said.

Gran-pere lapsed into a long silence, looking at the fading sunset. Then he looked around at Eddie again with some surprise. 'Did we eat yet? Wittles n rations?'

Eddie's heart sank. 'Yes, sir. At the table on the other side of the house.'

'Ah ask because if Ah'm gonna shoot some dirt, Ah usually shoot it d'recly after the night meal. Don't feel no urge, so Ah thought Ah'd ask.'

'No. We ate.'

'Ah. And what's your name?'

'Eddie Dean.'

'Ah.' The old man drew on his pipe. Twin curls of smoke drifted from his nose. 'And the brownie's yours?' Eddie was about to ask for clarification when Gran-pere gave it. 'The woman.'

'Susannah. Yes, she's my wife.'

'Ah.'

'Sir . . . Gran-pere . . . the Wolves?' But Eddie no longer believed he was going to get anything from the old guy. Maybe Suze could—

'As Ah recall, there was four of us,' Gran-pere said.

'Not five?'

'Nar, nar, although close enow so you could say a moit.' His voice had become dry, matter-of-fact. The accent dropped away a little. 'We 'us young and wild, didn't give a rat's red ass if we lived or died, do ya kennit. Just pissed enow to take a stand whether the rest of 'un said yes, no, or maybe. There 'us me . . . Pokey Slidell . . . who 'us my best friend . . . and there 'us Eamon Doolin and his wife, that redheaded Molly. She was the very devil when it came to throwin the dish.'

'The dish?'

'Aye, the Sisters of Oriza throw it. Zee's one. Ah'll make her show 'ee. They have plates sharpened all the way around except fer where the women hold on, do 'ee ken. Nasty wittit, they are, aye! Make a man witta bah look right stupid. You ort to see.'

Eddie made a mental note to tell Roland. He didn't know if there was anything to this dish-throwing or not, but he *did* know they were extremely short of weapons.

''Twas Molly killed the Wolf—'

'Not you?' Eddie was bemused, thinking of how truth and legend twisted together until there was no untangling them.

'Nar, nar, although' —Gran-pere's eyes gleamed— 'Ah might have said 'twas me on one time or another, mayhap to loosen a young lady's knees when they'd otherwise have stuck together, d'ye ken?'

'I think so.'

''Twas Red Molly did for it witter dish, that's the truth of it, but that's getting the cart out front of the horse. We seen their dust-cloud on the come. Then, mebbe six wheel outside of town, it split throg.'

'What's that? I don't understand.'

Gran-pere held up three warped fingers to show that the Wolves had gone three different ways.

'The biggest bunch — judgin by the dust, kennit — headed into town and went for Took's, which made sense because there were some'd thought to hide their babbies in the storage bin out behind. Tooky had a secret room way at the back where he kep' cash and gems and a few old guns and other outright tradeables he'd taken in; they don't call em Tooks for nothin, ye know!' Again the rusty, cackling chuckle. 'It were a good cosy, not even the folk who worked fer the old buzzard knew it were there, yet when the time come the Wolves went right to it and took the babbies and kilt anyone tried to stand in their way or even speak a word o' beggary to em. And then they whopped at the store with their light-sticks when they rode out and set it to burn. Burnt flat, it did, and they was lucky not to've lost the whole town, young sai, for the flames started out of them sticks the Wolves carry ain't like other fire, that can be put out with enough water. T'row water on these 'uns, they feed on it! Grow higher! Higher and hotter! Yer-bugger!'

He spat over the rail for emphasis, then looked at Eddie shrewdly.

'All of which Ah'm sayin is this: no matter how many in these parts my grandson conwinces to stand up and fight, or you and yer brownie, Eben Took won't never be among em. Tooks has kep' that store since time was toothless, and they don't ever mean to see it burned flat again. Once 'us enough for them cowardy custards, do 'ee foller?'

'Yes.'

'The other two dust-clouds, the biggest of em hied sout' for the ranches. The littlest come down East Rud toward the smallholds, which was where we were, and where we made our stand.'

The old man's face gleamed, memory-bound. Eddie did not glimpse the young man who had been (Gran-pere was too old for that), but in his rheumy eyes he saw the mixture of excitement and determination and sick fear which must have filled him that day. Must have filled them all. Eddie felt himself reaching out for it the way a hungry man will reach for food, and the old man must have seen some of this on his face, for he seemed to swell and gain vigor. Certainly this wasn't a reaction the old man had ever gotten from his grandson; Tian did not lack for bravery, say thankya, but he was a sodbuster for all that. *This* man, however, this Eddie of New

York . . . he might live a short life and die with his face in the dirt, but he was no sodbuster, by 'Riza.

'Go on,' Eddie said.

'Aye. So Ah will. Some of those comin toward us split off on River Rud, toward the little rice-manors that're there – you c'd see the dust – and a few more split off on Peaberry Road. Ah 'member Pokey Slidell turned to me, had this kind of sick smile on his face, and he stuck out his hand (the one didn't have his bah in it), and he said . . .'

7

What Pokey Slidell says under a burning autumn sky with the sound of the season's last crickets rising from the high white grass on either side of them is 'It's been good to know ya, Jamie Jaffords, say true.' He's got a smile on his face like none Jamie has ever seen before, but being only nineteen and living way out here on what some call the Rim and others call the Crescent, there's plenty he's never seen before. Or will ever see, way it looks now. It's a sick smile, but there's no cowardice in it. Jamie guesses he's wearing one just like it. Here they are under the sun of their fathers, and the darkness will soon have them. They've come to their dying hour.

Nonetheless, his grip is strong when he seizes Pokey's hand. 'You ain't done knowin me yet, Pokey,' he says.

'Hope you're right.'

The dust-cloud moils toward them. In a minute, maybe less, they will be able to see the riders throwing it. And, more important, the riders throwing it will be able to see them.

Eamon Doolin says, 'You know, I believe we ort to get in that ditch'—he points to the right side of the road—'an' snay down small-small. Then, soon's they go by, we can jump out and have at em.'

Molly Doolin is wearing tight black silk pants and a white silk blouse open at the throat to show a tiny silver reap charm: Oriza with her fist raised. In her own right hand, Molly holds a sharpened dish, cool blue titanium steel painted over with a delicate lacework of green spring rice. Slung over her shoulder is a reed pouch lined with silk. In it are five more plates, two of her own and three of her mother's. Her hair is so bright in the bright light that it looks as if her head is on fire. Soon enough it will be burning, say true.

'You can do what you like, Eamon Doolin,' she tells him. 'As for me, I'm going to stand right here where they can see me and shout my twin sister's name so they'll hear it plain.

They may ride me down but I'll kill one of 'un or cut the legs out from under one of their damn horses before they do, of that much I'll be bound.'

There's no time for more. The Wolves come out of the dip that marks the entrance to Arra's little smallhold patch, and the four Calla-folken can see them at last and there is no more talk of hiding. Jamie almost expected Eamon Doolin, who is mild-mannered and already losing his hair at twenty-three, to drop his bah and go pelting into the high grass with his hands raised to show his surrender. Instead, he moves into place next to his wife and nocks a bolt. There is a low whirring sound as he winds the cord tight-tight.

They stand across the road with their boots in the floury dust. They stand blocking the road. And what fills Jamie like a blessing is a sense of grace. This is the right thing to do. They're going to die here, but that's all right. Better to die than stand by while they take more children. Each one of them has lost a twin, and Pokey — who is by far the oldest of them — has lost both a brother and a young son to the Wolves. This is right. They understand that the Wolves may exact a toll of vengeance on the rest for this stand they're making, but it doesn't matter. This is right.

'Come on!' Jamie shouts, and winds his own bah — once and twice, then click. 'Come on, 'ee buzzards! 'Ee cowardy custards, come on and have some! Say Calla! Say Calla Bryn Sturgis!'

There is a moment in the heat of the day when the Wolves seem to draw no closer but only to shimmer in place. Then the sound of their horses' hooves, previously dull and muffled, grows sharp. And the Wolves seem to leap forward through the swarming air. Their pants are as gray as the hides of their horses. Dark-green cloaks flow out behind them. Green hoods surround masks (they must be masks) that turn the heads of the four remaining riders into the heads of snarling, hungry wolves.

'Four agin' four!' Jamie screams. 'Four agin' four, even up, stand yer ground, cullies! Never run a step!'

The four Wolves sweep toward them on their gray horses. The men raise their bahs. Molly — sometimes called Red Molly, for her famous temper even more than her hair — raises her dish over her left shoulder. She looks not angry now but cool and calm.

The two Wolves on the end have light-sticks. They raise them. The two in the middle draw back their fists, which are clad in green gloves, to throw something. Sneetches, Jamie thinks coldly. That's what them are.

'Hold, boys . . .' Pokey says. 'Hold . . . hold . . . now!'

He lets fly with a twang, and Jamie sees Pokey's bah-bolt pass just over the head of the Wolf second to the right. Eamon's strikes the neck of the horse on the far left. The beast gives a crazy whinnying cry and staggers just as the Wolves begin to close the final forty yards of distance. It crashes into its neighbor horse just as that second horse's rider throws the thing in his hand. It is indeed one of the sneetches, but it sails far off course and none of its guidance systems can lock onto anything.

Jamie's bolt strikes the chest of the third rider. Jamie begins a scream of triumph that dies in dismay before it ever gets out of his throat. The bolt bounces off the thing's chest just as it would have bounced off Andy's, or a stone in the Son of a Bitch field.

Wearing armor, oh you buggardly thing, you're wearing armor under that twice-damned—

The other sneetch flies true, striking Eamon Doolin square in the face. His head explodes in a spray of blood and bone and mealy gray stuff. The sneetch flies on maybe thirty grop, then whirls and comes back. Jamie ducks and hears it flash over his head, giving off a low, hard hum as it flies.

Molly has never moved, not even when she is showered with her husband's blood and brains. Now she screams 'THIS IS FOR MINNIE, YOU SONS OF WHORES!' and throws her plate. The distance is very short by now — hardly any distance at all — but she throws it hard and the plate rises as soon as it leaves her hand.

Too hard, dear, *Jamie thinks as he ducks the swipe of a light-stick (the light-stick is also giving off that hard, savage buzz).* Too hard, yer-bugger.

But the Wolf at which Molly has aimed actually rides into the rising dish. It strikes at just the point where the thing's green hood crosses the wolf-mask it wears. There is an odd, muffled sound — chump! — and the thing falls backward off its horse with its green-gauntleted hands flying up.

Pokey and Jamie raise a wild cheer, but Molly just reaches coolly into her pouch for another dish, all of them nestled neatly in there with the blunt gripping arcs pointed up. She is pulling it out when one of the light-sticks cuts the arm off her body. She staggers, teeth peeling back from her lips in a snarl, and goes to one knee as her blouse bursts into flame. Jamie is amazed to see that she is reaching for the plate in her severed hand as it lies in the dust of the road.

The three remaining Wolves are past them. The one Molly caught with her dish lies in the dust, jerking crazily, those gauntleted hands flying up and down into the sky as if it's trying to say, 'What can you do? What can you do with these damned sodbusters?'

The other three wheel their mounts as neatly as a drill-team of cavalry soldiers and race back toward them. Molly pries the dish from her own dead fingers, then falls backward, engulfed in fire.

'Stand, Pokey!' *Jamie cries hysterically as their death rushes toward them under the burning steel sky,* 'Stand, gods damn you!' *And still that feeling of grace as he smells the charring flesh of the Doolins. This is what they should have done all along, aye, all of them, for the Wolves* can *be brought down, although they'll probably not live to tell and these will take their dead* compadre *with them so none will know.*

There's a twang as Pokey fires another bolt and then a sneetch strikes him dead center and he explodes inside his clothes, belching blood and torn flesh from his sleeves, his cuffs, from the busted buttons of his fly. Again Jamie is drenched, this time by the hot stew that was his friend. He fires his own bah, and sees it groove the side of a gray horse. He knows it's useless to duck but he ducks anyway and something whirs over his head. One of the horses strikes him hard as it passes, knocking him into the ditch where Eamon proposed they hide. His bah flies from his hand. He lies there, open-eyed, not moving, knowing as they wheel their horses around again that there is nothing for it now but to play dead and hope they pass him by. They won't, of course they won't, but it's the only thing to do and so he does it, trying to give his eyes the glaze of death. In another few seconds, he knows, he won't have to pretend. He smells dust, he hears the crickets in the grass, and he holds onto these things, knowing they are the last things he will ever smell and hear, that the last thing he sees will be the Wolves, bearing down on him with their frozen snarls.

They come pounding back.

One of them turns in its saddle and throws a sneetch from its gloved hand as it passes. But as it throws, the rider's horse leaps the body of the downed Wolf, which still lies twitching in the road, although now its hands barely rise. The sneetch flies above Jamie, just a little too high. He can almost feel it hesitate, searching for prey. Then it soars on, out over the field.

The Wolves ride east, pulling dust behind them. The sneetch doubles back and flies over Jamie again, this time higher and slower. The gray horses sweep around a curve in the road fifty yards east and are lost to view. The last he sees of them are three green cloaks, pulled out almost straight and fluttering.

Jamie stands up in the ditch on legs that threaten to buckle beneath him. The sneetch makes another loop and comes back, this time directly toward him, but now it is moving slowly, as if whatever powers it is almost exhausted. Jamie scrambles back into the road, falls to his knees next to the burning remains of Pokey's body, and seizes his bah. This time he holds it by the end, as one might hold a Points mallet. The sneetch cruises toward him. Jamie draws the bah to his shoulder, and when the thing comes at him, he bats it out of the air as if it were a giant bug. It falls into the dust beside one of Pokey's torn-off shor'boots and lies there buzzing malevolently, trying to rise.

'There, you bastard!' Jamie screams, and begins to scoop dust over the thing. He is weeping. 'There, you bastard! There! There!' At last it's gone, buried under a heap of white dust that buzzes and shakes and at last becomes still.

Without rising — he doesn't have the strength to find his feet again, not yet, can still hardly believe he is alive — Jamie Jaffords knee-walks toward the monster Molly has killed . . . and it is dead now, or at least lying still. He wants to pull off its mask, see it plain. First he kicks at it with both feet, like a child doing a tantrum. The Wolf's body rocks from side to side, then lies still again. A pungent, reeky smell is coming from it. A rotten-smelling smoke is rising from the mask, which appears to be melting.

Dead, *thinks the boy who will eventually become Gran-pere, the oldest living human in the Calla.* Dead, aye, never doubt it. So garn, ye gutless! Garn and unmask it!

He does. Under the burning autumn sun he takes hold of the rotting mask, which feels like some sort of metal mesh, and he pulls it off, and he sees . . .

8

For a moment Eddie wasn't even aware that the old guy had stopped talking. He was still lost in the story, mesmerized. He saw everything so clearly it could have been *him* out there on the East Road, kneeling in the dust with the bah cocked to his shoulder like a baseball bat, ready to knock the oncoming sneetch out of the air.

Then Susannah rolled past the porch toward the barn with a bowl of chickenfeed in her lap. She gave them a curious look on her way by. Eddie woke up. He hadn't come here to be entertained. He supposed the fact that he *could* be entertained by such a story said something about him.

'And?' Eddie asked the old man when Susannah had gone into the barn. 'What did you see?'

'Eh?' Gran-pere gave him a look of such perfect vacuity that Eddie despaired.

'What did you *see?* When you took off the mask?'

For a moment that look of emptiness – the lights are on but no one's home – held. And then (by pure force of will, it seemed to Eddie) the old man came back. He looked behind him, at the house. He looked toward the black maw of the barn, and the lick of phosphor-light deep inside. He looked around the yard itself.

Frightened, Eddie thought. *Scared to death.*

Eddie tried to tell himself this was only an old man's paranoia, but he felt a chill, all the same.

'Lean close,' Gran-pere muttered, and when Eddie did: 'The only one Ah ever told was my boy Luke . . . Tian's Da', do 'ee ken. Years and years later, this was. He told me never to speak of it to anyone else. Ah said, "But Lukey, what if it could help? What if it could help t'next time they come?"'

Gran-pere's lips barely moved, but his thick accent had almost entirely departed, and Eddie could understand him perfectly.

'And he said to me, "Da', if 'ee really b'lieved knowin c'd help, why have 'ee not told afore now?" And Ah couldn't answer him, young fella, cos 'twas nothing but intuition kep' my gob shut. Besides, what good *could* it do? What do it *change?*'

'I don't know,' Eddie said. Their faces were close. Eddie could smell beef and gravy on old Jamie's breath. 'How can I, when you haven't told me what you saw?'

'"The Red King always finds 'is henchmen," my boy said, "It'd be good if no one ever knew ye were out there, better still if no one ever heard what ye *saw* out there, lest it get back to em, aye, even in Thunderclap." And Ah seen a sad thing, young fella.'

Although he was almost wild with impatience, Eddie thought it best to let the old guy unwind it in his own way. 'What was that, Gran-pere?'

'Ah seen Luke didn't entirely believe me. Thought his own Da' might just be a-storyin, tellin a wild tale about bein a Wolf-killer t'look tall. Although ye'd think even a halfwit would see that if Ah was goingter make a tale, Ah'd make it me that killed the Wolf, and not Eamon Doolin's wife.'

That made sense, Eddie thought, and then remembered Gran-pere at least hinting that he *had* taken credit more than once-upon-a, as Roland sometimes said. He smiled in spite of himself.

'Lukey were afraid someone else might hear my story and believe it. That it'd get on to the Wolves and Ah might end up dead fer no more than tellin a make-believe story. Not that it were.' His rheumy old eyes begged at Eddie's face in the growing dark. '*You* believe me, don't ya?'

Eddie nodded. 'I know you say true, Gran-pere. But who ...' Eddie paused. *Who would rat you out?* was how the question came to mind, but Gran-pere might not understand. 'But who would tell? Who did you suspect?'

Gran-pere looked around the darkening yard, seemed about to speak, then said nothing.

'Tell me,' Eddie said. 'Tell me what you—'

A large dry hand, a-tremor with age but still amazingly strong, gripped his neck and pulled him close. Bristly whiskers rasped against the shell of Eddie's ear, making him shudder all over and break out in gooseflesh.

Gran-pere whispered nineteen words as the last light died out of the day and night came to the Calla.

Eddie Dean's eyes widened. His first thought was that he now understood about the horses — all the gray horses. His second was *Of course. It makes perfect sense. We should have known.*

The nineteenth word was spoken and Gran-pere's whisper ceased. The hand gripping Eddie's neck dropped back into Gran-pere's lap. Eddie turned to face him. 'Say true?'

'Aye, gunslinger,' said the old man. 'True as ever was. Ah canna' say for all of em, for many sim'lar masks may cover many dif'runt faces, but—'

'No,' Eddie said, thinking of gray horses. Not to mention all those sets of gray pants. All those green cloaks. It made perfect sense. What was that old song his mother used to sing? *You're in the army now, you're not behind the plow. You'll never get rich, you son of a bitch, you're in the army now.*

'I'll have to tell this story to my dinh,' Eddie said.

Gran-pere nodded slowly. 'Aye,' he said, 'as ye will. Ah dun't git along well witta boy, ye kennit. Lukey tried to put t' well where Tian pointed wit' t' drotta stick, y' ken.'

Eddie nodded as if he understood this. Later, Susannah translated it for him: *I don't get along well with the boy, you understand. Lukey tried to put the well where Tian pointed with the dowsing stick, you see.*

'A dowser?' Susannah asked from out of the darkness. She had returned quietly and now gestured with her hands, as if holding a wishbone.

The old man looked at her, surprised, then nodded. 'The drotta, yar. Any ro', I argued agin' it, but after the Wolves came and tuk his sister, Tia, Lukey done whatever the boy wanted. Can 'ee imagine, lettin a boy nummore 'n seventeen site the well, drotta or no? But Lukey put it there and there *were* water, Ah'll give 'ee that, we all seen it gleam and smelt it before the clay sides give down and buried my boy alive. We dug him out but he were gone to the clearing, thrut and lungs all full of clay and muck.'

Slowly, slowly, the old man took a handkerchief from his pocket and wiped his eyes with it.

'The boy and I en't had a civil word between us since; that well's dug between us, do ya not see it. But he's right about wantin t' stand again the Wolves, and if you tell him anything for me, tell him his Gran-pere salutes him damn proud, salutes him big-big, yer-bugger! He got the sand o' Jaffords in his craw, aye! We stood our stand all those years agone, and now the blood shows true.' He nodded, this time even more slowly. 'Garn and tell yer dinh, aye! Every word! And if it seeps out . . . if the Wolves were to come out of Thunderclap early fer one dried-up old turd like me . . .'

He bared his few remaining teeth in a smile Eddie found extraordinarily gruesome.

'Ah can still wind a bah,' he said, 'and sumpin tells me yer brownie could be taught to throw a dish, shor' legs or no.'

The old man looked off into the darkness.

'Let 'un come,' he said softly. 'Last time pays fer all, yer-bugger. Last time pays fer all.'

CHAPTER VII

NOCTURNE, HUNGER

1

Mia was in the castle again, but this time was different. This time she did not move slowly, toying with her hunger, knowing that soon it would be fed and fed completely, that both she and her chap would be satisfied. This time what she felt inside was ravenous desperation, as if some wild animal had been caged up inside her belly. She understood that what she had felt on all those previous expeditions hadn't been hunger at all, not true hunger, but only healthy appetite. This was different.

His time is coming, she thought. *He needs to eat more, in order to get his strength. And so do I.*

Yet she was afraid – she was *terrified* – that it wasn't just a matter of needing to eat more. There was something she needed to eat, something forspecial. The chap needed it in order to . . . well, to . . .

To finish the becoming.

Yes! Yes, that was it, the becoming! And surely she would find it in the banquet hall, because *everything* was in the banquet hall – a thousand dishes, each more succulent than the last. She would graze the table, and when she found the right thing – the right vegetable or spice or meat or fish-roe – her guts and nerves would cry out for it and she would eat . . . oh she would *gobble* . . .

She began to hurry along faster yet, and then to run. She was vaguely aware that her legs were swishing together because she was wearing pants. Denim pants, like a cowboy. And instead of slippers she was wearing boots.

Shor'boots, her mind whispered to her mind. *Shor'boots, may they do ya fine.*

But none of this mattered. What mattered was eating, *gorging* (oh she was so hungry), and finding the right thing for the chap. Finding the thing that would both make him strong and bring on her labor.

She pelted down the broad staircase, into the steady beating murmur of the slo-trans engines. Wonderful smells should have overwhelmed her by now — roasted meats, barbecued poultry, herbed fish — but she couldn't smell food at all.

Maybe I have a cold, she thought as her shor'boots stut-tut-tuttered on the stairs. *That must be it, I must have a cold. My sinuses are all swollen and I can't smell anything—*

But she *could*. She could smell the dust and age of this place. She could smell damp seepage, and the faint tang of engine oil, and the mildew eating relentlessly into tapestries and curtains hung in the rooms of ruin.

Those things, but no food.

She dashed along the black marble floor toward the double doors, unaware that she was again being followed — not by the gunslinger this time but by a wide-eyed, tousle-haired boy in a cotton shirt and a pair of cotton shorts. Mia crossed the foyer with its red and black marble squares and the statue of smoothly entwined marble and steel. She didn't stop to curtsy, or even nod her head. That *she* should be so hungry was bearable. But not her chap. Never her chap.

What halted her (and only for a space of seconds) was her own reflection, milky and irresolute, in the statue's chrome steel. Above her jeans was a plain white shirt (*You call this kind a tee-shirt*, her mind whispered) with some writing on it, and a picture.

The picture appeared to be of a pig.

Never mind what's on your shirt, woman. The chap's what matters. You must feed the chap!

She burst into the dining hall and stopped with a gasp of dismay. The room was full of shadows now. A few of the electric torches still glowed, but most had gone out. As she looked, the only one still burning at the far end of the room stuttered, buzzed, and fell dark. The white forspecial plates had been replaced with blue ones decorated with green tendrils of rice. The rice plants formed the Great Letter **Zn**, which, she knew, meant eternity and *now* and also *come*, as in *come-commala*. But plates didn't matter. Decorations didn't matter. What mattered was that the plates and beautiful crystal glassware were empty and dull with dust.

No, not everything was empty; in one goblet she saw a dead black widow spider lying with its many legs curled against the red hourglass on its midsection.

She saw the neck of a wine-bottle poking from a silver pail and her stomach gave an imperative cry. She snatched it up, barely registering the fact that there was no water in the bucket, let alone ice; it was entirely dry. At least the bottle had weight, and enough liquid inside to slosh—

But before Mia could close her lips over the neck of the bottle, the smell of vinegar smote her so strongly that her eyes filled with water.

'Mutha-*fuck!*' she screamed, and threw the bottle down. 'You mutha-*fuckah!*'

The bottle shattered on the stone floor. Things ran in squeaking surprise beneath the table.

'Yeah, you *bettah* run!' she screamed. 'Get ye gone, whatever y'are! Here's Mia, daughter of none, and not in a good mood! Yet I *will* be fed! Yes! Yes I will!'

This was bold talk, but at first she saw nothing on the table that she *could* eat. There was bread, but the one piece she bothered to pick up had turned to stone. There was what appeared to be the remains of a fish, but it had putrefied and lay in a greenish-white simmer of maggots.

Her stomach growled, undeterred by this mess. Worse, something *below* her stomach turned restlessly, and kicked, and cried out to be fed. It did this not with its voice but by turning certain switches inside her, back in the most primitive sections of her nervous system. Her throat grew dry; her mouth puckered as if she had drunk the turned wine; her vision sharpened as her eyes widened and bulged outward in their sockets. Every thought, every sense, and every instinct tuned to the same simple idea: *food.*

Beyond the far end of the table was a screen showing Arthur Eld, sword held high, riding through a swamp with three of his knight-gunslingers behind him. Around his neck was Saita, the great snake, which presumably he had just slain. Another successful quest! Do ya fine! Men and their quests! Bah! What was slaying a magical snake to her? She had a chap in her belly, and the chap was hungry.

Hongry, she thought in a voice that wasn't her own. *It's be hongry.*

Behind the screen were double doors. She shoved through them, still unaware of the boy Jake standing at the far end of the dining hall in his underwear, looking at her, afraid.

The kitchen was likewise empty, likewise dusty. The counters were tattooed with critter-tracks. Pots and pans and cooking-racks were jumbled across the floor. Beyond this litter were four sinks, one filled with stagnant water that had grown a scum of algae. The room was lit by fluorescent tubes. Only a few still glowed steadily. Most of them flickered on and off, giving these shambles a surreal and nightmarish aspect.

She worked her way across the kitchen, kicking aside the pots and pans that were in her way. Here stood four huge ovens all a-row. The door of the third was ajar. From it came a faint shimmer of heat, as one might feel coming from a hearth six or eight hours after the last embers have burned out, and a smell that set her stomach clamoring all over again. It was the smell of freshly roasted meat.

Mia opened the door. Inside was indeed some sort of roast. Feeding on it was a rat the size of a tomcat. It turned its head at the clunk of the opening oven door and looked at her with black, fearless eyes. Its whiskers, bleary with grease, twitched. Then it turned back to the roast. She could hear the muttering smack of its lips and the sound of tearing flesh.

Nay, Mr Rat. It wasn't left for you. It was left for me and my chap.

'One chance, my friend!' she sang as she turned toward the counters and storage cabinets beneath them. 'Better go while you can! Fair warning!' Not that it would. Mr Rat be hongry, too.

She opened a drawer and found nothing but breadboards and a rolling pin. She considered the rolling pin briefly, but had no wish to baste her dinner with more rat-blood than she absolutely had to. She opened the cabinet beneath and found tins for muffins and molds for fancy desserts. She moved to her left, opened another drawer, and here was what she was looking for.

Mia considered the knives, took one of the meat-forks instead. It had two six-inch steel tines. She took it back to the row of ovens, hesitated, and checked the other three. They were empty, as she had known they would be. Something — some fate some providence some ka — had left fresh meat, but only enough for one. Mr Rat thought it was his. Mr Rat had made a mistake. She did not think he would make another. Not this side of the clearing, anyway.

She bent and once again the smell of freshly cooked pork filled her nose. Her lips spread and drool ran from the corners of her smile. This time Mr Rat didn't look around. Mr Rat had decided she was no threat. That was all right. She bent further forward, drew a breath, and impaled it on the meat-fork. Rat-kebab! She drew it out and held it up in front of her face. It squealed furiously, its legs spinning in the air, its head lashing back and forth, blood running down the meat-fork's handle to pool around her fist. She carried it, still writhing, to the sinkful of stagnant water and flipped it off the fork. It splashed into the murk and disappeared. For a moment the tip of its twitching tale stuck up, and then that was gone, too.

She went down the line of sinks, trying the faucets, and from the last one got a feeble trickle of water. She rinsed her bloody hand under it until the trickle subsided. Then she walked back to the oven, wiping her hand dry on the seat of her britches. She did not see Jake, now standing just inside the kitchen doors and watching her, although he made no attempt to hide; she was totally fixated on the smell of the meat. It wasn't enough, and not precisely what her chap needed, but it would do for the time being.

She reached in, grasped the sides of the roasting pan, then pulled back with a gasp, shaking her fingers and grinning. It was a grin of pain, yet not entirely devoid of humor. Mr Rat had either been a trifle more immune to the heat than she was, or maybe hongrier. Although it was hard to believe anyone or anything could be hongrier than she was right now.

'I'se *hongry!*' she yelled, laughing, as she went down the line of drawers, opening and closing them swiftly. 'Mia's one *hongry* lady, yessir! Didn't go to Morehouse, didn't go to *no* house, but I'se *hongry!* And my chap's hongry, too!'

In the last drawer (wasn't that always the way), she found the hotpads she'd been looking for. She hurried back to the oven with them in her hands, bent down, and pulled the roast out. Her laughter died in a sudden shocked gasp . . . and then burst out again, louder and stronger than ever. What a goose she was! What a damned silly-billy! For one instant she'd thought the roast, which had been done to a skin-crackling turn and only gnawed by Mr Rat in one place, was the body of a child. And yes, she supposed that a roasted pig *did* look a little bit like a child . . . a baby . . . someone's chap . . . but now that it was out and she could see the closed eyes and the charred ears and the baked apple in the open mouth, there was no question about what it was.

As she set it on the counter, she thought again about the reflection she'd seen in the foyer. But never mind that now. Her gut was a roar of famishment. She plucked a butcher's knife out of the drawer from which she had taken the meat-fork and cut off the place where Mr Rat had been eating, the way you'd cut a wormhole out of an apple. She tossed this piece back over her shoulder, then picked up the roast entire and buried her face in it.

From the door, Jake watched her.

When the keenest edge had been taken off her hunger, Mia looked around the kitchen with an expression that wavered between calculation and despair. What was she supposed to do when the roast was gone? What was she supposed to eat the next time this sort of hunger came? And where was she supposed to find what her chap really wanted, really needed? She'd do anything to locate that stuff and secure a good supply of it, that special food or drink or vitamin or whatever it was. The pork was close (close enough to put him to sleep again, thank all the gods and the Man Jesus), but not close enough.

She banged sai Piggy back into the roasting pan for the nonce, pulled the shirt she was wearing off over her head, and turned it so she could look at the front. There was a cartoon pig, roasted bright red but seeming not to mind; it was smiling blissfully. Above it, in rustic letters made to look like barnboard, was this: **THE DIXIE PIG, LEX AND 61ST**. Below it: **'BEST RIBS IN NEW YORK' —GOURMET MAGAZINE**.

The Dixie Pig, she thought. *The Dixie Pig. Where have I heard that before?*

She didn't know, but she believed she could find Lex if she had to. 'It be right there between Third and Park,' she said. 'That's right, ain't it?'

The boy, who had slipped back out but left the door ajar, heard this and nodded miserably. That was where it was, all right.

Well-a-well, Mia thought. *It all does fine for now, good as it can do, anyway, and like that woman in the book said, tomorrow's another day. Worry about it then. Right?*

Right. She picked up the roast again and began to eat. The smacking sounds she made were really not much different from those made by the rat. Really not much different at all.

2

Tian and Zalia had tried to give Eddie and Susannah their bedroom. Convincing them that their guests really didn't *want* their bedroom — that sleeping there would actually make them uncomfortable — hadn't been easy. It was Susannah who finally turned the trick, telling the Jaffordses in a hesitant, confiding voice that something awful had happened to them in the city of Lud, something so traumatic that neither of them could sleep easily in a house anymore. A barn, where you could see the door open to the outside world any time you wanted to take a look, was much better.

It was a good tale, and well told. Tian and Zalia listened with a sympathetic credulity that made Eddie feel guilty. A lot of bad things had happened to them in Lud, that much was true, but nothing which made either of them nervous about sleeping indoors. At least he guessed not; since leaving their own world, the two of them had only spent a single night (the previous) under the actual roof of an actual house.

Now he sat cross-legged on one of the blankets Zalia had given them to spread on the hay, the other two cast aside. He was looking out into the yard, past the porch where Gran-pere had told his tale, and toward the river. The moon flitted in and out of the clouds, first brightening the scene to silver, then darkening it. Eddie hardly saw what he was looking at. His ears were trained on the floor of the barn below him, where the stalls and pens were. She was down there somewhere, he was sure she was, but God, she was so *quiet*.

And by the way, who is she? Mia, Roland says, but that's just a name. Who is she really?

But it *wasn't* just a name. *It means* mother *in the High Speech*, the gunslinger had said.

It means *mother*.

Yeah. But she's not the mother of my kid. The chap is not my son.

A soft clunk from below him, followed by the creak of a board. Eddie stiffened. She was down there, all right. He'd begun to have his doubts, but she was.

He had awakened after perhaps six hours of deep and dreamless sleep to discover she was gone. He went to the barn's bay door, which they'd left open, and looked out. There she was. Even by moonlight he'd known that wasn't really Susannah down there in the wheelchair; not his Suze, not Odetta Holmes or Detta Walker, either. Yet she wasn't entirely unfamiliar. She—

You saw her in New York, only then she had legs and she knew how to use them. She had legs and she didn't want to go too close to the rose. She had her reasons for that, and they were good reasons, but you know what I think the real reason was? I think she was afraid it would hurt whatever it is she's carrying in her belly.

Yet he felt sorry for the woman below. No matter who she was or what she was carrying, she'd gotten herself into this situation while saving Jake Chambers. She'd held off the demon of the circle, trapping it inside her just long enough for Eddie to finish whittling the key he'd made.

If you'd finished it earlier — if you hadn't been such a damned little chickenshit — she might not even be in this mess, did you ever think of that?

Eddie had pushed the thought away. There was some truth to it, of course — he *had* lost his confidence while whittling the key, which was why it hadn't been finished when the time of Jake's drawing came — but he was done with that kind of thinking. It was good for nothing but creating a truly excellent array of self-inflicted wounds.

Whoever she was, his heart had gone out to the woman he saw below him. In the sleeping silence of the night, through the alternating shutters of moonlight and dark, she pushed Susannah's wheelchair first across the yard . . . then back . . . then across again . . . then left . . . then right. She reminded him a little of the old robots in Shardik's clearing, the ones Roland had made him shoot. And was that so surprising? He'd drifted off to sleep thinking of those robots, and what Roland had said of them: *They are creatures of great sadness, I think, in their own way. Eddie is going to put them out of their misery.* And so he had, after some persuasion: the one that looked like a many-jointed snake, the one that looked like the Tonka tractor he'd once gotten as a birthday present, the ill-tempered stainless-steel rat. He'd shot them all except for the last, some sort of mechanical flying thing. Roland had gotten that one.

Like the old robots, the woman in the yard below wanted to go someplace, but didn't know where. She wanted to get something, but didn't know what. The question was, what was he supposed to do?

Just watch and wait. Use the time to think up some other bullshit story in case one of them wakes up and sees her in the dooryard, pacing around in her wheelchair. More post-traumatic stress syndrome from Lud, maybe.

'Hey, it works for me,' he murmured, but just then Susannah had turned and wheeled back toward the barn, now moving with a purpose. Eddie had lain down, prepared to feign sleep, but instead of hearing her coming upstairs, he'd heard a faint cling, a grunt of effort, then the creak of boards going away toward the rear of the barn. In his mind's eye he saw her getting out of her chair and heading back there at her usual speedy crawl . . . for what?

Five minutes of silence. He was just beginning to get really nervous when there was a single squeal, short and sharp. It was so much like the cry of an infant that his balls pulled up tight and his skin broke out in goose-flesh. He looked toward the ladder leading down to the barn floor and made himself wait some more.

That was a pig. One of the young ones. Just a shoat, that's all.

Maybe, but what he kept picturing was the younger set of twins. Especially the girl. Lia, rhymes with Mia. No more than babies, and it was crazy to think of Susannah cutting a child's throat, totally insane, but . . .

But that's not *Susannah down there, and if you start thinking it is, you're apt to get hurt, the way you almost got hurt before.*

Hurt, hell. Almost *killed* was what he'd been. Almost gotten his face chewed off by the lobstrosities.

It was Detta who threw me to the creepy crawlies. This one isn't her.

Yes, and he had an idea — only an intuition, really — that this one might be a hell of a lot nicer than Detta, but he'd be a fool to bet his life on it.

Or the lives of the children? Tian and Zalia's children?

He sat there sweating, not knowing what to do.

Now, after what seemed an interminable wait, there were more squeaks and creaks. The last came from directly beneath the ladder leading to the loft. Eddie lay back again and closed his eyes. Not quite all the way, though. Peering through his lashes, he saw her head appear above the loft floor. At that moment the moon sailed out from behind a cloud and flooded the loft with light. He saw blood at the corners of her mouth, as dark as chocolate, and reminded himself to wipe it off her in the morning. He didn't want any of the Jaffords clan seeing it.

What I want to see is the twins, Eddie thought. *Both sets, all four, alive and well. Especially Lia. What else do I want? For Tian to come out of the barn with a frown on his face. For him to ask us if we heard anything in the night, maybe a fox or even one of those rock-cats they talk about. Because, see, one of the shoats has gone missing. Hope you hid whatever was left of it, Mia or whoever you are. Hope you hid it well.*

She came to him, lay down, turned over once and fell asleep — he could tell by the sound of her breathing. Eddie turned his head and looked toward the sleeping Jaffords home place.

She didn't go anywhere near the house.

No, not unless she'd wheeled her chair all the way through the barn and right out the back, that was. Gone around that way . . . slipped in a window . . . taken one of the younger twins . . . taken the little girl . . . taken her back to the barn . . . and . . .

She didn't do that. Didn't have the time, for one thing.

Maybe not, but he'd feel a lot better in the morning, just the same. When he saw all the kids at breakfast. Including Aaron, the little boy with the chubby legs and the little sticking-out belly. He thought of what his mother sometimes said when she saw a mother wheeling a little one like that along the street: *So cute! Looks good enough to eat!*

Quit it. Go to sleep!

But it was a long time before Eddie got back to sleep.

3

Jake awoke from his nightmare with a gasp, not sure where he was. He sat up, shivering, arms wrapped around himself. He was wearing nothing but a plain cotton shirt – too big for him – and flimsy cotton shorts, sort of like gym shorts, that were also too big for him. What . . .?

There was a grunt, followed by a muffled fart Jake looked toward these sounds, saw Benny Slightman buried up to the eyes under two blankets, and everything fell into place. He was wearing one of Benny's undershirts and a pair of Benny's undershorts. They were in Benny's tent. They were on the bluff overlooking the river. The riverbanks out here were stony, Benny had said, no good for rice but plenty good for fishing. If they were just a little bit lucky, they'd be able to catch their own breakfast out of the Devar-Tete Whye. And although Benny knew Jake and Oy would have to return to the Old Fella's house to be with their dinh and their ka-mates for a day or two, maybe longer, perhaps Jake could come back later on. There was good fishing here, good swimming a little way upstream, and caves where the walls glowed in the dark and the lizards glowed, too. Jake had gone to sleep well satisfied by the prospect of these wonders. He wasn't crazy about being out here without a gun (he had seen too much and done too much to ever feel entirely comfortable without a gun these days), but he was pretty sure Andy was keeping an eye on them, and he'd allowed himself to sleep deep.

Then the dream. The horrible dream. Susannah in the huge, dirty kitchen of an abandoned castle. Susannah holding up a squirming rat impaled on a meat-fork. Holding it up and laughing while blood ran down the fork's wooden handle and pooled around her hand.

That was no dream and you know it. You have to tell Roland.

The thought which followed this was somehow even more disturbing: *Roland already knows. So does Eddie.*

Jake sat with his knees against his chest and his arms linked around his shins, feeling more miserable than at any time since getting a good look at his Final Essay in Ms Avery's English Comp class. *My Understanding of the Truth*, it had been called, and although he understood it a lot better now – understood how much of it must have been called forth by what Roland called the touch – his first reaction had been pure horror. What he felt now wasn't so much horror as it was . . . well . . .

Sadness, he thought.

Yes. They were supposed to be ka-tet, one from many, but now their unity had been lost. Susannah had become another person and Roland didn't want her to know, not with Wolves on the way both here and in the other world.

Wolves of the Calla, Wolves of New York.

He wanted to be angry, but there seemed no one to be angry *at*. Susannah had gotten pregnant helping *him*, after all, and if Roland and Eddie weren't telling her stuff, it was because they wanted to protect her.

Yeah, right, a resentful voice spoke up. *They also want to make sure she's able to help out when the Wolves come riding out of Thunderclap. It'd be one less gun if she was busy having a miscarriage or a nervous breakdown or something.*

He knew that wasn't fair, but the dream had shaken him badly. The rat was what he kept coming back to; that rat writhing on the meat-fork. Her holding it up. And grinning. Don't want to forget that. *Grinning.* He'd touched the thought in her mind at that moment, and the thought had been *rat-kebab.*

'Christ,' he whispered.

He guessed he understood why Roland wasn't telling Susannah about Mia — and about the baby, what Mia called the chap — but didn't the gunslinger understand that something far more important had been lost, and was getting more lost every day this was allowed to go on?

They know better than you, they're grown-ups.

Jake thought that was bullshit. If being a grown-up really meant knowing better, why did his father go on smoking three packs of unfiltered cigarettes a day and snorting cocaine until his nose bled? If being a grown-up gave you some sort of special knowledge of the right things to do, how come his mother was sleeping with her masseuse, who had huge biceps and no brains? Why had neither of them noticed, as the spring of 1977 marched toward summer, that their kid (who had a nickname — Bama — known only to the housekeeper) was losing his fucking mind?

This isn't the same thing.

But what if it was? What if Roland and Eddie were so close to the problem they couldn't see the truth?

What is the truth? What is your understanding of the truth?

That they were no longer ka-tet, that was his understanding of the truth.

What was it Roland had said to Callahan, at that first palaver? *We are round, and roll as we do.* That had been true then, but Jake didn't think it was true now. He remembered an old joke people told when they got a blowout:

Well, it's only flat on the bottom. That was them now, flat on the bottom. No longer truly ka-tet — how could they be, when they were keeping secrets? And was Mia and the child growing in Susannah's stomach the only secret? Jake thought not. There was something else, as well. Something Roland was keeping back not just from Susannah but from all of them.

We can beat the Wolves if we're together, he thought. *If we're ka-tet. But not the way we are now. Not over here, not in New York, either. I just don't believe it.*

Another thought came on the heels of that, one so terrible he first tried to push it away. Only he couldn't do that, he realized. Little as he wanted to, this was an idea that had to be considered.

I could take matters into my own hands. I could tell her myself.

And then what? What would he tell Roland? How would he explain?

I couldn't. There'd be no explanation I could make or that he'd listen to. The only thing I could do—

He remembered Roland's story of the day he'd stood against Cort. The battered old squireen with his stick, the untried boy with his hawk. If he, Jake, were to go against Roland's decision and tell Susannah what had so far been held back from her, it would lead directly to his own manhood test.

And I'm not ready. Maybe Roland was — barely — but I'm not him. Nobody *is. He'd best me and I'd be sent east into Thunderclap alone. Oy would try to come with me, but I couldn't let him. Because it's death over there. Maybe for our whole ka-tet, surely for a kid all by himself.*

And yet still, the secrets Roland was keeping, that was *wrong.* And so? They'd be together again, all of them, to hear the rest of Callahan's story and — maybe — to deal with the thing in Callahan's church. What should he do then?

Talk to him. Try to persuade him he's doing the wrong thing.

All right. He could do that. It would be hard, but he could do it. Should he talk to Eddie as well? Jake thought not. Adding Eddie would complicate things even more. Let Roland decide what to tell Eddie. Roland, after all, was the dinh.

The flap of the tent shivered and Jake's hand went to his side, where the Ruger would have hung if he had been wearing the docker's clutch. Not there, of course, but this time that was all right. It was only Oy, poking his snout under the flap and tossing it up so he could get his head into the tent.

Jake reached out to pat the bumbler's head. Oy seized his hand gently in his teeth and tugged. Jake went with him willingly enough; he felt as if sleep were a thousand miles away.

Outside the tent, the world was a study in severe blacks and whites. A rock-studded slope led down to the river, which was broad and shallow at this point. The moon burned in it like a lamp. Jake saw two figures down there on the rocky strand and froze. As he did, the moon went behind a cloud and the world darkened. Oy's jaws closed on his hand again and pulled him forward. Jake went with him, found a four-foot drop, and eased himself down. Oy now stood above and just behind him, panting into his ear like a little engine.

The moon came out from behind its cloud. The world brightened again. Jake saw Oy had led him to a large chunk of granite that came jutting out of the earth like the prow of a buried ship. It was a good hiding place. He peered around it and down at the river.

There was no doubt about one of them; its height and the moonlight gleaming on metal were enough to identify Andy the Messenger Robot (Many Other Functions). The other one, though . . . who was the other one? Jake squinted but at first couldn't tell. It was at least two hundred yards from his hiding place to the riverbank below, and although the moonlight was brilliant, it was also tricky. The man's face was raised so he could look at Andy, and the moonlight fell squarely on him, but the features seemed to swim. Only the hat the guy was wearing . . . he knew the *hat* . . .

You could be wrong.

Then the man turned his head slightly, the moonlight sent twin glints back from his face, and Jake knew for sure. There might be lots of cowpokes in the Calla who wore round-crowned hats like the one yonder, but Jake had only seen a single guy so far who wore spectacles.

Okay, it's Benny's Da'. What of it? Not all parents are like mine, some of them get worried about their kids, especially if they've already lost one the way Mr Slightman lost Benny's twin sister. To hot-lung, Benny said, which probably means pneumonia. Six years ago. So we come out here camping, and Mr Slightman sends Andy to keep an eye on us, only then he wakes up in the middle of the night and decides to check on us for himself. Maybe he had his own bad dream.

Maybe so, but that didn't explain why Andy and Mr Slightman were having their palaver way down there by the river, did it?

Well, maybe he was afraid of waking us up. Maybe he'll come up to check on the tent now — in which case I better get back inside it — or maybe he'll take Andy's word that we're all right and head back to the Rocking B.

The moon went behind another cloud, and Jake thought it best to stay where he was until it came back out. When it did, what he saw filled him with the same sort of dismay he'd felt in his dream, following Mia through that deserted castle. For a moment he clutched at the possibility that this *was* a dream, that he'd simply gone from one to another, but the feel of the pebbles biting into his feet and the sound of Oy panting in his ear were completely undreamlike. This was happening, all right.

Mr Slightman wasn't coming up toward where the boys had pitched their tent, and he wasn't heading back toward the Rocking B, either (although Andy was, in long strides along the bank). No, Benny's father was wading *across* the river. He was heading dead east.

He could have a reason for going over there. He could have a perfectly good reason.

Really? What might that perfectly good reason be? It wasn't the Calla anymore over there, Jake knew that much. Over there was nothing but waste ground and desert, a buffer between the borderlands and the kingdom of the dead that was Thunderclap.

First something wrong with Susannah – his friend Susannah. Now, it seemed, something wrong with the father of his new friend. Jake realized he had begun to gnaw at his nails, a habit he'd picked up in his final weeks at Piper School, and made himself stop.

'This isn't fair, you know,' he said to Oy. 'This isn't fair at all.'

Oy licked his ear. Jake turned, put his arms around the bumbler, and pressed his face against his friend's lush coat. The bumbler stood patiently, allowing this. After a little while, Jake pulled himself back up to the more level ground where Oy stood. He felt a little better, a little comforted.

The moon went behind another cloud and the world darkened. Jake stood where he was. Oy whined softly. 'Just a minute,' Jake murmured.

The moon came out again. Jake looked hard at the place where Andy and Ben Slightman had palavered, marking it in his memory. There was a large round rock with a shiny surface. A dead log had washed up against it. Jake was pretty sure he could find this spot again, even if Benny's tent was gone.

Are you going to tell Roland?

'I don't know,' he muttered.

'Know,' Oy said from beside his ankle, making Jake jump a little. Or was it *no*? Was that what the bumbler had actually said?

Are you crazy?

He wasn't. There was a time when he'd thought he *was* crazy – crazy or going there in one hell of a hurry — but he didn't think that anymore. And sometimes Oy *did* read his mind, he knew it.

Jake slipped back into the tent. Benny was still fast asleep. Jake looked at the other boy — older in years but younger in a lot of the ways that mattered — for several seconds, biting his lip. He didn't want to get Benny's father in trouble. Not unless he had to.

Jake lay down and pulled his blankets up to his chin. He had never in his life felt so undecided about so many things, and he wanted to cry. The day had begun to grow light before he was able to get back to sleep.

CHAPTER VIII

TOOK'S STORE;
THE UNFOUND DOOR

1

For the first half hour after leaving the Rocking B, Roland and Jake rode east toward the smallholds in silence, their horses ambling side by side in perfect good fellowship. Roland knew Jake had something serious on his mind; that was clear from his troubled face. Yet the gunslinger was still astounded when Jake curled his fist, placed it against the left side of his chest, and said: 'Roland, before Eddie and Susannah join up with us, may I speak to you dan-dinh?'

May I open my heart to your command. But the subtext was more complicated than that, and ancient – pre-dating Arthur Eld by centuries, or so Vannay had claimed. It meant to turn some insoluble emotional problem, usually having to do with a love affair, over to one's dinh. When one did this, he or she agreed to do exactly as the dinh suggested, immediately and without question. But surely Jake Chambers didn't have love problems – not unless he'd fallen for the gorgeous Francine Tavery, that was – and how had he known such a phrase in the first place?

Meanwhile Jake was looking at him with a wide-eyed, pale-cheeked solemnity that Roland didn't much like.

'Dan-dinh – where did you hear that, Jake?'

'Never did. Picked it up from your mind, I think.' Jake added hastily: 'I don't go snooping in there, or anything like that, but sometimes stuff just comes. Most of it isn't very important, I don't think, but sometimes there are phrases.'

'You pick them up like a crow or a rustie picks up the bright things that catch its eye from the wing.'

'I guess so, yeah.'

'What others? Tell me a few.'

Jake looked embarrassed. 'I can't remember many. Dan-dinh, that means I open my heart to you and agree to do what you say.'

It was more complicated than that, but the boy had caught the essence. Roland nodded. The sun felt good on his face as they clopped along. Margaret Eisenhart's exhibition with the plate had soothed him, he'd had a good meeting with the lady-sai's father later on, and he had slept quite well for the first time in many nights. 'Yes.'

'Let's see. There's tell-a-me, which means — I think — to gossip about someone you shouldn't gossip about. It stuck in my head, because that's what gossip sounds like: tell-a-me.' Jake cupped a hand to his ear.

Roland smiled. It was actually *telamei*, but Jake had of course picked it up phonetically. This was really quite amazing. He reminded himself to guard his deep thoughts carefully in the future. There *were* ways that could be done, thank the gods.

'There's dash-dinh, which means some sort of religious leader. You're thinking about that this morning, I think, because of . . . is it because of the old Manni guy? Is he a dash-dinh?'

Roland nodded. 'Very much so. And his name, Jake?' The gunslinger concentrated on it. 'Can you see his name in my mind?'

'Sure, Henchick,' Jake said at once, and almost offhandedly. 'You talked to him . . . when? Late last night?'

'Yes.' That he *hadn't* been concentrating on, and he would have felt better had Jake not known of it. But the boy was strong in the touch, and Roland believed him when he said he hadn't been snooping. At least not on purpose.

'Mrs Eisenhart thinks she hates him, but you think she's only afraid of him.'

'Yes,' Roland said. 'You're strong in the touch. Much more so than Alain ever was, and much more than you were. It's because of the rose, isn't it?'

Jake nodded. The rose, yes. They rode in silence a little longer, their horses' hooves raising a thin dust. In spite of the sun the day was chilly, promising real fall.

'All right, Jake. Speak to me dan-dinh if you would, and I say thanks for your trust in such wisdom as I have.'

But for the space of almost two minutes Jake said nothing. Roland pried at him, trying to get inside the boy's head as the boy had gotten inside his (and with such ease), but there was nothing. Nothing at a—

But there was. There was a rat . . . squirming, impaled on something . . .

'Where is the castle she goes to?' Jake asked. 'Do you know?'

Roland was unable to conceal his surprise. His astonishment, really. And he supposed there was an element of guilt there, as well. Suddenly he understood . . . well, not everything, but much.

'There is no castle and never was,' he told Jake. 'It's a place she goes to in her mind, probably made up of the stories she's read and the ones I've told by the campfire, as well. She goes there so she won't have to see what she's really eating. What her baby needs.'

'I saw her eating a roasted pig,' Jake said. 'Only before she came, a rat was eating it. She stabbed it with a meat-fork.'

'Where did you see this?'

'In the castle.' He paused. 'In her dream. I was in her dream.'

'Did she see you there?' The gunslinger's blue eyes were sharp, almost blazing. His horse clearly felt some change, for it stopped. So did Jake's. Here they were on East Road, less than a mile from where Red Molly Doolin had once killed a Wolf out of Thunderclap. Here they were, facing each other.

'No,' Jake said. 'She didn't see me.'

Roland was thinking of the night he had followed her into the swamp. He had known she was someplace else in her mind, had sensed that much, but not quite where. Whatever visions he'd taken from her mind had been murky. Now he knew. He knew something else as well: Jake was troubled by his dinh's decision to let Susannah go on this way. And perhaps he was right to be troubled. But—

'It's not Susannah you saw, Jake.'

'I know. It's the one who still has her legs. She calls herself Mia. She's pregnant and she's scared to death.'

Roland said, 'If you would speak to me dan-dinh, tell me everything you saw in your dream and everything that troubled you about it upon waking. Then I'll give you the wisdom of my heart, such wisdom as I have.'

'You won't . . . Roland, you won't scold me?'

This time Roland was unable to conceal his astonishment. 'No, Jake. Far from it. Perhaps I should ask you not to scold *me*.'

The boy smiled wanly. The horses began to amble again, this time a little faster, as if they knew there had almost been trouble and wanted to leave the place of it behind.

2

Jake wasn't entirely sure how much of what was on his mind was going to come out until he actually began to talk. He had awakened undecided all over again concerning what to tell Roland about Andy and Slightman the Elder. In the end he took his cue from what Roland had just said – *Tell me everything you saw in your dream and everything that troubled you about it upon waking* – and left out the meeting by the river entirely. In truth, that part seemed far less important to him this morning.

He told Roland about the way Mia had run down the stairs, and about her fear when she'd seen there was no food left in the dining room or banqueting hall or whatever it was. Then the kitchen. Finding the roast with the rat battened on it. Killing the competition. Gorging on the prize. Then him, waking with the shivers and trying not to scream.

He hesitated and glanced at Roland. Roland made his impatient twirling gesture – go on, hurry up, finish.

Well, he thought, *he promised not to scold and he keeps his word.*

That was true, but Jake was still unable to tell Roland he'd actually considered spilling the beans to Susannah himself. He did articulate his principal fear, however: that with three of them knowing and one of them not, their ka-tet was broken just when it needed to be the most solid. He even told Roland the old joke, guy with a blowout saying *It's only flat on the bottom.* He didn't expect Roland to laugh, and his expectations were met admirably in this regard. But he sensed Roland was to some degree ashamed, and Jake found this frightening. He had an idea shame was pretty much reserved for people who didn't know what they were doing.

'And until last night it was even worse than three in and one out,' Jake said. 'Because you were trying to keep *me* out, as well. Weren't you?'

'No,' Roland said.

'No?'

'I simply let things be as they were. I told Eddie because I was afraid that, once they were sharing a room together, he'd discover her wanderings and try to wake her up. I was afraid of what might happen to both of them if he did.'

'Why not just tell her?'

Roland sighed. 'Listen to me, Jake. Cort saw to our physical training when we were boys. Vannay saw to our mental training. Both of them tried to teach us what they knew of ethics. But in Gilead, our fathers were responsible for teaching us about ka. And because each child's father was different, each of us emerged from our childhood with a slightly different idea of what ka is and what it does. Do you understand?'

I understand that you're avoiding a very simple question, Jake thought, but nodded.

'My father told me a good deal on the subject, and most of it has left my mind, but one thing remains very clear. He said that when you are unsure, you must let ka alone to work itself out.'

'So it's ka.' Jake sounded disappointed. 'Roland, that isn't very helpful.'

Roland heard worry in the boy's voice, but it was the disappointment that stung him. He turned in the saddle, opened his mouth, realized that some hollow justification was about to come spilling out, and closed it again. Instead of justifying, he told the truth.

'I don't know what to do. Would you like to tell me?'

The boy's face flushed an alarming shade of red, and Roland realized Jake thought he was being sarcastic, for the gods' sake. That he was angry. Such lack of understanding was frightening. *He's right*, the gunslinger thought. *We* are *broken. Gods help us.*

'Be not so,' Roland said. 'Hear me, I beg – listen well. In Calla Bryn Sturgis, the Wolves are coming. In New York, Balazar and his 'gentlemen' are coming. Both are bound to arrive soon. Will Susannah's baby wait until these matters have been resolved, one way or the other? I don't know.'

'She doesn't even look pregnant,' Jake said faintly. Some of the red had gone out of his cheeks, but he still kept his head down.

'No,' Roland said, 'she doesn't. Her breasts are a trifle fuller – perhaps her hips, as well – but those are the only signs. And so I have some reason to hope. I must hope, and so must you. For, on top of the Wolves and the business of the rose in your world, there's the question of Black Thirteen and how to deal with it. I think I know – I hope I know – but I must speak to Henchick again. And we must hear the rest of Pere Callahan's story. Have you thought of saying something to Susannah on your own?'

'I . . .' Jake bit his lip and fell silent.

'I see you have. Put the thought out of your mind. If anything other than death could break our fellowship for good, to tell without my sanction would do it, Jake. I am your dinh.'

'I know it!' Jake nearly shouted. 'Don't you think I know it?'

'And do you think I like it?' Roland asked, almost as heatedly. 'Do you not see how much easier all this was before . . .' He trailed off, appalled by what he had nearly said.

'Before we came,' Jake said. His voice was flat. 'Well guess what? We didn't *ask* to come, none of us.' *And I didn't ask you to drop me into the dark, either. To kill me.*

'Jake . . .' The gunslinger sighed, raised his hands, dropped them back to his thighs. Up ahead was the turning which would take them to the Jaffords smallhold, where Eddie and Susannah would be waiting for them. 'All I can do is say again what I've said already: when one isn't sure about ka, it's best to let ka work itself out. If one meddles, one almost always does the wrong thing.'

'That sounds like what folks in the Kingdom of New York call a copout, Roland. An answer that isn't an answer, just a way to get people to go along with what you want.'

Roland considered. His lips firmed. 'You asked me to command your heart.'

Jake nodded warily.

'Then here are the two things I say to you dan-dinh. First, I say that the three of us — you, me, Eddie — will speak an-tet to Susannah before the Wolves come, and tell her everything we know. That she's pregnant, that her baby is almost surely a demon's child, and that she's created a woman named Mia to mother that child. Second, I say that we discuss this no more until the time to tell her has come.'

Jake considered these things. As he did, his face gradually brightened with relief. 'Do you mean it?'

'Yes.' Roland tried not to show how much this question hurt and angered him. He understood, after all, why the boy would ask. 'I promise and swear to my promise. Does it do ya?'

'Yes! It does me fine!'

Roland nodded. 'I'm not doing this because I'm convinced it's the right thing but because *you* are, Jake. I—'

'Wait a second, whoa, wait,' Jake said. His smile was fading. 'Don't try to put all this on me. I never—'

'Spare me such nonsense.' Roland used a dry and distant tone Jake had seldom heard. 'You ask part of a man's decision. I allow it — *must* allow it — because ka has decreed you take a man's part in great matters. You opened this door when you questioned my judgment. Do you deny that?'

Jake had gone from pale to flushed to pale once more. He looked badly frightened, and shook his head without speaking a single word. *Ah, gods,* Roland thought, *I hate every part of this. It stinks like a dying man's shit.*

In a quieter tone he said, 'No, you didn't ask to be brought here. Nor did I wish to rob you of your childhood. Yet here we are, and ka stands to one side and laughs. We must do as it wills or pay the price.'

Jake lowered his head and spoke two words in a trembling whisper: 'I know.'

'You believe Susannah should be told. I, on the other hand, don't know *what* to do – in this matter I've lost my compass. When one knows and one does not, the one who does not must bow his head and the one who does must take responsibility. Do you understand me, Jake?'

'Yes,' Jake whispered, and touched his curled hand to his brow.

'Good. We'll leave that part and say thankya. You're strong in the touch.'

'I wish I wasn't!' Jake burst out.

'Nevertheless. Can you touch her?'

'Yes. I don't pry – not into her or any of you – but sometimes I do touch her. I get little snatches of songs she's thinking of, or thoughts of her apartment in New York. She misses it. Once she thought, "I wish I'd gotten a chance to read that new Allen Drury novel that came from the book club." I think Allen Drury must be a famous writer from her *when.*'

'Surface things, in other words.'

'Yes.'

'But you could go deeper.'

'I could probably watch her undress, too,' Jake said glumly, 'but it wouldn't be right.'

'Under these circumstances, it *is* right, Jake. Think of her as a well where you must go every day and draw a single dipperful to make sure the water's still sweet. I want to know if she changes. In particular I want to know if she's planning alleyo.'

Jake looked at him, round-eyed. 'To run away? Run away where?'

Roland shook his head. 'I don't know. Where does a cat go to drop her litter? In a closet? Under the barn?'

'What if we tell her and the other one gets the upper hand? What if *Mia* goes alleyo, Roland, and drags Susannah along with her?'

Roland didn't reply. This, of course, was exactly what he was afraid of, and Jake was smart enough to know it.

Jake was looking at him with a certain understandable resentment . . . but also with acceptance. 'Once a day. No more than that.'

'More if you sense a change.'

'All right,' Jake said. 'I hate it, but I asked you dan-dinh. Guess you got me.'

'It's not an arm-wrestle, Jake. Nor a game.'

'I know.' Jake shook his head. 'It feels like you turned it around on me somehow, but okay.'

I did turn it around on you, Roland thought. He supposed it was good none of them knew how lost he was just now, how absent the intuition that had carried him through so many difficult situations. *I did . . . but only because I had to.*

'We keep quiet now, but we tell her before the Wolves come,' Jake said. 'Before we have to fight. That's the deal?'

Roland nodded.

'If we have to fight Balazar first – in the other world – we still have to tell her before we do. Okay?'

'Yes,' Roland said. 'All right.'

'I hate this,' Jake said morosely.

Roland said, 'So do I.'

3

Eddie was sittin and whittlin on the Jaffordses' porch, listening to some confused story of Gran-pere's and nodding in what he hoped were the right places, when Roland and Jake rode up. Eddie put away his knife and sauntered down the steps to meet them, calling back over his shoulder for Suze.

He felt extraordinarily good this morning. His fears of the night before had blown away, as our most extravagant night-fears often do; like the Pere's Type One and Type Two vampires, those fears seemed especially allergic to daylight. For one thing, all the Jaffords children had been present and accounted for at breakfast. For another, there was indeed a shoat missing from the barn. Tian had asked Eddie and Susannah if they'd heard anything in the night, and nodded with gloomy satisfaction when both of them shook their heads.

'Aye. The mutie strains've mostly run out in our part of the world, but not in the north. There are packs of wild dogs that come down every fall. Two weeks ago they was likely in Calla Amity; next week we'll be shed of em and they'll be Calla Lockwood's problem. Silent, they are. It's not quiet I mean, but mute. Nothin in here.' Tian patted a hand against his throat. 'Sides, it ain't like they didn't do me at least *some* good. I found a hell of a big barn-rat out there. Dead as a rock. One of em tore its head almost clean off.'

'Nasty,' Hedda had said, pushing her bowl away with a theatrical grimace.

'You eat that porridge, miss,' Zalia said. 'It'll warm 'ee while you're hanging out the clothes.'

'Maw-Maw, *why-y-yy?*'

Eddie had caught Susannah's eye and tipped her a wink. She winked back, and everything was all right. Okay, so she'd done a little wandering in the night. Had a little midnight snack. Buried the leavings. And yes, this business of her being pregnant had to be addressed. Of course it did. But it would come out all right, Eddie felt sure of it. And by daylight, the idea that Susannah could ever hurt a child seemed flat-out ridiculous.

'Hile, Roland. Jake.' Eddie turned to where Zalia had come out onto the porch. She dropped a curtsy. Roland took off his hat, held it out to her, and then put it back on.

'Sai,' he asked her, 'you stand with your husband in the matter of fighting the Wolves, aye?'

She sighed, but her gaze was steady enough. 'I do, gunslinger.'

'Do you ask aid and succor?'

The question was spoken without ostentation – almost conversationally, in fact – but Eddie felt his heart give a lurch, and when Susannah's hand crept into his, he squeezed it. Here was the third question, the key question, and it hadn't been asked of the Calla's big farmer, big rancher, or big businessman. It had been asked of a sodbuster's wife with her mousy brown hair pulled back in a bun, a smallhold farmer's wife whose skin, although naturally dark, had even so cracked and coarsened from too much sun, whose housedress had been faded by many washings. And it was right that it should be so, perfectly right. Because the soul of Calla Bryn Sturgis was in four dozen smallhold farms just like this, Eddie reckoned. Let Zalia Jaffords speak for all of them. Why the hell not?

'I seek it and say thankya,' she told him simply. 'Lord God and Man Jesus bless you and yours.'

Roland nodded as if he'd been doing no more than passing the time of day. 'Margaret Eisenhart showed me something.'

'Did she?' Zalia asked, and smiled slightly. Tian came plodding around the corner, looking tired and sweaty, although it was only nine in the morning. Over one shoulder was a busted piece of harness. He wished Roland and Jake a good day, then stood by his wife, a hand around her waist and resting on her hip.

'Aye, and told us the tale of Lady Oriza and Gray Dick.'

''Tis a fine tale,' she said.

'It is,' Roland said. 'I'll not fence, lady-sai. Will 'ee come out on the line with your dish when the time comes?'

Tian's eyes widened. He opened his mouth, then shut it again. He looked at his wife like a man who has suddenly been visited by a great revelation.

'Aye,' Zalia said.

Tian dropped the harness and hugged her. She hugged him back, briefly and hard, then turned to Roland and his friends once more.

Roland was smiling. Eddie was visited by a faint sense of unreality, as he always was when he observed this phenomenon. 'Good. And will you show Susannah how to throw it?'

Zalia looked thoughtfully at Susannah. 'Would she learn?'

'I don't know,' Susannah said. 'Is it something I'm supposed to learn, Roland?'

'Yes.'

'When, gunslinger?' Zalia asked.

Roland calculated. 'Three or four days from now, if all goes well. If she shows no aptitude, send her back to me and we'll try Jake.'

Jake started visibly.

'I think she'll do fine, though. I never knew a gunslinger who didn't take to new weapons like birds to a new pond. And I must have at least one who can either throw the dish or shoot the bah, for we are four with only three guns we can rely on. And I like the dish. I like it very well.'

'I'll show what I can, sure,' Zalia said, and gave Susannah a shy look.

'Then, in nine days' time, you and Margaret and Rosalita and Sarey Adams will come to the Old Fella's house and we'll see what we'll see.'

'You have a plan?' Tian asked. His eyes were hot with hope.

'I will by then,' Roland said.

4

They rode toward town four abreast at that same ambling gait, but where the East Road crossed another, this one going north and south, Roland pulled up. 'Here I leave you for a little while,' he told them. He pointed north, toward the hills. 'Two hours from here is what some of the Seeking Folk call Manni Calla and others call Manni Redpath. It's their place by either name, a little town within the larger one. I'll meet with Henchick there.'

'Their dinh,' Eddie said.

Roland nodded. 'Beyond the Manni village, another hour or less, are a few played-out mines and a lot of caves.'

'The place you pointed out on the Tavery twins' map?' Susannah asked.

'No, but close by. The cave I'm interested in is the one they call Doorway Cave. We'll hear of it from Callahan tonight when he finishes his story.'

'Do you know that for a fact, or is it intuition?' Susannah asked.

'I know it from Henchick. He spoke of it last night. He also spoke of the Pere. I could tell you, but it's best we hear it from Callahan himself, I think. In any case, that cave will be important to us.'

'It's the way back, isn't it?' Jake said. 'You think it's the way back to New York.'

'More,' the gunslinger said. 'With Black Thirteen, I think it might be the way to everywhere and everywhen.'

'Including the Dark Tower?' Eddie asked. His voice was husky, barely more than a whisper.

'I can't say,' Roland replied, 'but I believe Henchick will show me the cave, and I may know more then. Meanwhile, you three have business in Took's, the general store.'

'Do we?' Jake asked.

'You do.' Roland balanced his purse on his lap, opened it, and dug deep. At last he came out with a leather drawstring bag none of them had seen before.

'My father gave me this,' he said absently. 'It's the only thing I have now, other than the ruins of my younger face, that I had when I rode into Mejis with my ka-mates all those years ago.'

They looked at it with awe, sharing the same thought: if what the gunslinger said was true, the little leather bag had to be hundreds of years old. Roland opened it, looked in, nodded. 'Susannah, hold out your hands.'

She did. Into her cupped palms he poured perhaps ten pieces of silver, emptying the bag.

'Eddie, hold out yours.'

'Uh, Roland, I think the cupboard's bare.'

'Hold out your hands.'

Eddie shrugged and did so. Roland tipped the bag over them and poured out a dozen gold pieces, emptying the bag.

'Jake?'

Jake held out his hands. From the pocket in the front of the poncho, Oy looked on with interest. This time the bag disgorged half a dozen bright gemstones before it was empty. Susannah gasped.

'They're but garnets,' Roland said, almost apologetically. 'A fair medium of exchange out here, from what they say. They won't buy much, but they *will* buy a boy's needs, I think.'

'Cool!' Jake was grinning broadly. 'Say thankya! Big-big!'

They looked at the empty sack with silent wonder, and Roland smiled. 'Most of the magic I once knew or had access to is gone, but you see a little lingers. Like soaked leaves in the bottom of a teapot.'

'Is there even more stuff inside?' Jake asked.

'No. In time, there might be. It's a grow-bag.' Roland returned the ancient leather sack to his purse, came out with the fresh supply of tobacco Callahan had given him, and rolled a smoke. 'Go in the store. Buy what you fancy. A few shirts, perhaps – and one for me, if it does ya; I could use one. Then you'll go out on the porch and take your ease, as town folk do. Sai Took won't care much for it, there's nothing he'd like to see so well as our backs going east toward Thunderclap, but he'll not shoo you off.'

'Like to see him try,' Eddie grunted, and touched the butt of Roland's gun.

'You won't need that,' Roland said. 'Custom alone will keep him behind his counter, minding his till. That, and the temper of the town.'

'It's going our way, isn't it?' Susannah said.

'Yes, Susannah. If you asked them straight on, as I asked sai Jaffords, they'd not answer, so it's best not to ask, not yet. But yes. They mean to fight. Or to let us fight for them. Which can't be held against them. Fighting for those who can't fight for themselves is our job.'

Eddie opened his mouth to tell Roland what Gran-pere had told him, then closed it again. Roland hadn't asked him, although that had been the reason he had sent them to the Jaffordses'. Nor, he realized, had Susannah asked him. She hadn't mentioned his conversation with old Jamie at all.

'Will you ask Henchick what you asked Mrs Jaffords?' Jake asked.

'Yes,' Roland said. 'Him I'll ask.'

'Because you know what he'll say.'

Roland nodded and smiled again. This was not a smile that held any comfort; it was as cold as sunlight on snow. 'A gunslinger never asks that question until he knows what the answer will be,' he said. 'We meet at the Pere's house for the evening meal. If all goes well, I'll be there just when the sun comes a-horizon. Are you all well? Eddie? Jake?' A slight pause. 'Susannah?'

They all nodded. Oy nodded, too.

'Then until evening. Do ya fine, and may the sun never fall in your eyes.'

He gigged his horse and turned off on the neglected little road leading north. They watched him go until he was out of sight, and as always when he was gone and they were on their own, the three of them shared a complex feeling that was part fear, part loneliness, and part nervous pride.

They rode on toward town with their horses a little closer together.

5

'Nayyup, nayyup, don'tchee bring that dairty bumble-beast in 'ere, don'tchee never!' Eben Took cried from his place behind the counter. He had a high, almost womanish voice; it scratched the dozy quiet of the mercantile like splinters of glass. He was pointing at Oy, who was peering from the front pocket of Jake's poncho. A dozen desultory shoppers, most of them women dressed in homespun, turned to look.

Two farm workers, dressed in plain brown shirts, dirty white pants, and zoris, had been standing at the counter. They backed away in a hurry, as if expecting the two outworlders carrying guns to immediately slap leather and blow sai Took all the way to Calla Boot Hill.

'Yessir,' Jake said mildly. 'Sorry.' He lifted Oy from the pocket of the poncho and set him down on the sunny porch, just outside the door. 'Stay, boy.'

'Oy stay,' the bumbler said, and curled his clockspring of a tail around his haunches.

Jake rejoined his friends and they made their way into the store. To Susannah, it smelled like ones she'd been in during her time in Mississippi: a mingled aroma of salted meat, leather, spice, coffee, mothballs, and aged cozenry. Beside the counter was a large wooden barrel with the top slid partway aside and a pair of tongs hanging on a nail nearby. From the keg came the strong and tearful smell of pickles in brine.

'No credit!' Took cried in that same shrill, annoying voice. 'Ah en't ever give credit to no one from away and Ah never will! Say true! Say thankya!'

Susannah grasped Eddie's hand and gave it a warning squeeze. Eddie shook it off impatiently, but when he spoke, his voice was as mild as Jake's had been. 'Say thankya, sai Took, we'd not ask it.' And recalled something he'd heard from Pere Callahan: 'Never in life.'

There was a murmur of approval from some of those in the store. None of them was any longer making even the slightest pretense of shopping. Took flushed. Susannah took Eddie's hand again and this time gave him a smile to go with the squeeze.

At first they shopped in silence, but before they finished, several people – all of whom had been at the Pavilion two nights before – said hello and asked (timidly) how they did. All three said they did fine. They got shirts, including two for Roland, denim pants, underwear singlets, and three sets of shor'boots which looked ugly but serviceable. Jake got a bag of candy, picking it out by pointing while Took put it in a bag of woven grass with grudging and disagreeable slowness. When he tried to buy a sack of tobacco and some rolling papers for Roland, Took refused him with all too evident pleasure. 'Nayyup, nayyup, Ah'll not sell smokeweed to a boy. Never have done.'

'Good idea, too,' Eddie said. 'One step below devil grass, and the Surgeon General says thankya. But you'll sell it to me, won't you, sai? Our dinh enjoys a smoke in the evening, while he's planning out new ways to help folks in need.'

There were a few titters at this. The store had begun to fill up quite amazingly. They were playing to a real audience now, and Eddie didn't mind a bit. Took was coming off as a shithead, which wasn't surprising. Took clearly *was* a shithead.

'Never seen no one dance a better commala than he did!' a man called from one of the aisles, and there were murmurs of assent.

'Say thankya,' Eddie said. 'I'll pass it on.'

'And your lady sings well,' said another.

Susannah dropped a skirtless curtsy. She finished her own shopping by pushing the lid a little further off the pickle barrel and dipping out an enormous specimen with the tongs. Eddie leaned close and said, 'I might have gotten something that green from my nose once, but I can't really remember.'

'Don't be grotesque, dear one,' Susannah replied, smiling sweetly all the while.

Eddie and Jake were content to let her assume responsibility for the dickering, which Susannah did with relish. Took tried his very best to overcharge her for their gunna, but Eddie had an idea this wasn't aimed at them specifically but was just part of what Eben Took saw as his job (or perhaps his sacred calling). Certainly he was smart enough to gauge the temperature of his clientele, for he had pretty much laid off nagging them by the time the trading was finished. This did not keep him from ringing their coins on a special square of metal which seemed reserved for that sole purpose, and holding Jake's garnets up to the light and rejecting one of them (which looked like all the others, so far as Eddie, Jake, and Susannah could see).

'How long'll 'ee be here, folks?' he asked in a marginally cordial voice when the dickering was done. Yet his eyes were shrewd, and Eddie had no doubt that whatever they said would reach the ears of Eisenhart, Overholser, and anyone else who mattered before the day was done.

'Ah, well, that depends on what we see,' Eddie said. 'And what we see depends on what folks show us, wouldn't you say?'

'Aye,' Took agreed, but he looked mystified. There were now perhaps fifty people in the roomy mercantile-and-grocery, most of them simply gawking. There was a powdery sort of excitement in the air. Eddie liked it. He didn't know if that was right or wrong, but yes, he liked it very well.

'Also depends on what folks want,' Susannah amplified.

'Ah'll tell you what they 'unt, brownie!' Took said in his shrill shards-of-glass voice. 'They 'unt peace, same as ever! They 'unt t'town t'still be here arter you four—'

Susannah seized the man's thumb and bent it back. It was dextrously done. Jake doubted if more than two or three *folken*, those closest to the counter, saw it, but Took's face went a dirty white and his eyes bulged from their sockets.

'I'll take that word from an old man who's lost most of his sense,' she said, 'but I won't take it from you. Call me brownie again, fatso, and I'll pull your tongue out of your head and wipe your ass with it.'

'Cry pardon!' Took gasped. Now sweat broke on his cheeks in large and rather disgusting drops. 'Cry 'er pardon, so Ah do!'

'Fine,' Susannah said, and let him go. 'Now we might just go out and sit on your porch for a bit, for shopping's tiring work.'

6

Took's General Store featured no Guardians of the Beam such as Roland had told of in Mejis, but rockers were lined up the long length of the porch, as many as two dozen of them. And all three sets of steps were flanked by stuffy-guys in honor of the season. When Roland's ka-mates came out, they took three rockers in the middle of the porch. Oy lay down contentedly between Jake's feet and appeared to go to sleep with his nose on his paws.

Eddie cocked a thumb back over his shoulder in Eben Took's general direction. 'Too bad Detta Walker wasn't here to shoplift a few things from the son of a bitch.'

'Don't think I wasn't tempted on her behalf,' Susannah said.

'Folks coming,' Jake said. 'I think they want to talk to us.'

'Sure they do,' Eddie said. 'It's what we're here for.' He smiled, his handsome face growing handsomer still. Under his breath he said, 'Meet the gunslingers, folks. Come-come-commala, shootin's gonna folla.'

'Hesh up that bad mouth of yours, son,' Susannah said, but she was laughing.

They're crazy, Jake thought. But if he was the exception, why was he laughing, too?

7

Henchick of the Manni and Roland of Gilead nooned in the shadow of a massive rock outcrop, eating cold chicken and rice wrapped in tortillas and drinking sof' cider from a jug which they passed back and forth between them. Henchick set them on with a word to what he called both The Force and The Over, then fell silent. That was fine with Roland. The old man had answered aye to the one question the gunslinger had needed to ask.

By the time they'd finished their meal, the sun had gone behind the high cliffs and escarpments. Thus they walked in shadow, making their way up a path that was strewn with rubble and far too narrow for their horses, which had been left in a grove of yellow-leaf quaking aspen below. Scores of tiny lizards ran before them, sometimes darting into cracks in the rocks.

Shady or not, it was hotter than the hinges of hell out here. After a mile of steady climbing, Roland began to breathe hard and use his bandanna to wipe the sweat from his cheeks and throat. Henchick, who appeared to be somewhere in the neighborhood of eighty, walked ahead of him with steady serenity. He breathed with the ease of a man strolling in a park. He'd left his cloak below, laid over the branch of a tree, but Roland could see no patches of sweat spreading on his black shirt.

They reached a bend in the path, and for a moment the world to the north and west opened out below them in gauzy splendor. Roland could see the huge taupe rectangles of graze-land, and tiny toy cattle. To the south and east, the fields grew greener as they marched toward the river lowlands. He could see the Calla village, and even – in the dreaming western distance – the edge of great forest through which they had come to get here. The breeze that struck them on this stretch of the path was so cold it made Roland gasp. Yet he raised his face into it gratefully, eyes mostly closed, smelling all the things that were the Calla: steers, horses, grain, river water, and rice rice rice.

Henchick had doffed his broad-brimmed, flat-crowned hat and also stood with his head raised and his eyes mostly closed, a study in silent thanks-giving. The wind blew back his long hair and playfully divided his waist-length beard into forks. They stood so for perhaps three minutes, letting the breeze cool them. Then Henchick clapped his hat back on his head. He looked at Roland. 'Do 'ee say the world will end in fire or in ice, gunslinger?'

Roland considered this. 'Neither,' he said at last. 'I think in darkness.'

'Do 'ee say so?'

'Aye.'

Henchick considered a moment, then turned to continue on up the path. Roland was impatient to get to where they were going, but he touched the Manni's shoulder, nevertheless. A promise was a promise. Especially one made to a lady.

'I stayed with one of the forgetful last night,' Roland said. 'Isn't that what you call those who choose to leave thy ka-tet?'

'We speak of the forgetful, aye,' Henchick said, watching him closely, 'but not of ka-tet. We know that word, but it is not our word, gunslinger.'

'In any case, I—'

'In any case, thee slept at the Rocking B with Vaughn Eisenhart and our daughter, Margaret. And she threw the dish for 'ee. I didn't speak of these things when we talked last night, for I knew them as well as you did. Any ro', we had other matters to discuss, did we not? Caves, and such.'

'We did.' Roland tried not to show his surprise. He must have failed, because Henchick nodded slightly, the lips just visible within his beard curving in a slight smile.

'The Manni have ways of knowing, gunslinger; always have.'

'Will you not call me Roland?'

'Nay.'

'She said to tell thee that Margaret of the Redpath Clan does fine with her heathen man, fine still.'

Henchick nodded. If he felt pain at this, it didn't show. Not even in his eyes. 'She's damned,' he said. His tone was that of a man saying *Looks like it might come off sunny by afternoon.*

'Are you asking me to tell her that?' Roland asked. He was amused and aghast at the same time.

Henchick's blue eyes had faded and grown watery with age, but there was no mistaking the surprise that came into them at this question. His bushy eyebrows went up. 'Why would I bother?' he asked. 'She knows. She'll have time to repent her heathen man at leisure in the depths of Na'ar. She knows that, too. Come, gunslinger. Another quarter-wheel and we're there. But it's upsy.'

8

Upsy it was, very upsy indeed. Half an hour later, they came to a place where a fallen boulder blocked most of the path. Henchick eased his way around it, dark pants rippling in the wind, beard blowing out sideways, long-nailed fingers clutching for purchase. Roland followed. The boulder was warm from the sun, but the wind was now so cold he was shivering.

He sensed the heels of his worn boots sticking out over a blue drop of perhaps two thousand feet. If the old man decided to push him, all would end in a hurry. And in decidedly undramatic fashion.

But it wouldn't, he thought. *Eddie would carry on in my place, and the other two would follow until they fell.*

On the far side of the boulder, the path ended in a ragged, dark hole nine feet high and five wide. A draft blew out of it into Roland's face. Unlike the breeze that had played with them as they climbed the path, this air was smelly and unpleasant. Coming with it, carried upon it, were cries Roland couldn't make out. But they were the cries of human voices.

'Is it the cries of folks in Na'ar we're hearing?' he asked Henchick.

No smile touched the old man's mostly hidden lips now. 'Speak not in jest,' he said. 'Not here. For you are in the presence of the infinite.'

Roland could believe it. He moved forward cautiously, boots gritting on the rubbly scree, his hand dropping to the butt of his gun — he always wore the left one now, when he wore any; below the hand that was whole.

The stench breathing from the cave's open mouth grew stronger yet. Noxious if not outright toxic. Roland held his bandanna against his mouth and nose with his diminished right hand. Something inside the cave, there in the shadows. Bones, yes, the bones of lizards and other small animals, but something else as well, a shape he knew—

'Be careful, gunslinger,' Henchick said, but stood aside to let Roland enter the cave if he so desired.

My desires don't matter, Roland thought. *This is just something I have to do. Probably that makes it simpler.*

The shape in the shadows grew clearer. He wasn't surprised to see it was a door exactly like those he'd come to on the beach; why else would this have been called Doorway Cave? It was made of ironwood (or perhaps ghostwood), and stood about twenty feet inside the entrance to the cave. It was six and a half feet high, as the doors on the beach had been. And, like those, it stood freely in the shadows, with hinges that seemed fastened to nothing.

Yet it would turn on those hinges easily, he thought. *Will turn. When the time comes.*

There was no keyhole. The knob appeared to be crystal. Etched upon it was a rose. On the beach of the Western Sea, the three doors had been marked with the High Speech: THE PRISONER on one, THE LADY OF THE SHADOWS on another, THE PUSHER on the third. Here were the hieroglyphs he had seen on the box hidden in Callahan's church:

'It means "unfound,"' Roland said.

Henchick nodded, but when Roland moved to walk around the door, the old man took a step forward and held out a hand. 'Be careful, or 'ee may be able to discover who those voices belong to for yourself.'

Roland saw what he meant. Eight or nine feet beyond the door, the floor of the cave sloped down at an angle of fifty or even sixty degrees. There was nothing to hold onto, and the rock looked smooth as glass. Thirty feet down, this slippery-slide disappeared into a chasm. Moaning, intertwined voices rose from it. And then one came clear. It was that of Gabrielle Deschain.

'*Roland, don't!*' his dead mother shrieked up from the darkness. '*Don't shoot, it's me! It's your m*—' But before she could finish, the overlapping crash of pistol shots silenced her. Pain shot up into Roland's head. He was pressing the bandanna against his face almost hard enough to break his own nose. He tried to ease the muscles in his arm and at first was unable to do so.

Next from that reeking darkness came the voice of his father.

'I've known since you toddled that you were no genius,' Steven Deschain said in a tired voice, 'but I never believed until yestereve that you were an idiot. To let him drive you like a cow in a chute! Gods!'

Never mind. These are not even ghosts. I think they're only echoes, somehow taken from deep inside my own head and projected.

When he stepped around the door (minding the drop now to his right), the door was gone. There was only the silhouette of Henchick, a severe man-shape cut from black paper standing in the cave's mouth.

The door's still there, but you can only see it from one side. And in that way it's like the other doors, too.

'A trifle upsetting, isn't it?' tittered the voice of Walter from deep in the Doorway Cave's gullet. 'Give it over, Roland! Better to give it over and die than to discover the room at the top of the Dark Tower is empty.'

Then came the urgent blare of Eld's Horn, raising gooseflesh on Roland's arms and hackles on the back of his neck: Cuthbert Allgood's final battle-cry as he ran down Jericho Hill toward his death at the hands of the barbarians with the blue faces.

Roland lowered the bandanna from his own face and began walking again. One pace; two; three. Bones crunched beneath his bootheels. At the third pace the door reappeared, at first side-to, with its latch seeming to bite into thin air, like the hinges on its other side. He stopped for a moment, gazing at this thickness, relishing the strangeness of the door just as he had relished the strangeness of the ones he'd encountered on the beach. And on the beach he had been sick almost to the point of death. If he moved his head forward slightly, the door disappeared. If he pulled it back again, it was there. The door never wavered, never shimmered. It was always a case of either/or, there/not there.

He stepped all the way back, put his splayed palms on the ironwood, leaned on them. He could feel a faint but perceptible vibration, like the feel of powerful machinery. From the dark gullet of the cave, Rhea of the Cöos screamed up at him, calling him a brat who'd never seen his true father's face, telling him his bit o' tail burst her throat with her screams as she burned. Roland ignored it and grasped the crystal doorknob.

'Nay, gunslinger, ye dare not!' Henchick cried in alarm.

'I dare,' Roland said. And he did, but the knob wouldn't turn in either direction. He stepped back from it.

'But the door was open when you found the priest?' he asked Henchick. They had spoken of this the previous night, but Roland wanted to hear more.

'Aye. 'Twas I and Jemmin who found him. Thee knows we elder Manni seek the other worlds? Not for treasure but for enlightenment?'

Roland nodded. He also knew that some had come back from their travels insane. Others never came back at all.

'These hills are magnetic, and riddled with many ways into many worlds. We'd gone out to a cave near the old garnet mines and there we found a message.'

'What kind of message?'

''Twas a machine set in the cave's mouth,' Henchick said. 'Push a button and a voice came out of it. The voice told us to come here.'

'You knew of this cave before?'

'Aye, but before the Pere came, it were called the Cave of Voices. For which reason thee now knows.'

Roland nodded and motioned for Henchick to go on.

'The voice from the machine spoke in accents like those of your ka-mates, gunslinger. It said that we should come here, Jemmin and I, and we'd find a door and a man and a wonder. So we did.'

'Someone left you instructions,' Roland mused. It was Walter he was thinking of. The man in black, who had also left them the cookies Eddie called Keeblers. Walter was Flagg and Flagg was Marten and Marten . . . was he Maerlyn, the old rogue wizard of legend? On that subject Roland remained unsure. 'And spoke to you by name?'

'Nay, he did not know s'much. Only called us the Manni-folk.'

'How did this someone know where to leave the voice machine, do you think?'

Henchick's lips thinned. 'Why must thee think it was a person? Why not a god speaking in a man's voice? Why not some agent of The Over?'

Roland said, 'Gods leave siguls. Men leave machines.' He paused. 'In my own experience, of course, Pa.'

Henchick made a curt gesture, as if to tell Roland to spare him the flattery.

'Was it general knowledge that thee and thy friend were exploring the cave where you found the speaking machine?'

Henchick shrugged rather sullenly. 'People see us, I suppose. Some mayhap watch over the miles with their spyglasses and binoculars. Also, there's the mechanical man. He sees much and prattles everlastingly to all who will listen.'

Roland took this for a yes. He thought someone had known Pere Callahan was coming. And that he would need help when he arrived on the outskirts of the Calla.

'How far open was the door?' Roland asked.

'These are questions for Callahan,' Henchick said. 'I promised to show thee this place. I have. Surely that's enough for ye.'

'Was he conscious when you found him?'

There was a reluctant pause. Then: 'Nay. Only muttering, as one does in his sleep if he dreams badly.'

'Then he can't tell me, can he? Not this part. Henchick, you seek aid and succor. This thee told me on behalf of all your clans. Help me, then! Help me to help you!'

'I do na' see how this helps.'

And it might not help, not in the matter of the Wolves which so concerned this old man and the rest of Calla Bryn Sturgis, but Roland had other worries and other needs; other fish to fry, as Susannah sometimes said. He stood looking at Henchick, one hand still on the crystal doorknob.

'It were open a bit,' Henchick said finally. 'So were the box. Both just a bit. The one they call the Old Fella, he lay facedown, there.' He pointed to the rubble- and bone-littered floor where Roland's boots were now planted. 'The box were by his right hand, open about this much.' Henchick held his thumb and forefinger perhaps two inches apart. 'Coming from it was the sound of the *kammen*. I've heard em before, but never s'strong. They made my very eyes ache and gush water. Jemmin cried out and begun walking toward the door. The Old Fella's hands were spread out on the ground and Jemmin treaded on one of em and never noticed.

'The door were only ajar, like the box, but a terrible light was coming through it. I've traveled much, gunslinger, to many *wheres* and many *whens*; I've seen other doors and I've seen todash tahken, the holes in reality, but never any light like that. It were black, like all the emptiness that ever was, but there were something red in it.'

'The Eye,' Roland said.

Henchick looked at him. 'An eye? Do 'ee say so?'

'I *think* so,' Roland said. 'The blackness you saw is cast by Black Thirteen. The red might have been the Eye of the Crimson King.'

'Who is he?'

'I don't know,' Roland said. 'Only that he bides far east of here, in Thunderclap or beyond it. I believe he may be a Guardian of the Dark Tower. He may even think he owns it.'

At Roland's mention of the Tower, the old man covered his eyes with both hands, a gesture of deep religious dread.

'What happened next, Henchick? Tell me, I beg.'

'I began to reach for Jemmin, then recalled how he stepped on the man's hand with his bootheel, and thought better of it. Thought, "Henchick, if thee does that, he'll drag you through with him."' The old man's eyes fastened on Roland's. 'Traveling is what we do, I know ye ken as much, and rarely are we afraid, for we trust The Over. Yet I were afraid of that light and the sound of those chimes.' He paused. 'Terrified of them. I've never spoken of that day.'

'Not even to Pere Callahan?'

Henchick shook his head.

'Did he not speak to you when he woke up?'

'He asked if he were dead. I told him that if he were so, so were we all.'

'What about Jemmin?'

'Died two years later.' Henchick tapped the front of his black shirt. 'Heart.'

'How many years since you found Callahan here?'

Henchick shook his head slowly back and forth in wide arcs, a Manni gesture so common it might have been genetic. 'Gunslinger, I know not. For time is—'

'Yes, in drift,' Roland said impatiently. 'How long would you *say*?'

'More than five years, for he has his church and superstitious fools to fill it, ye ken.'

'What did you do? How did thee save Jemmin?'

'Fell on my knees and closed the box,' Henchick said. ''Twas all I could think to do. If I'd hesitated even a single second I do believe I would ha' been lost, for the same black light were coming out of it. It made me feel weak and . . . and *dim*.'

'I'll bet it did,' Roland said grimly.

'But I moved fast, and when the lid of the box clicked down, the door swung shut. Jemmin banged his fists against it and screamed and begged to be let through. Then he fell down in a faint. I dragged him out of the cave. I dragged them both out. After a little while in the fresh air, both came to.' Henchick raised his hands, then lowered them again, as if to say *There you are*.

Roland gave the doorknob a final try. It moved in neither direction. But with the ball—

'Let's go back,' he said. 'I'd like to be at the Pere's house by dinnertime. That means a fast walk back down to the horses and an even faster ride once we get there.'

Henchick nodded. His bearded face was good at hiding expression, but Roland thought the old man was relieved to be going. Roland was a little relieved, himself. Who would enjoy listening to the accusing screams of one's dead mother and father rising out of the dark? Not to mention the cries of one's dead friends?

'What happened to the speaking device?' Roland asked as they started back down.

Henchick shrugged. 'Do ye ken bayderies?'

Batteries. Roland nodded.

'While they worked, the machine played the same message over and over, the one telling us that we should go to the Cave of Voices and find a man, a door, and a wonder. There was also a song. We played it once for the Pere, and he wept. You must ask him about it, for that truly is his part of the tale.'

Roland nodded again.

357

'Then the bayderies died.' Henchick's shrug showed a certain contempt for machines, the gone world, or perhaps both. 'We took them out. They were Duracell. Does thee ken Duracell, gunslinger?'

Roland shook his head.

'We took them to Andy and asked if he could recharge them, mayhap. He took them into himself, but when they came out again they were as useless as before. Andy said sorry. We said thankya.' Henchick rolled his shoulders in that same contemptuous shrug. 'We opened the machine — another button did that — and the tongue came out. It were this long.' Henchick held his hands four or five inches apart. 'Two holes in it. Shiny brown stuff inside, like string. The Pere called it a "cassette tape."'

Roland nodded. 'I want to thank you for taking me up to the cave, Henchick, and for telling me all thee knows.'

'I did what I had to,' Henchick said. 'And you'll do as 'ee promise. Wont'chee?'

Roland of Gilead nodded. 'Let God pick a winner.'

'Aye, so we do say. Ye speak as if ye knew us, once upon a season.' He paused, eyeing Roland with a certain sour shrewdness. 'Or is it just makin up to me that ye does? For anyone who's ever read the Good Book can thee and thou till the crows fly home.'

'Does thee ask if I play the toady, up here where there's no one to hear us but them?' Roland nodded toward the babbling darkness. 'Thou knows better, I hope, for if thee doesn't, thee's a fool.'

The old man considered, then put out his gnarled, long-fingered hand. 'Do 'ee well, Roland. 'Tis a good name, and a fair.'

Roland put out his right hand. And when the old man took it and squeezed it, he felt the first deep twinge of pain where he wanted to feel it least.

No, not yet. Where I'd feel it least is in the other one. The one that's still whole.

'Mayhap this time the Wolves'll kill us all,' said Henchick.

'Perhaps so.'

'Yet still, perhaps we're well-met.'

'Perhaps we are,' the gunslinger replied.

CHAPTER IX
THE PRIEST'S TALE CONCLUDED (UNFOUND)

1

'Beds're ready,' Rosalita Munoz said when they got back.

Eddie was so tired that he believed she'd said something else entirely — *Time to weed the garden*, perhaps, or *There's fifty or sixty more people'd like t'meet ye waitin up to the church*. After all, who spoke of beds at three in the afternoon?

'Huh?' Susannah asked blearily. 'What-say, hon? Didn't quite catch it.'

'Beds're ready,' the Pere's woman of work repeated. 'You two'll go where ye slept night before last; young soh's to have the Pere's bed. And the bumbler can go in with ye, Jake, if ye'd like; Pere said for me to tell 'ee so. He'd be here to tell you himself, but it's his afternoon for sick-rounds. He takes the Communion to em.' She said this last with unmistakable pride.

'Beds,' Eddie said. He couldn't quite get the sense of this. He looked around, as if to confirm that it was still midafternoon, the sun still shining brightly. 'Beds?'

'Pere saw 'ee at the store,' Rosalita amplified, 'and thought ye'd want naps after talking to all those people.'

Eddie understood at last. He supposed that at some point in his life he must have felt more grateful for a kindness, but he honestly couldn't remember when or what that kindness might have been. At first those approaching them as they sat in the rockers on the porch of Took's had come slowly, in hesitant little clusters. But when no one turned to stone or took a bullet in the head — when there was, in fact, animated conversation and actual laughter — more and more came. As the trickle became a flood, Eddie at last discovered what it was to be a public person. He was astounded by how difficult it was, how draining. They wanted simple answers to a

359

thousand difficult questions – where the gunslingers came from and where they were going were only the first two. Some of their questions could be answered honestly, but more and more Eddie heard himself giving weaselly politicians' answers, and heard his two friends doing the same. These weren't lies, exactly, but little propaganda capsules that sounded like answers. And everyone wanted a look straight in the face and a *Do ya fine* that sounded straight from the heart. Even Oy came in for his share of the work; he was petted over and over again, and made to speak until Jake got up, went into the store, and begged a bowl of water from Eben Took. That gentleman gave him a tin cup instead, and told him he could fill it at the trough out front. Jake was surrounded by townsfolk who questioned him steadily even as he did this simple chore. Oy lapped the cup dry, then faced his own gaggle of curious questioners while Jake went back to the trough to fill the cup again.

All in all, they had been five of the longest hours Eddie had ever put in, and he thought he would never regard celebrity in quite the same way again. On the plus side, before finally leaving the porch and heading back to the Old Fella's residence, Eddie reckoned they must have talked to everyone who lived in town and a good number of farmers, ranchers, cowpokes, and hired hands who lived beyond it. Word traveled fast: the outworlders were sitting on the porch of the General Store, and if you wanted to talk to them, they would talk to you.

And now, by God, this woman – this *angel* – was speaking of beds.

'How long have we got?' he asked Rosalita.

'Pere should be back by four,' she said, 'but we won't eat until six, and that's only if your dinh gets back in time. Why don't I wake you at five-thirty? That'll give ye time to wash. Does it do ya?'

'Yeah,' Jake said, and gave her a smile. 'I didn't know just talking to folks could make you so tired. And thirsty.'

She nodded. 'There's a jug of cool water in the pantry.'

'I ought to help you get the meal ready,' Susannah said, and then her mouth opened in a wide yawn.

'Sarey Adams is coming in to help,' Rosalita said, 'and it's nobbut a cold meal, in any case. Go on, now. Take your rest. You're all in, and it shows.'

2

In the pantry, Jake drank long and deep, then poured water into a bowl for Oy and carried it into Pere Callahan's bedroom. He felt guilty about being in here (and about having a billy-bumbler in here with him), but the bedcovers on Callahan's narrow bed had been turned down, the pillow had been plumped up, and both beckoned him. He put down the bowl and Oy quietly began to lap water. Jake undressed down to his new underwear, then lay back and closed his eyes.

Probably won't be able to actually sleep, he thought, *I wasn't ever any good at taking naps, even back when Mrs Shaw used to call me 'Bama.*

Less than a minute later he was snoring lightly, with one arm slung over his eyes. Oy slept on the floor beside him with his nose on one paw.

3

Eddie and Susannah sat side by side on the bed in the guest room. Eddie could still hardly believe this: not only a nap, but a nap in an actual bed. Luxury piled on luxury. He wanted nothing more than to lie down, take Suze in his arms, and sleep that way, but one matter needed to be addressed first. It had been nagging him all day, even during the heaviest of their impromptu politicking.

'Suze, about Tian's Gran-pere—'

'I don't want to hear it,' she said at once.

He raised his eyebrows, surprised. Although he supposed he'd known.

'We could get into this,' she said, 'but I'm tired. I want to go to sleep. Tell Roland what the old guy told you, and tell Jake if you want to, but don't tell me. Not yet.' She sat next to him, her brown thigh touching his white one, her brown eyes looking steadily into his hazel ones. 'Do you hear me?'

'Hear you very well.'

'Say thankya big-big.'

He laughed, took her in his arms, kissed her.

And shortly they were also asleep with their arms around each other and their foreheads touching. A rectangle of light moved steadily up their bodies as the sun sank. It had moved back into the true west, at least for the time being. Roland saw this for himself as he rode slowly down the drive to the Old Fella's rectory-house with his aching legs kicked free of the stirrups.

4

Rosalita came out to greet him. 'Hile, Roland – long days and pleasant nights.'

He nodded. 'May you have twice the number.'

'I ken ye might ask some of us to throw the dish against the Wolves, when they come.'

'Who told you so?'

'Oh . . . some little bird whispered it in my ear.'

'Ah. And would you? If asked?'

She showed her teeth in a grin. 'Nothing in this life would give me more pleasure.' The teeth disappeared and the grin softened into a true smile. 'Although perhaps the two of us together could discover some pleasure that comes close. Would 'ee see my little cottage, Roland?'

'Aye. And would you rub me with that magic oil of yours again?'

'Is it rubbed ye'd be?'

'Aye.'

'Rubbed hard, or rubbed soft?'

'I've heard a little of both best eases an aching joint.'

She considered this, then burst into laughter and took his hand. 'Come. While the sun shines and this little corner of the world sleeps.'

He came with her willingly, and went where she took him. She kept a secret spring surrounded by sweet moss, and there he was refreshed.

5

Callahan finally returned around five-thirty, just as Eddie, Susannah, and Jake were turning out. At six, Rosalita and Sarey Adams served out a dinner of greens and cold chicken on the screened-in porch behind the rectory. Roland and his friends ate hungrily, the gunslinger taking not just seconds but thirds. Callahan, on the other hand, did little but move his food from place to place on his plate. The tan on his face gave him a certain look of health, but didn't hide the dark circles under his eyes. When Sarey — a cheery, jolly woman, fat but light on her feet — brought out a spice cake, Callahan only shook his head.

When there was nothing left on the table but cups and the coffee pot, Roland brought out his tobacco and raised his eyebrows.

'Do ya,' Callahan said, then raised his voice. 'Rosie, bring this guy something to tap into!'

'Big man, I could listen to you all day,' Eddie said.

'So could I,' Jake agreed.

Callahan smiled. 'I feel the same way about you boys, at least a little.' He poured himself half a cup of coffee. Rosalita brought Roland a pottery cup for his ashes. When she had gone, the Old Fella said, 'I should have finished this story yesterday. I spent most of last night tossing and turning, thinking about how to tell the rest.'

'Would it help if I told you I already know some of it?' Roland asked.

'Probably not. You went up to the Doorway Cave with Henchick, didn't you?'

'Yes. He said there was a song on the speaking machine that sent them up there to find you, and that you wept when you heard it. Was it the one you spoke of?'

'"Someone Saved My Life Tonight," yes. And I can't tell you how strange it was to be sitting in a Manni cabin in Calla Bryn Sturgis, looking toward the darkness of Thunderclap and listening to Elton John.'

'Whoa, whoa,' Susannah said. 'You're way ahead of us, Pere. Last we knew, you were in Sacramento, it was 1981, and you'd just found out your friend got cut up by these so-called Hitler Brothers.' She looked sternly from Callahan to Jake and finally to Eddie. 'I have to say, gentlemen, that you don't seem to have made much progress in the matter of peaceful living since the days when I left America.'

'Don't blame it on me,' Jake said. 'I was in school.'

'And I was stoned,' Eddie said.

'All right, I'll take the blame,' Callahan said, and they all laughed.

'Finish your story,' Roland said. 'Maybe you'll sleep better tonight.'

'Maybe I will,' Callahan said. He thought for a minute, then said. 'What I remember about the hospital — what I guess everyone remembers — is the smell of the disinfectant and the sound of the machines. Mostly the machines. The way they beep. The only other stuff that sounds like that is the equipment in airplane cockpits. I asked a pilot once, and he said the navigational gear makes that sound. I remember thinking that night that there must be a hell of a lot of navigating going on in hospital ICUs.

'Rowan Magruder wasn't married when I worked at Home, but I guessed that must have changed, because there was a woman sitting in the chair by his bed, reading a paperback. Well-dressed, nice green suit, hose, low-heeled shoes. At least I felt okay about facing her; I'd cleaned up and combed up as well as I could, and I hadn't had a drink since Sacramento. But once we were actually face-to-face, I wasn't okay at all. She was sitting with her back to the door, you see. I knocked on the jamb, she turned toward me, and my so-called self-possession took a hike. I took a step back and crossed myself. First time since the night Rowan and I visited Lupe in that same joint. Can you guess why?'

'Of course,' Susannah said. 'Because the pieces fit together. The pieces *always* fit together. We've seen it again and again and again. We just don't know what the picture is.'

'Or can't grasp it,' Eddie said.

Callahan nodded. 'It was like looking at Rowan, only with long blond hair and breasts. His twin sister. And she laughed. She asked me if I thought I'd seen a ghost. I felt . . . surreal. As if I'd slipped into another of those other worlds, *like* the real one — if there is such a thing — but not quite the same. I felt this mad urge to drag out my wallet and see who was on the bills. It wasn't just the resemblance; it was her laughing. Sitting there beside a man who had her face assuming he had any face left at all under the bandages, and laughing.'

'Welcome to Room 19 of the Todash Hospital,' Eddie said.

'Beg pardon?'

'I only meant I know the feeling, Don. We all do. Go on.'

'I introduced myself and asked if I could come in. And when I asked it, I was thinking back to Barlow, the vampire. Thinking, *You have to invite them in the first time. After that, they can come and go as they please.* She told me of course I could come in. She said she'd come from Chicago to be with him in what she called "his closing hours." Then, in that same pleasant voice, she said, "I knew who you were right away. It's the scar on your hand. In his letters, Rowan said he was quite sure you were a religious man in your other life. He used to talk about people's other lives all the time, meaning before they started drinking or taking drugs or went insane or all three.

This one was a carpenter in his other life. That one was a model in her other life. Was he right about you?" All in that pleasant voice. Like a woman making conversation at a cocktail party. And Rowan lying there with his head covered in bandages. If he'd been wearing sunglasses, he would have looked like Claude Rains in *The Invisible Man.*

'I came in. I said I'd once been a religious man, yes, but that was all in the past. She put out her hand. I put out mine. Because, you see, I thought . . .'

6

He puts out his hand because he has made the assumption that she wants to shake with him. The pleasant voice has fooled him. He doesn't realize that what Rowena Magruder Rawlings is actually doing is raising *her hand, not putting it out. At first he doesn't even realize he has been slapped, and hard enough to make his left ear ring and his left eye water; he has a confused idea that the sudden warmth rising in his left cheek must be some sort of cocka-mamie allergy thing, perhaps a stress reaction. Then she is advancing on him with tears streaming down her weirdly Rowan-like face.*

'Go on and look at him,' *she says.* 'Because guess what? This is my *brother's other life! The only one he has left! Get right up close and get a good look at it. They poked out his eyes, they took off one of his cheeks — you can see the teeth in there, peekaboo! The police showed me photographs. They didn't want to, but I made them. They poked a hole in his heart, but I guess the doctors plugged that. It's his liver that's killing him. They poked a hole in that, too, and it's dying.'*

'Miss Magruder, I—'

'It's Mrs Rawlings,' *she tells him,* 'not that it's anything to you, one way or the other. Go on. Get a good look. See what you've done to him.'

'I was in California . . . I saw it in the paper . . .'

'Oh, I'm sure,' *she says.* 'I'm sure. But you're the only one I can get hold of, don't you see? The only one who was close to him. His other pal died of the Queer's Disease, and the rest aren't here. They're eating free food down at his flophouse, I suppose, or talking about what happened at their meetings. How it makes them feel. Well, Reverend Callahan — or is it Father? I saw you cross yourself — let me tell you how this makes* me *feel. It . . . makes . . . me . . . FURIOUS.' She is still speaking in the pleasant voice, but when he opens his mouth to speak again she puts a finger across his lips and there is so much force pressing back against his teeth in that single finger that he gives up. Let her talk, why not?*

It's been years since he's heard a confession, but some things are like riding a bicycle.

'He graduated from NYU cum laude,' *she says.* 'Did you know that? He took second in the Beloit Poetry Prize Competition in 1949, did you know that? As an undergraduate! He wrote a novel . . . a beautiful novel . . . and it's in my attic, gathering dust.'

Callahan can feel soft warm dew settling on his face. It is coming from her mouth.

'I asked him — no, begged him — to go on with his writing and he laughed at me, said he was no good. "Leave that to the Mailers and O'Haras and Irwin Shaws," he said, "people who can really do it. I'll wind up in some ivory-tower office, puffing on a meerschaum pipe and looking like Mr Chips."'

'And that would have been all right, too,' *she says,* 'but then he got involved in the Alcoholics Anonymous program, and from there it was an easy jump to running the flophouse. And hanging with his friends. Friends like you.'

Callahan is amazed. He has never heard the word friends *invested with such contempt.*

'But where are they now that he's down and going out?' *Rowena Magruder Rawlings asks him.* 'Hmmm? Where are all the people he cured, all the newspaper feature reporters who called him a genius? Where's Jane Pauley? She interviewed him on the* Today *show, you know. Twice! Where's that fucking Mother Teresa? He said in one of his letters they were calling her the little saint when she came to Home, well he could use a saint now, my brother could use a saint right now, some laying-on of hands, so where the hell is she?'*

Tears rolling down her cheeks. Her bosom rising and falling. She is beautiful and terrible. Callahan thinks of a picture he saw once of Shiva, the Hindu destroyer-god. Not enough arms, *he thinks, and has to fight a crazy, suicidal urge to laugh.*

'They're not here. There's just you and me, right? And him. He could have won a Nobel Prize for literature. Or he could have taught four hundred students a year for thirty years. Could have touched twelve thousand minds with his. Instead, he's lying here in a hospital bed with his face cut off, and they'll have to take up a subscription from his fucking flophouse to pay for his last illness — if you call getting cut to pieces an illness — and his coffin, and his burial.'

She looks at him, face naked and smiling, her cheeks gleaming with moisture and runners of snot hanging from her nose.

'In his previous other life, Father Callahan, he was the Street Angel. But this is his final other life. Glamorous, isn't it? I'm going down the hall to the canteen for coffee and a Danish. I'll be there for ten minutes or so. Plenty of time for you to have your little visit. Do me a favor and be gone when I get back. You and all the rest of his do-gooders make me sick.'

She leaves. Her sensible low heels go clicking away along the hall. It's not until they've faded completely and left him with the steady beeping of the machines that he realizes he's trembling all over. He doesn't think it's the onset of the dt's, but by God that's what it feels like.

When Rowan speaks from beneath his stiff veil of bandages, Callahan nearly screams. What his old friend says is pretty mushy, but Callahan has no trouble figuring it out.

'She's given that little sermon at least eight times today, and she never bothers to tell anyone that the year I took second in the Beloit, only four other people entered. I guess the war knocked a lot of the poetry out of folks. How you doing, Don?'

The diction is bad, the voice driving it little more than a rasp, but it's Rowan, all right. Callahan goes to him and takes the hands that lie on the counterpane. They curl over his with surprising firmness.

'As far as the novel goes . . . man, it was third-rate James Jones, and that's bad.'

'How you doing, Rowan?' Callahan asks. Now he's crying himself. The goddam room will be floating soon.

'Oh, well, pretty sucky,' says the man under the bandages. Then: 'Thanks for coming.'

'Not a problem,' Callahan says. 'What do you need from me, Rowan? What can I do?'

'You can stay away from Home,' Rowan says. His voice is fading, but his hands still clasp Callahan's. 'They didn't want me. It was you they were after. Do you understand me, Don? They were looking for you. They kept asking me where you were, and by the end I would have told them if I'd known, believe me. But of course I didn't.'

One of the machines is beeping faster, the beeps running toward a merge that will trip an alarm. Callahan has no way of knowing this but knows it anyway. Somehow.

'Rowan — did they have red eyes? Were they wearing . . . I don't know . . . long coats? Like trenchcoats? Did they come in big fancy cars?'

'Nothing like that,' Rowan whispers. 'They were probably in their thirties but dressed like teenagers. They looked like teenagers, too. These guys'll look like teenagers for another twenty years — if they live that long — and then one day they'll just be old.'

Callahan thinks, Just a couple of punks. Is that what he's saying? It is, it almost certainly is, but that doesn't mean the Hitler Brothers weren't hired by the low men for this particular job. It makes sense. Even the newspaper article, brief as it was, pointed out that Rowan Magruder wasn't much like the Brothers' usual type of victim.

'Stay away from Home,' Rowan whispers, but before Callahan can promise, the alarm does indeed go off. For a moment the hands holding his tighten, and Callahan feels a ghost of this man's old energy, that wild fierce energy that somehow kept Home's doors open in spite of all the times the bank account went absolutely flat-line, the energy that attracted men who could do all the things Rowan Magruder himself couldn't.

Then the room begins filling up with nurses, there's a doctor with an arrogant face yelling for the patient's chart, and pretty soon Rowan's twin sister will be back, this time possibly breathing fire. Callahan decides it's time to blow this pop-shop, and the greater pop-shop that

367

is New York City. The low men are still interested in him, it seems, very interested indeed, and if they have a base of operations, it's probably right here in Fun City, USA. Consequently, a return to the West Coast would probably be an excellent idea. He can't afford another plane ticket, but he has enough cash to ride the Big Gray Dog. Won't be for the first time, either. Another trip west, why not? He can see himself with absolute clarity, the man in Seat 29-C: a fresh, unopened package of cigarettes in his shirt pocket; a fresh, unopened bottle of Early Times in a paper bag; the new John D. MacDonald novel, also fresh and unopened, lying on his lap. Maybe he'll be on the far side of the Hudson and riding through Fort Lee, deep into Chapter One and nipping his second drink before they finally turn off all the machines in Room 577 and his old friend goes out into the darkness and toward whatever waits for us there.

7

'577,' Eddie said.

'Nineteen,' Jake said.

'Beg pardon?' Callahan asked again.

'Five, seven, and seven,' Susannah said. 'Add them, you get nineteen.'

'Does that mean something?'

'Put them all together, they spell mother, a word that means the world to me,' Eddie said with a sentimental smile.

Susannah ignored him. 'We don't know,' she said. 'You didn't leave New York, did you? If you had, you'd have never gotten that.' She pointed to the scar on his forehead.

'Oh, I left,' Callahan said. 'Just not quite as soon as I intended. My intention when I left the hospital really was to go back down to Port Authority and buy a ticket on the Forty bus.'

'What's that?' Jake asked.

'Hobo-speak for the farthest you can go. If you buy a ticket to Fairbanks, Alaska, you're riding on the Forty bus.'

'Over here, it'd be Bus Nineteen,' Eddie said.

'As I was walking, I got thinking about all the old times. Some of them were funny, like when a bunch of the guys at Home put on a circus show. Some of them were scary, like one night just before dinner when one guy says to this other one, "Stop picking your nose, Jeffy, it's making me sick" and Jeffy goes "Why don't you pick this, homeboy," and he pulls out this giant spring-blade knife and before any of us can move or even figure out what's happening, Jeffy cuts the other guy's throat. Lupe's screaming and I'm yelling "Jesus! Holy Jesus!" and the blood is spraying everywhere because he got the guy's carotid – or maybe it was the jugular – and then Rowan comes running out of the bathroom holding his pants up with one hand and a roll of toilet paper in the other, and do you know what he did?'

'Used the paper,' Susannah said.

Callahan grinned. It made him a younger man. 'Yer-bugger, he did. Slapped the whole roll right against the place where the blood was spurting and yelled for Lupe to call 211, which got you an ambulance in those days. And I'm standing there, watching that white toilet paper turn red, working its way in toward the cardboard core. Rowan said "Just think of it as the world's biggest shaving cut" and we started laughing. We laughed until the tears came out of our eyes.

'I was running through a lot of old times, do ya. The good, the bad, and the ugly. I remember – vaguely – stopping in at a Smiler's Market and getting a couple of cans of Bud in a paper sack. I drank one of them and kept on walking. I wasn't thinking about where I was going – not in my conscious mind, at least – but my feet must have had a mind of their own, because all at once I looked around and I was in front of this place where we used to go to supper sometimes if we were – as they say – in funds. It was on Second and Fifty-second.'

'Chew Chew Mama's,' Jake said.

Callahan stared at him with real amazement, then looked at Roland. 'Gunslinger, you boys are starting to scare me a little.'

Roland only twirled his fingers in his old gesture: *Keep going, partner.*

'I decided to go in and get a hamburger for old times' sake,' Callahan said. 'And while I was eating the burger, I decided I didn't want to leave New York without at least looking into Home through the front window. I could stand across the street, like the times when I swung by there after Lupe died. Why not? I'd never been bothered there before. Not by the vampires, not by the low men, either.' He looked at them. 'I can't tell you if I really believed that, or if it was some kind of elaborate, suicidal mind-game. I can recapture a lot of what I felt that night, what I said and how I thought, but not that.

'In any case, I never got to Home. I paid up and I went walking down Second Avenue. Home was at First and Forty-seventh, but I didn't want to walk directly in front of it. So I decided to go down to First and Forty-sixth and cross over there.'

'Why not Forty-eighth?' Eddie asked him quietly. 'You could have turned down Forty-eighth, that would have been quicker. Saved you doubling back a block.'

Callahan considered the question, then shook his head. 'If there was a reason, I don't remember.'

'There was a reason,' Susannah said. 'You wanted to walk past the vacant lot.'

'Why would I—'

'For the same reason people want to walk past a bakery when the dough-nuts are coming out of the oven,' Eddie said. 'Some things are just nice, that's all.'

Callahan received this doubtfully, then shrugged. 'If you say so.'

'I do, sai.'

'In any case, I was walking along, sipping my other beer. I was almost at Second and Forty-sixth when—'

'What was there?' Jake asked eagerly. 'What was on that corner in 1981?'

'I don't . . .' Callahan began, and then he stopped. 'A fence,' he said. 'Quite a high one. Ten, maybe twelve feet.'

'Not the one we climbed over,' Eddie said to Roland. 'Not unless it grew five feet on its own.'

'There was a picture on it,' Callahan said. 'I do remember that. Some sort of street mural, but I couldn't see what it was, because the street-lights on the corner were out. And all at once it hit me that wasn't right. All at once an alarm started going off in my head. Sounded a lot like the one that brought all the people into Rowan's room at the hospital, if you want to know the truth. All at once I couldn't believe I was where I was. It was nuts. But at the same time I'm thinking . . .'

8

At the same time he's thinking It's all right, just a few lights out is all it is, if there were vampires you'd see them and if there were low men you'd hear the chimes and smell rancid onions and hot metal. *All the same he decides to vacate this area, and immediately. Chimes or no chimes, every nerve in his body is suddenly out on his skin, sparking and sizzling.*

He turns and there are two men right behind him. There is a space of seconds when they are so surprised by his abrupt change of direction that he probably could have darted between them like an aging running back and gone sprinting back up Second Avenue. But he is surprised, too, and for a further space of seconds the three of them only stand there, staring.

There's a big Hitler Brother and a little Hitler Brother. The little one is no more than five-two. He's wearing a loose chambray shirt over black slacks. On his head is a baseball cap turned around backwards. His eyes are as black as drops of tar and his complexion is bad. Callahan immediately thinks of him as Lennie. The big one is maybe six-feet-six, wearing a Yankees sweatshirt, blue jeans, and sneakers. He's got a sandy mustache. He's wearing a fanny-pack, only around in front so it's actually a belly-pack. Callahan names this one George.

Callahan turns around, planning to flee down Second Avenue if he's got the light or if it looks like he can beat the traffic. If that's impossible, he'll go down Forty-sixth to the UN Plaza Hotel and duck into their lob—

The big one, George, grabs him by the shirt and yanks him back by his collar. The collar rips, but unfortunately not enough to set him free.

'No you don't, doc,' the little one says. 'No you don't.' Then bustles forward, quick as an insect, and before Callahan's clear on what's happening, Lennie has reached between his legs, seized his testicles, and squeezed them violently together. The pain is immediate and enormous, a swelling sickness like liquid lead.

'Like-at, niggah-lovvah?' Lennie asks him in a tone that seems to convey genuine concern, that seems to say 'We want this to mean as much to you as it does to us.' Then he yanks Callahan's testicles forward and the pain trebles. Enormous rusty saw-teeth sink into Callahan's belly and he thinks, He'll rip them off, he's already turned them to jelly and now he's going to rip them right off, there's nothing holding them on but a little loose skin and he's going to—

He begins to scream and George clamps a hand over his mouth. 'Quit it!' he snarls at his partner. 'We're on the fucking street, did you forget that?'

Even while the pain is eating him alive, Callahan is mulling the situation's queerly inverted quality: George is the big Hitler Brother in charge, not Lennie. George is the smart Hitler Brother. It's certainly not the way Steinbeck would have written it.

Then, from his right, a humming sound arises. At first he thinks it's the chimes, but the humming is sweet. It's strong, as well. George and Lennie feel it. And they don't like it.

'Whazzat?' Lennie asks. 'Did you hear sumpun?'

'I don't know. Let's get him back to the place. And keep your hands off his balls. Later you can yank em all you want, but for now just help me.'

One on either side of him, and all at once he is being propelled back up Second Avenue.

The high board fence runs past on their right. That sweet, powerful humming sound is coming from behind it. If I could get over that fence, I'd be all right, *Callahan thinks. There's something in there, something powerful and good. They wouldn't dare go near it.*

Perhaps this is so, but he doubts he could scramble over a board fence ten feet high even if his balls weren't blasting out enormous bursts of their own painful Morse Code, even if he couldn't feel them swelling in his underwear. All at once his head lolls forward and he vomits a hot load of half-digested food down the front of his shirt and pants. He can feel it soaking through to his skin, warm as piss.

Two young couples, obviously together, are headed the other way. The young men are big, they could probably mop up the street with Lennie and perhaps even give George a run for his money if they ganged up on him, but right now they are looking disgusted and clearly want nothing more than to get their dates out of Callahan's general vicinity as quickly as they possibly can.

'He just had a little too much to drink,' George says, smiling sympathetically, 'and then whoopsy-daisy. Happens to the best of us from time to time.'

They're the Hitler Brothers! *Callahan tries to scream.* These guys are the Hitler Brothers! They killed my friend and now they're going to kill me! Get the police! *But of course nothing comes out, in nightmares like this it never does, and soon the couples are headed the other way. George and Lennie continue to move Callahan briskly along the block of Second Avenue between Forty-sixth and Forty-seventh. His feet are barely touching the concrete. His Chew Chew Mama Swissburger is now steaming on his shirt.* Oh boy, he can even smell the mustard he put on it.

'Lemme see his hand,' George says as they near the next intersection, and when Lennie grabs Callahan's left hand, George says, 'No, dipstick, the other one.'

Lennie holds out Callahan's right hand. Callahan couldn't stop him if he tried. His lower belly has been filled with hot, wet cement. His stomach, meanwhile, seems to be quivering at the back of his throat like a small, frightened animal.

George looks at the scar on Callahan's right hand and nods. 'Yuh, it's him, all right. Never hurts to be sure. Come on, let's go, Faddah. Double-time, hup-hup!'

When they get to Forty-seventh, Callahan is swept off the main thoroughfare. Down the hill on the left is a pool of bright white light: Home. *He can even see a few slope-shouldered silhouettes, men standing on the corner, talking Program and smoking.* I might even know some of them, *he thinks confusedly.* Hell, probably do.

But they don't go that far. Less than a quarter of the way down the block between Second Avenue and First, George drags Callahan into the doorway of a deserted storefront with a FOR SALE OR LEASE *sign in both of its soaped-over windows. Lennie just kind of circles them, like a yapping terrier around a couple of slow-moving cows.*

'Gonna fuck you up, niggah-lovvah!' he's chanting. 'We done a thousand just like you,

gonna do a million before we're through, we can cut down any niggah, even when the niggah's biggah, that's from a song I'm writin', it's a song called "Kill All Niggah-Lovin Fags," I'm gonna send it to Merle Haggard when I'm done, he's the best, he's the one told all those hippies to squat n shit in their hats, fucking Merle's for America, I got a Mustang 380 and I got Hermann Goering's Luger, you know that, niggah-lovvah?'

'Shut up, ya little punkass,' George says, but he speaks with fond absentmindedness, reserving his real attention for finding the key he wants on a fat ring of them and then opening the door of the empty storefront. Callahan thinks, To him Lennie's like the radio that's always playing in an auto repair shop or the kitchen of a fast-food restaurant, he doesn't even hear him anymore, he's just part of the background noise.

'Yeah, Nort,' Lennie says, and then goes right on. 'Fuckin Goering's fuckin Luger, that's right, and I might blow your fuckin balls off with it, because we know the truth about what niggah-lovvahs like you are doin to this country, right, Nort?'

'Told you, no names,' George/Nort says, but he speaks indulgently and Callahan knows why: he'll never be able to give any names to the police, not if things go the way these douchebags plan.

'Sorry Nort but you niggah-lovvahs you fuckin Jewboy intellectuals are the ones fucking this country up, so I want you to think about that when I pull your fuckin balls right off your fuckin scrote—'

'The balls are the scrote, numbwit,' George/Nort says in a weirdly scholarly voice, and then: 'Bingo!'

The door opens. George/Nort shoves Callahan through it. The storefront is nothing but a dusty shadowbox smelling of bleach, soap, and starch. Thick wires and pipes stick out of two walls. He can see cleaner squares on the walls where coin-op washing machines and dryers once stood. On the floor is a sign he can just barely read in the dimness: TURTLE BAY WASHATERIA 'U WASH OR WE WASH EITHER WAY IT ALL COMES **KLEEN**!

All comes kleen, right, Callahan thinks. He turns toward them and isn't very surprised to see George/Nort pointing a gun at him. It's not Hermann Goering's Luger, looks more to Callahan like the sort of cheap .32 you'd buy for sixty dollars in a bar uptown, but he's sure it would do the job. George/Nort unzips his belly-pack without taking his eyes from Callahan — he's done this before, both of them have, they are old hands, old wolves who have had a good long run for themselves — and pulls out a roll of duct tape. Callahan remembers Lupe's once saying America would collapse in a week without duct tape. 'The secret weapon,' he called it. George/Nort hands the roll to Lennie, who takes it and scurries forward to Callahan with that same insectile speed.

'Putcha hands behind ya, niggah-reebop,' Lennie says.

Callahan doesn't.

George/Nort waggles the pistol at him. 'Do it or I put one in your gut, Faddah. You ain't never felt pain like that, I promise you.'

Callahan does it. He has no choice. Lennie darts behind him.

'Put em togetha, niggah-reebop,' *Lennie says.* 'Don'tchoo know how this is done? Ain'tchoo ever been to the movies?' *He laughs like a loon.*

Callahan puts his wrists together. There comes a low snarling sound as Lennie pulls duct-tape off the roll and begins taping Callahan's arms behind his back. He stands taking deep breaths of dust and bleach and the comforting, somehow childlike perfume of fabric softener.

'Who hired you?' *he asks George/Nort.* 'Was it the low men?'

George/Nort doesn't answer, but Callahan thinks he sees his eyes flicker. Outside, traffic passes in bursts. A few pedestrians stroll by. What would happen if he screamed? Well, he supposes he knows the answer to that, doesn't he? The Bible says the priest and the Levite passed by the wounded man, and heard not his cries, 'but a certain Samaritan . . . had compassion on him.' *Callahan needs a good Samaritan, but in New York they are in short supply.*

'Did they have red eyes, Nort?'

Nort's own eyes flicker again, but the barrel of the gun remains pointed at Callahan's midsection, steady as a rock.

'Did they drive big fancy cars? They did, didn't they? And how much do you think your life and this little shitpoke's life will be worth, once—'

Lennie grabs his balls again, squeezes them, twists them, pulls them down like window-shades. Callahan screams and the world goes gray. The strength runs out of his legs and his knees come totally unbuckled.

'Annnd hee's DOWN!' *Lennie cries gleefully.* 'Mo-Hammerhead A-Lee is DOWN! THE GREAT WHITE HOPE HAS PULLED THE TRIGGAH ON THAT LOUDMOUTH NIGGAH AND PUT IM ON THE CANVAS! I DON'T BELEEEEVE IT!' *It's a Howard Cosell imitation, and so good that even in his agony Callahan feels like laughing. He hears another wild purring sound and now it's his ankles that are being taped together.*

George/Nort brings a knapsack over from the corner. He opens it and rummages out a Polaroid One-Shot. He bends over Callahan and suddenly the world goes dazzle-bright. In the immediate aftermath, Callahan can see nothing but phantom shapes behind a hanging blue ball at the center of his vision. From it comes George/Nort's voice.

'Remind me to get another one, after. They wanted both.'

'Yeah, Nort, yeah!' *The little one sounds almost rabid with excitement now, and Callahan knows the real hurting's about to start. He remembers an old Dylan song called* 'A Hard Rain's A-Gonna Fall' *and thinks,* It fits. Better than 'Someone Saved My Life Tonight,' *that's for sure.*

He's enveloped by a fog of garlic and tomatoes. Someone had Italian for dinner, possibly while Callahan was getting his face slapped in the hospital. A shape looms out of the dazzle. The big guy. 'Doesn't matter to you who hired us,' says George/Nort. 'Thing is, we were hired, and as far as anyone's ever gonna be concerned, Faddah, you're just another niggah-lovvah like that guy Magruder and the Hitler Brothers done cleaned your clock. Mostly we're dedicated, but we will work for a dollar, like any good American.' He pauses, and then comes the ultimate, existential absurdity: 'We're popular in Queens, you know.'

'Fuck yourself,' Callahan says, and then the entire right side of his face explodes in agony. Lennie has kicked him with a steel-toed workboot, breaking his jaw in what will turn out to be a total of four places.

'Nice talk,' he hears Lennie say dimly from the insane universe where God has clearly died and lies stinking on the floor of a pillaged heaven. 'Nice talk for a Faddah.' Then his voice goes up, becomes the excited, begging whine of a child: 'Let me, Nort! C'mon, let me! I wanna do it!'

'No way,' George/Nort says. 'I do the forehead swastikas, you always fuck them up. You can do the ones on his hands, okay?'

'He's tied up! His hands're covered in that fuckin—'

'After he's dead,' George/Nort explains with a terrible patience. 'We'll unwrap his hands after he's dead and you can—'

'Nort, please! I'll do that thing you like. And listen!' Lennie's voice brightens. 'Tell you what! If I start to fuck up, you tell me and I'll stop! Please, Nort? Please?'

'Well . . .' Callahan has heard this tone before, too. The indulgent father who can't deny a favorite, if mentally challenged, child. 'Well, okay.'

His vision is clearing. He wishes to God it wasn't. He sees Lennie remove a flashlight from the backpack. George has pulled a folded scalpel from his fanny-pack. They exchange tools. George trains the flashlight on Callahan's rapidly swelling face. Callahan winces and slits his eyes. He has just enough vision to see Lennie swing the scalpel out with his tiny yet dexterous fingers.

'Ain't this gonna be good!' Lennie cries. He is rapturous with excitement. 'Ain't this gonna be so good!'

'Just don't fuck it up,' George says.

Callahan thinks, If this was a movie, the cavalry would come just about now. Or the cops. Or fucking Sherlock Holmes in H. G. Wells's time machine.

But Lennie kneels in front of him, the hardon in his pants all too visible, and the cavalry doesn't come. He leans forward with the scalpel outstretched, and the cops don't come. Callahan can smell not garlic and tomatoes on this one but sweat and cigarettes.

'Wait a second, Bill,' George/Nort says, 'I got an idea, let me draw it on for you first. I got a pen in my pocket.'

'Fuck that,' Lennie/Bill breathes. He stretches out the scalpel. Callahan can see the razor-sharp blade trembling as the little man's excitement is communicated to it, and then it passes from his field of vision. Something cold traces his brow, then turns hot, and Sherlock Holmes doesn't come. Blood pours into his eyes, dousing his vision, and neither does James Bond Perry Mason Travis McGee Hercule Poirot Miss Fucking Marple.

The long white face of Barlow rises in his mind. The vampire's hair floats around his head. Barlow reaches out. 'Come, false priest,' he's saying, 'learn of a true religion.' There are two dry snapping sounds as the vampire's fingers break off the arms of the cross his mother gave him.

'Oh you fuckin nutball,' George/Nort groans, 'that ain't a swastika, that's a fuckin cross! Gimme that!'

'Stop it, Nort, gimme a chance, I ain't done!'

Squabbling over him like a couple of kids while his balls ache and his broken jaw throbs and his sight drowns in blood. All those seventies-era arguments about whether or not God was dead, and Christ, look at him! Just look at him! How could there be any doubt?

And that is when the cavalry arrives.

9

'What exactly do you mean?' Roland asked. 'I would hear this part very well, Pere.'

They were still sitting at the table on the porch, but the meal was finished, the sun was down, and Rosalita had brought 'seners. Callahan had broken his story long enough to ask her to sit with them and so she had. Beyond the screens, in the rectory's dark yard, bugs hummed, thirsty for the light.

Jake touched what was in the gunslinger's mind. And, suddenly impatient with all this secrecy, he put the question himself: 'Were we the cavalry, Pere?'

Roland looked shocked, then actually amused. Callahan only looked surprised.

'No,' he said. 'I don't think so.'

'You didn't see them, did you?' Roland asked. 'You never actually saw the people who rescued you.'

'I told you the Hitler Brothers had a flashlight,' Callahan said. 'Say true. But these other guys, the cavalry . . .'

10

Whoever they are, they have a searchlight. *It fills the abandoned Washateria with a glare brighter than the flash of the cheapie Polaroid, and unlike the Polaroid, it's* constant. *George/Nort and Lennie/Bill cover their eyes. Callahan would cover his, if his arms weren't duct-taped behind him.*

'Nort, drop the gun! Bill, drop the scalpel!' The voice coming from the huge light is scary because it's scared. It's the voice of someone who might do damn near anything. 'I'm gonna count to five and then I'm gonna shoot the both of yez, which is what'chez deserve.' And then the voice behind the light begins to count not slowly and portentously but with alarming speed. 'Onetwothreefour—' It's as if the owner of the voice wants *to shoot,* wants *to hurry up and get the bullshit formality over with. George/Nort and Lennie/Bill have no time to consider their options. They throw down the pistol and the scalpel and the pistol goes off when it hits the dusty lino, a loud BANG like a kid's toy pistol that's been loaded with double caps. Callahan has no idea where the bullet goes. Maybe even into him. Would he even feel it if it did? Doubtful.*

'Don't shoot, don't shoot!' Lennie/Bill shrieks. 'We ain't, we ain't, we aint'—' Ain't what? Lennie/Bill doesn't seem to know.

'Hands up!' It's a different voice, but also coming from behind the sun-gun dazzle of the light. 'Reach for the sky! Right now, you momzers!*'*

Their hands shoot up.

'Nah, belay that,' says the first one. They may be great guys, Callahan's certainly willing to put them on his Christmas card list, but it's clear they've never done anything like this before. 'Shoes off! Pants off! Now! Right now!'

'What the fuck—' George/Nort begins. 'Are you guys the cops? If you're the cops, you gotta give us our rights, our fuckin Miranda—'

From behind the glaring light, a gun goes off. Callahan sees an orange flash of fire. It's probably a pistol, but it is to the Hitler Brothers' modest barroom .32 as a hawk is to a hummingbird. The crash is gigantic, immediately followed by a crunch of plaster and a puff of stale dust. George/Nort and Lennie/Bill both scream. Callahan thinks one of his rescuers — probably the one who didn't shoot — also screams.

'Shoes off and pants off! Now! Now! You better have em off before I get to thirty, or you're dead. Onetwothreefourfi—'

Again, the speed of the count leaves no time for consideration, let alone remonstrance. George/Nort starts to sit down and Voice Number Two says: 'Sit down and we'll kill you.'

And so the Hitler Brothers stagger around the knapsack, the Polaroid, the gun, and the flashlight like spastic cranes, pulling off their footgear while Voice Number One runs his suicidally rapid count. The shoes come off and the pants go down. George is a boxers guy while Lennie favors briefs of the pee-stained variety. There is no sign of Lennie's hardon; Lennie's hardon has decided to take the rest of the night off.

'Now get out,' Voice Number One says.

George faces into the light. His Yankees sweatshirt hangs down over his underwear shorts, which billow almost to his knees. He's still wearing his fanny-pack. His calves are heavily muscled, but they are trembling. And George's face is long with sudden dismayed realization.

'Listen, you guys,' he says, 'if we go out of here without finishing this guy, they'll kill us. These are very bad—'

'If you schmucks aren't out of here by the time I get to ten,' says Voice Number One, 'I'll kill you myself.'

To which Voice Number Two adds, with a kind of hysterical contempt: 'Gai cocknif en yom, you cowardly motherfuckers! Stay, get shot, who cares?'

Later, after repeating this phrase to a dozen Jews who only shake their heads in bewilderment, Callahan will happen on an elderly fellow in Topeka who translates gai cocknif en yom for him. It means go shit in the ocean.

Voice Number One starts reeling them off again: 'Onetwothreefour—'

George/Nort and Lennie/Bill exchange a cartoon look of indecision, then bolt for the door in their underwear. The big searchlight turns to follow them. They are out; they are gone.

'Follow,' Voice Number One says gruffly to his partner. 'If they get the idea to turn back—'

'Yeahyeah,' says Voice Number Two, and he's gone.

The brilliant light clicks off. 'Turn over on your stomach,' says Voice Number One.

Callahan tries to tell him he doesn't think he can, that his balls now feel roughly the size of teapots, but all that comes from his mouth is mush, because of his broken jaw. He compromises by rolling over on his left side as far as he can.

'Hold still,' says Voice Number One. 'I don't want to cut you.' It's not the voice of a man who does stuff like this for a living. Even in his current state, Callahan can tell that. The guy's breathing in rapid wheezes that sometimes catch in an alarming way and then start up again. Callahan wants to thank him. It's one thing to save a stranger if you're a cop or a fireman or a lifeguard, he supposes. Quite another when you're just an ordinary member of the greater public. And that's what his rescuer is, he thinks, both his rescuers, although how they came so well prepared he doesn't know. How could they know the Hitler Brothers' names? And exactly where were they waiting? Did they come in from the street, or were they in the abandoned laundrymat the whole time? Other stuff Callahan doesn't know. And doesn't really care. Because someone saved, someone saved, someone saved his life

tonight, and that's the big thing, the only thing that matters. George and Lennie almost had their hooks in him, din't they, dear, but the cavalry came at the last minute, just like in a John Wayne movie.

What Callahan wants to do is thank this guy. Where Callahan wants to be is safe in an ambulance and on his way to the hospital before the punks blindside the owner of *Voice Number Two* outside, or the owner of *Voice Number One* has an excitement-induced heart attack. He tries and more mush comes out of his mouth. Drunkspeak, what Rowan used to call gubbish. It sounds like fann-ou,

His hands are cut free, then his feet. The guy doesn't have a heart attack. Callahan rolls over onto his back again, and sees a pudgy white hand holding the scalpel. On the third finger is a signet ring. It shows an open book. Below it are the words Ex Libris. Then the searchlight goes on again and Callahan raises an arm over his eyes. 'Christ, man, why are you doing that?' It comes out Cry-mah, I-oo oonnat, but the owner of *Voice Number One* seems to understand.

'I should think that would be obvious, my wounded friend,' he says. 'Should we meet again, I'd like it to be for the first time. If we pass on the street, I would as soon go unrec-ognized. Safer that way.'

Gritting footsteps. The light is backing away.

'We're going to call an ambulance from the pay phone across the street—'

'No! Don't do that! What if they come back?' In his quite genuine terror, these words come out with perfect clarity.

'We'll be watching,' says *Voice Number One*. The wheeze is fading now. The guy's getting himself back under control. Good for him. 'I think it *is* possible that they'll come back, the big one was really quite distressed, but if the Chinese are correct, I'm now responsible for your life. It's a responsibility I intend to live up to. Should they reappear, I'll throw a bullet at them. Not over their heads, either.' The shape pauses. He looks like a fairly big man himself. Got a gut on him, that much is for sure. 'Those were the Hitler Brothers, my friend. Do you know who I'm talking about?'

'Yes,' Callahan whispers. 'And you won't tell me who you are?'

'Better you not know,' says Mr Ex Libris.

'Do you know who I am?'

A pause. Gritting steps. Mr Ex Libris is now standing in the doorway of the aban-doned laundrymat. 'No,' he says. Then, 'A priest. It doesn't matter.'

'How did you know I was here?'

'Wait for the ambulance,' says *Voice Number One*. 'Don't try to move on your own. You've lost a lot of blood, and you may have internal injuries.'

Then he's gone. Callahan lies on the floor, smelling bleach and detergent and sweet departed fabric softener. U wash or we wash, he thinks, either way it all comes kleen. His *testicles throb and swell. His jaw throbs and there's swelling there, too. He can feel his whole face tightening as the flesh puffs up. He lies there and waits for the ambulance and life or the return of the Hitler Brothers and death. For the lady or the tiger. For Diana's treasure or the deadly biter-snake. And some interminable, uncountable time later, red pulses of light wash across the dusty floor and he knows this time it's the lady. This time it's the treasure.*

This time it's life.

11

'And that,' Callahan said, 'is how I ended up in Room 577 of that same hospital that same night.'

Susannah looked at him, wide-eyed. 'Are you serious?'

'Serious as a heart attack,' he said. 'Rowan Magruder died, I got the living shit beaten out of me, and they slammed me back into the same bed. They must have had just about enough time to re-make it, and until the lady came with the morphine-cart and put me out, I lay there wondering if maybe Magruder's sister might not come back and finish what the Hitler Brothers had started. But why should such things surprise you? There are dozens of these odd crossings in both our stories, do ya. Have you not thought about the coincidence of Calla Bryn Sturgis and my own last name, for instance?'

'Sure we have,' Eddie said.

'What happened next?' Roland asked.

Callahan grinned, and when he did, the gunslinger realized the two sides of the man's face didn't quite line up. He'd been jaw-broke, all right. 'The storyteller's favorite question, Roland, but I think what I need to do now is speed my tale up a bit, or we'll be here all night. The important thing, the part you really want to hear, is the end part, anyway.'

Well, you may think so, Roland mused, and wouldn't have been surprised to know all three of his friends were harboring versions of the same thought.

'I was in the hospital for a week. When they let me out, they sent me to a welfare rehab in Queens. The first place they offered me was in Manhattan and a lot closer, but it was associated with Home — we sent people there sometimes. I was afraid that if I went there, I might get another visit from the Hitler Brothers.'

'And did you?' Susannah asked.

'No. The day I visited Rowan in Room 577 of Riverside Hospital and then ended up there myself was May 19th, 1981,' Callahan said. 'I went out to Queens in the back of a van with three or four other walking-wounded guys on May 25th. I'm going to say it was about six days after that, just before I checked out and hit the road again, that I saw the story in the *Post*. It was in the front of the paper, but not on the front page. TWO MEN FOUND SHOT TO DEATH IN CONEY ISLAND, the headline said. COPS SAY "IT LOOKS LIKE A MOB JOB." That was because the faces and hands had been burned with acid. Nevertheless, the cops ID'd both of them: Norton Randolph and William Garton, both of Brooklyn. There were photos. Mug shots; both of them had long records. They were my guys, all right. George and Lennie.'

'You think the low men got them, don't you?' Jake asked.

'Yes. Payback's a bitch.'

'Did the papers ever ID them as the Hitler Brothers?' Eddie asked. 'Because, man, we were still scarin each other with those guys when I came along.'

'There was some speculation about that possibility in the tabloids,' Callahan said, 'and I'll bet that in their hearts the reporters who covered the Hitler Brothers murders and mutilations knew it was Randolph and Garton — there was nothing afterward but a few halfhearted copycat cuttings — but no one in the tabloid press wants to kill the bogeyman, because the bogeyman sells papers.'

'Man,' Eddie said. 'You *have* been to the wars.'

'You haven't heard the last act yet,' Callahan said. 'It's a dilly.'

Roland made the twirling go-on gesture, but it didn't look urgent. He'd rolled himself a smoke and looked about as content as his three companions had ever seen him. Only Oy, sleeping at Jake's feet, looked more at peace with himself.

'I looked for my footbridge when I left New York for the second time, riding across the GWB with my paperback and my bottle,' Callahan said, 'but my footbridge was gone. Over the next couple of months I saw occasional flashes of the highways in hiding — and I remember getting a ten-dollar bill with Chadbourne on it a couple of times — but mostly they were gone. I saw a lot of Type Three Vampires and remember thinking that they were spreading. But I did nothing about them. I seemed to have lost the urge, the way Thomas Hardy lost the urge to write novels and Thomas Hart Benton lost the urge to paint his murals. "Just mosquitoes," I'd think. "Let them go.' My job was getting into some town, finding the nearest Brawny Man or ManPower or Job Guy, and also finding a bar where I felt comfortable. I favored places that looked like the Americano or the Blarney Stone in New York.'

'You liked a little steam-table with your booze, in other words,' Eddie said.

'That's right,' Callahan said, looking at Eddie as one does at a kindred spirit. 'Do ya! And I'd protect those places until it was time to move on. By which I mean I'd get tipsy in my favorite neighborhood bar, then finish up the evening — the crawling, screaming, puking-down-the-front-of-your-shirt part — somewhere else. *Al fresco*, usually.'

Jake began, 'What—'

'Means he got drunk outdoors, sug,' Susannah told him. She ruffled his hair, then winced and put the hand on her own midsection, instead.

'All right, sai?' Rosalita asked.

'Yes, but if you had somethin with bubbles in it, I surely would drink it.'

Rosalita rose, tapping Callahan on the shoulder as she did so. 'Go on, Pere, or it'll be two in the morning and the cats tuning up in the badlands before you're done.'

'All right,' he said. 'I drank, that's what it comes down to. I drank every night and raved to anyone who'd listen about Lupe and Rowan and Rowena and the black man who picked me up in Issaquena County and Ruta, who really might have been full of fun but who sure wasn't a Siamese cat. And finally I'd pass out.

'This went on until I got to Topeka. Late winter of 1982. That was where I hit my bottom. Do you folks know what that means, to hit a bottom?'

There was a long pause, and then they nodded. Jake was thinking of Ms Avery's English class, and his Final Essay. Susannah was recalling Oxford, Mississippi, Eddie the beach by the Western Sea, leaning over the man who had become his dinh, meaning to cut his throat because Roland wouldn't let him go through one of those magic doors and score a little H.

'For me, the bottom came in a jail cell,' Callahan said. 'It was early morning, and I was actually relatively sober. Also, it was no drunk tank but a cell with a blanket on the cot and an actual seat on the toilet. Compared to some of the places I'd been in, I was farting through satin. The only bothersome things were the name guy . . . and that song.'

12

The light falling through the cell's small chickenwire-reinforced window is gray, which consequently makes his skin gray. Also his hands are dirty and covered with scratches. The crud under some of his nails is black (dirt) and under some it's maroon (dried blood). He vaguely remembers tussling with someone who kept calling him sir, so he guesses that he might be here on the ever-popular Penal Code 48, Assaulting an Officer. All he wanted — Callahan has a slightly clearer memory of this — was to try on the kid's cap, which was very spiffy. He remembers trying to tell the young cop (from the look of this one, pretty soon they'll be hiring kids who aren't even toilet-trained as police officers, at least in Topeka) that he's always on the lookout for funky new lids, he always wears a cap because he's got the Mark of Cain on his forehead. 'Looksh like a crossh,' he remembers saying (or trying to say), 'but it'sh rilly the Marga-Gain.' Which, in his cups, is about as close as he can come to saying Mark of Cain.

Was really drunk last night, but he doesn't feel so bad as he sits here on the bunk, rubbing a hand through his crazy hair. Mouth doesn't taste so good — sort of like Ruta the Siamese Cat took a dump in it, if you wanted the truth — but his head isn't aching too badly. If only the voices would shut up! Down the hall someone's droning out a seemingly endless list of names in alphabetical order. Closer by, someone is singing his least favorite song: 'Someone saved, someone saved, someone saved my li-ife tonight . . .'

'Nailor! . . . Naughton! . . . O'Connor! . . . O'Shaugnessy! . . . Oskowski! . . . Osmer!'

He is just beginning to realize that he is the one singing when the trembling begins in his calves. It works its way up to his knees, then to his thighs, deepening and strengthening as it comes. He can see the big muscles in his legs popping up and down like pistons. What is happening to him?

'Palmer! . . . Palmgren!'

The trembling hits his crotch and lower belly. His underwear shorts darken as he sprays them with piss. At the same time his feet start snapping out into the air, as if he's trying to punt invisible footballs with both of them at the same time. I'm seizing, he thinks. This is probably it. I'm probably going out. Bye-bye blackbird. He tries to call for help and nothing comes out of his mouth but a low chugging sound. His arms begin to fly up and down. Now he's punting invisible footballs with his feet while his arms shout hallelujah, and the guy down the hall is going to go on until the end of the century, maybe until the next Ice Age.

'Peschier! . . . Peters! . . . Pike! . . . Polovik! . . . Rance! . . . Rancourt!'

Callahan's upper body begins to snap back and forth. Each time it snaps forward he *comes closer to losing his balance and falling on the floor. His hands fly up. His feet fly out. There is a sudden spreading pancake of warmth on his ass and he realizes he has just shot the chocolate.*

'Ricupero! . . . Robillard! . . . Rossi!'

He snaps backward, all the way to the whitewashed concrete wall where someone has scrawled BANGO SKANK *and* Just had my 19th Nervous Breakdown! *Then forward, this time with the full-body enthusiasm of a Muslim at morning prayers. For a moment he's staring at the concrete floor from between his naked knees and then he overbalances and goes down on his face. His jaw, which has somehow healed in spite of the nightly binges, rebreaks in three of the original four places. But, just to bring things back into perfect balance — four's the magic number — this time his nose breaks, too. He lies jerking on the floor like a hooked fish, his body fingerpainting in the blood, shit, and piss.* Yeah, I'm going out, *he thinks.*

'Ryan! . . . Sannelli! . . . Scher!'

But gradually the extravagant grand mal *jerks of his body moderate to* petit mal, *and then to little more than twitches. He thinks someone must come, but no one does, not at first. The twitches fade away and now he's just Donald Frank Callahan, lying on the floor of a jail cell in Topeka, Kansas, where somewhere farther down the hall a man continues working his way through the alphabet.*

'Seavey! . . . Sharrow! . . . Shatzer!'

Suddenly, for the first time in months, he thinks of how the cavalry came when the Hitler Brother were getting ready to carve him up there in that deserted laundrymat on East Forty-seventh. And they were really going to do it — the next day or the day after, someone would have found one Donald Frank Callahan, dead as the fabled mackerel and probably wearing his balls for earrings. But then the cavalry came and—

That was no cavalry, *he thinks as he lies on the floor, his face swelling up again,* meet the new face, same as the old face. That was Voice Number One and Voice Number Two. *Only that isn't right, either. That was two men, middle-aged at the least, probably getting a little on the old side. That was Mr Ex Libris and Mr Gai Cocknif En Yom, whatever that means. Both of them scared to death. And right to be scared. The Hitler Brothers might not have done a thousand as Lennie had boasted, but they had done plenty and killed some of them, they were a couple of human copperheads, and yes, Mr Ex Libris and Mr Gai Cocknif were absolutely right to be scared. It had turned out all right for them, but it might not have done. And if George and Lennie had turned the tables, what then? Why, instead of finding one dead man in the Turtle Bay Washateria, whoever happened in there first would have found three. That would have made the front page of the* Post *for sure! So those guys had risked their lives, and here was what they'd risked it for, six or eight months on down the line: a dirty emaciated* busted up asshole drunk, his underwear drenched with piss on one side and full of shit on the other. A daily drinker and a nightly drunk.

And that is when it happens. Down the hall, the steady slow-chanting voice has reached Sprang, Steward, and Sudby; in this cell up the hall, a man lying on a dirty floor in the long light of dawn finally reaches his bottom, which is, by definition, that point from which you can descend no lower unless you find a shovel and actually start to dig.

Lying as he is, staring directly along the floor, the dust-bunnies look like ghostly groves of trees and the lumps of dirt look like the hills in some sterile mining country. He thinks: What is it, February? February of 1982? Something like that. Well, I tell you what. I'll give myself one year to try and clean up my act. One year to do something – anything – to justify the risk those two guys took. If I can do something, I'll go on. But if I'm still drinking in February of 1983, I'll kill myself.

Down the corridor, the chanting voice has finally reached Targenfield.

13

Callahan was silent for a moment. He sipped at his coffee, grimaced, and poured himself a knock of sweet cider, instead.

'I knew how the climb back starts,' he said. 'I'd taken enough low-bottom drunks to enough AA meetings on the East Side, God knows. So when they let me out, I found AA in Topeka and started going every day. I never looked ahead, never looked behind. "The past is history, the future's a mystery," they say. Only this time, instead of sitting in the back of the room and saying nothing, I forced myself to go right down front, and during the introductions I'd say, "I'm Don C. and I don't want to drink anymore." I did want to, every day I wanted to, but in AA they have sayings for everything, and one of them is "Fake it till you make it." And little by little, I did make it. I woke up one day in the fall of 1982 and realized I really didn't want to drink anymore. The compulsion, as they say, had been lifted.

'I moved on. You're not supposed to make any big changes in the first year of sobriety, but one day when I was in Gage Park – the Reinisch Rose Garden, actually . . .' He trailed off, looking at them. 'What? Do you know it? Don't tell me you know the Reinisch!'

'We've been there,' Susannah said quietly. 'Seen the toy train.'

'That,' Callahan said, 'is amazing.'

'It's nineteen o'clock and all the birds are singing,' Eddie said. He wasn't smiling.

'Anyway, the Rose Garden was where I spotted the first poster. HAVE YOU SEEN CALLAHAN, OUR IRISH SETTER. SCAR ON PAW, SCAR ON FOREHEAD. GENEROUS REWARD. Et cetera, et cetera. They'd finally gotten the name right. I decided it was time to move on while I still could. So I went to Detroit, and there I found a place called The Lighthouse Shelter. It was a wet shelter. It was, in fact, Home without Rowan Magruder. They were doing good work there, but they were barely staggering along. I signed on. And that's where I was in December of 1983, when it happened.'

'When what happened?' Susannah asked.

It was Jake Chambers who answered. He knew, was perhaps the only one of them who *could* know. It had happened to him, too, after all.

'That was when you died,' Jake said.

'Yes, that's right,' Callahan said. He showed no surprise at all. They might have been discussing rice, or the possibility that Andy ran on ant-nomics. 'That's when I died. Roland, I wonder if you'd roll me a cigarette? I seem to need something a little stronger than apple cider.'

14

There's an old tradition at Lighthouse, one that goes back . . . jeez, must be all of four years (The Lighthouse Shelter has only been in existence for five). It's Thanksgiving in the gym of Holy Name High School on West Congress Street. A bunch of the drunks decorate the place with orange and brown crepe paper, cardboard turkeys, plastic fruit and vegetables. American reap-charms, in other words. You had to have at least two weeks' continuous sobriety to get on this detail. Also — this is something Ward Huckman, Al McCowan, and Don Callahan have agreed to among themselves — no wet brains are allowed on Decoration Detail, no matter how long they've been sober.

On Turkey Day, nearly a hundred of Detroit's finest alkies, hypes, and half-crazed homeless gather at Holy Name for a wonderful dinner of turkey, taters, and all the trimmings. They are seated at a dozen long tables in the center of the basketball court (the legs of the tables are protected by swags of felt, and the diners eat in their stocking feet). Before they dig in — this is part of the custom — they go swiftly around the tables ('Take more than ten seconds, boys, and I'm cutting you off,' Al has warned) and everyone says one thing they're grateful for. Because it's Thanksgiving, yes, but also because one of the principal tenets of the AA program is that a grateful alcoholic doesn't get drunk and a grateful addict doesn't get stoned.

It goes fast, and because Callahan is just sitting there, not thinking of anything in particular, when it's his turn he almost blurts out something that could have caused him trouble. At the very least, he would have been tabbed as a guy with a bizarre sense of humor.

'I'm grateful I haven't . . .' he begins, then realizes what he's about to say, and bites it back. They're looking at him expectantly, stubble-faced men and pale, doughy women with limp hair, all carrying about them the dirty-breeze subway station aroma that's the smell of the streets. Some already call him Faddah, and how do they know? How could they know? And how would they feel if they knew what a chill it gives him to hear that? How it makes him remember the Hitler Brothers and the sweet, childish smell of fabric softener? But they're looking at him. 'The clients.' Ward and Al are looking at him, too.

'I'm grateful I haven't had a drink or a drug today,' he says, falling back on the old faithful, there's always that to be grateful for. They murmur their approval, the man next to Callahan says he's grateful his sister's going to let him come for Christmas, and no one knows how close Callahan has come to saying 'I'm grateful I haven't seen any Type Three vampires or lost-pet posters lately.'

He thinks it's because God has taken him back, at least on a trial basis, and the power of Barlow's bite has finally been cancelled. He thinks he's lost the cursed gift of seeing, in other words. He doesn't test this by trying to go into a church, however — the gym of Holy Name High is close enough for him, thanks. It never occurs to him — at least in his conscious mind — that they want to make sure the net's all the way around him this time. They may be slow learners, Callahan will eventually come to realize, but they're not no learners.

Then, in early December, Ward Huckman receives a dream letter. 'Christmas done come early, Don! Wait'll you see this, Al!' Waving the letter triumphantly. 'Play our cards right, and boys, our worries about next year are over!'

Al McCowan takes the letter, and as he reads it his expression of conscious, careful reserve begins to melt. By the time he hands the letter to Don, he's grinning from ear to ear.

The letter is from a corporation with offices in New York, Chicago, Detroit, Denver, Los Angeles, and San Francisco. It's on rag bond so luxurious you want to cut it into a shirt and wear it next to your skin. It says that the corporation is planning to give away twenty million dollars to twenty charitable organizations across the United States, a million each. It says that the corporation must do this before the end of the calendar year 1983. Potential recipients include food pantries, homeless shelters, two clinics for the indigent, and a prototype AIDS testing program in Spokane. One of the shelters is Lighthouse. The signature is Richard P. Sayre, Executive Vice President, Detroit. It all looks on the up-and-up, *and the fact that all three of them have been invited to the corporation's Detroit offices to discuss this gift also seems on the up-and-up. The date of the meeting — what will be the date of Donald Callahan's death — is December 19th, 1983. A Monday.*

The name on the letterhead is THE SOMBRA CORPORATION.

15

'You went,' Roland said.

'We all went,' Callahan said. 'If the invitation had been for me alone, I never would've. But, since they were asking for all three of us . . . and wanted to give us a million dollars . . . do you have any idea what a million bucks would have meant to a fly-by-night outfit like Home or Lighthouse? Especially during the Reagan years?'

Susannah gave a start at this. Eddie shot her a nakedly triumphant look. Callahan clearly wanted to ask the reason for this byplay, but Roland was twirling his finger in that hurry-up gesture again, and now it really *was* getting late. Pressing on for midnight. Not that any of Roland's ka-tet looked sleepy; they were tightly focused on the Pere, marking every word.

'Here is what I've come to believe,' Callahan said, leaning forward. 'There is a loose league of association between the vampires and the low men. I think if you traced it back, you'd find the roots of their association in the dark land. In Thunderclap.'

'I've no doubt,' Roland said. His blue eyes flashed out of his pale and tired face.

'The vampires — those who aren't Type Ones — are stupid. The low men are smarter, but not by a whole lot. Otherwise I never would have been able to escape them for as long as I did. But then — finally — someone else took an interest. An agent of the Crimson King, I should think, whoever or whatever he is. The low men were drawn away from me. So were the vampires. There were no posters during those last months, not that I saw; no chalked messages on the sidewalks of West Fort Street or Jefferson Avenue, either. Someone giving the orders, that's what I think. Someone a good deal smarter. And a million dollars!' He shook his head. A small and bitter smile touched his face. 'In the end, that was what blinded me. Nothing but money. "Oh yes, but it's to do good!" I told myself . . . and we told each other, of course. "It'll keep us independent for at least five years! No more going to the

388

Detroit City Council, begging with our hats in our hands!" All true. It didn't occur to me until later that there's another truth, very simple: greed in a good cause is still greed.'

'What happened?' Eddie asked.

'Why, we kept our appointment,' the Pere said. His face wore a rather ghastly smile. 'The Tishman Building, 982 Michigan Avenue, one of the finest business addresses in the D. December 19th, 4:20 P.M.'

'Odd time for an appointment,' Susannah said.

'We thought so, too, but who questions such minor matters with a million dollars at stake? After some discussion, we agreed with Al – or rather Al's mother. According to her, one should show up for important appointments five minutes early, no more and no less. So we walked into the lobby of the Tishman Building at 4:10 P.M., dressed in our best, found Sombra Corporation on the directory board, and went on up to the thirty-third floor.'

'Had you checked this corporation out?' Eddie asked.

Callahan looked at him as if to say *duh*. 'According to what we could find in the library, Sombra was a closed corporation – no public stock issue, in other words – that mostly bought other companies. They specialized in high-tech stuff, real estate, and construction. That seemed to be all anyone knew. Assets were a closely guarded secret.'

'Incorporated in the US?' Susannah asked.

'No. Nassau, the Bahamas.'

Eddie started, remembering his days as a cocaine mule and the sallow thing from whom he had bought his last load of dope. 'Been there, done that,' he said. 'Didn't see anyone from the Sombra Corporation, though.'

But did he know that was true? Suppose the sallow thing with the British accent worked for Sombra? Was it so hard to believe that they were involved in the dope trade, along with whatever else they were into? Eddie supposed not. If nothing else, it suggested a tie to Enrico Balazar.

'Anyway, they were there in all the right reference books and yearlies,' Callahan said. 'Obscure, but there. And rich. I don't know exactly what Sombra is, and I'm at least half-convinced that most of the people we saw in their offices on the thirty-third floor were nothing but extras ... stage-dressing ... but there probably is an actual Sombra Corporation.

'We took the elevator up there. Beautiful reception area – French Impressionist paintings on the walls, what else? – and a beautiful reception-tionist to go with it. The kind of woman – say pardon, Susannah – if you're a man, you can almost believe that if you were allowed to touch her breast, you'd live forever.'

Eddie burst out laughing, looked sideways at Susannah, and stopped in a hurry.

'It was 4:17. We were invited to sit down. Which we did, feeling nervous as hell. People came and went. Every now and then a door to our left would open and we'd see a floor filled with desks and cubicles. Phones ringing, secretaries flitting hither and yon with files, the sound of a big copier. If it was a set-up — and I think it was — it was as elaborate as a Hollywood movie. I was nervous about our appointment with Mr Sayre, but no more than that. Extraordinary, really. I'd been on the run more or less constantly since leaving 'Salem's Lot eight years previous, and I'd developed a pretty good early-warning system, but it never so much as chirruped that day. I suppose if you could reach him via the Ouija board, John Dillinger would say much the same about his night at the movies with Anna Sage.

'At 4:19, a young man in a striped shirt and tie that looked just oh so Hugo Boss came out and got us. We were whisked down a corridor past some very upscale offices — with an upscale executive beavering away in every one, so far as I could see — and to double doors at the end of the hall. This was marked CONFERENCE ROOM. Our escort opened the doors. He said, "God luck, gentlemen." I remember that very clearly. Not *good* luck, but *god* luck. That was when my perimeter alarms started to go off, and by then it was far too late. It happened fast, you see. They didn't . . .'

16

It happens fast. They have been after Callahan for a long time now, but they waste little time gloating. The doors slam shut behind them, much too loudly and hard enough to shiver in their frames. Executive assistants who drag down eighteen thousand a year to start with close doors a certain way — with respect for money and power — and this isn't it. This is the way angry drunks and addicts on the jones close doors. Also crazy people, of course. Crazy people are ace doorslammers.

Callahan's alarm systems are fully engaged now, not pinging but howling, *and when he looks around the executive conference room, dominated at the far end by a large window giving a terrific view of Lake Michigan, he sees there's good reason for this and has time to think* Dear Christ — Mary, mother of God — how could I have been so foolish? *He can see thirteen people in the room. Three are low men, and this is his first good look at their heavy, unhealthy-looking faces, red-glinting eyes, and full, womanish lips. All three are smoking. Nine are Type Three vampires. The thirteenth person in the conference room is wearing a loud shirt and clashing tie, low-men attire for certain, but his face has a lean and foxy look, full of intelligence and dark humor. On his brow is a red circle of blood that seems neither to ooze nor to clot.*

There is a bitter crackling sound. Callahan wheels and sees Al and Ward drop to the floor. Standing to either side of the door through which they entered are numbers fourteen and fifteen, a low man and a low woman, both of them holding electrical stunners.

'Your friends will be all right, Father Callahan.'

He whirls around again. It's the man with the blood-spot on his forehead. He looks about sixty, but it's hard to tell. He's wearing a garish yellow shirt and a red tie. When his thin lips part in a smile, they reveal teeth that come to points. It's Sayre, Callahan *thinks.* Sayre, or whoever signed that letter. Whoever thought this little sting up.

'You, however, won't,' *he continues.*

The low men look at him with a kind of dull avidity: here he is, finally, their lost pooch with the burned paw and the scarred forehead. The vampires are more interested. They almost thrum within their blue auras. And all at once Callahan can hear the chimes. *They're faint, somehow damped down, but they're there. Calling him.*

Sayre — if that's his name — turns to the vampires. 'He's the one,' *he says in a matter-of-fact tone.* 'He's killed hundreds of you in a dozen versions of America. My friends' — *he gestures to the low men—* 'were unable to track him down, but of course they seek other, less suspecting prey in the ordinary course of things. In any case, he's here now. Go on, have at him. But don't kill him!'

He turns to Callahan. The hole in his forehead fills and gleams but never drips. It's an eye, Callahan *thinks,* a bloody eye. *What is looking out of it? What is watching, and from where?*

Sayre says, 'These particular friends of the King all carry the AIDS virus. You surely know what I mean, don't you? We'll let *that* kill you. It will take you out of the game forever, in this world and all the others. This is no game for a fellow like you, anyway. A false priest like you.'

Callahan doesn't hesitate. If he hesitates, he will be lost. It's not AIDS he's afraid of, but of letting them put their filthy lips on him in the first place, to kiss him as the one was kissing Lupe Delgado in the alley. They don't get to win. *After all the way he's come, after all the jobs, all the jail cells, after finally getting sober in Kansas,* they don't get to win.

He doesn't try to reason with them. There is no palaver. He just sprints down the right side of the conference room's extravagant mahogany table. The man in the yellow shirt, suddenly alarmed, shouts 'Get him! Get him!' Hands slap at his jacket — specially bought at Grand River Menswear for this auspicious occasion — but slip off. He has time to think The window won't break, it's made of some tough glass, anti-suicide glass, and it won't break . . . *and he has just time enough to call on God for the first time since Barlow forced him to take of his poisoned blood.*

'Help me! Please help me!' *Father Callahan cries, and runs shoulder-first into the window. One more hand slaps at his head, tries to tangle itself in his hair, and then it is gone. The window shatters all around him and suddenly he is standing in cold air, surrounded by flurries of snow. He looks down between black shoes which were also specially purchased for this auspicious occasion, and he sees Michigan Avenue, with cars like toys and people like ants.*

He has a sense of them — Sayre and the low men and the vampires who were supposed to infect him and take him out of the game forever — clustered at the broken window, staring with disbelief.

He thinks, This *does* take me out of it forever . . . doesn't it?

And he thinks, with the wonder of a child: This is the last thought I'll ever have. This is goodbye.

Then he is falling.

17

Callahan stopped and looked at Jake, almost shyly. 'Do you remember it?' he asked. 'The actual . . .' He cleared his throat. 'The dying?'

Jake nodded gravely. 'You don't?'

'I remember looking at Michigan Avenue from between my new shoes. I remember the sensation of standing there — seeming to, anyway — in the middle of a snow flurry. I remember Sayre behind me, yelling in some other language. Cursing. Words that guttural just about had to be curses. And I remember thinking, *He's frightened.* That was actually my last thought, that Sayre was frightened. Then there was an interval of darkness. I floated. I could hear the chimes, but they were distant. Then they came closer. As if they were mounted on some engine that was rushing toward me at terrible speed.

'There was light. I saw light in the darkness. I thought I was having the Kübler-Ross death experience, and I went toward it. I didn't care where I came out, as long as it wasn't on Michigan Avenue, all smashed and bleeding, with a crowd standing around me. But I didn't see how that could happen. You don't fall thirty-three stories, then regain consciousness.

'And I wanted to get away from the chimes. They kept getting louder. My eyes started to water. My ears hurt. I was glad I still had eyes and ears, but the chimes made any gratitude I might have felt pretty academic.

'I thought, *I have to get into the light,* and I lunged for it. I . . .'

18

He opens his eyes, but even before he does, he is aware of a smell. It's the smell of hay, but very faint, almost exhausted. A ghost of its former self, you might say. And he? Is he a ghost?

He sits up and looks around. If this is the afterlife, then all the holy books of the world, including the one from which he himself used to preach, are wrong. Because he's not in heaven or hell; he's in a stable. There are white wisps of ancient straw on the floor. There are cracks in the board walls through which brilliant light streams. It's the light he followed out of the darkness, he thinks. And he thinks, It's desert light. *Is there any concrete reason to think so? Perhaps. The air is dry when he pulls it into his nostrils. It's like drawing the air of a different planet.*

Maybe it is, *he thinks.* Maybe this is the Planet Afterlife.

The chimes are still there, both sweet and horrible, but now fading . . . fading . . . and gone. He hears the faint snuffle of hot wind. Some of it finds its way through the gaps between the boards, and a few bits of straw lift off from the floor, do a tired little dance, then settle back.

Now there is another noise. An arrhythmic thudding noise. Some machine, and not in the best of shape, from the sound. He stands up: It's hot in here, and sweat breaks immediately on his face and hands. He looks down at himself and sees his fine new Grand River Menswear clothes are gone. He is now wearing jeans and a blue chambray shirt, faded thin from many washings. On his feet is a pair of battered boots with rundown heels. They look like they have walked many a thirsty mile. He bends and feels his legs for breaks. There appear to be none. Then his arms. None. He tries snapping his fingers. They do the job easily, making little dry sounds like breaking twigs.

He thinks: Was my whole life a dream? Is this the reality? If so, who am I and what am I doing here?

And from the deeper shadows behind him comes that weary cycling sound: thud-THUD-thud-THUD-thud-THUD.

He turns in that direction, and gasps at what he sees. Standing behind him in the middle of the abandoned stable is a door. It's set into no wall, only stands free. It has hinges, but as far as he can see they connect the door to nothing but air. Hieroglyphs are etched upon it halfway up. He cannot read them. He steps closer, as if that would aid understanding. And in a way it does. Because he sees that the doorknob is made of crystal, and etched upon it is a rose. He has read his Thomas Wolfe: a stone, a rose, an unfound door; a stone, a rose, a door. There's no stone, but perhaps that is the meaning of the hieroglyph.

No, *he thinks.* No, the word is UNFOUND. Maybe I'm the stone.

He reaches out and touches the crystal knob. As though it were a signal (a sigul, he thinks)

the thudding machinery ceases. Very faint, very distant — far and wee — he hears the chimes. He tries the knob. It moves in neither direction. There's not even the slightest give. It might as well be set in concrete. When he takes his hand away, the sound of the chimes ceases.

He walks around the door and the door is gone. Walks the rest of the way around and it's back. He makes three slow circles, noting the exact point at which the thickness of the door disappears on one side and reappears on the other. He reverses his course, now going widdershins. Same deal. What the hell?

He looks at the door for several moments, pondering, then walks deeper into the stable, curious about the machine he heard. There's no pain when he walks, if he just took a long fall his body hasn't yet got the news, but Kee-rist is it ever hot in here!

There are horse stalls, long abandoned. There's a pile of ancient hay, and beside it a neatly folded blanket and what looks like a breadboard. On the board is a single scrap of dried meat. He picks it up, sniffs it, smells salt. Jerky, he thinks, and pops it into his mouth. He's not very worried about being poisoned. How can you poison a man who's already dead?

Chewing, he continues his explorations. At the rear of the stable is a small room like an afterthought. There are a few chinks in the walls of this room, too, enough for him to see a machine squatting on a concrete pad. Everything in the stable whispers of long years and abandonment, but this gadget, which looks sort of like a milking machine, appears brand new. No rust, no dust. He goes closer. There's a chrome pipe jutting from one side. Beneath it is a drain. The steel collar around it looks damp. On top of the machine is a small metal plate. Next to the plate is a red button. Stamped on the plate is this:

La Merk Industries
834789-AA-45-776019
DO NOT REMOVE SLUG
ASK FOR ASSISTANCE

The red button is stamped with the word ON. *Callahan pushes it. The weary thudding sound resumes, and after a moment water gushes from the chrome pipe. He puts his hands under it. The water is numbingly cold, shocking his overheated skin. He drinks. The water is neither sweet nor sour and he thinks,* Such things as taste must be forgotten at great depths. This—

'*Hello, Faddah.*'

Callahan screams in surprise. His hands fly up and for a moment jewels of water sparkle in a dusty sunray falling between two shrunken boards. He wheels around on the eroded heels of his boots. Standing just outside the door of the pump-room is a man in a hooded robe.

Sayre, *he thinks.* It's Sayre, he's followed me, he came through that damn door—

'*Calm down,' says the man in the robe.* '"Cool your jets," *as the gunslinger's new friend might say.' Confidingly:* 'His name is Jake, but the housekeeper calls him 'Bama.' And then, in the bright tone of one just struck by a fine idea, he says, 'I would show him to you! Both of them! Perhaps it's not too late! Come!' He holds out a hand. The fingers emerging from the robe's sleeve are long and white, somehow unpleasant. Like wax. When Callahan makes no move to come forward, the man in the robe speaks reasonably. 'Come. You can't stay here, you know. This is only a way station, and nobody stays here for long. Come.'*

'*Who are you?*'

The man in the robe makes an impatient tsking *sound. 'No time for all that, Faddah. Name, name, what's in a name, as someone or other said. Shakespeare? Virginia Woolf? Who can remember? Come, and I'll show you a wonder. And I won't touch you; I'll walk ahead of you. See?'*

He turns. His robe swirls like the skirt of an evening dress. He walks back into the stable, and after a moment Callahan follows. The pump-room is no good to him, after all; the pump-room is a dead end. Outside the stable, he might be able to run.

Run where?

Well, that's to see, isn't it?

The man in the robe raps on the free-standing door as he passes it. 'Knock on wood, Donnie be good!' he says merrily, and as he steps into the brilliant rectangle of light falling through the stable door, Callahan sees he's carrying something in his left hand. It's a box, perhaps a foot long and wide and deep. It looks like it might be made of the same wood as the door. Or perhaps it's a heavier version of that wood. Certainly it's darker, and even closer-grained.

Watching the robed man carefully, meaning to stop if he stops, Callahan follows into the sun. The heat is even stronger once he's in the light, the sort of heat he's felt in Death Valley. And yes, as they step out of the stable he sees that they are in a desert. Off to one side is a ramshackle building that rises from a foundation of crumbling sandstone blocks. It might once have been an inn, he supposes. Or an abandoned set from a Western movie. On the other side is a corral where most of the posts and rails have fallen. Beyond it he sees miles of rocky, stony sand. Nothing else but—

Yes! Yes, there is something! Two somethings! Two tiny moving dots at the far horizon!

'You see them! How excellent your eyes must be, Faddah!'

The man in the robe — it's black, his face within the hood nothing but a pallid suggestion — stands about twenty paces from him. He titters. Callahan cares for the sound no more than for the waxy look of his fingers. It's like the sound of mice scampering over bones. That makes no actual sense, but—

'Who are they?' Callahan asks in a dry voice. 'Who are *you*? Where is this place?'

The man in black sighs theatrically. 'So much backstory, so little time,' he says. 'Call me Walter, if you like. As for this place, it's a way station, just as I told you. A little rest stop between the hoot of your world and the holler of the next. Oh, you thought you were quite the far wanderer, didn't you? Following all those hidden highways of yours? But now, Faddah, you're on a *real* journey.'

'Stop calling me that!' Callahan shouts. His throat is already dry. The sunny heat seems to be accumulating on top of his head like actual weight.

'Faddah, Faddah, Faddah!' the man in black says. He sounds petulant, but Callahan knows he's laughing inside. He has an idea this man — if he is a man — spends a great deal of time laughing on the inside. 'Oh well, no need to be pissy about it, I suppose. I'll call you Don. Do you like that better?'

The black specks in the distance are wavering now; the rising thermals cause them to levitate, disappear, then reappear again. Soon they'll be gone for good.

'Who are they?' he asks the man in black.

'Folks you'll almost certainly never meet,' the man in black says dreamily. The hood shifts; for a moment Callahan can see the waxy blade of a nose and the curve of an eye, a small cup filled with dark fluid. 'They'll die under the mountains. If they don't die under the mountains, there are things in the Western Sea that will eat them alive. Dod-a-chock!' He laughs again. But—

But all at once you don't sound completely sure of yourself, my friend, Callahan thinks.

'If all else fails,' Walter says, 'this will kill them.' He raises the box. Again, faintly, Callahan hears the unpleasant ripple of the chimes. 'And who will bring it to them? Ka, of course, yet even ka needs a friend, a kai-mai. That would be you.'

'I don't understand.'

'No,' the man in black agrees sadly, 'and I don't have time to explain. Like the White Rabbit in *Alice*, I'm late, I'm late, for a very important date. They're following me, you

see, but I needed to double back and talk to you. Busy-busy-busy! Now I must get ahead of them again — how else will I draw them on? You and I, Don, must be done with our palaver, regrettably short though it has been. Back into the stable with you, amigo. Quick as a bunny!'

'What if I don't want to?' Only there's really no what-if about it. He's never wanted to go anyplace less. Suppose he asks this fellow to let him go and try to catch up with those wavering specks? What if he tells the man in black, 'That's where I'm supposed to be, where what you call ka wants me to be'? He guesses he knows. Might as well spit in the ocean.

As if to confirm this, Walter says, 'What you want hardly matters. You'll go where the King decrees, and there you will wait. If yon two die on their course — as they almost certainly must — you will live a life of rural serenity in the place to which I send you, and there you too will die, full of years and possibly with a false but undoubtedly pleasing sense of redemption. You'll live on your level of the Tower long after I'm bone-dust on mine. This I promise you, Faddah, for I have seen it in the glass, say true! And if they keep coming? If they reach you in the place to which you are going? Why, in that unlikely case you'll aid them in every way you can and kill them by doing so. It's a mind-blower, isn't it? Wouldn't you say it's a mind-blower?'

He begins to walk toward Callahan. Callahan backs toward the stable where the unfound door awaits. He doesn't want to go there, but there's nowhere else. 'Get away from me,' he says.

'Nope,' says Walter, the man in black. 'I can't go for that, no can do.' He holds the box out toward Callahan. At the same time he reaches over the top of it and grasps the lid.

'Don't!' Callahan says sharply. Because the man in the black robe mustn't open the box. There's something terrible inside the box, something that would terrify even Barlow, the wily vampire who forced Callahan to drink his blood and then sent him on his way into the prisms of America like a fractious child whose company has become tiresome.

'Keep moving and perhaps I won't have to,' Walter teases.

Callahan backs into the stable's scant shadow. Soon he'll be inside again. No help for it. And he can feel that strange only-there-on-one-side door waiting like a weight. 'You're cruel!' he bursts out.

Walter's eyes widen, and for a moment he looks deeply hurt. This may be absurd, but Callahan is looking into the man's deep eyes and feels sure the emotion is nonetheless genuine. And the surety robs him of any last hope that all this might be a dream, or a final brilliant interval before true death. In dreams — his, at least — the bad guys, the scary guys, never have complex emotions.

'I am what ka and the King and the Tower have made me. We all are. We're caught.'

Callahan remembers the dream-west through which he traveled: the forgotten silos, the *neglected sunsets and long shadows, his own bitter joy as he dragged his trap behind him, singing until the jingle of the very chains that held him became sweet music.*

'I know,' he says.

'Yes, I see you do. Keep moving.'

Callahan's back in the stable now. Once again he can smell the faint, almost exhausted aroma of old hay. Detroit seems impossible, a hallucination. So do all his memories of America.

'Don't open that thing,' *Callahan says,* 'and I will.'

'What an excellent Faddah you are, Faddah.'

'You promised not to call me that.'

'Promises are made to be broken, Faddah.'

'I don't think you'll be able to kill him,' *Callahan said.*

Walter grimaces. 'That's ka's business, not mine.'

'Maybe not ka, either. Suppose he's above ka?'

Walter recoils, as if struck. I've blasphemed, *Callahan thinks.* And with this guy, I've an idea that's no mean feat.

'No one's above ka, false priest,' *the man in black spits at him.* 'And the room at the top of the Tower is empty. I know it is.'

Although Callahan is not entirely sure what the man is talking about, his response is quick and sure. 'You're wrong. There is a God. He waits and sees all from His high place. He—'

Then a great many things happen at exactly the same time. The water pump in the alcove goes on, starting its weary thudding cycle. And Callahan's ass bumps into the heavy, smooth wood of the door. And the man in black thrusts the box forward, opening it as he does so. And his hood falls back, revealing the pallid, snarling face of a human weasel. (It's not Sayre, but upon Walter's forehead like a Hindu caste-mark is the same welling red circle, an open wound that never clots or flows.) And Callahan sees what's inside the box: he sees Black Thirteen crouched on its red velvet like the slick eye of a monster that grew outside God's shadow. And Callahan begins to shriek at the sight of it, for he senses its endless power: it may fling him anywhere or to the farthest blind alley of nowhere. And the door clicks open. And even in his panic — or perhaps below his panic — Callahan is able to think Opening the box has opened the door. *And he is stumbling backward into some other place. He can hear shrieking voices. One of them is Lupe's, asking Callahan why Callahan let him die. Another belongs to Rowena Magruder and she is telling him this is his other life, this is it, and how does he like it? And his hands come up to cover his ears even as one ancient boot trips over the other and he begins to fall backward, thinking it's Hell the man in black has pushed him into, actual Hell. And when his hands come up, the weasel-faced man thrusts the open box with its terrible glass ball into them. And the ball* moves. *It rolls like an actual eye in an invisible socket. And Callahan thinks,* It's alive, it's the stolen eye of some awful monster from beyond the world, and oh God, oh dear God, it is seeing me.

But he takes the box. It's the last thing in life he wants to do, but he is powerless to stop himself. Close it, you have to close it, *he thinks, but he is falling, he has tripped himself (or the robed man's ka has tripped him) and he's falling, twisting around as he goes down. From somewhere below him all the voices of his past are calling to him, reproaching him (his mother wants to know why he allowed that filthy Barlow to break the cross she brought him all the way from Ireland), and incredibly, the man in black cries 'Bon voyage, Faddah!' merrily after him.*

Callahan strikes a stone floor. It's littered with the bones of small animals. The lid of the box closes and he feels a moment of sublime relief . . . but then it opens again, very slowly, disclosing the eye.

'No,' Callahan whispers. 'Please, no.'

But he's not able to close the box — all his strength seems to have deserted him — and it will not close itself. Deep down in the black eye, a red speck forms, glows . . . grows. Callahan's horror swells, filling his throat, threatening to stop his heart with its chill. It's the King, *he thinks.* It's the Eye of the Crimson King as he looks down from his place in the Dark Tower. And he is seeing *me.*

'NO!' *Callahan shrieks as he lies on the floor of a cave in the northern arroyo country of Calla Bryn Sturgis, a place he will eventually come to love.* 'NO! NO! DON'T LOOK AT ME! OH FOR THE LOVE OF GOD, *DON'T LOOK AT ME!'*

But the Eye does look, and Callahan cannot bear its insane regard. That is when he passes out. It will be three days before he opens his own eyes again, and when he does he'll be with the Manni.

19

Callahan looked at them wearily. Midnight had come and gone, we all say thankya, and now it was twenty-two days until the Wolves would come for their bounty of children. He drank off the final two inches of cider in his glass, grimaced as if it had been corn whiskey, then set the empty tumbler down. 'And all the rest, as they say, you know. It was Henchick and Jemmin who found me. Henchick closed the box, and when he did, the door closed. And now what was the Cave of the Voices is Doorway Cave.'

'And you, Pere?' Susannah asked. 'What did they do with you?'

'Took me to Henchick's cabin – his *kra*. That's where I was when I opened my eyes. During my unconsciousness, his wives and daughters fed me water and chicken broth, squeezing drops from a rag, one by one.'

'Just out of curiosity, how many wives does he have?' Eddie asked.

'Three, but he may have relations with only one at a time,' Callahan said absently. 'It depends on the stars, or something. They nursed me well. I began to walk around the town; in those days they called me the Walking. Old Fella. I couldn't quite get the sense of where I was, but in a way my previous wanderings had prepared me for what had happened. Had toughened me mentally. I had days, God knows, when I thought all of this was happening in the second or two it would take me to fall from the window I'd broken through down to Michigan Avenue – that the mind prepares itself for death by offering some wonderful final hallucination, the actual semblance of an entire life. And I had days when I decided that *I* had finally become what we all dreaded most at both Home and Lighthouse: a wet brain. I thought maybe I'd been socked away in a moldy institution somewhere, and was imagining the whole thing. But mostly, I just accepted it. And was glad to have finished up in a good place, real or imagined.

'When I got my strength back, I reverted to making a living the way I had during my years on the road. There was no ManPower or Brawny Man office in Calla Bryn Sturgis, but those were good years and there was plenty of work for a man who wanted to work – they were big-rice years, as they do say, although stockline and the rest of the crops also did fine. Eventually I began to preach again. There was no conscious decision to do so – it wasn't anything I prayed over, God knows – and when I did, I discovered these people knew all about the Man Jesus.' He laughed. 'Along with The Over, and Oriza, and Buffalo Star . . . do you know Buffalo Star, Roland?'

'Oh yes,' the gunslinger said, remembering a preacher of the Buff whom he had once been forced to kill.

'But they listened,' Callahan said. 'A lot did, anyway, and when they offered to build me a church, I said thankya. And that's the Old Fella's story. As you see, you were in it . . . two of you, anyway. Jake, was that after you died?'

Jake lowered his head. Oy, sensing his distress, whined uneasily. But when Jake answered, his voice was steady enough. 'After the first death. Before the second.'

Callahan looked visibly startled, and he crossed himself. 'You mean it can happen more than once? Mary save us!'

Rosalita had left them. Now she came back, holding a 'sener high. Those which had been placed on the table had almost burned down, and the porch was cast in a dim and failing glow that was both eerie and a little sinister.

'Beds is ready,' she said. 'Tonight the boy sleeps with Pere. Eddie and Susannah, as you were night before last.'

'And Roland?' asked Callahan, his bushy brows raising.

'I have a cosy for him,' she said stolidly. 'I showed it to him earlier.'

'Did you,' Callahan said. 'Did you, now. Well, then, that's settled.' He stood. 'I can't remember the last time I was so tired.'

'We'll stay another few minutes, if it does ya,' Roland said. 'Just we four.'

'As you will,' Callahan said.

Susannah took his hand and impulsively kissed it. 'Thank you for your story, Pere.'

'It's good to have finally told it, sai.'

Roland asked, 'The box stayed in the cave until the church was built? Your church?'

'Aye. I can't say how long. Maybe eight years; maybe less. 'Tis hard to tell with certainty. But there came a time when it began to call to me. As much as I hated and feared that Eye, part of me wanted to see it again.'

Roland nodded. 'All the pieces of the Wizard's Rainbow are full of glammer, but Black Thirteen was ever told to be the worst. Now I think I understand why that is. It's this Crimson King's actual watching Eye.'

'Whatever it is, I felt it calling me back to the cave . . . and further. Whispering that I should resume my wanderings, and make them endless. I knew I could open the door by opening the box. The door would take me anywhere I wanted to go. And any*when!* All I had to do was concentrate.' Callahan considered, then sat down again. He leaned forward, looking at them in turn over the gnarled carving of his clasped hands. 'Hear me, I beg. We had a President, Kennedy was his name. He was assassinated some thirteen years before my time in 'Salem's Lot . . . assassinated in the West—'

'Yes,' Susannah said. 'Jack Kennedy. God love him.' She turned to Roland. 'He was a gunslinger.'

Roland's eyebrows rose. 'Do you say so?'

'Aye. And I say true.'

'In any case,' Callahan said, 'there's always been a question as to whether the man who killed him acted alone, or whether he was part of a larger conspiracy. And sometimes I'd wake in the middle of the night and think,

Why don't you go and see? Why don't you stand in front of that door with the box in your arms and think, Dallas, November 22nd, 1963? Because if you do that the door will open and you can go there, just like the man in Mr Wells's story of the time machine. And perhaps you could change what happened that day. If there was ever a watershed moment in American life, that was it. Change that, change everything that came after. Vietnam . . . the race riots . . . everything.'

'Jesus,' Eddie said respectfully. If nothing else, you had to respect the ambition of such an idea. It was right up there with the peg-legged sea captain chasing the white whale. 'But Pere . . . what if you did it and changed things for the *worse*?'

'Jack Kennedy was not a bad man,' Susannah said coldly. 'Jack Kennedy was a good man. A *great* man.'

'Maybe so. But do you know what? I think it takes a great man to make a great mistake. And besides, someone who came after him might have been a really bad guy. Some Big Coffin Hunter who never got a chance because of Lee Harvey Oswald, or whoever it was.'

'But the ball doesn't allow such thoughts,' Callahan said. 'I believe it lures people on to acts of terrible evil by whispering to them that they will do good. That they'll make things not just a little better but *all* better.'

'Yes,' Roland said. His voice was as dry as the snap of a twig in a fire.

'Do you think such traveling might actually be possible?' Callahan asked him. 'Or was it only the thing's persuasive lie? Its glammer?'

'I believe it's so,' Roland said. 'And I believe that when we leave the Calla, it will be by that door.'

'Would that I could come with you!' Callahan said. He spoke with surprising vehemence.

'Mayhap you will,' Roland said. 'In any case, you finally put the box — and the ball within — inside your church. To quiet it.'

'Yes. And mostly it's worked. Mostly it sleeps.'

'Yet you said it sent you todash twice.'

Callahan nodded. The vehemence had flared like a pine-knot in a fireplace and disappeared just as quickly. Now he only looked tired. And very old, indeed. 'The first time was to Mexico. Do you remember way back to the beginning of my story? The writer and the boy who believed?'

They nodded.

'One night the ball reached out to me when I slept and took me todash to Los Zapatos, Mexico. It was a funeral. The writer's funeral.'

'Ben Mears,' Eddie said. 'The *Air Dance* guy.'

'Yes.'

'Did folks see you?' Jake asked. 'Because they didn't see us.'

Callahan shook his head. 'No. But they sensed me. When I walked toward them, they moved away. It was as if I'd turned into a cold draft. In any case, the boy was there — Mark Petrie. Only he wasn't a boy any longer. He was in his young manhood. From that, and from the way he spoke of Ben — "There was a time when I would have called fifty-nine old" is how he began his eulogy — I'd guess that this might have been the mid-1990s. In any case, I didn't stay long . . . but long enough to decide that my young friend from all that long time ago had turned out fine. Maybe I did something right in 'Salem's Lot, after all.' He paused a moment and then said, 'In his eulogy, Mark referred to Ben as his father. That touched me very, very deeply.'

'And the second time the ball sent you todash?' Roland asked. 'The time it sent you to the Castle of the King?'

'There were birds. Great fat black birds. And beyond that I'll not speak. Not in the middle of the night.' Callahan spoke in a dry voice that brooked no argument. He stood up again. 'Another time, perhaps.'

Roland bowed acceptance of this. 'Say thankya.'

'Will 'ee not turn in, folks?'

'Soon,' Roland said.

They thanked him for his story (even Oy added a single, sleepy bark) and bade him goodnight. They watched him go and for several seconds after, they said nothing.

20

It was Jake who broke the silence. 'That guy Walter was *behind* us, Roland! When we left the way station, he was *behind* us! Pere Callahan, too!'

'Yes,' Roland said. 'As far back as that, Callahan was in our story. It makes my stomach flutter. As though I'd lost gravity.'

Eddie dabbed at the corner of his eye. 'Whenever you show emotion like that, Roland,' he said, 'I get all warm and squashy inside.' Then, when Roland only looked at him, 'Ah, come on, quit laughin. You know I love it when you get the joke, but you're embarrassing me.'

'Cry pardon,' Roland said with a faint smile. 'Such humor as I have turns in early.'

'Mine stays up all night,' Eddie said brightly. 'Keeps me awake. Tells me jokes. Knock-knock, who's there, icy, icy who, icy your underwear, yock-yock-yock!'

'Is it out of your system?' Roland asked when he had finished.

'For the time being, yeah. But don't worry, Roland, it always comes back. Can I ask you something?'

'Is it foolish?'

'I don't think so. I hope not.'

'Then ask.'

'Those two men who saved Callahan's bacon in the laundrymat on the East Side — were they who I think they were?'

'Who *do* you think they were?'

Eddie looked at Jake. 'What about you, O son of Elmer? Got any ideas?'

'Sure,' Jake said. 'It was Calvin Tower and the other guy from the book-shop, his friend. The one who told me the Samson riddle and the river riddle.' He snapped his fingers once, then twice, then grinned. 'Aaron Deepneau.'

'What about the ring Callahan mentioned?' Eddie asked him. 'The one with *Ex Libris* on it? I didn't see either of them wearing a ring like that.'

'Were you looking?' Jake asked him.

'No, not really. But—'

'And remember that we saw him in 1977,' Jake said. 'Those guys saved Pere's life in 1981. Maybe someone gave Mr Tower the ring during the four years between. As a present. Or maybe he bought it himself.'

'You're just guessing,' Eddie said.

'Yeah,' Jake agreed. 'But Tower owns a bookshop, so him having a ring with *Ex Libris* on it fits. Can you tell me it doesn't feel right?'

'No. I'd have to put it in the ninetieth percentile, at least. But how could they know that Callahan . . .' Eddie trailed off, considered, then shook his head decisively. 'Nah, I'm not even gonna get into it tonight. Next thing *we'll* be discussing the Kennedy assassination, and I'm tired.'

'We're all tired,' Roland said, 'and we have much to do in the days ahead. Yet the Pere's story has left me in a strangely disturbed frame of mind. I can't tell if it answers more questions than it raises, or if it's the other way around.'

None of them responded to this.

'We are ka-tet, and now we sit together an-tet,' Roland said. 'In council. Late as it is, is there anything else we need to discuss before we part from one another? If so, you must say.' When there was no response, Roland pushed back his chair. 'All right, then I wish you all—'

'Wait.'

It was Susannah. It had been so long since she'd spoken that they had nearly forgotten her. And she spoke in a small voice not much like her usual one. Certainly it didn't seem to belong to the woman who had told Eben Took that if he called her brownie again, she'd pull the tongue out of his head and wipe his ass with it.

'There might be something.'

That same small voice.

'Something else.'

And smaller still.

'I—'

She looked at them, each in turn, and when she came to the gunslinger he saw sorrow in those eyes, and reproach, and weariness. He saw no anger. *If she'd been angry,* he thought later, *I might not have felt quite so ashamed.*

'I think I might have a little problem,' she said. 'I don't see how it can be ... how it can possibly be ... but boys, I think I might be a little bit in the family way.'

Having said that, Susannah Dean/Odetta Holmes/Detta Walker/Mia daughter of none put her hands over her face and began to cry.

PART THREE
THE WOLVES

CHAPTER I

SECRETS

1

Behind the cottage of Rosalita Munoz was a tall privy painted sky-blue. Jutting from the wall to the left as the gunslinger entered, late on the morning after Pere Callahan had finished his story, was a plain iron band with a small disc of steel set eight inches or so beneath. Within this skeletal vase was a double sprig of saucy susan. Its lemony, faintly astringent smell was the privy's only aroma. On the wall above the seat of ease, in a frame and beneath glass, was a picture of the Man Jesus with his praying hands held just below his chin, his reddish locks spilling over his shoulders, and his eyes turned up to His Father. Roland had heard there were tribes of slow mutants who referred to the Father of Jesus as Big Sky Daddy.

The image of the Man Jesus was in profile, and Roland was glad. Had He been facing him full on, the gunslinger wasn't sure he could have done his morning business without closing his eyes, full though his bladder was. *Strange place to put a picture of God's Son*, he thought, and then realized it wasn't strange at all. In the ordinary course of things, only Rosalita used this privy, and the Man Jesus would have nothing to look at but her prim back.

Roland Deschain burst out laughing, and when he did, his water began to flow.

2

Rosalita had been gone when he awoke, and not recently: her side of the bed had been cold. Now, standing outside her tall blue oblong of a privy and buttoning his flies, Roland looked up at the sun and judged the time as not long before noon. Judging such things without a clock, glass, or pendulum had become tricky in these latter days, but it was still possible if you were careful in your calculations and willing to allow for some error in your result. Cort, he thought, would be aghast if he saw one of his pupils — one of his *graduated* pupils, a gunslinger — beginning such a business as this by sleeping almost until midday. And this *was* the beginning. All the rest had been ritual and preparation, necessary but not terribly helpful. A kind of dancing the rice-song. Now that part was over. And as for sleeping late ...

'No one ever deserved a late lying-in more,' he said, and walked down the slope. Here a fence marked the rear of Callahan's patch (or perhaps the Pere thought of it as God's patch). Beyond it was a small stream, babbling as excitedly as a little girl telling secrets to her best friend. The banks were thick with saucy susan, so there was another mystery (a minor one) solved. Roland breathed deeply of the scent.

He found himself thinking of ka, which he rarely did. (Eddie, who believed Roland thought of little else, would have been astounded.) Its only true rule was *Stand aside and let me work.* Why in God's name was it so hard to learn such a simple thing? Why always this stupid need to meddle? Every one of them had done it; every one of them had known Susannah Dean was pregnant. Roland himself had known almost since the time of her kindling, when Jake had come through from the house in Dutch Hill. Susannah herself had known, in spite of the bloody rags she had buried at the side of the trail. So why had it taken them so long to have the palaver they'd had last night? Why had they made such a *business* of it? And how much might have suffered because of it?

Nothing, Roland hoped. But it was hard to tell, wasn't it?

Perhaps it was best to let it go. This morning that seemed like good advice, because he felt very well. Physically, at least. Hardly an ache or a—

'I thought 'ee meant to turn in not long after I left ye, gunslinger, but Rosalita said you never came in until almost the dawn.'

Roland turned from the fence and his thoughts. Callahan was today dressed in dark pants, dark shoes, and a dark shirt with a notched collar. His cross lay upon his bosom and his crazy white hair had been partially tamed, probably with some sort of grease. He bore the gunslinger's regard for a little while and then said, 'Yesterday I gave the Holy Communion to those of the small-holds who take it. And heard their confessions. Today's my day to go out to the ranches and do the same. There's a goodish number of cowboys who hold to what they mostly call the cross-way. Rosalita drives me in the buckboard, so when it comes to lunch and dinner, you must shift for yourselves.'

'We can do that,' Roland said, 'but do you have a few minutes to talk to me?'

'Of course,' Callahan said. 'A man who can't stay a bit shouldn't approach in the first place. Good advice, I think, and not just for priests.'

'Would you hear *my* confession?'

Callahan raised his eyebrows. 'Do 'ee hold to the Man Jesus, then?'

Roland shook his head. 'Not a bit. Will you hear it anyway, I beg? And keep it to yourself?'

Callahan shrugged. 'As to keeping what you say to myself, that's easy. It's what we do. Just don't mistake discretion for absolution.' He favored Roland with a wintry smile. 'We Catholics save that for ourselves, may it do ya.'

The thought of absolution had never crossed Roland's mind, and he found the idea that he might need it (or that this man could give it) almost comic. He rolled a cigarette, doing it slowly, thinking of how to begin and how much to say. Callahan waited, respectfully quiet.

At last Roland said, 'There was a prophecy that I should draw three and that we should become ka-tet. Never mind who made it; never mind anything that came before. I won't worry that old knot, never again if I can help it. There were three doors. Behind the second was the woman who became Eddie's wife, although she did not at that time call herself Susannah . . .'

3

So Roland told Callahan the part of their story which bore directly upon Susannah and the women who had been before her. He concentrated on how they'd saved Jake from the doorkeeper and drawn the boy into Mid-World, telling how Susannah (or perhaps at that point she had been Detta) had held the demon of the circle while they did their work. He had known the risks, Roland told Callahan, and he had become certain – even while they were still riding Blaine the Mono – that she had not survived the risk of pregnancy. He had told Eddie, and Eddie hadn't been all that surprised. Then Jake had told *him*. Scolded him with it, actually. And he had taken the scolding, he said, because he felt it was deserved. What none of them had fully realized until last night on the porch was that Susannah herself had known, and perhaps for almost as long as Roland. She had simply fought harder.

'So, Pere — what do you think?'

'You say her husband agreed to keep the secret,' Callahan replied. 'And even Jake — who sees clearly—'

'Yes,' Roland said. 'He does. He did. And when he asked me what we should do, I gave him bad advice. I told him we'd be best to let ka work itself out, and all the time I was holding it in my hands, like a caught bird.'

'Things always look clearer when we see them over our shoulder, don't they?'

'Yes.'

'Did you tell her last night that she's got a demon's spawn growing in her womb?'

'She knows it's not Eddie's.'

'So you didn't. And Mia? Did you tell her about Mia, and the castle banqueting hall?'

'Yes,' Roland said. 'I think hearing that depressed her but didn't surprise her. There was the other — Detta — ever since the accident when she lost her legs.' It had been no accident, but Roland hadn't gone into the business of Jack Mort with Callahan, seeing no reason to do so. 'Detta Walker hid herself well from Odetta Holmes. Eddie and Jake say she's a schizophrenic.' Roland pronounced this exotic word with great care.

'But you cured her,' Callahan said. 'Brought her face-to-face with her two selves in one of those doorways. Did you not?'

Roland shrugged. 'You can burn away warts by painting them with silver metal, Pere, but in a person prone to warts, they'll come back.'

Callahan surprised him by throwing his head back to the sky and bellowing laughter. He laughed so long and hard he finally had to take his handkerchief from his back pocket and wipe his eyes with it. 'Roland, you may be quick with a gun and as brave as Satan on Saturday night, but you're no psychiatrist. To compare schizophrenia to *warts* . . . oh, my!'

'And yet Mia is real, Pere. I've seen her myself. Not in a dream, as Jake did, but with my own two eyes.'

'Exactly my point,' Callahan said. 'She's not an aspect of the woman who was born Odetta Susannah Holmes. She is *she*.'

'Does it make a difference?'

'I think it does. But here is one thing I can tell you for sure: no matter how things lie in your fellowship — your ka-tet — this must be kept a dead secret from the people of Calla Bryn Sturgis. Today, things are going your way. But if word got out that the female gunslinger with the brown skin might be carrying a demon-child, the *folken*'d go the other way, and in a hurry. With Eben Took leading the parade. I know that in the end you'll decide your course of action based on your own assessment of what the Calla needs, but the four of you can't beat the Wolves without help, no matter how good you are with such calibers as you carry. There's too much to manage.'

Reply was unnecessary. Callahan was right.

'What is it you fear most?' Callahan asked.

'The breaking of the tet,' Roland said at once.

'By that you mean Mia's taking control of the body they share and going off on her own to have the child?'

'If that happened at the wrong time, it would be bad, but all might still come right. *If* Susannah came back. But what she carries is nothing but poison with a heartbeat.' Roland looked bleakly at the religious in his black clothes. 'I have every reason to believe it would begin its work by slaughtering the mother.'

'The breaking of the tet,' Callahan mused. 'Not the death of your friend, but the breaking of the tet. I wonder if your friends know what sort of man you are, Roland?'

'They know,' Roland said, and on that subject said no more.

'What would you have of me?'

'First, an answer to a question. It's clear to me that Rosalita knows a good deal of rough doctoring. Would she know enough to turn the baby out before its time? And the stomach for what she might find?'

They would all have to be there, of course — he and Eddie, Jake, too, as little as Roland liked the thought of it. Because the thing inside her had surely quickened by now, and even if its time hadn't come, it would be dangerous. *And its time is almost certainly close*, he thought. *I don't know it for sure, but I feel it. I—*

The thought broke off as he became aware of Callahan's expression: horror, disgust, and mounting anger.

'Rosalita would never do such a thing. Mark well what I say. She'd die first.'

Roland was perplexed. 'Why?'

'Because she's a Catholic!'

'I don't understand.'

Callahan saw the gunslinger really did not, and the sharpest edge of his anger was blunted. Yet Roland sensed that a great deal remained, like the bolt behind the head of an arrow. 'It's abortion you're talking about!'

'Yes?'

'Roland ... Roland.' Callahan lowered his head, and when he raised it, the anger appeared to be gone. In its place was a stony obduracy the gunslinger had seen before. Roland could no more break it than he could lift a mountain with his bare hands. 'My church divides sins into two: venial sins, which are bearable in the sight of God, and mortal ones, which are not. Abortion is a mortal sin. It is murder.'

'Pere, we are speaking of a demon, not a human being.'

'So you say. That's God's business, not mine.'

'And if it kills her? Will you say the same then and so wash your hands of her?'

Roland had never heard the tale of Pontius Pilate and Callahan knew it. Still, he winced at the image. But his reply was firm enough. 'You who spoke of the breaking of your tet before you spoke of the taking of her life! Shame on you. *Shame.*'

'My quest — the quest of my ka-tet — is the Dark Tower, Pere. It's not saving this world we're about, or even this universe, but all universes. All of existence.'

'I don't care,' Callahan said. 'I *can't* care. Now listen to me, Roland son of Steven, for I would have you hear me very well. Are you listening?'

Roland sighed. 'Say thankya.'

'Rosa won't give the woman an abortion. There are others in town who could, I have no doubt — even in a place where children are taken every twenty-some years by monsters from the dark land, such filthy arts are undoubtedly preserved — but if you go to one of them, you won't need to worry about the Wolves. I'll raise every hand in Calla Bryn Sturgis against you long before they come.'

Roland gazed at him unbelievingly. 'Even though you know, as I'm sure you do, that we may be able to save a hundred other children? Human children, whose first task on earth would not be to eat their mothers?'

Callahan might not have heard. His face was very pale. 'I'll have more, do it please ya ... and even if it don't. I'll have your word, sworn upon the face of your father, that you'll never suggest an abortion to the woman herself.'

A queer thought came to Roland: Now that this subject had arisen — had pounced upon them, like Jilly out of her box — Susannah was no longer Susannah to this man. She had become *the woman*. And another thought: How many monsters had Pere Callahan slain himself, with his own hand?

As often happened in times of extreme stress, Roland's father spoke to

him. *This situation is not quite beyond saving, but should you carry on much further —*
should you give voice to such thoughts — it will be.

'I want your promise, Roland.'

'Or you'll raise the town.'

'Aye.'

'And suppose Susannah decides to abort herself? Women do it, and she's
very far from stupid. She knows the stakes.'

'Mia — the baby's true mother — will prevent it.'

'Don't be so sure. Susannah Dean's sense of self-preservation is very
strong. And I believe her dedication to our quest is even stronger.'

Callahan hesitated. He looked away, lips pressed together in a tight white
line. Then he looked back. '*You* will prevent it,' he said. 'As her dinh.'

Roland thought, *I have just been Castled.*

'All right,' he said. 'I will tell her of our talk and make sure she understands the position you've put us in. And I'll tell her that she must not tell
Eddie.'

'Why not?'

'Because he'd kill you, Pere. He'd kill you for your interference.'

Roland was somewhat gratified by the widening of Callahan's eyes. He
reminded himself again that he must raise no feelings in himself against
this man, who simply was what he was. Had he not already spoken to them
of the trap he carried with him wherever he went?

'Now listen to me as I've listened to you, for you now have a responsibility to all of us. Especially to "the woman."'

Callahan winced a little, as if struck. But he nodded. 'Tell me what you'd
have.'

'For one thing, I'd have you watch her when you can. Like a hawk! In
particular I'd have you watch for her working her fingers here.' Roland rubbed
above his left eyebrow. 'Or here.' Now he rubbed at his left temple. 'Listen
to her way of speaking. Be aware if it speeds up. Watch for her to start
moving in little jerks.' Roland snapped a hand up to his head, scratched it,
snapped it back down. He tossed his head to the right, then looked back
at Callahan. 'You see?'

'Yes. These are the signs that Mia is coming?'

Roland nodded. 'I don't want her left alone anymore when she's Mia.
Not if I can help it.'

'I understand,' Callahan said. 'But Roland, it's hard for me to believe that
a newborn, no matter who or what the father might have been—'

'Hush,' Roland said. 'Hush, do ya.' And when Callahan had duly hushed: 'What you think or believe is nothing to me. You've yourself to look out for, and I wish you well. But if Mia or Mia's get harms Rosalita, Pere, I'll hold you responsible for her injuries. You'll pay to my good hand. Do you understand that?'

'Yes, Roland.' Callahan looked both abashed and calm. It was an odd combination.

'All right. Now here's the other thing you can do for me. Comes the day of the Wolves, I'm going to need six *folken* I can absolutely trust. I'd like to have three of each sex.'

'Do you care if some are parents with children at risk?'

'No. But not all. And none of the ladies who may be throwing the dish — Sarey, Zalia, Margaret Eisenhart, Rosalita. They'll be somewhere else.'

'What do you want these six for?'

Roland was silent.

Callahan looked at him a moment longer, then sighed. 'Reuben Caverra,' he said. 'Reuben's never forgot his sister and how he loved her. Diane Caverra, his wife . . . or do 'ee not want couples?'

No, a couple would be all right. Roland twirled his fingers, gesturing for the Pere to continue.

'Cantab of the Manni, I sh'd say; the children follow him like he was the Pied Piper.'

'I don't understand.'

'You don't need to. They follow him, that's the important part. Bucky Javier and his wife . . . and what would you say to your boy, Jake? Already the town children follow him with their eyes, and I suspect a number of the girls are in love with him.'

'No, I need him.'

Or can't bear to have him out of your sight? Callahan wondered . . . but did not say. He had pushed Roland as far as was prudent, at least for one day. Further, actually.

'What of Andy, then? The children love him, too. And he'd protect them to the death.'

'Aye? From the Wolves?'

Callahan looked troubled. Actually it had been rock-cats he'd been thinking of. Them, and the sort of wolves that came on four legs. As for the ones that came out of Thunderclap . . .

'No,' Roland said. 'Not Andy.'

'Why not? For 'tisn't to fight the Wolves you want these six for, is it?'

'Not Andy,' Roland repeated. It was just a feeling, but his feelings were his version of the touch. 'There's time to think about it, Pere . . . and we'll think, too.'

'You're going out into the town.'

'Aye. Today and every day for the next few.'

Callahan grinned. 'Your friends and I would call it "schmoozing." It's a Yiddish word.'

'Aye? What tribe are they?'

'An unlucky one, by all accounts. Here, schmoozing is called commala. It's their word for damned near everything.' Callahan was a little amused by how badly he wanted to regain the gunslinger's regard. A little disgusted with himself, as well. 'In any case, I wish you well with it.'

Roland nodded. Callahan started up toward the rectory, where Rosalita already had harnessed the horses to the buckboard and now waited impatiently for Callahan to come, so they could be about God's work. Halfway up the slope, Callahan turned back.

'I do not apologize for my beliefs,' he said, 'but if I have complicated your work here in the Calla, I'm sorry.'

'Your Man Jesus seems to me a bit of a son of a bitch when it comes to women,' Roland said. 'Was He ever married?'

The corners of Callahan's mouth quirked. 'No,' he said, 'but His girl-friend was a whore.'

'Well,' Roland said, 'that's a start.'

4

Roland went back to leaning on the fence. The day called out to him to begin, but he wanted to give Callahan a head start. There was no more reason for this than there had been for rejecting Andy out of hand; just a feeling.

He was still there, and rolling another smoke, when Eddie came down the hill with his shirt flapping out behind him and his boots in one hand.

'Hile, Eddie,' Roland said.

'Hile, boss. Saw you talking with Callahan. Give us this day, our Wilma and Fred.'

Roland raised his eyebrows.

'Never mind,' Eddie said. 'Roland, in all the excitement I never got a chance to tell you Gran-pere's story. And it's important.'

'Is Susannah up?'

'Yep. Having a wash. Jake's eating what looks like a twelve-egg omelet.'

Roland nodded. 'I've fed the horses. We can saddle them while you tell me the old man's tale.'

'Don't think it'll take that long,' Eddie said, and it didn't. He came to the punchline – which the old man had whispered into his ear – just as they reached the barn. Roland turned toward him, the horses forgotten. His eyes were blazing. The hands he clamped on Eddie's shoulders – even the diminished right – were powerful.

'Repeat it!'

Eddie took no offense. 'He told me to lean close. I did. He said he'd never told anyone but his son, which I believe. Tian and Zalia know he was out there – or says he was – but they don't know what he saw when he pulled the mask off the thing. I don't think they even know Red Molly was the one who dropped it. And then he whispered . . .' Once again Eddie told Roland what Tian's Gran-pere claimed to have seen.

Roland's glare of triumph was so brilliant it was frightening. 'Gray horses!' he said. 'All those horses the exact same shade! Do you understand now, Eddie? Do you?'

'Yep,' Eddie said. His teeth appeared in a grin. It was not particularly comforting, that grin. 'As the chorus girl said to the businessman, we've been here before.'

5

In standard American English, the word with the most gradations of meaning is probably *run*. The Random House Unabridged Dictionary offers one hundred and eight options, beginning with 'to go quickly by moving the legs more rapidly than at a walk' and ending with 'melted or liquefied.' In the Crescent-Callas of the borderlands between Mid-World and Thunderclap, the blue ribbon for most meanings would have gone to *commala*. If the word were listed in the Random House Unabridged, the first definition (assuming they were assigned, as is common, in order of widest usage), would have been 'a variety of rice grown at the furthermost eastern edge of All-World.' The second one, however, would have been 'sexual intercourse.' The third would have been 'sexual orgasm,' as in *Dia 'ee come commala?* (The hoped-for reply being *Aye, say thankya, commala big-big.*) To wet the commala is to irrigate the rice in a dry time; it is also to masturbate. Commala is the commencement of some big and joyful meal, like a family feast (not the meal itself, do ya, but the moment of beginning to eat). A man who is losing his hair (as Garrett Strong was that season), is coming commala. Putting animals out to stud is damp commala. Gelded animals are dry commala, although no one could tell you why. A virgin is green commala, a menstruating woman is red commala, an old man who can no longer make iron before the forge is — say sorry — sof' commala. To stand commala is to stand belly-to-belly, a slang term meaning 'to share secrets.' The sexual connotations of the word are clear, but why should the rocky arroyos north of town be known as the commala draws? For that matter, why is a fork sometimes a commala, but never a spoon or a knife? There aren't a hundred and seventy-eight meanings for the word, but there must be seventy. Twice that, if one were to add in the various shadings. One of the meanings — it would surely be in the top ten — is that which Pere Callahan defined as *schmoozing.* The actual phrase would be something like 'come Sturgis commala,' or 'come Bryn-a commala.' The literal meaning would be to stand belly-to-belly with the community as a whole.

During the following five days, Roland and his ka-tet attempted to continue this process, which the outworlders had begun at Took's General Store. The going was difficult at first ('Like trying to light a fire with damp kindling,' Susannah said crossly after their first night), but little by little, the *folken* came around. Or at least warmed up to them. Each night, Roland and the Deans returned to the Pere's rectory. Each late afternoon or evening, Jake returned to the Rocking B Ranch. Andy took to meeting him at the place where the B's ranch-road split off from East Road and escorting him the rest of the way, each time making his bow and saying, 'Good evening, soh! Would you like your horoscope? This time of year is sometimes called Charyou Reap! You will see an old friend! A young lady thinks of you warmly!' And so on.

Jake had asked Roland again why he was spending so much time with Benny Slightman.

'Are you complaining?' Roland asked. 'Don't like him anymore?'

'I like him fine, Roland, but if there's something I'm supposed to be doing besides jumping in the hay, teaching Oy to do somersaults, or seeing who can skip a flat rock on the river the most times, I think you ought to tell me what it is.'

'There's nothing else,' Roland said. Then, as an afterthought: 'And get your sleep. Growing boys need plenty of sleep.'

'Why am I out there?'

'Because it seems right to me that you should be,' Roland said. 'All I want is for you to keep your eyes open and tell me if you see something you don't like or don't understand.'

'Anyway, kiddo, don't you see enough of us during the days?' Eddie asked him.

They *were* together during those next five days, and the days were long. The novelty of riding sai Overholser's horses wore off in a hurry. So did complaints of sore muscles and blistered butts. On one of these rides, as they approached the place where Andy would be waiting, Roland asked Susannah bluntly if she had considered abortion as a way of solving her problem.

'Well,' she said, looking at him curiously from her horse, 'I'm not going to tell you the thought never crossed my mind.'

'Banish it,' he said. 'No abortion.'

'Any particular reason why not?'

'Ka,' said Roland.

'Kaka,' Eddie replied promptly. This was an old joke, but the three of them laughed, and Roland was delighted to laugh with them. And with that, the subject was dropped. Roland could hardly believe it, but he was glad. The fact that Susannah seemed so little disposed to discuss Mia and the coming of the baby made him grateful indeed. He supposed there were things – quite a few of them – which she felt better off not knowing.

Still, she had never lacked for courage. Roland was sure the questions would have come sooner or later, but after five days of canvassing the town as a quartet (a quintet counting Oy, who always rode with Jake), Roland began sending her out to the Jaffords smallhold at midday to try her hand with the dish.

Eight days or so after their long palaver on the rectory porch – the one that had gone on until four in the morning – Susannah invited them out to the Jaffords smallhold to see her progress. 'It's Zalia's idea,' she said. 'I guess she wants to know if I pass.'

Roland knew he only had to ask Susannah herself if he wanted an answer to that question, but he was curious. When they arrived, they found the entire family gathered on the back porch, and several of Tian's neighbors, as well: Jorge Estrada and his wife, Diego Adams (in chaps), the Javiers. They looked like spectators at a Points practice. Zalman and Tia, the roont twins, stood to one side, goggling at all the company with wide eyes. Andy was also there, holding baby Aaron (who was sleeping) in his arms.

'Roland, if you wanted all this kept secret, guess what?' Eddie said.

Roland was not put out of countenance, although he realized now that his threat to the cowboys who'd seen sai Eisenhart throw the dish had been utterly useless. Country-folk talked, that was all. Whether in the border-lands or the baronies, gossip was ever the chief sport. *And at the very least,* he mused, *those humpies will spread the news that Roland's a hard boy, strong commala, and not to be trifled with.*

'It is what it is,' he said. 'The Calla-*folken* have known for donkey's years that the Sisters of Oriza throw the dish. If they know Susannah throws it, too — and well — maybe it's to the good.'

Jake said, 'I just hope she doesn't, you know, mess up.'

There were respectful greetings for Roland, Eddie, and Jake as they mounted the porch. Andy told Jake a young lady was pining for him. Jake blushed and said he'd just as soon not know about stuff like that, if that did Andy all right.

'As you will, soh.' Jake found himself studying the words and numbers stamped on Andy's midsection like a steel tattoo and wondering again if he was really in this world of robots and cowboys, or if it was all some sort of extraordinarily vivid dream. 'I hope this baby will wake up soon, so I do. And cry! Because I know several soothing cradle-songs—'

'Hush up, ye creakun steel bandit!' Gran-pere said crossly, and after crying the old man's pardon (in his usual complacent, not-a-bit-sorry tone of voice), Andy did. *Messenger, Many Other Functions,* Jake thought. *Is one of your other functions teasing folks, Andy, or is that just my imagination?*

Susannah had gone into the house with Zalia. When they came out, Susannah was wearing not one reed pouch, but two. They hung to her hips on a pair of woven straps. There was another strap, too, Eddie saw, running around her waist and holding the pouches snug. Like holster tie-downs.

'That's quite the hookup, say thankya,' Diego Adams remarked.

'Susannah thought it up,' Zalia said as Susannah got into her wheelchair. 'She calls it a docker's clutch.'

It wasn't, Eddie thought, not quite, but it was close. He felt an admiring smile lift the corners of his mouth, and saw a similar one on Roland's. And Jake's. By God, even Oy appeared to be grinning.

'Will it draw water, that's what *I* wonder,' Bucky Javier said. That such a question should even be asked, Eddie thought, only emphasized the difference between the gunslingers and the Calla-*folken*. Eddie and his mates had known from first look what the hookup was and how it would work. Javier, however, was a smallhold farmer, and as such, saw the world in a very different way.

You need us, Eddie thought toward the little cluster of men standing on the porch – the farmers in their dirty white pants, Adams in his chaps and manure-splattered shor'boots. *Boy, do you ever.*

Susannah wheeled to the front of the porch and folded her stumps beneath her so she appeared almost to be standing in her chair. Eddie knew how much this posture hurt her, but no discomfort showed on her face. Roland, meanwhile, was looking down into the pouches she wore. There were four dishes in each, plain things with no pattern on them. Practice-dishes.

Zalia walked across to the barn. Although Roland and Eddie had noted the blanket tacked up there as soon as they arrived, the others noticed it for the first time when Zalia pulled it down. Drawn in chalk on the barn-boards was the outline of a man – or a manlike being – with a frozen grin on his face and the suggestion of a cloak fluttering out behind him. This wasn't work of the quality produced by the Tavery twins, nowhere near, but those on the porch recognized a Wolf when they saw one. The older children oohed softly. The Estradas and the Javiers applauded, but looked apprehensive even as they did so, like people who fear they may be whistling up the devil. Andy complimented the artist ('whoever she may be,' he added archly), and Gran-pere told him again to shut his trap. Then he called out that the Wolves *he'd* seen were quite a spot bigger. His voice was shrill with excitement.

'Well, I drew it to man-size,' Zalia said (she had actually drawn it to *husband*-size). 'If the real thing turns out to make a bigger target, all to the good. Hear me, I beg.' This last came out uncertainly, almost as a question.

Roland nodded. 'We say thankya.'

Zalia shot him a grateful look, then stepped away from the outline on the wall. Then she looked at Susannah. 'When you will, lady.'

For a moment Susannah only remained where she was, about sixty yards from the barn. Her hands lay between her breasts, the right covering the left. Her head was lowered. Her ka-mates knew exactly what was going on in that head: *I aim with my eye, shoot with my hand, kill with my heart.* Their own hearts went out to her, perhaps carried by Jake's touch or Eddie's love, encouraging her, wishing her well, sharing their excitement. Roland watched fiercely. Would one more dab hand with the dish turn things in their favor? Perhaps not. But he was what he was, and so was she, and he wished her true aim with every last bit of his will.

She raised her head. Looked at the shape chalked on the barn wall. Still her hands lay between her breasts. Then she cried out shrilly, as Margaret Eisenhart had cried out in the yard of the Rocking B, and Roland felt his hard-beating heart rise. In that moment he had a clear and beautiful memory of David, his hawk, folding his wings in a blue summer sky and dropping at his prey like a stone with eyes.

'Riza!'

Her hands dropped and became a blur. Only Roland, Eddie, and Jake were able to mark how they crossed at the waist, the right hand seizing a dish from the left pouch, the left hand seizing one from the right. Sai Eisenhart had thrown from the shoulder, sacrificing time in order to gain force and accuracy. Susannah's arms crossed below her ribcage and just above the arms of her wheelchair, the dishes finishing their cocking arc at about the height of her shoulderblades. Then they flew, crisscrossing in midair a moment before thudding into the side of the barn.

Susannah's arms finished straight out before her; for a moment she looked like an impresario who has just introduced the featured act. Then they dropped and crossed, seizing two more dishes. She flung them, dipped again, and flung the third set. The first two were still quivering when the last two bit into the side of the barn, one high and one low.

For a moment there was utter silence in the Jaffordses' yard. Not even a bird called. The eight plates ran in a perfectly straight line from the throat of the chalked figure to what would have been its upper midsection. They were all two and a half to three inches apart, descending like buttons on a shirt. And she had thrown all eight in no more than three seconds.

'Do 'ee mean to use the dish against the Wolves?' Bucky Javier asked in a queerly breathless voice. 'Is that it?'

'Nothing's been decided,' Roland said stolidly.

In a barely audible voice that held both shock and wonder, Deelie Estrada said: 'But if that'd been a man, hear me, he'd be cutlets.'

It was Gran-pere who had the final word, as perhaps gran-peres should: 'Yer-*bugger!*'

6

On their way back out to the main road (Andy walked at a distance ahead of them, carrying the folded wheelchair and playing something bagpipey through his sound system), Susannah said musingly: 'I may give up the gun altogether, Roland, and just concentrate on the dish. There's an elemental satisfaction to giving that scream and then throwing.'

'You reminded me of my hawk,' Roland admitted.

Susannah's teeth flashed white in a grin. 'I *felt* like a hawk. Riza! O-*Riza!* Just saying the word puts me in a throwing mood.'

To Jake's mind this brought some obscure memory of Gasher ('Yer old pal, Gasher,' as the gentleman himself had been wont to say), and he shivered.

'Would you really give up the gun?' Roland asked. He didn't know if he was amused or aghast.

'Would you roll your own smokes if you could get tailor-mades?' she asked, and then, before he could answer: 'No, not really. Yet the dish is a lovely weapon. When they come, I hope to throw two dozen. And bag my limit.'

'Will there be a shortage of plates?' Eddie asked.

'Nope,' she said. 'There aren't very many fancy ones – like the one sai Eisenhart threw for you, Roland – but they've hundreds of practice-plates. Rosalita and Sarey Adams are sorting through them, culling out any that might fly crooked.' She hesitated, lowered her voice. 'They've all been out here, Roland, and although Sarey's brave as a lion and would stand fast against a tornado . . .'

'Hasn't got it, huh?' Eddie asked sympathetically.

'Not quite,' Susannah agreed. 'She's good, but not like the others. Nor does she have quite the same ferocity.'

'I may have something else for her,' Roland said.

'What would that be, sugar?'

'Escort duty, mayhap. We'll see how they shoot, day after tomorrow. A little competition always livens things up. Five o' the clock, Susannah, do they know?'

'Yes. Most of the Calla would turn up, if you allowed them.'

This *was* discouraging . . . but he should have expected it. *I've been too long out of the world of people,* he thought. *So I have.*

'No one but the ladies and ourselves,' Roland said firmly.

'If the Calla-*folken* saw the women throw well, it could swing a lot of people who are on the fence.'

Roland shook his head. He didn't *want* them to know how well the women threw, that was very nearly the whole point. But that the town knew they *were* throwing . . . that might not be such a bad thing. 'How good are they, Susannah? Tell me.'

She thought about it, then smiled. 'Killer aim,' she said. 'Every one.'

'Can you teach them that crosshand throw?'

Susannah considered the question. You could teach anyone just about anything, given world enough and time, but they had neither. Only thirteen days left now, and by the day the Sisters of Oriza (including their newest member, Susannah of New York) met for the exhibition in Pere Callahan's back yard, there would be only a week and a half. The crosshand throw had come naturally to her, as everything about shooting had. But the others . . .

'Rosalita will learn it,' she said at last. 'Margaret Eisenhart *could* learn it, but she might get flustered at the wrong time. Zalia? No. Best she throw one plate at a time, always with her right hand. She's a little slower, but I guarantee every plate she throws will drink something's blood.'

'Yeah,' Eddie said. 'Until a sneetch homes in on her and blows her out of her corset, that is.'

Susannah ignored this. 'We can hurt them, Roland. Thou knows we can.'

Roland nodded. What he'd seen had encouraged him mightily, especially in light of what Eddie had told him. Susannah and Jake also knew Granpere's ancient secret now. And, speaking of Jake . . .

'You're very quiet today,' Roland said to the boy. 'Is everything all right?'

'I do fine, thankya,' Jake said. He had been watching Andy. Thinking of how Andy had rocked the baby. Thinking that if Tian and Zalia and the other kids all died and Andy was left to raise Aaron, baby Aaron would probably die within six months. Die, or turn into the weirdest kid in the universe. Andy would diaper him, Andy would feed him all the correct stuff, Andy would change him when he needed changing and burp him if he needed burping, and there would be all sorts of cradle-songs. Each would be sung perfectly and none would be propelled by a mother's love. Or a father's. Andy was just Andy, Messenger Robot, Many Other Functions. Baby Aaron would be better off being raised by . . . well, by wolves.

This thought led him back to the night he and Benny had tented out (they hadn't done so since; the weather had turned chilly). The night he had seen Andy and Benny's Da' palavering. Then Benny's Da' had gone wading across the river. Headed east.

Headed in the direction of Thunderclap.

'Jake, are you sure you're okay?' Susannah asked.

'Yessum,' Jake said, knowing this would probably make her laugh. It did, and Jake laughed with her, but he was still thinking of Benny's Da'. The spectacles Benny's Da' wore. Jake was pretty sure he was the only one in town who had them. Jake had asked him about that one day when the three of them had been riding in one of the Rocking B's two north fields, looking out strays. Benny's Da' had told him a story about trading a beautiful true-threaded colt for the specs — from one of the lake-mart boats it had been, back when Benny's sissa had been alive, Oriza bless her. He had done it even though all of the cowpokes — even Vaughn Eisenhart himself, do ya not see — had told him such spectacles never worked; they were no more useful than Andy's fortunes. But Ben Slightman had tried them on, and they had changed everything. All at once, for the first time since he'd been maybe seven, he'd been able to really see the world.

He had polished his specs on his shirt as they rode, held them up to the sky so that twin spots of light swam on his cheeks, then put them back on. 'If I ever lose em or break em, I don't know what I'd do,' he'd said. 'I got along without such just fine for twenty years or more, but a person gets used to something better in one rip of a hurry.'

Jake thought it was a good story. He was sure Susannah would have believed it (assuming the singularity of Slightman's spectacles had occurred to her in the first place). He had an idea Roland would have believed it, too. Slightman told it in just the right way: a man who still appreciated his good fortune and didn't mind letting folks know that he'd been right about something while quite a number of other people, his boss among them, had been wide of the mark. Even Eddie might have swallowed it. The only thing wrong with Slightman's story was that it wasn't true. Jake didn't know what the real deal was, his touch didn't go that deep, but he knew that much. And it worried him.

Probably nothing, you know. Probably he just got them in some way that wouldn't sound so good. For all you know, one of the Manni brought them back from some other world, and Benny's Da' stole them.

That was one possibility; if pressed, Jake could have come up with half a dozen more. He was an imaginative boy.

Still, when added to what he'd seen by the river, it worried him. What kind of business could Eisenhart's foreman have on the far side of the Whye? Jake didn't know. And still, each time he thought to raise this subject with Roland, something kept him quiet.

And after giving him *a hard time about keeping secrets!*

Yeah, yeah, yeah. But—

But what, little trailhand?

But Benny, that was what. Benny was the problem. Or maybe it was Jake himself who was actually the problem. He'd never been much good at making friends, and now he had a good one. A real one. The thought of getting Benny's Da' in trouble made him feel sick to his stomach.

7

Two days later, at five o' the clock, Rosalita, Zalia, Margaret Eisenhart, Sarey Adams, and Susannah Dean gathered in the field just west of Rosa's neat privy. There were a lot of giggles and not a few bursts of nervous, shrieky laughter. Roland kept his distance, and instructed Eddie and Jake to do the same. Best to let them get it out of their systems.

Set against the rail fence, ten feet apart from each other, were stuffies with plump sharproot heads. Each head was wrapped in a gunnysack which had been tied to make it look like the hood of a cloak. At the foot of each guy were three baskets. One was filled with more sharproot. Another was filled with potatoes. The contents of the third had elicited groans and cries of protest. These three were filled with radishes. Roland told them to quit their mewling; he'd considered peas, he said. None of them (even Susannah) was entirely sure he was joking.

Callahan, today dressed in jeans and a stockman's vest of many pockets, ambled out onto the porch, where Roland sat smoking and waiting for the ladies to settle down. Jake and Eddie were playing draughts close by.

'Vaughn Eisenhart's out front,' the Pere told Roland. 'Says he'll go on down to Tooky's and have a beer, but not until he passes a word with 'ee.'

Roland sighed, got up, and walked through the house to the front. Eisenhart was sitting on the seat of a one-horse fly, shor'boots propped on the splashboard, looking moodily off toward Callahan's church.

'G'day to ya, Roland,' he said.

Wayne Overholser had given Roland a cowboy's broad-brimmed hat some days before. He tipped it to the rancher and waited.

'I guess you'll be sending the feather soon,' Eisenhart said. 'Calling a meeting, if it please ya.'

Roland allowed as how that was so. It was not the town's business to tell knights of Eld how to do their duty, but Roland would tell them what duty was to be done. That much he owed them.

'I want you to know that when the time comes, I'll touch it and send it on. And come the meeting, I'll say aye.'

'Say thankya,' Roland replied. He was, in fact, touched. Since joining with Jake, Eddie, and Susannah, it seemed his heart had grown. Sometimes he was sorry. Mostly he wasn't.

'Took won't do neither.'

'No,' Roland agreed. 'As long as business is good, the Tooks of the world never touch the feather. Nor say aye.'

'Overholser's with him.'

This was a blow. Not an entirely unexpected one, but he'd hoped Overholser would come around. Roland had all the support he needed, however, and supposed Overholser knew it. If he was wise, the farmer would just sit and wait for it to be over, one way or the other. If he meddled, he would likely not see another year's crops into his barns.

'I wanted ye to know one thing,' Eisenhart said. 'I'm in with 'ee because of my wife, and my wife's in with 'ee because she's decided she wants to hunt. This is what all such things as the dish-throwing comes to in the end, a woman telling her man what'll be and what won't. It ain't the natural way. A man's meant to rule his woman. Except in the matter of the babbies, o' course.'

'She gave up everything she was raised to when she took you to husband,' Roland said. 'Now it's your turn to give a little.'

'Don't ye think I know that? But if you get her killed, Roland, you'll take my curse with you when ye leave the Calla. If 'ee do. No matter how many children ye save.'

Roland, who had been cursed before, nodded. 'If ka wills, Vaughn, she'll come back to you.'

'Aye. But remember what I said.'

'I will.'

Eisenhart slapped the reins on the horse's back and the fly began to roll.

8

Each woman halved a sharproot head at forty yards, fifty yards, and sixty.

'Hit the head as high up into the hood as you can get,' Roland said. 'Hitting them low will do no good.'

'Armor, I suppose?' Rosalita asked.

'Aye,' Roland said, although that was not the entire truth. He wouldn't tell them what he now understood to be the entire truth until they needed to know it.

Next came the taters. Sarey Adams got hers at forty yards, clipped it at fifty, and missed entirely at sixty; her dish sailed high. She uttered a curse that was far from ladylike, then walked head-down to the side of the privy. Here she sat to watch the rest of the competition. Roland went over and sat beside her. He saw a tear trickling from the corner of her left eye and down her wind-roughened cheek.

'I've let ye down, stranger. Say sorry.'

Roland took her hand and squeezed it. 'Nay, lady, nay. There'll be work for you. Just not in the same place as these others. And you may yet throw the dish.'

She gave him a wan smile and nodded her thanks.

Eddie put more sharproot 'heads' on the stuffy-guys, then a radish on top of each. The latter were all but concealed in the shadows thrown by the gunnysack hoods. 'Good luck, girls,' he said. 'Better you than me.' Then he stepped away.

'Start from ten yards this time!' Roland called.

At ten, they all hit. And at twenty. At thirty yards, Susannah threw her plate high, as Roland had instructed her to do. He wanted one of the Calla women to win this round. At forty yards, Zalia Jaffords hesitated too long, and the dish she flung chopped the sharproot head in two rather than the radish sitting on top.

'*Fuck-commala!*' she cried, then clapped her hands to her mouth and looked at Callahan, who was sitting on the back steps. That fellow only smiled and waved cheerfully, affecting deafness.

She stamped over to Eddie and Jake, blushing to the tips of her ears and furious. 'Ye must tell him to give me another chance, say will ya please,' she told Eddie. 'I can do it, I know I can do it—'

Eddie put a hand on her arm, stemming the flood. 'He knows it, too, Zee. You're in.'

She looked at him with burning eyes, lips pressed so tightly together they were almost gone. 'Are you sure?'

'Yeah,' Eddie said. 'You could pitch for the Mets, darlin'.'

Now it was down to Margaret and Rosalita. They both hit the radishes at fifty yards. To Jake, Eddie murmured: 'Buddy, I would have told you that was impossible if I hadn't just seen it.'

At sixty yards, Margaret Eisenhart missed cleanly. Rosalita raised her plate over her right shoulder – she was a lefty – hesitated, then screamed '*Riza!*' and threw. Sharp-eyed though he was, Roland wasn't entirely sure if the plate's edge clipped the side of the radish or if the wind toppled it over. In either case, Rosalita raised her fists over her head and shook them, laughing.

'Fair-day goose! Fair-day goose!' Margaret began calling. The others joined in. Soon even Callahan was chanting.

Roland went to Rosa and gave her a hug, brief but strong. As he did so he whispered in her ear that while he had no goose, he might be able to find a certain long-necked gander for her, come evening.

'Well,' she said, smiling, 'when we get older, we take our prizes where we find them. Don't we?'

Zalia glanced at Margaret. 'What did he say to her? Did 'ee kennit?'

Margaret Eisenhart was smiling. 'Nothing you haven't heard yourself, I'm sure,' she said.

9

Then the ladies were gone. So was the Pere, on some errand or other. Roland of Gilead sat on the bottom porch step, looking downhill toward the site of the competition so lately completed. When Susannah asked him if he was satisfied, he nodded. 'Yes, I think all's well there. We have to hope it is, because time's closing now. Things will happen fast.' The truth was that he had never experienced such a confluence of events . . . but since Susannah had admitted her pregnancy, he had calmed nevertheless.

You've recalled the truth of ka to your truant mind, he thought. *And it happened because this woman showed a kind of bravery the rest of us couldn't quite muster up.*

'Roland, will I be going back out to the Rocking B?' Jake asked.

Roland considered, then shrugged. 'Do you want to?'

'Yes, but this time I want to take the Ruger.' Jake's face pinked a little, but his voice remained steady. He had awakened with this idea, as if the dreamgod Roland called Nis had brought it to him in his sleep. 'I'll put it at the bottom of my bedroll and wrap it in my extra shirt. No one needs to know it's there.' He paused. 'I don't want to show it off to Benny, if that's what you're thinking.'

The idea had never crossed Roland's mind. But what was in *Jake's* mind? He posed the question, and Jake's answer was the sort one gives when one has charted the likely course of a discussion well in advance.

'Do you ask as my dinh?'

Roland opened his mouth to say yes, saw how closely Eddie and Susannah were watching him, and reconsidered. There was a difference between keeping secrets (as each of them had in his own way kept the secret of Susannah's pregnancy) and following what Eddie called 'a hunch.' The request under Jake's request was to be on a longer rope. Simple as that. And surely Jake had earned the right to a little more rope. This was not the same boy who had come into Mid-World shivering and terrified and nearly naked.

'Not as your dinh,' he said. 'As for the Ruger, you may take it anywhere, and at any time. Did you not bring it to the tet in the first place?'

'Stole it,' Jake said in a low voice. He was staring at his knees.

'You took what you needed to survive,' Susannah said. 'There's a big difference. Listen, sugar — you're not planning to shoot anyone, are you?'

'Not planning to, no.'

'Be careful,' she said. 'I don't know what you've got in your head, but you be careful.'

'And whatever it is, you better get it settled in the next week or so,' Eddie told him.

Jake nodded, then looked at Roland. 'When are you planning to call the town meeting?'

'According to the robot, we have ten days left before the Wolves come. So . . .' Roland calculated briefly. 'Town gathering in six days. Will that suit you?'

Jake nodded again.

'Are you sure you don't want to tell us what's on your mind?'

'Not unless you ask as dinh,' Jake said. 'It's probably nothing, Roland. Really.'

Roland nodded dubiously and began rolling another smoke. Having fresh tobacco was wonderful. 'Is there anything else? Because, if there isn't—'

'There is, actually,' Eddie said.

'What?'

'I need to go to New York,' Eddie said. He spoke casually, as if proposing no more than a trip to the mercantile to buy a pickle or a licorice stick, but his eyes were dancing with excitement. 'And this time I'll have to go in the flesh. Which means using the ball more directly, I guess. Black Thirteen. I hope to hell you know how to do it, Roland.'

'Why do you need to go to New York?' Roland asked. 'This I *do* ask as dinh.'

'Sure you do,' Eddie said, 'and I'll tell you. Because you're right about time getting short. And because the Wolves of the Calla aren't the only ones we have to worry about.'

'You want to see how close to July fifteenth it's getting,' Jake said. 'Don't you?'

'Yeah,' Eddie said. 'We know from when we all went todash that time is going faster in that version of New York, 1977. Remember the date on the piece of *The New York Times* I found in the doorway?'

'June second,' Susannah said.

'Right. We're also pretty sure that we can't double back in time in that world; it's later every time we go there. Right?'

Jake nodded emphatically. 'Because that world's not like the others . . . unless maybe it was just being sent todash by Black Thirteen that made us feel that way?'

'I don't think so,' Eddie said. 'That little piece of Second Avenue between the vacant lot and maybe on up to Sixtieth is a very important place. I think it's a doorway. One big doorway.'

Jake Chambers was looking more and more excited. 'Not all the way up to Sixtieth. Not that far. Second Avenue between Forty-sixth and Fifty-fourth, that's what I think. On the day I left Piper, I felt something change when I got to Fifty-fourth Street. It's those eight blocks. The stretch with the record store on it and Chew Chew Mama, and The Manhattan Restaurant of the Mind. And the vacant lot, of course. That's the other end. It . . . I don't know . . .'

Eddie said, 'Being there takes you into a different world. Some kind of *key* world. And I think that's why time always runs one way—'

Roland held up his hand. 'Stop.'

Eddie stopped, looking at Roland expectantly, smiling a little. Roland was not smiling. Some of his previous sense of well-being had passed away. Too much to do, gods damn it. And not enough time in which to do it.

'You want to see how near time has run to the day the agreement becomes null and void,' he said. 'Have I got that right?'

'You do.'

'You don't need to go to New York physically to do that, Eddie. Todash would serve nicely.'

'Todash would do fine to check the day and the month, sure, but there's more. We've been dumb about that vacant lot, you guys. I mean *really* dumb.'

10

Eddie believed they could own the vacant lot without ever touching Susannah's inherited fortune; he thought Callahan's story showed quite clearly how it could be done. Not the rose; the rose was not to be owned (by them or anyone) but to be protected. And they could do it. Maybe.

Frightened or not, Calvin Tower had been waiting in that deserted laundrymat to save Pere Callahan's bacon. And frightened or not, Calvin Tower had refused – as of May 31st, 1977, anyway – to sell his last piece of real property to the Sombra Corporation. Eddie thought that Calvin Tower was, in the words of the song, holding out for a hero.

Eddie had also been thinking about the way Callahan had hidden his face in his hands the first time he mentioned Black Thirteen. He wanted it the hell out of his church . . . but so far he'd kept it anyway. Like the bookshop owner, the Pere had been holding out. How stupid they had been to assume Calvin Tower would ask millions for his lot! He *wanted* to be shed of it. But not until the right person came along. Or the right ka-tet.

'Suziella, you can't go because you're pregnant,' Eddie said. 'Jake, you can't go because you're a kid. All other questions aside, I'm pretty sure you couldn't sign the kind of contract I've been thinking about ever since Callahan told us his story. I could take you with me, but it sounds like you've got something you want to check into over here. Or am I wrong about that?'

'You're not wrong,' Jake said. 'But I'd almost go with you, anyway. This sounds really good.'

Eddie smiled. 'Almost only counts with grenados and horseshoes, kid. As for sending Roland, no offense, boss, but you're not all that suave in our world. You . . . um . . . lose something in the translation.'

Susannah burst out laughing.

'How much are you thinking of offering him?' Jake asked. 'I mean, it has to be *something*, doesn't it?'

'A buck,' Eddie said. 'I'll probably have to ask Tower to loan it to me, but—'

'No, we can do better than that,' Jake said, looking serious. 'I've got five or six dollars in my knapsack, I'm pretty sure.' He grinned. 'And we can offer him more, later on. When things kind of settle down on this side.'

'If we're still alive,' Susannah said, but she also looked excited. 'You know what, Eddie? You just might be a genius.'

'Balazar and his friends won't be happy if sai Tower sells us his lot,' Roland said.

'Yeah, but maybe we can persuade Balazar to leave him alone,' Eddie said. A grim little smile was playing around the corners of his mouth. 'When it comes right down to it, Roland, Enrico Balazar's the kind of guy I wouldn't mind killing twice.'

'When do you want to go?' Susannah asked him.

'The sooner the better,' Eddie said. 'For one thing, not knowing how late it is over there in New York is driving me nuts. Roland? What do you say?'

'I say tomorrow,' Roland said. 'We'll take the ball up to the cave, and then we'll see if you can go through the door to Calvin Tower's where and when. Your idea is a good one, Eddie, and I say thankya.'

Jake said, 'What if the ball sends you to the wrong place? The wrong version of 1977, or . . .' He hardly knew how to finish. He was remembering how *thin* everything had seemed when Black Thirteen had first taken them todash, and how endless darkness seemed to be waiting behind the painted surface realities around them. '. . . or someplace even farther?' he finished.

'In that case, I'll send back a postcard.' Eddie said it with a shrug and a laugh, but for just a moment Jake saw how frightened he was. Susannah must have seen it, too, because she took Eddie's hand in both of hers and squeezed it.

'Hey, I'll be fine,' Eddie said.

'You better be,' Susannah replied. 'You just better.'

CHAPTER II

THE DOGAN, PART 1

1

When Roland and Eddie entered Our Lady of Serenity the following morning, daylight was only a distant rumor on the northeast horizon. Eddie lit their way down the center aisle with a 'sener, his lips pressed tightly together. The thing they had come for was humming. It was a sleepy hum, but he hated the sound of it just the same. The church itself felt freaky. Empty, it seemed too big, somehow. Eddie kept expecting to see ghostly figures (or perhaps a complement of the vagrant dead) sitting in the pews and looking at them with otherworldly disapproval.

But the hum was worse.

When they reached the front, Roland opened his purse and took out the bowling bag which Jake had kept in his knapsack until yesterday. The gunslinger held it up for a moment and they could both read what was printed on the side: NOTHING BUT STRIKES AT MID-WORLD LANES.

'Not a word from now until I tell you it's all right,' Roland said. 'Do you understand?'

'Yes.'

Roland pressed his thumb into the groove between two of the floor-boards and the hidey-hole in the preacher's cove sprang open. He lifted the top aside. Eddie had once seen a movie on TV about guys disposing of live explosives during the London Blitz – *UXB*, it had been called – and Roland's movements now recalled that film strongly to his mind. And why not? If they were right about what was in this hiding place – and Eddie knew they were – then it *was* an unexploded bomb.

Roland folded back the white linen surplice, exposing the box. The hum rose. Eddie's breath stopped in his throat. He felt the skin all over his body grow cold. Somewhere close, a monster of nearly unimaginable malevolence had half-opened one sleeping eye.

The hum dropped back to its former sleepy pitch and Eddie breathed again.

Roland handed him the bowling bag, motioning for Eddie to hold it open. With misgivings (part of him wanted to whisper in Roland's ear that they should forget the whole thing), Eddie did as he was bidden. Roland lifted the box out, and once again the hum rose. In the rich, if limited, glow of the 'sener, Eddie could see sweat on the gunslinger's brow. He could feel it on his own. If Black Thirteen awoke and pitched them out into some black limbo . . .

I won't go. I'll fight to stay with Susannah.

Of course he would. But he was still relieved when Roland slipped the elaborately carved ghostwood box into the queer metallic bag they'd found in the vacant lot. The hum didn't disappear entirely, but subsided to a barely audible drone. And when Roland gently pulled the drawstring running around the top of the bag, closing its mouth, the drone became a distant whisper. It was like listening to a seashell.

Eddie sketched the sign of the cross in front of himself. Smiling faintly, Roland did the same.

Outside the church, the northeast horizon had brightened appreciably — there would be real daylight after all, it seemed.

'Roland.'

The gunslinger turned toward him, eyebrows raised. His left fist was closed around the bag's throat; he was apparently not willing to trust the weight of the box to the bag's drawstring, stout as it looked.

'If we were todash when we found that bag, how could we have picked it up?'

Roland considered this. Then he said, 'Perhaps the bag is todash, too.'

'Still?'

Roland nodded. 'Yes, I think so. Still.'

'Oh.' Eddie thought about it. 'That's spooky.'

'Changing your mind about revisiting New York, Eddie?'

Eddie shook his head. He was scared, though. Probably more scared than he'd been at any time since standing up in the aisle of the Barony Coach to riddle Blaine.

2

By the time they were halfway along the path leading to the Doorway Cave (*It's upsy*, Henchick had said, and so it had been, and so it was), it was easily ten o' the clock and remarkably warm. Eddie stopped, wiped the back of his neck with his bandanna, and looked out over the twisting arroyos to the north. Here and there he could see black, gaping holes and asked Roland if they were the garnet mines. The gunslinger told him they were.

'And which one have you got in mind for the kiddies? Can we see it from here?'

'As a matter of fact, yes.' Roland drew the single gun he was wearing and pointed it. 'Look over the sight.'

Eddie did and saw a deep draw which made the shape of a jagged double *S*. It was filled to the top with velvety shadows; he guessed there might be only half an hour or so at midday when the sun reached the bottom. Farther to the north, it appeared to dead-end against a massive rock-face. He supposed the mine entrance was there, but it was too dark to make out. To the southeast this arroyo opened on a dirt track that wound its way back to East Road. Beyond East Road were fields sloping down to fading but still green plots of rice. Beyond the rice was the river.

'Makes me think of the story you told us,' Eddie said. 'Eyebolt Canyon.'

'Of course it does.'

'No thinny to do the dirty work, though.'

'No,' Roland agreed. 'No thinny.'

'Tell me the truth: Are you really going to stick this town's kids in a mine at the end of a dead-end arroyo?'

'No.'

'The *folken* think you . . . that *we* mean to do that. Even the dish-throwing ladies think that.'

'I know they do,' Roland said. 'I want them to.'

'Why?'

'Because I don't believe there's anything supernatural about the way the Wolves find the children. After hearing Gran-pere Jaffords's story, I don't think there's anything supernatural about the *Wolves*, for that matter. No, there's a rat in this particular corn-crib. Someone who goes squealing to the powers that be in Thunderclap.'

'Someone different each time, you mean. Each twenty-three or twenty-four years.'

'Yes.'

'Who'd do that?' Eddie asked. 'Who *could* do that?'

'I'm not sure, but I have an idea.'

'Took? Kind of a handed-down thing, from father to son?'

'If you're rested, Eddie, I think we'd better press on.'

'Overholser? Maybe that guy Telford, the one who looks like a TV cowboy?'

Roland walked past him without speaking, his new shor'boots gritting on the scattered pebbles and rock-splinters. From his good left hand, the pink bag swung back and forth. The thing inside was still whispering its unpleasant secrets.

'Chatty as ever, good for you,' Eddie said, and followed him.

3

The first voice which arose from the depths of the cave belonged to the great sage and eminent junkie.

'Oh, wookit the wittle sissy!' Henry moaned. To Eddie, he sounded like Ebenezer Scrooge's dead partner in *A Christmas Carol*, funny and scary at the same time. 'Does the wittle sissy think he's going back to Noo-Ork? You'll go a lot farther than that if you try it, bro. Better hunker where you are . . . just do your little carvings . . . be a good little homo . . .' The dead brother laughed. The live one shivered.

'Eddie?' Roland asked.

'Listen to your brother, Eddie!' his mother cried from the cave's dark and sloping throat. On the rock floor, scatters of small bones gleamed. 'He gave up his life for you, his *whole life*, the least you could do is listen to him!'

'Eddie, are you all right?'

Now came the voice of Csaba Drabnik, known in Eddie's crowd as the Mad Fuckin Hungarian. Csaba was telling Eddie to give him a cigarette or he'd pull Eddie's fuckin pants down. Eddie tore his attention away from this frightening but fascinating gabble with an effort.

'Yeah,' he said. 'I guess so.'

'The voices are coming from your own head. The cave finds them and amplifies them somehow. Sends them on. It's a little upsetting, I know, but it's meaningless.'

'Why'd you let em kill me, bro?' Henry sobbed. 'I kept thinking you'd come, but you never did!'

'Meaningless,' Eddie said. 'Okay, got it. What do we do now?'

'According to both stories I've heard of this place — Callahan's and Henchick's — the door will open when I open the box.'

Eddie laughed nervously. 'I don't even want you to take the box out of the *bag*, how's that for chickenshit?'

'If you've changed your mind . . .'

Eddie was shaking his head. 'No. I want to go through with it.' He flashed a sudden, bright grin. 'You're not worried about me scoring, are you? Finding the man and getting high?'

From deep in the cave, Henry exulted, 'It's China White, bro! Them niggers sell the *best!*'

'Not at all,' Roland said. 'There are plenty of things I *am* worried about, but you returning to your old habits isn't one of them.'

'Good.' Eddie stepped a little farther into the cave, looking at the free-standing door. Except for the hieroglyphics on the front and the crystal knob with the rose etched on it, this one looked exactly like the ones on the beach. 'If you go around—?'

'If you go around, the door's gone,' Roland said. 'There *is* a hell of a drop-off, though . . . all the way to Na'ar, for all I know. I'd mind that, if I were you.'

'Good advice, and Fast Eddie says thankya.' He tried the crystal door-knob and found it wouldn't budge in either direction. He had expected that, too. He stepped back.

Roland said, 'You need to think of New York. Of Second Avenue in particular, I think. And of the time. The year of nineteen and seven-seven.'

'How do you think of a *year?*'

When Roland spoke, his voice betrayed a touch of impatience. 'Think of how it was on the day you and Jake followed Jake's earlier self, I suppose.'

Eddie started to say that was the wrong day, it was too early, then closed his mouth. If they were right about the rules, he *couldn't* go back to that day, not todash, not in the flesh, either. If they were right, time over there was somehow hooked to time over here, only running a little faster. If they were right about the rules . . . if there *were* rules . . .

Well, why don't you just go and see?

'Eddie? Do you want me to try hypnotizing you?' Roland had drawn a shell from his gunbelt. 'It can make you see the past more clearly.'

'No. I think I better do this straight and wide-awake.'

Eddie opened and closed his hands several times, taking and releasing deep breaths as he did so. His heart wasn't running particularly fast – was going slow, if anything – but each beat seemed to shiver through his entire body. Christ, all this would have been so much easier if there were just some controls you could set, like in Professor Peabody's Wayback Machine or that movie about the Morlocks!

'Hey, do I look all right?' he asked Roland. 'I mean, if I land on Second Avenue at high noon, how much attention am I going to attract?'

'If you appear in front of people,' Roland said, 'probably quite a lot. I'd advise you to ignore anyone who wants to palaver with you on the subject and vacate the area immediately.'

'That much I know. I meant how do I look clotheswise?'

Roland gave a small shrug. 'I don't know, Eddie. It's your city, not mine.'

Eddie could have demurred. *Brooklyn* was his city. Had been, anyway. As a rule he hadn't gone into Manhattan from one month to the next, thought of it almost as another country. Still, he supposed he knew what Roland meant. He inventoried himself and saw a plain flannel shirt with horn buttons above dark-blue jeans with burnished nickel rivets instead of copper ones, and a button-up fly. (Eddie had seen zippers in Lud, but none since.) He reckoned he would pass for normal on the street. New York normal, at least. Anyone who gave him a second look would think café waiter/artist-wannabe playing hippie on his day off. He didn't think most people would even bother with the first look, and that was absolutely to the good. But there *was* one thing he could add—

'Have you got a piece of rawhide?' he asked Roland.

From deep in the cave, the voice of Mr Tubther, his fifth-grade teacher, cried out with lugubrious intensity. 'You had potential! You were a wonderful student, and look at what you turned into! Why did you let your brother spoil you?'

To which Henry replied, in sobbing outrage: 'He let me die! He *killed* me!'

Roland swung his purse off his shoulder, put it on the floor at the mouth of the cave beside the pink bag, opened it, rummaged through it. Eddie had no idea how many things were in there; he only knew he'd never seen the bottom of it. At last the gunslinger found what Eddie had asked for and held it out.

While Eddie tied back his hair with the hank of rawhide (he thought it finished off the artistic-hippie look quite nicely), Roland took out what he called his swag-bag, opened it, and began to empty out its contents. There was the partially depleted sack of tobacco Callahan had given him, several kinds of coin and currency, a sewing kit, the mended cup he had turned into a rough compass not far from Shardik's clearing, an old scrap of map, and the newer one the Tavery twins had drawn. When the bag was empty, he took the big revolver with the sandalwood grip from the holster on his left hip. He rolled the cylinder, checked the loads, nodded, and snapped the cylinder back into place. Then he put the gun into the swag-bag, yanked the lacings tight, and tied them in a clove hitch that would come loose at a single pull. He held the bag out to Eddie by the worn strap.

At first Eddie didn't want to take it. 'Nah, man, that's yours.'

'These last weeks you've worn it as much as I have. Probably more.'

'Yeah, but this is New York we're talking about, Roland. In New York, everybody steals.'

'They won't steal from you. Take the gun.'

Eddie looked into Roland's eyes for a moment, then took the swag-bag and slung the strap over his shoulder. 'You've got a feeling.'

'A hunch, yes.'

'Ka at work?'

Roland shrugged. 'It's always at work.'

'All right,' Eddie said. 'And Roland – if I don't make it back, take care of Suze.'

'Your job is to make sure I don't have to.'

No, Eddie thought. *My job is to protect the rose.*

He turned to the door. He had a thousand more questions, but Roland was right, the time to ask them was done.

'Eddie, if you really don't want to—'

'No,' he said. 'I *do* want to.' He raised his left hand and gave a thumbs-up. 'When you see me do that, open the box.'

'All right.'

Roland speaking from behind him. Because now it was just Eddie and the door. The door with UNFOUND written on it in some strange and lovely language. Once he'd read a novel called *The Door Into Summer*, by . . . who? One of the science-fiction guys he was always dragging home from the library, one of his old reliables, perfect for the long afternoons of summer vacation. Murray Leinster, Poul Anderson, Gordon Dickson, Isaac Asimov, Harlan Ellison . . . Robert Heinlein. He thought it was Heinlein who'd written *The Door Into Summer*. Henry always ragging him about the books he brought home, calling him the wittle sissy, the wittle bookworm, asking him if he could read and jerk off at the same time, wanting to know how he could sit fuckin still for so long with his nose stuck in some made-up piece of shit about rockets and time machines. Henry older than him. Henry covered with pimples that were always shiny with Noxema and Stri-Dex. Henry getting ready to go into the Army. Eddie younger. Eddie bringing books home from the library. Eddie thirteen years old, almost the age Jake is now. It's 1977 and he's thirteen and on Second Avenue and the taxis are shiny yellow in the sun. A black man wearing Walkman earphones is walking past Chew Chew Mama's, Eddie can see him, Eddie knows the black man is listening to Elton John singing – what else? – 'Someone Saved My Life Tonight.' The sidewalk is crowded. It's late afternoon and people are going home after another day in the steel arroyos of Calla New York, where they grow money instead of rice, can ya say prime rate. Women looking amiably weird in expensive business suits and sneakers; their high heels are in their gunna because the workday is done and they're going home. Everyone seems to be smiling because the light is so bright and the air is so warm, it's summer in the city and somewhere there's the sound of a jackhammer, like on that old Lovin Spoonful song. Before him is a door into the summer of '77, the cabbies are getting a buck and a quarter on the drop and thirty cents every fifth of a mile thereafter, it was less before and it'll be more after but this is now, the dancing point of now. The space shuttle with the teacher on board hasn't blown up. John Lennon is still alive, although he won't be much longer if he doesn't stop messing with that wicked heroin, that China White. As for Eddie Dean, Edward Cantor Dean, he knows nothing about heroin. A few cigarettes are his only vice (other than trying to jack off, at which he will not be successful for almost another year). He's thirteen. It's 1977 and he has exactly four hairs on his chest, he counts them religiously each morning, hoping for big number five. It's the summer after the Summer of the Tall Ships. It's a late afternoon in the month of June and he can hear a happy tune. The tune is coming from the speakers over the doorway of the Tower of Power record shop, it's Mungo Jerry singing 'In the Summertime,' and—

Suddenly it was all real to him, or as real as he thought he needed it to be. Eddie raised his left hand and popped up his thumb: *let's go*. Behind him, Roland had sat down and eased the box out of the pink bag. And when Eddie gave him the thumbs-up, the gunslinger opened the box.

Eddie's ears were immediately assaulted by a sweetly dissonant jangle of chimes. His eyes began to water. In front of him, the free-standing door clicked open and the cave was suddenly illuminated by strong sunlight. There was the sound of beeping horns and the rat-a-tat-tat of a jackhammer. Not so long ago he had wanted a door like this so badly that he'd almost killed Roland to get it. And now that he had it, he was scared to death.

The todash chimes felt as if they were tearing his head apart. If he listened to that for long, he'd go insane. *Go if you're going*, he thought.

He stepped forward, through his gushing eyes seeing three hands reach out and grasp four doorknobs. He pulled the door toward him and golden late-day sunlight dazzled his eyes. He could smell gasoline and hot city air and someone's aftershave.

Hardly able to see anything, Eddie stepped through the unfound door and into the summer of a world from which he was now fan-gon, the exiled one.

4

It was Second Avenue, all right; here was the Blimpie's, and from behind him came the cheery sound of that Mungo Jerry song with the Caribbean beat. People moved around him in a flood – uptown, downtown, all around the town. They paid no attention to Eddie, partly because most of them were only concentrating on getting *out* of town at the end of another day, mostly because in New York, not noticing other people was a way of life.

Eddie shrugged his right shoulder, settling the strap of Roland's swag-bag there more firmly, then looked behind him. The door back to Calla Bryn Sturgis was there. He could see Roland sitting at the mouth of the cave with the box open on his lap.

Those fucking chimes must be driving him crazy, Eddie thought. And then, as he watched, he saw the gunslinger remove a couple of bullets from his gunbelt and stick them in his ears. Eddie grinned. *Good move, man.* At least it had helped to block out the warble of the thinny back on I-70. Whether it worked now or whether it didn't, Roland was on his own. Eddie had things to do.

He turned slowly on his little spot of the sidewalk, then looked over his shoulder again to verify the door had turned with him. It had. If it was like the other ones, it would now follow him everywhere he went. Even if it didn't, Eddie didn't foresee a problem; he wasn't planning on going far. He noticed something else, as well: that sense of darkness lurking behind everything was gone. Because he was really here, he supposed, and not just todash. If there were vagrant dead lurking in the vicinity, he wouldn't be able to see them.

Once more shrugging the swag-bag's strap further up on his shoulder, Eddie set off for The Manhattan Restaurant of the Mind.

5

People moved aside for him as he walked, but that wasn't quite enough to prove he was really here; people did that when you were todash, too. At last Eddie provoked an actual collision with a young guy toting not one briefcase but *two* – a Big Coffin Hunter of the business world if Eddie had ever seen one.

'Hey, watch where you're going!' Mr Businessman squawked when their shoulders collided.

'Sorry, man, sorry,' Eddie said. He was here, all right. 'Say, could you tell me what day—'

But Mr Businessman was already gone, chasing the coronary he'd probably catch up to around the age of forty-five or fifty, from the look of him. Eddie remembered the punchline of an old New York joke: 'Pardon me, sir, can you tell me how to get to City Hall, or should I just go fuck myself?' He burst out laughing, couldn't help it.

Once he had himself back under control, he got moving again. On the corner of Second and Fifty-fourth, he saw a man looking into a shop window at a display of shoes and boots. This guy was also wearing a suit, but looked considerably more relaxed than the one Eddie had bumped into. Also he was carrying only a single briefcase, which Eddie took to be a good omen.

'Cry your pardon,' Eddie said, 'but could you tell me what day it is?'

'Thursday,' the window-shopper said. 'The twenty-third of June.'

'1977?'

The window-shopper gave Eddie a little half-smile, both quizzical and cynical, plus a raised eyebrow. '1977, that's correct. Won't be 1978 for . . . gee, another six months. Think of that.'

Eddie nodded. 'Thankee-sai.'

'Thankee-*what*?'

'Nothing,' Eddie said, and hurried on.

Only three weeks to July fifteenth give or take, he thought. *That's cutting it too goddam close for comfort.*

Yes, but if he could persuade Calvin Tower to sell him the lot today, the whole question of time would be moot. Once, a long time ago, Eddie's brother had boasted to some of his friends that his little bro could talk the devil into setting himself on fire, if he really set his mind to it. Eddie hoped he still had some of that persuasiveness. Do a little deal with Calvin Tower, invest in some real estate, then maybe take a half-hour time-out and actually enjoy that New York groove a little bit. Celebrate. Maybe get a chocolate egg-cream, or—

The run of his thoughts broke off and he stopped so suddenly that someone bumped into him and then swore. Eddie barely felt the bump or heard the curse. The dark-gray Lincoln Town Car was parked up there again – not in front of the fire hydrant this time, but a couple of doors down.

Balazar's Town Car.

Eddie started walking again. He was suddenly glad Roland had talked him into taking one of his revolvers. And that the gun was fully loaded.

6

The chalkboard was back in the window (today's special was a New England Boiled Dinner consisting of Nathaniel Hawthorne, Henry David Thoreau, and Robert Frost – for dessert, your choice of Mary McCarthy or Grace Metalious), but the sign hanging in the door read SORRY WE'RE CLOSED. According to the digital bank-clock up the street from Tower of Power Records, it was 3:14 P.M. Who shut up shop at quarter past three on a weekday afternoon?

Someone with a special customer, Eddie reckoned. That was who.

He cupped his hands to the sides of his face and looked into The Manhattan Restaurant of the Mind. He saw the small round display table with the children's books on it. To the right was the counter that looked as if it might have been filched from a turn-of-the-century soda fountain, only today no one was sitting there, not even Aaron Deepneau. The cash register was likewise unattended, although Eddie could read the words on the orange tab sticking up in its window: NO SALE.

Place was empty. Calvin Tower had been called away, maybe there'd been a family emergency—

He's got an emergency, all right, the gunslinger's cold voice spoke up in Eddie's head. *It came in that gray auto-carriage. And look again at the counter, Eddie. Only this time why don't you actually use your eyes instead of just letting the light pour through them?*

Sometimes he thought in the voices of other people. He guessed lots of people did that – it was a way of changing perspective a little, seeing stuff from another angle. But this didn't feel like that kind of pretending. This felt like old long, tall, and ugly actually talking to him inside his head.

Eddie looked at the counter again. This time he saw the strew of plastic chessmen on the marble, and the overturned coffee cup. This time he saw the spectacles lying on the floor between two of the stools, one of the lenses cracked.

He felt the first pulse of anger deep in the middle of his head. It was dull, but if past experience was any indicator, the pulses were apt to come faster and harder, growing sharper as they did. Eventually they would blot out conscious thought, and God help anyone who wandered within range of Roland's gun when that happened. He had once asked Roland if this happened to him, and Roland had replied, *It happens to all of us.* When Eddie had shaken his head and responded that he wasn't like Roland – not him, not Suze, not Jake – the gunslinger had said nothing.

Tower and his special customers were out back, he thought, in that combination storeroom and office. And this time talking probably wasn't what they had in mind. Eddie had an idea this was a little refresher course, Balazar's gentlemen reminding Mr Tower that the fifteenth of July was coming, reminding Mr Tower of what the most prudent decision would be once it came.

When the word *gentlemen* crossed Eddie's mind, it brought another pulse of anger with it. That was quite a word for guys who'd break a fat and harmless bookstore owner's glasses, then take him out back and terrorize him. Gentlemen! Fuck-commala!

He tried the bookshop door. It was locked, but the lock wasn't such of a much; the door rattled in its jamb like a loose tooth. Standing there in the recessed doorway, looking (he hoped) like a fellow who was especially interested in some book he'd glimpsed inside, Eddie began to increase his pressure on the lock, first using just his hand on the knob, then leaning his shoulder against the door in a way he hoped would look casual.

Chances are ninety-four in a hundred that no one's looking at you, anyway. This is New York, right? Can you tell me how to get to City Hall or should I just go fuck myself?

He pushed harder. He was still a good way from exerting maximum pressure when there was a snap and the door swung inward. Eddie entered without hesitation, as if he had every right in the world to be there, then closed the door again. It wouldn't latch. He took a copy of *How the Grinch Stole Christmas* off the children's table, ripped out the last page (*Never liked the way this one ended, anyway*, he thought), folded it three times, and stuck it into the crack between the door and the jamb. Good enough to keep it closed. Then he looked around.

The place was empty, and now, with the sun behind the skyscrapers of the West Side, shadowy. No sound—

Yes. Yes, there was. A muffled cry from the back of the shop. *Caution, gentlemen at work*, Eddie thought, and felt another pulse of anger. This one was sharper.

He yanked the tie on Roland's swag-bag, then walked toward the door at the back, the one marked EMPLOYEES ONLY. Before he got there, he had to skirt an untidy heap of paperbacks and an overturned display rack, the old-fashioned drugstore kind that turned around and around. Calvin Tower had grabbed at it as Balazar's gents hustled him toward the storage area. Eddie hadn't seen it happen, didn't need to.

The door at the back wasn't locked. Eddie took Roland's revolver out of the swag-bag and set the bag itself aside so it wouldn't get in his way at a crucial moment. He eased the storage-room door open inch by inch, reminding himself of where Tower's desk was. If they saw him he'd charge, screaming at the top of his lungs. According to Roland, you *always* screamed at the top of your lungs when and if you were discovered. You might startle your enemy for a second or two, and sometimes a second or two made all the difference in the world.

This time there was no need for screaming or for charging. The men he was looking for were in the office area, their shadows once more climbing high and grotesque on the wall behind them. Tower was sitting in his office chair, but the chair was no longer behind the desk. It had been pushed into the space between two of the three filing cabinets. Without his glasses, his pleasant face looked naked. His two visitors were facing him, which meant their backs were to Eddie. Tower could have seen him, but Tower was looking up at Jack Andolini and George Biondi, concentrating on them alone. At the sight of the man's naked terror, another of those pulses went through Eddie's head.

There was the tang of gasoline in the air, a smell which Eddie guessed would frighten even the most stout-hearted shopowner, especially one presiding over an empire of paper. Beside the taller of the two men – Andolini – was a glass-fronted bookcase about five feet high. The door was swung open. Inside were four or five shelves of books, all the volumes wrapped in what looked like clear plastic dust-covers. Andolini was holding up one of them in a way that made him look absurdly like a TV pitchman. The shorter man – Biondi – was holding up a glass jar full of amber liquid in much the same way. Not much question about what it was.

'Please, Mr Andolini,' Tower said. He spoke in a humble, shaken voice. 'Please, that's a very valuable book.'

'Of course it is,' Andolini said. 'All the ones in the case are valuable. I understand you've got a signed copy of *Ulysses* that's worth twenty-six thousand dollars.'

'What's that about, Jack?' George Biondi asked. He sounded awed. 'What kind of book's worth twenty-six large?'

'I don't know,' Andolini said. 'Why don't you tell us, Mr Tower? Or can I call you Cal?'

'My *Ulysses* is in a safe-deposit box,' Tower said. 'It's not for sale.'

'But these are,' Andolini said. 'Aren't they? And I see the number 7500 on the flyleaf of this one in pencil. No twenty-six grand, but still the price of a new car. So here's what I'm going to do, Cal. Are you listening?'

Eddie was moving closer, and although he strove to be quiet, he made no effort whatever to conceal himself. And still none of them saw him. Had he been this stupid when he'd been of this world? This vulnerable to what was not even an ambush, properly speaking? He supposed he had been, and knew it was no wonder Roland had at first held him in contempt.

'I . . . I'm listening.'

'You've got something Mr Balazar wants as badly as you want your copy of *Ulysses*. And although these books in the glass cabinet are technically for sale, I bet you sell damned few of them, because you just . . . can't . . . bear

. . . to part with them. The way you can't bear to part with that vacant lot. So here's what's going to happen. George is going to pour gasoline over this book with *7500* on it, and I'm going to light it on fire. Then I'm going to take *another* book out of your little case of treasures, and I'm going to ask you for a verbal commitment to sell that lot to the Sombra Corporation at high noon on July fifteenth. Got that?'

'I—'

'If you give me that verbal commitment, this meeting will come to an end. If you *don't* give me that verbal commitment, I'm going to burn the second book. Then a third. Then a fourth. After four, sir, I believe my associate here is apt to lose patience.'

'You're fucking A,' George Biondi said. Eddie was now almost close enough to reach out and touch Big Nose, and still they didn't see him.

'At that point I think we'll just pour gasoline inside your little glass cabinet and set all your valuable books on f—'

Movement at last snagged Jack Andolini's eye. He looked beyond his partner's left shoulder and saw a young man with hazel eyes looking out of a deeply tanned face. The man was holding what looked like the world's oldest, biggest prop revolver. *Had* to be a prop.

'Who the fuck're—' Jack began.

Before he could get any further, Eddie Dean's face lit up with happiness and good cheer, a look that vaulted him way past handsome and into the land of beauty. '*George!*' he cried. It was the tone of one greeting his oldest, fondest friend after a long absence. '*George Biondi!* Man, you *still* got the biggest beak on this side of the Hudson! Good to see you, man!'

There is a certain hardwiring in the human animal that makes us respond to strangers who call us by name. When the summoning call is affectionate, we seem almost compelled to respond in kind. In spite of the situation they were in back here, George 'Big Nose' Biondi turned, with the beginning of a grin, toward the voice that had hailed him with such cheerful familiarity. That grin was in fact still blooming when Eddie struck him savagely with the butt of Roland's gun. Andolini's eyes were sharp, but he saw little more than a blur as the butt came down three times, the first blow between Biondi's eyes, the second above his right eye, the third into the hollow of his right temple. The first two blows provoked hollow thudding sounds. The last one yielded a soft, sickening smack. Biondi went down like a sack of mail, eyes rolling up to show the whites, lips puckering in a restless way that made him look like a baby who wanted to nurse. The jar tumbled out of his relaxing hand, hit the cement floor, shattered. The smell of gasoline was suddenly much stronger, rich and cloying.

Eddie gave Biondi's partner no time to react. While Big Nose was still twitching on the floor in the spilled gas and broken glass, Eddie was on Andolini, forcing him backward.

7

For Calvin Tower (who had begun life as Calvin Toren), there was no immediate sense of relief, no *Thank God I'm saved* feeling. His first thought was *They're bad; this new one is worse.*

In the dim light of the storage room, the newcomer seemed to merge with his own leaping shadow and become an apparition ten feet tall. One with burning eyeballs starting from their sockets and a mouth pulled down to reveal jaws lined with glaring white teeth that almost looked like fangs. In one hand was a pistol that appeared to be the size of a blunderbuss, the kind of weapon referred to in seventeenth-century tales of adventure as a machine. He grabbed Andolini by the top of his shirt and the lapel of his sport-coat and threw him against the wall. The hoodlum's hip struck the glass case and it toppled over. Tower gave a cry of dismay to which neither of the two men paid the slightest attention.

Balazar's man tried to wriggle away to his left. The new one, the snarling man with his black hair tied back behind him, let him get going, then tripped him and went down on top of him, one knee on the hoodlum's chest. He shoved the muzzle of the blunderbuss, the machine, into the soft shelf under the hoodlum's chin. The hoodlum twisted his head, trying to get rid of it. The new one only dug it in deeper.

In a choked voice that made him sound like a cartoon duck, Balazar's torpedo said, 'Don't make me laugh, slick — that ain't no real gun.'

The new one — the one who had seemed to merge with his own shadow and become as tall as a giant — pulled his machine out from under the hoodlum's chin, cocked it with his thumb, and pointed it deep into the storage area. Tower opened his mouth to say something, God knew what, but before he could utter a word there was a deafening crash, the sound of a mortar shell going off five feet from some hapless GI's foxhole. Bright yellow flame shot from the machine's muzzle. A moment later, the barrel was back under the hoodlum's chin.

'What do you think now, Jack?' the new one panted. 'Still think it's a fake? Tell you what *I* think: the next time I pull this trigger, your brains are going all the way to Hoboken.'

8

Eddie saw fear in Jack Andolini's eyes, but no panic. This didn't surprise him. It had been Jack Andolini who'd collared him after the cocaine mule-delivery from Nassau had gone wrong. This version of him was younger – ten years younger – but no prettier. Andolini, once dubbed Old Double-Ugly by the great sage and eminent junkie Henry Dean, had a bulging caveman's forehead and a jutting Alley Oop jaw to match. His hands were so huge they looked like caricatures. Hair sprouted from the knuckles. He looked like Old Double-Stupid as well as Old Double-Ugly, but he was far from dumb. Dummies didn't work their way up to become the second-in-command to guys like Enrico Balazar. And while Jack might not be that yet in this when, he *would* be by 1986, when Eddie would come flying back into JFK with about two hundred thousand dollars' worth of Bolivian marching-powder under his shirt. In that world, that where and when, Andolini had become *Il Roche*'s field-marshal. In this one, Eddie thought there was a very good chance he was going to take early retirement. From *everything*. Unless, that was, he played it perfectly.

Eddie shoved the barrel of the pistol deeper under Andolini's chin. The smell of gas and gunpowder was strong in the air, for the time being over-whelming the smell of books. Somewhere in the shadows there was an angry hiss from Sergio, the bookstore cat. Sergio apparently didn't approve of loud noises in his domain.

Andolini winced and twisted his head to the left. 'Don't, man . . . that thing's hot!'

'Not as hot as where you'll be five minutes from now,' Eddie said. 'Unless you listen to me, Jack. Your chances of getting out of this are slim, but not quite none. Will you listen?'

'I don't know you. How do you know us?'

Eddie took the gun out from beneath Old Double-Ugly's chin and saw a red circle where the barrel of Roland's revolver had pressed. *Suppose I told you that it's your ka to meet me again, ten years from now? And to be eaten by lobstrosities? That they'll start with the feet inside your Gucci loafers and work their way up?* Andolini wouldn't believe him, of course, any more than he'd believed Roland's big old revolver would work until Eddie had demonstrated the truth. And along this track of possibility – on this level of the Tower – Andolini might *not* be eaten by lobstrosities. Because this world was different from all the others. This was Level Nineteen of the Dark Tower. Eddie felt it. Later he would ruminate on it, but not now. Now the very act of thinking was difficult. What he wanted right now was to kill both of these men, then head over to Brooklyn and tune up on the rest of Balazar's tet. Eddie tapped the barrel of the revolver against one of Andolini's jutting cheekbones. He had to restrain himself from really going to work on that ugly mug, and Andolini saw it. He blinked and wet his lips. Eddie's knee was still on his chest. Eddie could feel it going up and down like a bellows.

'You didn't answer my question,' Eddie said. 'What you did instead was ask a question of your own. The next time you do that, Jack, I'm going to use the barrel of this gun to break your face. Then I'll shoot out one of your kneecaps, turn you into a jackhopper for the rest of your life. I can shoot off a good many parts of you and still leave you able to talk. And don't play dumb with me. You're not dumb – except maybe in your choice of employer – and I know it. So let me ask you again: Will you listen to me?'

'What choice do I have?'

Moving with that same blurry, spooky speed, Eddie swept Roland's gun across Andolini's face. There was a sharp crack as his cheekbone snapped. Blood began to flow from his right nostril, which to Eddie looked about the size of the Queens Midtown Tunnel. Andolini cried out in pain, Tower in shock.

Eddie socked the muzzle of the pistol back into the soft place under Andolini's chin. Without looking away from him, Eddie said: 'Keep an eye on the other one, Mr Tower. If he starts to stir, you let me know.'

'Who *are* you?' Tower almost bleated.

'A friend. The only one you've got who can save your bacon. Now watch him and let me work.'

'A-All right.'

Eddie Dean turned his full attention back to Andolini. 'I laid George out because George is stupid. Even if he could carry the message I need carried, he wouldn't believe it. And how can a man convince others of what he doesn't believe himself?'

'Got a point there,' Andolini said. He was looking up at Eddie with a kind of horrified fascination, perhaps finally seeing this stranger with the gun for what he really was. For what Roland had known he was from the very beginning, even when Eddie Dean had been nothing but a wetnose junkie shivering his way through heroin withdrawal. Jack Andolini was seeing a gunslinger.

'You bet I do,' Eddie said. 'And here's the message I want you to carry: Tower's off-limits.'

Jack was shaking his head. 'You don't understand. Tower has something somebody wants. My boss agreed to get it. He promised. And my boss always—'

'Always keeps his promises, I know,' Eddie said. 'Only this time he won't be able to, and that's not going to be his fault. Because Mr Tower has decided not to sell his vacant lot up the street to the Sombra Corporation. He's going to sell it to the ... mmm ... to the Tet Corporation, instead. Got that?'

'Mister, I don't know you, but I know my boss. He won't stop.'

'He will. Because Tower won't have anything to sell. The lot will no longer be his. And now listen even more closely, Jack. Listen ka-me, not ka-mai.' Wisely, not foolishly.

Eddie leaned down. Jack stared up at him, fascinated by the bulging eyes — hazel irises, bloodshot whites — and the savagely grinning mouth which was now the distance of a kiss from his own.

'Mr Calvin Tower has come under the protection of people more powerful and more ruthless than you could ever imagine, Jack. People who make *Il Roche* look like a hippie flower-child at Woodstock. You have to convince him that he has nothing to gain by continuing to harass Calvin Tower, and everything to lose.'

'I can't—'

'As for you, know that the mark of Gilead is on this man. If you ever touch him again — if you ever even step foot in this shop again — I'll come to Brooklyn and kill your wife and children. Then I'll find your mother and father, and I'll kill them. Then I'll kill your mother's sisters and your father's brothers. Then I'll kill your grandparents, if they're still alive. You I'll save for last. Do you believe me?'

Jack Andolini went on staring into the face above him — the bloodshot eyes, the grinning, snarling mouth — but now with mounting horror. The fact was, he *did* believe. And whoever he was, he knew a great deal about Balazar and about this current deal. About the current deal, he might know more than Andolini knew himself.

'There's more of us,' Eddie said, 'and we're all about the same thing: protecting . . .'. He almost said *protecting the rose*. '. . . protecting Calvin Tower. We'll be watching this place, we'll be watching Tower, we'll be watching Tower's friends — guys like Deepneau.' Eddie saw Andolini's eyes flicker with surprise at that, and was satisfied. 'Anybody who comes here and even raises his voice to Tower, we'll kill their whole families and them last. That goes for George, for 'Cimi Dretto, Tricks Postino . . . for your brother Claudio, too.'

Andolini's eyes widened at each name, then winced momentarily shut at the name of his brother. Eddie thought that maybe he'd made his point. Whether or not Andolini could convince Balazar was another question. *But in a way it doesn't even matter,* he thought coldly. *Once Tower's sold us the lot, it doesn't really matter what they do to him, does it?*

'How do you know so *much*?' Andolini asked.

'That doesn't matter. Just pass on the message. Tell Balazar to tell his friends at Sombra that the lot is no longer for sale. Not to them, it isn't. And tell him that Tower is now under the protection of folk from Gilead who carry hard calibers.'

'Hard—?'

'I mean folk more dangerous than any Balazar has ever dealt with before,' Eddie said, '*including* the people from the Sombra Corporation. Tell him that if he persists, there'll be enough corpses in Brooklyn to fill Grand Army Plaza. And many of them will be women and children. Convince him.'

'I . . . man, I'll try.'

Eddie stood up, then backed up. Curled in the puddles of gasoline and the strews of broken glass, George Biondi was beginning to stir and mutter deep in his throat. Eddie gestured to Jack with the barrel of Roland's pistol, telling him to get up.

'You better try hard,' he said.

9

Tower poured them each a cup of black coffee, then couldn't drink his. His hands were shaking too badly. After watching him try a couple of times (and thinking about a bomb-disposal character in *UXB* who lost his nerve), Eddie took pity on him and poured half of Tower's coffee into his own cup.

'Try now,' he said, and pushed the half-cup back to the bookshop owner. Tower had his glasses on again, but one of the bows had been twisted and they sat crookedly on his face. Also, there was the crack running across the left lens like a lightning bolt. The two men were at the marble counter, Tower behind it, Eddie perched on one of the stools. Tower had carried the book Andolini had threatened to burn first out here with him, and put it down beside the coffee-maker. It was as if he couldn't bear to let it out of his sight.

Tower picked up the cup with his shaking hand (no rings on it, Eddie noticed – no rings on either hand) and drained it. Eddie couldn't understand why the man would choose to drink such so-so brew black. As far as Eddie himself was concerned, the really good taste was the Half and Half. After the months he had spent in Roland's world (or perhaps whole years had been sneaking by), it tasted as rich as heavy cream.

'Better?' Eddie asked.

'Yes.' Tower looked out the window, as if expecting the return of the gray Town Car that had jerked and swayed away just ten minutes before. Then he looked back at Eddie. He was still frightened of the young man, but the last of his outright terror had departed when Eddie stowed the huge pistol back inside what he called 'my friend's swag-bag.' The bag was made of a scuffed, no-color leather, and closed along the top with lacings rather than a zipper. To Calvin Tower, it seemed that the young man had stowed the more frightening aspects of his personality in the 'swag-bag' along with the oversized revolver. That was good, because it allowed Tower to believe that the kid had been bluffing about killing whole hoodlum families as well as the hoodlums themselves.

'Where's your pal Deepneau today?' Eddie asked.

'Oncologist. Two years ago, Aaron started seeing blood in the toilet bowl when he moved his bowels. A younger man, he thinks "Goddam hemorrhoids" and buys a tube of Preparation H. Once you're in your seventies, you assume the worst. In his case it was bad but not terrible. Cancer moves slower when you get to be his age; even the Big C gets old. Funny to think of, isn't it? Anyway, they baked it with radiation and they say it's gone, but Aaron says you don't turn your back on cancer. He goes back every three months, and that's where he is. I'm glad. He's an old *cockuh* but still a hothead.'

I should introduce Aaron Deepneau to Jamie Jaffords, Eddie thought. *They could play Castles instead of chess, and yarn away the days of the Goat Moon.*

Tower, meanwhile, was smiling sadly. He adjusted his glasses on his face. For a moment they stayed straight, and then they tilted again. The tilt was somehow worse than the crack; made Tower look slightly crazy as well as vulnerable. 'He's a hothead and I'm a coward. Perhaps that's why we're friends – we fit around each other's wrong places, make something that's almost whole.'

'Say maybe you're a little hard on yourself,' Eddie said.

'I don't think so. My analyst says that anyone who wants to know how the children of an A-male father and a B-female mother turn out would only have to study my case-history. He also says—'

'Cry your pardon, Calvin, but I don't give much of a shit about your analyst. You held onto the lot up the street, and that's good enough for me.'

'I don't take any credit for that,' Calvin Tower said morosely. 'It's like this' —he picked up the book that he'd put down beside the coffee-maker— 'and the other ones he threatened to burn. I just have a problem letting things go. When my first wife said she wanted a divorce and I asked why, she said, "Because when I married you, I didn't understand. I thought you were a man. It turns out you're a packrat."'

'The lot is different from the books,' Eddie said.

'Is it? Do you really think so?' Tower was looking at him, fascinated. When he raised his coffee cup, Eddie was pleased to see that the worst of his shakes had subsided.

'Don't you?'

'Sometimes I dream about it,' Tower said. 'I haven't actually been in there since Tommy Graham's deli went bust and I paid to have it knocked down. And to have the fence put up, of course, which was almost as expensive as the men with the wrecking ball. I dream there's a field of flowers in there. A field of roses. And instead of just to First Avenue, it goes on forever. Funny dream, huh?'

Eddie was sure that Calvin Tower did indeed have such dreams, but he thought he saw something else in the eyes hiding behind the cracked and tilted glasses. He thought Tower was letting this dream stand for all the dreams he would not tell.

'Funny,' Eddie agreed. 'I think you better pour me another slug of that mud, beg ya I do. We'll have us a little palaver.'

Tower smiled and once more raised the book Andolini had meant to charbroil. 'Palaver. It's the kind of thing they're always saying in here.'

'Do you say so?'

'Uh-huh.'

Eddie held out his hand. 'Let me see.'

At first Tower hesitated, and Eddie saw the bookshop owner's face briefly harden with a misery mix of emotions.

'Come on, Cal, I'm not gonna wipe my ass with it.'

'No. Of course not. I'm sorry.' And at that moment Tower *looked* sorry, the way an alcoholic might look after a particularly destructive bout of drunkenness. 'I just . . . certain books are very important to me. And this one is a true rarity.'

He passed it to Eddie, who looked at the plastic-protected cover and felt his heart stop.

'What?' Tower asked. He set his coffee cup down with a bang. 'What's wrong?'

Eddie didn't reply. The cover illustration showed a small rounded building like a Quonset hut, only made of wood and thatched with pine boughs. Standing off to one side was an Indian brave wearing buckskin pants. He was shirtless, holding a tomahawk to his chest. In the background, an old-fashioned steam locomotive was charging across the prairie, boiling gray smoke into a blue sky.

The title of this book was *The Dogan*. The author was Benjamin Slightman Jr.

From some great distance, Tower was asking him if he was going to faint. From only slightly closer by, Eddie said that he wasn't. Benjamin Slightman Jr. Ben Slightman the Younger, in other words. And—

He pushed Tower's pudgy hand away when it tried to take the book back. Then Eddie used his own finger to count the letters in the author's name. There were, of course, nineteen.

10

He swallowed another cup of Tower's coffee, this time without the Half and Half. Then he took the plastic-wrapped volume in hand once more.

'What makes it special?' he asked. 'I mean, it's special to me because I met someone recently whose name is the same as the name of the guy who wrote this. But—'

An idea struck Eddie, and he turned to the back flap, hoping for a picture of the author. What he found instead was a curt two-line author bio: 'BENJAMIN SLIGHTMAN JR is a rancher in Montana. This is his second novel.' Below this was a drawing of an eagle, and a slogan: BUY WAR BONDS!

'But why's it special to *you?* What makes it worth seventy-five hundred bucks?'

Tower's face kindled. Fifteen minutes before he had been in mortal terror for his life, but you'd never know it looking at him now, Eddie thought. Now he was in the grip of his obsession. Roland had his Dark Tower; this man had his rare books.

He held it so Eddie could see the cover. '*The Dogan,* right?'

'Right.'

Tower flipped the book open and pointed to the inner flap, also under plastic, where the story was summarized. 'And here?'

'"*The Dogan,*"' Eddie read. '"A thrilling tale of the old west and one Indian brave's heroic effort to survive." So?'

'Now look at *this!*' Tower said triumphantly, and turned to the title page. Here Eddie read:

The Hogan
Benjamin Slightman Jr.

'I don't get it,' Eddie said. 'What's the big deal?'

Tower rolled his eyes. 'Look again.'

'Why don't you just tell me what—'

'No, look again. I insist. The joy is in the discovery, Mr Dean. Any collector will tell you the same. Stamps, coins, or books, the joy is in the discovery.'

He flipped back to the cover again, and this time Eddie saw it. 'The title on the front's misprinted, isn't it? *Dogan* instead of *Hogan.*'

Tower nodded happily. 'A hogan is an Indian home of the type illustrated on the front. A dogan is . . . well, nothing. The misprinted cover makes the book somewhat valuable, but now . . . look at this . . .'

He turned to the copyright page and handed the book to Eddie. The copyright date was 1943, which of course explained the eagle and the slogan on the author-bio flap. The title of the book was given as *The Hogan*, so that seemed all right. Eddie was about to ask when he got it for himself.

'They left the "Jr." off the author's name, didn't they?'

'Yes! *Yes!*' Tower was almost hugging himself. 'As if the book had actually been written by the author's *father!* In fact, once when I was at a bibliographic convention in Philadelphia, I explained this book's particular situation to an attorney who gave a lecture on copyright law, and this guy said that Slightman Jr.'s father might actually be able to assert right of ownership over this book because of a simple typographical error! Amazing, don't you think?'

'Totally,' Eddie said, thinking *Slightman the Elder*. Thinking *Slightman the Younger*. Thinking about how Jake had become fast friends with the latter and wondering why this gave him such a bad feeling now, sitting here and drinking coffee in little old Calla New York.

At least he took the Ruger, Eddie thought.

'Are you telling me that's all it takes to make a book valuable?' he asked Tower. 'One misprint on the cover, a couple more inside, and all at once the thing's worth seventy-five hundred bucks?'

'Not at all,' Tower said, looking shocked. 'But Mr Slightman wrote three really excellent Western novels, all taking the Indians' point of view. *The Hogan* is the middle one. He became a big bug in Montana after the war — some job having to do with water and mineral rights — and then, here is the irony, a group of Indians killed him. Scalped him, actually. They were drinking outside a general store—'

A general store named Took's, Eddie thought. *I'd bet my watch and warrant on it.*

'—and apparently Mr Slightman said something they took objection to, and . . . well, there goes your ballgame.'

'Do all your really valuable books have similar stories?' Eddie asked. 'I mean, some sort of coincidence makes them valuable, and not just the stories themselves?'

Tower laughed. 'Young man, most people who collect rare books won't even open their purchases. Opening and closing a book damages the spine. Hence damaging the resale price.'

'Doesn't that strike you as slightly sick behavior?'

'Not at all,' Tower said, but a telltale red blush was climbing his cheeks. Part of him apparently took Eddie's point. 'If a customer spends eight thousand dollars for a signed first edition of Hardy's *Tess of the D'Urbervilles*, it makes perfect sense to put that book away in a safe place where it can be admired but not touched. If the fellow actually wants to read the story, let him buy a Vintage paperback.'

'You believe that,' Eddie said, fascinated. 'You actually believe that.'

'Well . . . yes. Books can be objects of great value. That value is created in different ways. Sometimes just the author's signature is enough to do it. Sometimes – as in this case – it's a misprint. Sometimes it's a first print-run – a first edition – that's extremely small. And does any of this have to do with why you came here, Mr Dean? Is it what you wanted to . . . to palaver about?'

'No, I suppose not.' But what exactly *had* he wanted to palaver about? He'd known – it had all been perfectly clear to him as he'd herded Andolini and Biondi out of the back room, then stood in the doorway watching them stagger to the Town Car, supporting each other. Even in cynical, mind-your-own-business New York, they had drawn plenty of looks. Both of them had been bleeding, and both had had the same stunned *What the hell HAPPENED to me?* look in their eyes. Yes, then it had been clear. The book – and the name of the author – had muddied up his thinking again. He took it from Tower and set it facedown on the counter so he wouldn't have to look at it. Then he went to work regathering his thoughts.

'The first and most important thing, Mr Tower, is that you have to get out of New York until July fifteenth. Because they'll be back. Probably not those guys specifically, but some of the other guys Balazar uses. And they'll be more eager than ever to teach you and me a lesson. Balazar's a despot.' This was a word Eddie had learned from Susannah – she had used it to describe the Tick-Tock Man. 'His way of doing business is to always escalate. You slap him, he slaps back twice as hard. Punch him in the nose, he breaks your jaw. You toss a grenade, he tosses a bomb.'

Tower groaned. It was a theatrical sound (although probably not meant that way), and under other circumstances, Eddie might have laughed. Not under these. Besides, everything he'd wanted to say to Tower was coming back to him. He could do this dicker, by God. He *would* do this dicker.

'Me they probably won't be able to get at. I've got business elsewhere.

Over the hills and far away, may ya say so. Your job is to make sure they won't be able to get at you, either.'

'But surely . . . after what you just did . . . and even if they didn't believe you about the women and children . . .' Tower's eyes, wide behind his crooked spectacles, begged Eddie to say that he had really *not* been serious about creating enough corpses to fill Grand Army Plaza. Eddie couldn't help him there.

'Cal, listen. Guys like Balazar don't believe or disbelieve. What they do is test the limits. Did I scare Big Nose? No, just knocked him out. Did I scare Jack? Yes. And it'll stick, because Jack's got a little bit of imagination. Will Balazar be impressed that I scared Ugly Jack? Yes . . . but just enough to be cautious.'

Eddie leaned over the counter, looking at Tower earnestly.

'I don't want to kill kids, okay? Let's get that straight. In . . . well, in another place, let's leave it at that, in another place me and my friends are going to put our lives on the line to *save* kids. But they're *human* kids. People like Jack and Tricks Postino and Balazar himself, they're animals. Wolves on two legs. And do wolves raise human beings? No, they raise more wolves. Do male wolves mate with human women? No, they mate with female wolves. So if I had to go in there – and I would if I had to – I'd tell myself I was cleaning out a pack of wolves, right down to the smallest cub. No more than that. And no less.'

'My God he means it,' Tower said. He spoke low, and all in a breath, and to the thin air.

'I absolutely do, but it's neither here nor there,' Eddie said. 'The point is, they'll come after you. Not to kill you, but to turn you around in their direction again. If you stay here, Cal, I think you can look forward to a serious maiming at the very least. Is there a place you can go until the fifteenth of next month? Do you have enough money? I don't have any, but I guess I could get some.'

In his mind, Eddie was already in Brooklyn. Balazar guardian-angeled a poker game in the back room of Bernie's Barber Shop, everybody knew that. The game might not be going on during a weekday, but there'd be some-body back there with cash. Enough to—

'Aaron has some money,' Tower was saying reluctantly. 'He's offered a good many times. I've always told him no. He's also always telling me I need to go on a vacation. I think by this he means I should get away from the fellows you just turned out. He is curious about what they want, but he doesn't ask. A hothead, but a *gentleman* hothead.' Tower smiled briefly.

'Perhaps Aaron and I could go on a vacation together, young sir. After all, we might not get another chance.'

Eddie was pretty sure the chemo and radiation treatments were going to keep Aaron Deepneau up and on his feet for at least another four years, but this was probably not the time to say so. He looked toward the door of The Manhattan Restaurant of the Mind and saw the other door. Beyond it was the mouth of the cave. Sitting there like a comic-strip yogi, just a cross-legged silhouette, was the gunslinger. Eddie wondered how long he'd been gone over there, how long Roland had been listening to the muffled but still maddening sound of the todash chimes.

'Would Atlantic City be far enough, do you think?' Tower asked timidly.

Eddie Dean almost shuddered at the thought. He had a brief vision of two plump sheep – getting on in years, yes, but still quite tasty – wandering into not just a pack of wolves but a whole city of them.

'Not there,' Eddie said. 'Anyplace but there.'

'What about Maine or New Hampshire? Perhaps we could rent a cottage on a lake somewhere until the fifteenth of July.'

Eddie nodded. He was a city boy. It was hard for him to imagine the bad guys way up in northern New England, wearing those checkered caps and down vests as they chomped their pepper sandwiches and drank their Ruffino. 'That'd be better,' he said. 'And while you're there, you might see if you could find a lawyer.'

Tower burst out laughing. Eddie looked at him, head cocked, smiling a little himself. It was always good to make folks laugh, but it was better when you knew what the fuck they were laughing *at*.

'I'm sorry,' Tower said after a moment or two. 'It's just that Aaron *was* a lawyer. His sister and two brothers, all younger, are *still* lawyers. They like to boast that they have the most unique legal letterhead in New York, perhaps in the entire United States. It reads simply "DEEPNEAU."'

'That speeds things up,' Eddie said. 'I want you to have Mr Deepneau draw up a contract while you're vacationing in New England—'

'*Hiding* in New England,' Tower said. He suddenly looked morose. '*Holed up* in New England.'

'Call it whatcha wanna,' Eddie said, 'but get that paper drawn up. You're going to sell that lot to me and my friends. To the Tet Corporation. You're just gonna get a buck to start with, but I can almost guarantee you that in the end you'll get fair market value.'

He had more to say, lots, but stopped there. When he'd held his hand out for the book, *The Dogan* or *The Hogan* or whatever it was, an expression of miserly reluctance had come over Tower's face. What made the look unpleasant was the undercurrent of stupidity in it . . . and not very far under, either. *Oh God, he's gonna fight me on this. After everything that's happened, he's still gonna fight me on it. And why? Because he really* is *a packrat.*

'You can trust me, Cal,' he said, knowing trust was not exactly the issue. 'I set my watch and warrant on it. Hear me, now. Hear me, I beg.'

'I don't know you from Adam. You walk in off the street—'

'—and save your life, don't forget that part.'

Tower's face grew set and stubborn. 'They weren't going to kill me. You said that yourself.'

'They *were* gonna burn your favorite books. Your most valuable ones.'

'Not my *most* valuable. Also, that might have been a bluff.'

Eddie took a deep breath and let it out, hoping his suddenly strong desire to lean across the counter and sink his fingers into Tower's fat throat would depart or at least subside. He reminded himself that if Tower *hadn't* been stubborn, he probably would have sold the lot to Sombra long before now. The rose would have been plowed under. And the Dark Tower? Eddie had an idea that when the rose died, the Dark Tower would simply fall like the one in Babel when God had gotten tired of it and wiggled His finger. No waiting around another hundred or thousand years for the machinery running the Beams to quit. Just ashes, ashes, we all fall down. And then? Hail the Crimson King, lord of todash darkness.

'Cal, if you sell me and my friends your vacant lot, you're off the hook. Not only that, but you'll eventually have enough money to run your little shop for the rest of your life.' He had a sudden thought. 'Hey, do you know a company called Holmes Dental?'

Tower smiled. 'Who doesn't? I use their floss. *And* their toothpaste. I tried the mouthwash, but it's too strong. Why do you ask?'

'Because Odetta Holmes is my wife. I may look like Froggy the Gremlin, but in truth I'm Prince Fuckin Charming.'

Tower was quiet for a long time. Eddie curbed his impatience and let the man think. At last Tower said, 'You think I'm being foolish. That I'm being Silas Marner, or worse, Ebenezer Scrooge.'

Eddie didn't knew who Silas Marner was but he took Tower's point from the context of the discussion. 'Let's put it this way,' he said. 'After what you've just been through, you're too smart not to know where your best interests lie.'

'I feel obligated to tell you that this isn't just mindless miserliness on my part; there's an element of caution, as well. I know that piece of New York is valuable, *any* piece of Manhattan is, but it's not just that. I have a safe out back. There's something in it. Something perhaps even more valuable than my copy of *Ulysses*.'

'Then why isn't it in your safe-deposit box?'

'Because it's supposed to be here,' Tower said. 'It's *always* been here. Perhaps waiting for you, or someone like you. Once, Mr Dean, my family owned almost all of Turtle Bay, and . . . well, wait. Will you wait?'

'Yes,' Eddie said.

What choice?

11

When Tower was gone, Eddie got off the stool and went to the door only he could see. He looked through it. Dimly, he could hear chimes. More clearly he could hear his mother. 'Why don't you get out of there?' she called dolorously. 'You'll only make things worse, Eddie – you always do.'

That's my Ma, he thought, and called the gunslinger's name.

Roland pulled one of the bullets from his ear. Eddie noted the oddly clumsy way he handled it – almost pawing at it, as if his fingers were stiff – but there was no time to think about it now.

'Are you all right?' Eddie called.

'Do fine. And you?'

'Yeah, but . . . Roland, can you come through? I might need a little help.'

Roland considered, then shook his head. 'The box might close if I did. Probably *would* close. Then the door would close. And we'd be trapped on that side.'

'Can't you prop the damn thing open with a stone or a bone or something?'

'No,' Roland said. 'It wouldn't work. The ball is powerful.'

And it's working on you, Eddie thought. Roland's face looked haggard, the way it had when the lobstrosities' poison had been inside him.

'All right,' he said.

'Be as quick as you can.'

'I will.'

12

When he turned around, Tower was looking at him quizzically. 'Who were you talking to?'

Eddie stood aside and pointed at the doorway. 'Do you see anything there, sai?'

Calvin Tower looked, started to shake his head, then looked longer. 'A shimmer,' he said at last. 'Like hot air over an incinerator. Who's there? *What's* there?'

'For the time being, let's say nobody. What have you got in your hand?'

Tower held it up. It was an envelope, very old. Written on it in copperplate were the words *Stefan Toren* and *Dead Letter*. Below, carefully drawn in ancient ink, were the same symbols that were on the door and the box: ⌇⌇⌇⌇. *Now we might be getting somewhere*, Eddie thought.

'Once this envelope held the will of my great-great-great-grandfather,' Calvin Tower said. 'It was dated March nineteenth, 1846. Now there's nothing but a single piece of paper with a name written upon it. If you can tell me what that name is, young man, I'll do as you ask.'

And so, Eddie mused, *it comes down to another riddle*. Only this time it wasn't four lives that hung upon the answer, but all of existence.

Thank God it's an easy one, he thought.

'It's Deschain,' Eddie said. 'The first name will be either Roland, the name of my dinh, or Steven, the name of his father.'

All the blood seemed to fall out of Calvin Tower's face. Eddie had no idea how the man was able to keep his feet. 'My dear God in heaven,' he said.

With trembling fingers, he removed an ancient and brittle piece of paper from the envelope, a time traveler that had voyaged over a hundred and thirty-one years to this where and when. It was folded. Tower opened it and put it on the counter, where they could both read the words Stefan Toren had written in the same firm copperplate hand:

Roland Deschain, of Gilead
The line of ELD
GUNSLINGER

13

There was more talk, about fifteen minutes' worth, and Eddie supposed at least some of it was important, but the real deal had gone down when he'd told Tower the name his three-times-great-grandfather had written on a slip of paper fourteen years before the Civil War got rolling.

What Eddie had discovered about Tower during their palaver was dismaying. He harbored some respect for the man (for *any* man who could hold out for more than twenty seconds against Balazar's goons), but didn't like him much. There was a kind of willful stupidity about him. Eddie thought it was self-created and maybe propped up by his analyst, who would tell him about how he had to take care of himself, how he had to be the captain of his own ship, the author of his own destiny, respect his own desires, all that blah-blah. All the little code words and terms that meant it was all right to be a selfish fuck. That it was noble, even. When Tower told Eddie that Aaron Deepneau was his only friend, Eddie wasn't surprised. What surprised him was that Tower had any friends at all. Such a man could never be ka-tet, and it made Eddie uneasy to know that their destinies were so tightly bound together.

You'll just have to trust to ka. It's what ka's for, isn't it?

Sure it was, but Eddie didn't have to like it.

14

Eddie asked if Tower had a ring with *Ex Liveris* on it. Tower looked puzzled, then laughed and told Eddie he must mean *Ex Libris*. He rummaged on one of his shelves, found a book, showed Eddie the plate in front. Eddie nodded.

'No,' Tower said. 'But it'd be just the thing for a guy like me, wouldn't it?' He looked at Eddie keenly. 'Why do you ask?'

But Tower's future responsibility to save a man now exploring the hidden highways of multiple Americas was a subject Eddie didn't feel like getting into right now. He'd come as close to blowing the guy's mind as he wanted to, and he had to get back through the unfound door before Black Thirteen wore Roland away to a frazzle.

'Never mind. But if you see one, you ought to pick it up. One more thing and then I'm gone.'

'What's that?'

'I want your promise that as soon as *I* leave, *you'll* leave.'

Tower once more grew shifty. It was the side of him Eddie knew he could come to outright loathe, given time. 'Why . . . to tell you the truth, I don't know if I can do that. Early evenings are often a very busy time for me . . . people are much more prone to browse once the workday's over . . . and Mr Brice is coming in to look at a first of *The Troubled Air*, Irwin Shaw's novel about radio and the McCarthy era . . . I'll have to at least skim through my appointment calendar, and . . .'

He droned on, actually gathering steam as he descended toward trivialities.

Eddie said, very mildly: 'Do you like your balls, Calvin? Are you maybe as attached to them as they are to you?'

Tower, who'd been wondering about who would feed Sergio if he just pulled up stakes and ran, now stopped and looked at him, puzzled, as if he had never heard this simple one-syllable word before.

Eddie nodded helpfully. 'Your nuts. Your sack. Your stones. Your *cojones*. The old sperm-firm. Your *testicles*.'

'I don't see what—'

Eddie's coffee was gone. He poured some Half and Half into the cup and drank that, instead. It was very tasty. 'I told you that if you stayed here, you could look forward to a serious maiming. That's what I meant. That's probably where they'll start, with your balls. To teach you a lesson. As to when it happens, what that mostly depends on is traffic.'

'Traffic.' Tower said it with a complete lack of vocal expression.

'That's right,' Eddie said, sipping his Half and Half as if it were a thimble of brandy. 'Basically how long it takes Jack Andolini to drive back out to Brooklyn and then how long it takes Balazar to load up some old beater of a van or panel truck with guys to come back here. I'm hoping Jack's too dazed to just phone. Did you think Balazar'd wait until tomorrow? Convene a little brain-trust of guys like Kevin Blake and 'Cimi Dretto to discuss the matter?' Eddie raised first one finger and then two. The dust of another world was beneath the nails. 'First, they *got* no brains; second, Balazar doesn't trust em.

'What he'll do, Cal, is what any successful despot does: he'll react right away, quick as a flash. The rush-hour traffic will hold em up a little, but if you're still here at six, half past at the latest, you can say goodbye to your balls. They'll hack them off with a knife, then cauterize the wound with one of those little torches, those Bernz-O-Matics—'

'Stop,' Tower said. Now instead of white, he'd gone green. Especially around the gills. 'I'll go to a hotel down in the Village. There are a couple of cheap ones that cater to writers and artists down on their luck, ugly rooms but not that bad. I'll call Aaron, and we'll go north tomorrow morning.'

'Fine, but first you have to pick a town to go to,' Eddie said. 'Because I or one of my friends may need to get in touch with you.'

'How am I supposed to do that? I don't know any towns in New England north of Westport, Connecticut!'

'Make some calls once you get to the hotel in the Village,' Eddie said. 'You pick the town, and then tomorrow morning, before you leave New York, send your pal Aaron up to your vacant lot. Have him write the zip code on the board fence.' An unpleasant thought struck Eddie. 'You *have* zip codes, don't you? I mean, they've been invented, right?'

Tower looked at him as if he were crazy. 'Of course they have.'

''Kay. Have him put it on the Forty-sixth street side, all the way down where the fence ends. Have you got that?'

'Yes, but—'

'They probably won't have your bookshop staked out tomorrow morning – they'll assume you got smart and blew – but if they do, they won't have the lot staked out, and if they have the lot staked out, it'll be the Second Avenue side. And if they have the Forty-sixth Street side staked out, they'll be looking for you, not him.'

Tower was smiling a little bit in spite of himself. Eddie relaxed and smiled back. 'But . . .? If they're also looking for Aaron?'

'Have him wear the sort of clothes he doesn't usually wear. If he's a blue jeans man, have him wear a suit. If he's a suit man—'

'Have him wear blue jeans.'

'Correct. And sunglasses wouldn't be a bad idea, assuming the day isn't cloudy enough to make them look odd. Have him use a black felt-tip. Tell him it doesn't have to be artistic. He just walks to the fence, as if to read one of the posters. Then he writes the numbers and off he goes. And tell him for Christ's sake don't fuck up.'

'And how are you going to find us once you get to Zip Code Whatever?'

Eddie thought of Took's, and their palaver with the *folken* as they sat in the big porch rockers. Letting anyone who wanted to have a look and ask a question.

'Go to the local general store. Have a little conversation, tell anyone who's interested that you're in town to write a book or paint pictures of the lobster-pots. I'll find you.'

'All right,' Tower said. 'It's a good plan. You do this well, young man.'

I was made for it, Eddie thought but didn't say. What he said was, 'I have to be going. I've stayed too long as it is.'

'There's one thing you have to help me do before you go,' Tower said, and explained.

Eddie's eyes widened. When Tower had finished — it didn't take long — Eddie burst out, 'Aw, you're *shittin!*'

Tower tipped his head toward the door to his shop, where he could see that faint shimmer. It made the passing pedestrians on Second Avenue look like momentary mirages. 'There's a door there. You as much as said so, and I believe you. I can't see it, but I can see *something*.'

'You're insane,' Eddie said. 'Totally gonzo.' He didn't mean it — not precisely — but less than ever he liked having his fate so firmly woven into the fate of a man who'd make such a request. Such a *demand*.

'Maybe I am and maybe I'm not,' Tower said. He folded his arms over his broad but flabby chest. His voice was soft but the look in his eyes was adamant. 'In either case, this is my condition for doing all that you say. For falling in with *your* madness, in other words.'

'Aw, Cal, for God's sake! God and the Man Jesus! I'm only asking you to do what Stefan Toren's will *told* you to do.'

The eyes did not soften or cut aside as they did when Tower was waffling or preparing to fib. If anything, they grew stonier yet. 'Stefan Toren's dead and I'm not. I've told you my condition for doing what you want. The only question is whether or not—'

'Yeah, *yeah, YEAH!*' Eddie cried, and drank off the rest of the white stuff in his cup. Then he picked up the carton and drained that, for good measure. It looked like he was going to need the strength. 'Come on,' he said. 'Let's do it.'

15

Roland could see into the bookshop, but it was like looking at things on the bottom of a fast-running stream. He wished Eddie would hurry. Even with the bullets buried deep in his ears he could hear the todash chimes, and nothing blocked the terrible smells: now hot metal, now rancid bacon, now ancient melting cheese, now burning onions. His eyes were watering, which probably accounted for at least some of the wavery look of things seen beyond the door.

Far worse than the sound of the chimes or the smells was the way the ball was insinuating itself into his already compromised joints, filling them up with what felt like splinters of broken glass. So far he'd gotten nothing but a few twinges in his good left hand, but he had no illusions; the pain there and everywhere else would continue to increase for as long as the box was open and Black Thirteen shone out unshielded. Some of the pain from the dry twist might go away once the ball was hidden again, but Roland didn't think all of it would. And this might only be the beginning.

As if to congratulate him on his intuition, a baleful flare of pain settled into his right hip and began to throb there. To Roland it felt like a bag filled with warm liquid lead. He began to massage it with his right hand . . . as if *that* would do any good.

'Roland!' The voice was bubbly and distant – like the things he could see beyond the door, it seemed to be underwater – but it was unmistakably Eddie's. Roland looked up from his hip and saw that Eddie and Tower had carried some sort of case over to the unfound door. It appeared to be filled with books. 'Roland, can you help us?'

The pain had settled so deeply into his hips and knees that Roland wasn't even sure he could get up . . . but he did it, and fluidly. He didn't know how much of his condition Eddie's sharp eyes might have already seen, but Roland didn't want them to see any more. Not, at least, until their adventures in Calla Bryn Sturgis were over.

'When we push it, you pull!'

Roland nodded his understanding, and the bookcase slid forward. There was one strange and vertiginous moment when the half in the cave was firm and clear and the half still back in The Manhattan Bookstore of the Mind shimmered unsteadily. Then Roland took hold of it and pulled it through. It juddered and squalled across the floor of the cave, pushing aside little piles of pebbles and bones.

As soon as it was out of the doorway, the lid of the ghostwood box began to close. So did the door itself.

'No, you don't,' Roland murmured. 'No, you don't, you bastard.' He slipped the remaining two fingers of his right hand into the narrowing space beneath the lid of the box. The door stopped moving and remained ajar when he did. And enough was enough. Now even his *teeth* were buzzing. Eddie was having some last little bit of palaver with Tower, but Roland no longer cared if they were the secrets of the universe.

'Eddie!' he roared. 'Eddie, to me!'

And, thankfully, Eddie grabbed his swag-bag and came. The moment he was through the door, Roland closed the box. The unfound door shut a second later with a flat and undramatic clap. The chimes ceased. So did the jumble of poison pain pouring into Roland's joints. The relief was so tremendous that he cried out. Then, for the next ten seconds or so, all he could do was lower his chin to his chest, close his eyes, and struggle not to sob.

'Say thankya,' he managed at last. 'Eddie, say thankya.'

'Don't mention it. Let's get out of this cave, what do you think?'

'I think yes,' Roland said. 'Gods, yes.'

16

'Didn't like him much, did you?' Roland asked.

Ten minutes had passed since Eddie's return. They had moved a little distance down from the cave, then stopped where the path twisted through a small rocky inlet. The roaring gale that had tossed back their hair and plastered their clothes against their bodies was here reduced to occasional prankish gusts. Roland was grateful for them. He hoped they would excuse the slow and clumsy way he was building his smoke. Yet he felt Eddie's eyes upon him, and the young man from Brooklyn — who had once been almost as dull and unaware as Andolini and Biondi — now saw much.

'Tower, you mean.'

Roland tipped him a sardonic glance. 'Of whom else would I speak? The cat?'

Eddie gave a brief grunt of acknowledgment, almost a laugh. He kept pulling in long breaths of the clean air. It was good to be back. Going to New York in the flesh had been better than going todash in one way — that sense of lurking darkness had been gone, and the accompanying sense of *thinness* — but God, the place *stank*. Mostly it was cars and exhaust (the oily clouds of diesel were the worst), but there were a thousand other bad smells, too. Not the least of them was the aroma of too many human bodies, their essential polecat odor not hidden at all by the perfumes and sprays the *folken* put on themselves. Were they unconscious of how bad they smelled, all huddled up together as they were? Eddie supposed they must be. Had been himself, once upon a time. Once upon a time he couldn't wait to get back to New York, would have killed to get there.

'Eddie? Come back from Nis!' Roland snapped his fingers in front of Eddie Dean's face.

'I'm sorry,' he said. 'As for Tower . . . no, I didn't like him much. God, sending his *books* through like that! Making his lousy first editions part of his condition for helping to save the fucking universe!'

'He doesn't think of it in those terms . . . unless he does so in his dreams. And you know they'll burn his shop when they get there and find him gone. Almost surely. Pour gasoline under the door and light it. Break his window and toss in a grenado, either manufactured or homemade. Do you mean to tell me that never occurred to you?'

Of course it had. 'Well, maybe.'

It was Roland's turn to utter the humorous grunting sound. 'Not much *may* in that *be*. So he saved his best books. And now, in Doorway Cave, we have something to hide the Pere's treasure behind. Although I suppose it must be counted our treasure now.'

'His courage didn't strike me as real courage,' Eddie said. 'It was more like greed.'

'Not all are called to the way of the sword or the gun or the ship,' Roland said, 'but all serve ka.'

'Really? Does the Crimson King? Or the low men and women Callahan talked about?'

Roland didn't reply.

Eddie said, 'He may do well. Tower, I mean. Not the cat.'

'Very amusing,' Roland said dryly. He scratched a match on the seat of his pants, cupped the flame, lit his smoke.

'Thank you, Roland. You're growing in that respect. Ask me if I think Tower and Deepneau can get out of New York City clean.'

'Do you?'

'No, I think they'll leave a trail. *We* could follow it, but I'm hoping Balazar's men won't be able to. The one I worry about is Jack Andolini. He's creepy-smart. As for Balazar, he made a contract with this Sombra Corporation.'

'Took the king's salt.'

'Yeah, I guess somewhere up the line he did,' Eddie said. He had heard King instead of king, as in Crimson King. 'Balazar knows that when you make a contract, you have to fill it or have a damned good reason why not. Fail and word gets out. Stories start to circulate about how so-and-so's going soft, losing his shit. They've still got three weeks to find Tower and force him to sell the lot to Sombra. They'll use it. Balazar's not the FBI, but he *is* a connected guy, and . . . Roland, the worst thing about Tower is that in some ways, none of this is real to him. It's like he's mistaken his life for a life in one of his storybooks. He thinks things have *got* to turn out all right because the writer's under contract.'

'You think he'll be careless.'

Eddie voiced a rather wild laugh. 'Oh, I *know* he'll be careless. The question is whether or not Balazar will catch him at it.'

'We're going to have to monitor Mr Tower. Mind him for safety's sake. That's what you think, isn't it?'

'Yer-bugger!' Eddie said, and after a moment's silent consideration, both of them burst out laughing. When the fit had passed, Eddie said: 'I think we ought to send Callahan, if he'll go. You probably think I'm crazy, but—'

'Not at all,' Roland said. 'He's one of us . . . or *could* be. I felt that from the first. And he's used to traveling in strange places. I'll put it to him today. Tomorrow I'll come up here with him and see him through the doorway—'

'Let me do it,' Eddie said. 'Once was enough for you. At least for awhile.'

Roland eyed him carefully, then pitched his cigarette over the drop. 'Why do you say so, Eddie?'

'Your hair's gotten whiter up around here.' Eddie patted the crown of his own head. 'Also, you're walking a little stiff. It's better now, but I'd guess the old rheumatiz kicked in on you a little. Fess up.'

'All right, I fess,' Roland said. If Eddie thought it was no more than old Mr Rheumatiz, that was not so bad.

'Actually, I could bring him up tonight, long enough to get the zip code,' Eddie said. 'It'll be day again over there, I bet.'

'None of us is coming up this path in the dark. Not if we can help it.'

Eddie looked down the steep incline to where the fallen boulder jutted out, turning fifteen feet of their course into a tightrope-walk. 'Point taken.'

Roland started to get up. Eddie reached out and took his arm. 'Stay a couple of minutes longer, Roland. Do ya.'

Roland sat down again, looking at him.

Eddie took a deep breath, let it out. 'Ben Slightman's dirty,' he said. 'He's the tattletale. I'm almost sure of it.'

'Yes, I know.'

Eddie looked at him, wide-eyed. 'You *know*? How could you possibly—'

'Let's say I suspected.'

'*How?*'

'His spectacles,' Roland said. 'Ben Slightman the Elder's the only person in Calla Bryn Sturgis with spectacles. Come on, Eddie, day's waiting. We can talk as we walk.'

17

They couldn't, though, not at first, because the path was too steep and narrow. But later, as they approached the bottom of the mesa, it grew wider and more forgiving. Talk once more became practical, and Eddie told Roland about the book, *The Dogan* or *The Hogan*, and the author's oddly disputable name. He recounted the oddity of the copyright page (not entirely sure that Roland grasped this part), and said it had made him wonder if something was pointing toward the son, too. That seemed like a crazy idea, but—

'I think that if Benny Slightman was helping his father inform on us,' Roland said, 'Jake would know.'

'Are you sure he doesn't?' Eddie asked.

This gave Roland some pause. Then he shook his head. 'Jake suspects the father.'

'He told you that?'

'He didn't have to.'

They had almost reached the horses, who raised their heads alertly and seemed glad to see them.

'He's out there at the Rocking B,' Eddie said. 'Maybe we ought to take a ride out there. Invent some reason to bring him back to the Pere's . . .' He trailed off, looking at Roland closely. 'No?'

'No.'

'Why not?'

'Because this is Jake's part of it.'

'That's hard, Roland. He and Benny Slightman like each other. A lot.

If Jake ends up being the one to show the Calla what his Dad's been doing—'

'Jake will do what he needs to do,' Roland said. 'So will we all.'

'But he's still just a boy, Roland. Don't you see that?'

'He won't be for much longer,' Roland said, and mounted up. He hoped Eddie didn't see the momentary wince of pain that cramped his face when he swung his right leg over the saddle, but of course Eddie did.

CHAPTER III

THE DOGAN, PART 2

1

Jake and Benny Slightman spent the morning of that same day moving hay bales from the upper lofts of the Rocking B's three inner barns to the lower lofts, then breaking them open. The afternoon was for swimming and water-fighting in the Whye, which was still pleasant enough if one avoided the deep pools; those had grown cold with the season.

In between these two activities they ate a huge lunch in the bunkhouse with half a dozen of the hands (not Slightman the Elder; he was off at Telford's Buckhead Ranch, working a stock-trade). 'I en't seen that boy of Ben's work s'hard in my life,' Cookie said as he put fried chops down on the table and the boys dug in eagerly. 'You'll wear him plumb out, Jake.'

That was Jake's intention, of course. After haying in the morning, swimming in the afternoon, and a dozen or more barn-jumps for each of them by the red light of evening, he thought Benny would sleep like the dead. The problem was he might do the same himself. When he went out to wash at the pump — sunset come and gone by then, leaving ashes of roses deepening to true dark — he took Oy with him. He splashed his face clean and flicked drops of water for the animal to catch, which he did with great alacrity. Then Jake dropped to one knee and gently took hold of the sides of the billy-bumbler's face. 'Listen to me, Oy.'

'Oy!'

'I'm going to go to sleep, but when the moon rises, I want you to wake me up. Quietly, do 'ee ken?'

'Ken!' Which might mean something or nothing. If someone had been taking wagers on it, Jake would have bet on something. He had great faith in Oy. Or maybe it was love. Or maybe those things were the same.

476

'When the moon rises. Say moon, Oy.'

'Moon!'

Sounded good, but Jake would set his own internal alarm clock to wake him up at moonrise. Because he wanted to go out to where he'd seen Benny's Da' and Andy that other time. That queer meeting worried at his mind more rather than less as time went by. He didn't want to believe Benny's Da' was involved with the Wolves – Andy, either – but he had to make sure. Because it was what Roland would do. For that reason if no other.

2

The two boys lay in Benny's room. There was one bed, which Benny had of course offered to his guest, but Jake had refused it. What they'd come up with instead was a system by which Benny took the bed on what he called 'even-hand' nights, and Jake took it on 'odd-hand' nights. This was Jake's night for the floor, and he was glad. Benny's goosedown-filled mattress was far too soft. In light of his plan to rise with the moon, the floor was probably better. Safer.

Benny lay with his hands behind his head, looking up at the ceiling. He had coaxed Oy up onto the bed with him and the bumbler lay sleeping in a curled comma, his nose beneath his cartoon squiggle of a tail.

'Jake?' A whisper. 'You asleep?'

'No.'

'Me neither.' A pause. 'It's been great, having you here.'

'It's been great for me,' Jake said, and meant it.

'Sometimes being the only kid gets lonely.'

'Don't I know it . . . and I was *always* the only one.' Jake paused. 'Bet you were sad after your sissa died.'

'Sometimes I'm still sad.' At least he said it in a matter-of-fact tone, which made it easier to hear. 'Reckon you'll stay after you beat the Wolves?'

'Probably not long.'

'You're on a quest, aren't you?'

'I guess so.'

'For what?'

The quest was to save the Dark Tower in this where and the rose in the New York where he and Eddie and Susannah had come from, but Jake did not want to say this to Benny, much as he liked him. The Tower and the rose were kind of secret things. The ka-tet's business. But neither did he want to lie.

'Roland doesn't talk about stuff much,' he said.

A longer pause. The sound of Benny shifting, doing it quietly so as not to disturb Oy. 'He scares me a little, your dinh.'

Jake thought about that, then said: 'He scares me a little, too.'

'He scares my Pa.'

Jake was suddenly very alert. 'Really?'

'Yes. He says it wouldn't surprise him if, after you got rid of the Wolves, you turned on us. Then he said he was just joking, but that the old cowboy with the hard face scared him. I reckon that must have been your dinh, don't you?'

'Yeah,' Jake said.

Jake had begun thinking Benny had gone to sleep when the other boy asked, 'What was your room like back where you came from?'

Jake thought of his room and at first found it surprisingly hard to picture. It had been a long time since he'd thought of it. And now that he did, he was embarrassed to describe it too closely to Benny. His friend lived well indeed by Calla standards – Jake guessed there were very few smallhold kids Benny's age with their own rooms – but he would think a room such as Jake could describe that of an enchanted prince. The television? The stereo, with all his records, and the headphones for privacy? His posters of Stevie Wonder and The Jackson Five? His microscope, which showed him things too small to see with the naked eye? Was he supposed to tell this boy about such wonders and miracles?

'It was like this, only I had a desk,' Jake said at last.

'A *writing* desk?' Benny got up on one elbow.

'Well *yeah*,' Jake said, the tone implying *Sheesh, what else?*

'Paper? Pens? Quill pens?'

'Paper,' Jake agreed. Here, at least, was a wonder Benny could understand. 'And pens. But not quill. Ball.'

'Ball pens? I don't understand.'

So Jake began to explain, but halfway through he heard a snore. He looked across the room and saw Benny still facing him, but now with his eyes closed.

Oy opened *his* eyes – they were bright in the darkness – then winked at Jake. After that, he appeared to go back to sleep.

Jake looked at Benny for a long time, deeply troubled in ways he did not precisely understand . . . or want to.

At last, he went to sleep himself.

3

Some dark, dreamless time later, he came back to a semblance of wakefulness because of pressure on his wrist. Something pulling there. Almost painful. Teeth. Oy's.

'Oy, no, quittit,' he mumbled, but Oy would not stop. He had Jake's wrist in his jaws and continued to shake it gently from side to side, stopping occasionally to administer a brisk tug. He only quit when Jake finally sat up and stared dopily out into the silver-flooded night.

'Moon,' Oy said. He was sitting on the floor beside Jake, jaws open in an unmistakable grin, eyes bright. They *should* have been bright; a tiny white stone burned deep down in each one. '*Moon!*'

'Yeah,' Jake whispered, and then closed his fingers around Oy's muzzle. 'Hush!' He let go and looked over at Benny, who was now facing the wall and snoring deeply. Jake doubted if a howitzer shell would wake him.

'Moon,' Oy said, much more quietly. Now he was looking out the window. 'Moon, moon. Moon.'

4

Jake would have ridden bareback, but he needed Oy with him, and that made bareback difficult, maybe impossible. Luckily, the little border-pony sai Overholser had loaned him was as tame as a tabby-cat, and there was a scuffy old practice saddle in the barn's tackroom that even a kid could handle with ease.

Jake saddled the horse, then tied his bedroll behind, to the part Calla cowboys called the boat. He could feel the weight of the Ruger inside the roll – and, if he squeezed, the shape of it, as well. The duster with the commodious pocket in the front was hanging on a nail in the tackroom. Jake took it, whipped it into something like a fat belt, and cinched it around his middle. Kids in his school had sometimes worn their outer shirts that way on warm days. Like those of his room, this memory seemed far away, part of a circus parade that had marched through town . . . and then left.

That life was richer, a voice deep in his mind whispered.

This one is truer, whispered another, even deeper.

He believed that second voice, but his heart was still heavy with sadness and worry as he led the border-pony out through the back of the barn and away from the house. Oy padded along at his heel, occasionally looking up at the sky and muttering 'Moon, moon,' but mostly sniffing the crisscrossing scents on the ground. This trip was dangerous. Just crossing Devar-Tete Whye — going from the Calla side of things to the Thunderclap side — was dangerous, and Jake knew it. Yet what really troubled him was the sense of looming heartache. He thought of Benny, saying it had been great to have Jake at the Rocking B to chum around with. He wondered if Benny would feel the same way a week from now.

'Doesn't matter,' he sighed. 'It's ka.'

'Ka,' Oy said, then looked up. 'Moon. Ka, moon. Moon, ka.'

'Shut up,' Jake said, not unkindly.

'Shut up ka,' Oy said amiably. 'Shut up moon. Shut up Ake. Shut up Oy.' It was the most he'd said in months, and once it was out he fell silent. Jake walked his horse another ten minutes, past the bunkhouse and its mixed music of snores, grunts, and farts, then over the next hill. At that point, with the East Road in sight, he judged it safe to ride. He unrolled the duster, put it on, then deposited Oy in the pouch and mounted up.

5

He was pretty sure he could go right to the place where Andy and Slightman had crossed the river, but reckoned he'd only have one good shot at this, and Roland would've said pretty sure wasn't good enough in such a case. So he went back to the place where he and Benny had tented instead, and from there to the jut of granite which had reminded him of a partially buried ship. Once again Oy stood panting into his ear. Jake had no problem sighting on the round rock with the shiny surface. The dead log that had washed up against it was still there, too, because the river hadn't done anything but fall over the last weeks. There had been no rain whatever, and this was something Jake was counting on to help him.

He scrambled back up to the flat place where he and Benny had tented out. Here he'd left his pony tethered to a bush. He led it down to the river, then scooped up Oy and rode across. The pony wasn't big, but the water still didn't come up much higher than his fetlocks. In less than a minute, they were on the far bank.

It looked the same on this side, but wasn't. Jake knew it right away. Moonlight or no moonlight, it was darker somehow. Not exactly the way todash–New York had been dark, and there were no chimes, but there was a similarity, just the same. A sense of something waiting, and eyes that could turn in his direction if he was foolish enough to alert their owners to his presence. He had come to the edge of End-World. Jake's flesh broke out in goosebumps and he shivered. Oy looked up at him.

'S'all right,' Jake whispered. 'Just had to get it out of my system.'

He dismounted, put Oy down, and stowed the duster in the shadow of the round rock. He didn't think he'd need a coat for this part of his excursion; he was sweating, nervous. The babble of the river was loud, and he kept shooting glances across to the other side, wanting to make sure no one was coming. He didn't want to be surprised. That sense of presence, of *others*, was both strong and unpleasant. There was nothing good about what lived on this side of the Devar-Tete Whye; of that much Jake was sure. He felt better when he'd taken the docker's clutch out of the bedroll, cinched it in place, and then added the Ruger. The Ruger made him into a different person, one he didn't always like. But here, on the far side of the Whye, he was delighted to feel gunweight against his ribs, and delighted to be that person; that *gunslinger*.

Something farther off to the east screamed like a woman in life-ending agony. Jake knew it was only a rock-cat – he'd heard them before, when he'd been at the river with Benny, either fishing or swimming – but he still put his hand on the butt of the Ruger until it stopped. Oy had assumed the bowing position, front paws apart, head lowered, rump pointed skyward. Usually this meant he wanted to play, but there was nothing playful about his bared teeth.

'S'okay,' Jake said. He rummaged in his bedroll again (he hadn't bothered to bring a saddlebag) until he found a red-checked cloth. This was Slightman the Elder's neckerchief, stolen four days previous from beneath the bunkhouse table, where the foreman had dropped it during a game of Watch Me and then forgotten it.

Quite the little thief I am, Jake thought. *My Dad's gun, now Benny's Dad's snotrag. I can't tell if I'm working my way up or down.*

It was Roland's voice that replied. *You're doing what you were called here to do. Why don't you stop beating your breast and get started?*

Jake held the neckerchief between his hands and looked down at Oy. 'This always works in the movies,' he said to the bumbler. 'I have no idea if it works in real life . . . especially after weeks have gone by.' He lowered the neckerchief to Oy, who stretched out his long neck and sniffed it delicately. 'Find this smell, Oy. Find it and follow it.'

'Oy!' But he just sat there, looking up at Jake.

'This, Dumbo,' Jake said, letting him smell it again. 'Find it! Go on!'

Oy got up, turned around twice, then began to saunter north along the bank of the river. He lowered his nose occasionally to the rocky ground, but seemed a lot more interested in the occasional dying-woman howl of the rock-cat. Jake watched his friend with steadily diminishing hope. Well, he'd seen which way Slightman had gone. He could go in that direction himself, course around a little, see what there was to see.

Oy turned around, came back toward Jake, then stopped. He sniffed a patch of ground more closely. The place where Slightman had come out of the water? It could have been. Oy made a thoughtful *hoof*ing sound far back in his throat and then turned to his right – east. He slipped sinuously between two rocks. Jake, now feeling at least a tickle of hope, mounted up and followed.

6

They hadn't gone far before Jake realized Oy was following an actual path that wound through the hilly, rocky, arid land on this side of the river. He began to see signs of technology: a cast-off, rusty electrical coil, something that looked like an ancient circuit-board poking out of the sand, tiny shards and shatters of glass. In the black moonlight-created shadow of a large boulder, he spied what looked like a whole bottle. He dismounted, picked it up, poured out God knew how many decades (or centuries) of accumulated sand, and looked at it. Written on the side in raised letters was a word he recognized: Nozz-A-La.

'The drink of finer bumhugs everywhere,' Jake murmured, and put the bottle down again. Beside it was a crumpled-up cigarette pack. He smoothed it out, revealing a picture of a red-lipped woman wearing a jaunty red hat. She was holding a cigarette between two glamorously long fingers. PARTI appeared to be the brand name.

Oy, meanwhile, was standing ten or twelve yards farther along and looking back at him over one low shoulder.

'Okay,' Jake said. 'I'm coming.'

Other paths joined the one they were on, and Jake realized this was a continuation of the East Road. He could see only a few scattered boot-prints and smaller, deeper footprints. These were in places guarded by high rocks — wayside coves the prevailing winds didn't often reach. He guessed the bootprints were Slightman's, the deep footprints Andy's. There were no others. But there *would* be, and not many days from now, either. The prints of the Wolves' gray horses, coming out of the east. They would also be deep prints, Jake reckoned. Deep like Andy's.

Up ahead, the path breasted the top of a hill. On either side were fantas-tically misshapen organ-pipe cactuses with great thick barrel arms that seemed to point every which way. Oy was standing there, looking down at something, and once more seeming to grin. As Jake approached him, he could smell the cactus-plants. The odor was bitter and tangy. It reminded him of his father's martinis.

He sat astride his pony beside Oy, looking down. At the bottom of the hill on the right was a shattered concrete driveway. A sliding gate had been frozen half-open ages ago, probably long before the Wolves started raiding the borderland Callas for children. Beyond it was a building with a curved metal roof. Small windows lined the side Jake could see, and his heart lifted at the sight of the steady white glow that came through them. Not 'seners, and not lightbulbs, either (what Roland called 'sparklights'). Only fluores-cents threw that kind of white light. In his New York life, fluorescent lights made him think mostly of unhappy, boring things: giant stores where every-thing was always on sale and you could never find what you wanted, sleepy afternoons at school when the teacher droned on and on about the trade routes of ancient China or the mineral deposits of Peru and rain poured endlessly down outside and it seemed the Closing Bell would never ring, doctor's offices where you always wound up sitting on a tissue-covered exam table in your underpants, cold and embarrassed and somehow positive that you would be getting a shot.

Tonight, though, those lights cheered him up.

'Good boy!' he told the bumbler.

Instead of responding as he usually did, by repeating his name, Oy looked past Jake and commenced a low growl. At the same moment the pony shifted and gave a nervous whinny. Jake reined him, realizing that bitter (but not entirely unpleasant) smell of gin and juniper had gotten stronger. He looked around and saw two spiny barrels of the cactus-tangle on his right swiveling slowly and blindly toward him. There was a faint grinding sound, and dribbles of white sap were running down the cactus's central barrel. The needles on the arms swinging toward Jake looked long and wicked in the moonlight. The thing had smelled him, and it was hungry.

'Come on,' he told Oy, and booted the pony's sides lightly. The pony needed no further urging. It hurried downhill, not quite trotting, toward the building with the fluorescent lights. Oy gave the moving cactus a final mistrustful look, then followed them.

7

Jake reached the driveway and stopped. About fifty yards farther down the road (it was now very definitely a road, or had been once upon a time), train-tracks crossed and then ran on toward the Devar-Tete Whye, where a low bridge took them across. The *folken* called that bridge 'the causeway.' The older *folken*, Callahan had told them, called it the *devil's* causeway.

'The trains that bring the roont ones back from Thunderclap come on those tracks,' he murmured to Oy. And did he feel the tug of the Beam? Jake was sure he did. He had an idea that when they left Calla Bryn Sturgis — *if* they left Calla Bryn Sturgis — it would be along those tracks.

He stood where he was a moment longer, feet out of the stirrups, then headed the pony up the crumbling driveway toward the building. To Jake it looked like a Quonset hut on a military base. Oy, with his short legs, was having hard going on the broken-up surface. That busted-up paving would be dangerous for his horse, too. Once the frozen gate was behind them, he dismounted and looked for a place to tether his mount. There were bushes close by, but something told him they were *too* close. Too visible. He led the pony out onto the hardpan, stopped, and looked around at Oy. 'Stay!'

'Stay! Oy! Ake!'

Jake found more bushes behind a pile of boulders like a strew of huge and eroded toy blocks. Here he felt satisified enough to tether the pony. Once it was done, he stroked the long, velvety muzzle. 'Not long,' he said. 'Can you be good?'

The pony blew through his nose and appeared to nod. Which meant exactly nothing, Jake knew. And it was probably a needless precaution, anyway. Still, better safe than sorry. He went back to the driveway and bent to scoop the bumbler up. As soon as he straightened, a row of brilliant lights flashed on, pinning him like a bug on a microscope stage. Holding Oy in the curve of one arm, Jake raised the other to shield his eyes. Oy whined and blinked.

There was no warning shout, no stern request for identification, only the faint snuffle of the breeze. The lights were turned on by motion-sensors, Jake guessed. What came next? Machine-gun fire directed by dipolar computers? A scurry of small but deadly robots like those Roland, Eddie, and Susannah had dispatched in the clearing where the Beam they were following had begun? Maybe a big net dropping from overhead, like in this jungle movie he'd seen once on TV?

Jake looked up. There was no net. No machine-guns, either. He started walking forward again, picking his way around the deepest of the potholes and jumping over a washout. Beyond this latter, the driveway was tilted and cracked but mostly whole. 'You can get down now,' he told Oy. 'Boy, you're heavy. Watch out or I'll have to stick you in Weight Watchers.'

He looked straight ahead, squinting and shielding his eyes from the fierce glare. The lights were in a row running just beneath the Quonset's curved roof. They threw his shadow out behind him, long and black. He saw rock-cat corpses, two on his left and two more on his right. Three of them were little more than skeletons. The fourth was in a high state of decomposition, but Jake could see a hole that looked too big for a bullet. He thought it had been made by a bah-bolt. The idea was comforting. No weapons of super-science at work here. Still, he was crazy not to be hightailing it back toward the river and the Calla beyond it. Wasn't he?

'Crazy,' he said.

'Razy,' Oy said, once more padding along at Jake's heel.

A minute later they reached the door of the hut. Above it, on a rusting steel plate, was this:

NORTH CENTRAL POSITRONICS, LTD.
Northeast Corridor
Arc Quadrant

OUTPOST 16

Medium Security
VERBAL ENTRY CODE REQUIRED

On the door itself, now hanging crooked by only two screws, was another sign. A joke? Some sort of nickname? Jake thought it might be a little of both. The letters were choked with rust and eroded by God knew how many years of blowing sand and grit, but he could still read them:

WELCOME TO THE DOGAN

8

Jake expected the door to be locked and wasn't disappointed. The lever handle moved up and down only the tiniest bit. He guessed that when it had been new, there'd been no give in it at all. To the left of the door was a rusty steel panel with a button and a speaker grille. Beneath it was the word **VERBAL.** Jake reached for the button, and suddenly the lights lining the top of the building went out, leaving him in what at first seemed like utter darkness. *They're on a timer,* he thought, waiting for his eyes to adjust. *A pretty short one. Or maybe they're just getting tired, like everything else the Old People left behind.*

His eyes readapted to the moonlight and he could see the entry-box again. He had a pretty good idea of what the verbal entry code must be. He pushed the button.

'WELCOME TO ARC QUADRANT OUTPOST 16,' said a voice. Jake jumped back, stifling a cry. He had expected a voice, but not one so eerily like that of Blaine the Mono. He almost expected it to drop into a John Wayne drawl and call him little trailhand. 'THIS IS A MEDIUM SECURITY OUTPOST. PLEASE GIVE THE VERBAL ENTRY CODE. YOU HAVE TEN SECONDS. NINE ... EIGHT ...'

'Nineteen,' Jake said.

'INCORRECT ENTRY CODE. YOU MAY RETRY ONCE. FIVE
... FOUR ... THREE ...'

'Ninety-nine,' Jake said.

'THANK YOU.'

The door clicked open.

9

Jake and Oy walked into a room that reminded him of the vast control-
area Roland had carried him through beneath the city of Lud, as they had
followed the steel ball which had guided them to Blaine's cradle. This room
was smaller, of course, but many of the dials and panels looked the same.
There were chairs at some of the consoles, the kind that would roll along
the floor so that the people who worked here could move from place to
place without getting to their feet. There was a steady sigh of fresh air, but
Jake could hear occasional rough rattling sounds from the machinery driving
it. And while three-quarters of the panels were lighted, he could see a good
many that were dark. Old and tired: he had been right about that. In one
corner was a grinning skeleton in the remains of a brown khaki uniform.

On one side of the room was a bank of TV monitors. They reminded
Jake a little bit of his father's study at home, although his father had had
only three screens – one for each network – and here there were ... he
counted. Thirty. Three of them were fuzzy, showing pictures he couldn't
really make out. Two were rolling rapidly up and up, as if the vertical hold
had fritzed out. Four were entirely dark. The other twenty-one were
projecting pictures, and Jake looked at these with growing wonder. Half a
dozen showed various expanses of desert, including the hilltop guarded by
the two misshapen cactuses. Two more showed the outpost – the Dogan –
from behind and from the driveway side. Under these were three screens
showing the Dogan's interior. One showed a room that looked like a galley
or kitchen. The second showed a small bunkhouse that looked equipped to
sleep eight (in one of the bunks, an upper, Jake spied another skeleton).
The third inside-the-Dogan screen presented this room, from a high angle.
Jake could see himself and Oy. There was a screen with a stretch of the
railroad tracks on it, and one showing the Little Whye from this side, moon-

struck and beautiful. On the far right was the causeway with the train-tracks crossing it.

It was the images on the other eight operating screens that astounded Jake. One showed Took's General Store, now dark and deserted, closed up till daylight. One showed the Pavilion. Two showed the Calla high street. Another showed Our Lady of Serenity Church, and one showed the living room of the rectory . . . *inside* the rectory! Jake could actually see the Pere's cat, Snugglebutt, lying asleep on the hearth. The other two showed angles of what Jake assumed was the Manni village (he had not been there).

Where in hell's name are the cameras? Jake wondered. *How come nobody sees them?*

Because they were too small, he supposed. And because they'd been hidden. *Smile, you're on Candid Camera.*

But the church . . . the rectory . . . those were buildings that hadn't even *existed* in the Calla until a few years previous. And *inside? Inside* the rectory? Who had put a camera there, and when?

Jake didn't know when, but he had a terrible idea that he knew who. Thank God they'd done most of their palavering on the porch, or outside on the lawn. But still, how much must the Wolves — or their masters — know? How much had the infernal machines of this place, the infernal *fucking* machines of this place, recorded?

And transmitted?

Jake felt pain in his hands and realized they were tightly clenched, the nails biting into his palms. He opened them with an effort. He kept expecting the voice from the speaker-grille — the voice so much like Blaine's — to challenge him, ask him what he was doing here. But it was mostly silent in this room of not-quite-ruin; no sounds but the low hum of the equipment and the occasionally raspy whoosh of the air-exchangers. He looked over his shoulder at the door and saw it had closed behind him on a pneumatic hinge. He wasn't worried about that; from this side it would probably open easily. If it didn't, good old ninety-nine would get him out again. He remembered introducing himself to the *folken* that first night in the Pavilion, a night that already seemed a long time ago. *I am Jake Chambers, son of Elmer, the Line of Eld,* he had told them. *The ka-tet of the Ninety and Nine.* Why had he said that? He didn't know. All he knew was that things kept showing up again. In school, Ms Avery had read them a poem called 'The Second Coming,' by William Butler Yeats. There had been something in it about a hawk's turning and turning in a widening gyre, which was — according to Ms Avery — a kind of circle. But here things were in a spiral, not a circle.

For the Ka-Tet of Nineteen (or of the Ninety and Nine, Jake had an idea they were really the same), things were tightening up even as the world around them grew old, grew loose, shut down, shed pieces of itself. It was like being in the cyclone which had carried Dorothy off to the Land of Oz, where witches were real and bumhugs ruled. To Jake's heart it made perfect sense that they should be seeing the same things over and over, and more and more often, because—

Movement on one of the screens caught his eye. He looked at it and saw Benny's Da' and Andy the Messenger Robot coming over the hilltop guarded by the cactus sentries. As he watched, the spiny barrel arms swung inward to block the road – and, perhaps, impale the prey. Andy, however, had no reason to fear cactus spines. He swung an arm and broke one of the barrels off halfway down its length. It fell into the dust, spurting white goo. Maybe it wasn't sap at all, Jake thought. Maybe it was blood. In any case, the cactus on the other side swiveled away in a hurry. Andy and Ben Slightman stopped for a moment, perhaps to discuss this. The screen's resolution wasn't clear enough to show if the human's mouth was moving or not.

Jake was seized by an awful, throat-closing panic. His body suddenly seemed too heavy, as if it were being tugged by the gravity of a giant planet like Jupiter or Saturn. He couldn't breathe; his chest lay perfectly flat. *This is what Goldilocks would have felt like*, he thought in a faint and distant way, *if she had awakened in the little bed that was just right to hear the Three Bears coming back in downstairs.* He hadn't eaten the porridge, he hadn't broken Baby Bear's chair, but he now knew too many secrets. They boiled down to *one* secret. One monstrous secret.

Now they were coming down the road. Coming to the Dogan.

Oy was looking up at him anxiously, his long neck stretched to the max, but Jake could barely see him. Black flowers were blooming in front of his eyes. Soon he would faint. They would find him stretched out here on the floor. Oy might try to protect him, but if Andy didn't take care of the bumbler, Ben Slightman would. There were four dead rock-cats out there and Benny's Da' had dispatched at least one of them with his trusty bah. One small barking billy-bumbler would be no problem for him.

Would you be so cowardly, then? Roland asked inside his head. *But why would they kill such a coward as you? Why would they not just send you west with the broken ones who have forgotten the faces of their fathers?*

That brought him back. Most of the way, at least. He took a huge breath, yanking in air until the bottoms of his lungs hurt. He let it out in an explosive whoosh. Then he slapped himself across the face, good and hard.

'*Ake!*' Oy cried in a reproving — almost shocked — voice.

'S'okay,' Jake said. He looked at the monitors showing the galley and the bunkroom and decided on the latter. There was nothing to hide behind or under in the galley. There might be a closet, but what if there wasn't? He'd be screwed.

'Oy, to me,' he said, and crossed the humming room beneath the bright white lights.

10

The bunkroom held the ghostly aroma of ancient spices: cinnamon and clove. Jake wondered — in a distracted, back-of-the-mind way — if the tombs beneath the Pyramids had smelled this way when the first explorers had broken into them. From the upper bunk in the corner, the reclining skeleton grinned at him, as if in welcome. *Feel like a nap, little trailhand? I'm taking a long one!* Its ribcage shimmered with silky overlays of spiderweb, and Jake wondered in that same distracted way how many generations of spider-babies had been born in that empty cavity. On another pillow lay a jawbone, prodding a ghostly, ghastly memory from the back of the boy's mind. Once, in a world where he had died, the gunslinger had found a bone like that. And used it.

The forefront of his mind pounded with two cold questions and one even colder resolve. The questions were how long it would take them to get here and whether or not they would discover his pony. If Slightman had been riding a horse of his own, Jake was sure the amiable little pony would have whinnied a greeting already. Luckily, Slightman was on foot, as he had been last time. Jake would have come on foot himself, had he known his goal was less than a mile east of the river. Of course, when he'd snuck away from the Rocking B, he hadn't even been sure that he *had* a goal.

The resolve was to kill both the tin-man and the flesh-and-blood man if he was discovered. If he could, that was. Andy might be tough, but those bulging blue-glass eyes looked like a weak point. If he could blind him—

There'll be water if God wills it, said the gunslinger who now always lived in his head, for good and ill. *Your job now is to hide if you can. Where?*

Not in the bunks. All of them were visible in the monitor covering this room and there was no way he could impersonate a skeleton. Under one of the two bunk-stacks at the rear? Risky, but it would serve . . . unless . . .

Jake spied another door. He sprang forward, depressed the lever-handle, and pulled the door open. It was a closet, and closets made fine hiding places, but this one was filled with jumbles of dusty electronic equipment, top to bottom. Some of it fell out.

'Beans!' he whispered in a low, urgent voice. He picked up what had fallen, tossed it high and low, then shut the closet door again. Okay, it would have to be under one of the beds—

'WELCOME TO ARC QUADRANT OUTPOST 16,' boomed the recorded voice. Jake flinched, and saw another door, this one to his left and standing partway open. Try the door or squeeze under one of the two tiers of bunks at the rear of the room? He had time to try one bolt-hole or the other, but not both. 'THIS IS A MEDIUM SECURITY OUTPOST.'

Jake went for the door, and it was just as well he went when he did, because Slightman didn't let the recording finish its spiel. 'Ninety-nine,' came his voice from the loudspeakers, and the recording thanked him.

It was another closet, this one empty except for two or three moldering shirts in one corner and a dust-caked poncho slumped on a hook. The air was almost as dusty as the poncho, and Oy uttered three fast, delicate sneezes as he padded in.

Jake dropped to one knee and put an arm around Oy's slender neck. 'No more of that unless you want to get us both killed,' he said. 'You be quiet, Oy.'

'Kiyit Oy,' the bumbler whispered back, and winked. Jake reached up and pulled the door back to within two inches of shut, as it had been before. He hoped.

11

He could hear them quite clearly – *too* clearly. Jake realized there were mikes and speakers all over this place. The idea did nothing for his peace of mind. Because if he and Oy could hear *them* . . .

It was the cactuses they were talking about, or rather that Slightman was talking about. He called them boom-flurry, and wanted to know what had gotten them all fashed.

'Almost certainly more rock-cats, sai,' Andy said in his complacent, slightly prissy voice. Eddie said Andy reminded him of a robot named C3PO in *Star Wars*, a movie to which Jake had been looking forward. He had missed it by less than a month. 'It's their mating season, you know.'

'Piss on that,' Slightman said. 'Are you telling me boom-flurry don't know rock-cats from something they can actually catch and eat? Someone's been out here, I tell you. And not long since.'

A cold thought slipped into Jake's mind: had the floor of the Dogan been dusty? He'd been too busy gawking at the control panels and TV monitors to notice. If he and Oy had left tracks, those two might have noticed already. They might only be pretending to have a conversation about the cactuses while they actually crept toward the bunkroom door.

Jake took the Ruger out of the docker's clutch and held it in his right hand with his thumb on the safety.

'A guilty conscience doth make cowards of us all,' Andy said in his complacent, just-thought-you'd-like-to-know voice. 'That's my free adaptation of a—'

'Shut up, you bag of bolts and wires,' Slightman snarled. 'I—' Then he screamed. Jake felt Oy stiffen against him, felt his fur begin to rise. The bumbler started to growl. Jake slipped a hand around his snout.

'Let go!' Slightman cried out. 'Let go of me!'

'Of course, sai Slightman,' Andy said, now sounding solicitous. 'I only pressed a small nerve in your elbow, you know. There would be no lasting damage unless I applied at least twenty foot-pounds of pressure.'

'Why in the hell would you do that?' Slightman sounded injured, almost whiny. 'En't I doing all you could want, and more? En't I risking my life for my boy?'

'Not to mention a few little extras,' Andy said silkily. 'Your spectacles . . . the music machine you keep deep down in your saddlebag . . . and, of course—'

'You know why I'm doing it and what'd happen to me if I was found out,' Slightman said. The whine had gone out of his voice. Now he sounded dignified and a little weary. Jake listened to that tone with growing dismay. If he got out of this and had to squeal on Benny's Da', he wanted to squeal on a villain. 'Yar, I've taken a few little extras, you say true, I say thankya. Glasses, so I can see better to betray the people I've known all my life. A music machine so I won't have to hear the conscience you prate about so easy and can get to sleep at night. Then you pinch something in my arm that makes me feel like my by-Riza eyes are going to fall right out of my by-Riza *head*.'

'I allow it from the rest of them,' Andy said, and now his voice had changed. Jake once more thought of Blaine, and once more his dismay grew. What if Tian Jaffords heard *this* voice? What if Vaughn Eisenhart heard it? Overholser? The rest of the *folken*? 'They heap contumely on my head like hot coals and never do I raise a word o' protest, let alone a hand. "Go here, Andy. Go there, Andy. Stop yer foolish singing, Andy. Stuff yer prattle. Don't tell us of the future, because we don't want to hear it." So I don't, except of the Wolves, because they'd hear what makes em sad and I'd tell em, yes I would; to me each tear's a drop of gold. "You're nobbut a stupid pile of lights n wires," they say. "Tell us the weather, sing the babby to sleep, then get t'hell out o' here." And I allow it. Foolish Andy am I, every child's toy and always fair game for a tongue-whipping. But I won't take a tongue-whipping from *you*, sai. You hope to have a future in the Calla after the Wolves are done with it for another few years, don't you?'

'You know I do,' Slightman said, so low Jake could barely hear him. 'And I deserve it.'

'You and your son, both say thankya, passing your days in the Calla, both say commala! And that can happen, but it depends on more than the death of the outworlders. *It depends on my silence*. If you want it, I demand respect.'

'That's absurd,' Slightman said after a brief pause. From his place in the closet, Jake agreed wholeheartedly. A robot demanding respect *was* absurd. But so was a giant bear patrolling an empty forest, a Morlock thug trying to unravel the secrets of dipolar computers, or a train that lived only to hear and solve new riddles. 'And besides, hear me I beg, how can I respect you when I don't even respect myself?'

There was a mechanical click in response to this, very loud. Jake had heard Blaine make a similar sound when he – or it – had felt the absurd closing in, threatening to fry his logic circuits. Then Andy said: 'No answer, nineteen. Connect and report, sai Slightman. Let's have done with this.'

'All right.'

There were thirty or forty seconds' worth of keyboard-clatter, then a high, warbling whistle that made Jake wince and Oy whine far back in his throat. Jake had never heard a sound quite like it; he was from the New York of 1977, and the word *modem* would have meant nothing to him.

The shriek cut off abruptly. There was a moment's silence. Then: 'THIS IS ALGUL SIENTO. FINLI O' TEGO HERE. PLEASE GIVE YOUR PASSWORD. YOU HAVE TEN SEC—'

'Saturday,' Slightman replied, and Jake frowned. Had he ever heard that happy weekend word on this side? He didn't think so.

'THANK YOU. ALGUL SIENTO ACKNOWLEDGES. WE ARE ONLINE.' There was another brief, shrieking whistle. Then: 'REPORT, SATURDAY.'

Slightman told of watching Roland and 'the younger one' going up to the Cave of the Voices, where there was now some sort of door, very likely conjured by the Manni. He said he'd used the far-seer and thus gotten a very good look—

'Telescope,' Andy said. He had reverted to his slightly prissy, complacent voice. 'Such are called telescopes.'

'Would *you* care to make my report, Andy?' Slightman inquired with cold sarcasm.

'Cry pardon,' Andy said in a long-suffering voice. 'Cry pardon, cry pardon, go on, go on, as ye will.'

There was a pause. Jake could imagine Slightman glaring at the robot, the glare robbed of its ferocity by the way the foreman would have to crane his neck in order to deliver it. Finally he went on.

'They left their horses below and walked up. They carried a pink sack which they passed from hand to hand, as if 'twere heavy. Whatever was in it had square edges; I could make that out through the telescope far-seer. May I offer two guesses?'

'YES.'

'First, they might have been putting two or three of the Pere's most valuable books in safekeeping. If that's the case, a Wolf should be sent to destroy them after the main mission's accomplished.'

'WHY?' The voice was perfectly cold. Not a human being's voice, Jake was sure of that. The sound of it made him feel weak and afraid.

'Why, as an example, do it please ya,' Slightman said, as if this should have been obvious. 'As an example to the priest!'

'CALLAHAN WILL VERY SOON BE BEYOND EXAMPLES,' the voice said. 'WHAT IS YOUR OTHER GUESS?'

When Slightman spoke again, he sounded shaken. Jake hoped the traitor son of a bitch *was* shaken. He was protecting his son, sure, his only son, but why he thought that gave him the right—

'It may have been maps,' Slightman said. 'I've thought long and long that a man who has books is apt to have maps. He may have given em maps of the Eastern Regions leading into Thunderclap – they haven't been shy about saying that's where they plan to head next. If it is maps they took up there, much good may they do em, even if they live. Next year north'll be east, and likely the year after it'll swap places with south.'

In the dusty darkness of the closet Jake could suddenly see Andy watching Slightman make his report. Andy's blue electric eyes were flashing. Slightman didn't know – no one in the Calla knew – but that rapid flashing was the way DNF-44821-V-63 expressed humor. He was, in fact, laughing at Slightman.

Because he knows better, Jake thought. *Because he knows what's really in that bag. Bet a box of cookies that he does.*

Could he be so sure of that? Was it possible to use the touch on a robot?

If it can think, the gunslinger in his head spoke up, *then you can touch it.*

Well . . . maybe.

'Whatever it was, it's a damn good indication they really do plan to take the kids into the arroyos,' Slightman was saying. 'Not that they'd put em in *that* cave.'

'No, no, not *that* cave,' Andy said, and although his voice was as prissy-serious as ever, Jake could imagine his blue eyes flashing even faster. Almost stuttering, in fact. 'Too many voices in *that* cave, they'd scare the children! Yer-bugger!'

DNF-44821-V-63, Messenger Robot. *Messenger!* You could accuse Slightman of treachery, but how could anyone accuse Andy of it? What he did, what he *was*, had been stamped on his chest for the whole world to see. There it had been, in front of all of them. Gods!

Benny's Da', meanwhile, was plodding stolidly on with his report to Finli o' Tego, who was in some place called Algul Siento.

'The mine he showed us on the map the Taverys drew is the Gloria, and the Gloria en't but a mile off from the Cave of the Voices. But the bastard's trig. Can I give another guess?'

'YES.'

'The arroyo that leads to the Gloria Mine splits off to the south about a quarter-mile in. There's another old mine at the end of the spur. The Redbird Two, it's called. Their dinh is telling folks he means to put the kids in the Gloria, and I think he'll tell em the same at the meeting he's going to call later this week, the one where he asks leave to stand against the Wolves. But I b'lieve that when the time comes, he'll stick em in the Redbird instead. He'll have the Sisters of Oriza standing guard — in front and up above, as well — and ye'd do well not to underestimate those ladies.'

'HOW MANY?'

'I think five, if he puts Sarey Adams among em. Plus some men with bahs. He'll have the brownie throwing with em, kennit, and I hear she's good. Maybe best of all. But one way or the other, we know where the kids are going to be. Putting them in such a place is a mistake, but he don't know it. He's dangerous, but grown old in his thinking. Probably such a strategy has worked for him before.'

And it had, of course. In Eyebolt Canyon, against Latigo's men.

'The important thing now is finding out where he and the boy and the younger man are going to be when the Wolves come. He may tell at the meeting. If he don't, he may tell Eisenhart afterward.'

'OR OVERHOLSER?'

'No. Eisenhart will stand with him. Overholser won't.'

'YOU MUST FIND OUT WHERE THEY'LL BE.'

'I know,' Slightman said. 'We'll find out, Andy and I, and then make one more trip to this unblessed place. After that, I swear by the Lady Oriza and the Man Jesus, I've done my part. Now can we get out of here?'

'In a moment, sai,' Andy said. 'I have my own report to make, you know.'

There was another of those long, whistling shrieks. Jake ground his teeth and waited for it to be over, and finally it was. Finli o' Tego signed off.

'Are we done?' Slightman asked.

'Unless you have some reason to linger, I believe we are,' Andy said.

'Does anything in here seem different to you?' Slightman asked suddenly, and Jake felt his blood turn cold.

'No,' Andy said, 'but I have great respect for human intuition. Are you having intuition, sai?'

There was a pause that seemed to go on for at least a full minute, although Jake knew it must have been much shorter than that. He held Oy's head against his thigh and waited.

'No,' Slightman said at last. 'Guess I'm just getting jumpy, now that it's close. God, I wish it was over! I hate this!'

'You're doing the right thing, sai.' Jake didn't know about Slightman, but Andy's plummily sympathetic tone made him feel like gnashing his teeth.

'The *only* thing, really. 'Tisn't your fault that you're father to the only mate-less twin in Calla Bryn Sturgis, is it? I know a song that makes this point in particularly moving fashion. Perhaps you'd like to hear—'

'Shut up!' Slightman cried in a choked voice. 'Shut up, you mechanical devil! I've sold my goddam soul, isn't that enough for you? Must I be made sport of, as well?'

'If I've offended, I apologize from the bottom of my admittedly hypo-thetical heart,' Andy said. 'In other words, I cry your pardon.' Sounding sincere. Sounding as though he meant every word. Sounding as though butter wouldn't melt. Yet Jake had no doubt that Andy's eyes were flashing out in gales of silent blue laughter.

12

The conspirators left. There was an odd, meaningless jingle of melody from the overhead speakers (meaningless to Jake, at least), and then silence. He waited for them to discover his pony, come back, search for him, find him, kill him. When he had counted to a hundred and twenty and they hadn't returned to the Dogan, he got to his feet (the overdose of adrenaline in his system left him feeling as stiff as an old man) and went back into the control room. He was just in time to see the motion-sensor lights in front of the place switch off. He looked at the monitor showing the top of the rise and saw the Dogan's most recent visitors walking between the boom-flurry. This time the cactuses didn't move. They had apparently learned their lesson. Jake watched Slightman and Andy go, bitterly amused by the differ-ence in their heights. Whenever his father saw such a Mutt-and-Jeff duo on the street, he inevitably said *Put em in vaudeville*. It was about as close to a joke as Elmer Chambers could get.

When this particular duo was out of sight, Jake looked down at the floor. No dust, of course. No dust and no tracks. He should have seen that when he came in. Certainly *Roland* would have seen that. Roland would have seen everything.

Jake wanted to leave but made himself wait. If they saw the motion-lights glare back on behind them, they'd *probably* assume it was a rock-cat (or maybe what Benny called 'an armydillo'), but probably wasn't good enough. To pass the time, he looked at the various control panels, many of which had the LaMerk Industries name on them. Yet he also saw the familiar GE and IBM logos, plus one he didn't know – Microsoft. All of these latter gadgets were stamped MADE IN USA. The LaMerk products bore no such mark.

He was pretty sure some of the keyboards he saw – there were at least two dozen – controlled computers. What other gadgetry was there? How much was still up and running? Were there weapons stored here? He somehow thought the answer to this last question was no – if there *had* been weapons, they had no doubt been decommissioned or appropriated, very likely by Andy the Messenger Robot (Many Other Functions).

At last he decided it was safe to leave . . . if, that was, he was extremely careful, rode slowly back to the river, and took pains to approach the Rocking B the back way. He was nearly to the door when another question occurred to him. Was there a record of his and Oy's visit to the Dogan? Were they on videotape somewhere? He looked at the operating TV screens, sparing his longest stare for the one showing the control room. He and Oy were on it again. From the camera's high angle, anyone in the room would have to be in that picture.

Let it go, Jake, the gunslinger in his head advised. *There's nothing you can do about it, so just let it go. If you try poking and prying, you're apt to leave sign. You might even set off an alarm.*

The idea of tripping an alarm convinced him. He picked up Oy – as much for comfort as anything else – and got the hell out. His pony was exactly where Jake had left him, cropping dreamily at the bushes in the moonlight. There were no tracks in the hardpan . . . but, Jake saw, he wasn't leaving any himself. Andy would have broken through the crusty surface enough to leave tracks, but not him. He wasn't heavy enough. Probably Benny's Da' wasn't, either.

Quit it. If they'd smelled you, they would have come back.

Jake supposed that was true, but he still felt more than a little like Goldilocks tiptoeing away from the house of the Three Bears. He led his pony back to the desert road, then put on the duster and slipped Oy into the wide front pocket. As he mounted up, he thumped the bumbler a fairly good one on the saddle-horn.

'Ouch, Ake!' Oy said.

'Quit it, ya baby,' Jake said, turning his pony back in the direction of the river. 'Gotta be quiet, now.'

'Kiyit,' Oy agreed, and gave him a wink. Jake worked his fingers down through the bumbler's heavy fur and scratched the place Oy liked the best. Oy closed his eyes, stretched his neck to an almost comical length, and grinned.

When they got back to the river, Jake dismounted and peered over a boulder in both directions. He saw nothing, but his heart was in his throat all the way across to the other side. He kept trying to think what he would say if Benny's Da' hailed him and asked him what he was doing out here in the middle of the night. Nothing came. In English class, he'd almost always gotten A's on his creative-writing assignments, but now he was discovering that fear and invention did not mix. If Benny's Da' hailed him, Jake would be caught. It was as simple as that.

There was no hail – not crossing the river, not going back to the Rocking B, not unsaddling the horse and rubbing him down. The world was silent, and that was just fine with Jake.

13

Once Jake was back on his pallet and pulling the covers to his chin, Oy jumped up on Benny's bed and lay down, nose once more under his tail. Benny made a deep-sleep muttering sound, reached out, and gave the bumbler's flank a single stroke.

Jake lay looking at the sleeping boy, troubled. He liked Benny – his openness, his appetite for fun, his willingness to work hard when there were chores that needed doing. He liked Benny's yodeling laugh when something struck him funny, and the way they were evenly matched in so many things, and—

And until tonight, Jake had liked Benny's Da', too.

He tried to imagine how Benny would look at him when he found out that (a) his father was a traitor and (b) his friend had squealed on him. Jake thought he could bear anger. It was hurt that would be hard.

You think hurt's all it'll be? Simple hurt? You better think again. There aren't many props under Benny Slightman's world, and this is going to knock them all out from under him. Every single one.

Not my fault that his father's a spy and a traitor.

But it wasn't Benny's, either. If you asked Slightman, he'd probably say it wasn't even *his* fault, that he'd been forced into it. Jake guessed that was almost true. *Completely* true, if you looked at things with a father's eye. What was it that the Calla's twins made and the Wolves needed? Something in their brains, very likely. Some sort of enzyme or secretion not produced by singleton children; maybe the enzyme or secretion that created the supposed phenomenon of 'twin telepathy.' Whatever it was, they could take it from Benny Slightman, because Benny Slightman only *looked* like a singleton. Had his sister died? Well, that was tough titty, wasn't it? *Very* tough titty, especially for the father who loved the only one left. Who couldn't bear to let him go.

Suppose Roland kills him? How will Benny look at you then?

Once, in another life, Roland had promised to take care of Jake Chambers and then had let him drop into the darkness. Jake had thought there could be no worse betrayal than that. Now he wasn't so sure. No, not so sure at all. These unhappy thoughts kept him awake for a long time. Finally, half an hour or so before the first hint of dawn touched the horizon, he fell into a thin and troubled sleep.

CHAPTER IV

THE PIED PIPER

1

'We are ka-tet,' said the gunslinger. 'We are one from many.' He saw Callahan's doubtful look — it was impossible to miss — and nodded. 'Yes, Pere, you're one of us. I don't know for how long, but I know it's so. And so do my friends.'

Jake nodded. So did Eddie and Susannah. They were in the Pavilion today; after hearing Jake's story, Roland no longer wanted to meet at the rectory-house, not even in the back yard. He thought it all too likely that Slightman or Andy — maybe even some other as yet unsuspected friend of the Wolves — had placed listening devices as well as cameras there. Overhead the sky was gray, threatening rain, but the weather remained remarkably warm for so late in the season. Some civic-minded ladies or gents had raked away the fallen leaves in a wide circle around the stage where Roland and his friends had introduced themselves not so long ago, and the grass beneath was as green as summer. There were *folken* flying kites, couples promenading hand in hand, two or three outdoor tradesmen keeping one eye out for customers and the other on the low-bellied clouds overhead. On the bandstand, the group of musicians who had played them into Calla Bryn Sturgis with such brio were practicing a few new tunes. On two or three occasions, townsfolk had started toward Roland and his friends, wanting to pass a little time, and each time it happened, Roland shook his head in an unsmiling way that turned them around in a hurry. The time for so-good-to-meet-you politics had passed. They were almost down to what Susannah called the real nitty-gritty.

Roland said, 'In four days comes the meeting, this time I think of the entire town, not just the men.'

'Damn well told it ought to be the whole town,' Susannah said. 'If you're counting on the ladies to throw the dish and make up for all the guns we don't have, I don't think it's too much to let em into the damn hall.'

'Won't be in the Gathering Hall, if it's everyone,' Callahan said. 'There won't be room enough. We'll light the torches and have it right out here.'

'And if it rains?' Eddie asked.

'If it rains, people will get wet,' Callahan said, and shrugged.

'Four days to the meeting and nine to the Wolves,' Roland said. 'This will very likely be our last chance to palaver as we are now – sitting down, with our heads clear – until this is over. We won't be here long, so let's make it count.' He held out his hands. Jake took one, Susannah the other. In a moment all five were joined in a little circle, hand to hand. 'Do we see each other?'

'See you very well,' Jake said.

'Very well, Roland,' said Eddie.

'Clear as day, sug,' Susannah agreed, smiling.

Oy, who was sniffing in the grass nearby, said nothing, but he *did* look around and tip a wink.

'Pere?' Roland asked.

'I see and hear you very well,' Callahan agreed with a small smile, 'and I'm glad to be included. So far, at least.'

2

Roland, Eddie, and Susannah had heard most of Jake's tale; Jake and Susannah had heard most of Roland's and Eddie's. Now Callahan got both – what he later called 'the double feature.' He listened with his eyes wide and his mouth frequently agape. He crossed himself when Jake told of hiding in the closet. To Eddie the Pere said, 'You didn't mean it about killing the wives and children, of course? That was just a bluff?'

Eddie looked up at the heavy sky, considering this with a faint smile. Then he looked back at Callahan. 'Roland tells me that for a guy who doesn't want to be called Father, you have taken some very Fatherly stands just lately.'

'If you're speaking about the idea of terminating your wife's pregnancy—'

Eddie raised a hand. 'Let's say I'm not speaking of any one thing in particular. It's just that we've got a job to do here, and we need you to help us do it. The *last* thing we need is to get sidetracked by a lot of your old

Catholic blather. So let's just say yes, I was bluffing, and move on. Will that serve? *Father?*'

Eddie's smile had grown strained and exasperated. There were bright smudges of color on his cheekbones. Callahan considered the look of him with great care, and then nodded. 'Yes,' he said. 'You were bluffing. By all means let's leave it at that and move on.'

'Good,' Eddie said. He looked at Roland.

'The first question is for Susannah,' Roland said. 'It's a simple one: how are you feeling?'

'Just fine,' she replied.

'Say true?'

She nodded. 'Say true, say thankya.'

'No headaches here?' Roland rubbed above his left temple.

'No. And the jittery feelings I used to get — just after sunset, just before dawn — have quit. And look at me!' She ran a hand down the swell of her breasts, to her waist, to her right hip. 'I've lost some of the fullness. Roland ... I've read that sometimes animals in the wild — carnivores like wildcats, herbivores like deer and rabbits — reabsorb their babies if the conditions to have them are adverse. You don't suppose ...' She trailed off, looking at him hopefully.

Roland wished he could have supported this charming idea, but he couldn't. And withholding the truth within the ka-tet was no longer an option. He shook his head. Susannah's face fell.

'She's been sleeping quietly, so far as I can tell,' Eddie said. 'No sign of Mia.'

'Rosalita says the same,' Callahan added.

'You got dat jane watchin me?' Susannah said in a suspiciously Detta-like tone. But she was smiling.

'Every now and then,' Callahan admitted.

'Let's leave the subject of Susannah's chap, if we may,' Roland said. 'We need to speak of the Wolves. Them and little else.'

'But Roland—' Eddie began.

Roland held up his hand. 'I know how many other matters there are. I know how pressing they are. I also know that if we become distracted, we're apt to die here in Calla Bryn Sturgis, and dead gunslingers can help no one. Nor do they go their course. Do you agree?' His eyes swept them. No one replied. Somewhere in the distance was the sound of many children singing. The sound was high and gleeful and innocent. Something about commala.

'There *is* one other bit of business that we must address,' Roland said. 'It involves you, Pere. And what's now called the Doorway Cave. Will you go through that door, and back to your country?'

'Are you kidding?' Callahan's eyes were bright. 'A chance to go back, even for a little while? You just say the word.'

Roland nodded. 'Later today, mayhap you and I will take a little *pasear* on up there, and I'll see you through the door. You know where the vacant lot is, don't you?'

'Sure. I must have been past it a thousand times, back in my other life.'

'And you understand about the zip code?' Eddie asked.

'If Mr Tower did as you requested, it'll be written at the end of the board fence, Forty-sixth Street side. That was brilliant, by the way.'

'Get the number . . . and get the date, too,' Roland said. 'We have to keep track of the time over there if we can, Eddie's right about that. Get it and come back. Then, after the meeting in the Pavilion, we'll need you to go through the door again.'

'This time to wherever Tower and Deepneau are in New England,' Callahan guessed.

'Yes,' Roland said.

'If you find them, you'll want to talk mostly to Mr Deepneau,' Jake said. He flushed when they all turned to him, but kept his eyes trained on Callahan's. 'Mr Tower might be stubborn—'

'That's the understatement of the century,' Eddie said. 'By the time you get there, he'll probably have found twelve used bookstores and God knows how many first editions of *Indiana Jones's Nineteenth Nervous Breakdown*.'

'—but Mr Deepneau will listen,' Jake went on.

'Issen, Ake,' Oy said, and rolled over onto his back. 'Issen kiyet!'

Scratching Oy's belly, Jake said: 'If anyone can convince Mr Tower to do something, it'll be Mr Deepneau.'

'Okay,' Callahan replied, nodding. 'I hear you well.'

The singing children were closer now. Susannah turned but couldn't see them yet; she assumed they were coming up River Street. If so, they'd be in view once they cleared the livery and turned down the high street at Took's General Store. Some of the *folken* on the porch over there were already getting up to look.

Roland, meanwhile, was studying Eddie with a small smile. 'Once when I used the word *assume*, you told me a saying about it from your world. I'd hear it again, if you remember.'

Eddie grinned. '*Assume* makes an ass out of u *and* me – is that the one you mean?'

Roland nodded. 'It's a good saying. All the same, I'm going to make an assumption now – pound it like a nail – then hang all our hopes of coming out of this alive on it. I don't like it but see no choice. The assumption is that only Ben Slightman and Andy are working against us. That if we take care of them when the time comes, we can move in secrecy.'

'Don't kill him,' Jake said in a voice almost too low to hear. He had drawn Oy close and was petting the top of his head and his long neck with a kind of compulsive, darting speed. Oy bore this patiently.

'Cry pardon, Jake,' Susannah said, leaning forward and tipping a hand behind one ear. 'I didn't—'

'Don't *kill* him!' This time his voice was hoarse and wavering and close to tears. 'Don't kill Benny's Da'. *Please.*'

Eddie reached out and cupped the nape of the boy's neck gently. 'Jake, Benny Slightman's Da' is willing to send a hundred kids off into Thunderclap with the Wolves, just to spare his own. And you know how they'd come back.'

'Yeah, but in his eyes he doesn't have any choice because—'

'His choice could have been to stand with us,' Roland said. His voice was dull and dreadful. Almost dead.

'But—'

But what? Jake didn't know. He had been over this and over this and he still didn't know. Sudden tears spilled from his eyes and ran down his cheeks. Callahan reached out to touch him. Jake pushed his hand away.

Roland sighed. 'We'll do what we can to spare him. That much I promise you. I don't know if it will be a mercy or not – the Slightmans are going to be through in this town, if there's a town left after the end of next week – but perhaps they'll go north or south along the Crescent and start some sort of new life. And Jake, listen: there's no need for Ben Slightman to ever know you overheard Andy and his father last night.'

Jake was looking at him with an expression that didn't quite dare to be hope. He didn't care a hill of beans about Slightman the Elder, but he didn't want Benny to know it was him. He supposed that made him a coward, but he didn't want Benny to know. 'Really? For sure?'

'Nothing about this is for sure, but—'

Before he could finish, the singing children swept around the corner.

Leading them, silver limbs and golden body gleaming mellowly in the day's subdued light, was Andy the Messenger Robot. He was walking backward. In one hand was a bah-bolt wrapped in banners of bright silk. To Susannah he looked like a parade-marshal on the Fourth of July. He waved his baton extravagantly from side to side, leading the children in their song while a reedy bagpipe accompaniment issued from the speakers in his chest and head.

'Holy shit,' Eddie said. 'It's the Pied Piper of Hamelin.'

3

> '*Commala-come-one!*
> *Mamma had a son!*
> *Dass-a time 'at Daddy*
> *Had d' mos' fun!*'

Andy sang this part alone, then pointed his baton at the crowd of children. They joined in boisterously.

> '*Commala-come-come!*
> *Daddy had one!*
> *Dass-a time 'at Mommy*
> *Had d' mos' fun!*'

Gleeful laughter. There weren't as many kids as Susannah would have thought, given the amount of noise they were putting out. Seeing Andy there at their head, after hearing Jake's story, chilled her heart. At the same time, she felt an angry pulse begin to beat in her throat and her left temple. That he should lead them down the street like this! Like the Pied Piper, Eddie was right – like the Pied Piper of Hamelin.

Now he pointed his makeshift baton at a pretty girl who looked thirteen or fourteen. Susannah thought she was one of the Anselm kids, from the smallhold just south of Tian Jaffords's place. She sang out the next verse bright and clear to that same heavily rhythmic beat, which was almost (but not quite) a skip-rope chant:

> *'Commala-come-two!*
> *You know what to do!*
> *Plant the rice commala,*
> *Don't ye be . . . no . . . foo'!'*

Then, as the others joined in again, Susannah realized that the group of children *was* bigger than she'd thought when they came around the corner, quite a bit bigger. Her ears had told her truer than her eyes, and there was a perfectly good reason for that.

> *'Commala-come-two!* [they sang]
> *Daddy no foo'!*
> *Mommy plant commala*
> *cause she know jus' what to do!'*

The group looked smaller at first glance because so many of the faces were the same — the face of the Anselm girl, for instance, was nearly the face of the boy next to her. Her twin brother. Almost all the kids in Andy's group were twins. Susannah suddenly realized how eerie this was, like all the strange doublings they'd encountered caught in a bottle. Her stomach turned over. And she felt the first twinge of pain above her left eye. Her hand began to rise toward the tender spot.

No, she told herself, *I don't feel that.* She made the hand go back down. There was no need to rub her brow. No need to rub what didn't hurt.

Andy pointed his baton at a strutting, pudgy little boy who couldn't have been more than eight. He sang the words out in a high and childish treble that made the other kids laugh.

> *'Commala-come-t'ree!*
> *You know what t' be!*
> *Plant d' rice commala and*
> *d' rice'll make ya free!'*

To which the chorus replied:

> *'Commala-come-t'ree!*
> *Rice'll make ya free! When*
> *ya plant the rice commala You*
> *know jus' what to be!'*

Andy saw Roland's ka-tet and waved his baton cheerily. So did the children ... half of whom would come back drooling and roont if the parade-marshal had his way. They would grow to the size of giants, screaming with pain, and then die early.

'Wave back,' Roland said, and raised his hand. 'Wave back, all of you, for the sake of your fathers.'

Eddie flashed Andy a happy, toothy grin. 'How you doing, you cheap-shit Radio Shack dickweed?' he asked. The voice coming through his grin was low and savage. He gave Andy a double thumbs-up. 'How you doing, you robot psycho? Say fine? Say thankya! Say bite my bag!'

Jake burst out laughing at that. They all continued waving and smiling. The children waved and smiled back. Andy also waved. He led his merry band down the high street, chanting *Commala-come-four! River's at the door!*

'They love him,' Callahan said. There was a strange, sick expression of disgust on his face. 'Generations of children have loved Andy.'

'That,' Roland remarked, 'is about to change.'

4

'Further questions?' Roland asked when Andy and the children were gone. 'Ask now if you will. It could be your last chance.'

'What about Tian Jaffords?' Callahan asked. 'In a very real sense it was Tian who started this. There ought to be a place for him at the finish.'

Roland nodded. 'I have a job for him. One he and Eddie will do together. Pere, that's a fine privy down below Rosalita's cottage. Tall. Strong.'

Callahan raised his eyebrows. 'Aye, say thankya. 'Twas Tian and his neighbor, Hugh Anselm, who built it.'

'Could you put a lock on the outside of it in the next few days?'

'I could but—'

'If things go well no lock will be necessary, but one can never be sure.'

'No,' Callahan said. 'I suppose one can't. But I can do as you ask.'

'What's your plan, sugar?' Susannah asked. She spoke in a quiet, oddly gentle voice.

'There's precious little plan in it. Most times that's all to the good. The most important thing I can tell you is not to believe anything I say once we get up from here, dust off our bottoms, and rejoin the *folken*. Especially nothing I say when I stand up at the meeting with the feather in my hand. Most of it will be lies.' He gave them a smile. Above it, his faded blue eyes were as hard as rocks. 'My Da' and Cuthbert's Da' used to have a rule between em: first the smiles, then the lies. Last comes gunfire.'

'We're almost there, aren't we?' Susannah asked. 'Almost to the shooting.'

Roland nodded. 'And the shooting will happen so fast and be over so quick that you'll wonder what all the planning and palaver was for, when in the end it always comes down to the same five minutes' worth of blood, pain, and stupidity.' He paused, then said: 'I always feel sick afterward. Like I did when Bert and I went to see the hanged man.'

'I have a question,' Jake said.

'Ask it,' Roland told him.

'Will we win?'

Roland was quiet for such a long time that Susannah began to be afraid. Then he said: 'We know more than they think we know. *Far* more. They've grown complacent. If Andy and Slightman are the only rats in the woodpile, and if there aren't too many in the Wolfpack — if we don't run out of plates and cartridges — then yes, Jake, son of Elmer. We'll win.'

'How many is too many?'

Roland considered, his faded blue eyes looking east. 'More than you'd believe,' he said at last. 'And, I hope, many more than *they* would.'

5

Late that afternoon, Donald Callahan stood in front of the unfound door, trying to concentrate on Second Avenue in the year 1977. What he fixed upon was Chew Chew Mama's, and how sometimes he and George and Lupe Delgado would go there for lunch.

'I ate the beef brisket whenever I could get it,' Callahan said, and tried to ignore the shrieking voice of his mother, rising from the cave's dark belly. When he'd first come in with Roland, his eyes had been drawn to the books Calvin Tower had sent through. So many books! Callahan's mostly generous heart grew greedy (and a bit smaller) at the sight of them. His interest didn't last, however — just long enough to pull one at random and see it was *The Virginian*, by Owen Wister. It was hard to browse when your dead friends and loved ones were shrieking at you and calling you names.

His mother was currently asking him why he had allowed a vampire, a filthy bloodsucker, to break the cross she had given him. 'You was always weak in faith,' she said dolorously. 'Weak in the faith and strong for the drink. I bet you'd like one right now, wouldn't you?'

Dear God, would he ever. Whiskey. Ancient Age. Callahan felt sweat break on his forehead. His heart was beating double-time. No, *triple*-time.

'The brisket,' he muttered. 'With some of that brown mustard splashed on top of it.' He could even see the plastic squeeze-bottle the mustard came in, and remember the brand name. Plochman's.

'What?' Roland asked from behind him.

'I said I'm ready,' Callahan said. 'If you're going to do it, for God's love do it now.'

Roland cracked open the box. The chimes at once bolted through Callahan's ears, making him remember the low men in their loud cars. His stomach shriveled inside his belly and outraged tears burst from his eyes.

But the door clicked open, and a wedge of bright sunshine slanted through, dispelling the gloom of the cave's mouth.

Callahan took a deep breath and thought, *Oh Mary, conceived without sin, pray for us who have recourse to Thee.* And stepped into the summer of '77.

6

It was noon, of course. Lunchtime. And of course he was standing in front of Chew Chew Mama's. No one seemed to notice his arrival. The chalked specials on the easel just outside the restaurant door read:

HEY YOU, WELCOME TO CHEW-CHEW!

SPECIALS FOR JUNE 24

BEEF STROGANOFF
BEEF BRISKET (W/CABBAGE)
RANCHO GRANDE TACOS
CHICKEN SOUP

TRY OUR DUTCH APPLE PIE!

All right, one question was answered. It was the day after Eddie had come here. As for the next one . . .

Callahan put Forty-sixth Street at his back for the time being, and walked up Second Avenue. Once he looked behind him and saw the doorway to the cave following him as faithfully as the billy-bumbler followed the boy. He could see Roland sitting there, putting something in his ears to block the maddening tinkle of the chimes.

He got exactly two blocks before stopping, his eyes growing wide with shock, his mouth dropping open. They had said to expect this, both Roland *and* Eddie, but in his heart Callahan hadn't believed it. He'd thought he would find The Manhattan Restaurant of the Mind perfectly intact on this perfect summer's day, which was so different from the overcast Calla autumn he'd left. Oh, there might be a sign in the window reading GONE ON VACA-TION, CLOSED UNTIL AUGUST — something like that — but it would *be* there. Oh yes.

It wasn't, though. At least not much of it. The storefront was a burnt-out husk surrounded by yellow tape reading POLICE INVESTIGATION. When he stepped a little closer, he could smell charred lumber, burnt paper, and . . . very faint . . . the odor of gasoline.

An elderly shoeshine-boy had set up shop in front of Station Shoes & Boots, nearby. Now he said to Callahan, 'Shame, ain't it? Thank God the place was empty.'

'Aye, say thankya. When did it happen?'

'Middle of the night, when else? You think them goombars is gonna come t'row their Molly Coh'tails in broad daylight? They ain't geniuses, but they're smarter than that.'

'Couldn't it have been faulty wiring? Or maybe spontaneous combustion?'

The elderly shine-boy gave Callahan a cynical look. *Oh, please,* it said. He cocked a polish-smeared thumb at the smoldering ruin. 'You see that yella tape? You think they put yella tape says PERLICE INVESTIGATION around a place that spontaneously combust-you-lated? No way, my friend. No way José. Cal Tower was in hock to the bad boys. Up to his eyebrows. Everybody on the block knew it.' The shine-boy waggled his own eyebrows, which were lush and white and tangled. 'I hate to think about his loss. He had some very vallable books in the back, there. Ver-ry vallable.'

Callahan thanked the shine-boy for his insights, then turned and started back down Second Avenue. He kept touching himself furtively, trying to convince himself that this was really happening. He kept taking deep breaths of the city air with its tang of hydrocarbons, and relished every city sound, from the snore of the buses (there were ads for *Charlie's Angels* on some of them) to the pounding of the jackhammers and the incessant honking of horns. As he approached Tower of Power Records, he paused for a moment, transfixed by the music pouring from the speakers over the doors. It was an oldie he hadn't heard in years, one that had been popular way back in his Lowell days. Something about following the Pied Piper.

'Crispin St Peters,' he murmured. 'That was his name. Good God, say Man Jesus, I'm really here. *I'm really in New York!*'

As if to confirm this, a harried-sounding woman said, 'Maybe some people can stand around all day, but some of us are walking here. Think yez could move it along, or at least get over to the side?'

Callahan spoke an apology which he doubted was heard (or appreciated if it was), and moved along. That sense of being in a dream – an extraordinarily *vivid* dream – persisted until he neared Forty-sixth Street. Then he began to hear the rose, and everything in his life changed.

7

At first it was little more than a murmur, but as he drew closer, he thought he could hear many voices, *angelic* voices, singing. Raising their confident, joyful psalms to God. He had never heard anything so sweet, and he began to run. He came to the fence and laid his hands against it. He began to weep, couldn't help it. He supposed people were looking at him, but he didn't care. He suddenly understood a great deal about Roland and his friends, and for the first time felt a part of them. No wonder they were trying so hard to survive, and to go on! No wonder, when *this* was at stake! There was something on the other side of this fence with its tattered overlay of posters ... something so utterly and completely *wonderful* ...

A young man with his long hair held back in a rubber band and wearing a tipped-back cowboy hat stopped and clapped him briefly on the shoulder. 'It's nice here, isn't it?' the hippie cowboy said. 'I don't know just why, but it really is. I come once a day. You want to know something?'

Callahan turned toward the young man, wiping at his streaming eyes. 'Yes, I guess so.'

The young man brushed a hand across his brow, then his cheek. 'I used to have the world's worst acne. I mean, pizza-face wasn't even in it, I was *roadkill*-face. Then I started coming here in late March or early April, and . . . everything cleared up.' The young man laughed. 'The dermo guy my Dad sent me to says it's the zinc oxide, but I think it's this place. Something about this place. Do you hear it?'

Although Callahan's voice was ringing with sweetly singing voices – it was like being in Notre Dame cathedral, and surrounded by choirs – he shook his head. Doing so was nothing more than instinct.

'Nah,' said the hippie in the cowboy hat, 'me neither. But sometimes I *think* I do.' He raised his right hand to Callahan, the first two fingers extended in a V. 'Peace, brother.'

'Peace,' Callahan said, and returned the sign.

When the hippie cowboy was gone, Callahan ran his hand across the splintery boards of the fence, and a tattered poster advertising *War of the Zombies*. What he wanted more than anything was to climb over and see the rose . . . possibly to fall on his knees and adore it. But the sidewalks were packed with people, and already he had attracted too many curious looks, some no doubt from people who, like the hippie cowboy, knew a bit about the power of this place. He would best serve the great and singing force behind this fence (was it a rose? could it be no more than that?) by protecting it. And that meant protecting Calvin Tower from whoever had burned down his store.

Still trailing his hand along the rough boards, he turned onto Forty-sixth Street. Down at the end on this side was the glassy-green bulk of the UN Plaza Hotel. *Calla, Callahan*, he thought, and then: *Calla, Callahan, Calvin*. And then: *Calla-come-four, there's a rose behind the door, Calla-come-Callahan, Calvin's one more!*

He reached the end of the fence. At first he saw nothing, and his heart sank. Then he looked down, and there it was, at knee height: five numbers written in black. Callahan reached into his pocket for the stub of pencil he always kept there, then pulled off a corner of a poster for an off-Broadway play called *Dungeon Plunger, A Revue*. On this he scribbled five numbers.

He didn't want to leave, but knew he had to; clear thinking this close to the rose was impossible.

I'll be back, he told it, and to his delighted amazement, a thought came back, clear and true: *Yes, Father, anytime. Come-commala.*

On the corner of Second and Forty-sixth, he looked behind him. The door to the cave was still there, the bottom floating about three inches off the sidewalk. A middle-aged couple, tourists judging by the guide-books in their hands, came walking up from the direction of the hotel. Chatting to each other, they reached the door and swerved around it. *They don't see it, but they feel it*, Callahan thought. And if the sidewalk had been crowded and swerving had been impossible? He thought in that case they would have walked right through the place where it hung and shimmered, perhaps feeling nothing but a momentary coldness and sense of vertigo. Perhaps hearing, faintly, the sour tang of chimes and catching a whiff of something like burnt onions or seared meat. And that night, perhaps, they'd have transient dreams of places far stranger than Fun City.

He could step back through, probably should; he'd gotten what he'd come for. But a brisk walk would take him to the New York Public Library. There, behind the stone lions, even a man with no money in his pocket could get a little information. The location of a certain zip code, for instance. And – tell the truth and shame the devil – he didn't want to leave just yet.

He waved his hands in front of him until the gunslinger noticed what he was doing. Ignoring the looks of the passersby, Callahan raised his fingers in the air once, twice, three times, not sure the gunslinger would get it. Roland seemed to. He gave an exaggerated nod, then thumbs-up for good measure.

Callahan set off, walking so fast he was nearly jogging. It wouldn't do to linger, no matter how pleasant a change New York made. It couldn't be pleasant where Roland was waiting. And, according to Eddie, it might be dangerous, as well.

8

The gunslinger had no problem understanding Callahan's message. Thirty fingers, thirty minutes. The Pere wanted another half an hour on the other side. Roland surmised he had thought of a way to turn the number written on the fence into an actual place. If he could do that, it would be all to the good. Information was power. And sometimes, when time was tight, it was speed.

The bullets in his ears blocked the voices completely. The chimes got in, but even they were dulled. A good thing, because the sound of them was far worse than the warble of the thinny. A couple of days listening to that sound and he reckoned he'd be ready for the lunatic asylum, but for thirty minutes he'd be all right. If worse came to worst, he might be able to pitch something through the door, attract the Pere's attention, and get him to come back early.

For a little while Roland watched the street unroll before Callahan. The doors on the beach had been like looking through the eyes of his three: Eddie, Odetta, Jack Mort. This one was a little different. He could always see Callahan's back in it, or his face if he turned around to look, as he often did.

To pass the time, Roland got up to look at a few of the books which had meant so much to Calvin Tower that he'd made their safety a condition for his cooperation. The first one Roland pulled out had the silhouette of a man's head on it. The man was smoking a pipe and wearing a sort of gamekeeper's hat. Cort had had one like it, and as a boy, Roland had thought it much more stylish than his father's old dayrider with its sweat-stains and frayed tugstring. The words on the book were of the New York world. Roland was sure he could have read them easily if he'd been on that side, but he wasn't. As it was, he could read some, and the result was almost as maddening as the chimes.

'Sir-lock Hones,' he read aloud. 'No, *Holmes*. Like Odetta's fathername. Four ... short ... movels. Movels?' No, this one *was* an N. 'Four short *novels* by Sirlock Holmes.' He opened the book, running a respectful hand over the title page and then smelling it: the spicy, faintly sweet aroma of good old paper. He could make out the name of one of the four short novels — *The Sign of the Four*. Other than the words *Hound* and *Study*, the titles of the others were gibberish to him.

'A sign is a sigul,' he said. When he found himself counting the number of letters in the title, he had to laugh at himself. Besides, there were only sixteen. He put the book back and took up another, this one with a drawing of a soldier on the front. He could make out one word of the title: *Dead*. He looked at another. A man and woman kissing on the cover. Yes, there were always men and women kissing in stories; folks liked that. He put it back and looked up to check on Callahan's progress. His eyes widened slightly as he saw the Pere walking into a great room filled with books and what Eddie called Magda-seens ... although Roland was still unsure what Magda had seen, or why there should be so much written about it.

He pulled out another book, and smiled at the picture on the cover. There was a church, with the sun going down red behind it. The church looked a bit like Our Lady of Serenity. He opened it and thumbed through it. A *delah* of words, but he could only make out one in every three, if that. No pictures. He was about to put it back when something caught his eye. *Leaped* at his eye. Roland stopped breathing for a moment.

He stood back, no longer hearing the todash chimes, no longer caring about the great room of books Callahan had entered. He began reading the book with the church on the front. Or trying to. The words swam maddeningly in front of his eyes, and he couldn't be sure. Not quite. But, gods! If he was seeing what he thought he was seeing—

Intuition told him that this was a key. But to what door?

He didn't know, couldn't read enough of the words to know. But the book in his hands seemed almost to thrum. Roland thought that perhaps this book was like the rose . . .

. . . but there were black roses, too.

9

'Roland, I found it! It's a little town in central Maine called Stoneham, about forty miles north of Portland and . . .' He stopped, getting a good look at the gunslinger. 'What's wrong?'

'The chiming sound,' Roland said quickly. 'Even with my ears stopped up, it got through.' The door was shut and the chimes were gone, but there were still the voices. Callahan's father was currently asking if Donnie thought those magazines he'd found under his son's bed were anything a Christian boy would want to have, what if his mother had found them? And when Roland suggested they leave the cave, Callahan was more than willing to go. He remembered that conversation with his old man far too clearly. They had ended up praying together at the foot of his bed, and the three *Playboys* had gone into the incinerator out back.

Roland returned the carved box to the pink bag and once more stowed it carefully behind Tower's case of valuable books. He had already replaced the book with the church on it, turning it with the title down so he could find it again quickly.

They went out and stood side by side, taking deep breaths of the fresh air. 'Are you sure the chimes is all it was?' Callahan asked. 'Man, you looked as though you'd seen a ghost.'

'The todash chimes are *worse* than ghosts,' Roland said. That might or might not be true, but it seemed to satisfy Callahan. As they started down the path, Roland remembered the promise he had made to the others, and, more important, to himself: no more secrets within the tet. How quickly he found himself ready to break that promise! But he felt he was right to do so. He *knew* at least some of the names in that book. The others would know them, too. Later they would need to know, if the book was as important as he thought it might be. But now it would only distract them from the approaching business of the Wolves. If they could win that battle, then perhaps . . .

'Roland, are you quite sure you're okay?'

'Yes.' He clapped Callahan on the shoulder. The others would be able to read the book, and by reading might discover what it meant. Perhaps the story in the book was *just* a story . . . but how could it be, when . . .

'Pere?'

'Yes, Roland.'

'A novel is a story, isn't it? A made-up story?'

'Yes, a long one.'

'But make-believe.'

'Yes, that's what fiction means. Make-believe.'

Roland pondered this. *Charlie the Choo-Choo* had also been make-believe, only in many ways, many *vital* ways, it hadn't been. And the author's name had changed. There were many different worlds, all held together by the Tower. Maybe . . .

No, not now. He mustn't think about these things now.

'Tell me about the town where Tower and his friend went,' Roland said.

'I can't, really. I found it in one of the Maine telephone books, that's all. Also a simplified zip code map that showed about where it is.'

'Good. That's very good.'

'Roland, are you sure you're all right?'

Calla, Roland thought. *Callahan*. He made himself smile. Made himself clap Callahan on the shoulder again.

'I'm fine,' he said. 'Now let's get back to town.'

CHAPTER V

THE MEETING OF THE *FOLKEN*

1

Tian Jaffords had never been more frightened in his life than he was as he stood on the stage in the Pavilion, looking down at the *folken* of Calla Bryn Sturgis. He knew there were likely no more than five hundred – six hundred at the very outside – but to him it looked like a multitude, and their taut silence was unnerving. He looked at his wife for comfort and found none there. Zalia's face looked thin and dark and pinched, the face of an old woman rather than one still well within her childbearing years.

Nor did the look of this late afternoon help him find calm. Overhead the sky was a pellucid, cloudless blue, but it was too dark for five o' the clock. There was a huge bank of clouds in the southwest, and the sun had passed behind them just as he climbed the steps to the stage. It was what his Gran-pere would have called weirding weather; *omenish*, say thankya. In the constant darkness that was Thunderclap, lightning flashed like great sparklights.

Had I known it would come to this, I'd never have started it a-going, he thought wildly. *And this time there'll be no Pere Callahan to haul my poor old ashes out of the fire.* Although Callahan was there, standing with Roland and his friends – they of the hard calibers – with his arms folded on his plain black shirt with the notched collar and his Man Jesus cross hanging above.

He told himself not to be foolish, that Callahan *would* help, and the outworlders would help, as well. They were *there* to help. The code they followed demanded that they *must* help, even if it meant their destruction and the end of whatever quest they were on. He told himself that all he needed to do was introduce Roland, and Roland would come. Once before, the gunslinger had stood on this stage and danced the commala and won their hearts. Did Tian doubt that Roland would win their hearts again? In

518

truth, Tian did not. What he was afraid of in *his* heart was that this time it would be a death-dance instead of a life-dance. Because death was what this man and his friends were about; it was their bread and wine. It was the sherbet they took to clear their palates when the meal was done. At that first meeting — could it have been less than a month ago? — Tian had spoken out of angry desperation, but a month was long enough to count the cost. What if this was a mistake? What if the Wolves burned the entire Calla flat with their light-sticks, took the children they wanted one final time, and exploded all the ones that were left — old, young, in the middle — with their whizzing balls of death?

They stood waiting for him to begin, the gathered Calla. Eisenharts and Overholsers and Javiers and Tooks without number (although no twins among these last of the age the Wolves liked, aye-no, such lucky Tooks they were); Telford standing with the men and his plump but hard-faced wife with the women; Strongs and Rossiters and Slightmans and Hands and Rosarios and Posellas; the Manni once again bunched together like a dark stain of ink, Henchick their patriarch standing with young Cantab, whom all the children liked so well; Andy, another favorite of the kiddies, standing off to one side with his skinny metal arms akimbo and his blue electric eyes flashing in the gloom; the Sisters of Oriza bunched together like birds on fencewire (Tian's wife among them); and the cowboys, the hired men, the dayboys, even old Bernardo, the town tosspot.

To Tian's right, those who had carried the feather shuffled a bit uneasily. In ordinary circumstances, one set of twins was plenty to take the opopanax feather; in most cases, people knew well in advance what was up, and carrying the feather was nothing but a formality. This time (it had been Margaret Eisenhart's idea), three sets of twins had gone together with the hallowed feather, carrying it from town to smallhold to ranch to farm in a bucka driven by Cantab, who sat unusually silent and songless up front, clucking along a matched set of brown mules that needed precious little help from the likes of him. Oldest at twenty-three were the Haggengood twins, born the year of the last Wolf-raid (and ugly as sin by the lights of most folks, although precious hard workers, say thankya). Next came the Tavery twins, those beautiful map-drawing town brats. Last (and youngest, although eldest of Tian's brood) came Heddon and Hedda. And it was Hedda who got him going. Tian caught her eye and saw that his good (although plain-faced) daughter had sensed her father's fright and was on the verge of tears herself.

Eddie and Jake weren't the only ones who heard the voices of others in their heads; Tian now heard the voice of his Gran-pere. Not as Jamie was now, doddering and nearly toothless, but as he had been twenty years before: old but still capable of clouting you over the River Road if you sassed back or dawdled over a hard pull. Jamie Jaffords who had once stood against the Wolves. This Tian had from time to time doubted, but he doubted it no longer. Because Roland believed.

Garn, then! snarled the voice in his mind. *What is it fashes and diddles thee s' slow, oafing? 'Tis nobbut to say his name and stand aside, ennit? Then fer good or nis, ye can let him do a' rest.*

Still Tian looked out over the silent crowd a moment longer, their bulk hemmed in tonight by torches that didn't change — for this was no party — but only glared a steady orange. Because he wanted to say something, perhaps *needed* to say something. If only to acknowledge that he was partly to credit for this. For good or for nis.

In the eastern darkness, lightning fired off silent explosions.

Roland, standing with his arms folded like the Pere, caught Tian's eye and nodded slightly to him. Even by warm torchlight, the gunslinger's blue gaze was cold. Almost as cold as Andy's. Yet it was all the encouragement Tian needed.

He took the feather and held it before him. Even the crowd's breathing seemed to still. Somewhere far overtown, a rustie cawed as if to hold back the night.

'Not long since I stood in yon Gathering Hall and told 'ee what I believe,' Tian said. 'That when the Wolves come, they don't just take our children but our hearts and souls. Each time they steal and we stand by, they cut us a little deeper. If you cut a tree deep enough, it dies. Cut a town deep enough, that dies, too.'

The voice of Rosalita Munoz, childless her whole life, rang out in the fey dimness of the day with clear ferocity: 'Say true, say thankya! Hear him, *folken!* Hear him very well!'

'Hear him, hear him, hear him well' ran through the assembly.

'Pere stood up that night and told us there were gunslingers coming from the northwest, coming through Mid-Forest along the Path of the Beam. Some scoffed, but Pere spoke true.'

'Say thankya,' they replied. 'Pere said true.' And a woman's voice: 'Praise Jesus! Praise Mary, mother of God!'

'They've been among us all these days since. Any who's wanted to speak to em *has* spoke to em. They have promised nothing but to help—'

'And'll move on, leaving bloody ruin behind em, if we're foolish enough to allow it!' Eben Took roared.

There was a shocked gasp from the crowd. As it died, Wayne Overholser said: 'Shut up, ye great mouth-organ.'

Took turned to look at Overholser, the Calla's big farmer and Took's best customer, with a look of gaping surprise.

Tian said: 'Their dinh is Roland Deschain, of Gilead.' They knew this, but the mention of such legendary names still provoked a low, almost moaning murmur. 'From In-World that was. Would you hear him? What say you, *folken?*'

Their response quickly rose to a shout. '*Hear him! Hear him! We would hear him to the last! Hear him well, say thankya!*' And a soft, rhythmic crumping sound that Tian could not at first identify. Then he realized what it was and almost smiled. This was what the tromping of shor'boots sounded like, not on the boards of the Gathering Hall, but out here on Lady Riza's grass.

Tian held out his hand. Roland came forward. The tromping sound grew louder as he did. Women were joining in, doing the best they could in their soft town shoes. Roland mounted the steps. Tian gave him the feather and left the stage, taking Hedda's hand and motioning for the rest of the twins to go before him. Roland stood with the feather held before him, gripping its ancient lacquered stalk with hands now bearing only eight digits. At last the tromping of the shoes and shor'boots died away. The torches sizzled and spat, illuminating the upturned faces of the *folken*, showing their hope and fear; showing both very well. The rustie called and was still. In the east, big lightning sliced up the darkness.

The gunslinger stood facing them.

2

For what seemed a very long time looking was all he did. In each glazed and frightened eye he read the same thing. He had seen it many times before, and it was easy reading. These people were hungry. They'd fain buy something to eat, fill their restless bellies. He remembered the pieman who walked the streets of Gilead low-town in the hottest days of summer, and how his mother had called him seppe-sai on account of how sick such pies could make people. *Seppe-sai* meant the death-seller.

Aye, he thought, *but I and my friends don't charge.*

At this thought, his face lit in a smile. It rolled years off his craggy map, and a sigh of nervous relief came from the crowd. He started as he had before: 'We are well-met in the Calla, hear me, I beg.'

Silence.

'You have opened to us. We have opened to you. Is it not so?'

'Aye, gunslinger!' Vaughn Eisenhart called back. ''Tis!'

'Do you see us for what we are, and accept what we do?'

It was Henchick of the Manni who answered this time. 'Aye, Roland, by the Book and say thankya. Y'are of Eld, White come to stand against Black.'

This time the crowd's sigh was long. Somewhere near the back, a woman began to sob.

'Calla-*folken*, do you seek aid and succor of us?'

Eddie stiffened. This question had been asked of many individuals during their weeks in Calla Bryn Sturgis, but he thought to ask it here was extremely risky. What if they said no?

A moment later Eddie realized he needn't have worried; in sizing up his audience, Roland was as shrewd as ever. Some *did* in fact say no — a smattering of Haycoxes, a peck of Tooks, and a small cluster of Telfords led the antis — but most of the *folken* roared out a hearty and immediate *AYE, SAY THANKYA!* A few others — Overholser was the most prominent — said nothing either way. Eddie thought that in most cases, this would have been the wisest move. The most *politic* move, anyway. But this wasn't most cases; it was the most extraordinary moment of choice most of these people would ever face. If the Ka-Tet of Nineteen won against the Wolves, the people of this town would remember those who said no and those who said nothing. He wondered idly if Wayne Dale Overholser would still be the big farmer in these parts a year from now.

But then Roland opened the palaver, and Eddie turned his entire attention toward him. His *admiring* attention. Growing up where and how he had, Eddie had heard plenty of lies. Had told plenty himself, some of them very good ones. But by the time Roland reached the middle of his spiel, Eddie realized he had never been in the presence of a true genius of mendacity until this early evening in Calla Bryn Sturgis. And—

Eddie looked around, then nodded, satisfied.

And they were swallowing every word.

3

'Last time I was on this stage before you,' Roland began, 'I danced the commala. Tonight—'

George Telford interrupted. He was too oily for Eddie's taste, and too sly by half, but he couldn't fault the man's courage, speaking up as he did when the tide was so clearly running in the other direction.

'Aye, we remember, ye danced it well! How dance ye the mortata, Roland, tell me that, I beg.'

Disapproving murmurs from the crowd.

'Doesn't matter how I dance it,' Roland said, not in the least discommoded, 'for my dancing days in the Calla are done. We have work in this town, I and mine. Ye've made us welcome, and we say thankya. Ye've bid us on, sought our aid and succor, so now I bid ye to listen very well. In less of a week come the Wolves.'

There was a sigh of agreement. Time might have grown slippery, but even low *folken* could still hold onto five days' worth of it.

'On the night before they're due, I'd have every Calla twin-child under the age of seventeen there.' Roland pointed off to the left, where the Sisters of Oriza had put up a tent. Tonight there were a good many children in there, although by no means the hundred or so at risk. The older had been given the task of tending the younger for the duration of the meeting, and one or another of the Sisters periodically checked to make sure all was yet fine.

'That tent won't hold em all, Roland,' Ben Slightman said.

Roland smiled. 'But a bigger one will, Ben, and I reckon the Sisters can find one.'

'Aye, and give em a meal they won't ever forget!' Margaret Eisenhart called out bravely. Good-natured laughter greeted this, then sputtered before it caught. Many in the crowd were no doubt reflecting that if the Wolves won after all, half the children who spent Wolf's Eve on the Green wouldn't be able to remember their own names a week or two later, let alone what they'd eaten.

'I'd sleep em here so we can get an early start the next morning,' Roland said. 'From all I've been told, there's no way to know if the Wolves will come early, late, or in the middle of the day. We'd look the fools of the world if they were to come extra early and catch em right here, in the open.'

'What's to keep em from coming a *day* early?' Eben Took called out truculently. 'Or at midnight on what you call Wolf's Eve?'

'They can't,' Roland said simply. And, based on Jamie Jaffords's testimony, they were almost positive this was true. The old man's story was his reason for letting Andy and Ben Slightman run free for the next five days and nights. 'They come from afar, and not all their traveling is on horseback. Their schedule is fixed far in advance.'

'How do 'ee know?' Louis Haycox asked.

'Better I not tell,' Roland said. 'Mayhap the Wolves have long ears.'

A considering silence met this.

'On the same night – Wolf's Eve – I'd have a dozen bucka wagons here, the biggest in the Calla, to draw the children out to the north of town. I'll appoint the drivers. There'll also be child-minders to go with em, and stay with em when the time comes. And ye needn't ask me where they'll be going; it's best we not speak of that, either.'

Of course most of them thought they already knew where the children would be taken: the old Gloria. Word had a way of getting around, as Roland well knew. Ben Slightman had thought a little further – to the Redbird Two, south of the Gloria – and that was also fine.

George Telford cried out: 'Don't listen to this, *folken*, I beg ye! And even if 'ee *do* listen, for your souls and the life of this town, don't *do* it! What he's saying is madness! We've tried to hide our children before, *and it doesn't work!* But even if it did, they'd surely come and burn this town for vengeance' sake, burn it flat—'

'Silence, ye coward.' It was Henchick, his voice as dry as a whipcrack.

Telford would have said more regardless, but his eldest son took his arm and made him stop. It was just as well. The clomping of the shor'boots had begun again. Telford looked at Eisenhart unbelievingly, his thought as clear as a shout: *Ye can't mean to be part of this madness, can ye?*

The big rancher shook his head. 'No point looking at me so, George. I stand with my wife, and she stands with the Eld.'

Applause greeted this. Roland waited for it to quiet.

'Rancher Telford says true. The Wolves likely *will* know where the children have been bunkered. And when they come, my ka-tet will be there to greet them. It won't be the first time we've stood against such as they.'

Roars of approval. More soft clumping of boots. Some rhythmic applause. Telford and Eben Took looked about with wide eyes, like men discovering they had awakened in a lunatic asylum.

When the Pavilion was quiet again, Roland said: 'Some from town have agreed to stand with us, *folka* with good weapons. Again, it's not a thing you need to know about just now.' But of course the feminine construction told those who didn't already know about the Sisters of Oriza a great deal. Eddie once more had to marvel at the way he was leading them; cozy wasn't in it. He glanced at Susannah, who rolled her eyes and gave him a smile. But the hand she put on his arm was cold. She wanted this to be over. Eddie knew exactly how she felt.

Telford tried one last time. 'People, hear me! *All this has been tried before!*'

It was Jake Chambers who spoke up. 'It hasn't been tried by gunslingers, sai Telford.'

A fierce roar of approval met this. There was more stamping and clapping. Roland finally had to raise his hands to quiet it.

'Most of the Wolves will go to where they think the children are, and we'll deal with them there,' he said. 'Smaller groups may indeed raid the farms or ranches. Some may come into town. And aye, there may be some burning.'

They listened silently and respectfully, nodding, arriving ahead of him to the next point. As he had wanted them to.

'A burned building can be replaced. A roont child cannot.'

'Aye,' said Rosalita. 'Nor a roont heart.'

There were murmurs of agreement, mostly from the women. In Calla Bryn Sturgis (as in most other places), men in a state of sobriety did not much like to talk about their hearts.

'Hear me now, for I'd tell you at least this much more: We know exactly what these Wolves are. Jamie Jaffords has told us what we already suspected.'

There were murmurs of surprise. Heads turned. Jamie, standing beside his grandson, managed to straighten his curved back for a moment or two and actually puff up his sunken chest. Eddie only hoped the old buzzard would hold his peace over what came next. If he got muddled and contradicted the tale Roland was about to tell, their job would become much harder. At the very least it would mean grabbing Slightman and Andy early. And if Finli o' Tego – the voice Slightman reported to from the Dogan – didn't hear from these two again before the day of the Wolves, there would be suspicions. Eddie felt movement in the hand on his arm. Susannah had just crossed her fingers.

4

'There aren't living creatures beneath the masks,' Roland said. 'The Wolves are the undead servants of the vampires who rule Thunderclap.'

An awed murmur greeted this carefully crafted bit of claptrap.

'They're what my friends Eddie, Susannah, and Jake call *zombis*. They can't be killed by bow, bah, or bullet unless struck in the brain or the heart.' Roland tapped the left side of his chest for emphasis. 'And of course when they come on their raids, they come wearing heavy armor under their clothes.'

Henchick was nodding. Several of the other older men and women – *folken* who well remembered the Wolves coming not just once before but twice – were doing the same. 'It explains a good deal,' he said. 'But how—'

'To strike them in the brain is beyond our abilities, because of the helmets they wear under their hoods,' Roland said. 'But we saw such creatures in Lud. Their weakness is here.' Again he tapped his chest. 'The undead don't breathe, but there's a kind of gill above their hearts. If they armor it over, they die. That's where we'll strike them.'

A low, considering hum of conversation greeted this. And then Granpere's voice, shrill and excited: "Tis ever' word true, for dinna Molly Doolin strike one there hersel' wi' the dish, an' not even dead-on, neither, and yet the creetur' dropped down!'

Susannah's hand tightened on Eddie's arm enough for him to feel her short nails, but when he looked at her, she was grinning in spite of herself. He saw a similar expression on Jake's face. *Trig enough when the chips were down, old man*, Eddie thought. *Sorry I ever doubted you. Let Andy and Slightman go back across the river and report that happy horseshit!* He'd asked Roland if they (the faceless *they* represented by someone who called himself Finli o' Tego) would believe such tripe. *They've raided this side of the Whye for over a hundred years and lost but a single fighter*, Roland had replied. *I think they'd believe anything. At this point their really vulnerable spot is their complacence.*

'Bring your twins here by seven o' the clock on Wolf's Eve,' Roland said. 'There'll be ladies – Sisters of Oriza, ye ken – with lists on slateboards. They'll scratch off each pair as they come in. It's my hope to have a line drawn through every name before nine o' the clock.'

'Ye'll not drig no line through the names o' mine!' cried an angry voice from the back of the crowd. The voice's owner pushed several people aside and stepped forward next to Jake. He was a squat man with a smallhold rice-patch far to the south'ards. Roland scratched through the untidy storehouse of his recent memory (untidy, yes, but nothing was ever thrown away) and eventually came up with the name: Neil Faraday. One of the few who hadn't been home when Roland and his ka-tet had come calling . . . or not home to them, at least. A hard worker, according to Tian, but an even harder drinker. He certainly looked the part. There were dark circles under his eyes and a complication of burst purplish veins on each cheek. Scruffy, say bigbig. Yet Telford and Took threw him a grateful, surprised look. *Another sane man in bedlam*, it said. *Thank the gods.*

''Ay'll take 'een babbies anyro' and burn 'een squabbot town flat,' he said, speaking in an accent that made his words almost incomprehensible. 'But 'ay'll have one each o' my see', an' 'at'll stee' lea' me three, and a' best 'ay ain't worth squabbot, but my howgan *is*!' Faraday looked around at the townsfolk with an expression of sardonic disdain. 'Burn 'ee flat an' be damned to 'ee,' he said. 'Numb *gits*!' And back into the crowd he went, leaving a surprising number of people looking shaken and thoughtful. He had done more to turn the momentum of the crowd with his contemptuous and (to Eddie, at least) incomprehensible tirade than Telford and Took had been able to do together.

He may be shirttail poor, but I doubt if he'll have trouble getting credit from Took for the next year or so, Eddie thought. *If the store still stands, that is.*

'Sai Faraday's got a right to his opinion, but I hope he'll change it over the next few days,' Roland said. 'I hope you folks will help him change it. Because if he doesn't, he's apt to be left not with three kiddies but none at all.' He raised his voice and shaped it toward the place where Faraday stood, glowering. 'Then he can see how he likes working his tillage with no help but two mules and a wife.'

Telford stepped forward to the edge of the stage, his face red with fury. 'Is there nothing ye won't say to win your argument, you chary man? Is there no lie you won't tell?'

'I don't lie and I don't say for certain,' Roland replied. 'If I've given anyone the idea that I know all the answers when less than a season ago I didn't even know the Wolves existed, I cry your pardon. But let me tell you a story before I bid you goodnight. When I was a boy in Gilead, before the coming of the Good Man and the great burning that followed, there was a tree farm out to the east o' barony.'

'Whoever heard of farming *trees*?' someone called derisively.

Roland smiled and nodded. 'Perhaps not ordinary trees, or even iron-woods, but these were blossies, a wonderful light wood, yet strong. The best wood for boats that ever was. A piece cut thin nearly floats in the air. They grew over a thousand acres of land, tens of thousands of blosswood trees in neat rows, all overseen by the barony forester. And the rule, never even bent, let alone broken, was this: take two, plant three.'

'Aye,' Eisenhart said. ''Tis much the same with stock, and with *threaded* stock the advice is to keep four for every one ye sell or kill. Not that many could afford to do so.'

Roland's eyes roamed the crowd. 'During the summer season I turned ten, a plague fell on the blosswood forest. Spiders spun white webs over the upper branches of some, and those trees died from their tops down, rotting as they went, falling of their own weight long before the plague could get to the roots. The forester saw what was happening, and ordered all the good trees cut down at once. To save the wood while it was still worth saving, do you see? There was no more take two and plant three, because the rule no longer made any sense. The following summer, the blossy woods east of Gilead was gone.'

Utter silence from the *folken*. The day had drained down to a premature dusk. The torches hissed. Not an eye stirred from the gunslinger's face.

'Here in the Calla, the Wolves harvest babies. And needn't even go to the work of planting em, because — hear me — that's the way it is with men and women. Even the children know. "Daddy's no fool, when he plants the rice commala, Mommy knows just what to do."'

A murmur from the *folken*.

'The Wolves take, then wait. Take . . . and wait. It's worked fine for them, because men and women always plant new babies, no matter what else befalls. But now comes a new thing. Now comes plague.'

Took began, 'Aye, say true, ye're a plague all r—' Then someone knocked the hat off his head. Eben Took whirled, looked for the culprit, and saw fifty unfriendly faces. He snatched up his hat, held it to his breast, and said no more.

'If they see the baby-farming is over for them here,' Roland said, 'this last time they won't just take twins; this time they'll take every child they can get their hands on while the taking's good. So bring your little ones at seven o' the clock. That's my best advice to you.'

'What choice have you left em?' Telford asked. He was white with fear and fury.

Roland had had enough of him. His voice rose to a shout, and Telford fell back from the force of his suddenly blazing blue eyes. 'None that *you* have to worry about, sai, for your children are grown, as everyone in town knows. You've had your say. Now why don't you shut up?'

A thunder of applause and boot-stomping greeted this. Telford took the bellowing and jeering for as long as he could, his head lowered between his hunched shoulders like a bull about to charge. Then he turned and began shoving his way through the crowd. Took followed. A few moments later, they were gone. Not long after that, the meeting ended. There was no vote. Roland had given them nothing to vote on.

No, Eddie thought again as he pushed Susannah's chair toward the refreshments, cozy really wasn't in it at all.

5

Not long after, Roland accosted Ben Slightman. The foreman was standing beneath one of the torch-poles, balancing a cup of coffee and a plate with a piece of cake on it. Roland also had cake and coffee. Across the greensward, the children's tent had for the nonce become the refreshment tent. A long line of waiting people snaked out of it. There was low talk but little laughter. Closer by, Benny and Jake were tossing a springball back and forth, every now and then letting Oy have a turn. The bumbler was barking happily, but the boys seemed as subdued as the people waiting in line.

'Ye spoke well tonight,' Slightman said, and clicked his coffee cup against Roland's.

'Do you say so?'

'Aye. Of course they were ready, as I think ye knew, but Faraday must have been a surprise to ye, and ye handled him well.'

'I only told the truth,' Roland said. 'If the Wolves lose enough of their troop, they'll take what they can and cut their losses. Legends grow beards, and twenty-three years is plenty of time to grow a long one. Calla-*folken* assume there are thousands of Wolves over there in Thunderclap, maybe millions of em, but I don't think that's true.'

Slightman was looking at him with frank fascination. 'Why not?'

'Because things are running down,' Roland said simply, and then: 'I need you to promise me something.'

Slightman looked at him warily. The lenses of his spectacles twinkled in the torchlight. 'If I can, Roland, I will.'

'Make sure your boy's here four nights from now. His sister's dead, but I doubt if that untwins him to the Wolves. He's still very likely got what it is they come for.'

Slightman made no effort to disguise his relief. 'Aye, he'll be here. I never considered otten else.'

'Good. And I have a job for you, if you'll do it.'

The wary look returned. 'What job would it be?'

'I started off thinking that six would be enough to mind the children while we dealt with the Wolves, and then Rosalita asked me what I'd do if they got frightened and panicked.'

'Ah, but you'll have em in a cave, won't you?' Slightman asked, lowering his voice. 'Kiddies can't run far in a cave, even if they *do* take fright.'

'Far enough to run into a wall and brain themselves or fall down a hole in the dark. If one were to start a stampede on account of the yelling and the smoke and the fire, they might *all* fall down a hole in the dark. I've decided I'd like to have an even ten watching the kiddos. I'd like you to be one of em.'

'Roland, I'm flattered.'

'Is that a yes?'

Slightman nodded.

Roland eyed him. 'You know that if we lose, the ones minding the children are apt to die?'

'If I thought you were going to lose, I'd never agree to go out there with the kids.' He paused. 'Or send my own.'

'Thank you, Ben. Thee's a good man.'

Slightman lowered his voice even further. 'Which of the mines is it going to be? The Gloria or the Redbird?' And when Roland didn't answer immediately: 'Of course I understand if ye'd rather not tell—'

'It's not that,' Roland said. 'It's that we haven't decided.'

'But it'll be one or the other.'

'Oh, aye, where else?' Roland said absently, and began to roll a smoke.

'And ye'll try to get above them?'

'Wouldn't work,' Roland said. 'Angle's wrong.' He patted his chest above his heart. 'Have to hit em here, remember. Other places . . . no good. Even a bullet that goes through armor wouldn't do much damage to a *zombi*.'

'It's a problem, isn't it?'

'It's an *opportunity*,' Roland corrected. 'You know the scree that spreads out below the adits of those old garnet mines? Looks like a baby's bib?'

'Aye?'

'We'll hide ourselves in there. *Under* there. And when they ride toward us, we'll rise up and . . .' Roland cocked a thumb and forefinger at Slightman and made a trigger-pulling gesture.

A smile spread over the foreman's face. 'Roland, that's brilliant!'

'No,' Roland contradicted. 'Only simple. But simple's usually best. I think we'll surprise them. Hem them in and pick them off. It's worked for me before. No reason it shouldn't work again.'

'No. I suppose not.'

Roland looked around. 'Best we not talk about such things here, Ben. I know *you're* safe, but—'

Ben nodded rapidly. 'Say n' more, Roland, I understand.'

The springball rolled to Slightman's feet. His son held up his hands for it, smiling. 'Pa! Throw it!'

Ben did, and hard. The ball sailed, just as Molly's plate had in Granpere's story. Benny leaped, caught it one-handed, and laughed. His father grinned at him fondly, then glanced at Roland. 'They's a pair, ain't they? Yours and mine?'

'Aye,' Roland said, almost smiling. 'Almost like brothers, sure enough.'

6

The ka-tet ambled back toward the rectory, riding four abreast, feeling every town eye that watched them go: death on horseback.

'You happy with how it went, sugar?' Susannah asked Roland.

'It'll do,' he allowed, and began to roll a smoke.

'I'd like to try one of those,' Jake said suddenly.

Susannah gave him a look both shocked and amused. 'Bite your tongue, sugar — you haven't seen thirteen yet.'

'My Dad started when he was ten.'

'And'll be dead by fifty, like as not,' Susannah said sternly.

'No great loss,' Jake muttered, but he let the subject drop.

'What about Mia?' Roland asked, popping a match with his thumbnail. 'Is she quiet?'

'If it wasn't for you boys, I'm not sure I'd believe there even *was* such a jane.'

'And your belly's quiet, too?'

'Yes.' Susannah guessed everyone had rules about lying; hers was that if you were going to tell one, you did best to keep it short. If she had a chap in her belly – some sort of monster – she'd let them help her worry about it a week from tonight. If they were still able to worry about anything, that was. For the time being they didn't need to know about the few little cramps she'd been having.

'Then all's well,' the gunslinger said. They rode in silence for awhile, and then he said: 'I hope you two boys can dig. There'll be some digging to do.'

'Graves?' Eddie asked, not sure if he was joking or not.

'Graves come later.' Roland looked up at the sky, but the clouds had advanced out of the west and stolen the stars. 'Just remember, it's the winners who dig them.'

CHAPTER VI
BEFORE THE STORM

1

Rising up from the darkness, dolorous and accusatory, came the voice of Henry Dean, the great sage and eminent junkie. 'I'm in hell, bro! I'm in hell and I can't get a fix and *it's all your fault!*'

'How long will we have to be here, do you think?' Eddie asked Callahan. They had just reached the Doorway Cave, and the great sage's little bro was already shaking a pair of bullets in his right hand like dice – seven-come-eleven, baby need a little peace n quiet. It was the day after the big meeting, and when Eddie and the Pere had ridden out of town, the high street had seemed unusually quiet. It was almost as if the Calla was hiding from itself, overwhelmed by what it had committed itself to.

'I'm afraid it'll be awhile,' Callahan admitted. He was neatly (and nondescriptly, he hoped) dressed. In the breast pocket of his shirt was all the American money they'd been able to put together: eleven crumpled dollars and a pair of quarters. He thought it would be a bitter joke if he turned up in a version of America where Lincoln was on the single and Washington on the fifties. 'But we can do it in stages, I think.'

'Thank God for small favors,' Eddie said, and dragged the pink bag out from behind Tower's bookcase. He lifted it with both hands, began to turn, then stopped. He was frowning.

'What is it?' Callahan asked.

'There's something in here.'

'Yes, the box.'

'No, something in the *bag*. Sewn into the lining, I think. It feels like a little rock. Maybe there's a secret pocket.'

'And maybe,' Callahan said, 'this isn't the time to investigate it.'

Still, Eddie gave the object another small squeeze. It didn't *feel* like a stone, exactly. But Callahan was probably right. They had enough mysteries on their hands already. This one was for another day.

When Eddie slid the ghostwood box out of the bag, a sick dread invaded both his head and his heart. 'I hate this thing. I keep feeling like it's going to turn on me and eat me like a . . . a taco-chip.'

'It probably could,' Callahan said. 'If you feel something really bad happening, Eddie, shut the damn thing.'

'Your ass would be stuck on the other side if I did.'

'It's not as though I'm a stranger there,' Callahan said, eyeing the unfound door. Eddie heard his brother; Callahan heard his mother, endlessly hectoring, calling him Donnie. He'd always hated being called Donnie. 'I'll just wait for it to open again.'

Eddie stuffed the bullets into his ears.

'Why are you letting him do that, Donnie?' Callahan's mother moaned from the darkness. 'Bullets in your ears, that's *dangerous!*'

'Go on,' Eddie said. 'Get it done.' He opened the box. The chimes attacked Callahan's ears. And his heart. The door to everywhere clicked open.

2

He went through thinking about two things: the year 1977 and the men's room on the main floor of the New York Public Library. He stepped into a bathroom stall with graffiti on the walls (BANGO SKANK had been there) and the sound of a flushing urinal somewhere to his left. He waited for whoever it was to leave, then stepped out of the stall.

It took him only ten minutes to find what he needed. When he stepped back through the door into the cave, he was holding a book under his arm. He asked Eddie to step outside with him, and didn't have to ask twice. In the fresh air and breezy sunshine (the previous night's clouds had blown away), Eddie took the bullets from his ears and examined the book. It was called *Yankee Highways.*

'The Father's a library thief,' Eddie remarked. 'You're exactly the sort of person who makes the fees go up.'

'I'll return it someday,' Callahan said. He meant it. 'The important thing is I got lucky on my second try. Check page one-nineteen.'

Eddie did. The photograph showed a stark white church sitting on a hill above a dirt road. *East Stoneham Methodist Meeting Hall*, the caption said. *Built 1819.* Eddie thought: *Add em, come out with nineteen. Of course.*

He mentioned this to Callahan, who smiled and nodded. 'Notice anything else?'

Of course he did. 'It looks like the Calla Gathering Hall.'

'So it does. Its twin, almost.' Callahan took a deep breath. 'Are you ready for round two?'

'I guess so.'

'This one's apt to be longer, but you should be able to pass the time. There's plenty of reading matter.'

'I don't think I could read,' Eddie said. 'I'm too fucking nervous, pardon my French. Maybe I'll see what's in the lining of the bag.'

But Eddie forgot about the object in the lining of the pink bag; it was Susannah who eventually found that, and when she did, she was no longer herself.

3

Thinking 1977 and holding the book open to the picture of the Methodist Meeting Hall in East Stoneham, Callahan stepped through the unfound door for the second time. He came out on a brilliantly sunny New England morning. The church was there, but it had been painted since its picture had been taken for *Yankee Highways*, and the road had been paved. Sitting nearby was a building that hadn't been in the photo: the East Stoneham General Store. Good.

He walked down there, followed by the floating doorway, reminding himself not to spend one of the quarters, which had come from his own little stash, unless he absolutely had to. The one from Jake was dated 1969, which was okay. His, however, was from 1981, and that wasn't. As he walked past the Mobil gas pumps (where regular was selling for forty-nine cents a gallon), he transferred it to his back pocket.

When he entered the store — which smelled almost exactly like Took's — a bell jingled. To the left was a stack of Portland *Press*-Heralds, and the date gave him a nasty little shock. When he'd taken the book from the New York Public Library, not half an hour ago by his body's clock, it had been June 26th. The date on these papers was the 27th.

He took one, reading the headlines (a flood in New Orleans, the usual unrest among the homicidal idiots of the mideast) and noting the price: a dime. Good. He'd get change back from his '69 quarter. Maybe buy a piece of good old Made in the USA salami. The clerk looked him over with a cheerful eye as he approached the counter.

'That do it?' he asked.

'Well, I tell you what,' Callahan said. 'I could use a point toward the post office, if that does ya.'

The clerk raised an eyebrow and smiled. 'You sound like you're from these parts.'

'Do you say so, then?' Callahan asked, also smiling.

'Ayuh. Anyway, post office is easy. Ain't but a mile down this road, on your left.' He pronounced road *rud*, exactly as Jamie Jaffords might have done.

'Good enough. And do you sell salami by the slice?'

'I'll sell it just about any old way you want to buy it,' the clerk said amiably. 'Summer visitor, are you?' It came out *summah visitah*, and Callahan almost expected him to add *Tell me, I beg.*

'You could call me that, I guess,' Callahan said.

4

In the cave, Eddie fought against the faint but maddening jangle of the chimes and peered through the half-open door. Callahan was walking down a country road. Goody gumdrops for him. Meantime, maybe Mrs Dean's little boy *would* try having himself a bit of a read. With a cold (and slightly trembling) hand, he reached into the bookcase and pulled out a volume two down from one that had been turned upside down, one that would certainly have changed his day had he happened to grab it. What he came up with instead was *Four Short Novels of Sherlock Holmes*. Ah, Holmes, another great sage and eminent junkie. Eddie opened to *A Study in Scarlet* and began to read. Every now and then he found himself looking down at the box, where Black Thirteen pulsed out its weird force. He could just see a curve of glass. After a little bit he gave up trying to read, only looking at the curve of glass, growing more and more fascinated. But the chimes were fading, and that was good, wasn't it? After a little while he could hardly hear them at all. A little while after that, a voice crept past the bullets in his ears and began to speak to him.

Eddie listened.

5

'Pardon me, ma'am.'

'Ayuh?' The postmistress was a woman in her late fifties or early sixties, dressed to meet the public with hair of a perfect beauty-shop blue-white.

'I'd like to leave a letter for some friends of mine,' Callahan said. 'They're from New York, and they'd likely be General Delivery customers.' He had argued with Eddie that Calvin Tower, on the run from a bunch of dangerous hoods who would almost certainly still want his head on a stick, wouldn't do anything so dumb as sign up for mail. Eddie had reminded him of how Tower had been about his fucking precious first editions, and Callahan had finally agreed to at least try this.

'Summer folk?'

'Do ya,' Callahan agreed, but that wasn't quite right. 'I mean ayuh. Their names are Calvin Tower and Aaron Deepneau. I guess that isn't informa-tion you're supposed to give someone just in off the street, but—'

'Oh, we don't bother much about such things out in these parts,' she said. *Parts* came out *pahts.* 'Just let me check the list . . . we have so *many* between Memorial Day and Labor Day . . .'

She picked up a clipboard with three or four tattered sheets of paper on it from her side of the counter. Lots of hand-written names. She flicked over the first sheet to the second, then from the second to the third.

'Deepneau!' she said. 'Ayuh, there's that one. Now . . . just let me see if I can find t'other 'un . . .'

'Never mind,' Callahan said. All at once he felt uneasy, as though some-thing had gone wrong back on the other side. He glanced over his shoulder and saw nothing but the door, and the cave, and Eddie sitting there cross-legged with a book in his lap.

'Got somebody chasin ya?' the postlady asked, smiling.

Callahan laughed. It sounded forced and stupid to his own ears, but the postlady seemed to sense nothing wrong. 'If I were to write Aaron a note and put it in a stamped envelope, would you see that he gets it when he comes in? Or when Mr Tower comes in?'

'Oh, no need to buy a stamp,' said she, comfortably. 'Glad to do it.'

Yes, it *was* like the Calla. Suddenly he liked this woman very much. Liked her big-big.

Callahan went to the counter by the window (the door doing a neat do-si-do around him when he turned) and jotted a note, first introducing himself as a friend of the man who had helped Tower with Jack Andolini. He told Deepneau and Tower to leave their car where it was, and to leave some of the lights on in the place where they were staying, and then to move somewhere close by — a barn, an abandoned camp, even a shed. To do it immediately. *Leave a note with directions to where you are under the driver's side floormat of your car, or under the back porch step,* he wrote. *We'll be in touch.* He hoped he was doing this right; they hadn't talked things out this far, and he'd never expected to have to do any cloak-and-dagger stuff. He signed as Roland had told him to: *Callahan, of the Eld.* Then, in spite of his growing unease, he added another line, almost slashing the letters into the paper: *And make this trip to the post office your LAST. How stupid can you be???*

He put the note in an envelope, sealed it, and wrote AARON DEEPNEAU OR CALVIN TOWER, GEN'L DELIVERY on the front. He took it back to the counter. 'I'll be happy to buy a stamp,' he told her again.

'Nawp, just two cent' for the envelope and we're square.'

He gave her the nickel left over from the store, took back his three cents' change, and headed for the door. The ordinary one.

'Good luck to ye,' the postlady called.

Callahan turned his head to look at her and say thanks. He caught a glimpse of the unfound door when he did, still open. What he didn't see was Eddie. Eddie was gone.

6

Callahan turned to that strange door as soon as he was outside the post office. Ordinarily you couldn't do that, ordinarily it swung with you as neatly as a square-dance partner, but it seemed to know when you intended to step back through. Then you could face it.

The minute he was back the todash chimes seized him, seeming to etch patterns on the surface of his brain. From the bowels of the cave his mother cried, 'There-now, Donnie, you've gone and let that nice boy commit suicide! He'll be in purgie forever, and it's your fault!'

Callahan barely heard. He dashed to the mouth of the cave, still carrying the *Press-Herald* he'd bought in the East Stoneham General Store under one arm. There was just time to see why the box hadn't closed, leaving him a prisoner in East Stoneham, Maine, circa 1977: there was a thick book sticking out of it. Callahan even had time to read the title, *Four Short Novels of Sherlock Holmes*. Then he burst out into sunshine.

At first he saw nothing but the boulder on the path leading up to the mouth of the cave, and was sickeningly sure his mother's voice had told the truth. Then he looked left and saw Eddie ten feet away, at the end of the narrow path and tottering on the edge of the drop. His untucked shirt fluttered around the butt of Roland's big revolver. His normally sharp and rather foxy features now looked puffy and blank. It was the dazed face of a fighter out on his feet. His hair blew around his ears. He swayed forward . . . then his mouth tightened and his eyes became almost aware. He grasped an outcrop of rock and swayed back again.

He's fighting it, Callahan thought. *And I'm sure he's fighting the good fight, but he's losing.*

Calling out might actually send him over the edge; Callahan knew this with a gunslinger's intuition, always sharpest and most dependable in times of crisis. Instead of yelling he sprinted up the remaining stub of path and wound a hand in the tail of Eddie's shirt just as Eddie swayed forward again, this time removing his hand from the outcrop beside him and using it to cover his eyes in a gesture that was unmeaningly comic: *Goodbye, cruel world.*

If the shirt had torn, Eddie Dean would undoubtedly have been excused from ka's great game, but perhaps even the tails of homespun Calla Bryn Sturgis shirts (for that was what he was wearing) served ka. In any case the shirt didn't tear, and Callahan had held onto a great part of the physical strength he had built up during his years on the road. He yanked Eddie back and caught him in his arms, but not before the younger man's head struck the outcrop his hand had been on a few seconds before. His lashes fluttered and he looked at Callahan with a kind of stupid unrecognition. He said something that sounded like gibberish to Callahan: *Ihsay ahkin fly-oo ower.*

Callahan grabbed his shoulders and shook him. 'What? I don't understand you!' Nor did he much want to, but he had to make some kind of contact, had to bring Eddie back from wherever the accursed thing in the box had taken him. '*I don't . . . understand you!*'

This time the response was clearer: 'It says I can fly to the Tower. You can let me go. I *want* to go!'

'You can't fly, Eddie.' He wasn't sure that got through, so he put his head down – all the way, until he and Eddie were resting brow to brow, like lovers. 'It was trying to kill you.'

'No . . .' Eddie began, and then awareness came all the way back into his eyes. An inch from Callahan's own, they widened in understanding. '*Yes.*'

Callahan lifted his head, but still kept a prudent grip on Eddie's shoulders. 'Are you all right now?'

'Yeah. I guess so, at least. I was going along good, Father. Swear I was. I mean, the chimes were doing a number on me, but otherwise I was fine. I even grabbed a book and started to read.' He looked around. 'Jesus, I hope I didn't lose it. Tower'll scalp me.'

'You didn't lose it. You stuck it partway into the box, and it's a damned good thing you did. Otherwise the door would have shut and you'd be strawberry jam about seven hundred feet down.'

Eddie looked over the edge and went completely pale. Callahan had just time enough to regret his frankness before Eddie vomited on his new shor'boots.

7

'It crept up on me, Father,' he said when he could talk. 'Lulled me and then jumped.'

'Yes.'

'Did you get anything at all out of your time over there?'

'If they get my letter and do what it says, a great deal. You were right. Deepneau at least signed up for General Delivery. About Tower, I don't know.' Callahan shook his head angrily.

'I think we're gonna find that Tower talked Deepneau into it,' Eddie said. 'Cal Tower still can't believe what he's gotten himself into, and after what just happened to me – *almost* happened to me – I've got some sympathy for that kind of thinking.' He looked at what Callahan still had clamped under one arm. 'What's that?'

'The newspaper,' Callahan said, and offered it to Eddie. 'Care to read about Golda Meir?'

8

Roland listened carefully that evening as Eddie and Callahan recounted their adventures in the Doorway Cave and beyond. The gunslinger seemed less interested in Eddie's near-death experience than he was in the similarities between Calla Bryn Sturgis and East Stoneham. He even asked Callahan to imitate the accent of the storekeeper and the postlady. This Callahan (a former Maine resident, after all) was able to do quite well.

'Do ya,' said Roland, and then: 'Ayuh. Do ya, ayuh.' He sat thinking, one bootheel cocked up on the rail of the rectory porch.

'Will they be okay for awhile, do you think?' Eddie asked.

'I hope so,' Roland replied. 'If you want to worry about someone's life, worry about Deepneau's. If Balazar hasn't given up on the vacant lot, he has to keep Tower alive. Deepneau's nothing but a Watch Me chip now.'

'Can we leave them until after the Wolves?'

'I don't see what choice we have.'

'We could drop this whole business and go over there to East Overshoe and protect him!' Eddie said heatedly. 'How about that? Listen, Roland, I'll tell you exactly why Tower talked his friend into signing up for General Delivery: somebody's got a book he wants, that's why. He was dickering for it and negotiations had reached the delicate stage when I showed up and persuaded him to head for the hills. But Tower . . . man, he's like a chimp with a handful of grain. He won't let go. If Balazar knows that, and he probably does, he won't need a zip code to find his man, just a list of the people Tower did business with. I hope to Christ that if there *was* a list, it burned up in the fire.'

Roland was nodding. 'I understand, but we can't leave here. We've promised.'

Eddie thought it over, sighed, and shook his head. 'What the hell, three and a half more days over here, seventeen over there before the deal-letter Tower signed expires. Things'll probably hold together that long.' He paused, biting his lip. 'Maybe.'

'Is *maybe* the best we can do?' Callahan asked.

'Yeah,' Eddie said. 'For the time being, I guess it is.'

9

The following morning, a badly frightened Susannah Dean sat in the privy at the foot of the hill, bent over, waiting for her current cycle of contractions to pass. She'd been having them for a little over a week now, but these were by far the strongest. She put her hands on her lower belly. The flesh there was alarmingly hard.

Oh dear God, what if I'm having it right now? What if this is it?

She tried to tell herself this *couldn't* be it, her water hadn't broken and you couldn't go into genuine labor until that happened. But what did she actually know about having babies? Very little. Even Rosalita Munoz, a midwife of great experience, wouldn't be able to help her much, because Rosa's career had been delivering *human* babies, of mothers who actually looked pregnant. Susannah looked less pregnant now than when they'd first arrived in the Calla. And if Roland was right about *this* baby—

It's not a baby. It's a chap, and it doesn't belong to me. It belongs to Mia, whoever she is. Mia, daughter of none.

The cramps ceased. Her lower belly relaxed, losing that stony feel. She laid a finger along the cleft of her vagina. It felt the same as ever. Surely she was going to be all right for another few days. She *had* to be. And while she'd agreed with Roland that there should be no more secrets in their ka-tet, she felt she had to keep this one. When the fighting finally started, it would be seven against forty or fifty. Maybe as many as seventy, if the Wolves stuck together in a single pack. They would have to be at their very best, their most fiercely concentrated. That meant no distractions. It also meant that she must be there to take her place.

She yanked up her jeans, did the buttons, and went out into the bright sunshine, absently rubbing at her left temple. She saw the new lock on the privy – just as Roland had asked – and began to smile. Then she looked down at her shadow and the smile froze. When she'd gone into the privy, her Dark Lady had stretched out nine-in-the-morning long. Now she was saying that if noon wasn't here, it would be shortly.

That's impossible. I was only in there a few minutes. Long enough to pee.

Perhaps that was true. Perhaps it was Mia who had been in there the rest of the time.

'No,' she said. 'That can't be so.'

But Susannah thought it was. Mia wasn't ascendant – not yet – but she was rising. Getting ready to take over, if she could.

Please, she prayed, putting one hand out against the privy wall to brace herself. *Just three more days, God. Give me three more days as myself, let us do our duty to the children of this place, and then what You will. Whatever You will. But please—*

'Just three more,' she murmured. 'And if they do us down out there, it won't matter noway. Three more days, God. Hear me, I beg.'

10

A day later, Eddie and Tian Jaffords went looking for Andy and came upon him standing by himself at the wide and dusty junction of East and River Roads, singing at the top of his . . .

'Nope,' Eddie said as he and Tian approached, 'can't say lungs, he doesn't *have* lungs.'

'Cry pardon?' Tian asked.

'Nothing,' Eddie said. 'Doesn't matter.' But, by the process of association – lungs to general anatomy – a question had occurred to him. 'Tian, is there a doctor in the Calla?'

Tian looked at him with surprise and some amusement. 'Not us, Eddie. Gut-tossers might do well for rich folks who have the time to go and the money to pay, but when us gets sick, we go to one of the Sisters.'

'The Sisters of Oriza.'

'Yar. If the medicine's good – it usually be – we get better. If it ain't, we get worse. In the end the ground cures all, d'ye see?'

'Yes,' Eddie said, thinking how difficult it must be for them to fit roont children into such a view of things. Those who came back roont died eventually, but for years they just . . . lingered.

'There's only three boxes to a man, anyro'', Tian said as they approached the solitary singing robot. Off in the eastern distance, between Calla Bryn Sturgis and Thunderclap, Eddie could see scarves of dust rising toward the blue sky, although it was perfectly still where they were.

'Boxes?'

'Aye, say true,' Tian said, then rapidly touched his brow, his breast, and his butt. 'Headbox, titbox, shitbox.' And he laughed heartily.

'You say that?' Eddie asked, smiling.

'Well ... out here, between us, it does fine,' Tian said, 'although I guess no proper lady'd hear the boxes so described at her table.' He touched his head, chest, and bottom again. 'Thoughtbox, heartbox, ki'box.'

Eddie heard *key*. 'What's that last one mean? What kind of key unlocks your ass?'

Tian stopped. They were in plain view of Andy, but the robot ignored them completely, singing what sounded like opera in a language Eddie couldn't understand. Every now and then Andy held his arms up or crossed them, the gestures seemingly part of the song he was singing.

'Hear me,' Tian said kindly. 'A man is stacked, do ye ken. On top is his thoughts, which is the finest part of a man.'

'Or a woman,' Eddie said, smiling.

Tian nodded seriously. 'Aye, or a woman, but we use *man* to stand for both, because woman was born of man's breath, kennit.'

'Do you say so?' Eddie asked, thinking of some women's-lib types he'd met before leaving New York for Mid-World. He doubted they'd care for that idea much more than for the part of the Bible that said Eve had been made from Adam's rib.

'Let it be so,' Tian agreed, 'but it was Lady Oriza who gave birth to the first man, so the old folks will tell you. They say *Can-ah, can-tah, annah, Oriza:* "All breath comes from the woman."'

'So tell me about these boxes.'

'Best and highest is the head, with all the head's ideas and dreams. Next is the heart, with all our feelings of love and sadness and joy and happiness—'

'The emotions.'

Tian looked both puzzled and respectful. 'Do you say so?'

'Well, where I come from we do, so let it be so.'

'Ah.' Tian nodded as if the concept were interesting but only borderline comprehensible. This time instead of touching his bottom, he patted his crotch. 'In the last box is all what we'd call low-commala: have a fuck, take a shit, maybe want to do someone a meanness for no reason.'

'And if you *do* have a reason?'

'Oh, but then it wouldn't be meanness, would it?' Tian asked, looking amused. 'In that case, it'd come from the heartbox or the headbox.'

'That's bizarre,' Eddie said, but he supposed it wasn't, not really. In his mind's eye he could see three neatly stacked crates: head on top of heart, heart on top of all the animal functions and groundless rages people sometimes felt. He was particularly fascinated by Tian's use of the word *meanness*, as if it were some kind of behavioral landmark. Did that make sense, or didn't it? He would have to consider it carefully, and this wasn't the time.

Andy still stood gleaming in the sun, pouring out great gusts of song. Eddie had a vague memory of some kids back in the neighborhood, yelling out *I'm the Barber of Seville-a, You must try my fucking skill-a* and then running away, laughing like loons as they went.

'Andy!' Eddie said, and the robot broke off at once.

'Hile, Eddie, I see you well! Long days and pleasant nights!'

'Same to you,' Eddie said. 'How are you?'

'Fine, Eddie!' Andy said fervently. 'I always enjoy singing before the first seminon.'

'Seminon?'

'It's what we call the windstorms that come before true winter,' Tian said, and pointed to the clouds of dust far beyond the Whye. 'Yonder comes the first one; it'll be here either the day of Wolves or the day after, I judge.'

'The day of, sai,' said Andy. '"Seminon comin, warm days go runnin." So they say.' He bent toward Eddie. Clickings came from inside his gleaming head. His blue eyes flashed on and off. 'Eddie, I have cast a great horoscope, very long and complex, and it shows victory against the Wolves! A great victory, indeed! You will vanquish your enemies and then meet a beautiful lady!'

'I already *have* a beautiful lady,' Eddie said, trying to keep his voice pleasant. He knew perfectly well what those rapidly flashing blue lights meant; the son of a bitch was laughing at him. *Well*, he thought, *maybe you'll be laughing on the other side of your face a couple of days from now, Andy. I certainly hope so.*

'So you do, but many a married man has had his jilly, as I told sai Tian Jaffords not so long ago.'

'Not those who love their wives,' Tian said. 'I told you so then and I tell you now.'

'Andy, old buddy,' Eddie said earnestly, 'we came out here in hopes that you'd do us a solid on the night before the Wolves come. Help us a little, you know.'

There were several clicking sounds deep in Andy's chest, and this time when his eyes flashed, they almost seemed alarmed. 'I would if I could, sai,' Andy said, 'oh yes, there's nothing I like more than helping my friends, but there are a great many things I can't do, much as I might like to.'

'Because of your programming.'

'Aye.' The smug so-happy-to-see-you tone had gone out of Andy's voice. He sounded more like a machine now. *Yeah, that's his fallback position,* Eddie thought. *That's Andy being careful. You've seen em come and go, haven't you, Andy? Sometimes they call you a useless bag of bolts and mostly they ignore you, but either way you end up walking over their bones and singing your songs, don't you? But not this time, pal. No, I don't think so.*

'When were you built, Andy? I'm curious. When did you roll off the old LaMerk assembly line?'

'Long ago, sai.' The blue eyes flashing very slowly now. Not laughing anymore.

'Two thousand years?'

'Longer, I believe. Sai, I know a song about drinking that you might like, it's very amusing—'

'Maybe another time. Listen, good buddy, if you're thousands of years old, how is it that you're programmed concerning the Wolves?'

From inside Andy there came a deep, reverberant clunk, as though something had broken. When he spoke again, it was in the dead, emotionless voice Eddie had first heard on the edge of Mid-Forest. The voice of Bosco Bob when ole Bosco was getting ready to cloud up and rain all over you.

'What's your password, sai Eddie?'

'Think we've been down this road before, haven't we?'

'Password. You have ten seconds. Nine . . . eight . . . seven . . .'

'That password shit's very convenient for you, isn't it?'

'Incorrect password, sai Eddie.'

'Kinda like taking the Fifth.'

'Two . . . one . . . zero. You may retry once. Would you retry, Eddie?'

Eddie gave him a sunny smile. 'Does the seminon blow in the summertime, old buddy?'

More clicks and clacks. Andy's head, which had been tilted one way, now tilted the other. 'I do not follow you, Eddie of New York.'

'Sorry. I'm just being a silly old human bean, aren't I? No, I don't want to retry. At least not right now. Let me tell you what we'd like you to help us with, and you can tell us if your programming will allow you to do it. Does that sound fair?'

'Fair as fresh air, Eddie.'

'Okay.' Eddie reached up and took hold of Andy's thin metal arm. The surface was smooth and somehow unpleasant to the touch. Greasy. Oily.

Eddie held on nonetheless, and lowered his voice to a confidential level. 'I'm only telling you this because you're clearly good at keeping secrets.'

'Oh, yes, sai Eddie! No one keeps a secret like Andy!' The robot was back on solid ground and back to his old self, smug and complacent.

'Well . . .' Eddie went up on tiptoe. 'Bend down here.'

Servomotors hummed inside Andy's casing — inside what would have been his heartbox, had he not been a high-tech tin-man. He bent down. Eddie, meanwhile, stretched up even further, feeling absurdly like a small boy telling a secret.

'The Pere's got some guns from our level of the Tower,' he murmured. 'Good ones.'

Andy's head swiveled around. His eyes glared out with a brilliance that could only have been astonishment. Eddie kept a poker face, but inside he was grinning.

'Say true, Eddie?'

'Say thankya.'

'Pere says they're powerful,' Tian said. 'If they work, we can use em to blow the living bugger out of the Wolves. But we have to get em out north of town . . . and they're heavy. Can you help us load em in a bucka on Wolf's Eve, Andy?'

Silence. Clicks and clacks.

'Programming won't let him, I bet,' Eddie said sadly. 'Well, if we get enough strong backs—'

'I can help you,' Andy said. 'Where are these guns, sais?'

'Better not say just now,' Eddie replied. 'You meet us at the Pere's rectory early on Wolf's Eve, all right?'

'What hour would you have me?'

'How does six sound?'

'Six o' the clock. And how many guns will there be? Tell me that much, at least, so I may calculate the required energy levels.'

My friend, it takes a bullshitter to recognize bullshit, Eddie thought merrily, but kept a straight face. 'There be a dozen. Maybe fifteen. They weigh a couple of hundred pounds each. Do you know pounds, Andy?'

'Aye, say thankya. A pound is roughly four hundred and fifty grams. Sixteen ounces. "A pint's a pound, the world around." Those are big guns, sai Eddie, say true! Will they shoot?'

'We're pretty sure they will,' Eddie said. 'Aren't we, Tian?'

Tian nodded. 'And you'll help us?'

'Aye, happy to. Six o' the clock, at the rectory.'

'Thank you, Andy,' Eddie said. He started away, then looked back. 'You absolutely won't talk about this, will you?'

'No, sai, not if you tell me not to.'

'That's just what I'm telling you. The last thing we want is for the Wolves to find out we've got some big guns to use against em.'

'Of course not,' Andy said. 'What good news this is. Have a wonderful day, sais.'

'And you, Andy,' Eddie replied. 'And you.'

11

Walking back toward Tian's place — it was only two miles distant from where they'd come upon Andy — Tian said, 'Does he believe it?'

'I don't know,' Eddie said, 'but it surprised the shit out of him — did you feel that?'

'Yes,' Tian said. 'Yes, I did.'

'He'll be there to see for himself, I guarantee that much.'

Tian nodded, smiling. 'Your dinh is clever.'

'That he is,' Eddie agreed. 'That he is.'

12

Once more Jake lay awake, looking up at the ceiling of Benny's room. Once more Oy lay on Benny's bed, curved into a comma with his nose beneath his squiggle of tail. Tomorrow night Jake would be back at Father Callahan's, back with his ka-tet, and he couldn't wait. Tomorrow would be Wolf's Eve, but this was only the *eve* of Wolf's Eve, and Roland had felt it would be best for Jake to stay this one last night at the Rocking B. 'We don't want to raise suspicions this late in the game,' he'd said. Jake understood, but boy, this was sick. The prospect of standing against the Wolves was bad enough. The thought of how Benny might look at him two days from now was even worse.

Maybe we'll all get killed, Jake thought. *Then I won't have to worry about it.*

In his distress, this idea actually had a certain attraction.

'Jake? You asleep?'

For a moment Jake considered faking it, but something inside sneered at such cowardice. 'No,' he said. 'But I ought to try, Benny. I doubt if I'll get much tomorrow night.'

'I guess *not*,' Benny whispered back respectfully, and then: 'You scared?'

''Course I am,' Jake said. 'What do you think I am, crazy?'

Benny got up on one elbow. 'How many do you think you'll kill?'

Jake thought about it. It made him sick to think about it, way down in the pit of his stomach, but he thought about it anyway. 'Dunno. If there's seventy, I guess I'll have to try to get ten.'

He found himself thinking (with a mild sense of wonder) of Ms Avery's English class. The hanging yellow globes with ghostly dead flies lying in their bellies. Lucas Hanson, who always tried to trip him when he was going up the aisle. Sentences diagrammed on the blackboard: beware the misplaced modifier. Petra Jesserling, who always wore A-line jumpers and had a crush on him (or so Mike Yanko claimed). The drone of Ms Avery's voice. Outs at noon — what would be plain old lunch in a plain old public school. Sitting at his desk afterward and trying to stay awake. Was that boy, that neat Piper School boy, actually going out to the north of a farming town called Calla Bryn Sturgis to battle child-stealing monsters? Could that boy be lying dead thirty-six hours from now with his guts in a steaming pile behind him, blown out of his back and into the dirt by something called a sneetch? Surely that wasn't possible, was it? The housekeeper, Mrs Shaw, had cut the crusts off his sandwiches and sometimes called him 'Bama. His father had taught him how to calculate a fifteen per cent tip. Such boys surely did not go out to die with guns in their hands. Did they?

'I bet you get *twenty*!' Benny said. 'Boy, I wish I could be with you! We'd fight side by side! Pow! Pow! Pow! Then we'd reload!'

Jake sat up and looked at Benny with real curiosity. '*Would* you?' he asked. 'If you could?'

Benny thought about it. His face changed, was suddenly older and wiser. He shook his head. 'Nah. I'd be scared. Aren't you really scared? Say true?'

'Scared to death,' Jake said simply.

'Of dying?'

'Yeah, but I'm even more scared of fucking up.'

'You won't.'

Easy for you to say, Jake thought.

'If I have to go with the little kids, at least I'm glad my father's going, too,' Benny said. 'He's taking his bah. You ever seen him shoot?'

'No.'

'Well, he's good with it. If any of the Wolves get past you guys, he'll take care of them. He'll find that gill-place on their chests, and *pow!*'

What if Benny knew the gill-place was a lie? Jake wondered. False information this boy's father would hopefully pass on? What if he knew—

Eddie spoke up in his head, Eddie with his wise-ass Brooklyn accent in full flower. *Yeah, and if fish had bicycles, every fuckin river'd be the Tour de France.*

'Benny, I really have to try to get some sleep.'

Benny lay back down. Jake did the same, and resumed looking up at the ceiling. All at once he hated it that Oy was on Benny's bed, that Oy had taken so naturally to the other boy. All at once he hated everything about everything. The hours until morning, when he could pack, mount his borrowed pony, and ride back to town, seemed to stretch out into infinity.

'Jake?'

'What, Benny, *what?*'

'I'm sorry. I just wanted to say I'm glad you came here. We had some fun, didn't we?'

'Yeah,' Jake said, and thought: *No one would believe he's older than me. He sounds about . . . I don't know . . . five, or something.* That was mean, but Jake had an idea that if he wasn't mean, he might actually start to cry. He hated Roland for sentencing him to this last night at the Rocking B. 'Yeah, fun big-big.'

'I'm gonna miss you. But I'll bet they put up a statue of you guys in the Pavilion, or something.' *Guys* was a word Benny had picked up from Jake, and he used it every chance he got.

'I'll miss you, too,' Jake said.

'You're lucky, getting to follow the Beam and travel places. I'll probably be here in this shitty town the rest of my life.'

No, you won't. You and your Da' are going to do plenty of wandering . . . if you're lucky and they let you out of town, that is. What you're going to do, I think, is spend the rest of your life dreaming about this shitty little town. About a place that was home. And it's my doing. I saw . . . and I told. But what else could I do?

'Jake?'

He could stand no more. It would drive him mad. 'Go to sleep, Benny. And let *me* go to sleep.'

'Okay.'

Benny rolled over to face the wall. In a little while his breathing slowed.

A little while after that, he began snoring. Jake lay awake until nearly midnight, and then he went to sleep, too. And had a dream. In it Roland was down on his knees in the dust of East Road, facing a great horde of oncoming Wolves that stretched from the bluffs to the river. He was trying to reload, but both of his hands were stiff and one was short two fingers. The bullets fell uselessly in front of him. He was still trying to load his great revolver when the Wolves rode him down.

13

Dawn of Wolf's Eve. Eddie and Susannah stood at the window of the Pere's guest room, looking down the slope of lawn to Rosa's cottage.

'He's found something with her,' Susannah said. 'I'm glad for him.'

Eddie nodded. 'How you feeling?'

She smiled up at him. 'I'm fine,' she said, and meant it. 'What about you, sugar?'

'I'll miss sleeping in a real bed with a roof over my head, and I'm anxious to get to it, but otherwise I'm fine, too.'

'Things go wrong, you won't have to worry about the accommodations.'

'That's true,' Eddie said, 'but I don't think they're going to go wrong. Do you?'

Before she could answer, a gust of wind shook the house and whistled beneath the eaves. The seminon saying good day to ya, Eddie guessed.

'I don't like that wind,' she said. 'It's a wild-card.'

Eddie opened his mouth.

'And if you say anything about ka, I'll punch you in the nose.'

Eddie closed his mouth again and mimed zipping it shut. Susannah went to his nose anyway, a brief touch of knuckles like a feather. 'We've got a fine chance to win,' she said. 'They've had everything their own way for a long time, and it's made em fat. Like Blaine.'

'Yeah. Like Blaine.'

She put a hand on his hip and turned him to her. 'But things *could* go wrong, so I want to tell you something while it's just the two of us, Eddie. I want to tell you how much I love you.' She spoke simply, with no drama.

'I know you do,' he said, 'but I'll be damned if I know why.'

'Because you make me feel whole,' she said. 'When I was younger, I used to vacillate between thinking love was this great and glorious mystery and thinking it was just something a bunch of Hollywood movie producers made up to sell more tickets back in the Depression, when Dish Night kind of played out.'

Eddie laughed.

'Now I think that all of us are born with a hole in our hearts, and we go around looking for the person who can fill it. You ... Eddie, you fill me up.' She took his hand and began to lead him back to the bed. 'And right now I'd like you to fill me up the other way.'

'Suze, is it safe?'

'I don't know,' she said, 'and I don't care.'

They made love slowly, the pace only building near the end. She cried out softly against his shoulder, and in the instant before his own climax blotted out reflection, Eddie thought: *I'm going to lose her if I'm not careful. I don't know how I know that ... but I do. She'll just disappear.*

'I love you, too,' he said when they were finished and lying side by side again.

'Yes.' She took his hand. 'I know. I'm glad.'

'It's good to make someone glad,' he said. 'I didn't use to know that.'

'It's all right,' Susannah said, and kissed the corner of his mouth. 'You learn fast.'

14

There was a rocker in Rosa's little living room. The gunslinger sat in it naked, holding a clay saucer in one hand. He was smoking and looking out at the sunrise. He wasn't sure he would ever again see it rise from this place.

Rosa came out of the bedroom, also naked, and stood in the doorway looking at him. 'How're y' bones, tell me, I beg?'

Roland nodded. 'That oil of yours is a wonder.'

''Twon't last.'

'No,' Roland said. 'But there's another world — my friends' world — and maybe they have something there that will. I've got a feeling we'll be going there soon.'

'More fighting to do?'

'I think so, yes.'

'You won't be back this way in any case, will you?'

Roland looked at her. 'No.'

'Are you tired, Roland?'

'To death,' said he.

'Come back to bed a little while, then, will ya not?'

He crushed out his smoke and stood. He smiled. It was a younger man's smile. 'Say thankya.'

'Thee's a good man, Roland of Gilead.'

He considered this, then slowly shook his head. 'All my life I've had the fastest hands, but at being good I was always a little too slow.'

She held out a hand to him. 'Come ye, Roland. Come commala.' And he went to her.

15

Early that afternoon, Roland, Eddie, Jake, and Pere Callahan rode out the East Road – which was actually a north road at this point along the winding Devar-Tete Whye – with shovels concealed in the bedrolls at the backs of their saddles. Susannah had been excused from this duty on account of her pregnancy. She had joined the Sisters of Oriza at the Pavilion, where a larger tent was being erected and preparations for a huge evening meal were already going forward. When they left, Calla Bryn Sturgis had already begun to fill up, as if for a Fair-Day. But there was no whooping and hollering, no impudent rattle of firecrackers, no rides being set up on the Green. They had seen neither Andy nor Ben Slightman, and that was good.

'Tian?' Roland asked Eddie, breaking the rather heavy silence among them.

'He'll meet me at the rectory. Five o'clock.'

'Good,' Roland said. 'If we're not done out here by four, you're excused to ride back on your own.'

'I'll go with you, if you like,' Callahan said. The Chinese believed that if you saved a man's life, you were responsible for him ever after. Callahan had never given the idea much thought, but after pulling Eddie back from the ledge above the Doorway Cave, it seemed to him there might be truth in the notion.

'Better you stay with us,' Roland said. 'Eddie can take care of this. I've got another job for you out here. Besides digging, I mean.'

'Oh? And what might that be?' Callahan asked.

Roland pointed at the dust-devils twisting and whirling ahead of them on the road. 'Pray away this damned wind. And the sooner the better. Before tomorrow morning, certainly.'

'Are you worried about the ditch?' Jake asked.

'The ditch'll be fine,' Roland said. 'It's the Sisters' Orizas I'm worried about. Throwing the plate is delicate work under the best of circumstances. If it's blowing up a gale out here when the Wolves come, the possibilities for things to go wrong—' He tossed his hand at the dusty horizon, giving it a distinctive (and fatalistic) Calla twist. '*Delah.*'

Callahan, however, was smiling. 'I'll be glad to offer a prayer,' he said, 'but look east before you grow too concerned. Do ya, I beg.'

They turned that way in their saddles. Corn – the crop now over, the picked plants standing in sloping, skeletal rows – ran down to the rice-fields. Beyond the rice was the river. Beyond the river was the end of the borderlands. There, dust-devils forty feet high spun and jerked and sometimes collided. They made the ones dancing on their side of the river look like naughty children by comparison.

'The seminon often reaches the Whye and then turns back,' Callahan said. 'According to the old folks, Lord Seminon begs Lady Oriza to make him welcome when he reaches the water and she often bars his passage out of jealousy. You see—'

'Seminon married her sissa,' Jake said. 'Lady Riza wanted him for herself – a marriage of wind and rice – and she's still p.o.'d about it.'

'How did you know that?' Callahan asked, both amused and astonished.

'Benny told me,' Jake said, and said no more. Thinking of their long discussions (sometimes in the hayloft, sometimes lazing on the bank of the river) and their eager exchanges of legend made him feel sad and hurt.

Callahan was nodding. 'That's the story, all right. I imagine it's actually a weather phenomenon – cold air over there, warm air rising off the water, something like that – but whatever it is, this one shows every sign of going back where it came from.'

The wind dashed grit in his face, as if to prove him wrong, and Callahan laughed. 'This'll be over by first light tomorrow, I almost guarantee you. But—'

'Almost's not good enough, Pere.'

'What I was going to say, Roland, is that since I know almost's not good enough, I'll gladly send up a prayer.'

'Tell ya thanks.' The gunslinger turned to Eddie, and pointed the first two fingers of his left hand at his own face. 'The eyes, right?'

'The eyes,' Eddie agreed. 'And the password. If it's not nineteen, it'll be ninety-nine.'

'You don't know that for sure.'

'I know,' Eddie said.

'Still . . . be careful.'

'I will.'

A few minutes later they reached the place where, on their right, a rocky track wandered off into the arroyo country, toward the Gloria and Redbirds One and Two. The *folken* assumed that the buckas would be left here, and they were correct. They also assumed that the children and their minders would then walk up the track to one mine or the other. In this they were wrong.

Soon three of them were digging on the west side of the road, a fourth always standing watch. No one came – the *folken* from this far out were already in town – and the work went quickly enough. At four o'clock, Eddie left the others to finish up and rode back to town to meet Tian Jaffords with one of Roland's revolvers holstered on his hip.

16

Tian had brought his bah. When Eddie told him to leave it on the Pere's porch, the farmer gave him an unhappy, uncertain stare.

'He won't be surprised to see me packing iron, but he might have questions if he saw you with that thing,' Eddie said. This was it, the true beginning of their stand, and now that it had come, Eddie felt calm. His heart was beating slowly and steadily. His vision seemed to have clarified; he could see each shadow cast by each individual blade of grass on the rectory lawn. 'He's strong, from what I've heard. And very quick when he needs to be. Let it be my play.'

'Then why am I here?'

Because even a smart robot won't expect trouble if I've got a clodhapper like you with me was the actual answer, but giving it wouldn't be very diplomatic.

'Insurance,' Eddie said. 'Come on.'

They walked down to the privy. Eddie had used it many times during the last few weeks, and always with pleasure — there were stacks of soft grasses for the clean-up phase, and you didn't have to concern yourself with poison flurry — but he'd not examined the outside closely until now. It was a wood structure, tall and solid, but he had no doubt Andy could demolish it in short order if he really wanted to. If they gave him a chance to.

Rosa came to the back door of her cottage and looked out at them, holding a hand over her eyes to shield them from the sun. 'How do ya, Eddie?'

'Fine so far, Rosie, but you better go back inside. There's gonna be a scuffle.'

'Say true? I've got a stack of plates—'

'I don't think Rizas'd help much in this case,' Eddie said. 'I guess it wouldn't hurt if you stood by, though.'

She nodded and went back inside without another word. The men sat down, flanking the open door of the privy with its new bolt-lock. Tian tried to roll a smoke. The first one fell apart in his shaking fingers and he had to try again. 'I'm not good at this sort of thing,' he said, and Eddie understood he wasn't talking about the fine art of cigarette-making.

'It's all right.'

Tian peered at him hopefully. 'Do ya say so?'

'I do, so let it be so.'

Promptly at six o'clock (*The bastard's probably got a clock set right down to millionths of a second inside him*, Eddie thought), Andy came around the rectory-house, his shadow trailing out long and spidery on the grass in front of him. He saw them. His blue eyes flashed. He raised a hand in greeting. The setting sun reflected off his arm, making it look as though it had been dipped in blood. Eddie raised his own hand in return and stood up, smiling. He wondered if all the thinking-machines that still worked in this rundown world had turned against their masters, and if so, why.

'Just be cool and let me do the talking,' he said out of the corner of his mouth.

'Yes, all right.'

'Eddie!' Andy cried. 'Tian Jaffords! How good to see you both! And weapons to use against the Wolves! My! Where are they?'

'Stacked in the shithouse,' Eddie said. 'We can get a wagon down here once they're out, but they're heavy . . . and there isn't much room to move around in there . . .'

He stood aside. Andy came on. His eyes were flashing, but not in laughter now. They were so brilliant Eddie had to squint — it was like looking at flashbulbs.

'I'm sure I can get them out,' Andy said. 'How good it is to help! How often I've regretted how little my programming allows me to . . .'

He was standing in the privy door now, bent slightly at the thighs to get his metallic barrel of a head below the level of the jamb. Eddie drew Roland's gun. As always, the sandalwood grip felt smooth and eager against his palm.

'Cry your pardon, Eddie of New York, but I see no guns.'

'No,' Eddie agreed. 'Me either. Actually all I see is a fucking traitor who teaches songs to the kids and then sends them to be—'

Andy turned with terrible liquid speed. To Eddie's ears the hum of the servos in his neck seemed very loud. They were standing less than three feet apart, point-blank range. 'May it do ya fine, you stainless-steel bastard,' Eddie said, and fired twice. The reports were deafening in the evening stillness. Andy's eyes exploded and went dark. Tian cried out.

'NO!' Andy screamed in an amplified voice. It was so loud that it made the gunshots seem no more than popping corks by comparison. 'NO, MY EYES, I CAN'T SEE, OH NO, VISION ZERO, MY EYES, MY EYES—'

The scrawny stainless-steel arms flew up to the shattered sockets, where blue sparks were now jumping erratically. Andy's legs straightened, and his barrel of a head ripped through the top of the privy's doorway, throwing chunks of board left and right.

'NO, NO, NO, I CAN'T SEE, VISION ZERO, WHAT HAVE YOU DONE TO ME, AMBUSH, ATTACK, I'M BLIND, CODE 7, CODE 7, CODE 7!'

'Help me push him, Tian!' Eddie shouted, dropping the gun back into its holster. But Tian was frozen, gawking at the robot (whose head had now vanished inside the broken doorway), and Eddie had no time to wait. He lunged forward and planted his outstretched palms on the plate giving Andy's name, function, and serial number. The robot was amazingly heavy (Eddie's first thought was that it was like pushing a parking garage), but it was also blind, surprised, and off-balance. It stumbled backward, and suddenly the amplified words cut off. What replaced them was an unearthly shrieking siren. Eddie thought it would split his head. He grabbed the door and swung it shut. There was a huge, ragged gap at the top, but the door still closed flush. Eddie ran the new bolt, which was as thick as his wrist.

From within the privy, the siren shrieked and warbled.

Rosa came running with a plate in both hands. Her eyes were huge.

'What is it? In the name of God and the Man Jesus, *what is it?*'

Before Eddie could answer, a tremendous blow shook the privy on its foundations. It actually moved to the right, disclosing the edge of the hole beneath it.

'It's Andy,' he said. 'I think he just pulled up a horoscope he doesn't much care f—'

'*YOU BASTARDS!*' This voice was totally unlike Andy's usual three forms of address: smarmy, self-satisfied, or falsely subservient. '*YOU BASTARDS! COZENING BASTARDS! I'LL KILL YOU! I'M BLIND, OH, I'M BLIND, CODE 7! CODE 7!*' The words ceased and the siren recommenced. Rosa dropped her plates and clapped her hands over her ears.

Another blow slammed against the side of the privy, and this time two of the stout boards bowed outward. The next one broke them. Andy's arm flashed through, gleaming red in the light, the four jointed fingers at the end opening and closing spasmodically. In the distance, Eddie could hear the crazy barking of dogs.

'He's going to get out, Eddie!' Tian shouted, grabbing Eddie's shoulder. 'He's going to get out!'

Eddie shook the hand off and stepped to the door. There was another crashing blow. More broken boards popped off the side of the privy. The lawn was scattered with them now. But he couldn't shout against the wail of the siren, it was just too loud. He waited, and before Andy hammered the side of the privy again, it cut off.

'*BASTARDS!*' Andy screamed. '*I'LL KILL YOU! DIRECTIVE 20, CODE 7! I'M BLIND, ZERO VISION, YOU COWARDLY—*'

'Andy, Messenger Robot!' Eddie shouted. He had jotted the serial number on one of Callahan's precious scraps of paper, with Callahan's stub of pencil, and now he read it off. 'DNF-44821-V-63! Password!'

The frenzied blows and amplified shouting ceased as soon as Eddie finished giving the serial number, yet even the silence wasn't silent; his ears still rang with the hellish shriek of the siren. There was a clank of metal and the click of relays. Then: 'This is DNF-44821-V-63. Please give password.' A pause, and then, tonelessly: 'You ambushing bastard Eddie Dean of New York. You have ten seconds. Nine . . .'

'Nineteen,' Eddie said through the door.

'Incorrect password.' And, tin-man or not, there was no mistaking the furious pleasure in Andy's voice. 'Eight . . . seven . . .'

'Ninety-nine.'

'Incorrect password.' Now what Eddie heard was triumph. He had time to regret his insane cockiness out on the road. Time to see the look of terror which passed between Rosa and Tian. Time to realize the dogs were still barking.

'Five . . . four . . .'

Not nineteen; not ninety-nine. What else was there? What in the name of Christ turned the bastard off?

'. . . three . . .'

What flashed into his mind, as bright as Andy's eyes had been before Roland's big revolver turned them dark, was the verse scrawled on the fence around the vacant lot, spray-painted in dusty rose-pink letters: *Oh SUSANNAH-MIO, divided girl of mine, Done parked her RIG in the DIXIE PIG, in the year of—*

'. . . two . . .'

Not one or the other; *both.* Which was why the damned robot hadn't cut him off after a single incorrect try. He *hadn't* been incorrect, not exactly.

'*Nineteen-ninety-nine!*' Eddie screamed through the door.

From behind it, utter silence. Eddie waited for the siren to start up again, waited for Andy to resume bashing his way out of the privy. He'd tell Tian and Rosa to run, try to cover them—

The voice that spoke from inside the battered building was colorless and flat: the voice of a machine. Both the fake smarminess and the genuine fury were gone. Andy as generations of Calla-*folken* had known him was gone, and for good.

'Thank you,' the voice said. 'I am Andy, a messenger robot, many other functions. Serial number DNF-44821-V-63. How may I help?'

'By shutting yourself down.'

Silence from the privy.

'Do you understand what I'm asking?'

A small, horrified voice said, 'Please don't make me. You bad man. Oh, you bad man.'

'Shut yourself down *now.*'

A longer silence. Rosa stood with her hand pressed against her throat. Several men appeared around the side of the Pere's house, armed with various homely weapons. Rosa waved them back.

'DNF-44821-V-63, comply!'

'Yes, Eddie of New York. I will shut myself down.' A horrible self-pitying sadness had crept into Andy's new small voice. It made Eddie's skin crawl.

'Andy is blind and will shut down. Are you aware that with my main power cells ninety-eight per cent depleted, I may never be able to power up again?'

Eddie remembered the vast roont twins out at the Jaffords smallhold – Tia and Zalman – and then thought of all the others like them this unlucky town had known over the years. He dwelled particularly on the Tavery twins, so bright and quick and eager to please. And so beautiful. 'Never won't be long enough,' he said, 'but I guess it'll have to do. Palaver's done, Andy. Shut down.'

Another silence from within the half-busted privy. Tian and Rosa crept up to either side of Eddie and the three of them stood together in front of the locked door. Rosa gripped Eddie's forearm. He shook her off immediately. He wanted his hand free in case he had to draw. Although where he would shoot now that Andy's eyes were gone, he didn't know.

When Andy spoke again, it was in a toneless amplified voice that made Tian and Rosa gasp and step back. Eddie stayed where he was. He had heard a voice like this and words like this once before, in the clearing of the great bear. Andy's rap wasn't quite the same, but close enough for government work.

'*DNF-44821-V-63 IS SHUTTING DOWN! ALL SUBNUCLEAR CELLS AND MEMORY CIRCUITS ARE IN SHUTDOWN PHASE! SHUTDOWN IS 13 PER CENT COMPLETE! I AM ANDY, MESSENGER ROBOT, MANY OTHER FUNCTIONS! PLEASE REPORT MY LOCATION TO LAMERK INDUSTRIES OR NORTH CENTRAL POSITRONICS, LTD! CALL 1-900-54! REWARD IS OFFERED! REPEAT, REWARD IS OFFERED!*' There was a click as the message recycled. '*DNF-44821-V-63 IS SHUTTING DOWN! ALL SUBNUCLEAR CELLS AND MEMORY CIRCUITS ARE IN SHUTDOWN PHASE! SHUTDOWN IS 19 PER CENT COMPLETE! I AM ANDY—*'

'You *were* Andy,' Eddie said softly. He turned to Tian and Rosa, and had to smile at their scared-children's faces. 'It's all right,' he said. 'It's over. He'll go on blaring like that for awhile, and then he'll be done. You can turn him into a . . . I don't know . . . a planter, or something.'

'I think we'll tear up the floor and bury him right there,' Rosa said, nodding at the privy.

Eddie's smile widened and became a grin. He liked the idea of burying Andy in shit. He liked that idea very well.

17

As dusk ended and night deepened, Roland sat on the edge of the band-stand and watched the Calla-*folken* tuck into their great dinner. Every one of them knew it might be the last meal they'd ever eat together, that tomorrow night at this time their nice little town might lie in smoking ruins all about them, but still they were cheerful. And not, Roland thought, entirely for the sake of the children. There was great relief in finally deciding to do the right thing. Even when folk knew the price was apt to be high, that relief came. A kind of giddiness. Most of these people would sleep on the Green tonight with their children and grandchildren in the tent nearby, and here they would stay, their faces turned to the northeast of town, waiting for the outcome of the battle. There would be gunshots, they reckoned (it was a sound many of them had never heard), and then the dust-cloud that marked the Wolves would either dissipate, turn back the way it had come, or roll on toward town. If the last, the *folken* would scatter and wait for the burning to commence. When it was over, they would be refugees in their own place. Would they rebuild, if that was how the cards fell? Roland doubted it. With no children to build for — because the Wolves *would* take them all this time if they won, the gunslinger did not doubt it — there would be no reason. At the end of the next cycle, this place would be a ghost town.

'Cry your pardon, sai.'

Roland looked around. There stood Wayne Overholser, with his hat in his hands. Standing thus, he looked more like a wandering saddle-tramp down on his luck than the Calla's big farmer. His eyes were large and somehow mournful.

'No need to cry my pardon when I'm still wearing the dayrider hat you gave me,' Roland said mildly.

'Yar, but . . .' Overholser trailed off, thought of how he wanted to go on, and then seemed to decide to fly straight at it. 'Reuben Caverra was one of the fellas you meant to take to guard the children during the fight, wasn't he?'

'Aye?'

'His gut busted this morning.' Overholser touched his own swelling belly about where his appendix might have been. 'He lays home feverish and raving. He'll likely die of the bloodmuck. Some get better, aye, but not many.'

'I'm sorry to hear it,' Roland said, trying to think who would be best to replace Caverra, a hulk of a man who had impressed Roland as not knowing much about fear and probably nothing at all about cowardice.

'Take me instea', would ye?'

Roland eyed him.

'Please, gunslinger. I can't stand aside. I thought I could – that I must – but I can't. It's making me sick.' And yes, Roland thought, he *did* look sick.

'Does your wife know, Wayne?'

'Aye.'

'And says aye?'

'She does.'

Roland nodded. 'Be here half an hour before dawn.'

A look of intense, almost painful gratitude filled Overholser's face and made him look weirdly young. 'Thankee, Roland! Say thankee! Big-big!'

'Glad to have you. Now listen to me a minute.'

'Aye?'

'Things won't be just the way I told them at the big meeting.'

'Because of Andy, y' mean.'

'Yes, partly that.'

'What else? You don't mean to say there's *another* traitor, do 'ee? You don't mean to say that?'

'All I mean to say is that if you want to come with us, you have to roll with us. Do you ken?'

'Yes, Roland, very well.'

Overholser thanked him again for the chance to die north of town and then hurried off with his hat still in his hands. Before Roland could change his mind, perhaps.

Eddie came over. 'Overholser's coming to the dance?'

'Looks like it. How much trouble did you have with Andy?'

'It went all right,' Eddie said, not wanting to admit that he, Tian, and Rosalita had probably all come within a second of being toast. In the distance, they could still hear him bellowing. But probably not for much longer; the amplified voice was claiming shutdown was seventy-nine per cent complete.

'I think you did very well.'

A compliment from Roland always made Eddie feel like king of the world, but he tried not to show it. 'As long as we do well tomorrow.'

'Susannah?'

'Seems fine.'

'No . . .?' Roland rubbed above his left eyebrow.

'No, not that I've seen.'

'And no talking short and sharp?'

'No, she's good for it. Practiced with her plates all the time you guys were digging.' Eddie tipped his chin toward Jake, who was sitting by himself on a swing with Oy at his feet. 'That's the one I'm worried about. I'll be glad to get him out of here. This has been hard for him.'

'It'll be harder on the other boy,' Roland said, and stood up. 'I'm going back to Pere's. Going to get some sleep.'

'*Can* you sleep?'

'Oh, yes,' Roland said. 'With the help of Rosa's cat-oil, I'll sleep like a rock. You and Susannah and Jake should also try.'

'Okay.'

Roland nodded somberly. 'I'll wake you tomorrow morning. We'll ride down here together.'

'And we'll fight.'

'Yes,' Roland said. He looked at Eddie. His blue eyes gleamed in the glow of the torches. 'We'll fight. Until they're dead, or we are.'

CHAPTER VII

THE WOLVES

1

See this now, see it very well:

Here is a road as wide and as well-maintained as any secondary road in America, but of the smooth packed dirt the Calla-folk call oggan. Ditches for runoff border both sides; here and there neat and well-maintained wooden culverts run beneath the oggan. In the faint, unearthly light that comes before dawn, a dozen bucka waggons — they are the kind driven by the Manni, with rounded canvas tops — roll along the road. The canvas is bright clean white, to reflect the sun and keep the interiors cool on hot summer days, and they look like strange, low-floating clouds. The cumulus kind, may it do ya. Each waggon is drawn by a team of six mules or four horses. On the seat of each, driving, are either a pair of fighters or of designated child-minders. Overholser is driving the lead waggon, with Margaret Eisenhart beside him. Next in line comes Roland of Gilead, mated with Ben Slightman. Fifth is Tian and Zalia Jaffords. Seventh is Eddie and Susannah Dean. Susannah's wheelchair is folded up in the waggon behind her. Bucky and Annabelle Javier are in charge of the tenth. On the peak-seat of the last waggon are Father Donald Callahan and Rosalita Munoz.

Inside the buckas are ninety-nine children. The left-over twin — the one that makes for an odd number — is Benny Slightman, of course. He is riding in the last waggon. (He felt uncomfortable about going with his father.) The children don't speak. Some of the younger ones have gone back to sleep; they will have to be awakened shortly, when the waggons reach their destination. Ahead, now less than a mile, is the place where the path into the arroyo country splits off to the left. On the right, the land runs down a mild slope to the river. All the drivers keep looking to the east, toward the constant darkness that is Thunderclap. They are watching for an approaching dust-cloud. There is none. Not yet. Even the seminon winds

564

have fallen still. Callahan's prayers seem to have been answered, at least in that regard.

2

Ben Slightman, sitting next to Roland on the bucka's peak-seat, spoke in a voice so low the gunslinger could barely hear him. 'What will 'ee do to me, then?'

If asked, when the waggons set out from Calla Bryn Sturgis, to give odds on Slightman's surviving this day, Roland might have put them at five in a hundred. Surely no better. There were two crucial questions that needed to be asked and then answered correctly. The first had to come from Slightman himself. Roland hadn't really expected the man to ask it, but here it was, out of his mouth. Roland turned his head and looked at him.

Vaughn Eisenhart's foreman was very pale, but he took off his spectacles and met Roland's gaze. The gunslinger ascribed no special courage to this. Surely Slightman the Elder had had time to take Roland's measure and knew that he *must* look the gunslinger in the eye if he was to have any hope at all, little as he might like to do it.

'Yar, I know,' Slightman said. His voice was steady, at least so far. 'Know what? That *you* know.'

'Have since we took your pard, I suppose,' Roland said. The word was deliberately sarcastic (sarcasm was the only form of humor Roland truly understood), and Slightman winced at it: pard. Your pard. But he nodded, eyes still steady on Roland's.

'I had to figure that if you knew about Andy, you knew about me. Although he'd never have peached on me. Such wasn't in his programming.' At last it was too much and he could bear the eye-contact no longer. He looked down, biting his lip. 'Mostly I knew because of Jake.'

Roland wasn't able to keep the surprise out of his face.

'He changed. He didn't mean to, not as trig as he is — and as brave — but he did. Not toward me, toward my boy. Over the last week, week and a half. Benny was only . . . well, puzzled, I guess you'd say. He felt something but didn't know what it was. I did. It was like your boy didn't want to be around him anymore. I asked myself what could do that. The answer seemed pretty clear. Clear as short beer, do ya.'

Roland was falling behind Overholser's waggon. He flicked the reins over the backs of his own team. They moved a little faster. From behind them came the quiet sound of the children, some talking now but most snoring, and the muted jingle of trace. He'd asked Jake to collect up a small box of children's possessions, and had seen the boy doing it. He was a good boy who never put off a chore. This morning he wore a dayrider hat to keep the sun out of his eyes, and his father's gun. He rode on the seat of the eleventh waggon, with one of the Estrada men. He guessed that Slightman had a good boy, too, which had gone far toward making this the mess that it was.

'Jake was at the Dogan one night when you and Andy were there, passing on news of your neighbors,' Roland said. On the seat beside him, Slightman winced like a man who has just been punched in the belly.

'There,' he said. 'Yes, I could almost sense . . . or thought I could . . .' A longer pause, and then: '*Fuck.*'

Roland looked east. A little brighter over there now, but still no dust. Which was good. Once the dust appeared, the Wolves would come in a rush. Their gray horses would be fast. Continuing on, speaking almost idly, Roland asked the other question. If Slightman answered in the negative, he wouldn't live to see the coming of the Wolves no matter how fast their gray horses rode.

'If you'd found him, Slightman – if you'd found *my* boy – would you have killed him?'

Slightman put his spectacles back on as he struggled with it. Roland couldn't tell if he understood the importance of the question or not. He waited to see if the father of Jake's friend would live or die. He'd have to decide quickly; they were approaching the place where the waggons would stop and the children would get down.

The man at last raised his head and met Roland's eyes again. He opened his mouth to speak and couldn't. The fact of the matter was clear enough: he could answer the gunslinger's question, or he could look into the gunslinger's face, but he could not do both at the same time.

Dropping his gaze back to the splintery wood between his feet, Slightman said: 'Yes, I reckon we would have killed him.' A pause. A nod. When he moved his head a tear fell from one eye and splashed on the wood of the peak-seat's floor. 'Yar, what else?' Now he looked up; now he could meet Roland's eyes again, and when he did he saw his fate had been decided. 'Make it quick,' said he, 'and don't let me boy see it happen. Beg ya please.'

Roland flapped the reins over the mules' backs again. Then he said: 'I won't be the one to stop your miserable breath.'

Slightman's breath *did* stop. Telling the gunslinger that yes, he would have killed a twelve-year-old boy to protect his secret, his face had had a kind of strained nobility. Now it wore hope instead, and hope made it ugly. Nearly grotesque. Then he let his breath out in a ragged sigh and said, 'You're fooling with me. A-teasing me. You're going to kill me, all right. Why would you not?'

'A coward judges all he sees by what he is,' Roland remarked. 'I'd not kill you unless I had to, Slightman, because I love my own boy. You must understand that much, don't you? To love a boy?'

'Yar.' Slightman lowered his head again and began to rub the back of his sunburned neck. The neck he must have thought would end this day packed in dirt.

'But you have to understand something. For your own good and Benny's as much as ours. If the Wolves win, you *will* die. That much you can be sure of. "Take it to the bank," Eddie and Susannah say.'

Slightman was looking at him again, eyes narrowed behind his specs.

'Hear me well, Slightman, and take understanding from what I say. We're not going to be where the Wolves think we're going to be, and neither are the kiddies. Win or lose, this time they're going to leave some bodies behind. And win or lose, they'll know they were misled. Who was there in Calla Bryn Sturgis to mislead them? Only two. Andy and Ben Slightman. Andy's shut down, gone beyond the reach of their vengeance.' He gave Slightman a smile that was as cold as the earth's north end. 'But you're not. Nor the only one you care for in your poor excuse for a heart.'

Slightman sat considering this. It was clearly a new idea to him, but once he saw the logic of it, it was undeniable.

'They'll likely think you switched sides a-purpose,' Roland said, 'but even if you could convince them it was an accident, they'd kill you just the same. And your son, as well. For vengeance.'

A red stain had seeped into the man's cheeks as the gunslinger spoke – roses of shame, Roland supposed – but as he considered the probability of his son's murder at the hands of the Wolves, he grew white once more. Or perhaps it was the thought of Benny being taken east that did it – being taken east and roont. 'I'm sorry,' he said. 'Sorry for what I've done.'

'Balls to your sorry,' Roland said. 'Ka works and the world moves on.'

Slightman made no reply.

'I'm disposed to send you with the kids, just as I said I would,' Roland told him. 'If things go as I hope, you won't see a single moment's action. If things don't go as I hope, you want to remember Sarey Adams is boss of that shooting match, and if I talk to her after, you want to hope that she says you did everything you were told to do.' When this met with only more silence from Slightman, the gunslinger spoke sharply. 'Tell me you understand, gods damn you. I want to hear "Yes, Roland, I ken."'

'Yes, Roland, I ken very well.' There was a pause. 'If we *do* win, will the *folken* find out, do ee reckon? Find out about . . . me?'

'Not from Andy, they won't,' Roland said. 'His blabber's done. And not from me, if you do as you now promise. Not from my ka-tet, either. Not out of respect for you, but out of respect for Jake Chambers. And if the Wolves fall into the trap I've laid them, why would the *folken* ever suspect another traitor?' He measured Slightman with his cool eyes. 'They're innocent folk. Trusting. As ye know. Certainly ye used it.'

The flush came back. Slightman looked down at the floor of the peak-seat again. Roland looked up and saw the place he was looking for now less than a quarter of a mile ahead. Good. There was still no dust-cloud on the eastern horizon, but he could feel it gathering in his mind. The Wolves were coming, oh yes. Somewhere across the river they had dismounted their train and mounted their horses and were riding like hell. And from it, he had no doubt.

'I did it for my son,' Slightman said. 'Andy came to me and said they would surely take him. Somewhere over there, Roland—' He pointed east, toward Thunderclap. 'Somewhere over there are poor creatures called Breakers. Prisoners. Andy says they're telepaths and psychokinetics, and although I ken neither word, I know they're to do with the mind. The Breakers are human, and they eat what we eat to nourish their bodies, but they need other food, *special* food, to nourish whatever it is that makes *them* special.'

'Brain-food,' Roland said. He remembered that his mother had called fish brain-food. And then, for no reason he could tell, he found himself thinking of Susannah's nocturnal prowls. Only it wasn't Susannah who visited that midnight banquet hall; it was Mia. Daughter of none.

'Yar, I reckon,' Slightman agreed. 'Anyway, it's something only twins have, something that links them mind-to-mind. And these fellows – not the Wolves, but they who send the Wolves – take it out. When it's gone, the kids're idiots. Roont. It's *food*, Roland, do ya kennit? *That's* why they take em! To feed their goddamned *Breakers!* Not their bellies or their bodies, but their minds! And I don't even know what it is they've been set to break!'

'The two Beams that still hold the Tower,' Roland said.

Slightman was thunderstruck. And fearful. 'The Dark Tower?' He whispered the words. 'Do ya say so?'

'I do,' Roland said. 'Who's Finli? Finli o' Tego.'

'I don't know. A voice that takes my reports, is all. A taheen, I think — do you know what that is?'

'Do you?'

Slightman shook his head.

'Then we'll leave it. Mayhap I'll meet him in time and he'll answer to hand for this business.'

Slightman did not reply, but Roland sensed his doubt. That was all right. They'd almost made it now, and the gunslinger felt an invisible band which had been cinched about his middle begin to loosen. He turned fully to the foreman for the first time. 'There's always been someone like you for Andy to cozen, Slightman; I have no doubt it's mostly what he was left here for, just as I have no doubt that your daughter, Benny's sister, didn't die an accidental death. They always need one left-over twin, and one weak parent.'

'You can't—'

'Shut up. You've said all that's good for you.'

Slightman sat silent beside Roland on the seat.

'I understand betrayal. I've done my share of it, once to Jake himself. But that doesn't change what you are; let's have that straight. You're a carrion-bird. A rustie turned vulture.'

The color was back in Slightman's cheeks, turning them the shade of claret. 'I did what I did for my boy,' he said stubbornly.

Roland spat into his cupped hand, then raised the hand and caressed Slightman's cheek with it. The cheek was currently full of blood, and hot to the touch. Then the gunslinger took hold of the spectacles Slightman wore and jiggled them slightly on the man's nose. 'Won't wash,' he said, very quietly. 'Because of these. This is how they mark you, Slightman. This is your brand. You tell yourself you did it for your boy because it gets you to sleep at night. *I* tell *myself* that what I did to Jake I did so as not to lose my chance at the Tower . . . and that gets *me* to sleep at night. The difference between us, the *only* difference, is that I never took a pair of spectacles.' He wiped his hand on his pants. 'You sold out, Slightman. And you have forgotten the face of your father.'

'Let me be,' Slightman whispered. He wiped the slick of the gunslinger's spittle from his cheek. It was replaced by his own tears. 'For my boy's sake.'

Roland nodded. 'That's all this is, for your boy's sake. You drag him behind you like a dead chicken. Well, never mind. If all goes as I hope, you may live your life with him in the Calla, and grow old in the regard of your neighbors. You'll be one of those who stood up to the Wolves when the gunslingers came to town along the Path of the Beam. When you can't walk, he'll walk with you and hold you up. I see this, but I don't like what I see. Because a man who'll sell his soul for a pair of spectacles will resell it for some other prink-a-dee – even cheaper – and sooner or later your boy will find out what you are, anyway. The best thing that could happen to your son today is for you to die a hero.' And then, before Slightman could reply, Roland raised his voice and shouted. 'Hey, Overholser! Ho, the waggon! *Overholser!* Pull on over! We're here! Say thankya!'

'Roland—' Slightman began.

'No,' Roland said, tying off the reins. 'Palaver's done. Just remember what I said, sai: if you get a chance to die a hero today, do your son a favor and take it.'

3

At first everything went according to plan and they called it ka. When things began going wrong and the dying started, they called that ka, too. Ka, the gunslinger could have told them, was often the last thing you had to rise above.

4

Roland had explained to the children what he wanted of them while still on the common, under the flaring torches. Now, with daylight brightening (but the sun still waiting in the wings), they took their places perfectly, lining up in the road from oldest to youngest, each pair of twins holding hands. The buckas were parked on the left side of the road, their offside wheels just above the ditch. The only gap was where the track into the arroyo country split off from East Road. Standing beside the children in a stretched line were the minders, their number now swelled to well over a dozen with the addition of Tian, Pere Callahan, Slightman, and Wayne Overholser. Across from them, positioned in a line above the righthand ditch, were Eddie, Susannah, Rosa, Margaret Eisenhart, and Tian's wife, Zalia. Each of the women wore a silk-lined reed sack filled with plates. Stacked in the ditch below and behind them were boxes containing more Orizas. There were two hundred plates in all.

Eddie glanced across the river. Still no dust. Susannah gave him a nervous smile, which he returned in kind. This was the hard part – the scary part. Later, he knew, the red fog would wrap him up and carry him away. Now he was too aware. What he was aware of most was that right now they were as helpless and vulnerable as a turtle without its shell.

Jake came hustling up the line of children, carrying the box of collected odds and ends: hair ribbons, a teething infant's comfort-chewy, a whistle whittled from a yew-stick, an old shoe with most of the sole gone, a mate-less sock. There were perhaps two dozen similar items.

'Benny Slightman!' Roland barked. 'Frank Tavery! Francine Tavery! To me!'

'Here, now!' Benny Slightman's father said, immediately alarmed. 'What're you calling my son out of line f—'

'To do his duty, just as you'll do yours,' Roland said. 'Not another word.'

The four children he had called appeared before him. The Taverys were flushed and out of breath, eyes shining, still holding hands.

'Listen, now, and make me repeat not a single word,' Roland said. Benny and the Taverys leaned forward anxiously. Although clearly impatient to be off, Jake was less anxious; he knew this part, and most of what would follow. What Roland *hoped* would follow.

Roland spoke to the children, but loud enough for the strung-out line of child-minders to hear, too. 'You're to go up the path,' he said, 'and every few feet you leave something, as if 'twere dropped on a hard, fast march. And I expect *you* four to make a hard, fast march. Don't run, but just below it. Mind your footing. Go to where the path branches – that's half a mile – and no farther. D'you ken? *Not one step farther.*'

They nodded eagerly. Roland switched his gaze to the adults standing tensely behind them.

'These four get a two-minute start. Then the rest of the twins go, oldest first, youngest last. They won't be going far; the last pairs will hardly get off the road.' Roland raised his voice to a commanding shout. '*Children! When you hear this, come back! Come to me a-hurry!'* Roland put the first two fingers of his left hand into the corners of his mouth and blew a whistle so piercing that several children put their hands to their ears.

Annabelle Javier said, 'Sai, if you mean for the children to hide in one of the caves, why would you call them back?'

'Because they're not going into the caves,' Roland said. 'They're going down there.' He pointed east. 'Lady Oriza is going to take care of the children. They're going to hide in the rice, just this side of the river.' They all looked where he pointed, and so it was they all saw the dust at the same time.

The Wolves were coming.

5

'Our company's on the way, sugarpie,' Susannah said.

Roland nodded, then turned to Jake. 'Go on, Jake. Just as I say.'

Jake pulled a double handful of stuff from the box and handed it to the Tavery twins. Then he jumped the lefthand ditch, graceful as a deer, and started up the arroyo track with Benny beside him. Frank and Francine were right behind; as Roland watched, Francine let a little hat fall from her hand.

'All right,' Overholser said. 'I ken some of it, do ya. The Wolves'll see the cast-offs and be even surer the kids are up there. But why send the rest of em north at all, gunslinger? Why not just march em down to the rice right now?'

'Because we have to assume the Wolves can smell the track of prey as well as real Wolves,' Roland said. He raised his voice again. *'Children, up the path! Oldest first! Hold the hand of your partner and don't let go! Come back at my whistle!'*

The children started off, helped into the ditch by Callahan, Sarey Adams, the Javiers, and Ben Slightman. All the adults looked anxious; only Benny's Da' looked mistrustful, as well.

'The Wolves will start in because they've reason to believe the children are up there,' Roland said, 'but they're not fools, Wayne. They'll look for sign and we'll give it to em. If they smell — and I'd bet this town's last rice crop that they do — they'll have scent as well as dropped shoes and ribbons to look at. After the smell of the main group stops, that of the four I sent first will carry on yet awhile farther. It may suck em in deeper, or it may not. By then it shouldn't matter.'

'But—'

Roland ignored him. He turned toward his little band of fighters. They would be seven in all. *It's a good number*, he told himself. *A number of power.* He looked beyond them at the dust-cloud. It rose higher than any of the remaining seminon dust-devils, and was moving with horrible speed. Yet for the time being, Roland thought they were all right.

'Listen and hear.' It was Zalia, Margaret, and Rosa to whom he was speaking. The members of his own ka-tet already knew this part, had since old Jamie whispered his long-held secret into Eddie's ear on the Jaffordses' porch. 'The Wolves are neither men nor monsters; they're robots.'

'*Robots!*' Overholser shouted, but with surprise rather than disbelief.

'Aye, and of a kind my ka-tet has seen before,' Roland said. He was thinking of a certain clearing where the great bear's final surviving retainers had chased each other in an endless worry-circle. 'They wear hoods to conceal tiny twirling things on top of their heads. They're probably this wide and this long.' Roland showed them a height of about two inches and a length of about five. 'It's what Molly Doolin hit and snapped off with her dish, once upon a time. She hit by accident. We'll hit a-purpose.'

'Thinking-caps,' Eddie said. 'Their connection to the outside world. Without em, they're as dead as dogshit.'

'Aim here.' Roland held his right hand an inch above the crown of his head.

'But the chests ... the gills in the chests ...' Margaret began, sounding utterly bewildered.

'Bullshit now and ever was,' Roland said. 'Aim at the tops of the hoods.'

'Someday,' Tian said, 'I'm going to know why there had to be so much buggering bullshit.'

'I hope there *is* a someday,' Roland said. The last of the children – the youngest ones – were just starting up the path, obediently holding hands. The eldest would be perhaps an eighth of a mile up, Jake's quartet at least an eighth of a mile beyond that. It would have to be enough. Roland turned his attention to the child-minders.

'Now they come back,' he said. 'Take them across the ditch and through the corn in two side-by-side rows.' He cocked a thumb over his shoulder without looking. 'Do I have to tell you how important it is that the corn-plants not be disturbed, especially close to the road, where the Wolves can see?'

They shook their heads.

'At the edge of the rice,' Roland continued, 'take them into one of the streams. Lead them almost to the river, then have them lie down where it's tall and still green.' He moved his hands apart, his blue eyes blazing. 'Spread em out. You grown-ups get on the river side of em. If there's trouble – more Wolves, something else we don't expect – that's the side it'll come from.'

Without giving them a chance to ask questions, Roland buried his fingers in the corners of his mouth again and whistled. Vaughn Eisenhart, Krella Anselm, and Wayne Overholser joined the others in the ditch and began bellowing for the little 'uns to turn around and start back toward the road. Eddie, meanwhile, took another look over his shoulder and was stunned to see how far toward the river the dust-cloud had progressed. Such rapid movement made perfect sense once you knew the secret; those gray horses weren't horses at all, but mechanical conveyances disguised to *look* like horses, no more than that. *Like a fleet of government Chevvies,* he thought.

'Roland, they're coming fast! Like hell!'

Roland looked. 'We're all right,' he said.

'Are you sure?' Rosa asked.

'Yes.'

The youngest children were now hurrying back across the road, hand-in-hand, bug-eyed with fear and excitement. Cantab of the Manni and Ara, his wife, were leading them. She told them to walk straight down the middle of the rows and try not to even brush any of the skeletal plants.

'Why, sai?' asked one tyke, surely no older than four. There was a suspicious dark patch on the front of his overalls. 'Corn all picked, see.'

'It's a game,' Cantab said. 'A don't-touch-the-corn game.' He began to sing. Some of the children joined in, but most were too bewildered and frightened.

As the pairs crossed the road, growing taller and older as they came, Roland cast another glance to the east. He estimated the Wolves were still ten minutes from the other side of the Whye, and ten minutes should be enough, but gods, they were *fast!* It had already crossed his mind that he might have to keep Slightman the Younger and the Tavery twins up here, with them. It wasn't in the plan, but by the time things got this far, the plan almost always started to change. *Had* to change.

Now the last of the kids were crossing, and only Overholser, Callahan, Slightman the Elder, and Sarey Adams were still on the road.

'Go,' Roland told them.

'I want to wait for my boy!' Slightman objected.

'Go!'

Slightman looked disposed to argue the point, but Sarey Adams touched one elbow and Overholser actually took hold of the other.

'Come 'ee,' Overholser said. 'The man'll take care of yours same as he'll take care of his.'

Slightman gave Roland a final doubtful look, then stepped over the ditch and began herding the tail end of the line downhill, along with Overholser and Sarey.

'Susannah, show them the hide,' Roland said.

They'd been careful to make sure the kids crossed the ditch on the road's river side well down from where they had done their digging the day before. Now, using one of her capped and shortened legs, Susannah kicked aside a tangle of leaves, branches, and dead corn-plants — the sort of thing one would expect to see left behind in a roadside runoff ditch — and exposed a dark hole.

'It's just a trench,' she said, almost apologetically. 'There's boards over the top. Light ones, easy to push back. That's where we'll be. Roland's made a . . . oh, I don't know what you call it, we call it a periscope where I come from, a thing with mirrors inside it you can see through . . . and when the time comes, we just stand up. The boards'll fall away around us when we do.'

'Where's Jake and those other three?' Eddie asked. 'They should be back by now.'

'It's too soon,' Roland said. 'Calm down, Eddie.'

'I won't calm down and it's *not* too soon. We should at least be able to see them. I'm going over there—'

'No, you're not,' Roland said. 'We have to get as many as we can before they figure out what's going on. That means keeping our firepower over here, at their backs.'

'Roland, something's not right.'

Roland ignored him. 'Lady-sais, slide in there, do ya please. The extra boxes of plates will be on your end; we'll just kick some leaves over them.'

He looked across the road as Zalia, Rosa, and Margaret began to worm into the hole Susannah had disclosed. The path to the arroyo was now completely empty. There was still no sign of Jake, Benny, and the Tavery twins. He was beginning to think that Eddie was right; that something had gone amiss.

6

Jake and his companions reached the place where the trail split quickly and without incident. Jake had held back two items, and when they reached the fork, he threw a broken rattle toward the Gloria and a little girl's woven string bracelet toward the Redbird. *Choose,* he thought, *and be damned to you either way.*

When he turned, he saw the Tavery twins had already started back. Benny was waiting for him, his face pale and his eyes shining. Jake nodded to him and made himself return Benny's smile. 'Let's go,' he said.

Then they heard Roland's whistle and the twins broke into a run, despite the scree and fallen rock which littered the path. They were still holding hands, weaving their way around what they couldn't simply scramble over.

'Hey, don't run!' Jake shouted. 'He said not to run and mind your f—'

That was when Frank Tavery stepped into the hole. Jake heard the grinding, snapping sound his ankle made when it broke, knew from the horrified wince on Benny's face that he had, too. Then Frank let out a low, screaming moan and pitched sideways. Francine grabbed for him and got a hand on his upper arm, but the boy was too heavy. He fell through her grip like a sashweight. The thud of his skull colliding with the granite outcrop beside him was far louder than the sound his ankle had made. The blood which immediately began to flow from the wound in his scalp was brilliant in the early morning light.

Trouble, Jake thought. *And in our road.*

Benny was gaping, his cheeks the color of cottage cheese. Francine was already kneeling beside her brother, who lay at a twisted, ugly angle with his foot still caught in the hole. She was making high, breathless keening sounds. Then, all at once, the keening stopped. Her eyes rolled up in their sockets and she pitched forward over her unconscious twin brother in a dead faint.

'Come on,' Jake said, and when Benny only stood there, gawping, Jake punched him in the shoulder. 'For your father's sake!'

That got Benny moving.

7

Jake saw everything with a gunslinger's cold, clear vision. The blood splashed on the rock. The clump of hair stuck in it. The foot in the hole. The spittle on Frank Tavery's lips. The swell of his sister's new breast as she lay awkwardly across him. The Wolves were coming now. It wasn't Roland's whistle that told him this, but the touch. *Eddie*, he thought. *Eddie wants to come over here.*

Jake had never tried using the touch to send, but he did now: *Stay where you are! If we can't get back in time we'll try to hide while they go past BUT DON'T YOU COME DOWN HERE! DON'T YOU SPOIL THINGS!*

He had no idea if the message got through, but he *did* know it was all he had time for. Meanwhile, Benny was . . . what? What was *le mot juste?* Ms Avery back at Piper had been very big on *le mot juste*. And it came to him. Gibbering. Benny was gibbering.

'What are we gonna do, Jake? Man Jesus, *both* of them! They were fine! Just running, and then . . . what if the Wolves come? What if they come while we're still here? We better leave em, don't you think?'

'We're not leaving them,' Jake said. He leaned down and grabbed Francine Tavery by the shoulders. He yanked her into a sitting position, mostly to get her off her brother so Frank could breathe. Her head lolled back, her hair streaming like dark silk. Her eyelids fluttered, showing glabrous white beneath. Without thinking, Jake slapped her. And hard.

'Ow! *Ow!*' Her eyes flew open, blue and beautiful and shocked.

'Get up!' Jake shouted. 'Get off him!'

How much time had passed? How still everything was, now that the children had gone back to the road! Not a single bird cried out, not even a rustie. He waited for Roland to whistle again, but Roland didn't. And really, why would he? They were on their own now.

Francine rolled aside, then staggered to her feet. 'Help him . . . please, sai, I beg . . .'

'Benny. We have to get his foot out of the hole.' Benny dropped to one knee on the other side of the awkwardly sprawled boy. His face was still pale, but his lips were pressed together in a tight straight line that Jake found encouraging. 'Take his shoulder.'

Benny grasped Frank Tavery's right shoulder. Jake took the left. Their eyes met across the unconscious boy's body. Jake nodded.

'Now.'

They pulled together. Frank Tavery's eyes flew open — they were as blue and as beautiful as his sister's — and he uttered a scream so high it was soundless. But his foot did not come free.

It was stuck deep.

8

Now a gray-green shape was resolving itself out of the dust-cloud and they could hear the drumming of many hooves on hardpan. The three Calla women were in the hide. Only Roland, Eddie, and Susannah still remained in the ditch, the men standing, Susannah kneeling with her strong thighs spread. They stared across the road and up the arroyo path. The path was still empty.

'I heard something,' Susannah said. 'I think one of em's hurt.'

'Fuck it, Roland, I'm going after them,' Eddie said.

'Is that what Jake wants or what *you* want?' Roland asked.

Eddie flushed. He had heard Jake in his head — not the exact words, but the gist — and he supposed Roland had, too.

'There's a hundred kids down there and only four over there,' Roland said. 'Get under cover, Eddie. You too, Susannah.'

'What about you?' Eddie asked.

Roland pulled in a deep breath, let it out. 'I'll help if I can.'

'You're not going after him, are you?' Eddie looked at Roland with mounting disbelief. 'You're really not.'

Roland glanced toward the dust-cloud and the gray-green cluster beneath it, which would resolve itself into individual horses and riders in less than a minute. Riders with snarling wolf faces framed in green hoods. They weren't riding toward the river so much as they were swooping down on it.

'No,' Roland said. 'Can't. Get under cover.'

Eddie stood where he was a moment longer, hand on the butt of the big revolver, pale face working. Then, without a word, he turned from Roland and grasped Susannah's arm. He knelt beside her, then slid into the hole. Now there was only Roland, the big revolver slung low on his left hip, looking across the road at the empty arroyo path.

9

Benny Slightman was a well-built lad, but he couldn't move the chunk of rock holding the Tavery boy's foot. Jake saw that on the first pull. His mind (his cold, cold mind) tried to judge the weight of the imprisoned boy against the weight of the imprisoning stone. He guessed the stone weighed more.

'Francine.'

She looked at him from eyes which were now wet and a little blinded by shock.

'You love him?' Jake asked.

'Aye, with all my heart!'

He is *your heart*, Jake thought. *Good.* 'Then help us. Pull him as hard as you can when I say. Never mind if he screams, pull him anyway.'

She nodded as if she understood. Jake hoped she did.

'If we can't get him out this time, we'll have to leave him.'

'I'll *never!*' she shouted.

It was no time for argument. Jake joined Benny beside the flat white rock. Beyond its jagged edge, Frank's bloody shin disappeared into a black hole. The boy was fully awake now, and gasping. His left eye rolled in terror. The right one was buried in a sheet of blood. A flap of scalp was hanging over his ear.

'We're going to lift the rock and you're going to pull him out,' Jake told Francine. 'On three. You ready?'

When she nodded, her hair fell across her face in a curtain. She made no attempt to get it out of the way, only seized her brother beneath the armpits.

'Francie, don't hurt me,' he moaned.

'Shut up,' she said.

'One,' Jake said. 'You pull this fucker, Benny, even if it pops your balls. You hear me?'

'Yer-bugger, just *count.*'

'Two. *Three.*'

They pulled, crying out at the strain. The rock moved. Francine yanked her brother backward with all her force, also crying out.

Frank Tavery's scream as his foot came free was loudest of all.

10

Roland heard hoarse cries of effort, overtopped by a scream of pure agony. Something had happened over there, and Jake had done something about it. The question was, had it been enough to put right whatever had gone wrong?

Spray flew in the morning light as the Wolves plunged into the Whye and began galloping across on their gray horses. Roland could see them clearly now, coming in waves of five and six, spurring their mounts. He put the number at sixty. On the far side of the river, they'd disappear beneath the shoulder of a grass-covered bluff. Then they'd reappear, less than a mile away. They would disappear one last time, behind one final hill — all of them, if they stayed bunched up as they were now — and that would be the last chance for Jake to come, for all of them to get under cover.

He stared up the path, willing the children to appear — willing *Jake* to appear — but the path remained empty.

Wolves streaming up the west bank of the river now, their horses casting off showers of droplets which glittered in the morning sun like gold. Clods of earth and sprays of sand flew. Now the hoofbeats were an approaching thunder.

11

Jake took one shoulder, Benny the other. They carried Frank Tavery down the path that way, plunging ahead with reckless speed, hardly even looking down at the tumbles of rock. Francine ran just behind them.

They came around the final curve, and Jake felt a surge of gladness when he saw Roland in the ditch opposite, still Roland, standing watch with his good left hand on the butt of his gun and his hat tipped back from his brow.

'It's my brother!' Francine was shouting at him. 'He fell down! He got his foot caught in a hole!'

Roland suddenly dropped out of sight.

Francine looked around, not frightened, exactly, but uncomprehending. 'What—?'

'Wait,' Jake said, because that was all he knew to say. He had no other ideas. If that was true of the gunslinger as well, they'd probably die here.

'My ankle . . . burning,' Frank Tavery gasped.

'Shut up,' Jake said.

Benny laughed. It was shock-laughter, but it was also real laughter. Jake looked at him around the sobbing, bleeding Frank Tavery . . . and winked. Benny winked back. And, just like that, they were friends again.

12

As she lay in the darkness of the hide with Eddie on her left and the acrid smell of leaves in her nose, Susannah felt a sudden cramp seize her belly. She had just time to register it before an icepick of pain, blue and savage, plunged into the left side of her brain, seeming to numb that entire side of her face and neck. At the same instant the image of a great banquet hall filled her mind: steaming roasts, stuffed fish, smoking steaks, magnums of champagne, frigates filled with gravy, rivers of red wine. She heard a piano, and a singing voice. That voice was charged with an awful sadness. 'Someone saved, someone saved, someone saved my li-iife tonight,' it sang.

No! Susannah cried to the force that was trying to engulf her. And did that force have a name? Of course it did. Its name was Mother, its hand was the one that rocked the cradle, and the hand that rocks the cradle rules the w—

No! You have to let me finish this! Afterward, if you want to have it, I'll help you! I'll help you have it! But if you try to force this on me now, I'll fight you tooth and nail! And if it comes to getting myself killed, and killing your precious chap along with me, I'll do it! Do you hear me, you bitch?

For a moment there was nothing but the darkness, the press of Eddie's leg, the numbness in the left side of her face, the thunder of the oncoming horses, the acrid smell of the leaves, and the sound of the Sisters breathing, getting ready for their own battle. Then, each of her words articulated clearly from a place above and behind Susannah's left eye, Mia for the first time spoke to her.

Fight your fight, woman. I'll even help, if I can. And then keep your promise.

'Susannah?' Eddie murmured from beside her. 'Are you all right?'

'Yes,' she said. And she was. The icepick was gone. The voice was gone. So was the terrible numbness. But close by, Mia was waiting.

13

Roland lay on his belly in the ditch, now watching the Wolves with one eye of imagination and one of intuition instead of with those in his head. The Wolves were between the bluff and the hill, riding full-out with their cloaks streaming behind them. They'd all disappear behind the hill for perhaps seven seconds. *If*, that was, they stayed bunched together and the leaders didn't start to pull ahead. *If* he had calculated their speed correctly. *If* he was right, he'd have five seconds when he could motion Jake and the others to come. Or seven. *If* he was right, they'd have those same five seconds to cross the road. If he was wrong (or if the others were slow), the Wolves would either see the man in the ditch, the children in the road, or all of them. The distances would likely be too great to use their weapons, but that wouldn't much matter, because the carefully crafted ambush would be blown. The smart thing would be to stay down, and leave the kids over there to their fate. Hell, four kids caught on the arroyo path would make the Wolves more sure than ever that the rest of them were stashed farther on, in one of the old mines.

Enough thinking, Cort said in his head. *If you mean to move, maggot, this is your only chance.*

Roland shot to his feet. Directly across from him, protected by the cluster of tumbled boulders which marked the East Road end of the arroyo path, stood Jake and Benny Slightman, with the Tavery boy supported between them. The kid was bloody both north and south; gods knew what had happened to him. His sister was looking over his shoulder. In that instant they looked not just like twins but Kaffin twins, joined at the body.

Roland jerked both hands extravagantly back over his head, as if clawing for a grip in the air: *To me, come! Come!* At the same time, he looked east. No sign of the Wolves; good. The hill *had* momentarily blocked them all.

Jake and Benny sprinted across the road, still dragging the boy between them. Frank Tavery's shor'boots dug fresh grooves in the oggan. Roland could only hope the Wolves would attach no especial significance to the marks.

The girl came last, light as a sprite. 'Down!' Roland snarled, grabbing her shoulder and throwing her flat. 'Down, down, *down!*' He landed beside her and Jake landed on top of him. Roland could feel the boy's madly beating heart between his shoulderblades, through both of their shirts, and had a moment to relish the sensation.

Now the hoofbeats were coming hard and strong, swelling every second. Had they been seen by the lead riders? It was impossible to know, but they *would* know, and soon. In the meantime they could only go on as planned. It would be tight quarters in the hide with three extra people in there, and if the Wolves had seen Jake and the other three crossing the road, they would all no doubt be cooked where they lay without a single shot fired or plate thrown, but there was no time to worry about that now. They had a minute left at most, Roland estimated, maybe only forty seconds, and that last little bit of time was melting away beneath them.

'Get off me and under cover,' he said to Jake. 'Right now.'

The weight disappeared. Jake slipped into the hide.

'You're next, Frank Tavery,' Roland said. 'And be quiet. Two minutes from now you can scream all you want, but for now, keep your mouth shut. That goes for all of you.'

'I'll be quiet,' the boy said huskily. Benny and Frank's sister nodded.

'We're going to stand up at some point and start shooting,' Roland said. 'You three – Frank, Francine, Benny – stay down. Stay flat.' He paused. 'For your lives, *stay out of our way.*'

14

Roland lay in the leaf- and dirt-smelling dark, listening to the harsh breathing of the children on his left. This sound was soon overwhelmed by that of approaching hooves. The eye of imagination and that of intuition opened once more, and wider than ever. In no more than thirty seconds – perhaps as few as fifteen – the red rage of battle would do away with all but the most primitive seeing, but for now he saw all, and all he saw was exactly as he wanted it to be. And why not? What good did visualizing plans gone astray ever do anyone?

He saw the twins of the Calla lying sprawled like corpses in the thickest, wettest part of the rice, with the muck oozing through their shirts and pants. He saw the adults beyond them, almost to the place where rice became riverbank. He saw Sarey Adams with her plates, and Ara of the Manni — Cantab's wife — with a few of her own, for Ara also threw (although as one of the Manni-folk, she could never be at fellowship with the other women). He saw a couple of the men — Estrada, Anselm, Overholser — with their bahs hugged to their chests. Instead of a bah, Vaughn Eisenhart was hugging the rifle Roland had cleaned for him. In the road, approaching from the east, he saw rank upon rank of green-cloaked riders on gray horses. They were slowing now. The sun was finally up and gleaming on the metal of their masks. The joke of those masks, of course, was that there was more metal beneath them. Roland let the eye of his imagining rise, looking for other riders — a party coming into the undefended town from the south, for instance. He saw none. In his own mind, at least, the entire raiding party was here. And if they'd swallowed the line Roland and the ka-tet of the Ninety and Nine had paid out with such care, it *should* be here. He saw the bucka waggons lined up on the town side of the road and had time to wish they'd freed the teams from the traces, but of course this way it looked better, more hurried. He saw the path leading into the arroyos, to the mines both abandoned and working, to the honeycomb of caves beyond them. He saw the leading Wolves rein up here, dragging the mouths of their mounts into snarls with their gauntleted hands. He saw through their eyes, saw pictures not made of warm human sight but cold, like those in the Magda-seens. Saw the child's hat Francine Tavery had let drop. His mind had a nose as well as an eye, and it smelled the bland yet fecund aroma of children. It smelled something rich and fatty — the stuff the Wolves would take from the children they abducted. His mind had an ear as well as a nose, and it heard — faintly — the same sort of clicks and clunks that had emanated from Andy, the same low whining of relays, servomotors, hydraulic pumps, gods knew what other machinery. His mind's eye saw the Wolves first inspecting the confusion of tracks on the road (he *hoped* it looked like a confusion to them), then looking up the arroyo path. Because imagining them looking the other way, getting ready to broil the ten of them in their hide like chickens in a roasting pan, would do him no good. No, they were looking up the arroyo path. *Must* be looking up the arroyo path. They were smelling children — perhaps their fear as well as the powerful stuff buried deep in their brains — and seeing the few tumbled bits of trash and treasure their prey had left behind. Standing there on their mechanical horses. Looking.

Go in, Roland urged silently. He felt Jake stir a little beside him, hearing his thought. His prayer, almost. *Go in. Go after them. Take what you will.*

There was a loud *clack!* sound from one of the Wolves. This was followed by a brief blurt of siren. The siren was followed by the nasty warbling whistle Jake had heard out at the Dogan. After that, the horses began to move again. First there was the soft thud of their hooves on the oggan, then on the far stonier ground of the arroyo path. There was nothing else; these horses didn't whinny nervously, like those still harnessed to the buckas. For Roland, it was enough. They had taken the bait. He slipped his revolver out of its holster. Beside him, Jake shifted again and Roland knew he was doing the same thing.

He had told them the formation to expect when they burst out of the hide: about a quarter of the Wolves on one side of the path, looking toward the river, a quarter of their number turned toward the town of Calla Bryn Sturgis. Or perhaps a few more in that direction, since if there was trouble, the town was where the Wolves — or the Wolves' programmers — would reasonably expect it to come from. And the rest? Thirty or more? Already up the path. Hemmed in, do ya.

Roland began counting to twenty, but when he got to nineteen decided he'd counted enough. He gathered his legs beneath him — there was no dry twist now, not so much as a twinge — and then pistoned upward with his father's gun held high in his hand.

'For Gilead and the Calla!' he roared. 'Now, gunslingers! Now, you Sisters of Oriza! Now, now! Kill them! No quarter! Kill them all!'

15

They burst up and out of the earth like dragon's teeth. Boards flew away to either side of them, along with dry flurries of weeds and leaves. Roland and Eddie each had one of the big revolvers with the sandalwood grips. Jake had his father's Ruger. Margaret, Rosa, and Zalia each held a Riza. Susannah had two, her arms crossed over her breasts as though she were cold.

The Wolves were deployed exactly as Roland had seen them with the cool killer's eye of his imagination, and he felt a moment of triumph before all lesser thought and emotion was swept away beneath the red curtain. As always, he was never so happy to be alive as when he was preparing to deal death. *Five minutes' worth of blood and stupidity,* he'd told them, and here those five minutes were. He'd also told them he always felt sick afterward, and while that was true enough, he never felt so fine as he did at this moment of beginning; never felt so completely and truly himself. Here were the tag ends of glory's old cloud. It didn't matter that they were robots; gods, no! What mattered was that they had been preying on the helpless for generations, and this time they had been caught utterly and completely by surprise.

'Top of the hoods!' Eddie screamed, as in his right hand Roland's pistol began to thunder and spit fire. The harnessed horses and mules reared in the traces; a couple screamed in surprise. 'Top of the hoods, get the thinking-caps!'

And, as if to demonstrate his point, the green hoods of three riders to the right of the path twitched as if plucked by invisible fingers. Each of the three beneath pitched bonelessly out of their saddles and struck the ground. In Granpere's story of the Wolf Molly Doolin had brought down, there had been a good deal of twitching afterward, but these three lay under the feet of their prancing horses as still as stones. Molly might not have hit the hidden 'thinking-cap' cleanly, but Eddie knew what he was shooting for, and had.

Roland also began to fire, shooting from the hip, shooting almost casually, but each bullet found its mark. He was after the ones on the path, wanting to pile up bodies there, to make a barricade if he could.

'Riza flies true!' Rosalita Munoz shrieked. The plate she was holding left her hand and bolted across the East Road with an unremitting rising shriek. It clipped through the hood of a rider at the head of the arroyo path who was trying desperately to rein his horse around. The thing fell backward, feet up to heaven, and landed upside down with its boots in the road.

'Riza!' That was Margaret Eisenhart.

'For my brother!' Zalia cried.

'Lady Riza come for your asses, you bastards!' Susannah uncrossed her arms and threw both plates outward. They flew, screaming, crisscrossed in midair, and both found their mark. Scraps of green hooding fluttered down; the Wolves to whom the hoods had belonged fell faster and harder.

Bright rods of fire now glowed in the morning light as the jostling, struggling riders on either side of the path unsheathed their energy weapons. Jake shot the thinking-cap of the first one to unsheathe and it fell on its own bitterly sizzling sword, catching its cloak afire. Its horse shied sideways, into the descending light-stick of the rider to the direct left. Its head came off, disclosing a nest of sparks and wires. Now the sirens began to blat steadily, burglar alarms in hell.

Roland had thought the Wolves closest to town might try to break off and flee toward the Calla. Instead the nine on that side still left – Eddie had taken six with his first six shots – spurred past the buckas and directly toward them. Two or three hurled humming silvery balls.

'Eddie! Jake! Sneetches! Your right!'

They swung in that direction immediately, leaving the women, who were hurling plates as fast as they could pull them from their silk-lined bags. Jake was standing with his legs spread and the Ruger held out in his right hand, his left bracing his right wrist. His hair was blowing back from his brow. He was wide-eyed and handsome, smiling. He squeezed off three quick shots, each one a whipcrack in the morning air. He had a vague, distant memory of the day in the woods when he had shot pottery out of the sky. Now he was shooting at something far more dangerous, and he was glad. *Glad.* The first three of the flying balls exploded in brilliant flashes of bluish light. A fourth jinked, then zipped straight at him. Jake ducked and heard it pass just above his head, humming like some sort of pissed-off toaster oven. It would turn, he knew, and come back.

Before it could, Susannah swiveled and fired a plate at it. The plate flew straight to the mark, howling. When it struck, both it and the sneetch exploded. Shrapnel rained down in the corn-plants, setting some of them alight.

Roland reloaded, the smoking barrel of his revolver momentarily pointed down between his feet. Beyond Jake, Eddie was doing the same.

A Wolf jumped the tangled heap of bodies at the head of the arroyo path, its green cloak floating out behind it, and one of Rosa's plates tore back its hood, for a moment revealing the radar dish beneath. The thinking-caps of the bear's retinue had been moving slowly and jerkily; this one was spinning so fast its shape was only a metallic blur. Then it was gone and the Wolf went tumbling to the side and onto the team which had drawn Overholser's lead waggon. The horses flinched backward, shoving the bucka into the one behind, mashing four whinnying, rearing animals between. These tried to bolt but had nowhere to go. Overholser's bucka teetered, then overturned. The downed Wolf's horse gained the road, stumbled over the body of another Wolf lying there, and went sprawling in the dust, one of its legs jutting off crookedly to the side.

Roland's mind was gone; his eye saw everything. He was reloaded. The

Wolves who had gone up the path were pinned behind a tangled heap of bodies, just as he had hoped. The group of fifteen on the town side had been decimated, only two left. Those on the right were trying to flank the end of the ditch, where the three Sisters of Oriza and Susannah anchored their line. Roland left the remaining two Wolves on his side to Eddie and Jake, sprinted down the trench to stand behind Susannah, and began firing at the ten remaining Wolves bearing down on them. One raised a sneetch to throw, then dropped it as Roland's bullet snapped off its thinking-cap. Rosa took another one, Margaret Eisenhart a third.

Margaret dipped to get another plate. When she stood up again, a light-stick swept off her head, setting her hair on fire as it tumbled into the ditch. And Benny's reaction was understandable; she had been almost a second mother to him. When the burning head landed beside him, he batted it aside and scrambled out of the ditch, blind with panic, howling in terror.

'*Benny, no, get back!*' Jake cried.

Two of the remaining Wolves threw their silver deathballs at the crawling, screaming boy. Jake shot one out of the air. He never had a chance at the other. It struck Benny Slightman in the chest and the boy simply exploded outward, one arm tearing free of his body and landing palm-up in the road.

Susannah cut the thinking-cap off the Wolf which had killed Margaret with one plate, then did for the one who had killed Jake's friend with another. She pulled two fresh Rizas from her sacks and turned back to the oncoming Wolves just as the first one leaped into the ditch, its horse's chest knocking Roland asprawl. It brandished its sword over the gunslinger. To Susannah it looked like a brilliant red-orange tube of neon.

'*No you don't, muhfuh!*' she screamed, and slung the plate in her right hand. It sheared through the gleaming saber and the weapon simply exploded at the hilt, tearing off the Wolf's arm. The next moment one of Rosa's plates amputated its thinking-cap and it tumbled sideways and crashed to the ground, its gleaming mask grinning at the paralyzed, terrified Tavery twins, who lay clinging to each other. A moment later it began to smoke and melt.

Shrieking Benny's name, Jake walked across the East Road, reloading the Ruger as he went, tracking through his dead friend's blood without realizing it. To his left, Roland, Susannah, and Rosa were putting paid to the five remaining Wolves in what had been the raiding party's north wing. The raiders whirled their horses in jerky, useless circles, seeming unsure what to do in circumstances such as these.

'Want some company, kid?' Eddie asked him. On their right, the group

of Wolves who had been stationed on the town side of the arroyo path all lay dead. Only one of them had actually made it as far as the ditch; that one lay with its hooded head plowed into the freshly turned earth of the hide and its booted feet in the road. The rest of its body was wrapped in its green cloak. It looked like a bug that has died in its cocoon.

'Sure,' Jake said. Was he talking or only thinking? He didn't know. The sirens blasted the air. 'Whatever you want. They killed Benny.'

'I know. That sucks.'

'It should have been his fucking *father*,' Jake said. Was he crying? He didn't know.

'Agreed. Have a present.' Into Jake's hand Eddie dropped a couple of balls about three inches in diameter. The surfaces looked like steel, but when Jake squeezed, he felt some give — it was like squeezing a child's toy made out of hard, hard rubber. A small plate on the side read

'SNEETCH'
HARRY POTTER® MODEL

Serial # 465-11-AA HPJKR

CAUTION
EXPLOSIVE

To the left of the plate was a button. A distant part of Jake's mind wondered who Harry Potter was. The sneetch's inventor, more than likely.

They reached the heap of dead Wolves at the head of the arroyo path. Perhaps machines couldn't really be dead, but Jake was unable to think of them as anything else, tumbled and tangled as they were. Dead, yes. And he was savagely glad. From behind them came an explosion, followed by a shriek of either extreme pain or extreme pleasure. For the moment Jake didn't care which. All his attention was focused on the remaining Wolves trapped on the arroyo path. There were somewhere between eighteen and two dozen of them.

There was one Wolf out in front, its sizzling fire-stick raised. It was half-turned to its mates, and now it waved its light-stick at the road. *Except that's no light-stick*, Eddie thought. *That's a light-saber, just like the ones in the* Star Wars *movies. Only these light-sabers aren't special effects — they really kill. What the hell's going on here?* Well, the guy out front was trying to rally his troops, that much seemed clear. Eddie decided to cut the sermon short. He thumbed the button in one of the three sneetches he had kept for himself. The thing began to hum and vibrate in his hand. It was sort of like holding a joy-buzzer.

'Hey, Sunshine!' he called.

The head Wolf didn't look around and so Eddie simply lobbed the sneetch at it. Thrown as easily as it was, it should have struck the ground twenty or thirty yards from the cluster of remaining Wolves and rolled to a stop. It picked up speed instead, rose, and struck the head Wolf dead center in its frozen snarl of a mouth. The thing exploded from the neck up, thinking-cap and all.

'Go on,' Eddie said. 'Try it. Using their own shit against em has its own special pl—'

Ignoring him, Jake dropped the sneetches Eddie had given him, stumbled over the heap of bodies, and started up the path.

'Jake? Jake, I don't think that's such a good idea—'

A hand gripped Eddie's upper arm. He whirled, raising his gun, then lowering it again when he saw Roland. 'He can't hear you,' the gunslinger said. 'Come on. We'll stand with him.'

'Wait, Roland, wait.' It was Rosa. She was smeared with blood, and Eddie assumed it was poor sai Eisenhart's. He could see no wound on Rosa herself. 'I want some of this,' she said.

16

They reached Jake just as the remaining Wolves made their last charge. A few threw sneetches. These Roland and Eddie picked out of the air easily. Jake fired the Ruger in nine steady, spaced shots, right wrist clasped in left hand, and each time he fired, one of the Wolves either flipped backward out of its saddle or went sliding over the side to be trampled by the horses coming behind. When the Ruger was empty, Rosa took a tenth, screaming Lady Oriza's name. Zalia Jaffords had also joined them, and the eleventh fell to her.

While Jake reloaded the Ruger, Roland and Eddie, standing side by side, went to work. They almost certainly could have taken the remaining eight between them (it didn't much surprise Eddie that there had been nineteen in this last cluster), but they left the last two for Jake. As they approached, swinging their light-swords over their heads in a way that would have been undoubtedly terrifying to a bunch of farmers, the boy shot the thinking-cap off the one on the left. Then he stood aside, dodging as the last surviving Wolf took a halfhearted swing at him.

Its horse leaped the pile of bodies at the end of the path. Susannah was on the far side of the road, sitting on her haunches amid a litter of fallen green-cloaked machinery and melting, rotting masks. She was also covered in Margaret Eisenhart's blood.

Roland understood that Jake had left the final one for Susannah, who would have found it extremely difficult to join them on the arroyo path because of her missing lower legs. The gunslinger nodded. The boy had seen a terrible thing this morning, suffered a terrible shock, but Roland thought he would be all right. Oy — waiting for them back at the Pere's rectory-house — would no doubt help him through the worst of his grief.

'*Lady Oh-RIZA!*' Susannah screamed, and flung one final plate as the Wolf reined its horse around, turning it east, toward whatever it called home. The plate rose, screaming, and clipped off the top of the green hood. For a moment this last child thief sat in its saddle, shuddering and blaring out its alarm, calling for help that couldn't come. Then it snapped violently backward, turning a complete somersault in midair, and thudded to the road. Its siren cut off in mid-whoop.

And so, Roland thought, *our five minutes are over.* He looked dully at the smoking barrel of his revolver, then dropped it back into its holster. One by one the alarms issuing from the downed robots were stopping.

Zalia was looking at him with a kind of dazed incomprehension. 'Roland!' she said.

'Yes, Zalia.'

'Are they gone? *Can* they be gone? Really?'

'All gone,' Roland said. 'I counted sixty-one, and they all lie here or on the road or in our ditch.'

For a moment Tian's wife only stood there, processing this information. Then she did something that surprised a man who was not often surprised. She threw herself against him, pressing her body frankly to his, and covered his face with hungry, wet-lipped kisses. Roland bore this for a little bit, then held her away. The sickness was coming now. The feeling of useless-ness. The sense that he would fight this battle or battles like it over and over for eternity, losing a finger to the lobstrosities here, perhaps an eye to a clever old witch there, and after each battle he would sense the Dark

Tower a little farther away instead of a little closer. And all the time the dry twist would work its way in toward his heart.

Stop that, he told himself. *It's nonsense, and you know it.*

'Will they send more, Roland?' Rosa asked.

'They may have no more to send,' Roland said. 'If they do, there'll almost certainly be fewer of them. And now you know the secret to killing them, don't you?'

'Yes,' she said, and gave him a savage grin. Her eyes promised him more than kisses later on, if he'd have her.

'Go down through the corn,' he told her. 'You and Zalia both. Tell them it's safe to come up now. Lady Oriza has stood friend to the Calla this day. And to the line of Eld, as well.'

'Will ye not come yourself?' Zalia asked him. She had stepped away from him, and her cheeks were filled with fire. 'Will ye not come and let em cheer ye?'

'Perhaps later on we may all hear them cheer us,' Roland said. 'Now we need to speak an-tet. The boy's had a bad shock, ye ken.'

'Yes,' Rosa said. 'Yes, all right. Come on, Zee.' She reached out and took Zalia's hand. 'Help me be the bearer of glad tidings.'

17

The two women crossed the road, making a wide berth around the tumbled, bloody remains of the poor Slightman lad. Zalia thought that most of what was left of him was only held together by his clothes, and shivered to think of the father's grief.

The young man's shor'leg lady-sai was at the far north end of the ditch, examining the bodies of the Wolves scattered there. She found one where the little revolving thing hadn't been entirely shot off, and was still trying to turn. The Wolf's green-gloved hands shivered uncontrollably in the dust, as if with palsy. While Rosa and Zalia watched, Susannah picked up a largish chunk of rock and, cool as a night in Wide Earth, brought it down on the remains of the thinking-cap. The Wolf stilled immediately. The low hum that had been coming from it stopped.

'We go to tell the others, Susannah,' Rosa said. 'But first we want to tell thee well-done. How we do love thee, say true!'

Zalia nodded. 'We say thankya, Susannah of New York. We say thankya more big-big than could ever be told.'

'Yar, say true,' Rosa agreed.

The lady-sai looked up at them and smiled sweetly. For a moment Rosalita looked a little doubtful, as if maybe she saw something in that dark-brown face that she shouldn't. Saw that Susannah Dean was no longer here, for instance. Then the expression of doubt was gone. 'We go with good news, Susannah,' said she.

'Wish you joy of it,' said Mia, daughter of none. 'Bring them back as you will. Tell them the danger here's over, and let those who don't believe count the dead.'

'The legs of your pants are wet, do ya,' Zalia said.

Mia nodded gravely. Another contraction had turned her belly to a stone, but she gave no sign. ''Tis blood, I'm afraid.' She nodded toward the head-less body of the big rancher's wife. 'Hers.'

The women started down through the corn, hand-in-hand. Mia watched Roland, Eddie, and Jake cross the road toward her. This would be the dangerous time, right here. Yet perhaps not too dangerous, after all; Susannah's friends looked dazed in the aftermath of the battle. If she seemed a little off her feed, perhaps they would think the same of her.

She thought mostly it would be a matter of waiting her opportunity. Waiting . . . and then slipping away. In the meantime, she rode the contrac-tion of her belly like a boat riding a high wave.

They'll know where you went, a voice whispered. It wasn't a head-voice but a belly-voice. The voice of the chap. And that voice spoke true.

Take the ball with you, the voice told her. *Take it with you when you go. Leave them no door to follow you through.*

Aye.

18

The Ruger cracked out a single shot and a horse died.

From below the road, from the rice, came a rising roar of joy that was not quite disbelieving. Zalia and Rosa had given their good news. Then a shrill cry of grief cut through the mingled voices of happiness. They had given the bad, as well.

Jake Chambers sat on the wheel of the overturned waggon. He had unharnessed the three horses that were okay. The fourth had been lying with two broken legs, foaming helplessly through its teeth and looking to the boy for help. The boy had given it. Now he sat staring at his dead friend. Benny's blood was soaking into the road. The hand on the end of Benny's arm lay palm-up, as if the dead boy wanted to shake hands with God. What God? According to current rumor, the top of the Dark Tower was empty.

From Lady Oriza's rice came a second scream of grief. Which had been Slightman, which Vaughn Eisenhart? At a distance, Jake thought, you couldn't tell the rancher from the foreman, the employer from the employee. Was there a lesson there, or was it what Ms Avery, back at good old Piper, would have called FEAR, false evidence appearing real?

The palm pointing up to the brightening sky, *that* was certainly real.

Now the *folken* began to sing. Jake recognized the song. It was a new version of the one Roland had sung on their first night in Calla Bryn Sturgis.

'Come-come-commala
Rice come a-falla
I-sissa 'ay a-bralla
Dey come a-folla
We went to a-rivva
'Riza did us kivva . . .'

The rice swayed with the passage of the singing *folken,* swayed as if it were dancing for their joy, as Roland had danced for them that torchlit night. Some came with babbies in their arms, and even so burdened, they swayed from side to side. *We all danced this morning,* Jake thought. He didn't know what he meant, only that it was a true thought. *The dance we do. The only one we know. Benny Slightman? Died dancing. Sai Eisenhart, too.*

Roland and Eddie came over to him; Susannah, too, but she hung back a bit, as if deciding that, at least for the time being, the boys should be with the boys. Roland was smoking, and Jake nodded at it.

'Roll me one of those, would you?'

Roland turned in Susannah's direction, eyebrows raised. She shrugged, then nodded. Roland rolled Jake a cigarette, gave it to him, then scratched a match on the seat of his pants and lit it. Jake sat on the waggon wheel, taking the smoke in occasional puffs, holding it in his mouth, then letting it out. His mouth filled up with spit. He didn't mind. Unlike some things, spit could be got rid of. He made no attempt to inhale.

Roland looked down the hill, where the first of the two running men was just entering the corn. 'That's Slightman,' he said. 'Good.'

'Why good, Roland?' Eddie asked.

'Because sai Slightman will have accusations to make,' Roland said. 'In his grief, he isn't going to care who hears them, or what his extraordinary knowledge might say about his part in this morning's work.'

'Dance,' Jake said.

They turned to look at him. He sat pale and thoughtful on the waggon-wheel, holding his cigarette. 'This morning's dance,' he said.

Roland appeared to consider this, then nodded. 'His part in this morning's *dance*. If he gets here soon enough, we may be able to quiet him. If not, his son's death is only going to be the start of Ben Slightman's commala.'

19

Slightman was almost fifteen years younger than the rancher, and arrived at the site of the battle well before the other. For a moment he only stood on the far edge of the hide, considering the shattered body lying in the road. There was not so much blood, now – the oggan had drunk it greedily – but the severed arm still lay where it had been, and the severed arm told all. Roland would no more have moved it before Slightman got here than he would have opened his flies and pissed on the boy's corpse. Slightman the Younger had reached the clearing at the end of his path. His father, as next of kin, had a right to see where and how it had happened.

The man stood quiet for perhaps five seconds, then pulled in a deep breath and let it out in a shriek. It chilled Eddie's blood. He looked around for Susannah and saw she was no longer there. He didn't blame her for ducking out. This was a bad scene. The worst.

Slightman looked left, looked right, then looked straight ahead and saw Roland, standing beside the overturned waggon with his arms crossed. Beside him, Jake still sat on the wheel, smoking his first cigarette.

'*YOU!*' Slightman screamed. He was carrying his bah; now he unslung it. '*YOU DID THIS! YOU!*'

Eddie plucked the weapon deftly from Slightman's hands. 'No, you don't, partner,' he murmured. 'You don't need this right now, why don't you let me keep it for you.'

Slightman seemed not to notice. Incredibly, his right hand still made circular motions in the air, as if winding the bah for a shot.

'*YOU KILLED MY SON! TO PAY ME BACK! YOU BASTARD! MURDERING BAS—*'

Moving with the eerie, spooky speed that Eddie could still not completely believe, Roland seized Slightman around the neck in the crook of one arm, then yanked him forward. The move simultaneously cut off the flow of the man's accusations and drew him close.

'Listen to me,' Roland said, 'and listen well. I care nothing for your life or honor, one's been misspent and the other's long gone, but your son is dead and about *his* honor I care very much. If you don't shut up this second, you worm of creation, I'll shut you up myself. So what would you? It's nothing to me, either way. I'll tell em you ran mad at the sight of him, stole my gun out of its holster, and put a bullet in your own head to join him. What would you have? Decide.'

Eisenhart was badly blown but still lurching and weaving his way up through the corn, hoarsely calling his wife's name: '*Margaret! Margaret! Answer me, dear! Gi' me a word, I beg ya, do!*'

Roland let go of Slightman and looked at him sternly. Slightman turned his awful eyes to Jake. 'Did your dinh kill my boy in order to be revenged on me? Tell me the truth, soh.'

Jake took a final puff on his cigarette and cast it away. The butt lay smoldering in the dirt next to the dead horse. 'Did you even look at him?' he asked Benny's Da'. 'No bullet ever made could do that. Sai Eisenhart's head fell almost on top of him and Benny crawled out of the ditch from the . . . the horror of it.' It was a word, he realized, that he had never used out loud. Had never *needed* to use out loud. 'They threw two of their sneetches at him. I got one, but . . .' He swallowed. There was a click in his throat. 'The other . . . I would have, you ken . . . I tried, but . . .' His face was working. His voice was breaking apart. Yet his eyes were dry. And somehow as terrible as Slightman's. 'I never had a chance at the other 'n,' he finished, then lowered his head and began to sob.

Roland looked at Slightman, his eyebrows raised.

'All right,' Slightman said. 'I see how 'twas. Yar. Tell me, were he brave until then? Tell me, I beg.'

'He and Jake brought back one of that pair,' Eddie said, gesturing to the

Tavery twins. 'The boy half. He got his foot caught in a hole. Jake and Benny pulled him out, then carried him. Nothing but guts, your boy. Side to side and all the way through the middle.'

Slightman nodded. He took the spectacles off his face and looked at them as if he had never seen them before. He held them so, before his eyes, for a second or two, then dropped them onto the road and crushed them beneath one bootheel. He looked at Roland and Jake almost apologetically. 'I believe I've seen all I need to,' he said, and then went to his son.

Vaughn Eisenhart emerged from the corn. He saw his wife and gave a bellow. Then he tore open his shirt and began pounding his right fist above his flabby left breast, crying her name each time he did it.

'Oh, man,' Eddie said. 'Roland, you ought to stop that.'

'Not I,' said the gunslinger.

Slightman took his son's severed arm and planted a kiss in the palm with a tenderness Eddie found nearly unbearable. He put the arm on the boy's chest, then walked back toward them. Without the glasses, his face looked naked and somehow unformed. 'Jake, would you help me find a blanket?'

Jake got off the waggon wheel to help him find what he needed. In the uncovered trench that had been the hide, Eisenhart was cradling his wife's burnt head to his chest, rocking it. From the corn, approaching, came the children and their minders, singing 'The Rice Song.' At first Eddie thought that what he was hearing from town must be an echo of that singing, and then he realized it was the rest of the Calla. They knew. They had heard the singing, and they knew. They were coming.

Pere Callahan stepped out of the field with Lia Jaffords cradled in his arms. In spite of the noise, the little girl was asleep. Callahan looked at the heaps of dead Wolves, took one hand from beneath the little girl's bottom, and drew a slow, trembling cross in the air.

'God be thanked,' he said.

Roland went to him and took the hand that had made the cross. 'Put one on me,' he said.

Callahan looked at him, uncomprehending.

Roland nodded to Vaughn Eisenhart. 'That one promised I'd leave town with his curse on me if harm came to his wife.'

He could have said more, but there was no need. Callahan understood, and signed the cross on Roland's brow. The fingernail trailed a warmth behind it that Roland felt a long time. And although Eisenhart never kept his promise, the gunslinger was never sorry that he'd asked the Pere for that extra bit of protection.

20

What followed was a confused jubilee there on the East Road, mingled with grief for the two who had fallen. Yet even the grief had a joyful light shining through it. No one seemed to feel that the losses were in any way equal to the gains. And Eddie supposed that was true. If it wasn't your wife or your son who had fallen, that was.

The singing from town drew closer. Now they could see rising dust. In the road, men and women embraced. Someone tried to take Margaret Eisenhart's head away from her husband, who for the time being refused to let it go.

Eddie drifted over to Jake.

'Never saw *Star Wars*, did you?' he asked.

'No, told you. I was *going* to, but—'

'You left too soon. I know. Those things they were swinging – Jake, they were from that movie.'

'You sure?'

'*Yes*. And the Wolves . . . Jake, the Wolves themselves . . .'

Jake was nodding, very slowly. Now they could see the people from town. The newcomers saw the children – *all* the children, still here and still safe – and raised a cheer. Those in the forefront began to run. 'I know.'

'*Do* you?' Eddie asked. His eyes were almost pleading. 'Do you really? Because . . . man, it's so *crazy*—'

Jake looked at the heaped Wolves. The green hoods. The gray leggings. The black boots. The snarling, decomposing faces. Eddie had already pulled one of those rotting metal faces away and looked at what was beneath it. Nothing but smooth metal, plus lenses that served as eyes, a round mesh grille that doubtless served as a nose, two sprouted microphones at the temples for ears. No, all the personality these things had was in the masks and clothing they wore.

'Crazy or not, I know what they are, Eddie. Or where they come from, at least. Marvel Comics.'

A look of sublime relief filled Eddie's face. He bent and kissed Jake on the cheek. A ghost of a smile touched the boy's mouth. It wasn't much, but it was a start.

'The *Spider-Man* books,' Eddie said. 'When I was a kid I couldn't get enough of those things.'

'I didn't buy em myself,' Jake said, 'but Timmy Mucci down at Mid-Town Lanes used to have a terrible jones for the Marvel mags. *Spider-Man, The Fantastic Four, The Incredible Hulk, Captain America,* all of em. These guys . . .'

'They look like Dr Doom,' Eddie said.

'Yeah,' Jake said. 'It's not exact, I'm sure the masks were modified to make them look a little more like wolves, but otherwise . . . same green hoods, same green cloaks. Yeah, Dr Doom.'

'And the sneetches,' Eddie said. 'Have you ever heard of Harry Potter?'

'I don't think so. Have you?'

'No, and I'll tell you why. Because the sneetches are from the future. Maybe from some Marvel comic book that'll come out in 1990 or 1995. Do you see what I'm saying?'

Jake nodded.

'It's all nineteen, isn't it?'

'Yeah,' Jake said. 'Nineteen, ninety-nine, and nineteen-ninety-nine.'

Eddie glanced around. 'Where's Suze?'

'Probably went after her chair,' Jake said. But before either of them could explore the question of Susannah Dean's whereabouts any further (and by then it was probably too late, anyway), the first of the *folken* from town arrived. Eddie and Jake were swept into a wild, impromptu celebration – hugged, kissed, shaken by the hand, laughed over, wept over, thanked and thanked and thanked.

21

Ten minutes after the main body of the townsfolk arrived, Rosalita reluctantly approached Roland. The gunslinger was extremely glad to see her. Eben Took had taken him by the arms and was telling him – over and over again, endlessly, it seemed – how wrong he and Telford had been, how utterly and completely wrong, and how when Roland and his ka-tet were ready to move on, Eben Took would outfit them from stem to stern and not a penny would they pay.

'Roland!' Rosa said.

Roland excused himself and took her by the arm, leading her a little way up the road. The Wolves had been scattered everywhere and were now being mercilessly looted of their possessions by the laughing, deliriously happy *folken*. Stragglers were arriving every minute.

'Rosa, what is it?'

'It's your lady,' Rosa said. 'Susannah.'

'What of her?' Roland asked. Frowning, he looked around. He didn't see Susannah, couldn't remember when he *had* last seen her. When he'd given Jake the cigarette? That long ago? He thought so. 'Where is she?'

'That's just it,' Rosa said. 'I don't know. So I peeked into the waggon she came in, thinking that perhaps she'd gone in there to rest. That perhaps she felt faint or gut-sick, do ya. But she's not there. And Roland . . . her chair is gone.'

'Gods!' Roland snarled, and slammed his fist against his leg. 'Oh, *gods!*'

Rosalita took a step back from him, alarmed.

'Where's Eddie?' Roland asked.

She pointed. Eddie was so deep in a cluster of admiring men and women that Roland didn't think he would have seen him, but for the child riding on his shoulders; it was Heddon Jaffords, an enormous grin on his face.

'Are you sure you want to disturb him?' Rosa asked timidly. 'May be she's just gone off a bit, to pull herself back together.'

Gone off a bit, Roland thought. He could feel a blackness filling his heart. His sinking heart. She'd gone off a bit, all right. And he knew who had stepped in to take her place. Their attention had wandered in the aftermath of the fight . . . Jake's grief . . . the congratulations of the *folken* . . . the confusion and the joy and the singing . . . but that was no excuse.

'*Gunslingers!*' he roared, and the jubilant crowd quieted at once. Had he cared to look, he could have seen the fear that lay just beneath their relief and adulation. It would not have been new to him; they were always afraid of those who came wearing the hard calibers. What they wanted of such when the shooting was done was to give them a final meal, perhaps a final gratitude-fuck, then send them on their way and pick up their own peaceful farming-tools once more.

Well, Roland thought, *we'll be going soon enough. In fact, one of us has gone already. Gods!*

'*Gunslingers, to me! To me!*'

Eddie reached Roland first. He looked around. 'Where's Susannah?' he asked.

Roland pointed into the stony wasteland of bluffs and arroyos, then elevated his finger until it was pointing at a black hole just below the skyline. 'I think there,' he said.

All the color had drained out of Eddie Dean's face. 'That's Doorway Cave you're pointing at,' he said. 'Isn't it?'

Roland nodded.

'But the ball . . . Black Thirteen . . . she wouldn't even go *near* it when it was in Callahan's church—'

'No,' Roland said. '*Susannah* wouldn't. But she's not in charge anymore.'

'Mia?' Jake asked.

'Yes.' Roland studied the high hole with his faded eyes. 'Mia's gone to have her baby. She's gone to have her chap.'

'No,' Eddie said. His hands wandered out and took hold of Roland's shirt. Around them, the *folken* stood silently, watching. 'Roland, say no.'

'We'll go after her and hope we're not too late,' Roland said.

But in his heart, he knew they already were.

EPILOGUE:
THE DOORWAY CAVE

1

They moved fast, but Mia moved faster. A mile beyond the place where the arroyo path divided, they found her wheelchair. She had pushed it hard, using her strong arms to give it a savage beating against the unforgiving terrain. Finally it had struck a jutting rock hard enough to bend the left-hand wheel out of true and render the chair useless. It was a wonder, really, that she had gotten as far in it as she had.

'Fuck-commala,' Eddie murmured, looking at the chair. At the dents and dings and scratches. Then he raised his head, cupped his hands around his mouth, and shouted. '*Fight her, Susannah! Fight her! We're coming!*' He pushed past the chair and headed on up the path, not looking to see if the others were following.

'She can't make it up the path to the cave, can she?' Jake asked. 'I mean, her *legs* are gone.'

'Wouldn't think so, would you?' Roland asked, but his face was dark. And he was limping. Jake started to say something about this, then thought better of it.

'What would she want up there, anyway?' Callahan asked.

Roland turned a singularly cold eye on him. 'To go somewhere else,' he said. 'Surely you see that much. Come on.'

2

As they neared the place where the path began to climb, Roland caught up to Eddie. The first time he put his hand on the younger man's shoulder,

Eddie shook it off. The second time he turned — reluctantly — to look at his dinh. Roland saw there was blood spattered across the front of Eddie's shirt. He wondered if it was Benny's, Margaret's, or both.

'Mayhap it'd be better to let her alone awhile, if it's Mia,' Roland said.

'Are you crazy? Did fighting the Wolves loosen your *screws*?'

'If we let her alone, she may finish her business and be gone.' Even as he spoke the words, Roland doubted them.

'Yeah,' Eddie said, studying him with burning eyes, 'she'll finish her business, all right. First piece, have the kid. Second piece, kill my wife.'

'That would be suicide.'

'But she might do it. We have to go after her.'

Surrender was an art Roland practiced rarely but with some skill on the few occasions in his life when it had been necessary. He took another look at Eddie Dean's pale, set face and practiced it now. 'All right,' he said, 'but we'll have to be careful. She'll fight to keep from being taken. She'll kill, if it comes to that. You before any of us, mayhap.'

'I know,' Eddie said. His face was bleak. He looked up the path, but a quarter of a mile up, it hooked around to the south side of the bluff and out of sight. The path zigged back to their side just below the mouth of the cave. That stretch of the climb was deserted, but what did that prove? She could be anywhere. It crossed Eddie's mind that she might not even be up there at all, that the crashed chair might have been as much a red herring as the children's possessions Roland had had scattered along the arroyo path.

I won't believe that. There's a million ratholes in this part of the Calla, and if I believe that she could be in any of them . . .

Callahan and Jake had caught up and stood there looking at Eddie.

'Come on,' he said. 'I don't care who she is, Roland. If four able-bodied men can't catch one no-legs lady, we ought to turn in our guns and call it a day.'

Jake smiled wanly. 'I'm touched. You just called me a man.'

'Don't let it go to your head, Sunshine. Come on.'

3

Eddie and Susannah spoke and thought of each other as man and wife, but he hadn't exactly been able to take a cab over to Cartier's and buy her a diamond and a wedding band. He'd once had a pretty nice high school class ring, but that he'd lost in the sand at Coney Island during the summer he turned seventeen, the summer of Mary Jean Sobieski. Yet on their journeyings from the Western Sea, Eddie had rediscovered his talent as a woodcarver ('wittle baby-ass whittler,' the great sage and eminent junkie would have said), and Eddie had carved his beloved a beautiful ring of willow-green, light as foam but strong. This Susannah had worn between her breasts, hung on a length of rawhide.

They found it at the foot of the path, still on its rawhide loop. Eddie picked it up, looked at it grimly for a moment, then slipped it over his own head, inside his own shirt.

'Look,' Jake said.

They turned to a place just off the path. Here, in a patch of scant grass, was a track. Not human, not animal. Three wheels in a configuration that made Eddie think of a child's tricycle. What the hell?

'Come on,' he said, and wondered how many times he'd said it since realizing she was gone. He also wondered how long they'd keep following him if he kept on saying it. Not that it mattered. He'd go on until he had her again, or until he was dead. Simple as that. What frightened him most was the baby . . . what she called the chap. Suppose it turned on her? And he had an idea it might do just that.

'Eddie,' Roland said.

Eddie looked over his shoulder and gave him Roland's own impatient twirl of the hand: *let's go.*

Roland pointed at the track, instead. 'This was some sort of motor.'

'Did you hear one?'

'No.'

'Then you can't know that.'

'But I do,' Roland said. 'Someone sent her a ride. Or some*thing.*'

'You can't *know* that, goddam you!'

'Andy could have left a ride for her,' Jake said. 'If someone told him to.'

'Who would have told him to do a thing like that?' Eddie rasped.

Finli, Jake thought. *Finli o' Tego, whoever he is. Or maybe Walter.* But he said nothing. Eddie was upset enough already.

Roland said, 'She's gotten away. Prepare yourself for it.'

'Go fuck yourself!' Eddie snarled, and turned to the path leading upward. 'Come on!'

4

Yet in his heart, Eddie knew Roland was right. He attacked the path to the Doorway Cave not with hope but with a kind of desperate determination. At the place where the boulder had fallen, blocking most of the path, they found an abandoned vehicle with three balloon tires and an electric motor that was still softly humming, a low and constant *ummmmm* sound. To Eddie, the gadget looked like one of those funky ATV things they sold at Abercrombie & Fitch. There was a handgrip accelerator and handgrip brakes. He bent close and read what was stamped into the steel of the left one:

'SQUEEZIE-PIE' BRAKES, BY NORTH CENTRAL POSITRONICS.

Behind the bicycle-style seat was a little carry-case. Eddie flipped it up and was totally unsurprised to see a six-pack of Nozz-A-La, the drink favored by discriminating bumhugs everywhere. One can had been taken off the ring. She'd been thirsty, of course. Moving fast made you thirsty. Especially if you were in labor.

'This came from the place across the river,' Jake murmured. 'The Dogan. If I'd gone out back, I would have seen it parked there. A whole fleet of them, probably. I bet it *was* Andy.'

Eddie had to admit it made sense. The Dogan was clearly an outpost of some sort, probably one that predated the current unpleasant residents of Thunderclap. This was exactly the sort of vehicle you'd want to make patrols on, given the terrain.

From this vantage-point beside the fallen boulder, Eddie could see the battleground where they'd stood against the Wolves, throwing plates and lead. That stretch of East Road was so full of people it made him think of the Macy's Thanksgiving Day Parade. The whole Calla was out there partying, and oh how Eddie hated them in that moment. *My wife's gone because of you chickenshit motherfuckers*, he thought. It was a stupid idea, stupendously unkind, as well, yet it offered a certain hateful satisfaction. What was it that poem by Stephen Crane had said, the one they'd read back in high school? 'I like it because it is bitter, and because it is my heart.' Something like that. Close enough for government work.

Now Roland was standing beside the abandoned, softly humming trike, and if it was sympathy he saw in the gunslinger's eyes – or, worse, pity – he wanted none of it.

'Come on, you guys. Let's find her.'

5

This time the voice that greeted them from the Doorway Cave's depths belonged to a woman Eddie had never actually met, although he had heard of her – aye, much, say thankya – and knew her voice at once.

'She's gone, ye great dick-led galoot!' cried Rhea of the Cöos from the darkness. 'Taken her labor elsewhere, ye ken! And I've no doubt that when her cannibal baby finally comes out, it'll munch its mother north from the cunt, aye!' She laughed, a perfect (and perfectly grating) Witch Hazel cackle. 'No titty-milk fer this one, ye grobbut lost lad! This one'll have *meat!*'

'Shut up!' Eddie screamed into the darkness. 'Shut up, you . . . you fucking *phantom!*'

And for a wonder, the phantom did.

Eddie looked around. He saw Tower's goddamned two-shelf bookcase – first editions under glass, may they do ya fine – but no pink metal-mesh bag with MID-WORLD LANES printed on it; no engraved ghostwood box, either. The unfound door was still here, its hinges still hooked to nothing, but now it had a strangely dull look. Not just unfound but unremembered; only one more useless piece of a world that had moved on.

'No,' Eddie said. 'No, I don't accept that. The power is still here. *The power is still here.*'

He turned to Roland, but Roland wasn't looking at him. Incredibly, Roland was studying the books. As if the search for Susannah had begun to bore him and he was looking for a good read to pass the time.

Eddie took Roland's shoulder, turned him. 'What happened, Roland? Do you know?'

'What happened is obvious,' Roland said. Callahan had come up beside him. Only Jake, who was visiting the Doorway Cave for the first time, hung back at the entrance. 'She took her wheelchair as far as she could, then went on her hands and knees to the foot of the path, no mean feat for a woman who's probably in labor. At the foot of the path, someone – probably Andy, just as Jake says – left her a ride.'

'If it was Slightman, I'll go back and kill him myself.'

Roland shook his head. 'Not Slightman.' *But Slightman might know for sure,* he thought. It probably didn't matter, but he liked loose ends no more than he liked crooked pictures hanging on walls.

'Hey, bro, sorry to tell you this, but your poke-bitch is dead,' Henry Dean called up from deep in the cave. He didn't sound sorry; he sounded gleeful. 'Damn thing ate her all the way up! Only stopped long enough on its way to the brain to spit out her teeth!'

'*Shut up!*' Eddie screamed.

'The brain's the ultimate brain-food, you know,' Henry said. He had assumed a mellow, scholarly tone. Revered by cannibals the world over. That's quite the chap she's got, Eddie! Cute but *hongry.*'

'Be still, in the name of God!' Callahan cried, and the voice of Eddie's brother ceased. For the time being, at least, all the voices ceased.

Roland went on as if he had never been interrupted. 'She came here. Took the bag. Opened the box so that Black Thirteen would open the door. Mia, this is — not Susannah but Mia. Daughter of none. And then, still carrying the open box, she went through. On the other side she closed the box, closing the door. Closing it against us.'

'No,' Eddie said, and grabbed the crystal doorknob with the rose etched into its geometric facets. It wouldn't turn. There was not so much as a single iota of give.

From the darkness, Elmer Chambers said: 'If you'd been quicker, son, you could have saved your friend. It's your fault.' And fell silent again.

'It's not real, Jake,' Eddie said, and rubbed a finger across the rose. The tip of his finger came away dusty. As if the unfound door had stood here, unused as well as unfound, for a score of centuries. 'It just broadcasts the worst stuff it can find in your own head.'

'I was always hatin yo' guts, honky!' Detta cried triumphantly from the darkness beyond the door. 'Ain't I glad to be shed of you!'

'Like that,' Eddie said, cocking a thumb in the direction of the voice.

Jake nodded, pale and thoughtful. Roland, meanwhile, had turned back to Tower's bookcase.

'Roland?' Eddie tried to keep the irritation out of his voice, or at least add a little spark of humor to it, and failed at both. 'Are we boring you, here?'

'No,' Roland said.

'Then I wish you'd stop looking at those books and help me think of a way to open this d—'

'I know how to open it,' Roland said. 'The first question is where will it take us now that the ball is gone? The second question is where do we want to go? After Mia, or to the place where Tower and his friend are hiding from Balazar and *his* friends?'

'We go after Susannah!' Eddie shouted. 'Have you been listening to any of the shit those voices are saying? They're saying it's a cannibal! My wife could be giving birth to some kind of a cannibal monster *right now*, and if you think anything's more important than that—'

'The *Tower's* more important,' Roland said. 'And somewhere on the other side of this door there's a man whose *name* is Tower. A man who owns a certain vacant lot and a certain rose growing there.'

Eddie looked at him uncertainly. So did Jake and Callahan. Roland turned again to the little bookcase. It looked strange indeed, here in this rocky darkness.

'And he owns these books,' Roland mused. 'He risked all things to save them.'

'Yeah, because he's one obsessed motherfucker.'

'Yet all things serve ka and follow the Beam,' Roland said, and selected a volume from the upper shelf of the bookcase. Eddie saw it had been placed in there upside down, which struck him as a very un-Calvin Tower thing to do.

Roland held the book in his seamed, weather-chapped hands, seeming to debate which one to give it to. He looked at Eddie . . . looked at Callahan . . . and then gave the book to Jake.

'Read me what it says on the front,' he said. 'The words of your world make my head hurt. They swim to my eye easily enough, but when I reach my mind toward them, most swim away again.'

Jake was paying little attention; his eyes were riveted on the book jacket with its picture of a little country church at sunset. Callahan, meanwhile, had stepped past him in order to get a closer look at the door standing here in the gloomy cave.

At last the boy looked up. 'But . . . Roland, isn't this the town Pere Callahan told us about? The one where the vampire broke his cross and made him drink his blood?'

Callahan whirled away from the door. '*What?*'

Jake held the book out wordlessly. Callahan took it. Almost snatched it.

''*Salem's Lot,*' he read. 'A novel by Stephen King.' He looked up at Eddie, then at Jake. 'Heard of him? Either of you? He's not from my time, I don't think.'

Jake shook his head. Eddie began to shake his, as well, and then he saw something. 'That church,' he said. 'It looks like the Calla Gathering Hall. Close enough to be its twin, almost.'

'It also looks like the East Stoneham Methodist Meeting Hall, built in 1819,' Callahan said, 'so I guess this time we've got a case of triplets.' But his voice sounded faraway to his own ears, as hollow as the false voices which floated up from the bottom of the cave. All at once he felt false to himself, not real. He felt *nineteen*.

6

It's a joke, part of his mind assured him. *It must be a joke, the cover of this book says it's a novel, so—*

Then an idea struck him, and he felt a surge of relief. It was *conditional* relief, but surely better than none at all. The idea was that sometimes people wrote make-believe stories about real places. That was it, surely. Had to be.

'Look at page one hundred and nineteen,' Roland said. 'I could make out a little of it, but not all. Not nearly enough.'

Callahan found the page, and read this:

'"In the early days at the seminary, a friend of Father ..."' He trailed off, eyes racing ahead over the words on the page.

'Go on,' Eddie said. 'You read it, Father, or I will.'

Slowly, Callahan resumed.

'"... a friend of Father Callahan's had given him a blasphemous crewel-work sampler which had sent him into gales of horrified laughter at the time, but which seemed more true and less blasphemous as the years passed: *God grant me the SERENITY to accept what I cannot change, the TENACITY to change what I may, and the GOOD LUCK not to fuck up too often*. This in Old English script with a rising sun in the background.

'"Now, standing before Danny Glick's ... Danny Glick's mourners, that old credo ... that old credo returned."'

The hand holding the book sagged. If Jake hadn't caught it, it probably would have tumbled to the floor of the cave.

'You had it, didn't you?' Eddie said. 'You actually had a sampler saying that.'

'Frankie Foyle gave it to me,' Callahan said. His voice was hardly more than a whisper. 'Back in seminary. And Danny Glick . . . I officiated at his funeral, I think I told you that. That was when everything seemed to change, somehow. But this is a *novel*! A novel is *fiction*! How . . . how can it . . .'. His voice suddenly rose to a damned howl. To Roland it sounded eerily like the false voices that rose up from below. '*Damn it, I'm a REAL PERSON!*'

'Here's the part where the vampire broke your cross,' Jake reported. '""Together at last!" Barlow said, smiling. His face was strong and intelligent and handsome in a sharp, forbidding sort of way – yet, as the light shifted, it seemed—"'

'Stop,' Callahan said dully. 'It makes my head hurt.'

'It says his face reminded you of the bogeyman who lived in your closet when you were a kid. Mr Flip.'

Callahan's face was now so pale he might have been a vampire's victim himself. 'I never told anyone about Mr Flip, not even my mother. That can't be in that book. It just can't be.'

'It is,' Jake said simply.

'Let's get this straight,' Eddie said. 'When you were a kid, there *was* a Mr Flip, and you *did* think of him when you faced this particular Type One vampire, Barlow. Correct?'

'Yes, but—'

Eddie turned to the gunslinger. 'Is this getting us any closer to Susannah, do you think?'

'Yes. We've reached the heart of a great mystery. Perhaps *the* great mystery. I believe the Dark Tower is almost close enough to touch. And if the Tower is close, Susannah is, too.'

Ignoring him, Callahan was flipping through the book. Jake was looking over his shoulder.

'And you know how to open that door?' Eddie pointed at it.

'Yes,' Roland said. 'I'd need help, but I think the people of Calla Bryn Sturgis owe us a little help, don't you?'

Eddie nodded. 'All right, then, let me tell you this much: I'm pretty sure I *have* seen the name Stephen King before, at least once.'

'On the Specials board,' Jake said without looking up from the book. 'Yeah, I remember. It was on the Specials board the first time we went todash.'

'Specials board?' Roland asked, frowning.

'*Tower's* Specials board,' Eddie said. 'It was in the window, remember? Part of his whole Restaurant-of-the-Mind thing.'

Roland nodded.

'But I'll tell you guys something,' Jake said, and now he *did* look up from the book. 'The name was there when Eddie and I went todash, but it *wasn't* on the board the first time I went in there. The time Mr Deepneau told me the river riddle, it was someone else's name. It changed, just like the name of the writer on *Charlie the Choo-Choo*.'

'I *can't* be in a book,' Callahan was saying. 'I am *not* a fiction . . . am I?'

'Roland.' It was Eddie. The gunslinger turned to him. 'I need to find her. I don't care who's real and who's not. I don't care about Calvin Tower, Stephen King, or the Pope of Rome. As far as reality goes, she's all of it I want. *I need to find my wife.*' His voice dropped. 'Help me, Roland.'

Roland reached out and took the book in his left hand. With his right he touched the door. *If she's still alive,* he thought. *If we can find her, and if she's come back to herself. If and if and if.*

Eddie took Roland's arm. 'Please,' he said. 'Please don't make me try to do it on my own. I love her so much. Help me find her.'

Roland smiled. It made him younger. It seemed to fill the cave with its own light. All of Eld's ancient power was in that smile: the power of the White.

'Yes,' he said. 'We go.'

And then he said again, all the affirmation necessary in this dark place. '*Yes.*'

Bangor, Maine
December 15, 2002

AUTHOR'S NOTE

The debt I owe to the American Western in the composition of the *Dark Tower* novels should be clear without my belaboring the point; certainly the Calla did not come by the final part of its (slightly misspelled) name accidentally. Yet it should be pointed out that at least two sources for some of this material aren't American at all. Sergio Leone (*A Fistful of Dollars*, *For a Few Dollars More*, *The Good, The Bad, and The Ugly*, etc.) was Italian. And Akira Kurosawa (*The Seven Samurai*) was, of course, Japanese. Would these books have been written without the cinematic legacy of Kurosawa, Leone, Peckinpah, Howard Hawkes, and John Sturgis? Probably not without Leone. But without the others, I would argue there could *be* no Leone.

I also owe a debt of thanks to Robin Furth, who managed to be there with the right bit of information every time I needed it, and of course to my wife, Tabitha, who is still patiently giving me the time and light and space I need to do this job to the best of my abilities.

S.K.

AUTHOR'S AFTERWORD

Before you read this short afterword, I ask that you take a moment (may it do ya fine) to look again at the dedication page at the front of this story. I'll wait.

Thank you. I want you to know that Frank Muller has read a number of my books for the audio market, beginning with *Different Seasons*. I met him at Recorded Books in New York at that time and we liked each other immediately. It's a friendship that has lasted longer than some of my readers have been alive. In the course of our association, Frank recorded the first four *Dark Tower* novels, and I listened to them — all sixty or so cassettes — while preparing to finish the gunslinger's story. Audio is the perfect medium for such exhaustive preparation, because audio insists you absorb everything; your hurrying eye (or occasionally tired mind) cannot skip so much as a single word. That was what I wanted, complete immersion in Roland's world, and that was what Frank gave me. He gave me something more, as well, something wonderful and unexpected. It was a sense of newness and freshness that I had lost somewhere along the way; a sense of Roland and Roland's friends as *actual people*, with their own vital inner lives. When I say in the dedication that Frank heard the voices in my head, I am speaking the literal truth as I understand it. And, like a rather more benign version of the Doorway Cave, he brought them fully back to life. The remaining books are finished (this one in final draft, the last two in rough), and in large part I owe that to Frank Muller and his inspired readings.

I had hoped to have Frank on board to do the audio readings of the final three *Dark Tower* books (unabridged readings; I do not allow abridgments of my work and don't approve of them, as a rule), and he was eager to do them. We discussed the possibility at a dinner in Bangor during October of 2001, and in the course of the conversation, he called the *Tower* stories his absolute favorites. As he had read over five hundred novels for the audio market, I was extremely flattered.

Less than a month after that dinner and that optimistic, forward-looking discussion, Frank suffered a terrible motorcycle accident on a highway in California. It happened only days after discovering that he was to become a father for the second time. He was wearing his brain-bucket and that probably saved his life — motorcyclists please take note — but he suffered serious injuries nevertheless, many of them neurological. He won't be recording the final *Dark Tower* novels on tape, after all. Frank's final work will almost certainly be his inspired reading of Clive Barker's *Coldheart Canyon*, which was completed in September of 2001, just before his accident.

Barring a miracle, Frank Muller's working life is over. His work of rehabilitation, which is almost sure to be lifelong, has only begun. He'll need a lot of care and a lot of professional help. Such things cost money, and money's not a thing which, as a rule, freelance artists have a great deal of. I and some friends have formed a foundation to help Frank — and, hopefully, other freelance artists of various types who suffer similar cataclysms. All the income I receive from the audio version of *Wolves of the Calla* will go into this foundation's account. It won't be enough, but the work of funding The Wavedancer Foundation (*Wavedancer* was the name of Frank's sailboat), like Frank's rehabilitative work, is only beginning. If you've got a few bucks that aren't working and want to help insure the future of The Wavedancer Foundation, don't send them to me; send them to

The Wavedancer Foundation
c/o Mr Arthur Greene
101 Park Avenue
New York, NY 10001

Frank's wife, Erika, says thankya. So do I.

And Frank would, if he could.

Bangor, Maine
December 15, 2002